ELLIOTT "BEAR SCAT" SUTTA, MOUNTAIN MAN

Terry Grosz

WOLFPACK
PUBLISHING
— EST 2013 —

Print Edition
© Copyright 2017 Terry Grosz

Wolfpack Publishing
P.O. Box 620427
Las Vegas, NV 89162

ISBN: 978-1-64119-068-8

Table of Contents

DEDICATION

The first knowing revelation in my life occurred on the first day of school in the eighth grade. Into our classroom walked a new girl wearing a white blouse, a light blue skirt and sporting beautiful, long blond-colored hair with a slightly reddish tinge. For some reason I felt the strongest feelings rise up inside me that were almost physical upon seeing that new girl for the very first time in my life! Without any hesitation and with the most unusual feelings rising from deep inside, I turned to my friend Eugene Miller sitting alongside me in the classroom saying, "I am going to marry that girl someday!" Eugene just looked at me in amazement and said, "How are you going to do that? You are just a kid and you don't even know who she is." Then once again a 'voice' from somewhere inside of me rose up and I replied, "I don't know why I said what I just said, but I just somehow know in my heart that I am going to marry that girl someday."

I started dating 'that girl' named Donna Lee Larson during my junior year in high school and we were married on February the 3rd, 1963, while both of us were still in college. As these words are being put to print in 2017, we are still very happily married some 54 going on 55 years later…

My wife and very best friend, is without a doubt the most remarkable woman and one of the most wonderfully unusual people I have ever met in my 76 years of life! During our second date even as young as I was, I honest-to-God realized Donna was simply Heaven-sent just for me! I don't say that just because she may be reading these lines someday. But when one is blessed as was I by having by my side such a uniquely wonderful person who eventually became the co-author of my life, you just somehow know you are blessed! Throughout our lives together, I have come to realize that the exceptionalism she exhibits at every turn in our 'road of life' is not of this world! To me, Donna is a very rare human tapestry representing an exceptionalism that is always especially present in her love and caring for those who are around her. She constantly exhibits a uniquely shared love for me, her family and her friends. Her love and dedication for country and for those who provide for our many freedoms, is equal to that of those who wear the uniform and serve this wonderful country of ours! Her many times innocent and yet so perceptive understanding of life swirling around us on an everyday basis is uniquely present in everything she does. Donna's VERY special love and caring she has shown for me at EVERY juncture in our lives is just one of her many quiet trademarks of exceptionalism. Her faith in what tomorrow will bring; the room she has in her heart for those who have little or no love or caring in their own lives; her exceptional love for the world of humanity; her love for God's gifts found in the color of a wildflower, a bird's happy song, a sunrise in Colorado, the "whirr" of a hummingbird's wings in the spring, or a child's happy voice; the quiet happiness she finds when I hold her in my arms; the happiness found in holding a child, especially one of her own; and the innocence she shares with me in trying to understand my world of wildlife, are just some of the many 'gifts' she exhibits when in her presence.

It is to MY Renaissance woman for all seasons, the co-author of MY life, the love of MY life, and the very special woman whom I will love forever and a day, that I humbly dedicate this book...

ELLIOTT "BEAR SCAT" SUTTA, MOUNTAIN MAN

Terry Grosz

CHAPTER ONE — THE BIG BUCK AND A 'KILLER' MOVED AMONG THEM...

An eerily reddish-orange orb of a sun rose ominously above the great State of Missouri and soon the summer heat and humidity across the land became almost palpable. Off in a distance, a ten-point white-tailed buck deer still in velvet, peacefully feasted under a huge spreading oak tree on the plentiful mast crop scattered around its base, left over from the previous fall's 'natural harvest'. Then all of a sudden the quietly feeding deer's head shot up into the air in an alertness that came from surviving in an oftentimes predator rich environment! That and 10,000 years of survival genetics went into that alertness, moving the deer from quietly feeding under an oak tree into an all-of-a-sudden statuesque appearing presence. Every sensory nerve in the seven-year-old buck deer was now being tested in an effort to detect what his innate survival senses were 'warning'.

The early morning's breeze wafting across the landscape did not bring him anything other than those smells normally associated with his feeding presence in the field under the great oak tree. His eyes, which only saw in black and white not color, did not provide any early warning signs of suspicious movement in his surroundings other than that of the softly rustling grasses, tree leaves and bushes in the face of an oncoming storm. His 'mule-like' shaped ears developed over the last 10,000 years to provide hearing acuity of the highest degree for his species, especially when danger was near, brought him no such suspicious auditory evidence or other early warnings. The only out-of-the-ordinary element the great buck deer's body could detect was that there was a great storm brewing far to the northwest, if his senses correctly 'read' the barometric pressure changes now swirling around his massive body. Being of 'white-tail' genetics and collateral highly developed species survival instincts, the great buck carefully examined his nearby brushy surroundings at the edge of the meadow once again for any signs of danger. Then a slave to his empty stomach, he momentarily set carefulness and caution aside in favor of consuming more of the flavorful and abundant mast scattered around his feet. Lowering his head again, he adroitly picked up another of the energy rich nuts with his lips, moved it with his tongue to his molars and with a satisfying 'crunch', began enjoying the rich nut's flavor as he began quietly eating once again.

THUD! went the impact of a .33 caliber lead ball fired from a nearby Pennsylvania rifle, striking just behind the great deer's right front shoulder. As the high speed bullet tore through the deer's skin and flesh, it finally lodged deeply into his lungs in an explosion of destructive energy! The surprising explosive impact of the mushrooming speeding lead ball dropped the massive-sized deer to the ground in a heartbeat! A microsecond later, a chemical surge of adrenalin initiated by the physics of the bullet's explosive impact pumped into the deer's heart and spread throughout his circulatory system in two more now rapid heartbeats! With that surge of chemical into his bloodstream, the great buck found the power to leap back to his feet, took two lunges away from the **"BOOMING"** sound and the whitish black powder cloud of smoke surging his way from some nearby elderberry bushes, and then dropped to the ground beneath his feet to breathe no more!

Sixteen-year-old Elliott Sutta, son of Adam and Edna Sutta, small-time Jewish homesteaders among farmers and cattlemen near the Missouri town of Weldon Spring, just west of St. Louis, felt the comforting recoil of his dad's borrowed Pennsylvania rifle against his shoulder. That assuring recoil after hearing the report of his rifle being fired at a massive white-tailed buck, told him his long and arduous sneak upon the feeding monster-sized deer right at daylight had been successfully carried out. Jumping to his feet in excitement and looking past the small drifting away, whitish cloud of black powder smoke from his rifle, Elliott saw his quarry, the massive white-tailed buck on the ground kicking his last!

Remembering his dad's survival teachings learned during his military years on the frontier fighting Indians, instead of immediately running over to his kill site in the excitement of the moment, Elliott quickly reloaded his rifle. As he did, he continued looking all around for any signs of approaching hostile Indians or border ruffians who had heard him shoot and might be coming his way to investigate the shooting. Additionally, he alertly watched for signs of any approaching through the brush, black or grizzly bear or any other like in kind sounds of animal discovery. Sounds of discovery by bears conditioned to hearing someone shoot and smelling death in the air through their great abilities of smell, then somewhat later being 'treated' to a warm gut pile. For the next ten minutes after reloading his rifle and standing still as a stone and at the 'ready' for any signs of danger, Elliott did as his dad had taught him regarding surviving in a sometimes savage wilderness. Delayed danger could still be coming his way after he had made it known that he was in country, so he must always remain alert on the frontier.

Finally, Elliott in his excitement over his outstanding kill could stand himself no longer and trotted out to examine the great beast he had just slain. Standing over the body of the deer, Elliott's heart skipped a beat in the excitement of his first monster white-tailed buck deer kill! Elliott had killed many deer in his young life to date but none as magnificent as the one now lying dead at his feet! Since age twelve, Elliott's very stern, cautious and frontier-tested father had trusted him enough to allow him to go forth on his own and bring meat back for the family. As such, Elliott had listened intently to his father's frontier teachings and now, as a result of closely following those sage words of advice and with subsequent experiences gained on his own, was 'hickory' hard and locally renowned for being a seasoned hunter who allegedly 'could track a wounded red ant across a rock pile' and 'could shoot from the off-hand position a wood tick from the rump of a running mule deer at 50 yards'!

Looking down again, Elliott saw that the animal he had just killed was huge, weighing in around 350 pounds! Upon closer examination, Elliott could see from the bullet's entry point into the animal, he had made a clean kill, no meat would be wasted and one that his dad would be very proud of. Now the family would have enough to eat for the next few days, plus a small mountain of meat to preserve through smoking in his father's smokehouse or through his mother's canning process for consumption during the winter months.

It was only then that Elliott realized, after the excitement of the hunt, with the increasing winds blowing across the landscape there was every indication that a huge and dangerous looking storm front was developing to the northwest. He had been so intent on stalking such a giant-sized deer that morning that he had forgotten his father's earlier warning advice about watching the weather for the occurrence of violent summer thunderstorms so commonly found in Missouri during that time of the year. Finally getting his survival wits about him and really intelligently looking skyward for the first time, Elliott saw low hanging and ugly, huge rolling black and blue-black clouds that his frontier weather savvy now told him a dangerous thunderstorm was coming his way and he best make haste in gutting out his deer! Then 'both' of them had better retreat to some form of cover to avoid getting drenched with the oncoming deluge of rain, hit by lightning or both!

Laying his rifle down, Elliott quickly drew his dad's borrowed gutting knife and began the task of field-dressing his kill to avoid having the carcass bloat and starting to spoil in the Missouri summer heat, thereby ruining the meat. However, as he began his field-dressing chore, he kept one eye cocked on his surroundings for any sign of approaching wilderness danger and the other eye cocked on the now threatening and fast approaching, serious looking weather front rapidly bearing down upon him from out of the northwest.

As Elliott separated the eatable heart and liver from the rest of the entrails, he noticed that the storm's winds were now rapidly increasing, the smell of oncoming moisture was heavy in the air, and the low hanging ugly clouds now fast approaching were like none he had ever seen or experienced before. Throwing the heart and liver back into the now empty thoracic cavity to keep them from getting covered with dirt as he dragged his deer off into some nearby cover, he also became aware of an ominous sound like none he had ever heard before in his young life. Stopping midstride and wiping off his bloody and deer-fat covered hands on the fur of his kill, he glanced skyward again in wonder in the direction of the unusual storm front and sounds he was now seeing and hearing.

To his north, he could hear a sound like a thousand angry thunderstorms all rolled up into one and coming his way. THEN HE SAW IT! Coming his way was a huge funnel-shaped cloud of dirt and flying debris, undulating sideways, then rising and lowering as it moved along towards him! It was then that the magnitude of the danger began sinking into Elliott's thought processes, as the excitement over the earlier monster deer kill quickly subsided. THE ROARING SOUNDS HE HAD BEEN HEARING WAS AN APPROACHING TORNADO AND NOW IT SEEMED TO BE COMING RIGHT AT HIM!

Now almost in a panic over the oncoming violent weather event, Elliott grabbed his dad's precious rifle with one hand and reaching down, grabbed his deer by one of its velvet covered antlers and began dragging with difficulty his huge prize toward a small rocky outcropping at the edge of the meadow he now occupied. By now, Elliott's long hair was standing almost straight up in a fear like he had never before experienced and his heart was racing like he had never known in his young life! All around him trees were now whipping back and forth in the high winds. He could hear other close at hand trees being violently uprooted, torn asunder and crashing down around him, and the air was now full of limbs, dirt, leaves and parts of treetops flying through the air like cannon shot during a great land battle!

Finally realizing he could not drag his monster deer carcass quickly enough and still safely make his rocky outcropping before the tornado arrived, Elliott dropped the deer and raced for a small cave he saw in the rocky formation! With flying feet and racing heart, Elliott was now running through a tremendous howling wind, tons of flying debris and even flying rocks! Diving into the small sheltering opening in the rocky outcropping, Elliott discovered that his whole body would not fit into the small cave because it was partially filled with wood rat litter! But panic now overcame any common sense like looking for another place of safety, as Elliott frantically plowed headfirst into his small cave partially filled with wood rat crap and litter! By madly digging with his right hand, Elliott managed to remove enough litter so that he could drag most of his body into the small sheltering cave. That was except for the lower part of his legs and feet which were now hanging out in the open in front of the small cave!

By now, the roaring tornado was upon him as he tightly curled up as best as he could, making himself as small as possible and cowering at the back of his small cave in terror! It was then that Elliott looked past his exposed legs and feet saw his deer's carcass lifted up like it was walking in midair and disappearing into the swirling dust and airborne debris! Then his feet and lower legs were sandblasted by everything airborne as well! In pain, he tried dragging his legs up further into his body but all to no avail. There was just so much cover that his small cave provided and that did not include his lower legs and feet, so they continued taking a beating from all the flying debris the nearby tornado was generating…

It was then that 'a thousand thunderstorms of noise' was upon him and Elliott found himself calling out to his mother in fear, as the elements seemed to be trying to drag him bodily out from his small sheltering cave and whirl him away into the airborne violence just like it had done to his deer! Grabbing a small rocky protrusion at the head of his cave, Elliott hung on for dear life as the storm tried sucking him out from his rocky shelter! As he did, he found his legs slamming around uncontrollably at the entrance of his cave and the deep pain in his leg bones became so great that he finally passed out!

Somewhat later, Elliott awoke and found himself partway outside his small cave's entrance, battered, bruised and bleeding but still alive! The roaring sounds and violent winds were now gone and had been replaced by a drenching cold rain which had awakened him. Looking down at his painfully burning legs, Elliott saw that his moccasins had been sucked off his feet and his lower legs and feet were bloody and badly bruised! It was then that Elliott began laughing uncontrollably as he looked downward and realized that he still had all of his toes... But seeing that the cold rains washing over his lower legs and feet felt so comforting, he lay where he was as he gathered up his strength and wits about him. It was then that Elliott realized the killer tornado had not gotten him like it had the deer he had killed earlier. For that he found himself grateful and thanking the good Lord above, as his mother had always taught him to do for being spared and still alive from whatever deadly fury in life he had just experienced.

As the cooling rains subsided and as those clouds passed, the typical summer Missouri heat and humidity began returning to the landscape once again. Finally, Elliott found the wherewithal to crawl away from the front of his small cave, sit up and look at the surroundings around him in head-shaking wonder. Almost every deciduous tree that he could see around him was full of broken out tops and busted limbs, and most all lacked any remaining leaves whatsoever! The ground around him looked like someone had come by with a giant broom and swept most everything 'clean as a hound's tooth' down to the barren soil in many places. To the southeast of where he was sitting, Elliott could hear the sounds of a fading storm as it marched itself way away from the quiet countryside he had grown up in and had come to love.

Crawling back and reaching into his 'life-saving' cave, Elliott retrieved his father's rifle and carry bag holding his rifle balls, wadding, ball starter and powder horn. Then using his rifle as a crutch-like support, Elliott painfully stood on his damaged feet and legs and just dizzily swayed back and forth in pain for a few moments until he felt confident enough to try hobbling away from the area. That turned out to be a painful and slow adventure but using his dad's rifle as a support helped steady him along, bloody legs, bruised feet, ten bloodied toes and all.

THEN THE REALIZATION HIT HIM! The storm had moved down through the small valley in which he and his family lived! It was easy to see the direction the storm had taken by the path of destruction left behind and from what he could see through his eyes swimming in foot- and leg-caused pain, the tornado appeared to have been heading right for his folks' small homestead! Now beginning to worry about the rest of his family and finding his eyes filling with tears of apprehension and his heart filling with fear, Elliott half stumbled and staggered the three-eighths of a mile back to his folks' homestead. As he did, he found his heart filling with more and more fear and apprehension for every wobbling step he took, as his eyes filled with the scenes of absolute destruction surrounding him! Finally rounding a small finger of limbless and leafless trees, he got his first look at his homesite or what had been left after the tornado had passed right through the farmhouse and adjacent ranchlands…

Elliott broke out into a torrent of tears when he took his first real look at what remained of his homesite and discovered that his family's cabin in its entirety was no more! There was nothing left except a number of logs scattered around in what had been their front yard from the walls of the cabin and a few partial stone foundation walls! Their nearby barn however, with the exception of most all of its cedar shakes on the roof, was still standing but his home and everything else around, like their outhouse, springhouse, smokehouse, hog pen and chicken coop, was gone! With a barely beating heart, his eyes flooding with tears and growing fear over what he might find of his family members once he got closer, the 16-year-old boy, soon to quickly become a man with what he was now being forced to confront, continued hobbling down the hill towards the remains of his homesite.

Later that afternoon after a lot of looking, Elliott found his baby sister still wrapped up in her blanket with a tree limb driven clear through her smashed little body and slammed up against what was left of the giant oak tree whose limbs and leaves had once sheltered their cabin! His mother was discovered later, draped across a number of limbs in another nearby oak tree, minus both arms and her head! For the next hour, Elliott just lay at the bottom of that tree holding his mother's broken and dismembered body and cried until he found that after a while, he had no more tears to shed! In fact, when he removed her broken body from the tree, Elliott found that he was steeling-up inside with the realization his previous young life was gone and now he must carry on alone with just his memories… Carry on alone because no matter how hard he looked that day, Elliott never found the body of his father! The same went for all of their chickens, hogs, cattle and two milk cows in the area near their now mostly vanished homesite.

All that was now left of Elliott's family was a badly bruised 16-year-old Elliott and his 24-year-old brother, Jacob, who had left home years earlier not wanting to be a farmer like his father, and had gone off to make his fortune in the wild and adventurous fur trade in the wilderness of the West. That afternoon, Elliott found a shovel and buried his mother and baby sister together in the same grave alongside what was left of the great oak in what used to be part of their front yard. Elliott then discovered one petunia that had survived the tornado in his mother's destroyed flower garden and pathetically placed it on the fresh mound of dirt covering her and her shattered baby's body…

Utterly distraught over what the storm had left and emotionally drained by late afternoon, Elliott crawled into the haymow in their still standing barn holding his dad's two horses and four mules, and eventually drifted off into a fitful world of sleep... The next morning, Elliott discovered a lone chicken walking around in his old yard, which had somehow survived the tornado. Waking up to the rooster's crowing calls, Elliott's damaged feet and legs 'told' him that he had not dreamed about what had happened and what he had subsequently witnessed. Staggering out from the barn's haymow, Elliott found a pair of his father's old rubber boots he used when cleaning manure out from the horse and mule stalls, slipped them over his damaged feet and staggered out to meet what was the first day of the rest of his life. Once again, his eyes fell upon the devastation around him and then his eyes filled with the emotion of yesterday's moment in time, which brought him back to the current day's hard and cold reality. Then Elliott saw the lone rooster that had awakened him from his fitful sleep, missing a number of his feathers, pecking away at the lone petunia on his mother's grave and eating the same. That sad moment in time said it all to a young man now devoid of most of the rest of his life's hopes when it came to family...

Elliott later shot that offending rooster and cooked him over an open fire that evening. As if to further the young man's misery over the loss of his entire family save his older brother trapping somewhere out in the West, the rooster was so tough Elliott could hardly eat him. In fact during that sad and lonely supper, Elliott remembered just how good his mother's chicken and homemade noodle suppers used to taste and that brought a further flood of tears over the losses he had suffered. After his miserable chicken supper that evening, Elliott found a tin of bag balm in the hay barn that his father had used on the udders of their two milk cows, now also long gone in the tornado, and smeared the green-looking soothing greasy mixture over his badly cut and bruised feet and lower legs. Then another fitful night ensued as nightmare after nightmare surfaced in his dream world over the previous two days of his life-changing events.

The following day after Elliott let the two horses and four mules out in the morning to pasture and water, a revelation dawned on him. That day was his birthday and now he had just turned 17! Suffice to say, that was a birthday he would long remember... That was also the day Elliott finally came to grips with the fact that life as he once knew it was now long gone. Aside from his fur trapper brother who was hopefully still alive and hundreds of miles away, he had to move on if he wanted to find him and reunite once again as a family. However, to do so, he would need something more than a badly torn buckskin shirt, ragged looking pants, two riding horses, four plow mules, an old pair of his father's rubber boots, and a borrowed rifle, now his, if he wanted to move on with his life...

An hour later found Elliott with his shovel out in what used to be his mother's vegetable garden, digging up and around the fence posts still standing that had originally been used to support a wooden split-rail fence, now long gone thanks to the tornado. Many times in his earlier life he had heard his father talking about his "Posthole Bank". Over the years of hearing his folks talking about their Posthole Bank, Elliott finally came to realize what his folks were talking about. He finally figured that since there were few if any banks near their homestead and that his father did not trust those he knew of to safely keep what few dollars he had accumulated through crop and cattle sales, he had instituted his own system of 'banking', namely, a Posthole Bank.

With that in mind, Elliott spent the rest of his day digging fruitlessly around a number of posts hoping to find whatever existed in his father and mother's Posthole Bank. That he did because having no other close at hand living relatives that he knew of to help, he figured he would head west, join the fur trappers in the wilderness and in so doing, go looking for his brother Jacob in order to begin his life anew. But in order to do that, Elliott figured he would need some money to get started and provide for such travel out west. True, he had four mules he could sell but figured if there was any money in that Posthole Bank thing, he would avail himself of those resources as well to help him get a new start in life. Especially when it came to his travel, new clothing and much needed provisions for survival out west on the extreme frontier.

On Elliott's third day of digging up every remaining standing post on his folks' property, he had found nothing of interest but one hell of a huge-sized underground nest of pissed-off bumble bees and a mess of earthworms! Returning to his barn that evening and having eaten the last of his open fire roasted, tough as a horseshoe nail rooster chicken, he figured he might as well as move on with his life the next day, since there was nothing left on the home place for him unless he wanted to look at the backside of a mule every day for the rest of his life in order to make a living.

Then he saw it! There was only one post left standing on his folks' property that he had not previously dug up and he now spied it. Next to where the old outhouse once stood, there remained one lone cedar post standing all by itself. It was holding nothing up and was just standing there all by its 'lonesome' next to the 'borehole' of his family's outhouse. A family outhouse that had been lifted up by the tornado and vaporized, along with everything in the borehole as well… Grabbing up his shovel again, Elliott walked over to the post by their old outhouse and stood there, realizing just how foolish he had been over the last few days digging up every old post his father had sunken into the ground around their homestead. Shaking his head in disbelief of what he was doing one more time in possibly chasing a Posthole Bank fantasy, Elliott thrust his shovel into the ground around the old post soon to be removed and began digging. As he did, he noticed that the soil was looser around that post more so than any of the others he had dug up. Pulling up the now loosened post, Elliott continued digging until he had a hole dug down about two feet deep. About to give up in disgust and tired of smelling the tornado splattered-around 'poo' from the well-used outhouse, he thrust his shovel downward one more time in resignation and disgust.

It was then that the tip of his shovel made a loud 'clunking' sound when it hit something solid! Figuring with his luck it was just a rock, Elliott continued digging. Within moments, his shovel had partially unearthed what appeared to be the side of an old earthenware crock! Continuing to dig with a little more enthusiasm, Elliott finally unearthed a three-gallon earthenware crock with a heavy lid. Digging deeper so he could get his hands underneath the crock in order to lift it up out from the hole, Elliott was finally able to get his hands under the crock and attempt lifting it out from the hole. To his surprise, he found that he could not lift the crock from out of the hole because of its heavy weight!

Frustrated over the weight of the crock, Elliott took the tip of his shovel and pried off the crock's heavy lid. When he did, he almost fell into the hole he had just dug in amazement over what he was seeing... The three-gallon crock was almost clear full of silver dollars! Old Spanish silver dollars to be exact... Hardly believing his eyes, Elliott began dragging out handfuls of silver dollars and laying them alongside the hole until the crock was light enough so he could lift out the whole thing. Then just sitting down in amazement over what he was seeing, Elliott realized he had finally solved the mystery of his folks' Posthole Bank. Apparently over the years, his folks had been hoarding what dollars they had generated in crop, egg, butter, cream and livestock sales, and had been saving them up to buy more land, a larger herd of cattle or both.

Then it quietly dawned on Elliott that his parents were 'speaking to him from the grave' and giving him what he needed in order to start his new life on the Western frontier! In short, 'they' were giving him the wherewithal to begin anew, go forth and find his brother. Sitting there quietly in wonder, Elliott found his eyes once again misting up over his recent family losses, the great unknown facing him and now the magnitude of the quest to go into an almost unlimited wilderness land looking for one individual, namely his brother! Wiping his eyes so he could see better, Elliott began counting out the number of silver dollars. Seven-hundred and ninety-one Spanish silver dollars later, Elliott found himself looking upon a fortune in that day and age and now it was his!

Even in his young mind of just barely 17 years, he could see an omen of life in his chance discovery of that hoard of silver dollars. Realizing what he had just discovered and its extreme value, he quickly looked all around him to see if anyone else had seen what he had just uncovered. An hour later the Spanish silver dollars were hidden under a mound of hay in the barn, as Elliott made a supper from a cotton-tail rabbit he had shot hiding near their old barn. (Author's Note: At the edge of the western wilderness of the United States into the middle 1800's, the occurrence, use and acceptance of Spanish silver dollars left over from their earlier days of commerce when Spain owned the Louisiana Territory, was commonplace. Until the transfer of ownership of Louisiana from Spain to France in 1800-03, and then later to the United States by purchase from France in 1803, minted silver dollars from Spain during the heyday of the fur trade were still fairly commonly utilized in local commerce in large quantities that far west in the St. Louis area. Hence the common use of Spanish silver dollars as a medium of exchange because they were a form of hard, valuable and historically accepted currency, and because U.S. silver coinage during that time period on the Western frontier was scarce.)

The next day found Elliott with his horse and a trailing pack mule sporting panniers tied up to the hitching rail in front of Bailey's Country Store in Weldon Spring. Walking in the front door, Elliott was happily greeted by Don Bailey, Proprietor, saying how glad he was to see him after the storm and asking him how his folks and their property had fared when the big tornado came through. Elliott quietly replied that all of his kin had perished and he had yet to find his father's body. With those words, other folks gathered in the store shopping for their post-storm needs, got quiet out of respect for what Elliott had just shared with the proprietor.

"What are you going to do now, Boy?" asked Don.

"Since I have nothing left other than my folks' land, I plan on moving on after I take care of a few administrative issues related to that land," said Elliott flatly, not wanting to talk about it as he began looking at a stack of pants on a shelf since his had been torn mostly to sheds during the tornado as he lay in his cave shelter.

"Where are you going to go, Boy?" asked Don.

"I am going west into the fur trade and try and find my brother," said Elliott, as he laid two pairs of pants on the counter and then walked over to where the shirts were hung on a rack and began looking for several that were suitable in his size.

"What is going to happen to your place?" asked Don, as he continued peppering Elliott with questions.

"I aim to keep it. My Ma and sister are buried there next to where our cabin used to sit and I am sure my father's bones are out there on our land somewhere where the tornado dropped him as well. So I aim to keep it since it is paid for and my family is buried there. I aim to have our neighbor and family close friend farm and watch over my father's land until I return. Who knows, if I survive the fur trade and can find my brother, we both may come back, take it up once again, farm and live there," said Elliott, as he began looking at and then trying on a set of boots since all he had for footwear after the tornado had 'eaten' his moccasins was a pair of over-size rubber boots once belonging to his father.

"Damn, Boy! How are you going to pay for all of what you are stacking up on my counter?" asked Don with somewhat of a nosy and disbelieving edge beginning to show in his voice, knowing the young man shopping in his store was now more than likely without 'means'.

"I will manage. Now if you be so kind, I would like to take a look at that there heavy winter coat since I lost all of my clothing to that tornado," quietly replied Elliott.

By now, most of the people in the store were beginning to look at all the things Elliott was stacking up on the counter and wondering how a young man his age, without any folks or other means of support, was going to pay for such a mound of items. Then Elliott began picking out for purchasing several three-legged frying pans, two Dutch ovens, a coffee pot, all followed up with a slab of bacon, some coffee, sugar, metal cups, plates and some other cooking utensils. Then walking over to a glass-covered counter, he picked up for purchasing another cutting and gutting knife, a whetstone for sharpening his knives, along with fairly new Hawken, single-shot percussion, .52 caliber 'horse pistol' bullet molds, powder horn, wadding, ball starter, two tins of powder, two tins of No. 11 percussion caps, and 50 pre-cast .52 caliber-sized balls for the handgun he was about to purchase. Then remembering what he wanted to do with his farmland, he also requested from Don four sheets of writing paper and a pencil.

With those next to last selections of expensive weaponry, the busy-bodies in the store in a nosy sort of way quietly clustered around the front of the store to see how the young man without any visible means of support since the tornado had destroyed his farm and killed his kin, was going to pay for such a large and expensive set of purchases.

"That ought to do it for now," said Elliott quietly, as Don began ciphering out on paper with a pencil what Elliott owed for all the goods the young man needed to purchase.

After a few more moments ciphering, Don looked up from his figures saying, "That comes to $43.77, Elliott. How do you want to pay?" he asked with a quizzical look spreading across his face, realizing coming up with such a large sum of money was not easily done, especially from a now homeless kid with no kin to back him in such endeavors.

With several busy-bodies still looking on, their eyes got as large as dinner plates when Elliott took out 44 Spanish silver dollars from his shoulder carry-pouch and laid them on Don's counter in a glittering pile that was such, even the devil would have turned his head! *In fact, the devil did turn his head and that of several of his henchmen...*

"Whooo-ee! Where the hell, Boy, did you come by all of those Spanish silver dollars?" asked Don in amazement and with more than just a touch of greed ringing in the edge of his voice. When he spoke out in amazement over what he was seeing, Don also managed to get the nosy attention of everyone within hearing distance in his store as well...

Then realizing he probably never should have purchased all of those items in Don's local store but should have waited and purchased them elsewhere because of the obvious 'money-factor' issue, Elliott just quietly lied saying, "I earned them dollars over the years working for other folks who needed a strong back who knew how to chop and split their winter's supply of wood," he replied. Realizing his mistake in displaying a small hoard of silver dollars in front of the area's poorer residents, especially Don who was known for being slightly crooked in many of his dealings with the locals, Elliott swore at his stupidity under his breath for doing what he just did.

Don just continued looking at Elliott in disbelief, then quietly and without further fanfare, made change and returned those change coins to Elliott. But as he did, Elliott could see a strange look appearing in Don's eyes like he had never seen before in his dealings with the man over the years... Elliott then loaded his purchases into the panniers on his pack mule and left to go back to his hay barn. There he unpacked his purchases and placed them into the barn for safekeeping. Taking out his new pistol, one just like his father used to own and had taught him how to use, he went outside and began becoming familiar with its particular workings, including the loading and shooting at targets out behind the barn until he was comfortable with its mechanical, loading, shooting and aiming characteristics.

Then building an outside firepit behind the barn, Elliott began breaking in his cast iron cookware with grease from the full slab of bacon he had purchased at Don's store. Later that evening, Elliott sat out by his firepit after a supper of fried bacon and coffee and tried to remember what his mother and father's voices sounded like. Tearing up again over such thoughts, he wiped his eyes, let his outside fire burn out and then just sat there by the coals listening to see if he could possibly hear on the wind the voices of his mother and father once again or the soft cooing of his baby sister being excited over seeing him leaning over her in her crib...

Wrapping himself up in a couple of smelly horse blankets later that evening, Elliott crawled into a pile of hay at the back of the barn in one of the mule's stalls and after a long while lying there and thinking back over what he had lost in the way of his family members and his hopes and dreams, Elliott finally found a restless sleep. A restless sleep that comes from suffering a great human tragedy and the deep hurt and the collateral loss in one's soul such as Elliott was now suffering.

Around midnight, "SQUEAK" went a rusty hinge on one of the barn's doors as it was slowly opened! Having just minutes earlier gotten up and relieved himself at the back of the barn, the squeaking barn door's hinge found Elliott more than wide awake back at his sleeping stall over the mystery noise at the front door of his barn! Moments later, barely discernible in the reflected outside light of a half moon, Elliott could see the shadowy figures of two men carrying rifles entering his barn and slowly moving in his direction towards the back of the barn as if quietly looking for something or someone!

Quietly reaching over and feeling the comforting steel of his father's rifle standing up in the corner of the mule's stall where he had been sleeping earlier, Elliott wrapped his fingers around it and brought it up to his shoulder in preparation for any evil that might be coming his way! As he did, he found his heart racing just like it had done when he was almost dragged out from his small cave as the tornado had closely passed by his place of shelter just days earlier. Then he heard the whispered words, "Do you see that bastard anywhere, Don?" asked by a familiar sounding voice.

"No, but keep your voice down. If he is in here he will hear you and probably shoot first and ask questions later," said a voice that Elliott recognized as that of Don, the proprietor from their local country store in Weldon Spring! The one and same man who had given him a very strange, almost one of a greedy look, when he had paid for the goods he needed with a small hoard of Spanish silver dollars. "He may be just a kid now having just lost all of his kin and all but I am here to tell you, I have seen that boy shoot at a number of our local annual turkey shoots. If he gets a line of sight bead on you, you had better have well-developed angel wings," continued Don's hushed voice in the darkness of the barn.

"You sure he is in here?" came the familiar voice again that Elliott just couldn't put a name to.

"Don't know but the way I figure it, that kid won't be far away from all them Spanish silver dollars that he claims to have earned doing odd jobs and the one and same hoard that we aim to have for ourselves," replied Don, as the two men slowly walked by the darkened stall Elliott was hiding in obviously looking for him! As the two men slowly sneaked their ways past where Elliott was quietly standing at the back of his sleeping stall in the barn's pitch black darkness, the end of his Pennsylvania rifle was coldly trained on the dark shadow he figured was that of Don, his now ex-friend! Little did Elliott realize at the time, he was now rapidly being transformed from that of a lost and hurting young man into the world of that of an adult, whether he was ready for such a life-altering change or not...

"Maybe we ought to try the outhouse and see if the coins are cleverly hidden in that area. That is if it is still standing after that damn tornado went through the farm," said the strange voice. It was when those last words were spoken by the strange voice that Elliott recognized who was doing the talking. It was Caleb Jackson, the one and same neighbor who used to let his cattle and hogs run wild and in so doing, were found many times destroying his father's growing corn and wheat fields. The same neighbor that Elliott's father had little use for because of his slovenly habits, absence of humanity and lack of care or control over his livestock! With that realization coldly sinking into his inner being, Elliott quietly swung the end of his rifle barrel away from Don the country store owner, onto the darkened shape of Caleb and as he did, his trigger finger tightened in case the man turned and decided to investigate the darkened mule stall in which Elliott now steadfastly stood…

"OK, that outhouse suggestion of yours sounds like it might be a good one because he sure as hell isn't here in this here stinking of skunk smells barn and if he is, we would never see or find him in this damn dark barn anyway," whispered Don.

"Maybe we ought to set this damn old barn a-fire and smoke the kid out if he is hiding somewhere inside," said Caleb. "If we did, I doubt he would exit this here barn if it were on fire without that sack of Spanish silver you keep talking about. Then it would be ours to share and we could let that damn kid just burn up in the barn and we would be done with him and any questions our neighbors or the law might have regarding his disappearance," he continued. Then Caleb's voice droned on without waiting for Don's response to his 'barn burning' statement saying, "I aim to take all of his old man's cattle once we are through here and if nothing else, they should account for a few Spanish coins into our pockets from our neighbors who don't care where those cattle came from."

"And if we did and he burned up in the flames, how the hell would the two of us get our hands on all of that Spanish silver I know either he or his old man had squirreled away somewhere," said Don with a lilt of disgust in his voice over what his partner in crime was stupidly suggesting.

With that, the two armed men quietly left the barn for where they remembered the old outhouse stood so they could check it out. Relieved, Elliott sneaked off and retrieved his pistol from the back of the barn where he had left it on the stack of the rest of his scant provisions after his earlier practice shooting session. Then with a loaded pistol in hand since he potentially had two human targets to contend with since his rifle was a single shot, Elliott crawled back into the corner of his stall and waited in case the two would-be thieves looking for his silver dollars came back for him once again. Elliott again realized how foolish he had been in bringing all of that attention to what he had in the way of the coin of the realm into Don's store. He now realized he should have waited and spent that money in another town and then kept moving on so no one would be any the wiser regarding the wealth in silver dollars that he now possessed. As it turned out, the two men never came back that evening but left empty-handed. Little did either of those two men realize just how close they had come to meeting their Maker that morning in the cool darkness of the barn!

Realizing what he was now facing in the way of thieving neighbors who would hunt him down for his newfound wealth, Elliott figured it was just a matter of time before they returned and then what? Especially if the two men came back trying to steal his silver and he had to kill them to prevent them from doing so. Elliott then came to the sudden realization that if that happened, he would then have to deal with the kinfolk of those he had killed who would then be out after his hide as a matter of family pride and revenge. Either way, he would be figuratively looking at a 'snapping turtle in the mouth' were he to continue living in the barn at his parents' old home place...

The next morning right at daylight, Elliott was on his horse and speeding towards his nearest neighbor's homestead. Reining up in front of the man's barn where he could see Captain Elias Jacobson, his father's old commanding officer when he had served in the French and Indian Wars, working with his four boys. Elliott stepped from his saddle, removed some paper and pencil from one of his saddlebags and then walked over and warmly greeted the retired Army officer and family friend.

"Good morning, Elliott. I was sorry to hear about the passing of your folks and younger sister in the tornado. What can I do for you, Son?" asked Captain Jacobson.

"Captain Jacobson, I am getting ready to leave and go find my older brother. But when I do, I need to leave my father's farm, all 1,000 acres in good hands. My father always spoke highly of you and the good friend that you were and with that in mind, I have a proposition for you. I would like you and your sons to farm my land until I return. I am prepared to propose the two of us sign a "Transfer of Farming Rights and Transfer of Land" document that is good for a ten-year period or if and when until I return sometime in between. I would expect you to keep up any land taxes and in return, farm or raise cattle on my land as you chose for your own profit. Is that the kind of document you would find fair and be willing to sign?" asked Elliott, acting way beyond his 17 years of age.

"Holy cow, Elliott! Are you sure that is what you want to do?"

"Yes, Sir. My father respected and trusted you and so do I. I have the documents all written up and if you are in agreement to my terms and conditions, we can both sign them this day and make the temporary transfer of rights, right here and now," said Elliott.

Later riding back to his family's barn, Elliott took out his copy of the signed transfer agreement, folded it up and placed it inside a tobacco tin sealed with candle wax. Then he placed the tobacco tin inside a sealed earthenware crock and buried it on the northeast corner of his barn for later retrieval, if and when he survived his peregrinations out west in an effort to become a fur trapper and locate and reunite with his older brother.

Well, in light of his previous night's suspicious encounter, Elliott's father didn't raise a fool... By daylight the next morning so as to avoid a repeat nighttime encounter with those after his hoard of Spanish dollars, the 17-year-old kid, acting more like a man each passing hour, had packed and loaded his mules with his gear, mounted his riding horse, and trailing his animals who were also carrying his silver fortune, was on the road leading away from Weldon Spring and heading eventually for the city of St. Louis. There he figured he would outfit up with what he would need for an extended stay in the West trapping beaver and commence looking for his older brother. Elliott didn't know how to trap anything other than the skunks that always lived in his father's barn, but he figured he could team up with someone who knew what to do and then Elliott would be able to go forth into the wilderness, learn the trade of a fur trapper and become a Mountain Man. Little did Elliott realize the travails he would soon be facing leading such a rough and tumble life, not to mention surviving a dangerous existence out on the Western frontier, surrounded by fierce Indians who did not want any white men out there on their hunting grounds. Little did Elliott realize that the dangerous part of jumping from that of a young man into that of an adult in the sometimes violent West was a lot closer than he ever imagined and even more dangerous than he dreamed.

Pushing his stock train hard the next morning down the road so he and they would be long gone before anyone realized what had happened, Elliott headed southeasterly in the pre-dawn darkness towards the town of Creve Coeur in order to be rid of any nosy or thieving neighbors found in the Weldon Spring area. However in so doing, little did he realize just how easy it would be when it came to tracking several horses and mules all intermixed because of their different 'horseshoe' tracks. Especially if one was of an evil mind and an inclination to do so in order to come away Spanish silver rich...

Arriving in a secluded wooded area later in the day next to a stream, Elliott swung off the road into the timber and made camp. Hobbling his horses and mules, Elliott let them feed along the stream in the rich grasses found bankside while he built a small campfire and began making preparations for frying up some more of his slab bacon and heating up a pot of coffee. As he waited for some coals to develop so he could slow cook his bacon in his three-legged frying pan, Elliott made up his sleeping area under a dense stand of elderberry bushes a short distance away from his campfire. That way if the forming storm clouds in the northwest produced any rain, he and his sleeping gear would not get so wet by being under the covering vegetative canopy of the elderberry bushes. Then he stacked his riding and packsaddles near his sleeping area along with his mules' panniers and the rest of his provisions. Those items were soon covered with a canvas and by then, the coals in his campfire had burned down just enough for cooking his bacon up in his three-legged frying pan with its short legs without burning. Soon the night air around his campsite smelled pleasantly of frying bacon and fresh steaming coffee.

After his supper of wiggly, partially-cooked bacon just the way he liked it and several cups of steaming hot coffee, Elliott sat by the ebbing warmth of his campfire. There he watched the coals slowly burn down and begin dying out, thereby reducing the light around his campsite to just a warm glow. Sitting there in the quiet of the night, the ghosts of past times in Elliott's young life now began manifesting themselves throughout his thoughts. As he now saw it, all that remained from a good frontier life now past were two riding horses, four plow mules, a hoard of Spanish silver dollars, and a wealth of happy family memories. Then there was a flooding wealth of additional memories of his mother's soft voice and the many good smells emanating from her kitchen, especially when she made her wonderful homemade bread and pies. Those memories were soon replaced with those of his sister's soft cooing sounds and quick smiles that always appeared on her face when she saw Elliott leaning over and peering into her crib as he talked to her. Those flooding thoughts were soon followed with the rapidly fading memories of an older brother who always took time teaching a younger Elliott the finer points of hunting, picking up the great-eating snapping turtles without losing a finger, and how to tease a catfish out from its subterranean place of hiding in a slow-moving stream and onto a freshly baited hook. Lastly swirling around Elliott were those memories of his father and his constant teachings of his two boys about the finer points of frontier survival based on his military experiences fighting Indians on the frontier, belief in a supreme being, celebrating their own special Jewish religion, and the finer points of enjoying a good chew of some of their very own home-grown tobacco. It was then that Elliott, during those 'memory interludes', realized tears were once again streaming down his young face as the ghostly 'whispers' and fears of going it alone began manifesting themselves and in so doing, overrode the pleasant memories of the previous happy years he had once been sheltered and lived.

Almost ashamed at himself for still crying over something that no longer could be helped, Elliott quickly wiped the telltale moisture from the cheeks of his face with his shirt sleeve, grabbed his near at hand rifle, arose and headed for his sleeping gear stashed under the nearby dense stand of elderberry bushes. Laying his rifle down alongside his bedding as a learned matter of course, he returned to his horses and mules' picket line to make sure everything was still tightly tied off and secure. Satisfied with that important task, Elliott returned to his sleeping area. Crawling back under the overhanging elderberry limbs and nestling himself comfortably onto the dense layer of dropped dried leaves from past seasons as Nature's mattress, Elliott did as his father had taught him when out and about on the frontier. He reached out and placed his rifle within easy reach in case he was menaced in the night by a bear, and placed his new loaded pistol by his head in case he was about to be mortally bothered by one of his own kind. Slipping under his horse blankets after experiencing a hard emotional day in leaving his old home place, his buried remnants of his found family after the sweep of the tornado across his farm and his many years of happiness behind him maybe forever, Elliott slipped off into an exhausted and restless sleep. That Elliott did to the soothing sounds of a nearby gurgling creek flowing over its many rocks and small waterfalls…

"Do you see that little bastard anywhere?" whispered Caleb Jackson, as he sneaked into the edge of Elliott's darkened campsite after spending the day tracking an obviously intermixed trail of horse and mule tracks fleeing from the Weldon Spring area and heading southeasterly on the backcountry trails…

"Sure don't, but this time the little bastard is not going to leave us with our asses in our hands like he did earlier this morning when he skipped town afore we was ready to confront him and take away what is rightfully ours," replied Don.

With that, the two men sneaked silently past Elliott's picketed horses and mules and into his campsite proper, with any noises they were making being covered up by the sounds of the nearby flowing stream. Now that they were in Elliott's main campsite, the two men who had been trailing him since just after daylight once they realized Elliott had surprised them and had left his homesite even earlier, carried their rifles in an obvious 'deadly ready for any kind of action' position. With Caleb and Don carrying their rifles at the ready just in case they surprised Elliott and not wanting to take any chances, they were prepared to finally put a deadly mortal end to their hunt for the fabled stash of Spanish silver carried by the now homeless young man.

"Over there! I can see where he is sleeping over there under those bushes," hissed Caleb excitedly, as he pointed his rifle barrel in the direction in which he was looking for his partner-in-crime's benefit!

"Remember what I said about his shooting ability," whispered Don. "Make sure he does not have a chance to go for his rifle," he continued in a hushed and yet emotion-filled whisper, as he now also quietly headed in the direction in which Caleb was pointing his rifle barrel.

Caleb and Don in crouched-over sneak positions cautiously approached Elliott's sleeping blankets as the young man they were stalking lay mounded up under the elderberry bushes, sleeping heavily and not moving.

"Now!" yelled Caleb once they got close, as he fired in tandem with Don into the sleeping, mounded-up Elliott at such close range that the fire from the end of their rifle barrels blew forth and set fire to Elliott's old horse blanket sleeping covers!

KA-POW! went a single shot from a steadily held horse pistol from behind the bushes as its .52 caliber, heavy half-ounce lead slug tore into the side of Caleb's face with such force that once he hit the ground, even his beloved mother who spawned him would not have recognized or been able to have identified the exploded face of her once loved son!

BOOM! went a .33 caliber bullet quickly fired from a Pennsylvania rifle into a surprised and just standing there in amazement with a now empty rifle over what had just happened to his partner in crime, Don Bailey. After dropping his pistol once he had killed Caleb, Elliott hastily shouldered his rifle and fired into

Don's chest! The bullet fired from Elliott's rifle at such close range into Don's nearby chest tore through his heart and spine and then out the back side of his now falling body and smacked hard into the side of an American chestnut tree growing across the nearby creek!

It took a few minutes for Elliott's horses and mules to settle down after being so surprised by the four nearby explosions of quick firing weapons! However for Elliott, as he stepped out from behind the elderberry bushes where he had been hiding after hearing two horses reining up nearby and then seeing there were now two darkened figures making their ways through the nearby trees and bushes towards his campsite, then having to defend himself, he had other more important things on his mind. He had to quickly put out the fire on his sleeping blankets started when the two men had fired their rifles at point blank range into what they had figured was the sleeping figure of a young man underneath named Elliott Sutta. Elliott did so because he needed those horse blankets to sleep under in future nights while out on the trail. Plus, he didn't want the two packsaddles he had quickly placed under his bedcovers to look like he was sleeping there, to burn up as well because he may have need for them in the future to pack supplies. Or to hide them once again under his sleeping covers to make them look like there was a man sleeping underneath in order to fool anyone else looking to sneak up on him in the dark of the night and foolish enough to try and kill him where he slept…

However, once Elliott had put out his bedding fire, like his father had taught him he grabbed up his rifle and pistol and hastily reloaded them both so they would be ready to face any other oncoming dangers like a hungry varmint looking for a meal or a human varmint looking to cause him bodily harm. Then Elliott calmly stoked up the coals from his evening's fire, put on the coffee to boil and then he dragged off two dead and useless humans 50 yards away from his campsite for the varmints to find and enjoy. Then Elliott wandered off into the wood's darkness until he discovered the location of the two riding horses that had brought the two would-be killers into his camp and brought them over to where his livestock was picketed. Once there, Elliott tied off his two newest riding horses...

By now, Elliott's coffee was boiling away, so he sat the pot off on a rock to cool and began saddling up his horses and loading the packsaddles and panniers onto his mules. Then it was time for a few quiet moments around his campfire to savor his coffee, as the daylight began showing the rest of his world the start of 'a new day' to the east. Sitting there quietly, Elliott once again listened to see if he could hear any ghosts from his recent past reaching out to speak to him regarding his emergence into a 'new day' in the rest of his life. All he could hear was the far off four-note hooting call of a great horned owl and the leaves rustling in the trees as the morning's sun began heating up the earth and in so doing, brought forth a new day's soft breezes. A new day's breezes in the life of a 'young man' named Elliott Sutta, about to seek his fortune and destiny on the Western frontier as a Mountain Man and a 'young man' other than in his memory no more. As Elliott trailed his livestock out from the area that had just been the scene of deadly violence, a revelation and a reformation all in the same life-changing moment, he could hear what sounded like a sow black bear with two yearling cubs 50 yards away in the forest, fighting over a newfound 'breakfast' that someone had graciously left for them...

CHAPTER TWO: THE ODYSSEY BEGINS AND "FRIENDS"?

By noon on his second day of travel, Elliott found himself leading his string of horses and mules into the city of St. Louis from the west side. Never having been there in his life, he found himself amazed at all the new sights and sounds he was experiencing. The city streets were crowded with people going to and fro, the smells emanating from the city in general and surrounding industry befuddled one's nose, especially one who had lived in the clean air of the country all of his life, and the pace of human activity around Elliott almost fogged his mind. However, one place he rode by caught his eye and soon his livestock was tied up to the hitching rails in front of the huge, important looking building.

Moments later after unloading one of his mule's panniers and lifting out a heavy sack, Elliott struggled into the building with the sign high overhead proudly proclaiming, "First Mercantile Bank of St. Louis". Walking up to a bank clerk at an empty window, Elliott with some difficulty plopped his tote sack of Spanish silver dollars upon the counter with a heavy 'clinking' sound. Twenty minutes later, Elliott walked back out the door of the bank with a booklet in hand announcing that of a new patron with a bank account holding 300 Spanish silver dollars... It may not have been as secure as his father's Posthole Bank but being on the move like he expected to be as a future Mountain Man, that bank seemed to be the best solution for holding his heavy sack of silver coins. Plus if they were out of sight and mind, there would be no temptation for any of those he rode with in the future to get interested in the coins and light-fingered in dealing with them as well. With the remaining balance of Spanish silver dollars comfortably residing in his leather carry pouch, Elliott mounted back up onto his riding horse and began riding and trailing his livestock down the street looking for another specialized facility, as he had been instructed to do by the friendly bank clerk.

A half-hour later, Elliott had boarded his four riding horses and four mules in "Marshal Davis's Livery", which just happened to be right next door to "Ma Silvia Davis's Boarding House and Eatery". Because Elliott had not eaten anything since the night before, he found figuratively speaking, that 'his big guts were eating the little ones', so into the great smelling eatery he walked and was instantly met with many smells of sweat and filth from its many patrons, to the other great smells of pies being baked in the kitchen smelling just like those his mother used to make. Finding an empty table, he stood his Pennsylvania long rifle up against a nearby wall and was soon met by a Miss Betsy Davis, daughter of Ma Silvia, the proprietor as he later discovered, and ordered his breakfast. Several minutes later, his table was stacked high with pancakes, plates of wiggly bacon just as he liked it, hot coffee and a fresh from the oven blackberry pie! Never had Elliott seen such mounds of food and it didn't take him long to make little mounds of the big mounds that had been set before him…

But that was not what caught his eye as he was finishing his breakfast. Sitting just two tables away were five very heavily bearded men wearing buckskin clothing from head to toe. Their rifles were stacked against a nearby wall and were of a make and model that he had never seen before. Instead of being long and slender-barreled like that of his late father's Pennsylvania rifle, they were shorter in length, had a heavier octagonal-shaped barrel and instead of being a flintlock, they appeared to have a different firing mechanism that did not use a flint and flash pan system of ignition.

Intrigued over what he was seeing and realizing they must be the Mountain Man fur trappers he had heard so much about, Elliott carefully scanned their faces to see if one of the heavily bearded men was that of his long-lost brother, Jacob. Seeing the fur trappers, Elliott found that he was no longer interested in his almost finished breakfast and the 'big guts eating the little guts' situation, as he continued staring intently at the hard-looking and obviously seasoned fur trappers. All of the men appeared to be wearing at least two pistols, sporting a very obvious well-used tomahawk and a long-bladed sheath knife, whose knife sheath was made from what appeared to be a beaver's tail and was very heavily and colorfully beaded. Their moccasins were also heavily beaded as were their buckskin shirts. They were such magnificent specimens of Western men that Elliott could hardly take his eyes off them, as he found himself impolitely staring at the unusual looking men.

Then one of the fur trappers sensing they were being closely examined, turned and said, "What the hell are you looking at, Little Man?" said one of the men Elliott was staring at, who was sporting a massive beard with a mass of head hair that would have made a grizzly bear proud to be wearing.

Surprised over being caught staring which was not polite in that day and age, Elliott stammered out the words, "Sorry. I just have never seen anyone dressed like you fellas before."

"Well, when you get through looking, you can fill your bags underneath as well," continued "Bear Face" in a rough and sharp tone of voice, designed to warn Elliott off from what he had been doing.

Surprised over the giant of a man's reaction to Elliott's gawking, Elliott replied once again, "Sorry, I didn't mean to offend." Then Elliott turned away and began finishing his breakfast pie. That was when all of a sudden a large and dark shadow moments later fell across Elliott's breakfast table and when he looked up in surprise, he was further amazed in seeing one of

31

the fur trappers from the next set of tables standing over him looking kindly down at him.

"Don't mind him, Son. He ain't got no manners when it comes to being civil. In fact, if he ain't out roughing up a 'griz', he ain't happy. Name's "Muskrat". Well, that's what I am called anyways by my fellow trappers and friends. My given name by my now long-dead and beloved mother, bless her heart, is William Jackson Price. But as I said, my friends call me Muskrat. What's your 'handle', Son?" he asked in a soft tone of voice.

Still a little in shock over what was happening, Elliott squeaked out, "My name is Elliott Sutta and I am from Weldon Spring."

"Damn, Boy! You any relation to Jacob Sutta?" asked Muskrat in a surprised tone of voice.

For a moment, Elliott's heart skipped a beat or two upon hearing those words from Muskrat! "Uh, uh, yes! Jacob is my brother and I am looking for him! Do you know where he is?" asked Elliott, hardly able to believe what he was hearing coming from the fur trapper he just had the occasion to meet.

"Yeah, last time I seed him he was at Fort Union with his partner having their *'plus'* (a French word pronounced 'plews') graded and counted," said Muskrat. "You be anything like him, Boy, and you be one 'helluva' man! That man Jacob is part 'griz', part wildcat and part Blackfoot if we be talking about the same person," said Muskrat, with a surprised look still on his face over the 'chance' talking to another man's brother out in the damn middle of civilization.

"Sit down, Mr. Muskrat. Tell me about him because I haven't seen Jacob for over two years now. Now that our mother, father and sister were just killed by a tornado, I am looking for him. I am doing so because I don't have anyone other than my older brother left, and I really need to find him so we can be together again as family now that all of our kin are dead. In fact, I had hoped to go west and become a fur trapper myself. That way I can start a new life and at the same time, look for my brother," said Elliott with a newfound tone of hope rising up in his voice and heart.

"Well hell, Boy! Why don't you throw in with me and the rest of my fellow Free Trappers sitting over there having breakfast at our table? We just had one of our own killed by those murdering savages the Blackfoot jest last summer. In fact, we just came here to sell our furs in order to get a better price than the trading posts offer us out in the wilderness and look for a sixth partner to join up with us. Once we celebrate a little bit and provision-up at St. Louis's cheaper prices, we aim to go back to the Fort Union country and commence trapping beaver on the Upper Missouri, Yellowstone, Gallatin, Porcupine and other rivers, along with other fine furs come this fall as Free Trappers. If you be interested in joining up, let me talk to the rest of my fellow trappers and if you can carry your own share of the load, they may be interested in having you fill in for Bob, the man we jest lost last summer, as part of our crew," said Muskrat with a big welcoming smile on his face.

Elliott could hardly believe his ears over what he was hearing. Here was a chance to throw in with a number of experienced fur trappers, learn the 'trade' from them, eventually become a trapper himself, and maybe find his brother all in the same process! Looking up at Muskrat, Elliott said, "I don't know how to trap beaver or any of those other animals but that is why I came to St. Louis. I was hoping to hook up with some experienced fur trappers, learn the trade as I start my new life now that my folks are dead and maybe find my brother. Yes, I do have my own livestock and the money to outfit up with and would love to join up with you fellas. But I am not sure if they will have me, especially that large fellow with the long hair and huge beard," said Elliott with a sinking heart as he looked back over at the monster of a man, and he seemed to be just as ornery looking now as he was earlier when he caught Elliott gawking at his group of trappers.

"Let me worry about him. You see, Boy, your brother did me a favor once when I was outnumbered by a mess of mean-assed trappers all out having a rip-roaring good time. Being that Jacob stood up for me meant a lot to me and if I can return the favor, I will. Let me go over and talk with my friends and see what they have to say about having a greenhorn joining up with us," said Muskrat.

With that, he returned to his table with his friends, sat down and appeared to be seriously talking over his proposal with them as to Elliott joining up with them. In the meantime, Elliott tried to look all normal-like, as he investigated another slice of Miss Betsy's homemade pie, with his heart racing like his fastest horse over the potential opportunity of being able to join up with a group of experienced fur trappers and head out into the wilds of the frontier.

Then there was a loud roar of laughter coming from the fur trappers' table, as Muskrat rose and walked back over to Elliott. "If you can carry your load of what your share of the provisions would be, provide your own horses and mules along with any clothing and equipment you might need, then you are welcome to join us on our trip back to the Fort Union country and then into the upper reaches of the Upper Missouri and work as one of us. However, you need to be aware of the fact that some of the country we aim to beaver trap is crawling with them murdering Blackfeet and Gros Ventre Indians, killing son-of-a-bitches one and all when it comes to us white men," said Muskrat with a more than serious look on his face.

"I can do that," said Elliott, as his heart seemed to be skipping many beats over what he was now hearing, and he hoped his verbal responses back to Muskrat did not betray the joy and excitement in his voice over the adventure to come providing that he survived. "I already have my own riding horses and pack mules plus some provisions. Plus I have some money to purchase what you fellows think I need to acquire in the way of personal items as well as some money to throw into the 'pot' for what we all will need," continued Elliott with hope more than rising in his heart over what had been proposed and what lay ahead in his future at the hands of living with experienced trappers.

"Good! Now why don't you come on over and meet the rest of the boys and get acquainted," said Muskrat with a big happy grin spread clear across his heavily whiskered face.

Now Elliott really found his heart skipping many beats as he arose and followed Muskrat over to the table holding four other fur trappers, who had more than likely faced death many times in their lives and were now considering taking on a 'greenhorn', teaching him the ropes of being a fur trapper and expecting him to have any of their backs in their times of need as well.

"Boys, this is Elliott Sutta, younger brother to Jacob Sutta, "Wild Bill" McGinty's partner from up on the Big Muddy. Elliott, this here is Jacob Greer who is known to us as "Fish" because he seems to find himself falling in and ending up swimming in the trapping waters all the time. This here is Bob McGoon, also known to us as "Fingers" because he seems to all the time be finding his fingers getting 'whanged' in the traps he is setting more often than not. This here is Randy Stewart, also called "Biscuits" because if there are any Dutch oven biscuits around, he more often than not will have his hands full of them and shoving them into his big mouth two at a time. This last guy, who you already know since he ate your ass out for looking over at him, is called "Bear", whose real name is Jay Peterson. He is called Bear because he is as big as one, looks like one and most of the time because he won't take a bath, smells like one," said Muskrat with a big good-natured grin on his heavily bearded face, to the obvious laughter by the men at the table over the good-natured 'funny' he had just pulled on one of the members of his group…

With those introductions, Elliott shook hands all around and as he did, he looked each man he was introduced to directly into his eyes as his father had taught him to do whenever meeting anyone because the eyes never lied. He had also trained Elliott to make sure that when shaking another man's hand, he made sure that the man shaking his hand knew there was another man on the end of that handshake and not just a kid. That Elliott did that morning, making sure each and every man's hand that he shook in that group of fur trappers knew that he was not afraid of hard work, and his hard calloused handshake spoke volumes to that fact. Additionally, when Elliott shook each man's hand, he made sure that when they looked at him they could see they were dealing with a man despite his young age… However, when Elliott shook the hand of the man they called Bear, Elliott saw a look in his eyes that did not really register. In turn, when Bear looked at Elliott during the handshake, Elliott swore to himself inside that there was a man who was looking clear through him! But at least he smiled when he shook Elliott's hand, even though the look in his eyes did not…

For the next hour, Elliott sat at his new friends' table, drank a little whiskey along with them and got to know a little about the men. Muskrat he had liked right off the bat. He appeared to be open, very woods-wise and was going to make a great friend. As for Biscuits, Elliott found that he was funny with a sunny disposition and going to make an interesting fellow to get to know. Fish on the other hand was quieter than the rest and one that was harder to read. However, Elliott figured in time he would get to know him better and looked forward to the 'quiet one's' friendship. Fingers appeared to be the most serious of the bunch and seemed to have been the one in the group who had the highest number of life-threatening experiences among the lot of men. As for Bear, he was very hard to read, period! He was the leader of the group and it was evident that his word was the law of the land. To Elliott's way of thinking and on-the-spot evaluation, Bear was by far and away the fiercest of the bunch of his new fur trapper friends and on the other hand, felt that he could be the most dangerous if he was ever riled up.

For the next ten days, Elliott worked with his newfound friends making preparations for another year's work in the wilderness in the beaver trapping business. Right off the bat, Bear had all the men's livestock reshod in preparation for another hard year of living and working in the outback. During that process, he made sure each of the men's livestock had an extra set of shoes and nails. He did so when he discovered that Elliott had been taught by his dad to be a 'fair-to-middling' farrier. That way if an animal threw a shoe, they now had someone in their group who could re-shoe the animal in need of new footwear. Then a trip was made by all to several supply houses so worn out panniers could be replaced, and new beaver and wolf traps purchased to replace those previously lost, damaged or no longer useful. They also purchased mounds of dry provisions like beans, rice, dried fruit, flour and spices, which Elliott discovered could be purchased at St. Louis's cheaper prices rather than at the trading posts or rendezvous sites in the wilderness. Additionally, older model firearms and bullet mold blocks were replaced, cookware was replaced, three kegs of powder for all the men's rifles and pistols were purchased, along with tins of percussion caps and lastly several kegs of First Class Rum.

It was during that time that Elliott took time off from the group's preparations to meet with his liveryman and sell two of his father's mules and both of the riding horses that Don and Caleb had ridden into Elliott's camp with evil in their hearts and ended up becoming several meals to a sow black bear and her two hungry cubs. Additionally, the dead men's saddles were also sold to the liveryman who was more than happy with the purchases with no questions asked as to their previous ownership...

Returning to his group of newfound friends and trappers with sale of horse and mule money in his carry bag, along with his remaining Spanish silver dollars (other than what he held back in his St. Louis Posthole Bank account), Elliott made sure he more than provided his share of monetary resources when it came to purchasing the coming year's provisions. That he did because he was the youngest and most inexperienced of the group and wanted to show his newfound friends that even though being the youngest, he could carry a man's share of the load.

It was during one of those purchasing moments that Bear reached out and without warning or asking, took Elliott's Pennsylvania rifle in hand and carefully examined it. Then handing it back to a still surprised Elliott over the man's rather bold act of taking another man's rifle in hand, said, "Muskrat, take this here young fellow over to Jacob and Samuel's gun shop and see to it that he purchases an adequate rifle suitable of use and defense in the backcountry. One that will be sufficient of caliber designed for use out on the frontier, plus make sure he purchases all the other necessaries he will need for sustaining such a weapon once he is in the backcountry. I don't want any of us to fall to them damn savages because this greenhorn can't clear a charging Indian from his saddle with just one shot because he is using a rifle that won't even kill a pissant. Get him a Hawken if there is one available."

Muskrat acknowledged Bear's order with a nod of his head and then said, "Elliott, you and I need to hustle ourselves over to the best gun shop in town to see gunsmiths Jacob and Samuel Hawken and see if they have a newly finished Rocky Mountain Rifle available for sale. If they do, I suggest you trade in your Pennsylvania squirrel rifle for a man's rifle made by those brothers that is more suitable for the rough and tumble routinely found in the wilderness, either afoot or on horseback. Especially when the 'rough and tumble' rears its ugly head when it comes to riding through heavy timber and not hanging the barrel of your rifle up on every darn tree you go by like you will with that long and thin-barreled Pennsylvania rifle."

Elliott, upon hearing those 'trade in your rifle words', was not so sure he wanted to divest himself of one of the only things left that he still possessed that was 'family'. Concerned over what he was hearing, Elliott turned to Muskrat asking, "Muskrat, what is wrong with my Pennsylvania rifle? It served my dad and me up until now very well and did everything asked of it. Why not just save the money from buying another rifle and just keep this one?"

"Well, Elliott, the frontier is very rough on all sorts of gear including any kind of a firearm. Just riding through the dense brush and timber in our trapping areas will find you having all kinds of trouble with managing the control over the rifle you currently possess. First of all, it is delicately made and not really suited to stand up to the rough and tumble wear associated with living out in the wilderness. Second, its caliber is way too light for a many times required one-shot killing of charging buffalo, moose, elk and grizzly bear unless you are good enough to constantly be a 'head-shooter'. And to be quite frank, trying to head-shoot a large and dangerous critter from horseback or when the animal is charging you can be a bit of a challenge, especially when your life or that of a buddy is at stake. Lastly, the long barrel of your Pennsylvania rifle will be a clumsy pain in the ass when trying to ride through dense brush or away from a horde of Indians fresh after your scalp. You will just find that it will hang up on just about everything that you ride by. In short, you will need a rifle like mine if you want to survive fur trapping and all of its problems that occur almost on a daily basis. Like my rifle, you will need a heavy stocked .50 caliber rifle or larger, shooting a half-ounce lead ball behind about 20 or so grains of powder. That way you can easily make one-shot kills on either man or beast. Additionally, you will need one with a barrel length of no longer than 34 inches, so you can ride through heavy timber and brush without it being swept from your hands by every twig or branch. Now look at the heavy design of the barrel of my rifle compared to that of the light construction of yours. Bottom line, you need a rifle with a heavy octagonal barrel in order to survive rough everyday use, one with lower and heavier duty sights than you have on your rifle, preferably with a set trigger for more accurate shooting, and one using a more reliable percussion lock system instead of a flintlock system like you possess. Bear in mind that a flintlock firing system like yours will many times misfire during wet weather. In short, my new friend, if you want the best chance to survive out on the frontier, you better have the best 'smoke-pole' made by mankind, and what Jacob and Samuel Hawken are currently hand making are the best rifles made for us trappers."

Finally realizing his friend Muskrat knew the frontier and its demands made on the fur trapper better than he did, found the two of them somewhat later in a locally recommended gun shop smelling strongly of gun oil, wood smoke from their indoor stove and a pot of coffee that had been boiled too long. There Elliott was introduced by Muskrat to one of the local gunsmiths and gun builder of renown, one Jacob Hawken.

Elliott's friend Muskrat took the lead and explained to Jacob the need for Elliott to 'gun-up' for the demanding task that lay ahead of him as a soon to be fur trapper out in the heart of Indian country. Then stepping back and aware of Elliott's reluctance in trading his father's Pennsylvania rifle, Muskrat let Jacob work his 'selling magic' on the young man fast becoming experienced in the rough and tumble current day world of the fur trapper out on the Western frontier.

"Well, let's see," said Jacob, "where to begin? My brother, Samuel, and I have been in the gun making and repair business since the year of our Lord 1822. As such, we have learned a few things especially on what the fur trappers and buffalo hunters are telling us what they have experienced firsthand the demands the backcountry makes on weaponry and just how tough some of the critters are to kill that you will be going up against. Additionally, our users are telling us that cleaning a hard-charging Indian out from his saddle at over 150 yards with one of our fine long-range shooting rifles has a tendency to warn off the rest of the Indians and change their minds on tangling with our fur trapper or buffalo hunting friends equipped with our rifles. With that information from our users in general and the specific demands from the men afield reporting back to us, my brother and I have developed a new rifle which we call the "Rocky Mountain Rifle", because of its acceptance and now wide use by those making a living in the wilderness. Our new rifle is custom made one at a time, stoutly half-stocked and shorter than a Pennsylvania rifle like the one you are carrying. For example, our rifles are stocked with a hardwood while the wood used on rifles like you possess is maple, a softer wood. That makes the stocks and 'wrists' of our rifles much harder to break in light of the often times hard use found on the frontier. Our Rocky Mountain Rifle is of a heavier caliber than normally found in a number of the rifles commonly in use today and weighs about ten to eleven pounds. With that kind of weight, the rifle has little recoil, which makes the shooter a lot more accurate knowing there is little recoil to follow any shot taken. The rifle is also of the new percussion cap system which allows for quicker reloading and more dependability of firing every time during snowy or rainy weather, because it uses a No. 11, sealed percussion cap instead of a more exposed flash and pan system like on your Pennsylvania rifle. The reports we are getting back from the users in the field are that our rifle's .50 caliber ball behind a hefty charge of black powder, a greased patch and our slow twist rifling, is very capable of making one-shot kills on the elk, moose, buffalo and grizzly bear, many times at ranges out to 300-400 yards! My brother and I have also figured out that by using barrels made of a softer iron, we found a way to reduce black powder fouling considerably, making numerous long-range shots that are very accurate, more than possible. We are also finding that our new rifles made with our double set trigger system, a 33-34-inch barrel, and open blade sight in a .50 caliber, is just the ticket for one who has to carry such a weapon all day long, especially in the fur trade. We have also learned from our users that the system just described is very easily carried on horseback in dense timber and yet capably reaches out to distances of over 300 yards for normal shooting at either really large game animals or the fleet Indians as they come charging in or have surrounded the man with such a weapon. As I said earlier, each of our rifles is individually made by hand by either me or my brother and have a reputation for ruggedness, dependability and long-range accuracy. I don't know what else I can say for our invention other than our rifles will give its user a much better chance at killing a charging bull buffalo or mad as hell grizzly bear with one-shot kills or will clean a mad Indian clear out from his saddle when being struck by a ball from one of our guns," concluded Jacob with a proud look on his face.

The whole time Jacob was telling Elliott about the quality and abilities of their custom made rifles, he could swear he could hear the sixth sense 'frontier survival' urgings of his father in the back of his mind strongly advising him to trade in the older and less modern Pennsylvania rifle, because its better days were over and to do so for one of the newer guns just verbally advertised by

41

St. Louis gunmaker of renown, Jacob Hawken. With a sigh from deep inside of his being, Elliott stepped forward with his father's Pennsylvania rifle and gently laid it on the gunsmith's counter. Then as a final act of parting, Elliott let his hand slide down the rifle's slender barrel and across its scarred wooden stock showing its many years of hard family use. Then letting the tips of his fingers reverently slide slowly off the stock as his final act, he stepped back and prepared himself to meet a new day in the life and times of a fur trapper... A fur trapper who was properly armed and prepared for what the frontier would demand of him.

After stepping out back of the gun shop and firing one of the newer Rocky Mountain Rifles several times at a fixed target in the backyard, shortly thereafter found Elliott confidently purchasing one of the new .52 caliber Hawken rifles, bullet molds, extra ramrod, ball starter, 100 pre-cast lead balls for the rifle, powder, three tins of No. 11 caps, and one with double set triggers for better accuracy. Additionally at the urging of Muskrat, Elliott added a second percussion lock, .52 caliber pistol to his list of normally carried armament identical to the one he had purchased earlier in Don's store with Spanish silver dollars. This he did at Muskrat's urging, especially when it came to purchasing a pistol of the same caliber as that of his new rifle so their balls and percussion caps would be sensibly interchangeable. Additionally, Muskrat pointed out to Elliott that many times the trappers would be encountering superior numbers of hostile Indians. In those situations, carrying an extra pistol in his sash would be an added safety factor when possibly saving one's life in close quarter battles with the Indians. Then with a funny feeling still in his heart, Elliott consummated the deal in trading in his father's Pennsylvania .33 caliber musket for a .52 caliber Hawken Rocky Mountain Rifle and a like caliber Hawken pistol, along with some silver to cover the difference in cost, to aid in the beginning of his new life out on the frontier.

Two days later, Bear led his contingent of fur trappers and trailing livestock out from the civilization in St. Louis and into the wilds of the new frontier. As he did, he headed his contingent of fur trappers up the Mississippi River along its western bank until they arrived at the junction of the Missouri River. There they left the mighty Mississippi and headed in a northwesterly direction up the Missouri River, traveling all the while along its western bank. For the next month of their travels, the contingent of six heavily armed fur trappers, their six extra riding horses who were lightly packed and eight heavily packed mules continued moving in a northwesterly direction towards their eventual destination of Fort Union, located near the headwaters of the Missouri River.

Travel through the country constantly kept the party of trappers always within sight of numerous herds of buffalo, elk and even bands of bighorn sheep and antelope. Numerous times grizzly bears were sighted along the way feasting on buffalo carcasses or grazing on the luxurious stands of grasses along the river bottoms. However, because they were deep in Indian country, the fur trappers made sure their evening camps were located in the dense vegetation along the Missouri River to lessen the chance of discovery or encounters with the numerous local bands of Indians out hunting buffalo. By so doing, that made it hell on men and livestock in the evenings because of the hordes of buffalo flies and mosquitoes encountered in the bottomlands, but that was preferred to flying bullets and arrows from the always close at hand "Redman"!

Throughout their travels, Elliott grew to better know his fellow trappers and many a night was spent around a small campfire talking about the beaver country to which they were heading, the fierce winters in the northern reaches they would soon be encountering, the need to build a cabin once they arrived at their selected beaver trapping site for such a large group of trappers, the best way to cook buffalo or make Dutch oven biscuits, and the like. Additionally, many a day was spent with Elliott riding alongside his friend Muskrat, listening to all kinds of survival information from the experienced fur trapper. In so doing, Elliott learned about the various tribes of Indians and many of their cultural ways. He also learned from his friend about the various species of animals he would soon be encountering, how to read the weather in the northern reaches in which they would soon be living, how to trap beaver and other animals, techniques of skinning and care of pelts, how to read animal and Indian 'sign', how to correctly pack their animals, and how to recognize eatable plants like wild onions and including them in their everyday meals for the variety they offered. Elliott also discovered that the life of travel on the western plains was supremely to his liking and that each and every day he became more and more at ease with his choice of a new life. However, he did find that no matter how hard he tried, he could not get close to Bear or deeply comfortable whenever in his presence... Elliott found that there was just something about the man that was not endearing.

One evening just south of what his partners had identified as the Cannonball River, the men were on more than high alert. They had crossed numerous trails of unshod or Indian horses along the way and being deep in the heart of the country of the extremely dangerous Arikara Indians, remained on high alert. Playing it on the safe side, the men slipped into the densely vegetated Missouri River bottoms early one evening hoping to avoid such historically openly hostile Indians, two distant bunches of which had been sighted earlier. Once camp was made for that evening, the men double hobbled their horses to avoid any Indians slipping into their camp and stealing their valuable livestock and means of survival or making a livelihood. Then during supper of roasted buffalo meat, Dutch oven biscuits and coffee, Muskrat continued educating Elliott as to why the always deadly Arikara Indians were to be feared and never trusted.

In the story told by Muskrat over that evening's supper, apparently the U.S. Government some years earlier had invited one of the most beloved Arikara Indian chiefs back to Washington to impress him with the prowess of the ever-expanding white man and his population numbers that far exceeded those of the American Indians. In the process, that Indian chief died from contracting some sort of white man's disease and fearing the Arikara Indian

Nation's reaction to losing their favorite chief to the white man, the government didn't inform them of the chief's death until a year or so later! That devious behavior on the part of the white man so upset the entire Arikara Nation, that they subsequently went on the warpath with the now much-hated white man and had been killing the hell out of anyone white ever since that unfortunate tribal experience of losing one of their most beloved chiefs.

Elliott found those evening sessions involving the West's geography, its wildlife and the cultural histories of the various tribes in the lands they were traversing or going to trap in, extremely interesting and made it a point to commit to memory any and all information regarding the land and its use by its many native peoples. Also, information shared during those many evening sessions around a cup of First Class Rum or a pipe full of tobacco was the life and times of the beaver, trapping methods, grading of furs, best time to trap beaver (in the spring because of the animal's heavier winter coats), the meat value from beaver and muskrat as food items, and what a trapper could get in return for each beaver *plus* in trade at such trading posts like Fort Union. Sometimes so much great historical, native peoples or beaver trapping information was coming Elliott's way from his friend Muskrat that he thought his head would explode if he added any more facts to his brain. But all was welcome and he found that his new choice in life was exactly what he wanted to do the rest of his life. Well, that and staying alive, keeping his 'topknot', being a successful trapper, becoming a Mountain Man, and finding his brother alive and well so they could be family once again…

Making camp one evening in light of the heavy nearby Indian traffic out hunting buffalo, Muskrat brought in a second armload of wood and commented to Elliott that there appeared to be a huge thunderstorm coming their way that evening and make sure that he had selected a good sleeping site, one that would keep him as dry as possible if the coming summer rains were as heavy as was expected. Heeding Muskrat's weather observations, Elliott, like his partners, separated around their campsite and made their bedding sites under the spreading and dense needle heavy limbs of the numerous Western juniper trees in the heavily vegetated river bottoms. Scouting around, Elliott found a very bushy Western juniper tree a few feet further from their campfire than the rest of the men and began preparing to spread out his buffalo robe under the dense spreading tree's limbs. Crawling under the dense cover offered by the tree's low hanging limbs, Elliott spread out his buffalo robe that he had purchased back in St. Louis, spread out his bedding on top of the robe and then pulled the remainder of his heavy robe over his bedding in order to keep it dry. Standing back and surveying his well-hidden, somewhat distant bedding site, Elliott was more than pleased with himself. He was so well hidden under the dense tree limbs and their needles that he figured he would remain dry if Muskrat was correct about the oncoming summer thunderstorm expected sometime later that evening.

Making up the coffee, Elliott helped Fish with the rest of the supper's preparations and soon the only sounds around the campfire were those of hungry men doing what they loved the most, namely eating roasted buffalo, eating piping hot Dutch oven biscuits and drinking their favorite strong brew, namely 'trapper's coffee' that was so stout, it was reported that a mule shoe would stand upright in it if it had been properly brewed! An hour later, a strong breeze came up from out of the northwest and soon the trees began letting everyone know from all of their bending and bowing from the heavy winds that a 'strong blow' was coming. Soon the smell of moisture in the air was sensed, as all the trappers began covering up their saddles and other leather gear, making sure their horses and mules were well picketed, double hobbled and their individual sleeping areas were adequately sheltered for the drenching summer prairie thunderstorm rains that were soon to be upon them.

Then about 20 minutes later, as the men sat around their campfire enjoying their pipes and final cups of coffee, the first of the heavy and cold raindrops began spattering in the dust around their campsite as the warning flashes of oncoming lightning and the rumbling of distant thunder could be heard. With those warnings, the men snuffed out their pipes, grabbed up their weapons and headed for the shelter and cover of their previously selected scattered sleeping sites in order to avoid a cold soaking rain. Then as expected, the falling rain could be heard coming across the distant waving prairie grasses like an 'ocean wave' and then it was upon the trappers' camp with a vengeance of howling winds, flashes of close at hand bolts of lightning, the acrid smell of ozone hanging heavy in the air, and the almost constant rumbling 'claps' of thunder low overhead!

As the last of the flames from their campfire whipped about in the stiff winds from the storm, then began to die out in the deluge that followed, the men snuggled into their sleeping furs, each man warmly and dryly situated under the dense foliage of the densely growing Western junipers. Soon the men were in a typical violent summer thunderstorm out on the North American prairies consisting of increasing winds, flying leaves and rain coming across the land in almost horizontal drenching sheets! Moments later, 50 mile an hour winds whipped across the men's campsite and sheets of cold rain deluged the camp, putting out the remnants of their campfire and plunging their campsite into total noisy darkness except for the almost constant flashes of lightning! The fierce summer storm raged all night and at first, Elliott lay in his warm and dry bed under the spreading limbs of his sheltering tree listening to Mother Nature and all of her fury around him. Then after a hard 12-hour day in the saddle covering almost 30 miles, Elliott drifted off into a deep, warm and comfortably dry sleep with a full belly of buffalo and biscuits, amidst the whipping tree limbs, flying leaves and raindrops sailing by horizontally in the high winds around him.

Right at daylight in the stillness that comes after a fierce prairie thunderstorm has come and gone, Elliott awoke with a start! His well-developed sixth sense told him that something was dead wrong! Remembering what his father had taught him about wilderness survival and not making any kind of a knowing or discernible move or sound after awakening when feeling danger was close at hand or in the air, Elliott only moved his eyes around in the light's faintness trying to see what had keyed him so wide awake with such a start. However, he had chosen his sleeping area in the dense vegetation so well to avoid any incoming rains that he could see little around him with just his slight eye movements. Slowly reaching under his buffalo robe cover so no one on the outside looking on could see any sign of his movement, his fingers clasped around one of his pistols and he brought it forward so it would be handy if they had Arikara Indian danger close at hand. Then reaching back down under his sleeping furs, he brought forth his second pistol, remembering Muskrat's history lessons regarding numerous Indians in a close at hand fight and the need for multiple shots to protect oneself. If there was one Indian, there sure as hell would be more, so come all 'gunned up' when doing battle with their kind was the frontier survival lesson he had listened to and had learned well.

Still not being able to see much of their campsite in the morning's faint light because he had selected a sleeping area that was well covered and a short ways away from the main camp, he resorted to the use of his ears to see if he could detect what had awoken him with such a start. Remaining still as a stone, Elliott listened as hard as he could for any sign of close at hand danger or activity. Other than the still 'moaning' winds and the occasional heavy raindrops falling off his dripping wet tree branches onto the leather of his buffalo robe, he heard nothing out of the ordinary. Still, his well-developed sixth sense learned from growing up on the Missouri frontier as a young man had never been wrong in the past...

Then Elliott realized what it was that was bothering him! He could hear absolutely nothing, like other men moving around, Fish making a fire, Muskrat making biscuits, the nickering of a horse or anyone talking! The whole fur trappers' camp was as silent as a river rock lying in the bottom of a dry streambed! Reaching up slowly with his left hand and holding his pistol in his other at the ready, Elliott moved the closest heavy limbs away from his head so he could see better around his campsite. That was when Elliott, waking with a full bladder held under tight control due to his intense feeling that danger was close at hand, released its contents from between his legs and into his sleeping furs in an involuntary burst once he realized what he was seeing or more importantly, not seeing!

Quickly propping up onto his elbows and shoving his tree limbs forcefully aside, Elliott realized he was the only man in camp! The entire camp was vacant of any sign of life other than that which he provided! Every trapper was gone, the entire horse and mule herd was absent, no one was around their campfire, and everything that had been strewn around their campsite the evening before was now long gone! He was now totally alone in the river bottoms surrounded by a sea of grass, plenty of wind and a whole host of hostile Indians in country!

Exploding up out from his now urine-dampened bedding, Elliott looked all around just in case he had missed something and in so doing, saw nothing of any human existence other than a now long dead campfire... Elliott could not believe what he was seeing or not seeing! Sometime during the night, the rest of the men of his party had quietly gotten up under the cover of the noise and rain of the intense thunderstorm, deliberately loaded up all of their gear and horses, and had purposely left him alone and behind with apparently what they must have figured was little or no chance of survival!

Standing there in utter disbelief, Elliott came to the realization that such an event could have only been planned long in advance, and now there he stood deep in Arikara Indian country all alone and without a single horse to continue making his way. Then the realization truly dawned on him that he was TOTALLY alone and afoot in a sea of grass and knew not of where to go or how to EVEN get there!

Quickly slipping on his boots, Elliott began walking all around their camp looking for anything that had been left behind that could help fully explain what had just occurred or maybe even help him survive. There was no evidence of anything man-made left behind to help him survive, NOTHING! In fact, the only thing he found was a lot of horse and mule droppings along where their picket line had once been but that was it! All he had was what he possessed and that included very damn little in the way of survival gear. With a hopelessly sinking heart, Elliott walked back to his now wetted bed, pulled back his buffalo robe and wet bedding and took stock of his meager possessions.

Fortunately for him he still possessed his Hawken rifle, knife, powder horn, carry bag with just 13 lead balls, two pistols, a fire starter, some silver dollars, four ignition caps for his rifle, and a few bullet wads for his rifle or pistols. That was it! The rest of his gear of shot, powder, wads, tin of No. 11 caps, and his extra knife had been left in a carry bag under a canvas covering tossed over some of their saddles! That meant no matter what happened, he only had four shots with his rifle and one shot apiece with his pistols! The only clothing he had was what he was wearing since all the rest had gone the way of his horses, mules, equipment, clothing and the rest of his so called 'friends'...

Then Elliott found himself almost physically drawing up a growing fierce determination from within. To leave a man alone out on the prairie after stealing his horses was nothing short of a death sentence! Then adding to that misery, being left deep in Indian country afoot with every grizzly bear looking for any kind of a meal with only four shots for his rifle, and one could begin to see that the odds of survival didn't feel any too great no matter how one looked at it!

However, the bile started building up inside Elliott for what he considered being abandoned for no other reason than that of being a 'greenhorn'! That left him with a set of narrowed eyes and a stone cold deadly feeling starting to build up inside him like an erupting volcano over the futures of those who had left him in such terrible straits if he was ever to meet them again! Now for no other reason, he had to find a way to survive and make it to Fort Union, wherever the hell that was. Then to find those who had left him afoot and kill the entire lot starting with his 'friend' Muskrat, were the deadly feelings that were now pouring throughout every strand of his soul! Elliott knew he had been raised not to be a violent man but a just and honest and God-fearing man. However, he had already discovered that he could kill with the best of them under the right circumstances... Looking skyward, Elliott was heard to quietly utter the words, "Give me a hand, Lord." Then Elliott quietly closed many of the earlier chapters in his previous life to befriend people and become a fur trapper, turned back to his urine-soaked bedding site, and gathered unto him those few scraps which were still his...

Elliott "Bear Scat" Sutta, Mountain Man

CHAPTER THREE: TOUGH TIMES, PADDLEFISH EGGS AND "BEAR SCAT" GETS HIS NAME

All that Elliott knew was that Fort Union was somewhere on the upper reaches of the Missouri River, wherever that was. With only that as his 'compass', Elliott began his trek on foot northward following the Missouri River and all the while learning what it meant to be a Mountain Man alone in the wilderness and one who was going to survive and take back that which was his, the good Lord willing...

That first night alone in the wilderness, Elliott feasted on raw buffalo meat from a cow he had killed along the way. However in so doing, Elliott now realized he was down to just three shots left in his Hawken rifle! Elliott had observed numerous Indians riding by and hunting buffalo throughout the day so he did not dare risking a fire for fear of discovery and since he now only had three shots left in his rifle, joining Indians in battle was not an option! The next morning, he gorged himself on more raw buffalo meat and soon left the carcass to a pack of approaching prairie wolves, full well knowing he would be unable to defend the buffalo carcass against them with only three shots. Besides, he figured he still had many more miles to go in order to get to Fort Union and 'take care of' five previous 'friends' and fur trappers, and that alone was reason enough to conserve one's ammunition and make sure he survived!

For the next 15 days, Elliott trudged northward and westward looking for Fort Union until he 'plumb' wore out and had by then, literally walked out of his cheap store-bought boots purchased back at Don Bailey's Country Store in Weldon Spring before he had left that 'neck of the woods'. Cutting up his buffalo sleeping robe with his knife, Elliott made himself moccasin-like foot coverings and continued his long and lonely walk looking for some sign of friendly human habitation. As he continued walking northward, he faced terrible hunger on a daily basis as well as the fact that there was Indian sign everywhere, as it seemed they were hunting buffalo and gathering in their winter supplies of meat. Because of their numbers, that made it almost impossible for Elliott to hunt and kill any buffalo without drawing undue attention to his miserable and now starving condition. In fact, Elliott had lost so much weight because he had not been able to find anything to eat without bringing a horde of Indians down around him, that his 'store-bought' clothing, not designed for what he was experiencing, hung on his scarecrow-like body in the rags they had now become!

Finally, Elliott was able to kill only one more buffalo because two of his remaining ignition caps for his Hawken rifle had refused to fire and were now used up! That left him only two shots from his pistols and then he was only down to his knife as any type of defensive weapon. But for the moment, Elliott had food and for two days he did not leave the buffalo's carcass as he gorged himself on the raw meat, the first sustenance he had in the previous five days! By day three, the meat was becoming rancid, purple in color, slimy in consistency and basically uneatable even though he was still starving. It was then that Elliott had to leave because he knew the smell of rotting meat would soon be picked up by one of the routinely observed grizzly bears commonly foraging along the river and with only two pistol rounds left, tangling with a grizzly bear no matter how good a shooter he was was not an option.

The next four days found Elliott without anything to eat other than grass. Finally, Divine Providence provided an ambling skunk along the riverbank and Elliott was able to club it to death with the butt of his rifle! Even roasted, the meat from the skunk tasted of 'skunk smell', as did Elliott having been heavily sprayed in the act of killing the beast! Yet Elliott after his first meal in days, trekked on heading ever north and westerly along the Missouri River toward what he knew had to soon be Fort Union. Once there, he knew he would be fed but only after he had found and killed his five fur trapper 'friends', if they were at Fort Union or even still in country!

Three more days of travel without food now found Elliott more dead than alive, terribly sunburned through his tattered clothing, emaciated, covered with sores and hundreds of mosquito bites, not to mention exhausted! He had not eaten in three days and the last meal he had eaten was only half-cooked skunk meat that he had gagged down only to puke it right back up and in so doing, further dehydrated his already emaciated body! In short, to anyone observing the skeleton of a man shuffling along would quickly come to the realization that the barely moving scarecrow was not long for the world and would make scant magpie bait once he dropped and moved no more...

Resting along a riverbank unable to go any further, Elliott spied a grizzly bear along the bank of the Missouri River far ahead through his dizzying eyes, feasting on a great fish it had dragged up onto the bank. Waiting until the great bear had eaten its fill and had finally left its location, Elliott staggered and fell his way down to the site determined to eat what was left of the fish. When he arrived, he discovered the fish had died earlier of natural causes, bloated, floated onto the shoreline, and the bear had then discovered the odiferous carcass. Elliott could see the fish, a paddlefish of monster-sized proportions, had been a female as evidenced by the remaining rotten dark eggs spewing forth from a tear in the side of her rotting body. Hard as he tried and hungry as he was, Elliott found that he could not eat any of the stinking, maggot-infested, oily flesh falling off its bones, rotten fish.

Passing out from his hunger, Elliott dropped to the beach alongside the dead fish and moved no more for about an hour. Then awakening with terrible hunger pangs once again and with his face lying on the sand, looked out a few feet away from where his head now lay and observed a fresh bear scat oozing partially digested paddlefish eggs. Then the starving Elliott got an idea. He could see that lying alongside the great fish were numerous piles of bear scat filled with partially digested fish eggs. Starving as he was and through his hunger-crazed mind, Elliott figured if the bear had eaten the fish eggs and been able to digest most of them, that indicated they had been good to eat at that stage of its initial meal. Crawling over to a fresh wet pile of bear scat, Elliott poked around in the grizzly bear scat until he found one whole fish egg that was only partially digested. Taking the egg and smelling it, it only faintly reeked of the smell of fish. Then with 'swimming eyes', an indication of the advanced stages of starvation, Elliott took the partially digested paddlefish egg, placed it on his tongue and popped the egg with his teeth. The egg tasted fishy but when the oil squirted out from the tiny fish egg and covered part of his tongue, Elliott found himself in his condition of hunger relishing the food item… That discovery made, Elliott found himself busily picking out the largest-in-size paddlefish eggs from the grizzly bear scat deposited in great piles all around the partially eaten, monster-sized fish, and hungrily popping them one after another into his mouth! Soon because of his hunger, Elliott was using both hands to break apart the clumps of bear scat, picking out the best-looking eggs and eagerly passing them into his mouth. Being so hungry, that even included bits and chunks of bear poop going into his mouth as well… But at least it was something to eat and by that time, Elliott was ravenous with hunger and eating the rancid eggs was better than eating nothing at all. So before the afternoon was over, Elliott had raided every pile of bear scat for the nourishing paddlefish eggs they contained, partially digested or not!

"I ain't never seen anyone eat bear scat afore," came the voice of Jim Johnson from close behind Elliott, as the starving man continued picking through piles of bear scat for the partially digested fish eggs for the nourishment they were providing him.

Whirling around on his knees upon hearing the sound of a human voice, Elliott could see through a hazy set of eyes a white man fur trapper by the looks of his dress from head to toe in buckskins, holding his rifle in one hand and Elliott's previously dropped rifle in his other! Because of the advanced stages of starvation, Elliott's eyes could barely focus on the stranger standing there, watching him pulling out and eating partially digested fish eggs from the many piles of bear scat scattered around the huge dead paddlefish. But it was a white man's voice and sure as shooting, Elliott figured through his starvation-fogged brain that he had been saved!

Staggering to his feet and wobbling back and forth unsteadily on his legs, Elliott blurted out, "Damn, Man, thank you for saving me!"

"Well, you ain't saved yet. I got me a passel of Arikara hot on my trail and now they be on your trail as well, since you be a white man and all," said the fur trapper as he stepped off the bank and trotted over to Elliott. "Can ye still shoot, Man, because they be a-coming for me and now you as well, truth be known," said the fur trapper with a big floppy, wide-brimmed hat, as he looked back towards the prairie in the direction from whence he had just come. "Name's Jim Johnson and what be your handle, Stranger?" he asked as he continued looking back in the direction from whence he had just come.

"Name's Elliott Sutta and I only have my two loaded pistols," said Elliott, "but I am a damn good shot, so point me in the direction they are coming from and unless I miss my guess, I can get two of them before they get us," said Elliott.

"Damn, Man! You have one of the finest rifles a-goin in this here Hawken. Use it on those damn Indians as they come into range," said the trapper, as he turned and continued looking back in the direction from whence he had just come.

"I don't have any more powder, balls or caps," said Elliott, as he staggered down behind the riverbank for the cover it offered with the strange trapper, waiting for the pursuing Indians to show themselves.

"Hell, we have the same type of rifles. Use some of my powder and shot and load up your rifle while I lay here and keep an eye peeled," said the trapper as he tossed his 'Possibles bag' over to Elliott.

About then all hell broke loose! Back in the direction the fur trapper was looking and had just come, Elliott saw a storm of about 30 mounted yelling Indians riding down about ten other Indians who were on foot, doggedly following Johnson's tracks and running towards the two trapped trappers now hiding below the riverbank. By the time the dust had settled below the trappers, the two bunches of Indians had run into each other, and those ten Indians on foot chasing the trapper were quickly run down and killed as the unidentified mounted Indians continued swirling around the dead, whooping and yelling in victory over the 'coup' they had just counted.

"Damn, we be lucky, you and me," said Johnson, as he looked back towards the battle scene as the dust and the mounted Indians on their horses continued swirling around the ten dead Indians. "Looks like them damn Sioux caught those Arikara a-chasing me on foot and rode them down. Saved our bacon they did, that is unless they saw me a-running this-a-way and now they are a-coming after me as well," grimaced the fur trapper with the wide-brimmed hat.

Elliott by that time had reloaded his Hawken with powder and ball from the trapper who had run upon him eating fish eggs out from piles of grizzly bear scat. Now the two men lay low, hoping not to be discovered by the 30 or so Sioux Indians in the process of scalping the dead Arikara just 40 yards distant from the two hidden men! Finished with mutilating their slain dead enemies so that they could never enter "The Happy Hunting Grounds", the Sioux then gathered up the Arikara's nearby scattered horses, turned and rode off onto the prairie, oblivious to the two trappers huddled below the nearby riverbank awaiting their turn at the sure hands of death... (Author's Note: Many of the Plains tribes of Indians believed that if an Indian killed in battle was scalped or mutilated in such a way that part of his body was removed, he would roam forever outside The Happy Hunting Grounds looking for those lost pieces of his body, without which he could never enter such a revered place.)

For the rest of that day and into the night, both men out of fear of discovery by the nearby Sioux Indians remained hidden below the riverbank, not moving. Finally come the darkness, both men headed for the nearby river and drank deeply of the river's waters trying to refresh their dehydrated bodies after lying out in the hot prairie sun all day. That evening, no fire was chanced as each man gathered in armfuls of tall river grasses, made themselves beds and exhausted from the day's ordeal, crawled into their 'grass nests' beside the river's bank and slept deeply.

Just before daylight the following morning, Elliott awoke to something tugging on his foot. Waking after such a deep sleep because of the starvation factor and the emotions spawned by the closeness of death, first from the pursuing Arikara on foot and then the Sioux on horseback, it took a moment for Elliott's fogged brain to register the newest danger close at hand. Then Elliott snapped wide awake when he felt pain in his right foot! Instinctively grabbing his close at hand and now reloaded Hawken rifle, Elliott quickly sat up only to discover the darkened form of a huge grizzly bear 'mouthing' his foot!

BOOM! went Elliott's Hawken, as he felt an instant sharp pain in his foot upon discharging his rifle into the head of the great bear holding his foot in his mouth from just inches away! Lunging backwards in pain and terror all at the same time, Elliott heard his fellow trapper lying behind him yelling, "WHAT THE SAM HILL!" as he too exploded out from his deep sleep and into a close at hand world of wildlife violence in the making!

Both men scrambled away in terror from the perceived close at hand danger, ran to the riverside and then both stood there trying to figure out what the hell had just happened. Finally Elliott, sore right foot and all, figured out what had just occurred. Apparently a hungry grizzly bear, visiting the dead paddlefish site for some early morning's breakfast, had smelled a sleeping Elliott en route. Pausing to investigate another possible food source, the bear had ambled over to the sleeping trapper, smelled food and taking one of Elliott's feet in his mouth, began to take a bite. In so doing that aroused a once sleeping fur trapper and got the bear an instant faceful of fire from the end of a close at hand rifle barrel and a speeding lead ball through his forehead! Additionally, Elliott realized just how lucky he was as he stood there thinking back on what had just happened. When he felt the bear taking a sample of his foot, without thinking of anything but survival, Elliott had just grabbed his Hawken rifle and shot the bear in the face. Fortunately for Elliott, the huge Hawken slug barely missed his foot as it crashed into the bear's head. However the flame from the end of his rifle barrel, being so close to his foot, had burned his flesh severely around his ankle and foot! But at least, Elliott still had a foot and ankle and the bear had a bullet...

Working through the realization of what had just happened, both trappers found their heartbeats finally returning to a normal rate and then remembering where they both were, ran back to their protective riverbank and peered over the top to see if any nearby Indians were coming their way to investigate to see who had just fired a rifle over near the river. Not seeing anything moving about near the two trappers other than a small herd of buffalo, the trapper wearing the wide-brimmed hat turned to Elliott saying, "Well "Bear Scat", looks like ye not only saved your foot but provided the two of us some damn fine grizzly bear meat for our breakfast. Bear meat that may taste a little fishy but still some damn good tasting meat just the same."

Elliott just smiled over what his new friend had said, especially over the moniker he had just been given relative to his picking and eating fish eggs out from piles of grizzly bear scat. With that, Bear Scat replied with a like in kind grin saying, "Well, "Big Hat", since you mentioned it and seeing that there are no Indians nearby, what say we get a fire going and stake out some of those bear's steaks for our breakfast? Not to make a 'funny' but I am so hungry I could eat a bear," continued Elliott with a smile on his sunken in and gaunt-looking face, seconded by a soon to be welcoming 'growl' coming from his gut.

With those words, both men relieved they had survived the previous day's Indian danger and the grizzly bear who had 'come to breakfast' that morning, broke out into a welcome laughter in light of their dangers previously experienced together. That morning, both men gorged themselves on the open-fire roasted steaks from a summer fat grizzly bear which had come to breakfast uninvited. Later in the day with both men shouldering a hindquarter from the grizzly bear for future meals on the trail, they commenced their long walk towards where Big Hat knew Fort Union was located and a salvation of sorts in waiting provided they safely arrived there. However, in the back of Bear Scat's mind, arriving in Fort Union held another unfulfilled wish. As he saw it, he still had a deadly score to settle with Muskrat, Fish, Fingers, Biscuits and Bear for up and leaving him alone on the trail without the wherewithal for any chance of survival. Plus when it came to settling old scores, Bear Scat had a major score to settle with his old 'friend' Bear. Bear being the man and leader of the group of trappers whom Bear Scat blamed primarily for the planning and execution of his abandonment out on the plains to eventually act as magpie bait once he had succumbed to the rigors of survival out on the vast prairie…

.

CHAPTER FOUR: A BOY IN A "BULL BOAT" AND CAPTURED!

For the next eight days with Big Hat Johnson in the lead because he knew the way to Fort Union, followed by Bear Scat, the two men carefully trudged their ways north on foot through the territory of the deadly Arikara into that of the equally deadly Sioux. By then, Bear Scat had learned the story as to why his newfound trapper friend wore such a wide-brimmed hat. According to Big Hat, he was so fair-skinned that he sunburned easily out on the prairie and was constantly smearing bear grease over the burned portions of his skin to reduce the pain. So in order to preclude being sunburned badly around the neck and face, he had purchased a very wide-brimmed hat and had been wearing the same ever since. Then along came Elliott and just by chance and not knowing the name of the trapper who had just found and saved him, because of his big and unusual looking hat, had himself given Big Hat that moniker. As for Elliott's new name, it was obviously given to him by Big Hat after observing him eating paddlefish eggs from piles of bear scat like they were candy, after he had been abandoned by his 'friends' earlier and was in the process of caring for his starving body.

Come the morning of their ninth day of foot travel along the banks of the Missouri, Bear Scat heard what sounded like a desperate cry for help coming from out on the river! Turning and looking in the direction from whence had come the cry for help, Bear Scat observed a partially sunken and upside down Indian "Bull Boat" floating in the Missouri River. Clinging to one side of the Bull Boat appeared to be a young Indian boy struggling and yelling for help. Without a moment's hesitation, Bear Scat ran off the riverbank and down to the water's edge. There he quickly laid his Hawken in the sand and without another thought for his own safety and being a good swimmer, dove into the fast moving river waters! Swimming for all he was worth in the swift current, Bear Scat found himself being swept downstream just as fast as the young struggling Indian boy clinging for all he was worth to the side of his sinking Bull Boat!

However, still weakened from his many previous days of starvation, Bear Scat found that he was quickly tiring in the swift current as he approached the rapidly whirling and sinking boat. The panicked look in the young Indian boy's eyes told Bear Scat he was not long for hanging onto the sinking Bull Boat, so finding some inner strength, he redoubled his efforts and quickly closed the distance to the struggling young man. (Author's Note: A Bull Boat was a common means of travel for many Plains Indians living near riverine watercourses. The 'boat' itself was constructed by weaving and tying green willow limbs into a bowl-like inner structure. Then several bull buffalo hides (the largest in size) were stretched around the willow limb framing and tied on with leather strips. The bowl-like shaped craft was then used to cross waterways in order to get to the other side to hunt, gather wood, pick berries, dig up roots and the like. The Bull Boat was very light in weight, of shallow draft, could carry very heavy loads (upwards of a ton in some cases), and could be navigated in even the shallowest of waters. The craft was paddled by the person riding inside and was somewhat unmanageable directionally due to its rounded shape, and lack of a rudder and directional keel, especially in swifter flowing waters. Essentially, the Bull Boat is 'pulled' by an individual leaning over the side and with a pulling motion of the paddle or an oar, pulls the Bull Boat through the water in the direction the user wishes to go.)

THEN IT HAPPENED! The young Indian boy lost his hold on the side of the Bull Boat, gave one last yell for help and immediately slipped beneath the waves! But Bear Scat was only two strokes away and a heartbeat later he reached down where he had last seen the Indian boy slip beneath the waves and grabbed for where he had last been seen! Stretching his arm down as far as he could reach, Bear Scat felt his hands close on a long braid of hair and grabbed hold of it for all he was worth! With that and the extra weight and drag of the now drowning boy, Bear Scat felt himself being whirled even faster around in the river's currents and being not only swiftly dragged downstream but underwater as well!

It was then that Bear Scat glimpsed Big Hat running along the riverside yelling encouragement and trying to stay even with Bear Scat's perilous location in the river. Pulling for all he was worth, Bear Scat was able to finally drag the Indian boy's head above water, only to hear him sucking in huge gulps of air and water all at the same time. Choking, gagging and now struggling with Bear Scat in the panic of his near drowning experience, Bear Scat turned the Indian boy partially around so he could not fight his rescuer, grabbed him from behind and began swimming with one arm and dragging the boy with his other arm shoreward.

About then, Bear Scat saw Big Hat standing neck deep in the river's waters reaching out to him as the two swimmers drifted by in the river's swift currents. Reaching out at the last minute, Bear Scat grabbed Big Hat's powerfully strong extended hand and felt himself and the Indian boy being dragged bodily shoreward. Soon all three of them were beached on the shoreline, gasping, sucking and choking for air. But all appeared to now be safe and sound beached along the shoreline. Then out of the emotion of the moment, the Indian boy still scared witless, rose to his knees, began to cry, gesture with his hands and speak out loudly in his native tongue all at the same time. Bear Scat just smiled over the young man's emotional actions tied to the moment and looked over at Big

Hat for any interpretation of what such actions meant because he was unfamiliar with the boy's language, gestures and culture.

"Bear Scat, the boy is thanking The Great Spirit and you for saving his life," said a still winded Big Hat over his most recent lifesaving exertions with a big grin. Then Bear Scat realized why Big Hat had such a big grin on his face when he looked down at himself and discovered he was as naked as the day he was born! Then the realization as to what had happened causing him to be naked as a baby bird flashed through Bear Scat's mind. A combination of him losing so much weight when he was starving after being abandoned by his 'friends' and most of his cheap store-bought clothing having worn out during his earlier travails, had caused his pants and shirt to disintegrate and slip away in the swift moving Missouri River's 'grasping' currents when he was attempting to rescue the Indian boy...

Then the Indian boy pointed to something up on the river's bank and said something excitedly in his native tongue once again. That time upon hearing what the young Indian boy was saying caused Big Hat to jump up without explanation, run back to where both his and Bear Scat's rifles lay on the beach where he had jumped into the river to help in the rescue. Reaching both rifles, Big Hat reached down to grab up his, only to have a warning arrow strike the ground right next to his hand! When the arrow landed so close to Big Hat's hand, it caused him to jerk his hand away in alarm! When he did, little did he realize that hand movement away from his rifle had just saved his life!

When speaking in his native language, Big Hat having lived in and among the Sioux Tribes for many years, realized what the boy was initially saying after being dragged from the river. In that initial outburst after being removed from the river, the young boy was also talking out loud about seeing a number of his tribal members up on the riverbank on their horses watching on. Hearing those words, Big Hat figuring danger was close at hand, had made a run for his rifle left back on the beach only to have his effort to defend himself defeated by the close at hand arrival of an arrow

66

smacking into the sand by his hand as a warning not to pick up his rifle and defend himself.

Then down off the riverbank rode about 30 Indians all whooping and hollering over their discovery of one of their own being rescued, and the capture of two of the hated white men fur trappers! Soon the two trappers and the Indian boy just rescued from drowning were surrounded by a number of mounted and excited Sioux warriors! Without any weapon in hand with which to defend themselves, Big Hat cursed his stupidity in letting down his guard in Indian country, being that he should have known better being an experienced Mountain Man and all, as he and Bear Scat stood as still as a river rock and realized they were now as good as dead!

Then the surround of Indians began laughing as they began looking Bear Scat over. Bear Scat quickly realized because of the Indians' gestures and mannerisms, they were laughing at him over his scrawny sunburned body and obvious powder-burned right leg and foot, along with all of his nakedness.

It was then that the young man just rescued from drowning began frantically speaking to one very fierce and noble looking warrior with much fervor! As he did, Bear Scat could see an immediate change in the demeanor and temperament of the fierce looking warrior, as well as the rest of the men sitting ominously all around the trappers on their horses with their firearms still held at the ready.

Then Big Hat's face turned from its dour 'dead on arrival at being surrounded by fierce Sioux Indians' looks to one of wonder and then one carrying an immense smile of relief. Then Big Hat turned and said to Bear Scat, "This is truly our lucky day, my friend. It seems that you, from all of the Indian talk I am hearing, have just rescued a very highly respected tribal elder's son! Not only that, but these warriors watched the whole rescue taking place and are very impressed over your bravery, especially in rescuing one of their own and not just another white man! Not only that, but upon seeing another trapper walk out into a dangerous swiftly flowing river to aid in the rescue of one of their own and not just another white man trapper, has highly impressed this war party…"

Then the Indian warrior appearing to be the leader of the war party pulled the young just rescued Indian boy up onto the back of his horse. After that, he said something to some of the rest of his warriors and with those words, the two trappers soon found themselves pulled up onto the backs of two other Indians' horses as well. Lastly, two other Indians dismounted, picked up the two trappers' rifles, pistols and knives, mounted their horses and then the entire contingent with the fur trappers riding behind their captors, headed for the distant rolling Missouri River breaks holding a large stand of trees and a very large Indian encampment as evidenced by a collection of over 50 tipis.

"What is happening to us?" asked a concerned Bear Scat, looking over at Big Hat who was riding alongside on his Indian captor's horse.

"Don't know jest as of yet but appears we are being taken to their encampment for some reason. I don't know if it is to torture us or turn us over to their squaws to let them vent their wrath upon us. If the latter happens, be prepared to die a very slow and painful death. Whatever happens, Bear Scat, jest follow my lead, if we are allowed to live that long," said Big Hat. "But in the meantime, don't show any sign of fear or pain if we are to be tortured. The Sioux are big on courage and if we want to have any chance at living, we had better show nothing but lots of 'sand' around them, no matter whatever they choose to do with us."

About 15 minutes later, the contingent of warriors and their two captured fur trappers arrived at a rather large cluster of tipis scattered in and around the Missouri River breaks' stands of shade trees. Therein the trappers observed dozens of barking dogs, racks hung with strips of buffalo meat drying in the open air, women looking on in amazement at the incoming riders, dozens of little children nervously running for cover in the obvious presence of white men, and a number of staked out buffalo hides on the ground, all in the process of having their fat and meat scraped off as the hides were being prepared for making into robes or tipi covers. As the warriors dismounted, the group's leader had the two trappers dismount and through hand gestures indicated they were to follow him. Moments later they were introduced to what appeared to be a number of the encampment's war and civil chiefs. Then the war party's leader began telling the story of the boy's rescue, according to Big Hat who understood the language and was translating what he was hearing to Bear Scat. Then amidst a number of smiles and appreciative sounds being emanated from all who had gathered around to listen to the warrior's words, the trappers were then escorted to a lone tipi at the edge of the encampment and through more hand gestures instructed to enter. Upon entering the two men found the tipi empty with the exception of a number of sleeping furs arranged around the inside of the tipi. There the two trappers seated themselves on the sleeping furs and for the longest time the only activity was around the outside of their tipi, as numbers of women and men came and went after speaking to the two Indians standing outside their tipi.

Then Big Hat calmly turned to Bear Scat saying, "Bear Scat, you wanted to be a Mountain Man and fur trapper. Well, you are getting a taste of what can befall those of our kind if we are not alert to our surroundings and the good Lord above is not walking with us. That aside and if we live through this, you wanted me to teach you the travel and traditions of the fur trapper. Since I am still alive as are you, this is as good a time to teach you about what I know and what you will have to know, if you are to survive being a fur trapper out in the wilderness. When we rode into the Indian encampment, what did your senses tell you?"

"What?" replied Bear Scat upon hearing such a question during those most stressful times of their capture.

"A good fur trapper is always aware of his surroundings in every sense of the word, if he wishes to survive out in the wilderness with the beasts and generally mad-as-hell Indians over the trespassing white man. Once again, when we rode into this encampment, what did your senses tell you?" asked Big Hat.

"I don't know. I was too scared over being captured and brought into their camp to sense much of anything else other than my concern about seeing the next sunrise," replied a very nervous Bear Scat.

"Well, let your life's lessons begin even under these most trying of circumstances. If you want to survive out here on the frontier as a fur trapper, you need to start becoming aware of your total surroundings. I say that because the more and quicker you learn about your surroundings allows me, your partner, to also have a better chance of survival as well," quietly advised Big Hat. "Now when we rode towards this Indian encampment, my nose and ears told me there was an established Indian encampment nearby. When we were riding into this area and still about 100 yards away, I smelled wood smoke, the smell of rotting meat that had been discarded, human waste when we rode by many of the bushes nearby this campsite, steaming cooking pots as we got closer to the main encampment, burning meat fat dripping on the many fires' cook sites in camp, and numbers of barking dogs. I call that the 'smell of life'. The time will come when those smells will impact your senses when you are out on the trail in unfamiliar country and maybe, just maybe, alert you as to the nearness of an Indian encampment before either you see it or they see you, thereby possibly saving my life and yours!"

Thinking about Big Hat's survival words of wisdom, like some of those his father had imparted to him when he was younger, Bear Scat felt his face flushing hot in shame over what had just been said to him. True, he had asked Big Hat to teach him everything that he knew about the frontier, its animals, the Indians, and the art of being a fur trapper. In so doing, he now felt the embarrassment over his lack of understanding the importance of the simplest of senses that when perceived and correctly interpreted might just allow him or his close friend to live to see another day. From that day forward, if allowed to live through their current capture by the Sioux, Bear Scat vowed to never again let his guard down or ignore what his God-given senses were telling him...

About an hour later, all of a sudden there was a lot of outside noise and soon in walked three older women who through their gestures, made the two trappers stand up as the women then closely and quietly examined the men.

"What the hell are they doing?" asked Bear Scat, remembering the earlier words of warning spoken by Big Hat about the savage beatings the squaws could inflict upon their prisoners.

"Don't rightly know but appears to me they are looking us over rather carefully like they plan on doing something with or to us."

Even inside the darkened tipi, Bear Scat could feel himself turning red over his nakedness in front of the Indian women. But by then, he was so tired and emotionally drained that he just finally sat down on the deep pile of sleeping furs and regardless of being captured by members of the fierce Sioux nation or not, he soon fell into an exhausted sleep after his difficult swim in the swift flowing Missouri River and slow recovery over his almost being previously starved into eternity. For some reason however, before he fell fast asleep, he felt at least clean and better than he had for many days after his little swim. At least he wasn't all by himself, facing off with the animals on a daily basis and slowly starving in the process... *I will pick my friends better in the future,* were his last thoughts, as he drifted off into a deep and very welcome sleep.

******

"Wake up, Bear Scat. We have company and lots of 'em," said Big Hat somewhat later.

Waking up from one of the best sleeps he had had in many days, Bear Scat jumped up in front of at least five women who were all talking and poking their fingers at and laying them all over him all at the same time. Then he found not only himself standing there naked in front of God and everybody, but Big Hat himself was being stripped naked and forced to stand there in front of all the women like a baby 'jay bird' as well! Then as the two trappers stood there wondering what the hell was happening, they found

71

themselves being dressed in beautiful buckskin clothing from 'stem to stern'! Clothing that did not fit upon trying on was promptly removed and another pair of pants or shirt was tried on, until the gaggle of ladies found sufficient clothing to totally outfit each man! One thing that seemed to help was that Bear Scat and Big Hat were not large or really tall men, so the women seemed to be able to outfit each man without much difficulty from the clothing they had for other members of their families. Then the men found themselves being forced to sit on their sleeping furs and being fitted with several pairs of moccasins until moccasins were found that comfortably fit. Then the women were gone from their tipi and their clothes-fitting duties just as fast as they had arrived…

Sitting there comfortable as all get-out on his sleeping skins, Bear Scat asked Big Hat, "What the hell just happened? Why were we all dressed up?"

"Bear Scat, apparently you jest saved our bacon! By you jumping into that there river and saving their young Indian boy with such a show of courage on your part, is apparently keeping us from being killed outright by that bunch of warriors who captured us. Near as I can tell, because of that we are now being celebrated by this band over what you did and who you saved. It seems from all the talking that went on by those women who were dressing us up in new clothing you saved the only son of the most respected chief and tribal elder in this band of Lakota! The young man who you saved is named "Buffalo Horn", son of their respected war chief, "Buffalo Calf". It also seems from all of that there woman talk that their warriors were ready to attack and kill us until you jumped into that river and saved that there boy. Man, I am thinking that the two of us were destined to be partners by The Old Boy Upstairs after all the goodness that has been showered upon us this day. That is what I am thinking! I am damn proud to not only call you my friend and brother, but my new partner for the long haul as well, no matter what happens. What do you have to say to that, Bear Scat?" asked Big Hat with a big and yet almost sheepish grin spread clear across his prairie-weathered face.

Bear Scat just smiled over hearing those most welcome and genuine sounding words just spoken by his new friend, Big Hat. If he had his way, here is one friend he would never have to question as to his loyalty and friendship and one whom he would defend with his life. Then Bear Scat came to the realization that living and working out on the dangerous frontier not only required good survival senses and strongly bonded friendships but a hatful of good luck as well. So far to his way of thinking, he either had or was quickly in the process of developing all three of those required Mountain Man traits…

Then once again there was a great commotion of people gathering and talking outside the entrance to their tipi. Soon a giant of a fierce looking Indian ducked into the entrance to their tipi, stood up, all six-foot four inches of him, and just stared down at Bear Scat and Big Hat sitting on their sleeping furs.

Then in a booming voice in perfectly good English, the magnificent specimen of a man said, "I am Buffalo Calf, War Chief of the Bear Clan of the Hunkpapa nation of the Lakota. I have been told by my son and others that you saved him from drowning in the great river. For that I am pleased. You two follow me," and with that, the great chief briskly exited the tipi.

That moment caught both trappers by surprise, but then catching themselves both men quickly jumped up, exited the tipi and met Buffalo Calf patiently waiting outside for them. Then with the two now well-dressed trappers in tow, he briskly strode off towards several campfires which were surrounded with a large contingent of men, women and respectfully quiet children. Striding into a group of people who respectfully parted in order so the chief could make his way into the inner circle of people, Buffalo Calf and the two trappers were quietly seated by one campfire. Then several women began bringing the men platters of roasted buffalo meat as well as serving bowls full of meal and meat mixtures. Soon all three men were happily eating the great amounts of good and delicious tasting food being served, as well as watching in awe what was on going all around them. This being Bear Scat's first time in and among Indians in such a manner, he, in addition to putting away great amounts of food, did not let one cultural moment of celebration swirling around him go unnoticed for an instant… Figuring this was just one welcome experience in the life of a Mountain Man, Bear Scat drunk in everything his senses were 'presenting' to him. That Bear Scat did as Big Hat had earlier instructed since it was necessary for him to do so if he wished to survive as a fur trapper and Mountain Man…

Throughout the entire celebration of life swirling around them, Big Hat, familiar with the Sioux culture and traditions having trapped in their homeland and living among them for seven years, provided running interpretations to Bear Scat as the events unfolded so he could learn about the ways of the Sioux. After the evening's celebrations had ended and all of the speeches had been made by the Sioux dignitaries over the saving of Buffalo Horn, the two trappers were escorted back to their tipi and not long thereafter, both men with bellies full and heads swirling over their unbelievable good fortunes soon found themselves fast asleep.

The next morning's celebrations were more of the same with much feasting on buffalo and many speeches being made over the saving of Buffalo Calf's son, Buffalo Horn. Then Chief Buffalo Calf asked Big Hat why they were afoot instead of riding horses like all the rest of the white men seen in his country. Big Hat explained that his band of trappers had been killed, except for him, at their campsite by the Arikara in a surprise morning attack. He had survived by being out on a wood gathering chore and had been overlooked by the attacking Indians. After the attacking Indians had scalped all of his fellow trappers, looted and burned their camp, they left with all of the group's horses and mules. That left Big Hat afoot so he struck out for Fort Union, hoping he could survive the long trek. Two days of travel later, Big Hat advised he had been surprised by another smaller force of Arikara Indians and in the process of trying to escape by fleeing towards the Missouri River breaks to hide, discovered another trapper, namely Bear Scat. Then the band of pursuing Arikara were in turn ambushed by a band of

Sioux warriors and wiped out to a man. After the Indian danger had abated and the Sioux had ridden off not having discovered Big Hat, he confronted the just discovered lone trapper and obvious survivor of some sort of a calamity. Once they had a chance to get together and talk, Big Hat advised that Bear Scat was wandering alone after his band of trappers had abandoned him to starve or die out on the prairie. With those stories out and into the prairie winds, it was easy to see in the face of the chief that the story of deceit and deception perplexed him as to why one's own people would do so and then leave their own kind out alone on the prairie to wander off and die.

Then the great chief's face got all 'scrooched' up with an obvious 'burning' question and turning to Big Hat asked, "How come the "Squirrel Man" as he is now called by the women of my band, small as he is, is called Bear Scat after that of the droppings of the great bear?" Upon hearing that question coming from the great chief, Big Hat got a big grin on his face. Got a big knowing grin on his face because Big Hat knew the great chief, upon hearing the Bear Scat naming story, would be surprised and then in typical Indian cultural fashion, would be filled with mirth over such an unusual event leading up to acquiring such a strange name. So without hesitation Big Hat began speaking in the tongue of the Sioux. Not wanting to embarrass Bear Scat too much, Big Hat told the story about how Bear Scat was given his trapper name after being observed from afar hungrily picking and eating fish eggs out from fresh bear scat to avoid starving to death. Upon hearing that 'naming story', the chief broke out laughing until the tears just rolled uncontrollably down his cheeks!

Turning to Big Hat and Bear Scat after he had recovered his dignity over the funny story told by Big Hat about how Bear Scat Sutta had come by his Mountain Man name, the great chief said, "As long as the sun shines, the grass is green, the rivers flow and the buffalo roam, my friendship for the two of you will last until The Great Spirit reaches down for me and takes me up to join the rest of the "Cloud People". (Author's Note: The name given by the Plains Indians to those of their kind who have passed.) That friendship also means I will send out the word with runners to all of our other bands and let them know that the man who wears a big hat and the man who is so tough that he eats grizzly bear droppings are friends and are to be treated just like the rest of their Sioux Brothers."

Then the great chief surprised the two fur trappers with a very generous gift. That afternoon during another great feast, Chief Buffalo Calf presented the two horseless fur trappers with three horses from his own herd! At first Big Hat and Bear Scat were dumbfounded over the very generous gift. A generous gift especially in light of how much value Plains Indians placed in the personal ownership of their horses and horse herds. Big Hat told Buffalo Calf that the two trappers could in no way repay him for the very generous and life-giving gift of his three horses. It was then that the chief pointed to his son, Buffalo Horn, and advised that his woman could no longer have children and by saving his one and only son and future leader of the Sioux from drowning in the great Missouri River, the debt had already been repaid. The chief then also had his men return the Hawken rifles, pistols and knives they had taken when the fur trappers had been captured, along with additional supplies of powder and balls for their firearms for their trip that lay ahead. Fortunately, Big Hat still had two tins of No. 11 caps in his 'Possibles bag', so the men found themselves armed and now fully ready to face the wilderness once again.

The next day after another great feast in their honor for their acts of bravery in rescuing his son, Big Hat and Bear Scat thanked the chief for his hospitality and once again hit the trail heading northwest towards Fort Union and whatever destiny awaited the two fur trappers and now very close friends. However when the two men saddled their gift horses from Buffalo Calf with obviously commandeered cavalry saddles provided by the chief, they noticed old blood stains on each of the saddles… Upon those discoveries, Big Hat made a gesture of silence with his index finger to his lips to Bear Scat over the obvious grief that had befallen the original owners of the blood-stained saddles... Nodding in understanding over Big Hat's gesture for silence, Bear Scat once again came to realize that life out in the wilderness could be wonderful and reveling, that was if one lived through many of the dangers it had to offer...

For the next seven days, Big Hat and Bear Scat continued traveling northwesterly in the direction Big Hat knew Fort Union to be located. As they did, they feasted their eyes on the hundreds of small herds of buffalo dotting the grassy plains, extensive herds of elk and antelope, and smaller herds of bighorn sheep dotting the sea of grass known as the northern prairies. With such a natural abundance of wildlife around the two trappers at every turn in the trail on a daily basis, they had no problem in procuring their meals while traveling in and among the great herds of wildlife. (Author's Note: To my reader-hunters, originally numerous bighorn sheep dotted the prairies as grazers before they were reduced in numbers by white man and Indian shooters relishing their excellent tasting meat for food and hides that once tanned, turned supple, which were much desired by Indian women for the fine clothing it produced. Under such heavy and selective shooting pressures, the bighorns soon had their natural home ranges on the prairies much reduced or totally eliminated, to just those surviving populations in the more rugged Rocky Mountain regions. However history would in later years find those bighorn sheep populations even further decimated by a new population of protein-starved gold and silver miners. Today the bighorn sheep's home ranges are no longer those in the seas of grasses out on the prairies, but rather in the rugged mountain chains where forage is found from much-reduced human pressures.)

During one of their evenings while getting ready for their supper of roasting buffalo hump ribs over an open fire, Bear Scat all of a sudden got really serious and quiet. Noticing Bear Scat's 'sea change' in demeanor after being advised that the two of them were only one day out from their destination of Fort Union, Big

Hat asked Bear Scat what was on his mind and troubling him. For the longest time Bear Scat just looked into the fire roasting away at their fat-spattering hump ribs and then finally replied.

"Big Hat, I am still a man on a life and death mission. I have no remaining family other than my older brother and fellow mountain man, Jacob Sutta, and now you. The last I heard from one of my previous partners before he abandoned me with all of the rest of that party out on the prairie, was that Jacob and his partner "Wild Bill" McGinty, were bringing their beaver *'plus'* into Fort Union for grading and sale. I am hoping to find him there this summer and join up with him so we can be together once again as family. Barring that and if he is not there, I aim to 'cold-track' him and follow his trail for as long as I can in an attempt to find him and become a part of his trapping group. If I can find him, I would hope you would join up with us as well because I now consider you as my brother as well as my dearest of friends. But regardless of where my brother goes, I hope to 'cold-track' him until I find him and we are reunited. I wish to do so because that is what my parents would want me to do under the circumstances and something I most desire." Then Bear Scat paused as he took time to turn their hump ribs so they would not burn or flame-up from all of the dripping fat dropping in rivulets into their open fire.

Finished with his rib turning chore, Bear Scat paused as if gathering up his thoughts on what and how he wanted to say next. "Then there is this other thing sticking in my craw. My first partners lured me into the wilderness as a fellow trapper and I thought friend in their group of trappers. So much so that I more than provided way more than my share of the money for our provisions back in St. Louis, since I was relying on them to show me the way and teach me about the fur trade in my new life as a trapper. There while along the trail during one hell of a thunderstorm and heavy rainfall being used as a cover, they as the evil group they were, quietly in the dead of night, up and left me, sneaking away as they did without leaving me hardly any means of survival. I had no food or horses to get around, very little ammunition and no idea as to where I was and which way to go. To me by so doing, they knew they had left me out on the prairie to wander until I was killed or die with no means of survival, and in short nothing more than a death sentence did I face. I almost starved to death before you stumbled upon me in my rather wretched condition and what a godsend you turned out to be! With that in mind, you need to know that in addition to finding my brother, I intend to hunt down my earlier partners no matter where they be and kill the lot of them for sentencing me to death out on the open prairie. Just so you understand, that is where it is with me. I am on a mission to find and reunite with my brother and then seek out and kill, as opportunity allows, my earlier partners for their role in trying to kill me, in addition to my beaver trapping. I won't blame you if upon hearing what I plan on doing to my previous partners, if you want to up and leave me to fend for myself as well. But I feel strongly that I must do both things before I die, or at least die trying. Besides, I do not long for them to find some other unfortunate and subject him to the same fate as they handed out to me back on the trail."

With those words out and in the open, Bear Scat looked over at his friend Big Hat for any sign of his reaction to such a set of diverse and possibly dangerous missions. "Well, as I seed it, you being such a great shot and all, I would say you don't need no help in that arena when it comes to caring for yourself. However, after watching those Sioux squaws back at Buffalo Calf's camp looking you over when you were bare-assed naked, I had best go along with you in your vision quest to keep you out of trouble. I will do so for no other reason than to keep any other squaws from looking upon you in your nakedness and laughing themselves silly over what my partner bodily possesses because that is all the good Lord gave him. Count me in, Bear Scat! I agree, any varmint who leaves someone out on this here prairie to die deserves to have some 'air' let into his miserable carcass as well," said Big Hat, with a quiet look of grim determination spelled clear across his weathered and sunburned face.

With that out and into the evening air, Bear Scat and his partner and brother now united in a 'joint' vision quest, enjoyed their roasted buffalo hump ribs, streaming fat-grease and all, out under the starlit wilderness sky…

CHAPTER FIVE: FORT UNION, A FRESH START AND THE HUNT BEGINS

Around noon the following day, Bear Scat got his first look at the storied Fort Union. He was amazed at what he was looking at clear out there near the confluence of the headwaters of the Missouri and Yellowstone Rivers in the middle of the wilderness! As the two trappers rode into the establishment's area drinking in its most welcome view, Bear Scat could see nothing but humanity and horseflesh hustle and bustle going on all around the fort. There were groups of buckskin-dressed trappers racing their horses out on a nearby open field, other trappers were gathered around and cheering on a wrestling match between two burly fur trappers, and off to one side of the fort, other groups of men were intensely involved in shooting competitions between trappers. As for Indians, the entire area was spotted with dozens of tipis around the fort and numerous gaily dressed of their kind streamed easily into and out from the fort. Off to the northwest of the fort and across the river, Bear Scat could see several flat-bottomed boats ferrying arriving caravans of trappers heading for the grounds of the fort. Fur trappers who had been trapping further west of the fort and were just now arriving after spending a year's worth of trapping further out west, with their horses and mules heavily loaded with packs of furs and hides. Then sitting by several docks out on the

Missouri River were two keelboats anchored with all kinds of loading of packs of furs, buffalo robes and hides thereon, and the unloading of needed provisions for the fort also going on around the boats by streams of men as well.

As for the fort, after seeing nothing but a sea of prairie grasses for many weeks and herds of buffalo from horizon to horizon, the fort and its surrounding grounds looked huge, impressive and mighty fine to the untrained eyes of Bear Scat, never having seen such an enterprise out in the middle of nowhere. As for Big Hat who had been there before, he just smiled over finally being safely there and in watching his partner Bear Scat marveling over what he was seeing for the first time in the way of Western civilization located so far out in the wilderness. But therein lay an upcoming problem for both of the trappers. They had nothing in the way of supplies or provisions needed for the life of a fur trapper other than three Indian horses and their individual weapons! Additionally, they were both on a vision quest to not only continue their lives as fur trappers, but seeking out one man in particular for family reunification and five others needing to 'meet their Maker'!

About an hour later found Big Hat and Bear Scat riding their horses through the very heavy and wide wooden front gates of Fort Union. Immediately behind the front gates in the inner courtyard and facing them and anyone else wanting to enter was a cannon aimed at the entrance to forbid the entry of those not wanted. Behind the cannon lay the inner courtyard surrounded by the fort's high walls, which were rimmed with narrow walkways so guards could constantly patrol and watch over the fort's outer surroundings for any signs of danger. Stopping and quietly sitting on his horse, Bear Scat let his eyes sweep around the inner courtyard lying before him. Immediately his eyes fastened upon a great house lying directly to his front, obviously for someone of great importance. Then as his eyes continued sweeping around the inner walls of the fort at the other sights, he saw blacksmith shops, warehouses, other buildings for the fort's employees to reside within, and conspicuously center to the inner courtyard was a large cast iron structure called a fur press. The fur press Bear Scat figured was utilized to compress the raw furs and hides into tight bundles for easier packing and shipping on the nearby keelboats for their trip downstream to the St. Louis fur houses.

Then Bear Scat saw Big Hat riding his horse over to the distinguished looking house, towards an important looking man standing on the porch watching over the inner courtyard's fur grading activities. Bear Scat saw Big Hat dismount his horse, walk over to the porch and up its steps to warmly greet the important looking man standing on the porch. Then Big Hat yelled over at Bear Scat and told him to come on over and meet Mr. Kenneth McKenzie, Factor for Fort Union.

Bear Scat rode his horse over to the important looking house, dismounted and tied his steed to the hitching rail. Walking up the steps, Big Hat began introducing him to the important looking man Bear Scat had observed earlier standing on the porch watching over the inner courtyard's busy activities.

"Bear Scat, I would like you to meet my friend Mr. Kenneth McKenzie, Factor or the overall manager for the American Fur Company here at Fort Union," said Big Hat.

"Welcome, Mr. Bear Scat. Or may I just call you Bear Scat, as does my good friend here, Big Hat?" asked McKenzie with a welcoming smile.

"Well, that is the name Big Hat gave me so I guess I am stuck with it," replied Bear Scat with a good natured grin over his rather unusual but well-earned fur trapper moniker.

"Well, I have heard worse names within the fur trapper community, but yours I think is the most distinctive, unusual and I would bet storied that I have ever heard," said McKenzie with a friendly grin. Then he continued saying, "I can tell from the looks of amazement 'spelled clear across your face' about the fort that I need to provide you some information relative to our being and function. I say that since I anticipate you two are more than likely, based on what little 'kit' you and Big Hat arrived with, once provisioned from my stores, are going to try and become one of my numerous groups of "Free Trappers"."

Looking over at Big Hat with a 'business' grin of understanding, McKenzie continued saying, "Let me see, how and where to begin? This here fort is really not a fort in the military sense of the word. It is a trading post established in the year of our Lord 1828, at the request of the Assinboine Nation. Its owner is New York businessman John Jacob Astor of the American Fur Company. This post is located near the confluence of the headwaters of the Missouri and Yellowstone Rivers, where it is close to the fur trapping and trading opportunities. It was established to service the fur trade industry, not only at the fur trapper level but to also provide services to the Indian fur trade as well, which is huge. As such, this post provides a fur trade purchasing service and provides supplies to members of the Assinboine, Plains Cree, Mandan, Arikara, Hidatsa, Blackfeet or Piegans, and Chippewa Nations, plus those of our company as well as the class of Free Trappers. However we do find ourselves in direct and serious competition with the Hudson's Bay Company to our northwest and further north into Canada."

Then pausing while he took out a plug of chewing tobacco from his coat pocket, bit off a chunk and moved it around between his teeth and gums, McKenzie began again once his chew had been comfortably settled saying, "The fur industry is huge because a lot of the cloth and clothing in Europe is of poor quality or not as warm and colorful as is that from our animals' furs and robes. In fact from our first year of being in business, we shipped back to our fur houses in St. Louis over 25,000 smaller furs like beaver, fox, muskrat, raccoon, bobcat, coyote, wolf, mink, and river otter, as well as buffalo and bear robes. This year with more trappers pouring into this country, and almost limitless numbers of available fur bearing animals at every creek, marsh and field, we hope to do an even bigger business, especially since we are now even better known to all of the tribes in this area. Those tribal trappers I have since learned are by far and away the largest suppliers of our raw furs and robes in the entire fur industry. However something I have also come to understand of late and is more important is the value of the indigenous women to the fur trade. They are the ones who are doing the pelting and tanning of the skins and hides, and are the ones pushing their menfolk to trade those furs for such things we commonly have in our society like metal pots, pans, kettles, knives, bolts of cloth, and glass beads for what is lacking in their culture. It seems the Indians have an almost inexhaustible desire for the modern day goods of the white man, which understandably makes their lives easier. That plus they are bringing us skins, furs and hides which they consider insignificant and of low value since they exist everywhere in 'their' world. That they do for what they consider significant and of higher value in the ways of white man's guns, brightly colored glass beads, cooking ware, gunpowder, lead, knives, and metal to make their arrow points, which are always in short supply in their cultures. We in turn are trading everyday items of lower value from our society for expensive furs to be sold in an almost inexhaustible market in Europe. Either way, it appears to be good for business for both sides and for that I am pleased, as is Mr. Astor."

All of a sudden McKenzie paused in his business ramblings saying, "I am sorry! I forgot my manners. The two of you Free Trappers are invited to my home this evening for supper. There we can discuss the business that the two of you came here to discuss and enjoy some very fine victuals provided by my Chinese cooks. Additionally, since I see the two of you arrived with just the clothing on your backs and rifles in hand, I assume you had a spate of bad luck and lost all of your kit. Not to worry on your part. With the arrival of the keelboats on the Missouri River's "Spring Rush", my warehouses are bulging at the seams and you two shall have the pick of the lot because of your poor condition, before the rest of the hordes come looking to provision up for their year in the field. (Author's Note: The "Spring Rush" refers to the high waters in the Missouri River caused by the short periods of spring rains and snowmelt runoff in what became the State of Montana on the Big

Muddy, Poplar, Wolf, Porcupine and Yellowstone Rivers, just to name a few of the watersheds. Most ship captains realized that to safely navigate the Missouri carrying heavy loads in their vessels, they needed high water flows in order to avoid that river's many hidden sand bars, shallows, floating dead winter-killed buffalo that had fallen through the thin spring ice while crossing the river, and other navigational obstacles. Hence most successful vessels navigated upstream during the high water flows carrying supplies to upstream forts and trading posts, and avoided trying to do so during low water flows represented during the summer and early fall months.) Additionally, since I see you have no bedding, you are to stay in one of my houses normally reserved for my company's *Engagés* to stay in until I can get the two of you provisioned. Now I must run for I see I have a squabble going on over at the fur sorting and grading tables that I must settle between my men and that pair of just arriving Free Trappers from the field."

With that, McKenzie headed down his steps and trotted off across the courtyard to settle the squabble over the number or quality of the furs being sorted from the newly arriving Free Trappers. In the meantime, Bear Scat's head just spun like a dusty whirlwind had spun by with him in the middle over what all he had just learned. He not only had gotten a thumbnail sketch of Fort Union and the fur trade in general but what he eventually came to understand was a look at the human side of a well-known and highly respected Factor in the trade as well. That plus a look at a future businessman that he and Big Hat would be dealing with if they survived and were successful as Free Trappers coming back to Fort Union annually to trade and re-provision.

That evening, Big Hat and Bear Scat were Factor McKenzie's sole supper guests. There they were treated to roast buffalo, fried potatoes with onions grown in Fort Union's nearby garden, Dutch oven biscuits slathered in wild plum jam, real homemade butter, pickled beets and for dessert, apple cobbler smothered in cow's cream! Big Hat and Bear Scat could hardly believe their eyes nor could their stomachs. Both men gorged themselves since they had been eating fairly light while out on the trail and as a result, both men later paid the price. Throughout most of that evening after such a magnificent supper, both men found each other sitting side by side on the nearest two-hole outhouse with bad cases of the 'green-apple goose-step' from all of the rich food just consumed! Especially from that of the many more than generous helpings of the rich cow's cream slathered all over their cobbler!

After such a wonderful supper, Factor McKenzie got down to the 'brass tacks' when it came to the needed business at hand concerning his newest arriving and nearly destitute Free Trappers. He began their meeting by saying, "Since I saw the two of you coming into the fort's courtyard with only the clothing on your backs and obviously riding two Indian ponies and trailing a third, what do you lads need in the way of provisions and how do you want to settle up with the company regarding the acquisition of those provisions?" Typical of Factor McKenzie, he got right down to business straight away like any good businessman who knew his trade.

Big Hat began by saying, "Mr. McKenzie, we plan on staying in country and trapping our ways on some of the big rivers further west of here. Then come the late spring after that first trapping season, we plan on coming back here to sell our furs and celebrate another year of keeping our 'topknots'. Additionally, try keeping a family wish alive for Bear Scat here in locating his brother and then moving once again back into the country we wish to explore and trap in the late fall, winter and early spring. However, as you 'seed', we were unfortunately waylaid in our coming here by two different sets of evil factors and now need some help if we are to continue in country as Free Trappers. Bottom line, we will need some better livestock than we rode in on and total re-supply if we are to survive as trappers and be successful in what we wish to do."

"Alright, as I told the two of you back on my porch earlier this afternoon, you are in luck. We have just received our year's supply of provisions and I now make them available to the two of you on a first-come basis. I will do so since you men need everything and in so doing, I will give you 'the pick of the litter' when it comes to my available supplies. Big Hat, I have known you from past years of working together and as far as I am concerned, you are an honest and honorable man, so your credit is always good with me. As for you, Bear Scat, by which means do you wish to repay me for any goods received or do you as well wish to have me 'carry' you for the upcoming trapping season?" asked McKenzie in a gracious sort of way.

Reaching into his carry bag, Bear Scat took out his booklet from the First Mercantile Bank of St. Louis regarding his Spanish silver dollar deposit saying, "I have $300 in my bank in St. Louis that I brought from my parents' farm and deposited there. I wish to use that money to help in getting Big Hat and myself outfitted for this next trapping season. However I do not know how to get that money up here to pay you for those supplies that we need."

"That is not hard for me to do since our company uses that same bank. I will get one of my Clerks to sit down with you, draft up a letter of release to your bank which will allow my St. Louis fur house to withdraw the funds you want released, and that way we will be square," advised McKenzie. "If you go over the amount that you have banked, then I will carry that balance on what you need on my books and you can settle up with me upon your return from this coming trapping season. Now tomorrow before I open up my warehouses for trade and everyone makes a rush for their annual supplies, the two of you need to go into those warehouses and provision up. I will let one of my Clerks know of our arrangement and then the two of you can help yourselves to what you will need for the coming trapping season without competition from all the other trappers and Indians pushing and shoving while they look for and purchase the same things," said McKenzie.

With that business out of the way and in full agreement of the parties, Bear Scat took his leave during the interlude of conversation and began asking questions of McKenzie relating to some of his most pressing concerns and desires. "Mr. McKenzie, do you know a Free Trapper named Jacob Sutta? He is my older brother and if you know him, is he here on-site now and if not, do you know of his whereabouts?"

"Sure do!" said McKenzie. "I had supper with Jacob and his partner, Wild Bill McGinty, not more than two weeks ago! They came in with a lame horse, traded that one in for a good one, sold off their furs, got their provisions and headed back out, because they had a long ways to go to get to their desired new trapping grounds before the beaver were all trapped out. In fact, they took out almost two years' worth of supplies, saying they were headed up onto the upper reaches of the Porcupine River and were not sure they could make it back by next summer with their furs. I told the two of them that they might be asking for trouble by trying to trap those waters so far north. Trouble because other American trappers have reported the Hudson's Bay Company trappers are coming down from Canada and are working those same trapping waters in the upper reaches of the Porcupine as well. That being the case, I think your brother and his partner Wild Bill, are heading for some clashes between themselves and some of those damn French-Canadian Hudson's Bay trappers in the form of trap stealing and theft of catches in the field. Additionally that is in the heart of the territory of the dreaded Gros Ventre Indians, and they seem only to cater to the wishes of the Hudson's Bay people and not us Americans. Additionally if the two of you follow in those two trappers' footsteps in order to reunite some family ties, you may run into a mess of renegade Piegans or Blackfeet. That can be bad for one's health because they can be killing son-of-a-bitches if they are riled up as well. I told Jacob and Wild Bill the same thing but they seemed determined to trap those waters for the 'blanket-sized' beaver reported to be in that area. (Author's Note: "Blanket-sized" was 'period' terminology identifying very large in size and therefore the more valuable, adult beaver.) There were only the two of them and I reminded them that they more than likely would be easy targets for those groups of mean-as-hell Indians or mean-assed grizzly bears known to heavily inhabit that area. However that brother of yours just laughed over my words of caution and said they would be back in the summer to trade in their furs and I had better have a large supply of Fourth Class Rum on hand or else, after trying to scare them away from what they have heard are some real First Class beaver trappings."

Upon hearing those most welcome words about McKenzie's firsthand and current knowledge of his brother, Bear Scat's eyes lit up and just glistened with tears of eventual reunion hope. Then he looked over at Big Hat saying, "I guess it is the Porcupine River for us as well, Partner. Any problem if we head in that direction, wherever the hell that is?" asked Bear Scat.

"You know me, Partner. I am in this one for the distance that it takes to make it happen. However with that in mind, I would say all of your bank money will be used up and then some when it comes to purchasing all of the provisions that we will need for that faraway adventure. I passed through that area a number of years back and it is a fer piece and all through Gros Ventre and Blackfeet country as well. Like McKenzie says, those damn Gros Ventre are killing sons-a-bitches if I remember correctly and don't cotton much at all to us white folk from America tramping across their ancestral lands uninvited, trapping and killing off all of their game," said Big Hat with a grin over the possible coming adventure spelled clear across his weathered face. Then Big Hat paused as if thinking ahead of the possible trip north to the trapping grounds of the Porcupine saying, "Bear Scat, I think we need to consider looking for a couple more compatible partners if we are to safely navigate that area and return to Fort Union next summer with our 'topknots'."

"Whatever it takes is what it takes," replied Bear Scat quietly. "As you know, Jacob is my brother and only living kin. I aim to see him once again afore I pass and that is that. However, you being my friend and all, I don't want to expose you to any more undue dangers than necessary. If you would like, I could seek out another partner while here at the fort who is willing and able to go clear out to the Porcupine and then go looking for my brother as well as trapping for a living. That way I wouldn't be dragging you in front of a Gros Ventre's speeding lead ball or iron-tipped arrow point."

"Don't you ever doubt my friendship with you, damn you Bear Scat! I am here to do for you what you would do for me if I were in like circumstances. So don't you walk on that ground ever again in my presence unless you want a damn fist-sized knot on the side of your damn thick head," replied Big Hat in a tone and tenor of voice that read 'finality of discussion' regarding life's dangerous circumstances up on the Porcupine!

"I am sorry for speaking out of turn like that, Big Hat. I just didn't want to drag you into something that was of my doing and getting you killed or shot all to hell," quietly said an admonished Bear Scat.

"Nuff said on that matter," replied Big Hat as he settled back down on his 'rump of ruffled feathers'... "However, I think while I am here, I will be looking for some of my old compatriots who might be in the need of a couple good partners. If I can find any, it would do us good to have them and their extra rifles along for all our own safety. Plus if that area has a lot of 'blanket-sized' beaver running around, that could just be the added incentive to drag someone else along with us into 'hell's kitchen' in the heart of that mean-assed Indian territory." Realizing Big Hat's frontier wisdom regarding the 'extra rifles coming along for the company it offered', Bear Scat nodded his head in support over Big Hat's thinking.

"Now in addition to that matter, Mr. McKenzie, do you by chance know of a group of five trappers headed up by a rather large and mean-looking individual named "Bear"? My best guess is they would have arrived within the last two weeks sometime, needing more supplies as well," inquired Bear Scat.

"Do you have any more information other than just a mean-looking trapper named "Bear"?" asked McKenzie. "I ask because it is amazing just how many of you fur trappers are the size of a bear, smell like one and possess a mean-assed attitude and moniker to match."

"I do," responded Bear Scat. "When I first met this bunch of trappers, it was when they were back in St. Louis selling their furs. I met a man named William Price who went by the name "Muskrat". He in turn discovering that I wanted to be a fur trapper and at the same time be on the lookout for my brother, requested of his group that I be allowed to join them on their return trip to this area. When his group said it would be alright if I joined their party of trappers, Muskrat subsequently introduced me to his friends. When he did, there was a man named Bob McGoon also known as "Fingers", another man named Randy Stewart or "Biscuits", another named Jacob Greer the group called "Fish", and lastly a man named Jay Peterson, who went by the moniker of "Bear". It is that group of trappers that I am looking for in particular. I am looking for that group of men because one night during a heavy rain and violent thunderstorm, they quietly robbed me of everything that I owned while I was sleeping, slipped away and left me afoot out on the prairie in Indian country with little more than my name to just up and die. I intend to hunt down that group of trappers and if I catch them, kill the entire lot anyway that I can. That is if God is willing because none of them deserve to live for what they did to another human being, namely me!"

For the longest moment after Bear Scat had finished speaking, the only thing that one could hear in the great dining room of the Factor's home was the rhythmic ticking of the giant grandfather clock in the corner of the room. Then realizing just how determined Bear Scat was by the tone and tenor of his voice regarding his mission to set things right according to the unwritten code of those living out on the frontier, McKenzie said, "Yes, now that I think about it, I do remember that bunch of trappers of which you speak. I remember them because they did not like the prices I offered for their furs late one spring and said they would take them to St. Louis and be robbed there instead of being robbed out here by me and my "Mountain Prices" on the frontier. (Author's Note: "Mountain Prices" referred to what the trading posts out on the frontier charged for goods and supplies. They referred to those prices charged with anywhere from a 700-1,000% markup on the prices of goods over and above the prices charged for the same items back in civilization. Traders found it necessary to charge such exorbitant prices to offset their losses in getting such supplies way out onto the frontier.) Yes, now that I think about it, I do remember that bunch," replied McKenzie somewhat quietly, as if not wishing to get involved in a blood feud between his trappers and his good business sense!

"Any idea where they were heading?" asked Bear Scat quietly, with a tone of 'deadly' in his voice and with a foreboding, narrow-eyed look of destiny in his eyes.

"All I know was they were heading west out to some river somewhere in the heart of Gros Ventre country," replied McKenzie. "But if you lads are heading as far west as the Porcupine, you very well might run across that bunch. If not there, maybe you will run across those fellows when they are coming back to Fort Union next summer and are traveling along the Missouri as they so often wont to do. Lastly, if not there, maybe back here at Fort Union when the two of you groups of trappers come back to resupply for the coming trapping season," replied McKenzie trying to be helpful. Then as an afterthought McKenzie said, "Now that I think about it, those fellows got their supplies and headed out the next day after they had arrived at the fort, almost as if they were being cold tracked. Yeah, now that I think about it, they acted real guilty like they had done something wrong and wanted to quickly get into the wilderness to get away from the stain of it all or anyone who might be trailing them…"

Those thoughtful and informational responses from McKenzie seemed to satisfy Bear Scat, especially now that he knew those he was after were now long gone and 'in the wind'. However, what that group of five former 'friends' had done to him was never far from his mind or the bile that remained in his soul. With those issues out in the wind and settled for now, there were handshakes all around and then Big Hat and Bear Scat retired to their sleeping quarters because the trappers knew their next week at the fort would be a busy one gathering up all they needed and preparing for the coming trapping season. After all, the mission to find his brother and the ugly issue of 'doing unto others who had done unto him' now being 'in the wind', the two of them still had to make a living doing what they wanted to do, causing them to begin just thinking in the present...for now. At that moment in time, it was obvious to McKenzie that their thinking for now was directed towards the upper reaches of the Porcupine River and whatever fortunes of 'beaver, brother or both' that would bring.

After having breakfast with the fort's employees the following morning and then making one more visit to the outhouse to rid themselves of the final intestinal vestiges of ultra-rich, triple helpings of fresh cow's cream from the previous night's supper, Big Hat and Bear Scat headed for the Clerks' quarters. There they hooked up with one of the fort's Clerks and out they went to Fort Union's resident horse and mule herds located outside its protective walls that were for sale. There Big Hat and Bear Scat bartered off their Indian ponies and with their various credits proffered by McKenzie, purchased two spirited riding horses, two more ordinary riding horses (cost less) for reserve in case one of their main riding horses was injured or killed by a grizzly bear or stolen by Indians, and four ordinary but hell-for-stout pack mules. Then with their Clerk and selected livestock in tow, it was off to the blacksmith shops to get their just purchased livestock in line with the other trappers so they could be reshod. Leaving their animals, they then headed for one of the fort's warehouses to shop for and stock up on provisions needed for the coming trapping season before they were opened up for 'shopping' by the hordes of trappers and Indians waiting to start the trading they needed to do.

That was when Big Hat's value as a mentor and partner really shone at being an experienced fur trapper. Big Hat knew from previous years of experience as a trapper in the wilderness what they would need for a year afield and it wasn't long before the two trappers began looking at selecting a small mountain of the much-needed supplies. However before they began, Big Hat pulled Bear

Scat aside and just like Bear Scat's father used to do with him, began instructing him as to the 'how and whys' of provision selection for such a long absence from any easy form of re-supply. That he did because Bear Scat had earlier requested of Big Hat that every time a unique fur trapping and fur trade learning opportunity arose, he be taught every aspect of the trade of becoming a good fur trapper and backcountry survivalist. Having come from living a 'hard-scrabble' earlier life, Bear Scat already had developed an innate ability to realize the life of a fur trapper on the frontier would mean he would be facing twin challenges of hardship and danger. He also realized that in order for him to become a successful Mountain Man, he would need to possess a set of learned wilderness skills and personal attributes. Possess learned wilderness skills like mastery of his rifle and pistol, being able to swim and swim well especially in icy waters, be a successful mountain climber, be able to handle himself when armed and unarmed conflict was called for, possess skills with his knife and tomahawk, being able to supply his food through his acumen as a hunter, being able to read not only animal but human sign, horsemanship, and most of all being a trapper able to survive under the frontier's extreme conditions. Bear Scat also had begun to realize that those needed personal attributes of a fur trapper on the frontier where any form of help was always distant, included physical, mental and emotional strength, as well as endurance along with a will to live and survive that was every bit as strong as the steel on his rifle barrel. That was why Bear Scat had requested from Big Hat that he be taught every aspect of being a fur trapper and one who could live through those challenges experienced by a fur trapper.

As Big Hat walked the aisles between the stacks, boxes, kegs and bags of goods in the warehouses making his selections of provisions, Bear Scat stored them off to one side for later retrieval. Even more importantly, Bear Scat had an almost unbelievably keen mind for not only facts, figures and justification for needs but for retention of the same as well. As Big Hat had items pulled from the shelves and stacks, Bear Scat was committing to memory such needs for the day in case he was on his own and maybe would not have an experienced Big Hat as a partner. Not having such an experienced mentor as Big Hat in the future, such as often happened or was the case in the many times violent unexplored West of the fur trapper or Western explorer, where every moment was more times than not, pregnant with peril...

Initially and before they were all picked over, Big Hat went right to the firearms section of the warehouse like a man on a mission. With a Clerk in tow recording his picks, amounts of items needed and respective costs, Big Hat made sure right off the bat that he selected two of the Lancaster rifles made in England (most popular Mountain Man rifle), .52 caliber rifles valued at $16.50 each. Then turning to Bear Scat who had a questioning look on his face since the two of them already possessed the same caliber of rifles, only they were Hawken rifles made in St. Louis, responded to the 'look' he was getting from his younger partner by saying, "Bear Scat, where we are going we will be in the heart of the territory of the dreaded Gros Ventre and Blackfeet Indians. We are but two in number and the only way we will have any chance of surviving if we tangle with any of the above groups of Indians, is to be heavily armed since we more than likely will be outnumbered and must be straight shooting in our performance. We both are damn fine shooters with our current rifles but just imagine what our survival chances will be if we have twice the rifle firepower than our attackers will expect from just two lone trappers."

Then Big Hat walked over to the cases displaying various types and calibers of pistols. There Big Hat selected four single shot, percussion cap system pistols of .52 caliber, valued at $10 apiece. Once again, Big Hat got a wondering look from his younger and inexperienced partner as to why the purchase of four pistols, since they already possessed several like in kind pistols of their own. Grinning over his younger partner's questioning looks again, Big Hat said, "Bear Scat, once again we are but two trappers in an unforgiving land of fierce adversaries and larger numbers of them than us. No matter how we look at it, once we run dry with our long guns and the Indians see that, they will be upon us like flies on a dead buffalo in the hot July sun. When that happens, all we will have left to defend ourselves are our pistols. However since we now each possess four pistols, imagine the surprise any close-in attacking Indians will discover when they run into our multiple blazing pistols. Now you can see why I wanted the extra firepower. Additionally notice they are of the same caliber as are our rifles. That makes our casting of balls and using the same powders and caps we would normally use on our rifles just that much more practical and efficient. I value my 'topknot' and I am sure you do so as well. With these purchases we just guaranteed our wearing a full head of hair just a mite longer if we are ever attacked and called upon to defend our lives or the lives of those around us."

Following those selections, Big Hat headed over to the section of their warehouse holding all the assorted 'necessaries' needed to accompany any firearms purchases. There he selected four eight-pound sheets of lead-corked, air tight canisters holding four pounds each of Best powder at $1.50 per pound of powder. Without hesitation, Big Hat then selected ten tins of No. 11 percussion caps for use on either their rifles or pistols, 30 pounds of lead 'pigs' at $1 per pound so one could cast their own bullets while afield, 100 pre-cast .52 caliber balls for interchangeable use in either their rifles or pistols at $1 per pound, a bullet-casting kettle and ladle at $4, and two sets of .52 caliber mold blocks for casting rifle and pistol balls while afield at $4 each. Finished with those selections and looking over at his partner, Big Hat could see his acknowledgment of understanding for those purchases in Bear Scat's eyes as being necessary for the trip ahead. Seeing that Bear Scat fully comprehended the value of those purchases and needing no further explanation, Big Hat moved on to the next counter of what he considered 'necessaries'. There he selected gun worms or wipers, ball screws, extra parts for the locks on their rifles and pistols, tools with which to repair their firearms, extra powder horns, three canisters of patches, and two extra ramrods at $1 each for their rifles in case any were broken in the field. Once again, Big Hat looked over at his younger partner to see if any looks he got required explanation of the latest selections. Seeing acknowledgement once again and understanding of said selections in Bear Scat's eyes, Big Hat moved on with his provision 'shopping'. Standing there quietly thinking over his selections, Big Hat finally seemed satisfied with his choices of the personal protection and sporting items and amounts that he had selected for purchase.

Then with the Clerk leading the way over to the trapping necessaries, Big Hat selected 20 St. Louis-style, steel, double spring, rectangular jaws without teeth, hand forged by Mr. Hill, five-pound beaver traps with six-foot chains holding double swivels at $9 each! Then almost as an afterthought, Big Hat moved over to the larger jawed traps with teeth and selected six Newhouse #14 toothed traps designed for wolf and mountain lion-sized animals. Turning to Bear Scat, Big Hat said, "If the St. Louis-style beaver traps made by Hill are not ever available whenever you are ordering, I would suggest that you select Newhouse #4 traps weighing around five pounds each. As for the Newhouse #14-sized traps, we will need those for the trapping of wolves once we are frozen out from trapping our 'finer furs' like beaver. Wolf pelts taken during the dead of winter will be in their prime and fetch us top dollar back at any trading post." Those traps Big Hat purchased respectively cost $9 and $10 each. Then Big Hat selected two spools of trap wire costing $2.50 per spool, so the traps could be wired down to their anchors in order to prevent loss of such valuable items.

Looking over at Bear Scat, Big Hat could see another questioning look in his partner's eyes. "What?" said Big Hat.

"We will have to catch a lot of beaver in order to pay for everything you have selected based on these Mountain Prices. That being the case, why don't we buy at least 40 beaver traps instead of just 20 so we could catch more beaver?" asked Bear Scat.

"Bear Scat, a good beaver trapper will only need about six to eight traps a day in which to successfully run his trap line. However, in order to allow for trap loss, theft from Indians and breakage, a smart trapper will keep at least ten traps per trapper in his inventory. Just so you learn and understand, it will take a good trapper a full day with six to eight traps to find suitable places to make a beaver set, make his rounds, skin out his catch, flesh them out, and stretch and hoop them for drying before the day is done. If there are large 'blanket-sized' beaver in the numbers everyone talks about up on the Porcupine, that tells me the beaver populations up there are very healthy and mature. That being the case, as skilled trappers we should catch a beaver in every set. I don't mean to brag but I am a damn good trapper of beaver if I say so myself, so not to worry about coming back to Fort Union with way more beaver in value than we will spend here this day for our supplies, Mountain Prices or not."

Seeing that explanation was sufficient for his partner learning the fur trade, Big Hat followed the Clerk to the cooking section of the warehouse with Bear Scat in tow. Once there, Big Hat selected six sheet-iron kettles at $2.25 per pound, three six-quart Dutch ovens and two sets of cooking irons to hang cooking pots over an open fire at $2 each. Those selections were quickly followed by an assortment of stirring spoons, tin cups, plates and eating utensils for $6. Stepping over to the immediate next section of the warehouse, Big Hat selected three square axes at $2.50 each. Then at Big Hat's request to the Clerk, the trio went over to the tool section and there Big Hat selected two square shovels, two saws and six files for another $18. During those specific selections, the learning Bear Scat having come from a frontier farm earlier in his life saw the need for what Big Hat was selecting for their extended trapping and cabin-building foray to come and held his tongue.

Following that bit of shopping, the Clerk took the two trappers over to a rather large section of the warehouse housing knives of every sort and size. "AHA!" said Big Hat with an approving smile over the next section of the warehouse. "Bear Scat, next to me, your horse and firearms, this section of the warehouse is the most important part of life to anyone working out on the frontier, white man or Indian alike! Being without a good knife is like being without a good woman to have in one's life. However, I see a lot of cheap 'scalpers' here in this section and those are the kind we do not want or have any use for. If for some reason I am not around and you are out and on your own, always make sure you have a good knife in reach and it had better be the kind I am looking for, or I will kick your ass for not listening to what I am trying to teach you. THERE THEY ARE! Look at that bunch of knives over there, Bear Scat. Those are the ones I am looking for, namely, Thomas Wilson Sheer Steel knives made in Sheffield, England. Those are some of the best butcher and scalper knives made from the finest steel the English have to offer. Remember, Bear Scat, a trapper always has a need for a knife or knives that are style-wise country-made, heavy enough for chopping, yet small enough to be used as a 'scalper' or general purpose knife. These Thomas Wilson knives are some of the best. In fact when my previous camp of fellow fur trappers were ambushed by those damn stinking Arikara, I had one hell of a set of this kind of knives made from the finest steel the English had to offer. I suppose some damn squaw has those great knives now, chopping buffalo bones apart for the marrow contained therein. Bear Scat, we are going to pick up a number of these, namely some skinning knives, butcher knives, what I call cooking knives, and some smaller assorted ones as well. Knives are essential to a trapper and if the truth be known, hardly less valid to an Indian as well. Whoa, lookee-here! I am also going to take three of this type of knife as well. See here, Bear Scat, I will have the blacksmith re-grind this knife for our purposes of skinning out the beaver we catch. I will have the blacksmith re-grind these three knives so the bevel is only on one side of the knife. That way when we are skinning out our beaver that reduces the danger of slashing a hole in the hide which subtracts from its value back here at Fort Union. Oh, we also need to pick up three butcher's steels as well in order to keep the edges on our knives," said Big Hat, who was like a kid in a St. Louis candy store while he was in the knife section of the warehouse! But that same level of excitement and their intrinsic values was also being infused into the memory banks of his still learning fur trapper disciple, namely Bear Scat, as well.

Following that, at Big Hat's request to the Clerk, it was off to the blankets and clothing sections of the warehouse. By now, Bear Scat's head was swimming over how much he needed to learn and what was needed just to get started in making a living out on the frontier as a trapper, and they still weren't finished with their preparations! Remembering how quickly his previous store-bought clothing had fallen apart under the rigors of hard use out on the frontier, Bear Scat eagerly watched as Big Hat now went 'shopping' for the necessary clothing needed to survive the Western weather, which would be in addition to what they made for each other from tanned animal skins while out on the trapping grounds. Big Hat, like a man on a mission, quickly picked out eight, 2½-point blankets at $7 each, eight horse and mule blankets at $6 each, four heavy capotes at $5 each for the extreme winter weather they would soon be facing trapping in the northern latitudes, blue cloth at $4 per yard (for clothing repairs), and three-piece fitted, "Linsey-woolsy" shirts.

Upon the selections of the English-made shirts instead of the long-wearing buckskins, Bear Scat's face reflected another questioning look. Catching his partner's questioning looks over purchasing shirts that would more than likely quickly wear out and fall apart on the rough and tumble frontier, Big Hat said, "Those shirts will be worn in the summer months when the wearing of buckskin is too hot to do so. Plus they will be worn underneath our buckskin shirts come winter for the added warmth they will bring." With that explanation, Bear Scat smiled his understanding and then on and on it went until Bear Scat's head was swimming again over the wide selections of items, numbers of each needed, and trading post costs at the exorbitant Mountain Prices of 700-1,000% higher compared to purchasing the same items back in St. Louis!

Following that, Big Hat and Bear Scat headed to the basic supplies section of another warehouse and selected 30 pounds of brown cone sugar at $1 a pound, 60 pounds of green coffee beans at $1.25 per pound (needed to be cooked or burned in the bottom of a Dutch oven and then ground before they would make good coffee), 20 pounds of raisins at $1.50 per pound, and on it went for the needed amounts of flour, salt, pepper, dried beans, rice, cooking spices, moccasin awls, spools of thread, spurs, spools of brass wire to repair broken or cracked rifle stocks, bolts of gray cloth, kegs of Fourth Class Rum, iron buckles, leather strapping for repairs, packsaddles, panniers, a 100-foot spool of cotton lead rope, extra fire steels, dried fruit, washing soap, straight razors (contrary to beliefs, most Mountain Men shaved; there was a head lice epidemic in the general population in those days and by shaving, that kept the head louse 'habitat' on one's body to a minimum), shaving soap, several tins of 'bag balm' to treat saddle and pack sores on their animals, two crocks of bear grease (for cooking), two whetstones, and eight first quality 'carrots' of James River chewing and smoking tobacco, weight about three pounds each. (Author's Note: Tobacco in those days to facilitate easy measurement for valuation and safe travel in horse or mule packs, was tightly rolled and then wrapped with a heavy twine until the lump of rolled tobacco resembled a long, wrapped carrot.) Such numbers and selections of provisions were gathered up until Bear Scat thought his head was going to explode off into the air over so many facts, needs and figures! At the end of their big 'shopping' day, Big Hat was satisfied his purchases would last out their trapping year out on the frontier and any other needs they required that arose while out on the trail.

Then it was off to the fort's blacksmith shops where all the recently acquired riding horses and pack mules were located in the process of having their old shoes removed and replaced with new ones. Then Big Hat had the blacksmiths make an additional set of shoes for each of their animals in case they threw any shoes while out on the trail. Also while at the blacksmiths, Big Hat had any and all of their animals' teeth checked to see if they needed to have them 'floated'. Following that, Big Hat explained what he wanted in the way of re-grinding his three Thomas Wilson knives so there would only be a bevel on one side of the knife which made the skinning of beaver less apt to having its hide slashed by the skinner. Then it was back to another warehouse for the needed farrier tools in case horse or mule shoes needed replacing while out in the field once Big Hat discovered that Bear Scat was also a skilled farrier, a trade he had learned on his father's farm. When all the shopping for a year's supplies were completed, Big Hat and Bear Scat discovered they owed the American Fur Company $316.53 over and above the 300 Spanish silver dollars Bear Scat had back in a bank in St. Louis for which he had executed a withdrawal draft! But neither man blanched over what they owed because First Class beaver *'plus'* or "Made Beaver", were bringing around $6 each that year and the frontier rivers and waterways were crawling with the furry rodents, especially reportedly on the upper reaches of the Porcupine River where they were headed! (Author's Note: A "Made Beaver" was a measurement and medium of exchange at most trading posts. A Made Beaver was a prime quality skin from an adult beaver. In most trading posts and at rendezvous, it was considered a standard unit of trade. For example, ten Made Beaver could be used to purchase one trade rifle or one Made Beaver could trade for 1½ pounds of powder, a hatchet, a good coat, a brass kettle, or two pounds of cone sugar and the like.)

The following day, Big Hat and Bear Scat spent most of the day at the fort's fur grading tables. That was done by Big Hat in order to teach Bear Scat the proper method of fleshing and mounting of beaver skins whose quality of work was evidenced by the numbers, conditions and grades of furs submitted by the various arriving trappers. While there, Bear Scat also got a lesson in the different species of fur bearers he would also be encountering and the different values offered by the fort's fur buyers by species, quality and constantly shifting market demands.

In the late afternoon, Big Hat saw to it that Bear Scat got his fur trade knowledge increased as indicated by a sample of trade values offered at Fort Union. There he discovered that trading in an ordinary riding horse would get the horse's owner a Northwest fusil rifle with 100 rounds of ammunition or a 'carrot' of tobacco weighing about three pounds. Or if Bear Scat and Big Hat traded in a buffalo or large bearskin robe, they could receive in trade knives, kettles or ammunition depending on the quality of their submission. Bear Scat also discovered that his newly acquired taste for Fourth Class Rum, per keg, would cost him up to ten Made Beaver skins! Finally after several days of being 'schooled' by Big Hat on the frontier marketplace, Bear Scat was reminded that everything they would need to purchase that far out on the frontier cost between 700 and up to 1,000 times what a like item would have cost one to purchase in St. Louis, and many times those items purchased out on the frontier were of a poorer quality!

Anxious to get underway on his mission to hopefully find his brother on the upper reaches of the Porcupine River and just as anxious to learn the practical aspects and trade of a fur trapper, Bear Scat kept pushing Big Hat for a departure date from Fort Union. However having been there before, Big Hat would not leave until he was convinced everything they needed in order to get their work done afield was accomplished. Finally Big Hat figured they were more than ready to go and let Bear Scat know they would leave two days later! Bear Scat was beside himself in excitement when Big Hat announced their departure date, and the night before leaving for the dangerous and mostly unexplored wilds of the West, barely slept a wink! Barely slept a wink because he was soon to be onto his new life as a fur trapper, hopefully heading into an area where he might find his brother and be reunited once again, have a chance to see some new country, and lastly, send those five fur trappers who had left him to die out on the prairie on their ways to hell as well...

Come the day of their departure from Fort Union into the wilds of the frontier, McKenzie had Big Hat and Bear Scat over at his home for breakfast as was his tradition with his Free Trappers and other people of note. There they had bacon, fresh eggs, Dutch oven biscuits, coffee, and an apple pie made from previously soaked-in-water dried apples. However, that time both men passed on slathering their pie with fresh cow's cream upon remembering what had happened to them in the outhouse the last time they had imbibed great amounts of such a creamy and unfamiliar substance to their intestines that were used to mostly lean meat and in great quantities...

Wolfing down his breakfast in excitement, Bear Scat was more than ready to go and finally the long-awaited moment in time came. After packing their horses and mules, Big Hat and Bear Scat walked their loaded animals to the river and boarded the flat-bottomed boats used to ferry them across the Missouri River to the far west side and finally drop them off at the very edge of the 'wilds' in what is the modern-day State of Montana. Once ashore on the western side of the Missouri River, Big Hat took the lead leading a lightly packed, extra riding horse, trailed by two fully loaded mules as he headed westerly along the northern side of the Missouri River. Following closely behind came Bear Scat leading his packed extra riding horse, trailed by two heavily loaded pack mules as well. To Bear Scat, they were now off on an adventure of a lifetime into a land of the unknowns...

Bear Scat carried across his saddle his Hawken rifle, the one he had traded his father's Pennsylvania rifle for back in St. Louis at the Hawken gun shop, carried two single shot pistols in his sash, and had two additional single shot pistols attached to holsters on his close at hand trailing packhorse. He also had a fully loaded Lancaster rifle in a scabbard attached to his trailing riding horse in case a need for defense from man or beast arose. Big Hat figured since there were only two of them and they were going into hostile Indian country basically alone and right off the bat, they had best go heavily armed and be ready for any kind of an eventuality. Especially since the odds they would be facing if discovered by hostile Indians would be grave when it came to the numbers of attackers faced. Hence, the close at hand 'artillery' each trapper carried in hand and on horse as they ventured into the largely unknown Indian territory. That type of defensive armament Big Hat had provided for since he had been unable to find anyone of character or work ethic that he trusted to add as extra partners from the pool of trappers back at Fort Union.

By the end of that first long day of travel alongside the northern bank of the Missouri River found Big Hat and Bear Scat making camp near where the confluence of the Big Muddy River flowed into the Missouri. Moving off the prairie where they and any campfire they had could be seen for miles by maybe those with evil intent in their hearts, Big Hat and Bear Scat moved into the deeper brush along the Missouri and made camp. The first thing done was to unpack all of their animals and let them roll around on the ground and scratch the many itches they had developed on their backs during that first day of travel under the heavy packs full of provisions and the like. As the two men stacked and covered all of their packs against the threat of any afternoon or evening thunderstorms and prepared to set up their campsite, they let the horses and mules feed and water in the rich grasses alongside the river. Then when Bear Scat prepared to lay out their sleeping furs, the lessons in living out on the frontier were verbally provided once again by Big Hat.

"Bear Scat, anytime you prepare to make camp, make sure that you set up in a place that has lots of available water, wood, shade and space. For example, don't place our sleeping robes where you now have them placed. Always set up your camp and sleeping furs on the northeastern side of a cottonwood tree if at all possible so you can block out the midday sun. But when you do, make sure you do not do so under its branches. If it rains, the large leaves in the tree will be dripping water drops on you for hours, soaking everything you have in that area. Additionally, when you bring in the wood for our campfire, make sure you bring in a mess of green brush and tree limbs for night use as well. That way with green branches come dark when the camp is soon plagued with buffalo gnats, blue flies and mosquitoes, burning such greenery of some sort will provide clouds of smoke and help in keeping the bugs away so we won't be so pestered. Plus by burning such greenery at night, it won't be seen by any other travelers and the smell of smoke will help in keeping the grizzly bears out of our campsite."

Come dusk that first day, the horses and mules were brought in from 'putting on the feed bag', double hobbled to preclude any nearby Indians who had seen them from stealing away any of their valuable stock animals, and then picketed so they could continue feeding throughout the darkness if they so desired. Big Hat, as Bear Scat prepared their supper, made sure all of their weapons were brought into camp and placed strategically in and around their sleeping area and campfire just in case they had surprise visitors of the uninvited kind.

While Bear Scat made a small-sized fire and staked over it some venison steaks from a deer that Big Hat had shot earlier in the day along the trail, Big Hat brought in several more armloads of wood that he had picked up lying nearby. Then Bear Scat began making coffee from previously burned and crushed green coffee beans and Dutch oven biscuits, while Big Hat inspected the horses and mules making sure they were properly hobbled and that their picket ropes remained securely tied. Shortly thereafter, the men quietly ate their supper and visited over the day's events. Bear Scat still found himself excited over what they had observed while traveling along the trail in the ways of the many herds of buffalo, elk, deer and wolves they had passed. Big Hat on the other hand, having seen such natural wonders before during his last seven years as a fur trapper, just smiled over his young quickly learning partner's exuberance over the life of a trapper. Soon the rigors of the day's travels, the dimming light from the campfire and with venison-filled bellies and the understanding that the next day's travels would be just as energy draining, found the two men heading for their individual sleeping furs for a good night's rest. Within moments, the soft snoring of Big Hat could be heard by Bear Scat, as he lay there snuggly covered by his buffalo sleeping robe and dreaming of tomorrow's adventures that he would soon be facing in seeing new country for the very first time and being just another day closer to the possibility of being united on the upper reaches of the Porcupine River with his brother...

"OOOPHF—OOOPHF—UMMMPH—UMMMPH," went the all too familiar rumbling sounds of an approaching boar grizzly bear! A hungry grizzly bear, an animal that to this day has no fear of man and was the pre-eminent predator in the old West, had been traveling along the Missouri River and winding nearby horses and mules, moved inland to investigate the smells that told him the possibility of dinner was near at hand! Stalking up on a picketed and dozing horse, the great bear attacked in a rush without a single moment's hesitation! At one of the last moments of that horse's life as he awakened realizing a grizzly bear was near upon him, he reared back in terror, snapping his picket rope just as the now standing bear's savage jaws closed over the horse's neck near the back of his skull!

With a bone shattering "CRUNCH", the horse's death knell rent the evening's air, as did the sounds of the rest of the panicked livestock's now raring, snorting and jerking in abject panic against their picket ropes! As they did, they loudly made known their terror at having such a savage meat eater in their previously quiet and sleepy midst! A quiet midst now being shattered by another horse's dying scream as its spine was being crushed by the bear's savagely biting jaws and its neck's flesh ripped in long gashes by two sets of massive and powerful front paws with dagger-like six-inch claws!

Bear Scat's deep sleep was instantly replaced with his own terror at being awoken by such rendering screams of a nearby animal being rent into pieces in the savage claws and jaws of a ten-foot-tall grizzly bear weighing in at almost 1,000 pounds! In that next microsecond, Bear Scat shot almost vertically straight up out from his sleeping robe while in a lying position and then dropped back down with a heavy "THUMP"! Still partly asleep and waking all at the same time to the wilderness's 'music' of one wild animal tearing another one to pieces, Bear Scat's budding survival instincts began rapidly kicking in. With the sounds of a near at hand 'killing' ringing in his ears, Bear Scat desperately scrambled around groping on the ground in the almost total heavily vegetated river bottoms' darkness alongside his bedding for the comforting feel of the steel of his Hawken rifle! Finally feeling his fingers touching and then quickly closing around the comforting cold steel of the barrel of his rifle, Bear Scat leapt to his feet and faced the savage tearing sounds coming from the almost pitch-black area of their livestock's picket line. As he did, he could feel the hairs along his arms and on his head standing up in fear of the terrible rendering sounds of one unseen animal roaring forth in all of its savagery, and another being rendered alive and asunder all at the same violent moment in time!

During Bear Scat's terror-filled microsecond of time, Big Hat, upon hearing the sounds of a dying horse renting the air, the savage growling of a grizzly bear in the height of his killing moments, and the tremendous snapping and crashing of the limbs of the trees and brush in the killing zone, found those sounds quickly translated into the mind of the experienced trapper! Grabbing his rifle, jumping up like he had been shot from a cannon, Big Hat took three quick steps in the direction of the life and death battle between the bear and one of his horses, and RAN RIGHT INTO A LOW HANGING COTTONWOOD LIMB THE SIZE OF A LARGE MAN'S FOREARM AND BETWEEN HIS SPEED OF FORWARD MOVEMENT AND THE UNMOVING SOLID WOOD OF THE LIMB, BIG HAT WAS KNOCKED SENSELESS INTO A JUMBLED HEAP UPON THE GROUND!

Simultaneously, Bear Scat ran through the 'grabbing and scratching' limbs of the brush separating the trappers' earlier campsite and the livestock's picket line in darkness that was so complete he could not see anything! However he kept running in the direction of the noise from the diminishing battle sounds in the dense 'face-grabbing' and blinding brush, as the horse at that very moment in time died in the great bear's rapidly biting jaws and locked tight front paws wrapped around its quarry!

Bear Scat smashed through the remaining barrier of brush, bursting onto the scene of battle at a dead run and in the blackness, RAN FULL SPEED RIGHT ONTO THE VERY BACK OF THE GRIZZLY BEAR WHOSE JAWS WERE STILL CLAMPED VISE-LIKE AROUND THE NECK OF THE HORSE! THE BEAR, THINKING HE WAS NOW BEING 'ATTACKED' FROM BEHIND, RELEASED HIS HOLD ON THE NECK OF THE NOW DEAD HORSE, WHIRLED, SWUNG HIS GREAT, HEAVILY CLAWED RIGHT PAW IN THE DARKNESS IN THE DIRECTION OF HIS 'ATTACKER' AND KNOCKED ASUNDER WHAT HAD JUST PLOWED INTO HIS BACKSIDE! "WHOOOOMP!" went the powerfully swung paw as it landed on the 'thing attacking' him, sending 'it' into the dark beyond like 'it' had been launched from a giant slingshot, bleeding and out cold to the rest of the world and everything else going violently on around it!

However, simultaneously with the swipe of the great bear's massive and 'armed' paw onto the side of the head of its 'attacker' came a loud **BOOOM!**, as Bear Scat realizing that he had run by mistake into what was killing one of their horses, had the quick sense and reaction to pull the trigger on his fully cocked and ready to fire Hawken! When Bear Scat fired, the Hawken rifle's .52 caliber, half-ounce slug of soft lead literally exploded through the great bear's head and exited out the far side of its skull in a shower of bone, tissue, teeth, blood and gray matter! That 'mushroomed' bullet then continued on its way, slamming into a cottonwood limb as thick as a large man's forearm that was already covered with Big Hat's fresh blood and blew it clear in half! With that, the broken portion of the huge limb dropped down and landed upon the head of the trapper lying out cold on the ground below, opening up another gash on the far side of his already badly damaged forehead!

The next thing Bear Scat remembered of the previous night's events was waking up with a head which felt like it was floating around off his neck somewhere else! Then through still blurred eyes, Bear Scat saw a Steller's jay standing on an overhead limb just feet away peering down at him as he lay on the ground in a drying pool of blood looking to see if the 'thing' on the ground was something good to eat. Slowly rising up on one elbow, Bear Scat was aware that he was dripping blood from his face and head! Additionally, he felt like he had when he had been shoeing one of his father's mules as a younger man and the animal had kicked backwards, hitting him squarely in his head so violently that the hoof had left a permanent dent in the frontal bone of his forehead...

Finally slowly sitting up, Bear Scat felt like his head was about to fall off and quickly laid back down until the 'fuzzy' in his head had settled down somewhat. Then more slowly the second time, he sat back up and through hazy peering eyes through a slight film of blood, saw Big Hat stumbling towards him, rifle in one hand and holding his head with his other hand in obvious pain! Then Big Hat gave one big stumble and fell directly on top of Bear Scat and both men were once again flattened out on the blood-stained ground. A few minutes later Bear Scat was able to rise and stand although somewhat wobbly as he did so. Reaching out, Bear Scat studied himself against a nearby cottonwood sapling until he began feeling like he just might live. Then realizing his friend Big Hat was lying close by near his feet, Bear Scat staggered over to his friend, dripping blood from his head and face all the way. Dropping heavily down to his knees, Bear Scat reached over and lifted Big Hat up into a sitting position and it was then that the two men got a real good look at one another for the very first time that morning...

"Bear Scat, what the Sam Hill happened to your face? You have three deep claw marks running clear across your face and another deep gouge running clear across the side of your head just above your ear!" said Big Hat in surprise.

"I was going to ask you the same thing, Big Hat. You have a deep gouge clear across your entire forehead! Then another one on the side of your head like a big log dropped down on the side of your head! Damn, Man, you are a mess!" said Bear Scat, followed up with an 'I'm glad you are still alive' grin on his still somewhat bloody and dried blood-encrusted face.

"Well, you damn sure ain't no beauty winner neither when it comes to your looks," said Big Hat with a grin twisted in pain. "Your head is all swelled up like one of our Dutch ovens and with them claw marks all across your ugly mug, you ain't never going to get a woman to look at you other than maybe an ugly old Indian woman," said Big Hat, happy at least to see his young partner still alive. A young partner still alive who had just survived another life-taking experience even worse than when he had been previously abandoned out on the prairie by his earlier partners and 'friends' to just up and die.

"What the hell happened?" asked Big Hat as he stood up again, leaned against a cottonwood tree to steady himself up from his bad case of the 'wobbles' and an injured head that felt like he had been on a big drunk.

"Well, I woke up last night with one of our horses screaming out in pain and hearing what I figured was a bear attacking him on the picket line. I remember grabbing my rifle and running towards all the noise of a big battle between one of our horses and a bear. Then in the dark, I ran right into something huge, alive and furry like a bull buffalo, and then I saw blue, red and yellow sparks and don't remember much of anything else until just a few moments ago. That was when I began coming around and seeing you stumbling over towards me with blood all over your head and shirt, and one eye almost closed on the other side of your head where something else hit you. Other than that, I am not sure what the hell happened other than some sort of critter attacked us in the night and got into our string of horses and mules," said Bear Scat, as he tried not moving his head very much when he talked because of the 'lightning strikes-like pain' that he felt throughout the top of his head when he did.

"I had better go look after our horses. You just sit there because the more you move around, the more blood you are losing from that head and facial wound," said Big Hat.

Bear Scat hurt so much that he didn't argue with his partner, just knelt, then lay back down on the ground and continued bleeding like a 'stuck hog'. With that, Big Hat, using his rifle as a walking stick, began walking slowly over to where the picket line had been. When he left, Bear Scat just closed his eyes and fell asleep from the loss of blood from his wounds and did not move one bit until Big Hat came back later and awakened him.

"Bear Scat, get up! We need to get you over to the fire I built and get you cleaned up," said Big Hat. When Bear Scat could focus his eyes better, he saw that Big Hat had some of their recently purchased gray cloth from Fort Union wrapped around his head to stem the flow of blood from his head wound caused by a low hanging limb that he had run full bore into. With that, Big Hat helped Bear Scat stumble over to their campfire and sit down on a saddle brought over to the fire to be used as a chair. Then Big Hat took some cold water from the nearby river and began washing Bear Scat's bloody head off. Soon the application of rags dipped in the cold river water began reviving Bear Scat and then he had a full cup of rum thrust into his hands and was told to drink it by Big Hat. The first drink of rum did not go down very well and Bear Scat, not really used to drinking, immediately vomited back up what he had just gulped down without really thinking through what he was doing!

"Keep drinking the rest of that rum, Bear Scat. Because what I have to do next is going to be right damn painful. I have washed out your wounds but now I must clean them out with some rum to make sure your meat does not rot and then sew you up with one of our moccasin awls and some thread! So best you get a mess of this here rum down your gullet or you are going to hurt like a 'sum-bitch' once I began using this here big needle to sew up your ugly as a mule's hind end face," said Big Hat.

Bear Scat finally managed to get down the cup of rum but when Big Hat approached with another cup full of rum and poured some of it into one of Bear Scat's facial wounds where the grizzly bear had clawed him across the face, he passed out from the instant burning pain! It was some time later when Bear Scat woke up after passing out when his facial wounds had been doused with the high proof rum. When he did, his face felt like it was on fire! His face felt like it was on fire because Big Hat had since stitched up the three long grizzly bear claw gouge marks across his face and the one long claw-tear across the side of his head just above his ear while he was still passed out. As for the bruising along the entire side of his head where the bear had head-slapped him when he had run full tilt into the back of the horse-killing grizzly, there was not much Big Hat could do other than have Bear Scat lay down on his sleeping robes and try sleeping off the throbbing and burning pain, which he did.

Later in the day, Bear Scat came around and felt better in his head all for except the side of his now badly swollen face. It was all stitched up by Big Hat but he wasn't a doctor, and Bear Scat would have to live with a grizzly bear claw-scarred face the rest of his life! But feeling steadier on his feet than earlier, it was Bear Scat's turn to doctor up Big Hat's swollen face and head. Under Big Hat's 'frontier-doctoring' instructions, Bear Scat cleaned out Big Hat's now blood-clotted wounds with liberal applications of rum and the tip of his knife flicking off the bigger pieces of clotted blood! Then Bear Scat stitched up Big Hat's two long head wounds like he himself had been stitched up, closing the gashes with a 'whip stitch' he had learned to use on his parents' farm to sew up their larger animals that had also been wounded. Now both men had swollen heads the size of one of their six-quart Dutch ovens from all the tissue damage and additional injuries caused by using a larger in size leather awl and thick thread designed for sewing rough leather together, not tender facial and head tissues!

It was then over another cup of rum that stayed down that time that Big Hat told Bear Scat what he had figured happened between the two of them when the grizzly bear had struck. Big Hat began by telling Bear Scat that one of the largest grizzly bears he had ever seen in his life had somehow slipped into their camp the evening before apparently smelling the nearby picketed horses and mules. The bear then had attacked one of their riding horses and in that noisy fight to the death, Big Hat had jumped up from his sleeping robes only half awake, took off running to save the horse, ran into an unseen in the darkness low hanging limb and knocked himself out. When that happened, he took no further part in the fight. However as he patched together the rest of the events, Bear Scat had then jumped up with his rifle and bravely run in the dark of the night into a fight of monster proportions trying to protect their horses. Pausing to take a sip of rum from his cup, Big Hat said that from what he could tell from the fight scene and all of the tracks in the battle area, Bear Scat mistakenly had run full bore into the back of the attacking bear in the dark of the night! The bear figuring it was under attack had turned and with a massive swipe by one of his front paws had slapped Bear Scat across the side of his head, knocking him 'clear and hell a-gone' from the fight! But just before Bear Scat had been knocked out of the fight, he had apparently by dumb luck slammed the end of his rifle barrel luckily up against the side of the bear's head! When he did, he was violently struck in the head with the bear's massive paw, causing Bear Scat through his inadvertent reflex actions to pull the trigger on his fully cocked Hawken rifle, killing the bear instantly.

Then Big Hat got to laughing but tenderly through his damaged face saying, "Near as I can figure it from there, your bullet went clear through that bear's head and 'dead-hit' that same damn low hanging limb I ran into in the dark. When that big ole bullet hit the limb, it blew it clear off and the damned big-ole thing dropped down onto the side of my head as I laid out cold below. So near as I can figure, that is how I got swiped twice in the head by the same damn limb!"

"Now if you be up to it, we need to butcher out parts of that damn horse-killing bear for our eats for the next few days and then drag the damn thing off and dump him into the river so other hungry critters don't come nosing around looking for an easy meal. Then we need to take the best steaks off my riding horse afore he bloats any further and then drag him off and dump him into the river as well, so we don't attract any more of them damn hungry bears our way," said Big Hat.

For the next two hours, the two tender-faced and still gimpy men managed to find and round up all of their horses and mules who had broken their picket ropes and fled the scene during the earlier bear and horse battle. Thankfully, they had been doubled hobbled and were prevented from wandering very far away. Once all the horses and mules, minus the dead one, were back on the new picket line, the work continued. First the dead horse was cut into two pieces, its best steaks removed from its hindquarters and then the mules were used to drag the horse's parts to the water's edge. There the horse parts were slipped into the waters so it would not attract any more bears to camp and allowed to drift off downstream. Then the bear had a number of heavy with fat steaks removed for the trappers' future meals and it too was dragged off, with some difficulty because the mules did not like the smell of the bear being towed so closely behind them, and it too was dumped into the river so it could float away and not attract any other hungry bears into the trappers' campsite as well.

For the next three days, the two all 'gowed-up' trappers stayed quietly around their camp and let the healing process begin on Bear Scat's torn and bruised face and Big Hat's head and damaged forehead. However neither mother of each of the trappers would have recognized them as one of her own because of their swollen heads and wound-draining, badly damaged faces...

By the end of that third day of healing around their camp, Big Hat said, "Bear Scat, I need to return to Fort Union and replace the horse that we lost. I need to do so because if we lose another horse to a critter or accident that leaves us dangerously exposed without adequate transport. Plus if we have a good year beaver trapping, we may need an extra horse just to transport additional packs of beaver skins back to Fort Union for trade. I say that because on a good year we each should account for at least 120 to 140 beaver each and with the Porcupine being as good a beaver ground as some say, maybe even more. With that in mind, I best leave tomorrow morning and ride back to Fort Union to see if I can purchase another good horse on credit and then I will 'hightail' it right back here. I will make a fast trip because we still have a far piece to go to get to the upper reaches of the Porcupine. Once there we can scout around for your brother and if unsuccessful in that endeavor, we ourselves need to search out good beaver trapping areas because we still have to make a living. Additionally the two of us need to build ourselves a winter cabin afore the snows begin flying. After all, we still need to trap a passel of beaver afore next summer if we are to survive as trappers out here in this Indian-ridden wilderness. Also while there I will look around Fort Union and see if any of my old buddies from years past are wandering around and may consider throwing their lot in with us. If I am successful in so doing, that would sure increase our chances of survival while trapping as a larger group of trappers than just the two of us out there all by our lonesome."

Bear Scat just nodded gently in agreement and said nothing in order not to 'fire up' the burning pain he was still feeling in his badly torn face and the throbbing aches emanating from the side of his badly bruised and now infected head. Since Big Hat had said what needed saying, both men just quietly sat there by their campfire and tried ignoring their similar ailing faces and heads. Later that evening while eating supper, both men got some satisfaction while eating grizzly bear steaks previously removed from the same damn bear that had caused them all of their physical miseries!

The next morning right at daylight, Big Hat saddled up his reserve horse and after several words of warning about caring for the remaining livestock and staying on the lookout for any marauding Blackfeet Indians, disappeared on his way back to Fort Union to see if he could purchase another riding horse and maybe round up several additional good partners to round out their preferred 'safety in numbers' plan. Bear Scat, now with a badly infected face, just headed for his sleeping furs and managed to sleep away the rest of the day. That evening after sleeping most of the day away trying to heal up, Bear Scat saw to the horses and mules as they fed along the riverbank and allowed them to water as well. Then remembering what Big Hat had taught him about traveling or camping in Indian Territory, he double hobbled all of the mules and horses to preclude any Indians sneaking into their camp and easily running off their valuable animals. However that double hobbling of all of their livestock created some problems in the doing. By so doing, Bear Scat had to bend over in order to hobble all of their livestock. When he did that caused all the blood to run to his head and into the damaged tissue, causing him a great and burning pain every time he bent over! Then after another grizzly bear steak supper, Bear Scat retired early still feeling the aftereffects of having received a badly damaged face subsequent to being badly clawed in a fight with a bear many times his size and coming out badly on the losing end...

However, continuing to practice what he was fast learning about becoming and surviving as a Mountain Man in the wilderness, before lying down in his sleeping furs for the night he took several additional precautions. First he laid one of his rifles right alongside his sleeping furs so it would be ready for instant retrieval and use if it became 'hostile Indian or mean-assed grizzly bear' necessary. Secondly, he laid one of his fully loaded pistols at the head of his sleeping furs for instant retrieval and another loaded pistol right alongside his sleeping furs in case none of his other weapons, for whatever reason, became available in the case of an emergency or had failed to fire. Then with the soothing sounds of the nearby quietly flowing Missouri River and the soft shuffling noises of the horses and mules along their picket line, Bear Scat soon found himself drifting off to sleep. Drifted off to sleep because he was secure in the knowledge that he 'was ready for 'bear', and that his fellow trapping partner and mentor should return by the following evening hopefully with another riding horse and maybe even several more partners to assist in their Porcupine River trapping endeavor.

All of a sudden hours later, Bear Scat's eyes flew wide open sensing some kind of danger was close at hand! Remembering what his father had taught both him and his older brother about frontier survival, he moved nothing other than his eyelids upon sensing what he suspected was some sort of nearby danger. Bear Scat could hear the nearby picketed horses nervously shuffling their feet and his mules making their soft-sounding verbal noises when someone was near at hand that they recognized as strangers! By now, Bear Scat's hand had surreptitiously retrieved the pistol he laid earlier at his side before drifting off to sleep and had since quietly pulled that weapon out of sight under his buffalo sleeping robe. Then with his sleeping robe muffling any metallic sounds, he quietly cocked its hammer back so it would be ready for action if called upon. Following that action, Bear Scat slowly moved his other searching hand out from under the sleeping robe until it clutched the comforting wooden and metal handle of his other pistol lying near his head and quietly slipped it under his buffalo sleeping robe as well. Moments later, its hammer was also fully cocked and ready for any kind of deadly action if called upon. After filling both hands with a cocked and fully loaded pistol and still without discernibly moving his head as he had been taught as a young man when possibly facing dangers on the frontier, he began by just swinging his eyes from side to side in the darkness looking for what he perceived as a nearby danger so as not to alert anyone or anything that he was now alerted to their or its presence.

THEN HE SAW IT! Kneeling by the edge of his almost totally out campfire, he saw a shadowy figure that appeared to be a kneeling figure of a man holding a rifle! But it was still so dark what he thought he was seeing could have been just some of the woodpile that he had stacked up by their campfire earlier in the day. However his budding Mountain Man instincts still told him danger was close at hand, so he kept his eyes swinging from side to side around his sleeping area without moving any other part of his body to see if there were any other signs of danger closer at hand.

THEN THERE IT WAS AGAIN! That time the faint shadowy darkened lump that appeared to be that of a kneeling man holding a rifle in the darkness by the campfire MOVED! That movement was just so slight that one with a less keen eye would have missed such a subtle movement. But Bear Scat had observed what he construed to be that of a rifle barrel moving so subtly as the suspected form of a person holding it slightly shifted his kneeling position to one that was more comfortable!

Then another darkened figure of a man 'melted' in alongside the first suspected form of a kneeling human and knelt down! Then a third form of a darkened human being appeared alongside what bear scat figured were the first two unknown humans! By now Bear Scat could feel the hairs on his arms standing straight up and the hairs on the back of his neck beginning to rise as well. Bear Scat also discovered that the healing fresh wounds on the sides of his face and head, in light of the mystery events now swirling around him, for some reason no longer hurt or seemed to bother him…

Then all of the suspected darkened figures started quietly sneaking towards the area where the two trappers had laid out their sleeping furs! However the three silently sneaking figures stopped at Big Hat's sleeping area first and Bear Scat could hear the metallic stabbing sounds of knives being thrust violently through the furs and into the ground underneath! Realizing no one was sleeping under those furs, all three darkened humanoid figures now briskly but still silently 'melted' across the ground towards Bear Scat's sleeping area! Slinking right up to the side of where Bear Scat's sleeping furs were bunched up, he saw the upraised flashing glint of two knives in the faint moonlight that was filtering through the dense canopy of a cottonwood tree under which he had been sleeping.

Realizing what was coming next, a surprisingly calm but determined Bear Scat, quickly learning the survival ways of a

Mountain Man, did what he knew he must to do. As both darkened human figures slightly leaned over him in order to stab their knives down upon the 'sleeping' fur trapper's covered body form, their world blew up in their faces! **BOOM—BOOM!** went two quick shots fired upward from beneath his sleeping furs, as Bear Scat discharged both of his .52 caliber pistols into the two figures bending over to stab him from just two feet away! When Bear Scat fired, the flames from the ends of both of his pistol barrels immediately set his bedding alight, as it was blown upward and away from him by the two quick explosive and concussive pistol shots fired from under the furs! Immediately both men previously leaning over Bear Scat's sleeping furs were blown violently backwards like a giant hand had just struck both assailants! That was especially so when the soft lead, .52 caliber, half-ounce lead balls blew through both men's chests and out their backs, causing tremendous tissue and bone damage as they smashed their ways through their bodies, spewing their essence out the other side!

Ignoring the immediate burning pain felt on both of his arms from the concussive and flaming back blasts when he fired the two pistols from under his sleeping furs, Bear Scat became instantly aware that the third figure was now running right at him with what appeared to be an upraised spear! Dropping his now empty pistols, Bear Scat quickly reached for his Hawken rifle still lying by his side! He instantly felt the comforting wood and cold steel as his fingers immediately tightened around it. But the third man with what appeared to be an upraised spear in the pale moonlight was by then too close for him to raise his long barreled rifle upward and shoot him in time before he had plunged his spear into Bear Scat! Bear Scat did the next best thing instinctively by violently sweeping his heavy Hawken rifle barrel just above ground level, thereby tangling up the feet of his fast oncoming assailant. When he did, that tripped the onrushing man, causing him to violently stumble and then plunge right over the top of a now sitting upright in his burning sleeping furs trapper!

When the onrushing man was swept off his feet by the end of the heavy Hawken rifle barrel, that caused him to lose his balance and plunge the end of his spear into the ground just short of a sitting Bear Scat, splintering the spear's handle in the process! That caused the onrushing man to totally lose his balance, sail right over the top of Bear Scat and slam into the ground on the other side! However the adrenalin was now up in his system by that moment in time and he quickly regained his composure, turned around from his sitting position on the ground and quickly drew his hunting knife to stab a still sitting close at hand Bear Scat!

BOOM! went the now quickly retrieved rifle leveled at the assailant's face from just two feet away by a still sitting Bear Scat! At that range, the speeding lead ball vaporized the assailant's head, and the following stream of flame from being fired from such close quarters instantly 'fried' the blood all over what remained of the man's neck, down to the top of his shoulders! In fact, the now headless man just sat there like a human in real life, as his heart pumped blood out from the arteries in the dead man's neck two more heartbeats worth and then remained stilled for all time...

Except for the nervous stamping and shuffling of the trappers' livestock's feet over the nearby surprising sounds of shooting and now the fresh smell of blood, one could only hear the sinister four-note hooting call of a great horned owl disturbed by all the commotion in the cottonwood grove of trees just below the trappers' camp. Even in that intense emotional moment of time and residual fear, Bear Scat strangely remembered what his once friend and now enemy, 'Muskrat', had told him one evening around their campfire before he and the rest of his compatriots had abandoned him out on the prairie to die on his first trip to Fort Union as a 'greenhorn' fur trapper. That story which he had been told by 'Muskrat' about the calls of a great horned owl in the culture of the mighty Sioux had stuck in his memory. The gist of that story being that a nation of Sioux Indians greatly feared that animal, who believed that anyone upon hearing those calls meant there was death close at hand in the wind...

Remembering once again some of what his father, an old French and Indian War veteran, had taught him about wilderness survival, Bear Scat quickly rummaged around in the darkness, found his 'Possibles bag' and immediately reloaded both of his pistols. Shoving them under his sash in case there were more enemies about, he walked over to his old firepit, found a few live embers and placed some dry grass and a handful of small limbs over them. Moments later he was able to build up his new fire so he could make sense of and be able to see what the hell had just occurred. There by the light of the fire, Bear Scat discovered three dead Indians! Not recognizing what tribe they had come from, he dragged their bodies off to one side of their campsite and left them for Big Hat, an experienced fur trapper and one knowledgeable in Indian lore and local tribal dress, to identify when he returned the next day from Fort Union. The rest of that night Bear Scat just sat by his fire with two loaded pistols and rifle on the lookout for anyone else who just happened to wander by and be in the market for some good horseflesh, as had been the previous three 'good' Indians...

Around four in the afternoon the following day, Bear Scat heard the familiar call of "Hello the camp" from his arriving mentor and fellow trapper, Big Hat. Soon Big Hat rode into view trailing another riding horse and sporting a big grin of being successful. Riding into camp, Big Hat lightly stepped out from his saddle, instantly smelled burned hair and noticed that Bear Scat's burned buffalo sleeping robe was hanging in the branches of a tree airing out. "Bear Scat, what the hell happened to your sleeping robe?" asked a surprised Big Hat over what he was seeing.

A half-hour later, Bear Scat's story of his close call with death was out 'in the wind' and all Big Hat could do was shake his head in amazement. Here he was finding that his 'greenhorn' partner wasn't as 'green' as he had originally thought! In fact, Bear Scat's survival instincts were showing signs of maturation on the part of his partner that never ceased amazing Big Hat. Then Bear Scat took Big Hat over to where he had dumped the three attackers' bodies and there Big Hat identified them as being Indians from the dreaded Blackfeet Nation. Shortly thereafter their bodies were dumped into the Missouri River to drift the way of the previous grizzly bear and horse carcasses and in so doing, reducing any subsequent recriminations over their killings by the Blackfeet since they would never know who they were.

Then Big Hat continued Bear Scat's frontier education by asking him, "Did you locate where the Indian attackers had tied off and left their horses before they had attacked our camp?" Bear Scat just looked blankly at Big Hat, realizing he had not even figured on the Indians having any horses or if they did, where they had left them prior to attacking the camp. Bear Scat then realized he still had a ways to go in the learning department when it came to thinking like an experienced Mountain Man. That was especially when it came to thinking through the events and realizing his job had not been completed until he had also recovered the Indians' valuable horses and anything else of value they may have left.

Later with Big Hat cold tracking the three dead Indians away from their camp and teaching Bear Scat a thing or two about the art of tracking in the process, he soon found the three Indian attackers' horses tied up in a grove of trees a short distance from the trappers' campsite along with four additional horses still carrying heavy packs of beaver furs! Not only teaching Bear Scat how to cold track Indians, Big Hat had also brought forth the common sense facts that the dead men had valuable horses and that one should always go looking for them after their killing. In so doing, Bear Scat learned an important lesson in retrieving valuable riding horses and that sometimes there might also be a surprise bonus when dealing with Indians. Especially when it came to anticipating the possibility the Indians may have earlier killed other fur trappers and had stolen their valuable furs as well! Now through such cold tracking and searching the two trappers were now not only richer in riding and packhorses but in some dead trappers' valuable fur wealth as well! By late afternoon and back at camp with the extra horses and now valuable beaver furs from some long dead fur trappers, Bear Scat began to slowly realize the way of a Mountain Man was many faceted and to think in that manner would not only lengthen one's life out on the frontier but could many times enrich it materially as well...

After a supper of roasted buffalo hump ribs from a cow buffalo who had wandered too close to the trappers' camp and had fallen to a single rifle shot from Bear Scat's Hawken rifle, the men happily feasted. Sitting around their campfire later smoking their pipes, Big Hat provided another one of his many wilderness lessons to his young fur trapping partner so he would be better prepared to survive in their chosen professions. Exhaling a long stream of pipe smoke, Big Hat said, "Bear Scat, let the fire go for a bit and sit down so I can share some of what I have learned about our profession with you. Way back in '07, Manuel Vasquez, a St. Louis businessman, understanding the potential value existing in the fur trade on the upper reaches of the Missouri River and the surrounding river systems after hearing about what Lewis and Clark had to say about the abundance of beaver they had seen on their 2½-year expedition trip to the Pacific Coast, put together a contingent of fur trappers and headed north up the Missouri River. That Vasquez did to see if there would be any value in establishing a trading post that far north and trading with the Indians. Upon reaching a point where the Big Horn River entered the Yellowstone River during his subsequent exploratory travels, Vasquez built a fort and trading post so he could trade with the local tribes of Indians. When he was ready for business, he made it a policy to only trade his goods with the Flathead and Crow Nations and not the Blackfeet. He did not trade with the Blackfeet because he did not trust them and considered them to be treacherous and warlike Indians to all white men and many tribes of his fellow man. When he followed through with such trade practices, that meant the Flatheads and the Crow Indians, bitter enemies of the Blackfeet, were allowed to trade in their furs and buffalo robes for firearms. Then armed with those new firearms and now being better armed than the Blackfeet who had no such firearms, went to war with their natural and lifelong enemies. In so doing, the Flatheads and the Crow waged war successfully against the Blackfeet. As a result of Vasquez's non-firearms trade policies with the Blackfeet causing them to lose many Indian wars with the Flatheads and the Crow, aroused a bitter hatred against the whites by the Blackfeet nation that has since existed."

Pausing to re-light his pipe, Big Hat continued his historical training of Bear Scat regarding concerns he should have regarding different tribes in the area in which they would be trapping. "As you know, we are now deep in the land of the Blackfeet and Gros Ventre Indian Nations. Both of these tribes have little regard for the likes of us and what they consider our outright trespass trapping and hunting on their ancestral lands. That is why you must learn to recognize which Indians we might be facing at any time from a distance based on their dress. For to fail to do so and master that skill will get one or both of us killed at some point in time as long as we remain upon what they consider their ancestral homelands. Now this time you won out in a match between three of them Blackfeet red devils along with the uses of your quick senses and good shooting eye. However the next time, they may be displaying your hair tied onto the mane of one of their riding horses and be carrying your Hawken or Lancaster rifles if your senses betray you and your shooting eye is not as good as it was during this instance," said Big Hat in a very serious tone of voice. As for Bear Scat in this latest lesson on wilderness survival, not a single word spoken by Big Hat was lost on him, having realized the importance of what had just been said by one experienced in the cultures and histories of the land upon which they both were challenging...

"Now," said Big Hat, "we have a far piece to go to reach the Upper Porcupine and see if we can locate that brother of yours. I suggest we ready our gear and supplies for that trip and head out in the morrow at daylight for that area. Besides, in addition to locating your brother we must find a good beaver trapping area that is off the beaten path of the local Indians so we don't run into trouble with their kind, as well as find the time to build a cabin to hole up into come the winter's icy blasts. What say you, Bear Scat, to that proposal?"

Bear Scat just broadly grinned now that his face was starting to heal up and feeling somewhat better over the opportunity to once again hit the trail into a new territory en route the upper reaches of the Porcupine River. En route the upper reaches of the Porcupine River, reported home to numerous 'blanket-sized' beaver, their fur trapping destination for the coming year, a continuation of his learning the fur trade, and the last reported destination of his older brother according to McKenzie and the eventual long sought-after family reunion. Daylight the next morning found the two trappers now trailing four heavily packed horses carrying packs of beaver furs, four mules carrying a year's supplies for living out in the wilderness, and an additional five riding horses. Crossing the Big Muddy River at a shallow ford, the two men and their pack string then proceeded westward along the northern bank of the Missouri River as they headed for their final destination on the Porcupine River and a possible family reunion with Jacob Sutta, older brother to Elliott Bear Scat Sutta...

*****

One month earlier, Jacob Sutta, older brother to Elliott Bear Scat Sutta, and Jacob's partner Wild Bill McGinty, after spending a day in the saddle upon leaving Fort Union, made their first camp on the north bank of the Missouri River near the confluence of the Big Muddy River. As Wild Bill began preparing the two men's supper, Jacob Sutta took up his rifle and walked over to the confluence of the Big Muddy and began hunting around for a deer for camp meat in that river's dense riverbank vegetation. As he did Jacob could not help but noticing all of the beaver sign along the banks and floating within the Big Muddy's waters. Forgetting the deer hunting for the moment, Jacob took the time to investigate all of the beaver sign he was seeing. There were beaver slides everywhere, signs of cottonwood and willows that had been cut down and dragged into the river for food abounded, and many of the river's muddy banks were covered with beaver tracks going to and from. Looking riverward Jacob also noticed numerous chewed willow and cottonwood branches floating in the river's waters along with numerous leaves floating thereon, evidencing much ongoing beaver feeding activity further upstream. So much so that he began walking northward along the river's bank continuing to examine the numerous signs of beaver and the freshness of their activities.

Later that afternoon while looking for fresh beaver sign, Jacob killed a fat mule deer doe, removed her hindquarters and backstraps, left the rest for the meat-eating critters and then carried the deer's quarters back to his camp along the Missouri. That evening during supper, Jacob shared his newly discovered beaver-activity findings with his partner saying, "Bill, that there Big Muddy is alive with beaver sign of every kind. I took the time to walk the banks of the river and everywhere I looked, there was fresh beaver sign and lots of it!"

"What are you getting at?" asked Wild Bill, as he was having trouble mouthing a large a piece of still piping hot venison and in so doing, trying not to burn his lips or tongue on the meat in the process.

"Well, after hearing all the talk about 'blanket-sized' beaver everywhere on the upper reaches of the Porcupine River, you and I had decided that was where we were a-going for the coming year's trappings. But with what I saw today and I would imagine there is more of the same upstream, I have been a-thinking. Why should we go any further west to get to the Porcupine, when it appears there is one hell of a lot of beaver right here on the Big Muddy. Plus by not going so far west, we would have a shorter distance traveling back to Fort Union with our furs than coming clear back from the Porcupine. Additionally, we would have less hostile Indian country to traverse coming back from the Big Muddy than the Porcupine, and lastly we shouldn't have all the problems associated with the Hudson's Bay Company trappers that are reported trapping some of that country just north of the Porcupine in Canada. I think it is something we need to think about," continued Jacob Sutta.

Finally managing to get past the 'piping hot' on the piece of meat he was trying to chew, Wild Bill said, "Jacob, your thinking has gotten us to where we are today as trappers. It has gotten us out of trouble with the Indians several times and has taken us into some of the finest beaver trapping this neck of the woods has offered. I say we go with your gut and if that is your way of thinking, we turn north tomorrow and trap the Big Muddy instead of going clear over to the Porcupine. Besides, hopefully that beaver trapping water over on the Porcupine won't be trapped out by next year and we can then go clear over there and trap those waters plus see some more of this great country. Well, that is providing those damn Blackfeet don't lift our hair in the meantime if we go up the Big Muddy and cross trails with them because there be a passel of them living up there as well."

The next morning found Jacob Sutta and Wild Bill McGinty traveling up the eastern side of the Big Muddy instead of traveling much further west to the Porcupine River and its trapping grounds. As they did both men were convinced even further that they had made the right choice because if anything, the good beaver sign continued unabated and became even more in evidence the further north they traveled. The rest of that year found Jacob Sutta and Wild Bill McGinty very successfully trapping beaver along the Big Muddy and in a number of its tributaries. As Jacob had predicted, there was no need to go clear over and trap the upper reaches of the Porcupine River when they had all the beaver they could trap on the much closer Muddy River and its drainages.

******

Several weeks later found Big Hat Johnson and Bear Scat Sutta camping in the very same campsite that had been used by Jacob Sutta and Wild Bill McGinty just weeks earlier. From that location, that pair was en route the upper reaches of the Porcupine River looking for Bear Scat's older brother, one Jacob Sutta, reported to be there beaver trapping on its headwaters with his partner Wild Bill McGinty...

CHAPTER SIX: TRAPPING THE "PORCUPINE"

Two days' travel later, found Big Hat and Bear Scat crossing the Poplar River and quietly camping on its western bank without incident. Two more days of travel found the two fur trappers still heading westerly as they crossed the shorter-in-length Wolf River. There they rested for two days and let their horses and mules put on the 'feed-bag' on the rich prairie grasses. Over the next four days found Big Hat and Bear Scat ducking into the Missouri River bottoms numerous times as they continued heading westward towards the Porcupine, dodging several nearby bands of Indians out on the prairie hunting buffalo. Finally the two men reached the Porcupine River as Big Hat remembered it having been there in 1807, after coming up the Missouri River with Vasquez as a very young fur trapper. There the two men crossed the river over to its western side and then headed north traveling close along the river looking for beaver sign and the dense cover its river bottoms offered to avoid the almost continuous bands of Gros Ventre Indians observed out hunting buffalo off in a distance on the prairie.

Remembering McKenzie's words back at Fort Union regarding the possible whereabouts of Bear Scat's older brother Jacob, he was told the last that McKenzie had heard was that he and his partner were heading for the hoped-for untapped upper reaches of the

Porcupine River. With those words of encouragement as to Jacob's whereabouts on his mind, Big Hat and Bear Scat continued north on the Porcupine checking out the river's waters and marshy areas around the cottonwoods and stands of willows looking for beaver sign as they headed ever northward for the river's headwaters. However with Big Hat teaching Bear Scat along the way the art of tracking, the two men looked for any sign of shod horses in the area that may have belonged to Jacob and Wild Bill. They also realized that any signs of shod horses in the area could also be the possible signs of other white trappers in the area and maybe even those from the reported Hudson's Bay Company trapper competition trapping their ways down from Canada. However as it turned out, the lower reaches of the Porcupine were almost barren of any sign of shod horses. In fact, those few shod horse tracks being discovered mixed in with so many unshod horse tracks, Big Hat just figured those few shod horses were being ridden by Indians who had killed its white owners or had somehow stolen the horses from other trappers. But their 'looking for sign' efforts were not in vain because Bear Scat, being the able pupil he was, was a very quick learner and in just a few short days of training was well on his way to mastering the fine art of tracking. Bear Scat was still having problems telling by the depth of the horse's tracks whether or not it had been ridden or was just trailed, and the difference of a white man's moccasin track from that of an Indian by the way they placed their feet, but he was an eager learner and learning fast. So much so that Big Hat now had Bear Scat in the lead and 'reading' what he saw on the ground first, with Big Hat providing a follow-up critique in each instance of difficult sign being discovered and examined.

One afternoon where Big Hat figured they were just below where the Porcupine River's headwaters originated, they passed a set of low lying hills to their west. Big Hat had Bear Scat draw up from the lead and called him back to where he was sitting on his horse in front of his trailing pack string. Pointing to the ground at some very faint horse tracks as a result of being blurred by a previous late afternoon thunderstorm leading into the adjacent timbered hills, Big Hat said, "Bear Scat, you rode over these here shod tracks. Leave your pack string here with me and follow these old tracks to see where they are going, for as you can see they are all from shod horses. Plus being near the Porcupine's headwaters as we are, didn't you say the last word you heard was that was where he and his partner were supposed to be trapping? If so, those tracks may just be from your brother and his trapping partner."

Handing the reins of his trailing pack string to Big Hat without a word being spoken in his excitement, Bear Scat bailed off his horse and leading it on foot so he could see the faint tracks better, began tracking the several sets of shod horse tracks leading into a distant long draw heading into a small set of rolling and timbered hills. As Bear Scat sped away following the faint horse tracks at a trot, Big Hat had to smile. Two weeks ago, Bear Scat couldn't track a bull moose through a mud flat. Now he was tracking just like an Indian at a trot with eyes not missing a single clue spelled out on the ground. Seeing that, Big Hat smiled a large appreciative smile over how fast Bear Scat had learned an artful trade, namely that of tracking an animal or human and did so with almost an Indian's instinct and precision! *Yes, Bear Scat was well on his way to learning an artful attribute that was required if he was to become a successful Mountain Man*, thought Big Hat with a smile...

Sitting there out in the open on his horse but keeping an eye 'slicked' as to what was going on around him so he didn't get surprised by a hostile band of Indians, Big Hat watched Bear Scat disappear into a finger of timber leading into the rolling hills. Moments after he had disappeared into that line of timber, Big Hat saw Bear Scat quickly reappear and wave him over to where he was standing. Slowly walking their two strings of animals over to where Bear Scat stood with his rifle now held at the ready like danger was close at hand, Big Hat, upon seeing such exhibited defensive behavior taken by his partner, fingered the rifle lying across his saddle in case its quick use was also called upon.

THEN IT HAPPENED! Big Hat quickly drew up short his string of horses and mules and just looked all around like a long-tailed weasel would look for a just-scented nearby deer mouse! Drawing in a 'snoot full' of the foul-smelling air once again to make sure of what he had originally thought, Big Hat, experienced Mountain Man that he was, detected the faint sickly sweet smell of death, and the smell was that of the unique smell associated with a human and not that of a long dead animal! Drawing in several more deep breaths through his nose, Big Hat confirmed in his mind that his original assessments as to the sickly sweet smells lying heavy in the air were correct. Without a doubt, they were indeed the smells of a dead human or humans…

Placing his right hand now on the forestock of his Hawken rifle for immediate retrieval if needed, Big Hat more cautiously continued riding forward trailing the two pack strings. Finally riding up alongside Bear Scat, he could see a look of disbelief flooded clear across his young partner's face. Then it dawned on Big Hat, with such a look of disbelief on Bear Scat's face and the now stronger-than-ever smell of a dead human or humans reeking through the air, could only mean one thing. Maybe the dead human smell coupled with the strange looks on Bear Scat's face meant that he had found his long-lost brother and he was the one dead and smelling up the countryside! Thinking the worst possible, Big Hat said, "Bear Scat, why the strange looks spelled clear across that ugly, bear clawed-up mug of yours? Ain't you ever smelled the smell of death afore?"

"Big Hat, you are not going to believe what I just found partway up this draw. There are three bloated fur trappers' bodies lying up there and they belong to men whom I knew at one time and considered my friends named Bob "Fingers" McGoon, Randy "Biscuits" Steward and Jacob "Fish" Greer. They along with William "Muskrat" Price and Jay "Bear" Peterson were the group of fur trappers I met in St. Louis when I first arrived in that city. They are the same group that I was asked to join because I wanted to be a fur trapper and come looking in the wilderness for my brother. That same group of men who later quietly took everything I owned one night during a furious thunderstorm and dumped me out on the prairie the following morning with hardly anything that would have allowed me to survive! From the looks of their powder burns and their entry wounds, all three men were shot at close range in the back of their heads and left where they fell! Whoever did such a thing didn't even bother to give them a decent Christian burial..."

"Bear Scat, are you telling me these are the same trappers who abandoned you out on the prairie so long ago before you and I met up along the Missouri River, when I saw you eating those fish eggs out from those fresh piles of bear scat alongside that huge bloated paddlefish carcass?" asked an incredulous looking Big Hat.

"Those three are the 'one and same' of those who were once my friends and after what they did to me, I swore I would someday hunt them down and kill the lot of them. But here are three of those bastards and someone has beaten me to killing them before I could draw a bead on any of them. Not only that, but take a look up into the head of this draw in that copse of pines. There is a freshly built cabin sitting up there with a ready built horse corral and no one around using it!"

"What? Get down, you damned fool!" said Big Hat upon seeing the cabin for the first time, placing them well within rifle range, as he bailed off his horse and began quickly pulling their two pack strings of animals into the nearby line of timber for the protection it would offer if someone at that cabin was of a mind to put a speeding lead ball into them. For a second, Bear Scat stood his ground not understanding why Big Hat had reacted so, then realizing he was out in the open of maybe those who had killed the three men and were still residing in the cabin watching them, he too sprinted for the protective cover offered by the line of timber, dragging his horse along with him in the process!

Tying off their livestock out of sight in the timber, Big Hat and Bear Scat, curious as they were, began circling around and behind the cabin, examining it for any sign of habitation or danger as they went. Seeing the cabin's front and rear doors flung wide open and not seeing any other signs of life, the two men with their rifles held at the ready, finally cautiously approached the cabin. Taking quick peeks inside the darkened cabin through the open doors, the two men saw or heard nothing other than the softly blowing winds around the area. Finally Big Hat took a quick step into the cabin with his rifle at the ready in case the killers of the three dead men were hidden therein. The cabin proved to be as empty as all get-out and showed no signs of recent or current habitation. For all intents and purposes, the cabin had just been built so recently that it still smelled of green, fresh-cut pine timbers. Other than that, there had never even been a fire built in the fireplace at the far end of the cabin or any other sign that it had ever been lived in! Standing there inside a well-built and perfectly habitable cabin with no sign of current use baffled the two men. In fact, the cabin was so new that whoever had built such fine living quarters hadn't even spent the time to build any beds inside or add any tables or chairs! The inside of the perfectly good cabin was as barren as a 'sucked hound's tooth' after a good meal.

Walking outside questioning in their minds what they had just discovered, the two men walked over to the hell-for-stout and well-built corral, and only saw old sign of its use by any livestock with no fresh droppings, indicating the cabin builders for whatever reason were now long gone. Shaking their heads once again in wonder over what they had just seen, Big Hat and Bear Scat walked back to the three bloated bodies dumped at the edge of the tree line. There Big Hat observed that it appeared all three men had been lined up and shot in the back of their heads at very close range! Shaking his head in disbelief over such an outrage, Big Hat said, "Bear Scat, do you see any sign of the other two men from this group that dumped you out on the prairie to die? Because from the looks of all the tracks in the area, there were originally five men here who came and built that there cabin. But for some reason, the 'bear crapped in the clover', hard feelings developed and ended up with three of the five men being shot at close range by either one or both of the remaining two men of the group."

"I don't see any more bodies and I didn't smell anything out of the ordinary when we walked around the cabin thinking maybe the Indians had done such a dirty deed. That being said, I figured maybe the other two got into a fight with these three and killed the lot. Then realizing how this killing looked, got the hell out of the country so no other trappers would stumble upon these killings and go looking for the killers in order to settle up the score as our code of frontier justice requires," quietly said Bear Scat, as he continued constantly looking all around for any signs of danger as he had been taught to do while out in the wilderness by his friend and mentor, Big Hat.

"Well, let us grab a couple of shovels and bury these poor buggers afore some damn grizzly comes wandering along, gets used to eating humans and then once finished with these three, comes looking for us as well," said Big Hat as he headed for one of the mules packing their shovels. Two hours later, Fingers, Fish and Biscuits had been laid to rest and a huge pile of rocks had been gathered up and laid over their communal grave site to preclude the critters from digging them up and eating them. Following that, the two men tied off their pack strings out of sight in the deep timber, mounted up and with Big Hat now in the lead, began tracking the old sets of two ridden horses followed by a fairly long pack string, as it showed signs of hurriedly leaving the area of death and heading southwest further into the wilderness. For three hours the two men trailed the obviously fast moving string of horses based on their strides and in the end, finally gave up following them because they showed no signs of slowing down as they were obviously from all of their sign, leaving the immediate area for good. Finally Big Hat reined up and just sat there looking long and hard in the direction in which the two fleeing men and their pack string had ridden. There the trail of murderers ended in a mile-wide swath of ground that had been chewed up by thousands of hooves from a stampeding herd of buffalo. From where the two trappers sat upon their horses, no matter how good a tracker one was, it would be sheer folly to try and keep tracking anyone under the land's conditions lying before them. In short, those murderers were long gone and now both they and their evil deeds were 'in the wind'...

"There is no use in continuing to track these fellows by the looks of it. They are heading for places other than remaining here for some reason. I am sure they could have buried their dead just as easily as we buried the three men and no one would have been any the wiser. But I am also convinced they have totally left this area for another place in order to hide out from what they did. Maybe they are heading for the Musselshell and then from there onto a rendezvous somewhere further to the south. If they did, that sure would preclude any awkward questions being asked back at Fort Union by friends of those three dead men as to what had happened to them. That is too bad they got away before we arrived and discovered what had happened. No two ways about it, those two skunks deserve to be killed for how they killed those three men back there and for what they did to you, Bear Scat," said Big Hat slowly, as he continued watching for any sign of discovery by Indians, being that the two of them were now out on the open prairie and in front of 'God and everybody'.

Several hours before dusk, the two men arrived back at the freshly built and uninhabited cabin and their still tied-off pack strings awaiting their return. Standing there and looking up at the just-finished and never lived-in cabin, Big Hat said, "Bear Scat, what say you to the two of us taking over that cabin since the other two trappers from 'Hell' seem to have 'skedaddled' for good? That would sure allow us to have a nice place to live in during the harsh northern latitude's winters, save us one hell of a lot of work in building our own cabin and by so doing, allow us to move in and then get going on our trapping preparations and get to looking for your brother all at the same time?"

"I think that would be fine with me. I didn't look forward to all the work that went with that cabin building anyway. Plus we have a fine corral adjacent that spring that will hold all of our stock, provide all of our drinking and horse water, we are down here out of the wind, and we would appear to be off the beaten trails frequently utilized by the local bands of Indians from what I can see. That certainly fits the space, water, grass and firewood requirements you always taught me to look for," said Bear Scat, as he continued casting his eyes to all points of the compass as if looking for Muskrat and Bear to come back and suddenly appear at any minute. Knowing what those two had more than likely done to the other three now dead men, if he chanced seeing Bear and Muskrat coming into his life again, Bear Scat figured he had 'just the right kind of medicine to apply to Bear and Muskrat's brand of evil sickness'...

With the decision made as to their new 'home' for the next ten or eleven months, the two men brought their livestock into the cabin area and began unloading their packs. While Big Hat unloaded the animals and watered them in the nearby spring by the corrals, Bear Scat cleaned out any animal refuse left behind in the cabin in the absence of its original builders. Then after Big Hat let the livestock out to graze nearby after being hobbled, he gave Bear Scat a hand at building an outdoor firepit for much of their outside cooking during good weather events. Once finished with that chore, the two men took their axes and went right behind their new home and cut a small mountain of firewood from the abundant dead insect-killed trees and hauled it back down to the outside now rocked-in firepit and stacked it nearby. By then it was time to bring in the livestock and house them in their new home inside the hell-for-stout corral, while Bear Scat began preparations of the men's supper of coffee, Dutch oven biscuits and the last of their deer meat from a doe deer shot two days earlier and now beginning to smell just a little strongly of 'past due'...

Later, not being familiar with the Indian traffic in their area, the men retired to their cabin and stacked a number of saddles and packs up behind the inside of the front and rear doors, so no hostile Indians who came to discover them could just burst into the cabin in surprise and start shooting. Then the men stationed a rifle near each window opening and door in case shooting would be called

139

for. Finally staking out their bedding areas inside the cabin, each man made sure there were two loaded pistols within easy reach of their sleeping areas just in case the packs and saddles stacked up behind the doors were insufficient to stop any entry by those who were unwanted... Sleep soon came easily to each man after a long, hard, emotional and trying first day in their new home. But at least they now had a stoutly built home deep in good beaver country and for that the two trappers were very thankful.

Daylight the following day found Bear Scat, the designated camp cook, stoking up an outside fire and after roasting their green coffee beans and crushing the same in the bottom of one of their cooking pots, setting the always welcome coffee pot on the hanging irons over the fire to boil. Following that, Bear Scat mixed up his biscuit dough for his Dutch oven biscuits to round out the men's breakfast. However his Hawken rifle was close by, leaning against a nearby sitting log which had been brought down the day before and placed near the firepit. Additionally, there was a Lancaster rifle leaning against the front of the cabin for easy access, in case some nosy Indian smelling the wood smoke from their morning's campfire found himself ambling in to investigate the neighborhood's newest inhabitants...

Then the "**BOOMING**" sound of a rifle being fired from up behind the cabin told Bear Scat to dig out several of his three-legged frying pans and get them warming up over a bed of coals, because Big Hat never missed when it came to killing a deer, buffalo, bighorn sheep or elk, or blowing a mad charging Indian out from his saddle. About 40 minutes later, Big Hat came around the north side of their cabin dragging a nice fat doe deer with a big grin spread across his face saying, "Bear Scat, is that coffee a-boiling and are the biscuits ready? If so, let me at them because I am so damn hungry I could eat my weight in this here deer I just dragged in."

Grinning, Bear Scat dug into one of their panniers, dragged out several metal plates and soon the two hungry men were feasting on Dutch oven biscuits and steaming, stout as an angry mule's kick, trapper's brand of coffee. After breakfast, the two men working in concert, skinned the deer and saved the skin so it could be made into a window covering once it had been 'shaved and tanned'. Then a meat pole was fastened between two near-at-hand aspens and the deer's carcass strung up so it could cool out and form a glaze, much to the happiness of a pair of hungry and always trusting gray jays...

Finished with that chore, Big Hat turned and said, "Bear Scat, we need to saddle up and get moving. Near as I can figure, you won't rest until we explore the last few miles of the upper reaches of the Porcupine to see if your brother and Wild Bill have a camp, dugout or a cabin somewhere up in that neck of the woods. That way if we find them, we can throw in with them for the extra firepower that would represent, and we could share our cabin and the beaver trapping waters with them as well, if they don't have a good place to winter-out. Also by doing it that way, we could 'kill two birds with one stone' regarding finding your brother, increasing our safety with the increased firepower, and do our beaver trapping as well. What do you have to say to that suggestion?" asked Big Hat.

Six hours of searching later found Big Hat and Bear Scat sitting on their horses at the headwaters of the Porcupine with no Jacob Sutta or Wild Bill McGinty in sight. Neither man in sight because they had earlier turned off at the confluence of the big muddy river and traveled north to beaver trap, instead of trapping on the upper reaches of the further west porcupine, as had been reported earlier by Mckenzie back at one of the fort union suppertime conversations...

Obviously disappointed, Bear Scat tried holding back his tears of frustration with the wipe of his buckskin shirt sleeve across his eyes and then turning said, "Big Hat, we are burning daylight. My brother for some reason is obviously not here, so we best get going on with the rest of our lives by returning to our cabin and start getting squared away for what lies ahead of us before we can even set one beaver trap. What do you think, since you know this country better than I and know more of what lies ahead of us in this fall beaver trapping thing than I?"

"Bear Scat, just because Jacob is not here, I am sure there is some sort of an explanation for his absence. I have found that the trappers working this and any other beaver country are a pretty independent lot. It doesn't take much to turn their heads and head them down a different trail than the one they had originally planned on taking. I say let us get back to our cabin and begin getting ready for this fall and spring's beaver trapping. The way I see it, like you, we have a mountain of work ahead of us before we can set a single trap. So we best get on with our necessary chores and my teachings when it comes to 'learning you' about beaver trapping and the fur trade. After all, something might happen to me sooner than later and before that happens, you had best be ready to make a living by learning how to survive in this here wild and sometimes dangerous land," said Big Hat with a characteristic good-natured grin, signaling he was ready to get on with the rest of their lives as he knew it.

Somewhat later in the day found the two trappers back at their cabin. First in the line of business was hobbling the horses and mules and letting them out to feed and water. Then grabbing a shovel, Bear Scat commenced digging out and rocking up their adjacent free-flowing spring with nearby rocks so they would have an improved good and clean water source for drinking and cooking, as well as the animals having a rocked-up and structured place in which several at a time could water. As Bear Scat tended to his work around the spring, Big Hat began cutting aspen saplings, digging holes and setting four posts near the south side of their cabin. Then with a spool of their heavy duty twine purchased back at Fort Union, lashed a number of smaller and more limber poles throughout a now framed-up area. Standing back and admiring his work, Big Hat looked forward to the day when his new meat drying and smoking racks would be heavy with strips of delicious buffalo meat being processed into life-sustaining jerky to be used when they were out on the trail either beaver trapping or out on the plains hunting buffalo or other big game animals.

That evening, Bear Scat once again put on their coffee pot to boil with several handfuls of just roasted and crushed coffee beans tossed in for good stout makings. Then he saw to it that the biscuit dough was prepared and his Dutch ovens warmed up with bear fat from the jugs purchased back at Fort Union melting inside so there would be grease for the biscuit makings. That was followed with heavy slabs of meat freshly cut from their hanging deer tossed into two three-legged frying pans sitting over a low bed of coals, which soon were sizzling away and filling the night's air with wonderful smells! Soon the two men had drawn up their sitting logs closer around the campfire with their Hawken rifles close at hand and were doing what hungry and hard-working men do best, namely eating what they loved out in the country and night air in which they happily existed.

After a hearty breakfast of coffee, deer steak and Dutch oven biscuits, the next day found the two men hard at work up on the hillside in the timber behind their cabin. There with a single buck saw, they began cutting down a number of dead pine and Douglas fir trees, bucked them into manageable lengths and after a short lunch of cold deer steak left over from breakfast and Dutch oven biscuits also left over, hooked up two mules and began dragging the dead timber down and placing the shortened logs into a pile near the cabin for winter use when the snows were too deep in which to go 'logging'. By nightfall there were two dead-tired men and two worn-out mules, but off to the side of their cabin had risen a pile of uncut logs that would carry the trappers safely through the winter months when the vast country in which they lived was buried under feet of snow and blanketed with sub-zero temperatures, making any kind of travel difficult and many times even dangerous.

The following day found two stove-up trappers from all their hard work 'logging' the day before, sitting around a warm campfire warming up and working out the 'kinks' in their muscles and backs.

Once again after a short but 'venison-heavy' fulfilling breakfast, the men loaded up all four of their mules with dual panniers and headed for the nearby densely wooded and heavily vegetated Porcupine River bottoms. There the two men spent the morning with the blue flies, buffalo gnats and hordes of mosquitoes, cutting rich Timothy hay and stuffing the panniers full of the greenery. Then while one trapper continued cutting emergency supplies of the protein-rich hay, the other took the mule trains back to their cabin and spread the hay out on a grassy flat near the cabin to dry out and cure. For the next two days the 'hay' detail continued on, until the two trappers figured they had enough emergency feed for their livestock when the snows got too deep for the horses and mules to easily reach their feed sources. Several days later after the hay had sufficiently dried, it was gathered up and stuffed ceiling high into a storage shed that had been built by the previous 'owners' and attached to the north end of their cabin. This winter hay preparation was one lesson Bear Scat took to heart, once he realized from his northern latitudes-experienced trapping partner just how important it would become if their horses were too 'poorly' and unable to travel in the winter because of the lack of feed. He then realized just how important it was in having to suffer the blue flies, mosquitoes and buffalo gnats collecting hay in the summer months if one needed winter transportation, and that became problematic because the stock was too poor to travel for want of an emergency food supply. So a valuable lesson was learned regarding the value of a hay supply harvested from the river bottoms during the summer months in readiness for whatever weather 'Old Man Winter' blew their way...

Following the end of their 'haying' detail, Bear Scat was detailed to go out and kill another deer for their meals. Kill another deer because the two hard-working men had already consumed most of the entire boned-out deer Big Hat had killed just several days before! Two hours later, Bear Scat returned carrying the hindquarter from the massive buck deer he had killed just over the hill behind their cabin. However the deer was so large he had to bring it out in quarters! As he did, his mind drifted back to his days as a young man when he had killed a huge white-tailed deer on his father's farm only to have a tornado 'whirl off' with his deer's entire carcass. Forgetting the unfortunate loss of the earlier white-tailed buck to a tornado, as he rounded the cabin with his prize 'ham of deer', Bear Scat observed Big Hat just finishing up processing the deer hide from his earlier deer kill and beginning to tack it onto the window frame he had just built, so their cabin could have some light filtered through the thinly trimmed and shaved deer hide and yet keep out most of the cold and wind come winter. Hanging his hindquarter up on the meat pole, Bear Scat headed for their cold running spring, guzzled down enough water to satisfy a camel, and then headed back up onto his mountain to retrieve another quarter of the deer he had just killed before any critter, especially the always pesky grizzly bears who feared no man, discovered it just lying there and added the rest of its carcass to its menu...

As he did, Big Hat, a man indentured by his drunken father early on in life in order to have more money to purchase whiskey, learned a trade as a carpenter and later that of a blacksmith. Putting those learned skills while under the employ of another as a young man, Big Hat headed back into the aspen grove with an ax and a saw. Shortly thereafter, one could hear the ringing of an ax and the 'singing' of a saw. By late afternoon, Big Hat had returned from his aspen grove carrying several armloads of stout poles. Big Hat, arriving back at the cabin after one of his aspen grove trips hauling large limbs and poles, had to smile over watching the gray jays feasting on the fat from the two hindquarters and a section of venison ribs all now hanging from their meat pole from Bear Scat's earlier deer kill. Then into their cabin he went with his arms full of long poles, and soon one could hear sawing and such noises coming from inside the trappers' cabin, along with the sounds of a happily singing, albeit off-key, Big Hat.

An hour later, Bear Scat tiredly rounded the north end of their cabin carrying the last section of the over 275-pound mule deer buck he had killed, along with the entire hide which he figured they could scrape, tan and then use for the other window covering on their cabin. Hoisting up the last section of his deer so it could also cool out and glaze, Bear Scat turned just in time to see Big Hat emerging from their cabin. "Bear Scat, come over and take a look," said Big Hat with a 'come hither' gesture with his arm and right hand. Nodding his head in understanding over Big Hat's 'come hither' gesture, a tired Bear Scat from all of his exertions walking back and forth over the small mountain behind their cabin hauling heavy quarters of his big deer back to the meat pole, walked over to the front door of the cabin and into its darkened and cool interior. Big Hat, with a much-satisfied grin, pointed over to the side of the cabin where Bear Scat previously had his sleeping furs spread out on the hard dirt-packed floor. There in all of its glory stood a newly constructed bedframe made from aspen poles with a crisscrossed rope 'matting' for a mattress! No longer would Bear Scat have to sleep on a cold and damp dirt floor in the future! Then casting his eyes over to where Big Hat slept in the cabin, there stood a copy of a handmade bedframe with a crisscrossed rope mattress as well! Then swinging his eyes over towards their mud, stone and stick fireplace located on the north side of their cabin, Bear Scat saw a crude homemade table with two tall log rounds which had been cut from their winter woodpile seated at each side of the table acting as sitting stools. Then his eyes swung around the inside of their cabin and he noticed that the packs of beaver furs that the Blackfeet Indians during the Missouri River incident had taken from some poor damn fur trapper now long dead, were now up off the floor and sitting on aspen log supports to keep them dry and vermin free. Additionally, their bags of flour, salt, spices, rice, beans, and dried fruit were now hanging up off the floor in the cabin's rafters so they would remain vermin- and spoilage-free as well. Looking over at Big Hat and his big self-satisfied grin in the dim light of their cabin, Bear Scat said, "I think I am through hauling deer meat for the day. Now I plan on making us one hell of a supper and if I can get it right as my father taught me many years ago when cooking or baking with Dutch ovens, I will make us a raisin and apple from our dried apples, Dutch oven cobbler to celebrate what we have accomplished this fine day. I might also add we have some Fourth Class Rum that probably ought to be served along with our meal this evening in celebration for what we have accomplished. What say you, Big Hat?" Without a single word, Big Hat walked over to one of their kegs of rum, took out two cups from his homemade cupboard, filled both cups to the rims, and with a big grin said, "I don't think we need to wait for supper, do we?"

That evening with a special supper of Dutch oven biscuits coated with sugar scraped off from their supply of dark sugar cones, all the fresh, fried in bear fat venison backstraps one could eat, coffee that was so strong it would make a mule piss backwards, and a Dutch oven raisin and apple cobbler that would knock one's eyes out at 20 feet, its crust was so flaky and sweet, the men partook until they almost floundered, then they went back for seconds...

Later that night with the sounds of a heavy rain drumming off their deeply sodded roof, the crackling sounds of nearby lightning strikes and the almost constant rumbling of the thunderclaps from high overhead, the two exhausted but well-fed men slept soundly on their new beds under their heavy sleeping furs. That they did as the Fourth Class Rum did its duty and salved the most grievous of sore joints and muscles from their many days of hard labor. Perhaps the two men should have not imbibed so much rum, but one would not know that based on the snoring taking place in the cabin still smelling of fresh-cut pine...

The next morning, Bear Scat, with a hammering head from the previous evening's celebration with 'demon rum', stumbled out from his wonderful new bed realizing he had not put any dry wood aside in light of the evening's surprise heavy thunderstorm. That would make for a harder start to his breakfast fire detail, so he hurriedly dressed, slipped on his moccasins, routinely grabbed his Hawken just in case a need arose and quietly slipped outside so as not to awaken Big Hat. Doing as he always did under Big Hat's frontier survival training, he slowly stepped outside but not before looking all around for any signs of danger. Nothing out of the ordinary stirred around except for the two magpies flying away in alarm from off the deer meat hanging on the meat pole upon seeing him exiting through the front door of the cabin. Looking over at his firepit, he could not even see any steam arising from his bed of coals it had rained so hard the evening before. Shaking his head and realizing he was going to have to walk out into the nearby forest and scrounge up some dry wood, he turned and walked under the still heavily dripping trees. Finding an old pitchy pine stump, he took his knife and cut off a number of pitch-laden chunks of wood, gathered them into his arms along with his rifle, and walked back to their cabin's firepit so he could get a fire going and make a bed of coals so he could make Big Hat's favorite breakfast, namely anything just so they were accompanied with piping hot Dutch oven biscuits slathered with honey from a crock full of the 'sweet-gooey' they had purchased when they had been shopping in Fort Union's warehouse earlier in the summer.

Walking back to the firepit, Bear Scat laid down his pitch sticks on a large flat boulder beside his main cooking area and went to lay his Hawken against one of the nearby sitting logs in case any danger showed its hand. Turning, his eyes routinely swept their livestock corral and then moved back to his firepit and the pitch sticks. SON-OF-A-BITCH! THEIR HORSES WERE ALL GONE! The balky, stubborn and cantankerous mules were still in the corral but every damn horse was absent the corral! "BIG HAT, GET YOUR ASS OUT HERE AND RIGHT NOW!" yelled Bear Scat. Grabbing up his Hawken from the sitting log, Bear Scat's eyes quickly scanned all around him in case those who had stolen their horses during the night and had used the cover of the thunderstorm's noises to do so, were still dangerously close at hand. Fortunately no one of such dangerous horse-stealing 'color' could to be seen! About then Big Hat, naked as a baby jay bird, burst forth from the front door of their cabin with his Hawken in hand and more or less ready for what he figured was a fight close at hand, rum-soaked brain from the night before or not!

"What the hell is the problem?" he bellowed in a cranky sounding tone of voice over being woken up so abruptly and still feeling some of the effects from the previous night's numerous cups of rum.

"Our horses have been stolen!" said Bear Scat, as he took off running over to the corral to see what he could see in the way of tracks or any other kind of clues as to the thieves. Arriving at the still closed corral gate, he looked down for any sign that would 'speak' to him. Sure as all get-out, there were six sets of moccasin footprints in and around the damp soil of the corral. Then looking over at their nearby cabin where they kept all of the bridles for the horses and mules hanging from the log walls, Bear Scat noticed that a number of the bridles were missing! About then, Big Hat arrived and he too began looking all around the corral in an attempt to 'read' from the maze of footprints as to what had occurred during the dark of the night and more than likely at the height of the covering thunderstorm's noises.

"At least six of them red devils and damned if they hadn't discovered our whereabouts and waited until they had the cover of that damn thunderstorm last night to pull off their raid," he slowly said through gritted teeth, as his rum-fogged mind now became a thing of the past in light of the desperate situation they were immediately facing being afoot and horseless while deep in Indian country!

As for Bear Scat, his mind was really endlessly churning as well! Once again, it was as if he had been left out on the vast prairie after a violent thunderstorm had covered up an evil act with all of its noise and heavy rainfall! Only this time, the thieves had made a fatal mistake. This time, Bear Scat found himself a lot more mentally and emotionally experienced in how to react to a pending disaster, namely the loss of one's transportation and only true means of escape from danger. Once again, Bear Scat found himself tightening up inside with bitter determination to right an evil wrong. Turning, he calmly walked back to their cabin, entered and walked over to his sleeping area. There he loaded his 'Possibles bag' with a tin of percussion caps, about 50 .52 caliber lead balls, oiled patches and then pulled two full powder horns from hanging off the wall, because his Hawken 'ate' powder with the best of them when called upon. Then slipping his tomahawk's handle through his back sash and putting two pistols into his front sash, he checked his belt knife and then turned to leave. As he did, he found Big Hat now fully clothed and gathering up his 'war gear' for the fight to the death they both knew was coming! Fight to the death because both Big Hat and Bear Scat realized that without their horses, they were 'dead men walking' in the heart of Indian country inhabited by the deadly Blackfeet and killing Gros Ventre Indians...

"If you are ready, Bear Scat, we need to be moving. Whoever stole our horses has one hell of a headstart over us, but I will teach you a little ground-eating trick that is familiar to all of us experienced and skilled trappers. Let us get going and you do as I do," said Big Hat.

Out the cabin's front door and after closing it behind them, off streamed the two trappers at a trot hot on the rain-washed stolen horses' trail. That was when Bear Scat got another lesson in the many times desperate life and times of a Mountain Man fur trapper. For the first 100 yards, Big Hat trotted along the trail of the stolen horses. Then after running 100 yards, he stopped and walked the next 50 yards as he rested up and got his wind back. Then after walking those 50 steps, Big Hat once again took off at a ground-eating trot for another 100 yards. This trapper's maneuver, designed to cover lots of ground in a short period of time and arrive at one's destination in fairly good shape and in a ready-to-fight condition, went on all day and into the darkness when the trail of the stolen horses was lost due to the lack of light.

That evening, the two desperate trappers went without the use of any fire for fear of warning the horse thieves they were being tailed in case they were watching their back trail. Thus the two trappers spent a cold and sleepless night upon the previous rainstorm's dampened ground. By daylight the next morning, Bear Scat was now in the lead tracking the stolen horses. That he did while the more experienced Big Hat was trailing his partner with the sole purpose of watching the terrain to their front looking for those they were pursuing, and trying to spot any ambush that might have been planned for anyone trailing their stolen livestock with the hope of getting them back.

A second cold night followed the first, as darkness once again stopped their pursuit of the Indian horse thieves. Indian horse thieves, if the unshod ponies running along with their shod stolen stock said anything as to the identity of the horse thieves. By now, hunger, fatigue and the evening's cold was taking its toll of the two horseless trappers still in a desperate pursuit. However the grim determination found within both men and the bile the stolen horses' event created carried them resolutely through another cold and sleepless night. Day three of the pursuit began as had day two. Bear Scat, least experienced in Indian ambushes, led the way as the lead tracker and Big Hat brought up the rear with searching eyes sweeping every possible ambush point lying ahead of them in case the horse thieves figured they were being pursued and were now lying in wait in order to kill their pursuers. As in the previous days' of pursuit on foot, the two trappers employed the running of 100 yards and then resting for the following 50 yards, trapper's distance-covering technique throughout the day. However by day three, Big Hat had roughly figured the general direction of travel the horse thieves were now taking. Additionally, the horse thieves were now walking their stolen horses as if no longer fearing any kind of pursuit, so instead of directly following the tracks, the trappers were now cutting crosscountry and intercepting the tracks further down the line still moving in their last basic direction of travel. By so doing, Big Hat figured that would throw off anyone watching their back trail, especially if they did not see anyone directly trailing behind the tracks they had just left.

Daylight on day four of the pursuit found the trappers trailing their human prey through a densely forested area. All of a sudden both men simultaneously stopped dead in their tracks and then quickly took cover on both sides of the horses' trail! Looking over at Big Hat, Bear Scat could see him holding his index finger up to his nose indicating for Bear Scat to smell the air. However, by now with all the wilderness training he had been continuously receiving from Big Hat, Bear Scat was now using all of his senses to stay alive as he had been taught. In so doing, just moments before, Bear Scat had smelled wood smoke and that was why he had dived off the trail in case those using a fire were the targets of their chase and might see him coming. That was also why Big Hat had gestured with his finger to his nose, telling Bear Scat to smell and realize they were close to someone burning wood who were more than likely the targets of their long chase and unawares of the close hands of death in the air...

Moments later, Big Hat crawled over to Bear Scat, as he continued looking down the line of travel evidenced by all the now fresh shod and unshod horse tracks. Bear Scat on the other hand, for some reason, was no longer tired or hungry but he did have a powerful thirst developing, as evidenced by his now dry throat. Using the many trees in the area, the two trappers began crawling toward the smell of wood smoke and in so doing, found it getting stronger and stronger smelling. About 30 minutes later, the two still crawling forward trappers could hear the 'nickering' sounds many horses made when they were picketed all together and not being familiar with each other, as well as the guttural sounding talk of the Indians. Listening for a while to the unseen foe talking, Big Hat leaned over and whispered, "Blackfeet, and they are heading for the Hudson's Bay Company's trading post on the Frenchman River in Canada in order to sell the stolen horses and buy more guns and whiskey! Also from what I can determine in their discussions, they are a bunch of Blackfeet Indians hired by that Hudson's Bay Company's trading post to travel America's beaver trapping areas, killing any American trappers encountered and stealing their furs and horses in the process. Then they take what they have stolen back to Canada and sell them at that Hudson's Bay Company trading post on the Frenchman River with the encouragement of that trading post's *Bourgeois*. Apparently that trading post's *Bourgeois* feels that if his Indians kill enough of our trappers and steal the American trappers' horses and pelts that will reduce his competition. Well, we are just going to see about this mess and in less time than it takes to tell about it after the dust settles and the killing field has a few more inhabitants..."

Then the two trappers could smell the smells of cooking meat. Now Bear Scat could feel the hunger pangs coming back and overriding his excitement over what he felt about the battle soon to come. Soon the trappers could hear the excited talk of men feasting on cooked meat and enjoying life. Those happy noises of hungry men went on for about an hour and then the noises around the horse thieves dimmed down and then died out altogether adding to the evening's quietness.

After a long while with no human noises coming from the Blackfeet's camp ahead in the deep timber, Big Hat crawled back over to Bear Scat saying, "I think the entire camp has eaten their fill and now all of them have gone to sleep for the evening. Check the caps on your rifle and pistols to make sure they are ready to go. I will sneak up on one side of those sleeping men and you stay just off to my right so we don't shoot ourselves in a crossfire. Wait until I yell so all of the sleeping men jump up making them better and easier targets to hit. Between the two of us we only have six shots so don't miss. You shoot those to my right and I will take care of those to my left. When we start, use your rifle to fire the first shot, then drop it, quick draw your pistols for your next two shots and aim for the biggest part of anyone standing nearest to you! That way we should be able to get them all. Now cock your rifle and pistols so all you have to is pull the trigger and that way by not cocking them when we are alongside where they are sleeping, none of their light sleepers will hear the metallic 'clicks' when we cock them. Now let's go and be damn quiet in everything that you do, or they will be up and on us like a mess of stirred-up hornets and I don't relish the thought of that!" said Big Hat.

For the next 20 minutes, the two men silently crawled up to the edge of what they soon discovered was a camp full of sleeping

Indians wrapped up in their blankets. Then continuing to crawl even closer, Big Hat quietly gestured with hand signals for Bear Scat to separate slightly away from him and move more to the right, so they would not put each other into a deadly crossfire once the shooting started. Finally in position where both men could cover all of the sleeping Indians once they jumped to their feet in alarm, both men quietly stood up and took their 'ready' positions. Once standing, the two trappers raised their rifles, took aim where they figured their first target would be standing once surprised and at that moment in time, the trappers were now not more than ten feet away from every sleeping Indian. Then Big Hat looked over at a very determined-looking Bear Scat once more to make damn sure he was ready to take several men's lives and satisfied over what he was seeing on the face of his younger partner, loudly yelled, "HEY!"

Even though Bear Scat was more than ready with his finger on the trigger of his Hawken rifle, he was surprised over how fast all six sleeping Indians, upon hearing Big Hat yell, exploded up from the ground and looked right at them! **BOOM—BOOM!** went the two quick-shooting Hawken rifles and immediately two Indians on the receiving end of those soft lead balls fired from such close ranges, exploded blood and guts all over their blankets lying behind them! Then in quick succession, after dropping their now empty rifles, one could hear the .52 caliber pistols sounding off almost in a rolling thunder! **BOOM—BOOM—BOOM—CLICK!** One of Bear Scat's pistols had somehow lost its percussion cap when he had quickly jerked it from his sash and it had misfired! Five Indians died immediately, as the huge .52 caliber soft lead balls smashed and tore their ways through each of the recipient's bones and vitals. In almost every case, the rifle and pistol balls had mushroomed so violently in the Indians' bodies that they instantly dropped into crumpled and bleeding heaps upon the ground! However, the one Indian who avoided being killed along with his brethren, attempted to escape when Bear Scat's pistol had misfired.

In a panic, that Indian man, a short fat warrior, ran directly at Bear Scat in utter confusion and wide-eyed panic!

Dropping both of his pistols, Bear Scat quickly reached behind his back, immediately withdrew his tomahawk and in one violent swing with a force of energy he knew not from whence it came, slammed its blade directly under the fleeing man's chin as he attempted to run off into the darkness! When he did, the full force of Bear Scat's adrenalin-driven tomahawk tore clear through the man's soft tissue in his throat and then slammed into his spine with such force, that it was severed completely and almost lopped off the man's head except for a small piece of tissue barely holding it on! When that happened, the fat warrior's escape speed spun his almost headless body right around and into Bear Scat with his blood from severed arteries momentarily pumping blood up and all over Bear Scat's head, face and shirt, knocking him to the ground in the process!

Big Hat, seeing the spew of blood spraying high into the air momentarily masking Bear Scat and his once-terrified and now dead fleeing Indian in the light of the Indians' campfire and then seeing his partner slammed onto the ground in the collision, yelled out in panic thinking it was Bear Scat who had been killed! Running over to his friend, Big Hat was tremendously relieved upon seeing Bear Scat jumping up from the inadvertent collision and then having his heart almost stopping, upon seeing his friend completely covered frontally with blood and for a moment not realizing it was from the just tomahawk-killed Indian and not that of his partner!

Later that morning when things had died down and emotions had returned to a more or less normal state, Big Hat and Bear Scat feasted hungrily on the remains of the now dead Indians' breakfast of roasted buffalo. Then using the dead Indians' sleeping furs, both men slept an exhausted sleep through the rest of that day and deep into the next morning's hours. However, in so doing, both men awoke about the same time in the morning itching and scratching their bodies almost raw. Soon they both realized that had picked up a terrible case of lice from the dead Indians' blankets!

Finally rising unable to sleep anymore over all the itching and scratching with the lice finding new sources of a white man's blood, the trappers let all of the Indians' horses loose to roam wild. That they did to confuse any other Indian kin from figuring out what had happened to their like in kind and coming looking for the ones who may have done them in. However when it came to retrieving their own horses, they discovered an 'equine gold mine'! Their 11 horses stolen from out of their corrals by the Blackfeet Indians had now turned into 20! Seeing that, Big Hat figured the just-killed Blackfeet Indians had been busy on the trapping grounds of the American frontier when it came to their killing, horse stealing and beaver pack acquisitions! That moment of realization occurred when Bear Scat, returning from dragging the last dead Indian off to join the rest of his kind for the grizzly bears and wolves to enjoy, discovered a pile of packsaddles and 18 complete packs of beaver skins! When Bear Scat made Big Hat aware of their newly discovered wealth in beaver packs, he could hardly believe his ears. As such, between the acquisition of nine additional horses and the 18 packs of beaver skins, they had become wealthy men overnight! Then coupled with the eight packs of beaver furs back at their cabin taken from the Indians who had sneaked into Bear Scat's camp when he was alone and healing up from being paw-swiped across the face by a marauding grizzly bear, the two of them were more than rich. Especially if they took in the fact that they had yet to set a single beaver trap and had their whole trapping season yet ahead of them on the Porcupine…

Taking back all of their horses and the other discovered nine the Indians had taken off some unfortunate trapper, the two trappers rode bareback back towards their cabin by several routes and up and down two creeks to confuse anyone else who might be trailing them and their now large herd of shod horses. However, Bear Scat got another unique and never to be forgotten lesson in wilderness survival when he observed that Big Hat's scratching from the louse infestation he had picked up from sleeping in the dead Indians' blankets, got the better of him. Finally Big Hat called over to Bear Scat when they approached a flat piece of ground covered with numerous black ant mounds saying, "Follow my lead, Bear Scat, and do just exactly as I do or you will pay the price from the 'little people'." With that, Big Hat stopped his horse, dismounted and stripped bare-assed naked out in front of a surprised Bear Scat, God and anybody else who might be taking a gander! Bear Scat figuring his partner had lost his mind, just watched in wonder and then eventually surprise, when Big Hat took his louse-infected clothing, walked over to an ant mound and stirred it up until it just swarmed with big, mad-as-hell, black ants. Then Big Hat took his highly louse-infected clothing and draped it all over the mound of swarming ants and stirred it gently all around until it was just swarming with angry ants. Now that he had the ants' attention, Big Hat laid his garments down and left it for the ants to explore and do their thing. Then without another word, he walked over to another ant mound that was not as badly stirred up and taking his time, gently lay down right at the edge of the mound and let the black ants crawl all over him. By doing it that way, one found the ants crawling all over one's body exploring it out as they routinely looked for food items. Looked for food items such as lice, which were quickly snapped right up wherever they were discovered crawling over Big Hat's inert body and taken back into the ant mound to feed their larvae. Finally it dawned on Bear Scat that what Big Hat was doing was allowing the ants to crawl all over his body and cleanse him of the tiny crawling and biting louse-parasites. After a while and figuring the ants had caught all of his lice on one side of his body, Big Hat slowly turned over so as not to arouse the ants and let them have at his other side and in his more than full head of hair. When he did, he looked up at a still surprised over what was occurring Bear Scat and told him to dismount and do the same thing. Otherwise he would be bringing his lice back to their cabin and then both of them would continue to be infested. Finally figuring out what Big Hat was doing and his excellent but rather unorthodox reason for doing so, Bear Scat slid off his horse and did likewise. After about an hour lying alongside a black ant mound out in the middle of the prairie in the hot sun, he too was uniquely cleansed as was his clothing which had been draped over another nearby stirred-up ant mound, as Big Hat had so instructed!

Dressing, the two men mounted their horses and once again headed for their cabin, all the while watching the ridge tops looking out for any of those who would do them harm. Finally arriving back at their cabin, the two men dismounted, put their horses back into their corral and tied up their new nine acquisitions to the corral rail. Then hauling into the cabin all of their newly acquired packs of beaver skins, they were placed at the rear of their cabin until they could build some more platforms to get them up off the damp dirt flooring inside their cabin. Next, in came all of the packsaddles and bridles to preclude anyone else from running off with their valuable horse gear. Finally, Big Hat took his saw and headed for their nearby aspen grove as Bear Scat began digging new postholes so they could enlarge the size of their corral to comfortably hold their nine new additions. Both men later commented that when they were working and sweating at their jobs, unlike before when such activity aroused the body lice's biting activity, no biting had been felt as a result of their ant 'baths' out on the prairie to rid themselves of such a scourge... (Author's Note: A lesson that Bear Scat Sutta never forgot, and in his later years, relished and never tired of telling that 'ant mound' story to anyone who would stand still long enough to listen to a Mountain Man's tale about a bare-assed Big Hat, a real hardened Mountain Man and himself, lying in and among the black ants, letting them cleanse their bodies of the biting lice he and Big Hat had picked up after sleeping in the blankets of the Indians they had just killed for stealing their horses.)

Come evening time found Bear Scat making up a supper of coffee and Dutch oven biscuits, as Big Hat hauled over to the corral the last of the new posts and rails needed to expand the livestock corral. Then as the men quietly ate their supper, the horses were let out in two hobbled groups one at a time, since the trappers only had enough hobbles for half of their horses so they could feed. Once that group was finished feeding, they were brought back to the corral, watered and then enclosed therein. By then it was almost dark as the other half of the hobbled horses were let out to feed as well. That required the trappers to build a fire so they could keep an eye on the late feeding horses. Finally they were brought back into camp, watered and hitched to the corral railing for the night. Finally satisfied over the work accomplished, two very tired trappers went to bed. But when they retired, they did so with several packs stacked behind the inside of the doors, just in case someone who was not personally invited came looking with evil intent in his heart to settle the score over his lost kin...

The following morning right at dawn found Bear Scat shouldering his Hawken rifle and heading out onto the long sloping timbered hill behind their cabin. Bear Scat hadn't been gone more than 20 minutes when Big Hat, placing corral posts into the holes Bear Scat had dug the previous evening into the ground, heard Bear Scat shoot one shot and then silence. Starting to worry after about another hour had transpired without the reappearance of Bear Scat, Big Hat returned to the cabin, picked up his Hawken rifle and 'Possibles bag' and started out the door. Just as he exited the cabin, he ran into a much-bloodied Bear Scat with a big grin on his face and a huge elk hindquarter slung over his shoulder that was still dripping blood.

Suffice to say, breakfast that morning featured all the elk steak one could tuck away, followed by Dutch oven biscuits slathered with honey, and steaming hot, strong as an angry mule's kick, trapper's coffee. Then as Big Hat worked off his huge breakfast finishing up on the new corral extension, Bear Scat made five more trips back onto his hillside, so he could bring back the remainder of the elk he had just shot. As he did, the quarters of still bloody meat were hung from their meat pole to cool out and glaze. Once the elk meat had cooled out, a number of steaks were cut from one of the animal's hams and taken inside the cabin where it would store longer for future meals because it was cooler. The remainder of the elk was then boned out, cut into thin strips, hung from Big Hat's meat smoking rack, and an aspen fire with smoke initiated so the meat would smoke-up and dry into energy-rich jerky.

All the next day was spent by the two trappers chasing magpies off their meat rack and casting up a small mountain of .52 caliber lead balls for use in their lead-eating Hawken rifles and their single shot horse pistols of the same caliber. Following that, numerous trips with their four mules carrying panniers were made down to the Porcupine again, as more Timothy grasses were cut and laid out on the grassy flat by their cabin to cure for horse and mule feed during the worst of the winter when grazing out on the open range became difficult because of drifting snow. When those grasses had later cured, they were also added to their cache of hay since they now had a larger herd of most valuable horses to care for. Additionally, while the men were streamside gathering in hay, they cut a mess of green willows, brought them back to their cabin, built a small smoke fire, and smoked their beaver traps to destroy the metal and man smells. However when the men did that, they kept their Hawken rifles close at hand and each one wore two pistols in case the small smoke column smoking the beaver traps attracted Indian visitors of the worst kind...

One morning several days later found the two men out on the prairie trailing all four of their mules with their packsaddles. To the trappers' way of thinking, they were now going to do something they enjoyed doing very much. Locating a small herd of buffalo watering down on the Porcupine and sneaking up on the same from downwind so the older cows, who had a much better ability to smell man, remained unawares of the approaching dangers, one quick and well-placed shot each from the men's two Hawken and Lancaster rifles resulted in four fat cow buffalo kicking their last. With the noise of the shooting, smells of fresh blood and now that of man, the small herd of buffalo ambled off to a less noisy neighborhood and took their afternoon drinks elsewhere along the Porcupine River.

Then the 'cutting and gutting' work began, but first Bear Scat got introduced to a much-appreciated and age-old Plains Indian and Mountain Man tradition! Approaching one of the younger looking cow buffalos, Big Hat took out one of his longer bladed Thomas Wilson knives and opened up the cow with a quick thrust and slice just below the last rib. When he did, the animal's large liver was exposed and with another expert thrust, cut off a large chunk of organ tissue from one of the liver's lobes. Holding the bloody organ meat in his hand and with a grin seeing the strange look on Bear Scat's face, Big Hat greedily took several bites from the warm and still quivering chunk of obviously raw meat! After making many satisfying noises while eating his large chunk of meat, Big Hat finished his warm liver with gusto. It was then that Big Hat saw the incredulous looks spread clear across Bear Scat's face over what he had just done to such a bloody piece of raw meat! Without a moment's hesitation, Big Hat thrust his hands deep into the cavity of the buffalo once again, grabbed the remaining liver and lopped off another double fist-sized chunk of the organ meat, withdrew it from the bloody cavity, and handed it to Bear Scat! For a moment, Bear Scat just stood there looking at the bloody offering trying to figure out what to do. Then Big Hat said, "Bear Scat, take this and enjoy it. It is rich in minerals, which is one of the things we are missing in our daily lean meat diets and it is more than good for you." For another long moment, Bear Scat just stood there looking at the bloody and still dripping chunk of meat and then trusting Big Hat, limply took the offering. "Taste it. You will find that you will like it and in the future when we kill any buffalo, you will find yourself looking eagerly for such a good tasting and healthy for you treat from the first kill of buffalo of the day," said a grinning Big Hat with fresh blood now besmirched all over his lower chin! Bear Scat's first tepid bite was soon followed by more that were eagerly taken as he found himself rather enjoying the warm and easy to eat meat. Soon the two men had gorged themselves on the rich organ meat and now both of the men sported bloody lower faces that came from eating such raw and delicious meat... (Author's Note: In

1975 as the Division of Law Enforcement's Senior Resident Agent for the U.S. Fish and Wildlife Service over the States of North and South Dakota, during the annual elk and bison herd's culling operations at Sully's Hill National Game Preserve (created by President Theodore Roosevelt), located near Devils Lake, North Dakota, the Author, a college-trained wildlife biologist as well, along with other officers, officially culled out through shooting a number of bison and elk. Being a trained wildlife biologist who took a keen interest in experiencing all aspects of wild game, as well as an amateur U.S. historian of the Old West, I opened up one of the freshly killed buffalo as was done during the early days, cut off pieces of the animal's liver and partook of such raw and bloody organ meat as had the Indians and Mountain Men of old. I found the still warm and quivering raw liver to be profoundly strongly tasting of minerals and yet after eating a fist-sized chunk of said meat, also discovered it to be strangely filling and not difficult to eat or swallow. However, six hours later, the gas generated from eating raw bison liver turned out to be less than tolerable in a public place and yet a historically interesting experience. However, when one is out on the Plains amidst 'a sea of grass, plenty of wind and the ghosts of the Old West, anything went if you get my gist...)

Four hours later all the mules were heavily loaded with the front and rear quarters of the critters just killed, along with a small mound of the excellent eating when roasted buffalo hump ribs as they headed back to the men's cabin. For the next two days, Big Hat's smoking racks were loaded with strips of delicious drying buffalo meat being made into jerky for the long fall and spring months out on the beaver trapping trail. Additionally the men feasted to their hearts content on buffalo meat and hump ribs until they could hardly hold anymore! Two more buffalo hunting trips were made before the men felt they had enough jerky and heavily smoked ribs in their deerskin bags hanging from the rafters in their cabin, along with numerous slabs of smoked buffalo ribs hanging from pegs cut and driven into carved out holes in the inside walls of their cabin, to carry them through some of the winter's worst of times they knew was soon in coming.

One frosty morning two weeks later as Bear Scat prepared the men's breakfast, a chore he loved plus he was the better cook between the two men, Big Hat walked out from the cabin to go to the bathroom and just then quietly stood there as if testing the air and 'sensing' the moment in time. Then he said, "Bear Scat, tomorrow we head out to the beaver trapping grounds we previously scouted out and you are going to get a lesson on how to trap and skin beaver. I think it is time. With these last three hard frosts we have had, that will start bringing the beaver into their prime and that is when we need to trap them in order to get the best price for our catch. We will need to take only one mule with its panniers, maybe 20 of our beaver traps, a shovel, an ax, a spool of wire and a bottle of that castoreum we purchased way back when we were gathering up our provisions for this trip at Fort Union. We also need to take two of those special Thomas Wilson skinning knives I had the blacksmith alter back at Fort Union especially for us. You know, the ones with the special bevel on just one side that will make cutting the hide a whole lot less likely when we are skinning out our catch. That special adaptation will really become even more important when we are doing the skinning during colder weather and our fingers are not working as well as they should. We will also need to take along a saddlebag of our jerky as well. That way if we get surprised by Indians and have to spend a night out on the trail hidden in the brush somewhere, we at least have something good to eat. That is if we are still alive. We also need to take our reserve Lancaster rifles and fasten them to our pack mule so we have at least four good rifles to long-range shoot if we are challenged by a number of Indians. Additionally, make sure your 'Possibles bag' is fully loaded with what you will need for a good long fight if we get into one with the Indians, and plan on bringing and wearing both of your pistols and your tomahawk. Say, when will breakfast be ready? I am so hungry I could almost eat one of those horses we took away from those Blackfeet Indians some time back."

After a quick breakfast of just biscuits and coffee, the men saddled up their horses and prepared one mule for their first day of beaver trapping of the year. Then heading out right at daylight with Big Hat in the lead and Bear Scat trailing their mule, the men made their ways across the open prairie and down to the nearby Porcupine River for the cover it offered from any evil eyes who might be watching them moving about. An hour later the two men were at one of the river's marshy areas they had previously scouted out and were determined to trap in light of all of the beaver sign, numerous active beaver houses dotting the ponded areas, currently maintained dams, and many swimming critters they had observed in the adjacent riverine areas a month earlier. They would have arrived at their destination at an earlier hour but a huge herd of buffalo had come between them and their trapping grounds while on their way to water. So the men had to ride way around the shaggy beasts to avoid any kind of conflict with the sometimes aggressive animals.

Riding along behind Big Hat trailing their heavily loaded mule carrying all of what they figured they would need to begin setting and running their trap line, Bear Scat never let his eyes miss anything Big Hat was showing or telling him. Finally Big Hat saw a spot that he liked, heavy with many signs of beaver activity, dismounted and walked back to Bear Scat with an 'I am happy to be beaver trapping once again' smile spread clear across his face.

"Bear Scat, I want you to pay careful attention to what I am about to show you. As a beaver trapper, you are the one who is the most vulnerable to surprise attack from any renegade Indians who happen along and spot you out in the water setting or tending your traps. That is because your thinking will be preoccupied with your trap setting and you will not really be looking out for any kind of danger that happens by. Second, being that you are out there many times waist high in the water and deep mud, staggering around as a trapper, you must leave your rifle and pistols behind for fear of them ending up in the water if you stumble or step into an unseen deep muskrat hole. Therefore, the life of the trapper wading about in the water is wholly dependent on the sharp eye and good sense of the remaining trapper still on his horse and acting as a lookout for the man in the water running the trap line."

With those words of caution and warning, Big Hat paused and let them sink into his inexperienced but proving more and more capable and dependable with each passing day, younger partner. With that, Big Hat handed Bear Scat his rifle and the two pistols removed from his sash. Seeing that he more than had his young partner's rapt attention with those moves of disarmament, Big Hat continued on with his trapping lessons. Walking back to the mule's panniers, Big Hat withdrew a beaver trap, a hand ax and a short length of trap wire. Walking over to a large clump of willows growing along the edge of the beaver pond, Big Hat chopped down a dead willow stick that was about four feet in length and two inches in diameter. Then he had Bear Scat ride and walk the horses and mule over to where Big Hat had pointed to the edge of the beaver pond, at a muddy and much-disturbed area littered with many tracks and fallen leaves that had been dropped as green branches were being dragged into the beaver pond.

"Bear Scat, from where you are sitting on your horse watching out for any signs of danger, I want you to look at this disturbed area along the edge of the pond. See all the beaver tracks made in the mud while they were dragging fresh-cut willow and cottonwood saplings and branches into the water? They are doing so for fresh food to eat and also to stick the ends of the larger saplings and branches into the mud and underwater where they have set up their winter food caches. By placing them deep underwater, that helps in keeping the food material fresh and precludes them from being eaten by the many moose we have in the area. Then come winter, all they have to do is swim out from their beaver house over to their cache, grab a branch or two and then take them back to inside their beaver house and eat away. This they can do while under 'Old Man Winter's' deep snow and ice. But in order to get fresh food or fresh branches and limbs for their winter's cache, they have to come ashore and walk about cutting down and dragging such greenery back to the water. When they do, that is our clue as to where to set our traps," said Big Hat seeing he still had Bear Scat's rapt attention.

Then with a quick look around making sure any nearby signs of danger were non-existent, Big Hat began his beaver trapping lessons once again. "Now watch what I am about to do and don't miss anything I am about to show you. I am telling you this because I will only set one trap. Then because you are a younger man than me and not as arthritic as I am from wading about these so many years in icy cold waters, this daily trapping routine will become your responsibility as long as we are a team. I don't like the cold water and even colder mud that one has to wade around in, and because you need to learn how to do this, it is best learned by doing so yourself. Therefore, you will be scouting out and setting all the rest of our traps," said Big Hat, as he carefully examined his partner's face to see if his field lessons were still being recorded in his memory banks. Then as an afterthought said, "Besides, my rheumatism isn't getting any better and it takes me longer and longer every morning just to warm up my bones and get these tired old legs a-moving. So now you get to earn these same afflictions all of us old Mountain Men carry with us on a daily basis."

Satisfied over what he was seeing in his partner's level of attention, Big Hat walked back to their mule, removed a trap from the pannier and unwound the chain wrapped around his five-pound, St. Louis-style beaver trap. Then walking back, he sat the trap on the bank of the beaver pond a short distance away from where all the beaver sign had been seen in the mud by the beaver slide to avoid leaving any more of his scent than possible. There he depressed the trap's springs on each end of the rectangular-jawed trap simultaneously with his feet and engaged the trap's 'dog' in the 'pan notch'. Then with a big sigh over the cold water and mud to come, Big Hat stepped out into the pond's waters and walked over to where the beaver's slide entered the water. Taking the still open-jawed trap, Big Hat carefully laid it down on a hard ground surface adjacent the beaver slide area under about four inches of water. Taking his hand, he gently swirled the water around where the trap had been laid until the swirled muddy water had thinly coated the trap with a light film of mud and hidden the whole trap completely. Then taking the blunt end of his hand ax, Big Hat drove one end of a wooden stick he had cut down previously deeply into the mud, leaving a substantial amount of the wood sticking out from the water. With that, Big Hat carefully slipped the ring at the end of the trap's chain over the top of the end of the wooden stick, letting it slide down the stick until it was resting on the bottom of the pond. Taking his short piece of trap wire, Big Hat then tied the ring on the end of the trap's chain to the wooden stick. That way if the beaver somehow was able to pull up the long wooden stake anchored in the deep end of the pond before he drowned because of the weight of the trap, the valuable trap would still remain attached to the wooden stick and could be more easily spotted floating in the water and retrieved. Besides, by using an old dried wooden stake, the beaver was less apt to try chewing through it and attempt to escape with the hard-to-replace heavy trap. Walking back to where he had set the trap in the shallow water, Big Hat took out his knife and cut off a green willow branch from the nearby clump of willows growing at the edge of the beaver pond, scraped off all the green bark so a beaver would not want to chew on it and walked back to the trap site. There he stuck the willow twig into the bank where the tip of the willow twig would be diagonally hanging right over the pan of the beaver trap lying directly below in about four inches of water. Satisfied over his set, Big Hat removed a small bottle of castoreum purchased back at Fort Union from his 'Possibles bag' and taking a short twig, dipped it into the bottle of liquid. Then taking the small twig that had been dipped into the bottle of castoreum, Big Hat daubed the liquid-laden twig onto the very tip of the stick hanging diagonally over the water over the trap.

Walking back out from the water a dozen or so steps away from where his trap had been set so as not to leave any more human scent than necessary, Big Hat walked over to where Bear Scat was sitting on his horse doing double duty as a guard and learning about what had been demonstrated out in the water of the beaver pond. "Now," said Big Hat, "beaver are very territorial. If they smell the scent of another beaver in their pond, they will come right over to investigate. By daubing the castoreum on the end of that stick placed so it hangs over the open jaws of the trap, any beaver smelling the strange beaver scent will come over to investigate. The way I set that trap, the beaver should come over to investigate the strange beaver smell in his home waters, swim to the end of that castoreum-daubed stick, stand on the bottom of the pond so he can reach up, grab the stick and pull it over to his nose so he can smell who left the strange beaver smell other than him. When he drops his feet in order to stand so he can reach out, grab and smell the stick, his feet should be on top of the pan of the trap. When that happens, the trap will explode closed and we will have a beaver with one or both of its feet in the trap. In a panic, the beaver will swim away from where the trap just slammed on his foot or feet and head out into what he thinks is the safety of the deeper water. However he can only swim the six-foot length of the trap's chain and no further. That is because the heavy wooden stake I drove into the bottom of the pond will keep the beaver from swimming no further than the length of the trap's chain. There he will continue trying to swim away in panic, all the while held from doing so because of the trap being fastened to that heavy wooden stake. Soon the five-pound weight of the trap and chain will drag the soon to be exhausted beaver underwater and drown the beast. When we return, if we have done a good job in setting the trap, we should have a $6 beaver drowned and dead in our trap. So ends your lesson, Bear Scat, and now it will be your turn to set the rest of our traps while I sit comfortably on my horse looking out for danger and watching you get wet and cold the rest of the day," said Big Hat with a grin.

By around four o'clock in the afternoon, Bear Scat had managed to locate 13 other likely looking beaver trapping sites and had managed to set all 13 traps with only occasional words of encouragement or direction coming from his mentor, Big Hat. Tiredly emerging from the cold waters and even colder mud of the beaver pond after his thirteenth and last beaver trap set for the day, Bear Scat found Big Hat smiling at the nearly flawless trap-setting performance of his younger partner. It now had become apparent to Big Hat that his less experienced partner had a quick mind like the 'snap' of a beaver trap and once told how to do something, did so with precision and dedication to the moment.

However, as a tired and wet Bear Scat was soon to discover, his day work was not done. The two trappers had barely ridden a quarter of their way back along their newly set trap line, when they began seeing dead beaver already in their previously set traps! Bear Scat could hardly believe his eyes that he had already caught a beaver in one of his very first set beaver traps. Bailing off his horse in excitement over his first catch, Bear Scat waded out to his drowned beaver, a large one, removed it from the trap and headed back to shore with a proud grin that was as wide as the beaver pond he was splashing around in. Wading ashore with a 'blanket-sized' beaver weighing over 90 pounds, Bear Scat held its heavy body proudly up in the air as if Big Hat could not see what his partner had just caught.

Grinning broadly over Bear Scat's enthusiasm, Big Hat slipped off his horse after taking another long look around for any sign of danger and then walked over to his rapidly learning partner and gave him a big congratulatory slap on his back! "Way to go, Bear Scat! However, now the work starts. Hand me that beaver, then go over and remove your Hawken rifle from your horse so you can now stand watch and learn your next lesson in what it takes to become a Mountain Man."

With that advice quickly followed and with Bear Scat now watching intently over the two of them, Big Hat gave him his latest lesson in being a fur trapper out on the frontier. "Now watch carefully, for if you make a wrong slip up in this skinning process, you are going to cost us nothing but money back at the trading post when this fur is graded," said Big Hat, as he took out one of his specially modified Thomas Wilson skinning knives, rolled the beaver over on his back on the pond's grassy bank and began. "Alright, Bear Scat, there is a right and wrong way to do this. I will show you the way I want it done. Anything less and we will lose money. Now watch carefully as I slit the skin of this here beaver down the length of the animal's belly. That cut made and done, I will now make transverse slits along the insides of each of the beaver's legs and then I am going to cut off each of its feet. OK, now I am going to cut off and save the tail, because roasted they are a real treat because of their fatty content, and I am going to save the body as well. Also, if one needs a new knife sheath, a beaver's tail makes a right presentable one once tanned and smoked. Now, beaver are very good eating and I always keep the first-caught beaver of any trapping season for a traditional 'good luck' meal at the end of the first day of any trapping season. Plus as you are now going to learn, a real Mountain Man learns to 'waste not, want not' as the 'Good Book' says and your blessed mother always reminded you. Next, using one of our special knives, I am going to carefully remove the skin from our critter and throw it and the meaty beaver's body into one of our panniers. That done, we need to 'run' the rest of our previously set trap line because I have to believe that is not our last beaver caught this fine day. But first you need to go and set that trap again as I taught you earlier, because where there is one beaver there will always be another until we trap out this area. Then when we do that, we pick up our stakes and move on into another likely looking area and start the trapping process all over again."

Before that day in the field was done, Bear Scat had caught another eight beaver in his freshly set traps! As Big Hat had so instructed, he showed Bear Scat one time on how he wanted things done in the skinning detail and then it was Bear Scat's turn to do as he had been taught. In so doing and in the manner he was being taught by Big Hat, Bear Scat found himself learning the fur trapper trade by huge leaps and bounds! Tiredly riding back into their cabin site late that afternoon, Big Hat took care of their day's livestock and also saw to it that the rest of their animals were allowed to leave the corral so they could also feed and water. While that work was ongoing, Bear Scat prepared their evening meal with some guidance from Big Hat on cooking beaver meat for his first time and how to correctly roast the tails they had brought back to camp. However as Bear Scat quickly learned, they only brought back to camp that which they could eat. As for the remainder of the skinned beaver carcasses, they were tossed into the bushes along the trap line for the critters to eat out in the field and not brought back to their cabin and left lying around to attract the always hungry and troublesome grizzly bears...

After supper and things had been cleaned up and put away, Bear Scat looked forward after a hard, wet and cold day's work in the field to stretching out in his sleeping furs and letting his still cold legs from all the wading in the beaver ponds, warm up. However to his surprise, the way, life and times of the fur trapper got in the way once again! "Alright, Bear Scat, get your miserable carcass over here. We still have some work that needs doing," said Big Hat with a knowing grin over Bear Scat dragging his weary bottom. Bear Scat tiredly walked over to where Big Hat was pulling their freshly skinned beaver skins out from the pannier and with an armload of wet hides, headed for their cabin. Soon Big Hat had a fire going in their fireplace and three beeswax candles burning brightly, as he sat Bear Scat down and began providing even more instruction as to what needed to be done with their fresh beaver skins.

First Big Hat showed Bear Scat how to use one of their heavier, less sharp knives and laying out a beaver skin on their floor on top of a tanned deerskin, used the dull knife to remove all vestiges of fat and meat left on the flesh side of the skin, which if left unattended would eventually cause rotting to occur. As Big Hat provided instruction in the art of 'de-fatting' a fresh beaver skin, he made sure Bear Scat was aware that a pelt from a beaver is always heavy with fat. Therefore to properly pelt a beaver skin, all of the fat and any pieces of meat must be removed or the skin may rot in those places where scraps of tissue remained. Once Bear Scat had mastered that duty to Big Hat's satisfaction, Big Hat went out from their cabin to a large pile of previously gathered and stored green willow limbs. Coming back into their cabin, Big Hat showed Bear Scat how to make 18- to 36-inch willow hoops according to the size of the now prepared fresh beaver skin and with the spools of twine they had purchased back in Fort Union, tied the pelts through small slits made in the edges of the skin to the willow branch hoops so they could dry. Then Big Hat said, "Bear Scat, we will let these skins dry into a flat, round *'plus'* and when they do, they will generally resist any attacks by insects providing we have done our job correctly in fleshing out the hides, and makes it easier for us to place into packs when we are getting ready to transport them to the trading post."

FINALLY Bear Scat got to head for his sleeping furs and soon was dead to the world, still 'pond water' cold legs and feet as well! However he found himself stirring before daybreak as his biological clock awakened and alerting him that it was time to get up, go to the bathroom, get a fire going, and start their breakfast so the two of them could face another full day. Face another full day because once the traps had been set, they had to be tended on a daily basis or the carcasses would become food to prey animals or discovery and theft by the local Indians. After a breakfast of coffee and Dutch oven biscuits slathered in honey, the two trappers riding their horses and trailing a pack mule carrying panniers, made their ways back to their familiar beaver trapping grounds and trap line. However as they did, they tried leaving their cabin site by different exits every time so as not to leave a distinguishable white man's shod horse trail leading right back to their camp and a corral full of valuable horseflesh, not to mention a cabin full of a white man's highly desirable provisions.

As the winter season finally began closing in on the trappers, they continued their trapping without let-up. But as Big Hat had so advised, Bear Scat continued as their primary trapper and Big Hat, being more experienced with Indians and some of their local warring tactics when it came to attacking white men trappers, remained as Bear Scat's sole guard when he was out and about setting and running their trap line in the cold, late fall waters and even now colder mud it seemed in the bottom of the ponds. However they had done very well when it came to trapping beaver that fall season. Bear Scat had learned his trapping techniques very well and in the beaver-rich waters they were trapping, he averaged almost a beaver per trap because he had become so skillful in reading the beaver's sign and the setting of his traps. So much so that he had managed to trap over 30 river otter as well in his beaver sets, and they now had over 240 dried beaver *plus'* back at their cabin that Bear Scat had caught in his first trapping season! Additionally, the trappers still had the eight packs of beaver skins from the three Indians that had ambushed Bear Scat back on the Missouri River, and the 18 packs of beaver skins they had discovered when they had the run-in with the six horse-stealing Blackfeet Indians early on in their arrival at their current cabin site! Lastly, they would still have the spring trapping season in which they would be trapping the even higher grades of beaver because of the better pelage the beaver had grown due to the long winter's cold. In short, the two trappers were now horse and beaver-pack rich, that is if they could manage to keep their hair and get all of those riches back to the trading post come summer.

Big Hat and Bear Scat kept trapping right up to freeze-up and then they pulled their traps because trapping the beaver under the ice was difficult. The following day, the two trappers trailing all four of their pack mules headed out into the nearest buffalo herd and killed four cow buffalos. Then they spent the remainder of the day skinning and quartering their kills. Come dusk, they headed back to their cabin with four heavily loaded and complaining mules over the weight of the loads of meat they were carrying. Back at camp because of the volume of meat they now possessed, the two men constructed two more meat poles to accommodate the hanging stocks of fresh buffalo quarters and since the weather was now colder than 'Billy Hell', they could just let the meat hang in the air since there was no worry over the vast stocks of buffalo meat spoiling.

Then due to the arriving freezing winter weather and fiercely howling winds driving the temperatures even lower, the two trappers spent a number of their hours when not caring for their livestock, feeding them the emergency hay and breaking the ice in the spring so they could water, and packing their beaver skins for the summer trip back to the trading post. On the warmer of days when the winds were not howling, the two men folded each of their beaver skins in half with the fur side in. Then using the butt end of one of their heavier winter woodpile Douglas fir logs, the two men placed 60 *'plus'* to a bundle (each *'plus'* weighed between a pound and a pound-and-a-half) and using another woodpile log as a pry, lifted the heavier log end up, slid the bundle of furs under the lifted log and then laid it back down on the *'plus'* so they would be even more compressed. Then the bundle of compressed furs weighing between 90-100 pounds, was tightly tied four ways with deer hide stripping. Then once the bundle of compressed furs was tightly tied, the pry log was used again to lift up the heavier Douglas fir log and the bundle of compressed and tied-up furs was removed, and the process repeated for each bundle of furs needing to be compressed for easier transport. Lastly, each pack of furs numbering around 60 pelts to a pack, was then wrapped up in previously tanned deer hides to protect the valuable furs from being soiled when transported the long distance back to Fort Union, and from all the packing upon the horses and unpacking at the end of each day while along the trail. Depending upon the fur prices back at the trading post, each bundle of furs would be worth $300-600 per pack! Then when transported back to the trading post, each horse or mule would be expected to carry two packs, weighing between 90 and 100 pounds each.

One morning while getting ready to go deer hunting so the trappers could acquire more deer hides to be tanned and then used to wrap around each bundle of furs to protect them from the rains and dirt along the trail, Bear Scat was busy with making breakfast. Busy making Dutch oven biscuits, frying buffalo steaks and watching so his pot of coffee would not boil over when all of a sudden, he heard a low whistle coming from Big Hat who had just exited their cabin and was standing at its doorway. Bear Scat, all engrossed with his breakfast preparations, paid little heed to Big Hat until he low whistled once again. Looking up from his biscuit-checking detail making sure they would not burn in the Dutch ovens, he could see that Big Hat was obviously looking past him in his bent-over cooking position. Realizing there was something of interest behind him if Big Hat's cold stare meant anything, Bear Scat took a quick look over his shoulder and then whipped his eyes back to the cooking fire upon burning his fingers on the cast iron Dutch oven lid he had just removed in order to check his biscuits!

Then realizing what big hat had been staring at and what he had just seen, bear scat slowly turned around to see six Gros Ventre warriors who had quietly sneaked up from behind him in the fresh snow and were standing not ten feet away, all with leveled rifles upon both him and big hat! Slowly raising his right arm in the universal sign of greeting as Big Hat had taught him to do when meeting any Indians and forcing a smile, Bear Scat said, "Welcome, do any of you speak English?"

For the longest moment in time in Bear Scat's young life, not a single Indian moved, said anything or had any kind of a facial change showing friendliness! Finally, one of the Indian men and apparently the leader of the group, without taking his eyes off or the end of his rifle barrel away from covering Bear Scat, grunted out something to the rest of his compatriots in his native tongue. Instantly two warriors ran up to Big Hat and jerked his rifle out from his hands as well as his pistol out from his sash! As they disarmed Big Hat, two other Indians ran up to Bear Scat and one of the men jerked Bear Scat's pistol out from his sash and the other man snatched up Bear Scat's Hawken from the nearby sitting log. Then he let out a loud yell of exultation over capturing a very fine rifle and counting coup on a white man, as he raised his trophy rifle overhead for all the world to see!

Then the fierce looking Indian confronting Bear Scat, the one with a savage looking knife scar running across his nose and onto one cheek, smiled a wicked looking smile, lowered his rifle and then pointing his hand and fingers on his right hand at his mouth and moving it back and forth away and towards his mouth grunted "UMMPH—UMMPH"! Bear Scat instantly realized that the man was hungry and wanted to be fed. Also realizing that to make just one wrong move would get both him and Big Hat killed outright, he smiled and gestured to a nearby sitting log near the fire upon which the man was to sit and then chancing his next move, abruptly turned his back on his Indian antagonist like he was no big worry. Then Bear Scat reached for one of the plates warming by the fire and commenced loading up the plate with food just like he would do if he were feeding Big Hat. He knew he was taking a big risk in turning his back on the obviously unfriendly Indian but as far as he was concerned, they were already dead men so nothing ventured, nothing gained...at least until he could come up with a battle plan that would extricate the two trappers from the situation they now found themselves embroiled in!

Turning around with a plate full of steaming meat and two Dutch oven biscuits, he gambled as he formulated his battle plan and handed the plate to the scar-faced Indian like it was an everyday event around his cooking fire. Then turning back toward the firepit, he took up the remaining plate lying on a warming rock next to the fire, filled it with a steaming chunk of meat, two biscuits, turned and offered that plate full of food to the next closest Indian standing alongside the one with the knife scar running across part of his face. Instantly both men grabbed the plates and with their fingers, began wolfing down their food. When they did, Bear Scat taking another bold gamble, picked up a coffee cup sitting near his boiling coffee pot, lifted it high into the air so all could see saying in a loud voice, "Big Hat, I need four more coffee cups and four more plates." When he did he heard the Indian seated right next to him on the sitting log, quickly put his plate down, grab up his rifle and stuck it forcefully into Bear Scat's ribs, grunting out something in a language the trapper did not understand! But Bear Scat's plan for action had now been formulated and holding his breath expecting the blast of a rifle bullet slamming into his body, just ignored the rifle barrel sticking in his ribs and took the coffee cup he had been holding up and waved it in an obvious gesture for Big Hat to make his move in procuring more eating utensils so the rest of the Indians could be fed. Following that and finding himself coldly calculating his next move full well knowing it might be his last, Bear Scat grabbed up the coffee pot, casually poured a steaming cup of coffee, turned, moved the rifle barrel away from his guts with his hand like it was nothing to worry about and smiling, handed the cup of coffee to the scar-faced Indian holding the rifle. When he did, he saw a look of surprise fly across "Scar Face's" face and then realizing how cold he was and in need of some white man's hot coffee, laid the rifle back down and eagerly took the cup of coffee. Then he sat back down on his sitting log, took a sip of the hot brew, grunted his satisfaction and began wolfing his food down once again.

Then seeing Big Hat still standing outside of their cabin and being held under two leveled rifle barrels, Bear Scat once again held up the remaining coffee cup and said, "Big Hat, I need four more plates and coffee cups." Only that time after asking Big Hat for more eating utensils, Bear Scat turned to Scar Face saying, "I need more cups," as he gestured with the empty cup. Then it must have dawned on the one with the scarred face what was needed, for he said something to the two men holding Big Hat under their rifle barrels and then the two Indians let Big Hat go inside the cabin. Then as if nothing other than a prayer meeting was occurring, Bear Scat took his remaining coffee cup, filled it with coffee, turned and casually handed it to the other Indian sitting alongside the scar-faced one still wolfing down his plate of steaming hot food.

About then, Big Hat walked out the front door of the cabin bringing the extra plates and cups and several more chunks of buffalo meat from inside their cabin. When he arrived at the firepit, Bear Scat whispered to a bent-over Big Hat in the act of putting the cups and plates down on their warming rock, "Be ready," and then taking a handful of clattering plates which muffled his spoken words to Big Hat, began serving the other two Indians now standing behind Scar Face with dour looks on their faces as well. Soon he had four Indians on the sitting log behind him eating, as he continued cooking and serving them just as fast as they emptied their plates. Then since Big Hat was now helping Bear Scat making up more dough for Dutch oven biscuits, the other two Indians came over to the firepit and sat on the opposite side on a sitting log and were served cooked buffalo meat and freshly made biscuits as well. Only this time, Bear Scat only served those Indians half-cups full of his steaming coffee…by design…

Within a few short moments, the Indians had gone through all of the Dutch oven biscuits like 'crap through a goose'. Then Bear Scat could see their hungry and envious eyes following his every biscuit making move, as he refilled both Dutch ovens with raw biscuit dough, which indicated soon there would be more of the highly anticipated and much-favored biscuits on the way. When he did, Bear Scat knew he could turn out Dutch oven biscuits approximately every three minutes in his hot Dutch ovens… Big Hat also realized at that moment in time that Bear Scat turned out his Dutch oven biscuits every three minutes, once his ovens were up and baking and with that in mind, he tensed up for what was coming…

Approximately three minutes later, it was Dutch oven biscuits served too hot to hold all around to the biscuit-loving Indians. When each Indian had a plateful of biscuits, Big Hat also made the rounds with piping hot buffalo steak, half-cooked just as the Indians seemed to love it. As Big Hat kept the steaks flowing, Bear Scat removed the steaming coffee pot and began refilling the eagerly extended coffee cups just as fast as he could. He purposely filled the two Indians' eagerly extended cups on Big Hat's side of the firepit first, then returned to the four Indians sitting on his side of the firepit. As he did, he purposely stood in the middle of his four Indians and through a 'ready to fill gesture', made the near at hand Indians on his side of the fire shove out their empty coffee cups towards him in order to have their cups filled. When Bear Scat made such a 'ready to serve gesture', every Indian on his sitting log eagerly thrust out his coffee cup for the white man's much anticipated brew, not realizing it was the devil's brew...

That was when Mountain Man Bear Scat Sutta's heart hardened in the face of the trappers' sure death to follow once all the Indians sitting around them had eaten their fill! "Whooosh!" Went the contents from the coffee pot, as the boiling hot liquid was violently flung across all four of the closely sitting Indians' faces on Bear Scat's side of the firepit! Amidst their screams of pain and surprise, bear scat took his heavy coffee pot and hit scar face so hard on the side of his head that he felt the bones give way and saw gray matter squirting out from the crack in his skull! Bear Scat's knife, which had not been taken from him when he had been disarmed of his rifle and pistol, then flashed and was driven clear up to the handle into the right eye socket of the next Indian in line still holding his face where the scalding coffee had been splashed before he could make any kind of a defensive move! Indian number three still standing and screaming like a banshee as he held both hands over his boiling hot coffee-scalded eyeballs, then had Bear Scat's long-bladed knife plunged clear to the handle guards deeply into the man's left ear, dropping him instantly to the ground! Indian number four in line had partially recovered from bending over screaming in pain over a scalded face, as he sensed the danger seeing Bear Scat in action. That Indian turned to resist, only to have Bear Scat's knife shoved clear to his spine at the base of his neck! That Indian joined his compatriots on the snowy ground as well, to move no more other than to bodily quiver in his death throes!

179

BOOM! went an explosion from behind Bear Scat, as he felt his left leg knocked out from under him and down he went, just as he had plunged his knife into the last standing Indian on his side of the fire! However that put him in range of his Hawken rifle that had been taken from him earlier and propped up against a sitting log right next to the now dead Indian with the scarred face. Quickly grabbing his rifle, he turned while sitting on his rump just in time to spine shoot an Indian on the other side of the firepit trying to kill Big Hat with his tomahawk! That after having his shot taken at Big Hat knocked aside at the last moment by that fiercely fighting trapper and in so doing, hitting Bear Scat in his leg! Then except for the nervous snorting of their mules and shuffling of feet from the always skittish horses when they smelled blood and lots of it, it was all over and quiet reigned, except for the heavy breathing of two emotion filled trappers who had just stared down their deaths one more time!

Then Big Hat was standing over Bear Scat with a worried look on his face. "How badly you hit?" he asked in a deeply concerned tone of voice.

"Don't rightly know," said Bear Scat, as he grabbed the burning spot on his thigh and when he pulled his hand away, it was covered with blood!

Dropping down on his one knee, Big Hat said, "Roll over so I can have a look." When Bear Scat rolled over, he could feel Big Hat's rough hands on his leg and then heard him happily bellow out, "Whoo-ee! It is just a flesh wound. It will be painful but sure as shooting, one that will not slow you down after a few weeks of healing up and some of my good cooking."

"You might as well as kill me now if I have to eat any of your cooking," said a much-relieved Bear Scat. "But if that is my fate, I am going to make you taste what you cook before I try it," he said with a grin.

An hour later with Bear Scat limping around his beloved firepit, he pulled his fresh batch of Dutch oven biscuits and yelled out for Big Hat to get his butt over for some grub. Up from below their cabin Bear Scat could see Big Hat coming at the typical trapper's trot with an armload of wood. Arriving, he said, "How is that patch job I did on your leg holding out?"

"I am getting around but I think I sure could use some of that rum in my coffee if you would be so kind and bring me some," Bear Scat replied with a grin of anticipation. After a slightly rum-soaked breakfast, the two fur trappers dragged the six dead Indians off with their horses into a distant ravine away from their camp and for the next two days, a pack of wolves argued day and night it seemed over who was going to get the next 'wishbone'... As for the Indians' horses, they were taken down to the Porcupine River and released at different points along the waterway so they could scatter, run wild and confuse anyone looking for their riders if they were ever recaptured, as to their Indian owners' whereabouts or the reason for their absence...

Later that night over several more cups of rum, the two trappers sat across the table from one another inside their cabin, quietly listening to the wood snapping and crackling as it burned in their fireplace. Finally Big Hat spoke saying, "Bear Scat, when you gave me a heads-up earlier this morning about you getting ready to fight and then I saw you making that fresh batch of biscuits for that greedy bunch of red bastards, I just knew whatever you had in mind, I only had about three more minutes left to live. Figuring only three more minutes to live because that was how long it usually took for your biscuits to bake and being that we were so outnumbered by our Indian adversaries, no matter what we tried, we were goners. Never in a million years did I figure you going into battle with just our coffee pot! By the way, the old one is no longer worth a damn it is so bent in and now that I think about it, it was a good idea you had to replace several of our pots and pans when back at Fort Union earlier in the year in case anything happened to them out on the trail. Anyway, when you blew those glutinous chaps up with the flying scalding coffee, I stuck the meat fork I was dishing out meat with into that one bastard's eye and into his brain! Then I grabbed the other one beside me before he could get up off that sitting log. But he was stronger than a bull and nearly jerked me clear off my feet and was putting a hurt on me afore you broke him down with that spinal shot from your Hawken rifle. I thank you for that because if you had been just a few seconds later in taking that shot, that bastard would have killed me with his tomahawk! How you put away those other four poor bastards all by your lonesome I will never know, but I do know one thing. You have come a long way since your fish egg-eating days out from those piles of bear scat along the Missouri River. I am proud to call you my friend and brother and if you never find that wayward brother of yours, I would be proud to claim you as one of my own..." Bear Scat found that he had no words to say after Big Hat had spoken so profoundly and genuinely from his heart. However, he found that no further words were needed... That night, both Mountain Men slept like babies, firm in their convictions that they both had made the right choice of lifestyles and partners...

The next morning, the two trappers awoke to find a fresh foot of powder snow upon the ground. As Bear Scat limped around, he managed to build a roaring fire in their fireplace and began his preparations for making a hearty breakfast. As he did, Big Hat prepared their gear and horses for a trapping trip of another sort out on the now cold as all get-out, sea of grasses, snow-covered prairie. After breakfast and dressed for the extreme cold, the two trappers rode out the back way from their cabin and up and over the long timbered ridge leading out onto the prairie on the far side of their mountain range. Finally locating a small herd of buffalo near a finger of timber, Bear Scat shot a cow, dropping her with just one shot. Riding up to the dead buffalo, both trappers just sat there on their horses for about ten minutes watching all around making sure there was no danger nearby. That they did making sure if any Indians had heard them shoot and came over to investigate as to who was doing the shooting, the two trappers would have time to set up their defense in the near at hand tree line. Seeing no outside surprise visitors riding their way, Big Hat remained on his horse as

Bear Scat sorely dismounted because of his flesh wound and slowly walked back to the mule he had been trailing. Removing a pair of Newhouse No. 14 wolf traps from the pannier, he returned to the dead buffalo, laid his traps on top of the animal and then commenced opening up the buffalo, spilling out its guts so it would bleed out and scent up the area with the smell of a 'free meal'. Then taking his hand ax, Bear Scat drove two long steel 'picket pins' deeply into the hard ground with a wolf trap's chain attached to each so any animal so trapped could not escape with their valuable trap. Then sloshing several handfuls of stomach contents, blood and bodily juices over the traps now lightly covered with snow, Bear Scat's wolf sets were complete. Returning to the dead buffalo, Bear Scat cut even more deeply into the side of the animal, removed two large slices of the warm and quivering liver, giving one chunk to Big Hat and took the other for himself. There the two trappers quietly consumed the warm and bloody chunks of mineral-rich liver with relish. Finally Bear Scat took a double handful of snow over to Big Hat sitting on his horse acting as their sentry, so he could 'snow-wash' the sticky blood off his hands and face, as Bear Scat soon did the same.

Mounting his horse, Bear Scat nodded his head at Big Hat letting him know he was ready to go, and off rode the two trappers until they came upon another small herd of feeding buffalo a short distance away. Once again, Bear Scat dropped another buffalo with a single shot from his deadly accurate Hawken rifle. Like as before, he hurriedly reloaded his Hawken rifle before he slipped from his saddle and duplicated what he had done earlier in setting out another pair of wolf traps. This procedure was followed throughout the entire morning until they had killed five buffalo and set out their ten wolf traps around the five carcasses which were used as a lure and attractant for any hungry wolf who happened to be in country. Collaterally at each buffalo carcass, the trappers feasted on warm buffalo liver until they had gorged themselves on the tender mineral-laden organ meat and were finally satiated. By now, fresh snow was once again falling and low, ugly gray and black-looking clouds foretold that another major blow from out of the northwest was in the works. With that weather warning in mind, the two trappers beat a hasty retreat back to their cabin by another route so as not to leave a well-traveled trail right back to their cabin for any hostile, outside and unwanted visitors to easily follow.

The rest of that day was quietly spent casting more bullets for their 'lead-eating' guns, and cutting and stacking wood next to their cabin for use in their fireplace for when the snows deepened. Lastly just before the end of the day, Big Hat and Bear Scat hobbled their horses and mules and let them out to graze on a nearby windswept hillside. Then after breaking the ice in their spring so the horses and mules could water, they were herded back into the corral, had their hobbles removed and put 'to bed' for the night. With those chores out of the way, the two now wet and cold trappers headed for their cabin in order to dry out and warm up. Since both men were still full from all the fresh buffalo liver eaten earlier during the day when out setting their wolf traps, a cup of rum each served as their supper meal that evening.

The following morning, the wind just howled around the corners of the trappers' cabin, the snow flew every which way and the temperature dropped way below zero, as the first blizzard of the season was now upon them. The remainder of that first winter in the wilderness for Mountain Man trappers Big Hat and Bear Scat out on the Porcupine went pretty much the same. That winter's daily sameness included buffalo hunts for fresh meat, tending their very successful wolf traps, cooking meals, cutting wood, tanning wolf hides, and taking care of their valuable livestock… Collateral with those duties were those associated with keeping a wary eye out for visitors of the worst kind.

Months later with the first vestiges of spring rearing its welcome head and Bear Scat's first spring beaver trapping season as a Mountain Man found him more than raring to go. Once again in preparation for spring trapping, the men saw to it that their 'Possibles bags' were flush with two handfuls of pre-cast .52

caliber lead balls, a tin of percussion caps, greased wadding, fire steels and the like, along with extra horns of powder, smoked beaver traps, sharpened knives, and the appropriate clothing for the often snow-wet weather and high waters soon to be encountered. Come the appointed first day of trapping, Bear Scat had breakfast ready to go and both men in keen anticipation of what was to come, bolted down their food, mounted their horses and trailing a mule carrying a pannier with all the kinds of equipment needed for trapping, the two trappers headed for their chosen trapping grounds for the spring trapping season on the Porcupine.

Riding along and finding the first well-used beaver slide of the season, Bear Scat bailed off his horse, trotted back to the mule now being trailed by Big Hat, removed a trap from the pannier and headed for the water. However, upon stepping into the icy cold water of the beaver pond and sinking slightly into the very cold mud, after catching his breath in shock, Bear Scat proceeded in making his first beaver trap set of the season. Eighteen sets later and by late in the afternoon, Bear Scat had finished making trap sets now with little or no feeling in his soaked feet and legs from being immersed in icy spring waters for most of the day. Then mounting his horse and with Big Hat trailing, letting Bear Scat run the trap line, back the two trappers went riding along their previously set trap line. By the time they had finally arrived back at their first set, Bear Scat happily discovered that he had already caught eight beaver in his previously set traps! To say the day was a success was an understatement, even though Bear Scat still had all the skinning on-site to do. Upon finishing those skinning duties and saving two very large beaver carcasses for their 'lucky' and celebratory meal that evening of the first spring trapping day, the trappers finally left the field and tiredly headed for their cabin.

Later back at their cabin, Bear Scat, still excited over the day's very successful trapping results, bailed off his horse so as to get started on their supper and promptly badly rolled his ankle on a rock! For the rest of that evening cooking their supper, he hobbled around in pain on his rolled ankle, as Big Hat tended to all the caring for their livestock and fleshing and hooping all of their fresh pelts. However, for the next 13 days, sore ankle or not, Bear Scat still totally ran the trappers' trap line as Big Hat proudly watched his partner, who he now considered a fully-fledged Mountain Man doing what he did best and loved the most!

By day 30 of their spring trapping operation on the Porcupine, Bear Scat had phenomenally trapped another 121 beaver and as was now quite evident due to his declining take, most of the beaver had by now been trapped out from their immediate trapping area! On that last day of trapping in their original beaver-rich area, Bear Scat only caught four beaver in their 20 trap sets! Standing at their last trap on their old trap line, Big Hat moved his horse forward until he was alongside Bear Scat saying, "Bear Scat, we are going to pull all of our 20 traps and move on up the Porcupine to another area richer in beaver. This area has been trapped out and we need to move on in order to continue trapping all of these spring-prime beaver before they go out of their prime and then we are done for this spring's season."

Bear Scat nodded his approval of the decision made by the more experienced Big Hat and by the end of that day, having trapped out their original trapping grounds, the trappers had decided to move on upstream to better waters not previously trapped and continue on for about another month. Then they would stop once the beaver went out of their prime, return to their camp to pack up all of their gear and furs, and head for Fort Union to trade in their year's catch and celebrate. Then maybe while back at Fort Union in between trapping seasons, possibly run into Bear Scat's brother Jacob, and be reunited once again as family!

Big Hat headed the two of them home by another route that evening, one that they had never taken before in order to return to their camp from the wooded northern side. Riding up into the cool of the dense pine forest as Big Hat headed their horses and mule for their cabin, he all of a sudden abruptly reined up his horse hard as he spotted something on the ground that caught his keen and experienced eyes. Quickly stepping off his horse, Big Hat dropped to his knees and carefully began examining the mystery trail just discovered. All of a sudden he jumped back up from examining the trail, vaulted into the saddle and said, "Bear Scat! Follow me, I think we have a serious problem!" Without any further explanation, he kicked his horse hard in its flanks and sped off heading for their cabin located about a half-mile away. Bear Scat followed as fast as he could, pulling and tugging on the reins of his cantankerous slow-moving mule, making it move as fast as he would run. However it wasn't long before Big Hat was out of sight as he raced for their cabin. Meanwhile, Bear Scat followed as fast as he could, leading a mule who would have nothing of running fast back to their cabin...

Finally Bear Scat pulled into the area of the cabin only to find Big Hat standing in front of their cabin, with his rifle in hand and with a scowl running clear across his face! "They cleaned us out, Bear Scat! They took everything that wasn't tied down and then some!" he bellowed. "If I catch those sons-a-bitches I am going to personally kill the lot! That includes your brother if he is one of the ones who cleaned us out! If he is one of those stealing bastards, I will shoot him squarely between his evil eyes!" ranted Big Hat, so mad that he was spitting spittle out the corners of his mouth with every angry word he uttered.

Then Bear Scat turned in his saddle and realized EVERY HORSE AND MULE THEY OWNED WAS NOW MISSING FROM THEIR CORRAL! Quickly stepping off his horse and running past a highly fuming Big Hat, he ran into their cabin. Damned if Big Hat wasn't right! Everything of value was now long gone. That included all of their many packs of furs, their food supplies, the extra powder kegs, their remaining kegs of rum, their pigs of lead, EVERYTHING! The only things the mysterious robbers had left were the men's sleeping furs. No two ways about it, their entire year's worth of hard labor trapping beaver, wolves and river otters had vanished, along with their stolen horses and mules!

"It is too damned late in the day to follow the trail now, but we had better have our asses mashed in our saddles come daylight and be hot on their trail. If not, all will surely be lost when it comes to tracking the lot down and disposing of them whoever they are, so we can get our livestock, provisions and furs back. When I first crossed their trail fleeing the area, I noticed every horse and mule hoofprint was that of a shod animal. They weren't no blamed Indians, I know that. If I were a betting man, I would say some Hudson's Bay men had come into our beaver trapping area looking for better trappings, saw us trapping and put two and two together. Then waiting until we were afield running our trap line, they backtracked our horses right back to our cabin, helped themselves to our riding and pack stock, loaded up everything else we had, and skedaddled afore we returned. My guess is they have a good day's start on us and from looking at all of them tracks, I would say from the hoof spacing, they were more than moving out and on down the line in order to escape any pursuit by us! Dag-nabbit, Bear Scat! I never figured we would run into such problems from the Indians and our own kind by coming up here and trapping on the Porcupine. I knew we might run across some savages but just figured there wouldn't be that damned many. Then now, we have our own kind making our lives miserable. Well, them whoever done it ain't seen nothing yet!" snapped Big Hat in a state of 'mean-assed and pissed-off' all at the same time like Bear Scat had never seen before. However Bear Scat had seen worse times in his life and just coldly decided whoever took the fruits of their livelihood would pay the price if he had his druthers, and he would save his 'mean' and control his feelings when and until the culprits were well within his rifle range...

Daylight the next morning found Big Hat in the lead as head tracker and Bear Scat hard on the trail of those who had just robbed them blind. Once the sun was high in the sky, Big Hat stopped, got off his horse and began walking and examining the trail left by the thieves of all the fruits of their year's trapping labors and the two trappers' entire horse and mule herd. After about a half-hour of walking the trail and carefully examining the individual prints as if looking for something out of the ordinary, Big Hat once again mounted up and turning to Bear Scat said, "Near as I can tell, there are four sets of hoofprints telling me the animals leaving those deeper than normally expected hoofprints are being ridden! That being said, once again the two of us are outnumbered. But right now I don't care if it is ten against the two of us, those thieves don't know who the hell they have messed with and if we can catch them, they are for damned sure going to wish they hadn't been caught by the two of us!"

By day's end and when it got too dark to continue tracking the thieves, Big Hat and Bear Scat stopped for the night so their horses could graze, water and rest. As for the two trappers, they had jerky for supper and then sat side by side throughout the long night hours using their body warmth with each other to keep warm in the late spring weather. However by dawn the next morning, Big Hat had figured out where the four men and thieves might be heading and he now was cutting crosscountry in a northwesterly direction towards the closest Canadian trading post located along the Frenchman River just inside Canada.

That second evening of pursuit, the two trappers made a cold camp once again. Then when darkness descended upon them, they once again huddled together for the warmth that offered under a large conifer. Long about ten in the evening, Bear Scat had to go to the bathroom, quietly got up so he wouldn't wake Big Hat and walked off a few paces to urinate. Looking skyward at all the clear night's stars, he wondered if any one of the stars he was looking at was his long dead mother, father or younger sister looking down on him... Finishing, he put everything back where it belonged, turned to walk back to where Big Hat was resting and then, saw the light of what he first figured was a star where it should not have been on the far hillside! Then Bear Scat suddenly realized that 'stars' aren't normally found on a distant hillside...

"Big Hat, I have found the men we have been after!" he yelled out, and then put his hand over his mouth. as if anyone around the distant light could have heard him blurting out his surprising words of discovery to his sleeping partner! With those words of surprise over his discovery ringing in the night air, Bear Scat could hear Big Hat jumping up in surprise and walking over to where Bear Scat's dark form was standing staring off at a distant faint flickering light.

"Where exactly are you looking, Partner?" asked Big Hat.

"Over there to the northwest. See on that far mountainside that small dot of light. I think that is a small fire of some sort!" said a really starting to get excited Bear Scat over his discovery.

"Sure as hell, you are right! Bear Scat, you may have spotted the campfire of those bastards we have been trailing for two days! That sure would be the direction they should be traveling if they were heading for that trading post on the Frenchman River in Canada. That would sure be my bet if those bastards wanted to trade in our furs and sell our horses at the first available location. That is the closest trading post I know of and they have been heading for Canada ever since we got on their trail," said Big Hat quietly, but with a tone of discovery satisfaction ringing throughout the tone and tenor of his voice.

Two hours later and still a good quarter-mile away from what was now the clear light of a campfire, Big Hat and Bear Scat could hear loud raucous voices of a distant celebration in full swing, if all the whooping and hollering was any sign or indication that someone was having one hell of a good time! As they crept closer, the two now quietly sneaking trappers could hear much laughter and loud talking but still could not make out what was being said. That was until Big Hat stopped and turning to Bear Scat saying, "No wonder we can't understand what the dickens they are saying. Bear Scat, they are speaking in French! No wonder we couldn't understand them. Plus that sure as hell fits into what I figured early on, that whoever stole all of our stuff were more than likely other fur trappers from the Hudson's Bay Company. That certainly is now confirmed in my mind, being they are speaking French and all," said Big Hat with just a tingle of excitement now sounding in his voice. Following those words from his partner, it was then that

Bear Scat heard the distinctive loud 'click' of Big Hat's Hawken being set at 'full cock' for what he assumed was the righteous killing to come for what the Frenchmen had done to them in stealing all of their supplies and livestock...

About 20 more minutes of sneaking in more closely to the culprits, found Big Hat and Bear Scat quietly looking on into a well-lit campsite with its huge fire, and what Big Hat figured were four very drunk French Canadian fur trappers. Then sure as hell, Bear Scat spied their own horses in among the suspect thieves' horses tied off on a long nearby picket line. Additionally, over by the horse and mule picket line was a huge mound of fur packs, packsaddles, provisions, and riding saddles belonging to Big Hat and Bear Scat...

"I say we walk right into their camp and being as drunk as they are on our rum, they won't be able to defend themselves and I say we kill the lot!" said Big Hat with a decisive coldness in the tone and tenor of his voice.

"No! I have a better idea. Let them get so damned drunk that they can't stand. Then we make our move and that way, no one will get hit with some damn stray bullet like I did back when the Gros Ventre hit our camp before we killed the lot," said Bear Scat in a determined sounding tone of voice. "Besides, these men are almost helpless with all the rum they have consumed, and I don't cotton to killing any man who can't defend himself no matter what he is guilty of doing," quietly said Bear Scat. Those wise words from Bear Scat gave Big Hat pause and then through a smile, the very first one he had on his face since their pursuit had begun, he realized that his younger partner was not only truly special but thinking way beyond his years...

About an hour later, the last French Canadian fur trapper had passed out stone cold from all the rum he had consumed, and he too joined the rest of his partners dead drunk and passed out cold around their campfire! Carefully sneaking into the thieves' camp, Big Hat and Bear Scat quietly removed all of their weapons and piled them up over by the horse and mule picket lines, so if any of the French Canadians came around seeing the two strangers in their camp, there would be no gunplay. Then Big Hat and Bear Scat loaded all of their furs, provisions, the one remaining keg of rum, and everything else that had been taken from their cabin, back onto all their horses and mules. As Big Hat began quietly moving the entire string of heavily loaded animals away from the French Canadians' camp, including the thieves' own four riding horses, Bear Scat got an idea. Since according to Big Hat they weren't far from the Canadian trading post, he got an evil and great get-even idea. Sneaking back into the fur trappers' camp, Bear Scat quietly removed each of the four drunken and out like a river rock, Frenchmen's moccasins. Then he threw all of their footwear into their fire. Bear Scat just figured if they wanted to pursue both him and his partner, they would have to do it barefooted! Plus it would be easier to walk the few remaining miles to the Canadian trading post than to go all the way back to his and Big Hat's cabin barefooted, hence his little simple plan of less than lethal revenge as had been initially considered…

The rest of that night, Bear Scat and Big Hat rode their horses and trailed their now larger than ever string of livestock, which included the French Canadians' riding horses, out of the country. That they were able to do because horses could see quite easily in the darkness and the two trappers wanted to be out of any form of pursuit, if they had their druthers come the next morning when the effects of drinking too much rum by the Frenchmen had worn off! Also, Bear Scat figured by so doing, it was different than when Bear and his group of fur trappers had abandoned him in Indian country, with him not knowing where to go and not having a horse to get there. Here the French Canadians had but a short distance to go to get to their trading post. Additionally, the Indians in Canada were friendly to the white Canadian fur trappers, so there would be no danger from run-ins with any Indians like it would have been when Bear Scat had been abandoned and staggering around on his own on the prairie.

Two days later, Big Hat and Bear Scat arrived back at their cabin during the evening hours. The next morning right at daylight, Big Hat and Bear Scat had loaded the remaining things the French Canadians had left behind when they had raided the trappers' cabin, and were heading due south towards the Missouri River and eventually Fort Union. Big Hat figured spring fur trapping was over for the year along the Porcupine, and there was no use letting the now sober and likely mad as hell French Canadians walk out to their trading post, get new horses and come after the trappers who had 'robbed the Hudson's Bay Company robbers blind' of their own livestock!

******

Two weeks before Big Hat and Bear Scat left the upper reaches of the Porcupine River en route Fort Union with their furs, Jacob Sutta and Wild Bill McGinty had already arrived at that trading post! Those two trappers had a very successful trapping venture on the beaver waters on the upper reaches of the closer at hand to Fort Union, Big Muddy River and were now ready to cash in their hard-won goods from all their hard-won efforts. However, due to the many close calls they had and were continuing to have with the local bands of Blackfeet Indians, they had decided not to further 'chance' their luck and had safely left the area with a big load of furs. Arriving at Fort Union shortly thereafter because of the shorter distance they had to travel in order to get there from their trapping grounds on the Big Muddy and in particular because of the high prices beaver furs were commanding, Jacob and Bill decided to make a 'life change' in their move as businessmen and in their future trapping geography.

Both Jacob Sutta and Wild Bill McGinty figured with the exceptionally high prices commanded by beaver furs on the frontier that year, they would command even much higher prices down in St. Louis if they could just be safely delivered and not lost along the way because of Indian attacks. With that in mind and supported by their huge load of high quality beaver *'plus'*, both men figured they could become rich men once their furs were sold to the St. Louis fur houses! Additionally, both men had been making a go of it on the frontier for several years living the rugged, without any kind of frills, frontier life and figured maybe a little time back in civilization under less trying conditions might be most welcome. That was especially so if they weren't dodging a mess of mad Indians, feeling the cold steel of an arrow tip into one's back, experiencing a speeding lead ball meant for any white fur trapper, or the many times icy cold and constant contact of the northern clime's beaver trapping waters.

With those thoughts under consideration, Jacob and Bill sold off their horses and mules to Fort Union and the rest of their gear other than their furs to other fur trappers in need of such trappings. Taking those monies, after a week's celebration at Fort Union with other fellow friends and trappers, they purchased their way back down the Missouri on one of the fort's returning supply keelboats and left the following day on the spring rush of high waters for the fur capital of the West in St. Louis for the promise of bigger and better things...

Watching the view of Fort Union receding from where Jacob and Bill sat on the superstructure of the keelboat slowly drifting down the Missouri River, both men felt an evident release of many emotions. For several years the northern reaches of the Missouri River's tributary river systems had been a very good home and 'provider' to the two men now safely drifting downstream. However those years of dodging and worrying about the violent and vicious Blackfeet and Gros Ventre Indian menace had taken their toll on the two men. Being constantly supremely aware of the safety ramifications of everything they did, from simply going to the bathroom to eating and having to be constantly on the alert avoiding mortal conflict with the always hungry mean-assed grizzly bears and seemingly always hostile local inhabitants out on the frontier, had taken its mental and physical toll. Both men's faces showed the deep furrows of worry, possessed skin hardened by the constant baking prairie sun and winds, all evidenced by the deeply rooted physiological and physical effects of many times experiencing hunger and the constant hard work related to becoming successful in the beaver fur trapping trade. Yes, maybe some time back in the West's outer reaches of civilization in St. Louis might be just what was long overdue and needed. However to the keen-eyed observer watching Jacob and Bill's demeanor, fiercely examining eyes and intense pleasure subtly shown as they experienced the watering herds of buffalo, the herds of elk along the shoreline, the running bands of antelope, the occasional grizzly bear seeking food along the shoreline, and the sea of grass waving in the winds as they slowly drifted by, indicated their love affair with the wilderness and desire to remain a distinct part of it was not over or out from their systems by a long shot...

******

When Big Hat and Bear Scat reached the Missouri River on their travels back to Fort Union with their load of furs, it was with extreme relief. Herding along their 28 heavily loaded horses and mules while out in plain view of the numerous bands of Indians traversing the prairie was nerve-racking at the very least to the two trappers. Especially so if any bands of Indians got a glimpse of 28 valuable animals being moved along and protected by only two trappers! Then while Bear Scat watched their very evident back trail covered with the tracks of shod horses for any Indians who had discovered such a telling trail, Big Hat saw to unloading the tired animals, hobbling the lot and letting them out to graze out of sight in the rich, densely vegetated river bottoms. Finally with the advent of darkness masking the visible horse and mule trail, Bear Scat rode into their campsite for the evening after watching their back trail, dismounted, tended to his horse and then began making preparations for a much-anticipated supper.

After a light supper because the men dared not shoot any game along the way for fear of bringing unwanted attention to their heavily loaded, largely unguarded pack string, the two men made a small defensive fort out of the packs of beaver furs, tossed down their sleeping furs and then sat by their small fire making sure that someone was not subsequently 'dogging' them and their valuable pack string. For the next four days, Big Hat kept the long pack string adjacent the Missouri River so if any Indians were sighted, they could quickly head into the cover the river bottoms offered and be out of sight. Come day five of their travels, the two trappers hove into sight of the welcome Fort Union and the safety it offered for such weary fur trappers. Shortly thereafter arriving at the edge of the Missouri River, a flatboat was hailed from the fort's side of the river and was soon ferrying men, horses and mules safely across the river to Fort Union.

Standing on the fort's walkway on the inside walls looking on in disbelief at the long 28-horse and mule pack string heading for the front gate, the Company Clerk left the walkway and made his way down to the main courtyard so he could welcome the obvious Free Trappers in their arrival. Standing there looking on not believing how just two trappers had managed to safely arrive with such a huge pack string and wondering where they had acquired so many horses and mules, the Company Clerk just shook his head in disbelief. However, he was happy just the same for the business it was bringing his company in the ways of valuable furs, sale of extra horse and mule flesh, or both.

Moving all of their pack string inside the gates of the fort, Big Hat tiredly dismounted and was greeted by his friend from times past, the fort's Company Clerk or number two man-in-charge of the fort.

"Big Hat, you old 'scudder', how in the dickens did you and your partner come by so many horses and mules? If I remember correctly, when the two of you left for the reaches of the Upper Porcupine, your pack string was one hell of a lot shorter than it is today, like just eight horses and mules."

"Well, Calvin, that is one hell of a story best shared around one of your fort's home-cooked suppers and several rounds of your best rum," said Big Hat, as he shook his old friend's hand like it was a pump handle indicating just how happy he was to be safely behind its heavy wooden gates with his entire pack string, its huge loads of furs, and his and his partner's 'top-knot'.

"You have a deal. You know Mr. McKenzie's tradition. There will be a special supper for each and every Free Trapper who has survived the wilderness and brings his furs or extra livestock to trade here at the fort. By the way, Mr. McKenzie is not here. He left a few days back on one of our returning supply keelboats to go back to St. Louis to conduct some urgent business. So I am in charge until he gets back on the next keelboat bringing up some more supplies," said the Clerk.

"Well, let's get down to business," said Big Hat. "Me and my partner, Bear Scat over there, owe Mr. McKenzie for some supplies he advanced us last fall, and I need to get that debt out from my 'craw' so I can feel better about where we stand and are no longer obliging to any man."

"Well, you will be glad to hear that beaver prices have gone clear through the roof. It seems every man in Europe has to have a beaver hat in order to be fashionable in their society, and Mr. Astor just can't seem to ship enough of them enough across the ocean to meet their demands. So when you left last fall the average for a good adult-sized *'plus'* or Made Beaver was around $3. Today's prices here at the fort are running around $4 per good adult-sized Made Beaver *'plus'*!" advised the Company Clerk.

"Well, that is good news," said Big Hat, as he got a funny look on his face overhearing the magnitude of those words. "Say, we owe Mr. McKenzie around $300 for the provisions he advanced us from last year. Have your fur graders and sorters just unload enough furs from our pack animals to settle up on that debt. Then have them stop unloading any more furs until I have a chance to talk things over with my partner Bear Scat," said Big Hat with that strange look still on his face, like he was chewing on a piece of buffalo meat just too big to comfortably swallow… A strange look that Big Hat always got when he was mulling over a better idea in his head and needed to discuss it with his partner Bear Scat before 'he pulled the trigger'.

"OK," said the Clerk with a wondering look crossing his face as well over Big Hat's change in temperament when he heard about the higher beaver prices. Then he continued saying, "After you finish talking with Mr. Bear Scat, you need to get back to me. You two have one hell of a mess of furs to be counted and graded if you decide to sell them here. That will take some time so don't dally around and leave me hanging, especially if other Free Trappers arrive with big loads as well."

Big Hat walked over to Bear Scat who was trying to keep their herd of animals from eating all of Mr. McKenzie's flowers around the Factor's House in his special flower garden without a great deal of success. "Bear Scat, we need to talk. The Clerk tells me our furs are worth $4 for a Made Beaver because of the demand for beaver from those folks living in Europe. With that in mind, we could take the remainder of our furs after we settle up with McKenzie for what he advanced us from last year, and take them overland ourselves to St. Louis to sell. If we did that, we could make one hell of a lot more than we can here for the price of our furs. That is if you be interested in taking that chance and doing that. With what I figure in my head, based on the prices the Clerk just stated to me and the numbers of furs that we still have after paying off McKenzie, if we took our furs to St. Louis and sold them there to the fur house, we could probably become rich men."

"But what about finding my brother? Jacob and his partner Wild Bill could be on their way from wherever they were trapping to Fort Union as we speak, and if we up and went to St. Louis, we would miss him when he arrived here at Fort Union," said Bear Scat with a world of concern rising up in his voice.

About then the Clerk was walking back from speaking to his group of pelt counters and graders and overheard Bear Scat's concerns. "Excuse me, but did you say 'Jacob'? Would that be Jacob Sutta and Wild Bill McGinty you were mentioning? Because if you were speaking about Jacob Sutta and Wild Bill McGinty,

Bear Scat, you missed them by several days. They are on their ways to St. Louis as we speak on one of our keelboats with Mr. McKenzie. Jacob and his partner figured they could get a better price for their furs down there, as well as spend some time in civilization away from the colder weather, mad Indians and ever-numerous bears at every turn in the trail. They didn't say anything about coming back here to this neck of the woods for next year's trapping season either," said the Clerk trying to be helpful.

"Damn!" said Bear Scat in utter frustration. "Now what the hell can I do to run down that brother of mine before I end up dying of old age or get eaten by some damn old hungry grizzly bear?"

"Speaking of the devil," said Big Hat. "As I suggested earlier, I was just thinking about us going to St. Louis with all of these valuable furs because by doing so, we could end up rich men at the prices the Clerk quoted me for our beaver *'plus'* here, and I can imagine what they would bring down there. Then along the Clerk comes and tells us that your brother is on his way as we speak to St. Louis to sell his furs. Maybe we could cross trails down there with him if you were willing to head south with our furs. What say you to that suggestion, Bear Scat?"

"If you are sure we could sell our furs for almost double of what they were last fall, I say we take our chances with the Indians and head south. I wonder if Jacob has had enough of this fur trapping thing and is heading down to St. Louis and then back to our farm. If he is, I could maybe find him back on our farm one hell of a lot easier than I can way out here on this never-ending frontier," said Bear Scat with just a lilt of hope in his voice over the whereabouts of his brother.

"Then let us do as I suggested. Besides, I could use some time back in civilization myself where not everybody is after our hair, our livestock or our furs," said Big Hat with one of his characteristic grins. "Plus I could have the chance to eat someone else's cooking beside yours," he said with another wide grin on his face over the 'funny' he had just pulled on his friend and fellow Mountain Man.

That evening at supper with Big Hat's friend Calvin, the fort's Company Clerk, Bear Scat learned about the whole story as to how he had just missed Jacob by a few days before he and his partner had set sail for St. Louis. Disappointed as all get-out over just missing his brother, Bear Scat continued thinking just maybe his brother was heading back to the farm and if so, he could be found there more easily than chasing after him throughout the wilds of the entire frontier...

For the next week, Big Hat and Bear Scat celebrated around and in the fort with old friends and new acquaintances who were also fur trappers. It was also during that period of time that the two men found time to gather in from the fort's warehouses a number of needed provisions for their month-long forthcoming trip to St. Louis. Additionally Big Hat rounded up three of his old fur trapper acquaintances desiring to quit the fur trade by going to St. Louis, selling their furs and then retiring on a quiet farm somewhere in Missouri. When Bear Scat heard that information about having three more men to accompany them south to St. Louis he was pleased. Bear Scat was pleased because that meant in addition to his and Big Hat's guns, they would have three more shooters in case they ran into a mess of killing Arikara or Sioux Indians on their trip through those tribal lands as they headed south.

CHAPTER SEVEN: ST. LOUIS AND "WHITE EAGLE"

Come the appointed departure date set for heading down to St. Louis, found Big Hat and Bear Scat leading with difficulty their 28 head of fully packed mules and horses, along with other fur trappers' friends who also wanted to go to St. Louis, namely Dee Barbea, Paul Barbea and David Hager with their pack strings of 12 horses. No two ways about it, with 40 horses and mules in the trappers' pack strings they could be asking for trouble if sighted by the always 'horse-hungry' Sioux or Arikara Indians whose territories the trappers had to traverse in order to get down to distant St. Louis…

For the next six days, the five fur trappers heading south and easterly made good time with their heavily loaded and long string of pack animals. As they did, they stayed as close to the Missouri River and its bottoms for the cover it offered as much as possible to avoid the roving eyes of Sioux Indians whose lands they were initially moving through. At the end of each day, a cow buffalo was killed from the many animals feeding in the area for meat, and all that shooting was done by Bear Scat who was the best shooter in the bunch. By so doing, only one shot was fired daily in killing the 'supper' buffalo which luckily did not garner any attention from any nearby Indians who might have heard just the one shot being fired and come to investigate. Plus with all the winds that blew daily out on the prairie, hearing one shot would have been problematic due to sound dissipation unless the Indians were close at hand to the one doing the shooting. Additionally, many Indians were out on a daily basis harvesting buffalo for their winter stores and their hides which were used for trade or staples within their own societies, so as a result the sounds of shooting were common, allowing the long livestock train of trappers to almost make it to the present-day city of Bismarck, North Dakota, without incident. There they separated from the river above that future city site and moved westward to avoid discovery by the inhabitants of the well-known, numerous earthen-mounded Mandan villages scattered along that portion of the Missouri River.

Then south of the clustered Mandan villages, the five trappers once again headed back easterly to the protective cover of the Missouri River breaks as they made their way towards the distant city of St. Louis. At day's end, as Bear Scat shot his one cow 'supper' buffalo, the five men quickly butchered out the animal taking the best parts and then the group melted into the heavy vegetation of the Missouri River breaks with their pack strings and made camp for the evening. As Bear Scat began preparing supper for the whole party, the other four men unloaded all of their animals, examined them for any sores being caused by poorly adjusted packs or riding saddles, hobbled the animals, and let them out to feed under the watchful eyes of Dee and Paul Barbea to preclude any of them from wandering off, being stampeded by the numerous herds of buffalo, or being stolen by any nearby Indian. As the men laid out their sleeping furs around their campsite, the air around the fur trappers' campfire began taking on the great smells of roasting slabs of buffalo meat fat dripping into the fire, Dutch oven biscuits and the aromatic smells of coffee wafting through the cooling evening's air.

Shortly thereafter, supper was had by all, as the hungry men did what they did best when it came to eating half-cooked buffalo meat and piping hot biscuits fresh out from a Dutch oven. Then as the men later sat around their campfire smoking their pipes and talking, they drained the rest of the two-gallon coffee pot as many yarns were spun and much laughter was heard! Finally, the ashes from the men's pipes were tapped out on the ground, the horses and mules were brought into camp from their feedgrounds for safekeeping, hobbled, and then as their campfire crackled away its last into smoking red coals and then hot ashes, the men retired to their sleeping furs. However, as each man settled in for the night, he was careful to place his rifle close at hand and lay a pistol near his head since they were still deep in Lakota Indian country.

The next morning right at daylight found Bear Scat at a rebuilt campfire with staked over the fire slabs of buffalo meat cooking away still dripping blood and fat droplets, Dutch oven biscuits doing what they did best over their beds of coals, and the coffee pot steaming away its aromatic smells into the early morning air. As Bear Scat scurried around preparing the trappers' morning meal, the rest of the men packed and saddled up all of the horses and mules as they stood patiently tied to their two long picket lines. Once the men had finished with their packing and saddling duties, they adjourned to the fire and waited for the breakfast to be served, like bear cubs waiting to be fed. They did not have long to wait because the much breakfast cooking-practiced Bear Scat soon had the victuals onto their plates and cups of steaming hot coffee served to all. Soon the only sounds heard around the camp besides the wood crackling in the firepit were the sounds hungry men made doing what they like doing best, namely eating semi-cooked buffalo meat and biscuits washed down with their style of trapper's strong and bitter tasting coffee in the morning's cool air.

Making his second round of serving more biscuits and steaming hot chunks of buffalo meat to the men, the group heard the distant heavy rumbling of a nearby buffalo herd lumbering off out onto the prairie adjacent the trappers' campsite. Looking up from his serving detail, all Bear Scat could see was the billowing of dust lingering in the morning's air where the feeding buffalo had once quietly fed nearby. Then cutting up the last of the staked buffalo meat, Bear Scat served the remainder to the still hungry men, as evidenced by their outstretched arms holding forth their empty plates with big grins smeared across their faces. Smiling back, Bear Scat stirred the fire one more time before he sat down on his sitting log around the campfire to finish the last of his breakfast as well. When he did, he chanced a look at the horse and mules' picket lines, then glanced out onto the prairie still heavy with dust from the fast-leaving herd of buffalo just in time to see about 30 heavily armed and serious-looking Sioux Indians emerging out from the buffalos' dust in a long line and riding slowly towards the fur trappers' campsite! The trappers had just been discovered!

"GRAB YOUR GUNS, BOYS!" mumbled Bear Scat through a partial mouthful of food, as he tossed his plate off to one side, quickly grabbed up his Hawken and stood facing the line of Indians slowly and deliberately riding right at the trappers' camp, now not more than 30 yards distant! A mad scramble followed those words of warning as each man rushed for his weapons upon Bear Scat's command, which reeked of close at hand danger! When they did, the long, angry-looking line of Indian horsemen stopped and held their ground. The heavily outnumbered fur trappers, upon looking over the overwhelming number of Indians confronting them, simultaneously realized today would more than likely be their last day on earth if the 'grim looks' spelled across each Indian warrior's face 'said' anything in the 'warning' department...

All of a sudden, one of the Indian horsemen bailed off his horse and began running right at bear scat! Bear Scat quickly cocked his Hawken to full cock expecting the worst, when all of a sudden he recognized the Indian running right at him, as the rest of the Indian horsemen remained seated and stoically looking at the unfolding event taking place! It was then that Bear Scat realized the young Indian warrior running right at him was unarmed and none other than buffalo horn, the Indian boy in the sinking bull boat that he had rescued from drowning in the Missouri river the year before!

"BEAR SCAT!" yelled the young man, as he ran right up to his friend and savior from his Bull Boat experience many months earlier on the Missouri River! Then Buffalo Horn gave Bear Scat a big and warm embrace saying, "It is good to see my old friend once again."

Seeing there was no danger, Bear Scat let the fully cocked hammer down on his rifle just as Big Hat told all the other men to put down their weapons because the group of Indians still sitting there stoically in their saddles looking on were their friends. Then Chief Buffalo Calf dismounted and strode right up to Bear Scat, grabbed him by his forearm in a typical Indian hand-and-arm shake saying, "My old friend, we meet again." Then turning he said something in the Lakota language and five of his men peeled off from his line of still stoic-looking warriors and disappeared back onto the prairie from whence they had just arrived. Then turning back and facing Bear Scat, Chief Buffalo Calf said in his perfectly clear English, "Bear Scat, my warriors and I are hungry. Will you and the rest of your white man friends share your food with us?"

Moments later, digging around in their nearby packs, Bear Scat and David Hager dug out their extra coffee pot, another Dutch oven, flour for more biscuit makings, and all of the rest of their plates and coffee cups. Then Bear Scat hurriedly turned to his biscuit making duties, just as the five Indians who had left earlier came back into the trappers' camp with the backstraps and two hindquarters from a freshly butchered buffalo they had killed earlier from the herd that had been quietly feeding nearby. True to course, after one of their own had been killed within their ranks and the smell of blood hung heavy in the air, the rest of the small herd had stampeded off, raising such a dust cloud that they had even alerted the trappers. It was then that the Indians, after killing the buffalo, had smelled the smoke from the nearby trappers' campfire and came over to investigate. As Dee and Paul Barbea butchered out the buffalo's hindquarters just brought to the trappers' camp by the Indians into individual slabs of meat for cooking, Big Hat went off and brought back to the campfire more firewood. Soon the staked-out buffalo meat over the fire was sizzling fat juices, the three biscuit making Dutch ovens were emitting great smells, and the now two coffee pots were beginning to steam away filling the air with their great smelling aromatics...

Two hours later, all 30 of the Indians had eaten all they could hold. Then as the rest of the fur trappers cleaned up their camp and began packing and loading up all of their animals with their packs of furs and equipment, Chief Buffalo Calf asked Bear Scat what were he and his four other trappers doing crossing through Sioux Indian country. Especially since they were now about to enter the country of the dreaded and white man-hating Arikara Indians just a short distance further to their south. Bear Scat explained that he and his friends were heading to the white man's very large city called St. Louis to sell their beaver furs, and he would then try and find his only living relative, his brother who was in that city selling his furs as they spoke.

For the longest time Chief Buffalo Calf just looked closely at Bear Scat and finally said, "If the five of you go through the country of the white man-hating Arikara, you all will be killed and your horses, mules and furs will be stolen by those bad Indians."

Bear Scat looked at the chief for a few long moments thinking over what he had just advised and then said, "Chief Buffalo Calf, we have no choice. That is where the great white man fur buyer lives. So if we trappers are to sell our furs in St. Louis that is where we must go in order to do so. Plus if I ever hope to find my brother who is just as important to me as your son is to you, I must go through the dangerous Arikara Indian country in order to do so."

For the longest time Chief Buffalo Calf just looked closely at Bear Scat as if trying to determine the depth of his friend's determination to go to the white man's city and possibly be killed for his foolish efforts in the process. Then Chief Buffalo Calf said, "If that is your wish, then since you saved my one and only son, I will save you and all of your friends. To do so Chief Buffalo Calf and his warriors will ride with you until you are no longer in danger from being in the country of the bad Indians, to make sure that you will live to sell your furs and see your brother again. That is my wish." Then the great Sioux chief just looked at Bear Scat with a large smile on his face and a twinkle in his eyes as if he had something else on his mind as well...

Bear Scat just stood there looking back at the chief and hardly believing what he was hearing. Then he said, "Chief, that is a long way to go and I can't guarantee the safety of any of your men if the Arikara attack us."

"If they attack me and my men, they can just go and join their own 'Cloud People'," said the chief with a look in his eyes that meant what he said. Then he continued saying, "My men will kill the buffalo for our meals while on this trip, but you must make us your biscuits for every meal," he said with a big grin, "because my men know to protect you will mean there will be biscuits for all of them at every meal..."

For the next week until the group had passed through the lands of the dreaded Arikara, the Sioux warriors safely escorted the trappers along the way. Several times, the Arikara were seen at a distance but upon seeing the size of the group traveling through their land, just melted away into the forever-waving prairie grasses. Finally out of harm's way, the Sioux made plans for their departure but not before the trappers rearranged the loads their horses were carrying, so that Bear Scat and Big Hat could return the favor the chief had bestowed upon those two trappers when they had been captured afoot a year earlier by the Sioux. By rearranging their loads, Big Hat and Bear Scat were able to send the chief back to his people with extra Dutch ovens, a coffee pot, bags of green coffee beans, cones of brown sugar, an extra keg of powder, three 'carrots' of smoking tobacco, 30 pounds of lead pigs, and the two extra Lancaster rifles with accessories that Big Hat and Bear Scat had purchased earlier as extra protection when in the lands of the Blackfeet and Gros Ventre, along with three horses to replace those the chief had generously given to them when he had captured the two men earlier... Bear Scat saw personally that Buffalo Horn, the young man he had rescued from drowning on the Missouri River, received one of the much-coveted by the Indians and white man alike, Lancaster rifles with all of its needed accessories and spare locks...

Moments later after presenting to the chief all of the white man's much-valued supplies and horses, Bear Scat saw Chief Buffalo Calf walk over and stand by Bear Scat's main riding horse doing something near the horse's head. Curious, Bear Scat walked over to where Chief Buffalo Calf, Buffalo Horn his son, and five other Sioux warriors were doing something unusual to his horse. Walking around the rear of his main riding horse so he could see better as to what was going on, Bear Scat saw Chief Buffalo Calf doing something with the mane on his horse. Moving in even more closely, Bear Scat observed Chief Buffalo Calf tying the last of five white bald eagle tail feathers into his horse's mane. Sensing the nearness of Bear Scat, Chief Buffalo Calf turned and said, "Bear Scat, from now on among my people, you are not to be known as Bear Scat but carry the name of "White Eagle". Within a few moons, after my riders have spread the tale of Bear Scat across our lands to our other peoples, wherever you ride with the eagle's white tail feathers in your horse's mane, you will be protected as one of our own by the power of The Great Spirit and the word of Chief Buffalo Calf of the Lakota!"

By now, seeing the gathering of Sioux by Bear Scat's horse and the looks of amazement on Bear Scat's face, the other trappers moved in more closely so they could hear and see what was occurring between a Mountain Man and the Indians. As they moved in more closely, they heard Chief Buffalo Calf saying, "No longer will you be known among our people as Bear Scat but will have the name of a great warrior named "White Eagle"! As long as your horse wears these sacred white tail feathers of the great white-headed eagle, you will be able to move among my people and their lands as one of them and without fear of any harm coming to you from them. My riders will also spread the word of Chief Buffalo Calf to our Northern Cheyenne Brothers as well. So if The Great Spirit finds you in the land of the Northern Cheyenne, they will also respect and honor my friendship with you as well. Then you may move among them as their brother as well without any fear from harm or concern over your well-being." With the finish of that eagle feather-tying ceremony and the great chief's words, Chief Buffalo Calf and Buffalo Horn physically bid Bear Scat farewell with a warm embrace, mounted their horses and then the entire group rode off to the north on the way back to their home. For the longest time, Bear Scat watched his friends ride across the prairie. Then he saw them pause on the far horizon, turn, raise their arms in a final salute and then they were gone...

That was when Bear Scat heard Big Hat say, "Well, that was pretty special if I say so myself. You might want to really watch over those white eagle tail feathers tied to your horse's mane in the future and make sure they remain attached, Bear Scat. If what Chief Buffalo Calf said is true, we just might find ourselves being welcomed by the mighty Sioux or the Northern Cheyenne if we find ourselves in their backyard in the near future instead of having to dodge hot lead or flying arrows or having our hair lifted." Without saying a word, Bear Scat walked back to his horse and closely examined how the bases of the eagle feathers had been so expertly tied into his horse's mane. *Just like Bear Scat*, thought Big Hat, *he doesn't miss a damn thing, especially any opportunity to learn...* For the next 43 days, the party of trappers headed southward then easterly towards the city of St. Louis without further incident, other than a few horse wrecks and several run-ins with stampeding herds of buffalo that came too close to their caravan for comfort.

Finally the trappers began running across small outlying farms as they neared St. Louis and then other similar caravans of trappers heading northwesterly along the Missouri River as they headed out into the great frontier on their fur trapping adventures, or as they too neared the city called "The Gateway to the West" bringing in their furs to sell at the "The Fur Capital of the West".

******

In fact, one very long and heavily loaded caravan of over 80 men were seen at a distance heading in a northwesterly direction who were unknown at the time by Big Hat and company, but were those men of William Sublette's 'brigade-rendezvous' group heading for the Green River Valley in the present-day State of Wyoming on a rendezvous and trapping expedition mounted by the newly established Rocky Mountain Fur Company. Within that fur brigade were none other than one Jacob Sutta and Wild Bill McGinty…

******

The first things Big Hat's trappers noticed as they entered the city of St. Louis later in the afternoon other than strings and groups of fur trappers coming and going, unlike the prairie, was the constant hum of noise, hordes of people not dressed like fur trappers moving about, and the sickly sweet smell of the city that hung heavy in the air! However that aside, found Bear Scat examining almost every man's face near him as he looked for the familiar face belonging to that of his brother. Soon as they moved deeper into the city, there were so many faces to look at, that Bear Scat finally gave up in frustration looking for his brother and settled down to the business at hand. After stopping and getting directions, Big Hat set his caravan of horses and mules heading for the American Fur Company at Tenth and Lockett Streets.

Reining up in front of the American Fur Company's fur house, Bear Scat stayed with their 28 horses and mules as did the rest of his group with their valuable furs, as Big Hat went inside seeking counting and grading assistance from the fur company's Clerks. Minutes later, five men, strongly smelling of sweat, animal grease from all the processing of pelts they were responsible for, and that of rancid decay from poorly processed pelts, welcomed the men sitting patiently outside on their horses still looking all around in amazement at the hordes of humanity streaming by them on the muddy streets. Soon all the men and their heavily laden animals were welcomed inside a vast warehouse and once there, the unloading of the packs of furs began in earnest as the five fur house men, having done this many times in their lives, skillfully and expertly began unloading, counting and grading the trappers' furs. As they did, the trappers watched every move of the counting and grading process, since their continuation in the fur trade as Free Trappers depended on the monetary outcome of that counting and grading process going on before and around them.

Several hours later, the counting, grading and sorting work was done and the warehouse foreman called the team of trappers into his Clerk's office to settle up with the men with drafts to be drawn on the First Mercantile Bank of St. Louis in compensation for their individual lots of furs. When it came time for Big Hat and Bear Scat to settle up with the American Fur Company, the Clerk cutting the draft for redemption from the bank did not believe his eyes over the figures he had been given. With a questioning look in his eyes over the amount of fur that only two trappers had brought in, he called the warehouse foreman over for a quiet consultation over the numbers he had been given. That he did because he knew from years of work in the fur business that the average number of beaver furs submitted by all other trappers only numbered between 120 and 130 beaver successfully trapped and pelted per trapping season per trapper. There the warehouse foreman was heard to say, "Yep, the figures from my graders and sorters are correct. Those figures are 'as right as rain'," he advised. Shaking his head once again over the numbers, back the Clerk went to his desk and began cutting the draft to the bank for the amount of furs just purchased by John Jacob Astor's American Fur Company from just two trappers named Big Hat and Bear Scat. For the 2,172 mostly beaver furs that Big Hat and Bear Scat had brought forth at $6 per pelt on the average, the two trappers eventually found themselves holding a bank draft in the amount of $13,032! Neither man had ever seen so much money soon to come their way for a year's endeavors as fur trappers, and both just looked at each other in amazement like they had just eaten a live toad! That they did with the realization

211

the fur buyers were unaware of how they came by so many beaver skins. Furs in their total numbers submitted to the fur company that the two men had acquired in part from a number of Indians who had stolen them from other trappers, as well as from a number of furs acquired from a number of thieving French Canadian fur trappers. It was only then both fur trappers got really big grins on their faces realizing their decision to come to St. Louis to trade in their furs for the higher prices that they garnered had been the best decision they could have made...

In short, between Big Hat and Bear Scat, with Bear Scat doing almost all of the trapping once he had learned the technique of beaver trapping, had in one trapping season trapped 612 beaver and river otter on their own! Then they had been the recipients of four horses carrying eight packs of beaver *'plus'* from the three Gros Ventre who had attacked Bear Scat one morning, while Big Hat was away at Fort Union purchasing another horse to replace the one he had lost to a hungry grizzly bear. Big Hat, upon his return with Bear Scat in tow, discovered and recovered the three Indian attackers' hidden horses as well, as they also discovered four horses carrying full packs of beaver pelts the Indians had more than likely taken from other trappers they had surprised and killed. Later it was discovered that those four horses carrying eight packs of beaver *'plus'* numbered 480! Lastly, when the six Blackfeet Indians had stolen all of Big Hat and Bear Scat's horses, once they had been run down and killed and all of their own livestock recovered, Bear Scat had discovered another 18 packs of beaver *'plus'* those Indians had taken from other less fortunate trappers that they had more than likely killed in the process. Those packs of beaver *'plus'* once unloaded and counted back at the American Fur Company warehouse in St. Louis, numbered 1,080! So, it was easy to see why the company Clerk had a bad case of the 'BIG EYE' upon seeing so many pelts being brought in from the field and sold by just two trappers! It was also easy to see why Big Hat Johnson and Bear Scat Sutta, upon seeing a bank draft for $13,032, a fortune in that day and age, looked like they both had just eaten a live toad!

However, ultimately the 'luck of the draw' was not with Bear Scat when asked for his name so it could be put upon the joint draft along with Big Hat Johnson's. When the Clerk heard the last name of 'Sutta', he quickly looked up and asked Bear Scat if he was any relation to Jacob Sutta! Bear Scat almost wet himself upon hearing that question, which indicated that the Clerk knew of his sought-after brother and maybe even where he was currently located. "Yes I am! Jacob Sutta is my older brother. Do you know where he is staying here in town?" Bear Scat excitedly asked.

"I don't think he is here anymore. I overheard him talking to several other trappers when they were here a short while ago selling their furs about moving back onto the frontier in a newer trapping area, one that was not crawling with mean-assed Blackfeet and Gros Ventre Indians. If I remember correctly, they had just signed on with William Sublette of the new **Rocky Mountain Fur Company** along with 80 other fur trappers and were soon to be heading back out to trap somewhere way far west of here in a place they called the **Green River Valley...**"

Upon hearing those words, Bear Scat's heart just sank. "Did he say where this Green River Valley place was located?" he hopefully asked.

"No. Not that I remember as to where exactly they was a-going. Just somewhere out west of here in the wilderness with that Sublette fellow and all his other company trappers is all I can remember. But as I understood it, that new fur company is also signing up another group of trappers as we speak and soon going to send another fur brigade into the Rocky Mountains to trap beaver as well. They have been running an ad in the *Missouri Republican* newspaper for a number of days now requesting that all interested men sign up for this upcoming beaver trapping expedition soon to leave the St. Louis area. Other than that, that was all that I can remember," he said. Suffice to say, Bear Scat was crestfallen...

213

Later it was off to the bank where Bear Scat in his earlier days before becoming a Mountain Man, had deposited his Spanish silver dollars recovered from his father's Posthole Bank before making his ill-fated move teaming up with Muskrat and his bunch of outlaws as they headed for Fort Union in order to trap points west of that trading post's location. After depositing their American Fur Company draft in the bank, Bear Scat asked the teller to check their records and see if one Jacob Sutta had an account with them. That search turned up negative and once again Bear Scat, hoping for a successful long-shot at finding any clues regarding his brother, was turned away disappointed.

Then it was off to the nearest livery stable where Big Hat and Bear Scat sold off their entire horse herd minus their original four riding horses and four hell-for-stout mules. Those they kept so when they returned to the fur trade, they would have dependable stock on which to ride and use as pack animals. However, with their saddlebags now bulging with 'coin of the realm' from the sale of so many dependable horses slung over their shoulders for safekeeping and their four riding horses and four mules now boarded at the local livery, off the two Mountain Men headed with their Hawken rifles in hand for a nearby boarding house advertising, "All You Can Eat At Ma Sylvia's — 50 Cents!"

There Bear Scat and Big Hat were soon joined by their travel partners, Dee and Paul Barbea and David Hager. Since none of the men had eaten all day in their eagerness to get into St. Louis out from any kind of harm's way and sell their furs, Ma Sylvia found that she did not charge enough for those five men when it came to all they could eat for just 50 cents… That evening, the five fur trappers rented rooms at Ma Sylvia's and retired after a long but relaxing day. However, by midnight, Big Hat and Bear Scat had removed the bedcovers from their uncomfortable beds and slept more comfortably on the floor of the boarding house…

Arising at daylight, Big Hat and Bear Scat were soon found seated at a table at Ma Sylvia's once again for breakfast. There the two men almost foundered on large helpings of pancakes, pork sausage, hot coffee which both of the men found too weak for their tastes, and all the homemade apple pie they could pack away. However, between forkfuls of chow, the two men found time to discuss their next move as fur trappers. As to be expected, Bear Scat was 'all hot and bothered' to follow that 80-man contingent of fur trappers they had spotted leaving St. Louis on the day he and his fellow trappers had arrived in St. Louis. Bear Scat figured his brother was in that bunch of men and his best chance of reuniting with him was to pursue and stay as close to his 'cold tracks' as possible. Additionally, by following that first fur brigade into their Green River Valley-reported destination, that narrowed the fur trapping search area in which to find his brother. Big Hat, figuring no differently plus wanting to see some new country other than that filled with white man-hating Blackfeet and Gros Ventre Indians, like back in the Fort Union area, readily agreed with Bear Scat.

With that, the two men set out on foot after breakfast to find out where the newly established Rocky Mountain Fur Company had set up their hiring location for new trappers, as the Clerk back at the fur warehouse had so advised. They discovered that the hiring of another 40 fur trappers for a trip out west was the talk of the town and they were soon directed to the Rocky Mountain Fur Company's hiring site located near the *Missouri Republican* newspaper's office. There Big Hat and Bear Scat met David Jackson, one of the original owners of the fur company and soon made arrangements to accompany the 40 or so men heading out west on a fur trapping expedition, but as Free Trappers. With their obvious experience as Mountain Men, David Jackson more than welcomed the two men into his coming expedition, knowing experienced fur trappers would be good for the economic health of his new company come the annual rendezvous soon to be held. With those economic considerations in mind, he quickly hired the two men to accompany the next fur brigade heading west to a place called the Green River Valley.

Later back at Ma Sylvia Davis's for lunch, Bear Scat and Big Hat met up with the other three men of their party and the group settled in for another wonderful home-cooked, all you could eat, meal. During the meal, Big Hat and Bear Scat advised their group that they had just hired on with David Jackson of the new Rocky Mountain Fur Company for their upcoming trip to the Green River Valley country. Then the discussion quickly devolved into if the other three men wished to join up in the group and go west to the Green River Valley in order to continue their fur trapping profession. David Hager quickly advised he wished to continue fur trapping and would 'throw his hat' into the Big Hat and Bear Scat ring for another round of trapping adventures. However, Dee and Paul Barbea, both family men, wished to take their trapping monies garnered during their last trip, return home to their wives, Nancy and Daisy, buy some more land and continue the rest of their lives as quiet country farmers. They made it pretty clear that they figured as fur trappers, they had dodged enough arrows, speeding lead balls, mean-assed grizzlies, and horse wrecks to last them for a lifetime. The son and father team figured with their earnings, they both could afford to purchase even more land back home, become gentlemen farmers and were going to do so. The rest of that morning and afternoon found the five men having a good time together eating, for once, all they could hold while not worrying about getting ambushed by Indians or interrupted by a mean-assed and hungry grizzly bear while enjoying their meals.

The next morning after breakfast, Big Hat, Bear Scat and David Hager parted company with Dee and Paul Barbea, wishing them the best of luck and shortly thereafter, found themselves heading for a nearby supply store to lay in the needed provisions for the planned beaver trapping trip out west. Once there, Big Hat had Bear Scat head for the cooking section of the supply warehouse as his first order of business. That he did because Bear Scat was his designated camp cook and he liked his partner's style of Dutch oven biscuits. Since Bear Scat had given most of his cookware to Chief Buffalo Calf earlier on their trip down to St. Louis, he had to start all over again from scratch in the cooking department. Selecting what he needed from off the shelves, Bear Scat kept Big

Hat and David Hager busy piling up his selections just as fast as he picked out what he figured were needed items. Those items included three Lodge Dutch ovens (two for biscuit making, one for cooking), three three-legged frying pans, hanging irons for holding pots and Dutch ovens over the firepit, roasting skewers, plates, pots, cups, eating utensils, an assortment of Thomas Wilson cutting, skinning and slicing knives made in Sheffield, England, of the finest steel in the day, three jugs of bear grease for cooking, eight 'carrots' of tobacco, four scarlet cloth blankets, 100 pounds of green coffee beans, 12 bars of soap, shaving soap, extra straight razors, and on it went.

Then it was David's turn to make his selections since he was new to the group of men and Big Hat and Bear Scat wanted to make sure he had the 'fixings needed to grace his gut' as Big Hat so aptly put it. Soon sacks of green coffee beans, pinto beans, rice, dried apples, raisins, flour, brown sugar cones, salt, black pepper, red pepper flakes, jugs of honey, three kegs of Fourth Class Rum, dried garlic, tins of oysters, corked bottles of castoreum, tins of bag balm to treat sores and abrasions on the animals and men, and the like decorated David's pile of what he figured were needed items for the year afield. Bear Scat looked over at Big Hat to see if the looks on his face reflected the items he figured they needed for a year afield were in David's pile of items and the satisfactory look he got back was assuring.

Then Big Hat stepped over to his part of the selection process, selecting three new and extra Lancaster rifles since they had given their extras to Chief Buffalo Calf and his son for safely escorting them through Arikara Indian country, four kegs of Number One grade powder, new .52 caliber bullet molds, 50 pounds of lead pigs, 300 pre-cast .52 caliber lead balls, ten tins of No. 11 percussion caps for their rifles and pistols, spools of cotton lead rope, extra saddle blankets to replace their worn-out ones, bolts of common gray cloth for clothing repairs, fire steels, needle and thread, spools of brass wire to repair gunstocks, extra gun locks and trigger sets, extra ramrods, casting pots to render lead pigs for bullet making, two capotes per man since their old ones needed replacing, extra leather strapping, and so it went. They did not replace any beaver or wolf traps though, since David and Big Hat still had all of their traps from previous years. The same went for the men's axes, shovels and saws which they still retained from the previous year afield. Then Bear Scat remembered something that he had always craved from his previous time in the backcountry and found himself scouting around in the supply house until he found what he had been looking for. Soon back he came toting a 20-pound wooden keg of hard rock candy… Using the money they had received from the previous sale of their horse herd paid for the three men's year's supplies with plenty left over.

Then the men were off to the livery stables where they had all of their horses and mules reshod for the coming trip into the outback. Big Hat also had the blacksmith make separate sets of shoes for each individual animal and purchased extra horseshoe nails, files and hoof picks as well. Since they still had their farrier tools and being that Bear Scat was proficient in the shoeing of horses and mules, the men figured they were all set except for 'floating' the teeth on their livestock as was needed and so ordered. The liveryman was also advised to check out all of their riding and packsaddles and make any necessary repairs as well, which was done.

Then it was back to Ma Sylvia's boarding house and a final 'last day in town' celebration supper. Knowing full well there would soon be hard times out on the trail and sometimes meals could be a bit skimpy, the men made sure they had all the wonderful homemade pie they could put away that evening…and then some.

CHAPTER EIGHT: TRAILS WEST TO THE GREEN RIVER VALLEY

Come the day of departure, David Jackson, new part-owner of the Rocky Mountain Fur Company, led the company's second contingent of fur trappers out from St. Louis in a long, heavily loaded stream of horseflesh and gaily bedecked humanity of Company and Free Trappers. From the temporary assembly point of people and animals across the river, flatboats took the trappers and their livestock to the west bank of the Mississippi River and once the pack train and riders had all been ferried across and reassembled, they once again formed up and in a long string headed northward along the west bank of the Mississippi until they reached where the Missouri River entered the mighty Mississippi. There they changed course and continued their travels along the western bank of the Missouri River through the hundreds of small herds of buffalo, elk, deer, antelope and the occasional grizzly bear until they reached the sandy, shallow and full of quicksand pits near the shore, Platte River. There they headed westward until they arrived at the confluence of the North Platte and thence headed northwesterly along that waterway until they arrived at the Sweetwater River in current-day Wyoming. From there the contingent of fur trappers and supply pack train headed westerly over the South Pass and then northwesterly towards the group's

219

final destination of the Green River Valley country, home to some of the finest beaver trapping in the Rocky Mountains! There David Jackson set up camp with his partner William Sublette, who had arrived earlier with his fur brigade of 80 trappers, since dispersed earlier to trapping grounds at different locations.

After a day's rest and letting the livestock graze in the lush stream bottoms, Jackson began assigning the various groups of trappers from his fur brigade to different areas north and west of the Green River Valley so they would not be competing with one another or have overlapping trapping locations. As it so turned out, Big Hat, Bear Scat and David Hager were assigned an area in the southwestern portion of the current State of Wyoming by David Jackson near the current-day town of Fort Bridger, to trap along the "Muddy" and "Little Muddy River" systems and their tributaries.

Arriving in their newly designated trapping area five days later, the three men were greeted with rolling hills, numerous watered draws and swales lined with cottonwood trees, all dotted heavily with beaver ponds, active dams, swimming animals and conical beaver houses! Sitting on his horse, Big Hat looked over the area with approving eyes over the numerous signs of beaver activity in the many gentle draws and watered swales. However, seeing an absence of big stands of conifers in the lowlands, the trio traveled from cottonwood stand to cottonwood stand of trees until Big Hat found a likely looking draw away from the north wind. In the end, Big Hat selected a likely looking draw where a south-facing dugout could be built into a nearby hillside that was adjacent to a fresh water supply and a sheltered location for a livestock corral that was pretty much out of sight and off any beaten old Indian trail.

Making camp in a long grassy draw out from the wind, the men unloaded their packs, hobbled their livestock, and turned them out to water and graze in an adjacent grassy bottom. Unfamiliar with any Indian traffic or occupation in the area, the men made a ring of packs as a defense perimeter around a dense grove of cottonwood trees adjacent a small bluff. Then leaving camp shortly thereafter on a meat hunting trip, Bear Scat killed a cow buffalo not a 100 yards from their temporary campsite. At the kill site, he removed the backstraps and hump ribs, and with difficulty loaded the hindquarters onto his pack mule and headed back to camp. When he arrived, he found David and Big Hat industriously beginning to dig out a dugout home for the three of them to live in a steeply vertically sloped hillside.

Knowing what his duties were, Bear Scat unloaded the buffalo meat onto a grassy area so the meat would not get dirty, finished unpacking his mule, hobbled it, and released it so it could feed and water with the rest of the nearby quietly feeding livestock. Then figuring out where the entrance to their dugout would be located, Bear Scat got out his shovel and dug a firepit close by. Scouting around, he dragged in a number of rocks from a nearby side hill and lined his firepit. Trading his shovel for an ax, Bear Scat began cutting up loose limbs of wood from under the grove of adjacent cottonwood trees and hauling the wood over to a woodpile being built up next to his firepit. Finished with those duties, he rustled around in the various packs, removed one of his previously broken-in cast iron Dutch ovens and sat it over next to his now blazing fire. Then back to the packs he went and retrieved his hanging irons and roasting steels. Assembling the hanging irons over the fire, a coffee pot filled with water from a nearby beaver pond was soon set to heating over the fire, as Bear Scat began making up his biscuit dough. Setting the dough off to one side to rise on a nearby downed cottonwood log near the warmth of the fire, Bear Scat butchered out and cleaned up a sizeable amount of buffalo meat, since his group of trappers had not eaten anything since breakfast. The buffalo meat was then skewered upon the roasting steels and placed over a raked-out mess of the fire's coals. Smearing some buffalo fat into the bottom of his hot Dutch oven, he waited until the fat had melted and he had sufficient grease in the bottom of his heated Dutch. Then into the bottom of the Dutch went a number of hand-formed biscuits. Sitting the Dutch over another bed of coals, he then placed the Dutch's lid, just heated up and removed from the open fire, onto the Dutch oven and placed a shovelful of live coals on top of the lid so his biscuits could begin baking. Following that, into the coffee pot went two liberal handfuls of rough ground green coffee beans previously roasted and then he adjusted the buffalo meat a little lower over the fire so it would now cook faster. Soon the coffee pot was emitting small puffs of steam, the buffalo meat was sizzling and dripping fat into the fire, and removing the hot coals that covered the Dutch oven's lid, Bear Scat found that his biscuits were now golden brown and smelling Heavenly! Turning to his two fur trapper friends who had turned into 'badgers' as they dug out the hillside for their future homesite, he said, "Hey, chow is ready! If you guy don't come and get it. I am going to throw it out!"

Moments later, here came two heavily sweating fur trappers turned 'badgers', with big grins on their faces as they could see and smell the chow waiting for them. Making sure their rifles were laid alongside the nearby cottonwood logs Bear Scat had dragged next to their outdoor cooking firepit to sit upon, the three men using their knives, cut off hunks of still steaming chunks of buffalo meat and ignoring the heat of the meat, hungrily shoveled it into their mouths, along with a bite of some of the fluffiest Dutch oven biscuits one ever laid a set of lips to! Dutch oven biscuits made even more Heavenly by Bear Scat who had scattered a small amount of brown sugar cone scrapings and powdered cinnamon over their tops...

A half-hour later supper was done. The sun was setting low in the west, the trappers' 'little friends' were making their immediate presence known with their incessant humming sounds, even though the men were leaving clouds of pipe smoke hanging in the dew-heavy evening air, along with the smoke from their campfire doing its best to keep the buzzing insects at bay as well. "Those biscuits were damn good tonight. Suppose we could have some more of the same with our breakfast?" asked David with a full grin and now a belly to match.

"David, Bear Scat is our designated camp cook because even a starving grizzly bear or a damn skinny badger would not even touch any victuals that I would make. But the one thing I have demanded of his mangy old hide is that he makes his brand of biscuits at every meal. Because if he doesn't, then I get to be the cook and he knows if that happens he will be out scratching crap with the sage hens in order to get enough to eat," said Big Hat with a knowing grin in response to David's request for more biscuits come the morrow.

About then the mosquitoes got to be a bit much as the fire began dying down, so the men knocked the ashes out from their pipes and headed for their sleeping furs, which had been set up behind their piles of packs in case some mangy old Indian tried taking them on when he should have known better. Daylight the next morning found the trappers' camp covered in a heavy foggy mist as the men busied themselves around camp making ready for another day. Big Hat and David were already hard at work digging out a cave in the nearby hillside, as Bear Scat tended to his coffee and biscuit making while slabs of buffalo meat sizzled merrily over the dry, almost smokeless cottonwood fire. However, this day Bear Scat had gathered up a mess of green cottonwood branches near his fire so if the mosquitoes got busy once again come evening time, he would smoke them out with a mess of burning and heavily smoking green leaves and branches.

Shortly thereafter, breakfast was ready and the men ate heartily knowing the work they were facing that day digging out a home in the side of the bank and the bracing work that would be required with stout cottonwood posts the deeper they dug into the hillside. For the next five days, the men labored digging out their dugout so it would be roomy enough for stashing all of their furs, provisions, sleeping furs, saddles and the like. Once they had sufficiently dug out a roomy earthen area within the streambank's hillside and shored up the same with green cottonwood poles, then they began making an adjacent vertical log palisade that was roofed over with cottonwood logs and covered with two feet of dirt which had been recovered from their cave's digging operations. Then as a finishing touch, Big Hat built an earthen, mud, stone and log fireplace within their log palisade, so the heat from any such fires would warm up the inside living area and provide for inside cooking when the weather was so foul that it precluded any outside cooking.

Finished with their 'home' for the year, the men set about building a corral right next to their dugout, allowing the men to more closely watch over their valuable livestock. Four days of digging postholes and cutting down and dragging into the area the right-sized, green cottonwood logs occupied the men's time from daylight until dark. Finally the corral was finished and the horses and mules had a new home. But for the men, the work was still far from being done and the trapping season would soon be upon them! The following week was spent cutting down nearby dry cottonwood trees, sectioning them and dragging the same into a winter woodpile located right next to their dugout, but laid out in such a manner so no hostile Indian could use the pile of logs as a means to hide behind and ambush the trappers. In fact, the men had yet to see any sign of Indians, which suited them just fine. However, before they had left the main party of trappers earlier in the summer, David Jackson had pulled Big Hat aside and warned him that the beaver trapping area into which they were being sent was smack dab in the Southern Paiute area and they were some of the best horse thieves going. In fact in Jackson's mind, the Southern Paiute Indians were even better horse thieves than the much-renowned Apaches living in the Southwest! Additionally he warned Big Hat to make sure if they had Ute Indian problems, make sure none of his trappers were ever captured alive because if they were, their deaths would be slow and painful in coming...

One morning as the three trappers were sitting around eating breakfast by the warmth of their outside fire, Big Hat said, "Boys, I don't figure we will have to cut and cure any winter hay this year. The country we are in is such that I figure with this wind that always seems to be blowing across the land, it should keep a lot of these hills and hillsides blown clear of snow all winter long, allowing our stock to freely feed even during the worst weather. Besides, we have so many low swales in and around the cottonwood groves, there should be plenty of feed year round no matter how bitter the winter gets. Plus if the weather in this neck of the woods gets so bad that there is nothing on the ground for our livestock to eat, we can always cut cottonwood bark and use that as feed for our stock in a pinch until the weather improves. That being said, I figure we are almost ready to begin fall trapping with all the cold mornings we have been experiencing lately. I figure we best get our traps out so they can be smoked to get rid of a lot of the human smell. Additionally, we need to finish building the rest of our meat-smoking racks and get us a mess of buffalo smoked and bagged-up so we have some jerky to eat when times get tough and we are out and on the trail, or find ourselves in among a pile of Indians and can't build a fire to cook up some grub."

Breaking camp the next morning found Bear Scat and David heading out to kill some buffalo as they trailed all four of their hell-for-stout mules so as to bring back as much meat as possible at one setting. In the meantime, Big Hat remained back at their campsite and finished building their meat racks and hauling in some good smoking wood, so when the other two men returned with mules loaded with meat, he could get to the smoking of the meat once it was cut into thin strips. Later that afternoon when David and Bear Scat returned, their mules labored under the loads of buffalo meat that they carried. Then as David and Bear Scat cut the rich buffalo meat into thin strips, Big Hat got busy with his meat hanging, fire maintenance and smoking duties. Soon the three large meat racks that Big Hat had constructed sagged heavily under the amount of meat being hung for smoking and drying. It was then that the real work began in tending the smoky fire to keep it going but not letting it get too hot so that it cooked the meat. In addition, that and chasing off all the black-billed magpies so they would not eat the curing meat or crap all over it. Then once the meat was sufficiently dried and smoked, it was hung from the support posts in the dugout in tanned deerskin bags to avoid its spoiling from the cave's dampness or becoming vermin-ridden. Two additional buffalo hunting trips by Bear Scat and David Hager and the resultant meat-smoking operations furnished the trappers with all the jerky they would require for the remainder of the year.

Then one morning when Big Hat exited their dugout, he looked skyward and seeing his breath hanging heavy in the air exclaimed, "Boys, today we need to venture forth and see what we can do to reduce the beavers living in this area. I think we need to get going and set out our traps and on the way back, visit those willow patches next to our camp and bring in a mess of willow limbs so we can hoop what we catch and get it on its way to drying out all right and proper-like."

Bear Scat looked up from his cooking activities at his friend Big Hat and had to grin. He had figured any day now his friend would come forth from their dugout and make such a pronouncement and to his way of thinking, he was more than ready to get trapping underway as well! About then David emerged from the brush where he had 'been taking care of his daily business' saying, "Damn, I am hungry! What's for breakfast, Bear Scat? I hope there is plenty for the two of you because now that I am emptied out, I could eat an entire bull buffalo all by myself!" About 30 minutes later, a light breakfast had been served and once done, their horses had been saddled and two of their mules had been saddled with two panniers apiece to carry all their beaver traps and other assorted gear needed to begin running their beaver trapping line. However before the men left camp, Big Hat made sure they were carrying the right 'artillery' in case they ran into any Paiutes who disagreed with the trappers being out beaver trapping in their homeland and backyard.

That in mind, Big Hat took the lead figuring he would begin the day by selecting the beaver trapping sites. In so doing, he carried two horse pistols in his sash and his trusted Hawken rifle in hand. Behind him trailed Bear Scat who was the designated trapper for the group. Bear Scat also carried two single shot horse pistols safely tucked away in his sash and a Hawken rifle as well. Trailing directly behind Bear Scat were two fully loaded mules sporting loaded panniers. In those panniers were all the tools, traps and other equipment the men would need for the day's trapping activities. However, Bear Scat's lead mule also sported in a scabbard a reserve Lancaster rifle just in case things got a little hot with some of their local 'neighbors' and a little extra firepower was needed. Lastly, David Hager brought up the rear carrying two horse pistols in his sash and his Lancaster rifle as well. No two ways about it, if confronted in a fair fight, the three trappers were prepared to make themselves known as to the accurate shooters they were in the many times often violent Indian world...

As they had been since their first arrival in the area, the three trappers were amazed over the amount of beaver sign that abounded in just about every waterway or grove of willows, aspens or cottonwoods they occasioned! So much so that Big Hat had Bear Scat setting out his first traps just a mere 300 yards away from their campsite! Usually a trapper only carried six to eight traps in which to make his daily sets because of the five pounds of weight the individual traps sported. That morning, Big Hat had Bear Scat load 20 beaver traps into the mule's panniers and by noon that first day, all 20 traps had been easily set out because of so much beaver sign in the area! Upon finishing their beaver sets for the day, the three men rode further ahead along several other potential beaver-filled waterways, scouting out their next day's trap setting regimen if it was required. However because of so much beaver sign in their immediate area, Big Hat called off any further scouting as being unnecessary. He figured when they had trapped out an area, it was just a simple matter of pulling one's traps in the trapped-out area and then moving on to the next potential site, and beginning all over once again since there were so many beaver in their area!

Finished with their first day's beaver sets, Big Hat had the men backtrack along their trap line only to discover they already had 13 drowned beaver in their 20 traps by the time they had finished setting their last one! As Big Hat sat on his horse watching out and over for the two trappers in the water and on the ground setting traps and skinning out freshly trapped beaver, he had to smile to himself. The country was full of beaver just waiting to be trapped, the weather was perfectly cool and beautiful, the country was stunning in its natural beauty, and the three men were working as smoothly as a well-greased turning wagon wheel. Leaving all the skinned-out beaver carcasses along the trap line for the predators to clean up, with the exception of the three fattest ones saved for their first beaver meat meal for the season, the men headed back for their camp via skirting a large patch of willows. At the willow patch, the men cut and filled a pannier with limber willow branches in which to hoop their catches and then they headed back to camp.

Back at camp as David and Big Hat skinned out the last three fat beaver and handed their carcasses over to Bear Scat to cook, he built up his fire in preparation for a celebration supper over their first day's successes. Taking the three skinned-out beaver carcasses, Bear Scat deboned out the meat and placed a portion of the best chunk meat into a 16-quart Dutch oven and set it over the fire on his hanging irons to cook, along with a mess of previously soaking pinto beans, black pepper, red pepper flakes and dried garlic. Within an hour, the hearty smell of heavily spiced cooking pinto beans mixed in with chunks of beaver meat began filling the air around their outside campfire. The remaining chunks of beaver meat were skewered on the roasting irons interspersed with wild onions dug from a nearby hillside a day previously by Bear Scat, once he discovered the aromatic bounty lying just inches beneath the soil ready for harvest! Then the coffee pot was set on the back side of the fire on a hanging iron to slow boil. Into another Dutch oven went several handfuls of dried raisins, scrapings from brown sugar cones and powdered cinnamon with previously soaking rice, which was also set on the cooler end of the firepit to slow cook into a gooey, sweet mixture to help quell Big Hat's sweet tooth. Lastly, Bear Scat fired up his biscuit makings as the last part in his preparation for a celebratory supper feast celebrating their first day's successful trapping beaver in the southern portion of the Green River Valley.

In the meantime while Bear Scat was preparing his big celebration supper, Big Hat and David finished skinning, defatting and removing any remaining meat on the 13 fresh beaver skins. Then tying together willow branches into hoops varying in size from 20 inches to several 'blanket-sized' 36-inch hoops, made small slits on the edges of the skinned-out pelts and using twine purchased back in St. Louis for just such operations, tied the stretched hides to the willow hoops so they could dry in a fully extended position. Then the hooped skins were stood up along the inside walls of their dugout to begin the drying process.

Finished with their pelting chores, Big Hat took one of their kegs of rum outside with several cups and sat on his sitting log by the fire with a drink in hand as he watched Bear Scat work his magic with their supper. Soon David had also washed up with some of the lye soap purchased back in St. Louis when they went 'provision' shopping so he didn't smell like beaver fat, took his place on his sitting log by the fire and with a cup of rum in hand, watched Bear Scat as he rustled himself around their campfire finishing out his supper's preparations. However, lying alongside each man and another within quick reach of Bear Scat, lay a trusty rifle, just in case 'others' came uninvited to their great-smelling supper...

Finally Bear Scat took the skewers of beaver meat and wild onions and staked them out over the coals at the end of the firepit for slow roasting, and soon the air was blessed with the smell of beaver fat dripping onto the coals and in essence, smoke-roasting the meat along with the wild onions. Soon all three men were pulling the chunks of roasted beaver meat and cooked wild onions off the skewers and gobbling down the piping hot beaver and lip-smacking toasted onions! Once that snack was gone, out came the plates which were ladled full of slow-cooked and heavily spiced beaver meat with pinto beans also mixed with the wild onions and piping hot Dutch oven biscuits. Man, now there was no happy talk going on around the campfire but just the lip-smacking sounds hungry men make doing what they loved doing best out in a small slice of God's country in the clean evening air. Finally, the finale to their special supper was presented when out came the steaming hot rice, sugar cone, cinnamon and now plumped-up and cooked raisin mixture dessert, which was served in the men's drinking cups. Following that, the only sounds the rest of that evening event came from the wood crackling in the fire, accompanied by the sounds of metal spoons clanking around in metal cups, as each man spooned his treat over his lips and past his gums -- look out stomach, here it comes... Finally, the men sat quietly drinking their cups of trapper's coffee liberally dosed with rum, as the men sat there quietly listening to a nearby herd of buffalo 'grunting' and carrying on. So ended the first day of trapping in the most extreme southwestern portion of the Green River Valley by Big Hat, Bear Scat and David "Are there any more biscuits?" Hager.

For the next 42 days, the three trappers worked from daylight until way into the dark's hours trapping, skinning and hooping beaver until the inside of their dugout was crammed with dried packs of beaver *'plus'* and inside walls lined and ceiling timbers hung heavy with more hooped and drying-out skins. By that time of the season, Bear Scat found himself every morning breaking a skim of ice on every pond or waterway in which he entered and set his traps. Mornings required the men to wear their capotes against the Green River Valley's cold winds, sounds of Canada geese and sandhill cranes could be heard overhead flying south, and the herds of buffalo were now beginning to sport longer and denser coats against the winter's coming cold.

Day 43 found the three trappers huddled around the firepit having just hot coffee and biscuits for breakfast. As they had done many mornings before, Big Hat led the group followed by Bear Scat trailing a loaded mule and David bringing up the rear, always on the watch for Indians attacking them from the back side of their little trappers' caravan. Having trapped out the beaver nearest their campsite, found the men now trapping the waterways almost a mile away from their camp. Moving into another new beaver trapping area, Big Hat now let Bear Scat seek out the new beaver trapping sites by himself as he remained the vigilant horsed sentinel always on the lookout for any kind of discovery by hostile Southern Paiutes.

Taking the lead and riding with his head down and watching the water's edge for sign of beaver 'runs' or 'slides', Bear Scat upon seeing a promising beaver slide area, dismounted, grabbed one of their five-pound beaver traps from a mule's pannier and began his trap-setting regimen. Opening the jaws of the trap by stepping on both sides of the springs with his feet, Bear Scat then carefully engaged the 'dog' in the 'pan notch'. Holding the heavy trap in hand, he walked in the pond's waters the last few yards to the trap site in order to reduce his scent over the area in which he wanted to make a set. Then carefully setting the trap on a firm bottom in about four inches of water, he swirled the muddy waters over the trap concealing it. Walking away from the trap set laying down the trap's chain as he went, he stepped out into the deeper water of the pond and laid the end of the chain where he could recover the chain with the ring of iron on the end of the length of chain moments later. Then walking over to a willow patch, Bear Scat took his hand ax and began cutting a heavy dead willow branch from along the bank. His intention was to use the long heavy willow stick as an anchor point out in the deeper water, after the willow had been placed through the ring on the end of the trap's chain and driven deeply into the pond's bottom with the top of the stick remaining out of the water. That way once the beaver was trapped and tried swimming off into the deeper waters to escape, that anchored trap ring around the willow stick precluded him from doing so.

As Bear Scat began noisily cutting the dead willow with his ax, he heard out in the dense willow thicket surrounding him a loud "OU-WAHH—OU-WAHH"! Pausing in his stick-whacking with his ax, he quietly listened for the strange sounds coming from the willow patch by the beaver pond. Standing there quietly knee deep in water and mud, he no longer heard the loud and rather unusual noises coming from the patch of willows. Starting to really feel the cold from the icy water and mud sinking into the bones of his feet and legs, Bear Scat commenced cutting and whacking the dead willow stick he needed for his trap's anchor once again, and ignored the strange deep moaning mystery sounds of "OU-WAHH—OU-WAHH" every time he continued striking his ax against the dead willow stick as he continued chopping it off for his trap anchor post.

The second time Bear Scat began driving the dead willow stick deeply into the mud in the beaver pond's bottom even Big Hat heard the strange low moaning sounds over the eternally blowing winter winds. Curious over the sounds, he swung his horse in that direction so he would be facing the strange sounds emanating out from the dense willow thicket. All of a sudden as Bear Scat continued noisily driving his wooden trap anchor stake out into the mud of the beaver pond, Big Hat and David heard a tremendous crashing sound coming from the willow patch and the loud brush-crashing noise was coming their way! All of a sudden, a rare for the area, huge bull moose in rut exploded out from the willow patch, charged across the shallow beaver pond's waters throwing water every which way and before Big Hat could make any kind of a move, the mad moose lowered its massive antlers and charged right into the side of big hat's horse with a loud "THUD"! When it did in its full energy and testosterone-charged collision, it bowled over big hat and his horse in an instant! Big Hat's horse went down screaming out in pain having been slammed in its ribs by the moose's antlers, and Big Hat trying to swing up his Hawken in defense, was knocked clear off his horse. When Big Hat was sent flying through the air, he ended up landing face down hard on the semi-frozen ground with a bone-crunching "THUD"!

David on the other hand, sitting on his horse nearby, was instantly bucked off high into the air by his horse which, being fearful of soon to be sexually mounted by a 1,500-pound moose, EXPLODED IN PANIC! Bear Scat, standing there seeing his whole world blowing up around him, felt his hair rising up on the back of his neck as the bull moose now standing only 15 feet away, turned in his direction and with a red-eyed testosterone-fueled glare in his eyes, lowered his head and charged! Trying to scramble

away from the now charging and splashing moose hurtling his way, Bear Scat tried to run, only to find the deep mud in the beaver pond was doing nothing but clutching at his feet like that of a giant octopus! Realizing to run would only invite a full body slam like Big Hat had sustained, Bear Scat whirled and did the only thing he could do. Quickly drawing his single shot pistol from his sash, he took quick aim at the monster coming right at him with his head down in a full charge! In so doing, Bear Scat aimed right at the base of the animal's neck in the split second he had just before impact with the hard-charging moose and pulled the trigger —
BOOM!

Upon impact from the now starting to fall but still slamming forward from its inertia Bull Moose, Bear Scat felt himself being 'crunched' into and then felt himself flying through the air and landing hard, butt down at the edge of the beaver pond. "snap!" Went the previously set beaver trap painfully right on his hind end upon which he had just landed after being slammed into by the hard-charging moose! Painful as it was, Bear Scat soon discovered that was the least of his worries! The sharpshooting by Bear Scat's heavy .52 caliber bullet had luckily hit the moose's spine right at the base of its skull. Upon the bullet's powerful impact from such close range, that caused the charging moose to drive its head deeply into the bottom of the beaver pond with such force, that it lifted up the entire rear end of the charging moose, flipped it clear over the animal's antlered head now stuck into the bottom of the pond, and landed its hind end directly on top of Bear Scat!

"WHOOOMP!" went the moose's hind end right on top of Bear Scat, smashing him violently into the mud of the beaver pond, squashing him flat as a flounder and in the process, driving his whole body completely under water deeply into the pond's muddy bottom! Moments later, that was when Bear Scat felt the hands of David "Are there any more biscuits?" Hager, grabbing him by his buckskin shirt and pulling him bodily out from under the 1,500-pound moose with superhuman strength brought on by an adrenalin rush! Pulling a blowing mud and water from his lungs and mouth

Bear Scat, they both scrambled like a couple of scared all to hell land crabs up the bank and away from the heretofore body-slamming moose. Then David picked up his previously dropped and now stock-cracked Hawken rifle, smashed when he had hit the ground after being tossed violently off his horse, ran back into the pond and shot the moose at close range just to make sure no one else got mashed by a flying moose! Then the only sounds one could hear were those from a flock of noisy black-billed magpies scared off from eating a dead skunk a few yards away. Well, maybe that plus the sounds of three trappers' loudly beating hearts scared them off as well...

'God-o-Friday', Bear Scat hurt so badly that all he could do was crawl around on the ground like a gutshot prairie dog and just groaned every time he made any kind of a physical movement after being 'moose-mashed'. In fact, if he hadn't been smashed deeply into the forgiving mud by the flying 1,500-pound moose, he more than likely would have been hurt even more and possibly killed. As for David, he had a badly sprained back that hurt so badly from being unexpectedly bucked off his horse and landing poorly, that it caused him to involuntarily urinate into his buckskin pants. About then, here came Big Hat limping along, bleeding like a stuck hog from a badly broken nose received when he had landed face first on the semi-frozen ground after being tossed off his horse. As he limped along, he had an extreme look of worry over what had happened to his two now badly 'dinged-up' compatriots. Moments later, all the trappers had a chance to get their winds back, look each over and realized that everyone would live except for the poor damn old moose, who had made a bad mistake in charging the wrong group of men. Then Big Hat got to laughing and shortly thereafter so did David, as both men saw that Bear Scat still had a five-pound beaver trap's jaws, one that he had previously set and then had the misfortune of being hurled onto the top of its open jaws by the moose, still snapped tightly to his ass...

The rest of that day was a bit of a mess for the three trappers. Big Hat's horse was so 'gowed' up that it couldn't be ridden after being body-slammed by the irate moose, so Big Hat with his bad leg was forced to go it afoot and 'mouth breathe' all the way back to their cabin because of a smashed flat, dried blood-clogged nose. David's back was so badly sprained that he could not mount or ride his horse and found it easier to just stagger along and walk back to their campsite with Big Hat. However, he had to put his Hawken with the cracked stock into the mule's pannier and take the reserve Lancaster rifle for the protection that functioning rifle provided. As for Bear Scat, he had a big blood blister on his butt! A large blood blister from where the previously set five-pound beaver trap had snapped its jaws across his tender hind end when he had landed directly upon it after being slammed into by an irate and in full rut moose... Additionally Bear Scat had a badly sprained shoulder when almost the full weight of the moose had landed on top of him after he had pulled off a lucky spinal shot. But by the end of the day, the men had managed to set out their new trap line because they had caught all of the highly territorial beaver from the area previously utilized in their first trap line. Plus they had managed to skin out the six newly caught beaver they had trapped the same day after they had set out their new trap line. However for some reason, the skinning process took longer than normal...

As the men retired to their campsite later that afternoon, Big Hat figured out loud to himself why they had such a memorable run-in with the moose. Big Hat figured when Bear Scat had been chopping a dried willow stick for his trap's anchor pole, that the moose in rut heard the wood being whacked with the ax. In the moose's testosterone-fueled state of mind, being in rut and all, he must have figured those whacking sounds were coming from another moose's antlers smacking the woody brush announcing a challenge and that he was in a mood for a fight. Not one to duck a challenge, the 'monster moose in the marsh' in a blind fury charged out from the dense patch of willows and upon seeing Big Hat sitting on a moose-sized animal, namely his horse, must have figured that was his challenger and charged. The rest of the morning's events spoke for themselves. That night, the trappers sure enjoyed eating a big moose supper, courtesy of the moose that had kicked the hell out of the three of them, 'gowed' up one of their horses and saw to it that he had caused the busting of a stock on one of their precious, hard to replace in the field, Hawken rifles... But David being crafty as he was, managed to repair the broken-at-the-wrist rifle stock with an ample amount of brass wire being tightly wrapped heavily around the damaged area of wood. Then he took a piece of fresh deerskin, wrapped it tightly around that portion of the cracked stock, sewed it tightly in place and then set the rifle near their fireplace where the deerskin could dry. When it did, the deerskin had shrunk around the split rifle stock and was now almost as hard as the wood it surrounded, thereby preserving the stock on a once again functioning rifle.

However after supper, it was a 'moose' of another color, as Bear Scat had to put two small sticks up Big Hat's broken and smashed flat nose and painfully pull it back open so he could nose breathe. That field operation was accompanied by Big Hat's howls of agony heard ringing clear across the quiet of their nearby meadow! Bear Scat was soon told in rather colorful language that he was no frontier doctor upon completion of the 'operation'! That was especially so after Big Hat's feet had finally landed back down on earth, after having his smashed-flat nose pulled back into some semblance of a nose so the cartilage underneath could heal and he could nose breathe once again...

The following day dawned clear and colder as winter was making an early appearance in the southern reaches of the Green River Valley. Moving very slowly around his campfire because of his still stiff back, Bear Scat finally managed to fix a breakfast of coffee and only one batch of his Dutch oven biscuits. He would have made more biscuits but his back 'complained' every time he lifted up the heavy cast iron Dutch oven, so he gave up his biscuit making. Staggering out from their dugout next exited Big Hat. What a mess of the morning he made with a blood-encrusted front of his buckskin shirt on display, hobbling along on a considerably stiffened-up leg, displaying two of the prettiest black eyes one ever saw, and sporting a nose that was now 'human-looking' but was the size of a man's fist! Lastly, David staggered out from the dugout using his reserve Lancaster rifle as a support since the deerskin was still in its final stages of drying on the cracked stock of his Hawken, all the while walking around in a stooped-over position favoring his badly sprained and sored-up back.

Taking that scene of disrepair in stride, Bear Scat, the least hurt other than his pride since he was still sporting a rather large blood blister on his right cheek that needed lancing so he could comfortably ride on a horse, managed to enter their dugout. He later staggered forth carrying a partial keg of rum. Several cups of rum later mixed with a little coffee seemed to go a long way in fixing up what ailed each trapper... With breakfast such as it was done and a mess of jerky placed in each man's saddlebag to keep 'the big guts from eating the little guts' since breakfast had been so skimpy, the trio made ready to run their newest trap line. However, not before Bear Scat had to drop his buckskins and have Big Hat lance his rather large beaver trap-caused blood blister with his rather large hunting knife so he could sit in his saddle and be able to ride out to their trap line in some comfort. But not before Big Hat had also rather roughly rubbed a generous amount of bag balm into the lanced area on Bear Scat's bottom, for medicinal purposes of course. The grumpy looks on Bear Scat's highly embarrassed face however, especially during the bag balm application, pretty well silenced any further snide or rude comments coming from his two grinning compatriots...

Moments later, a slightly dinged-up caravan of trappers moved down from their campsite and headed for their new trap line. As they did, the rum's earlier soothing effects continued manifesting itself and by the time the three trappers had arrived at their new trap line, not a lot of pain was felt by any one of the three men. Once again with Big Hat serving as the lone sentinel over the almost defenseless Bear Scat checking and setting the traps, David painfully stepped out from his saddle already seeing a drowned beaver floating in their first trap. Since he was the group's designated skinner because of his deftness and expertise with a knife when skinning out a beaver, David followed Bear Scat over to the trap site and waited for him to retrieve and bring to shore the dead beaver. When he finally had the dead beaver in hand, David deftly slit the beaver up the center of his belly and made transverse cuts along each of the animal's legs in preparation to removing the pelt from the carcass. As David quickly removed the beaver's hide, he made sure he cut off its fat tail and tossed the hide and the tail member into the trailing mule's pannier. That way, by day's end there would be a few more beaver tails in the pannier suitable for a supper of roasted tail come time for their evening meal. In the meantime, Bear Scat reset his trap in the same place because the immediate area still had a number of beaver residing therein, daubed some castoreum on the lure stick over the now set trap, and then walked out from the pond's cold waters heading for his horse.

Moments later, the highly efficient but all 'gowed-up' trapping team was onto the next trap site, where another dead beaver was graced with the same skinning treatment by David, as Bear Scat reset and baited the trap. For the next three trap sites, beaver were found in every trap and by now with each man limbering up from his injuries suffered the day before, the highly efficient trio made better and better time in removing the dead beaver, skinning out the same and resetting their traps. As the trappers headed for trap site number six along their newly established trap line, each man's memory temporarily flashed back to that area and the almost fatal run-in the day before that they had with the sex-crazed moose in full rut.

Approaching the site where the remains of the moose's body had been left after the trappers had just removed its backstraps and hindquarters after all was said and done, Bear Scat noticed there were no scavenging birds like magpies or crows as of yet discovered feeding upon the moose's carcass remains. *That was strange,* thought Bear Scat. *The scavenger birds always discover any animal's carcass in just a short period of time after that animal had been killed and left for the critters to feed upon,* he thought.

Looking down from atop his horse as he passed by the moose's carcass, Bear Scat could see that the moose had been badly scavenged during their absence from the area. *Damn, I know the birds didn't do that,* thought Bear Scat, as he dismounted from his now really getting nervous 'crow-hopping' horse and walked over to check his obviously nearby empty beaver trap.

Walking right up to the beaver trap without giving it any thought, Bear Scat could see only the foot of a beaver still firmly clenched between the jaws of the trap. Kneeling down so he could examine the trap with the foot still firmly clenched between the jaws, Bear Scat could see that the body of the beaver had obviously been chewed off at the foot! Then looking all around the trap, Bear Scat could see where the muddy bottom had been all stirred up showing the signs of a fight and there was blood and beaver fur spread all over the area around the trap site! Then looking down in the soft mud next to the bank, Bear Scat froze! There in the mud just as pretty as you please, were the front claw marks on a huge footprint of a bear! *That damn bear and a grizzly from the size of its claw marks left in the mud, found my beaver in the trap and chewed him right out from it, only leaving his foot!* thought Bear Scat.

Damn, that is a footprint from a huge grizzly bear sure as shooting! thought Bear Scat again, as he quickly stood back up and began quickly looking all around for any sign of bear danger close at hand. Then looking over at the badly scavenged moose carcass once again he thought, *That's what caused all the damage to the remainder of that moose's carcass. Sure as hell is hot, the carcass had been discovered by a grizzly bear and scavenged. No wonder there aren't any birds on the carcass.* ***Holy crap, if there are no birds on this carcass that means only one thing! That damn bear is nearby and still guarding the remains of the carcass!*** thought Bear Scat, as he NOW wildly looked all around the dense willow brush ringing the beaver's pond! Quickly stepping out from the beaver pond with bear danger in mind, Bear Scat yelled for Big Hat to be on the alert. "A grizzly bear has been on the moose's carcass and even ate a beaver right out from my trap," yelled Bear Scat as he quickly began removing his beaver trap from that immediate area. He knew it would not do for him to make a beaver set right next to a now bear-scavenged moose carcass. *In fact, he probably never should have set a trap there in the first place,* he thought...

Deep in the dense adjoining willow patch the next thing Bear Scat heard was a loud roar of a maddened grizzly bear just awakened in his daybed, after hearing Bear Scat yelling out his warning to Big Hat and David that there was a bear in the area! Grabbing his beaver trap and taking off running for the safety of his nervous horse, Bear Scat could hear the loud crashing of a huge animal busting through the nearby clump of willows behind him, and **IT WAS COMING HIS WAY!**

Running like the wind for his nearby and now showing signs of extreme nervousness horse, Bear Scat could see that reaching his horse would not be an option upon seeing his horse quickly shying away from him out of fear. Upon hearing the loud roaring of an oncoming bear crashing through the willows, the other horses and the lone mule were now making like a 'rodeo' and trying to get the hell out of there no matter what their individual riders were trying to do with them! Realizing he was trapped without his horse, Bear Scat headed for the only nearby cottonwood tree growing in the area. Reaching the tree just as a roaring maddened grizzly bear, rudely awakened from its daybed, burst from his willow patch and upon seeing a near at hand fleeing Bear Scat, made for him in an instant! In two giant maddened leaps, with the grizzly bear rapidly gaining on him from the sounds of it, Bear Scat jumped for the small cottonwood tree trunk and began scrambling up through its limbs as fast as a squirrel being pursued by a fisher could go!

"WHOOOMP!" went a huge female grizzly bear's right paw as the bear arrived at the tree just split-seconds too late to execute a killing blow on the madly fleeing trapper, as Bear Scat literally flew up the trunk of the 30-foot tall cottonwood! But Bear Scat was just a second too slow as the bear's right front paw took a swipe at the quickly disappearing fur trapper, RIPPING OUT THE BOTTOM

OF HIS BUCKSKINS AND IN THE PROCESS, LEAVING A FOUR-CLAW GOUGE MARK ACROSS THE FLEEING TRAPPER'S HIND END, SHREDDING THE REAR END OF HIS BUCKSKINS AND PREVIOUSLY TRAP-DAMAGED HIND END IN THE PROCESS! "OWHEEE!" yelled Bear Scat in pain as he felt his bottom being ripped open by the grizzly bear's furious clawed-paw swipe! Furious over not catching the fleeing trapper who had disturbed the great bear's sleep after gorging on the remains of the dead moose in the beaver pond and being an adult grizzly bear, unable to climb the tree after him, the trapper found his problem had not decreased but had increased twofold!

The adult grizzly bear maybe could not climb the tree but her two two-year-old cubs, also now involved in the chase, sure as hell could and following the lead of their mom, up the tree they climbed hot after what their mom could not catch! On just desperate instinct, Bear Scat tried kicking the head of the closest bear cub climbing up right after him, only to lose his moccasin in a vicious bite from the closest following two-year-old. Having enough of that crap plus there was no more tree trunk left in which he could climb any higher, Bear Scat drew his pistol from his sash. **BOOM!** went Bear Scat's pistol, shooting the closest cub after him in the face from two feet away! Killing him instantly, that 200-pound cub dropped out from the tree like a stone! However Bear Scat was now without any powder or ball in which to reload, since he had only brought one of his pistols along that day! Swinging the butt of his now empty pistol at the head of the next cub climbing up the tree and hot after him, explosion from his pistol earlier or not, Bear Scat had his pistol grabbed by the bear's jaw full of teeth and torn out from his hand! Grabbing his knife in desperation, Bear Scat prepared to knife the still madly climbing bear in the face if it got any closer. As it turned out, that was his last remaining option because there was no more tree trunk that was thick enough to hold him onto which to climb...

BOOM—BOOM! went two rifles almost simultaneously, fired by Big Hat and David from a short distance away! The large cub in the tree still trying to get at Bear Scat instantly turned and bit at his side where one of the fired .52 caliber balls had hit its mark! That bear although mortally struck, instantly shimmied back down the tree crying out in pain and died seconds later at the tree's base! However, the huge sow only turned and bit at her side where the lead ball fired at her had struck and thinking Bear Scat was the one who had inflicted her pain, began tearing great chunks of bark from the tree with her teeth in her frustration at being unable to get at the man perched precariously above in the tree just feet away from her still viciously swinging paw armed with five six-inch claws!

BOOM—BOOM! went two more shots fired from two hastily reloaded rifles. That time both lead balls struck home, causing the sow grizzly to stagger off a short distance from the base of the tree holding a trapped Bear Scat, and then biting and tearing at the ground with her front paws in frustration, soon lay still in death! Watching from his treetop, Bear Scat waited until he saw that both Big Hat and David had reloaded and with them slowly walking toward the presumed dead sow, he began painfully sliding back down the tree through a slippery 'slide' of his own blood pouring profusely from his previously claw-damaged hind end!

Standing there holding onto the tree trunk and dizzy over the pain he was feeling in his 'last part over the fence', Bear Scat saw his two partners walk over to the sow and make sure she was dead before they came over to see how he was doing. "WHOO-EEE," said Big Hat, once he got closer to Bear Scat and could see the claw damage done to his hind end through the ripped open seat of his buckskins! "Damn, Bear Scat! From the looks of it, you now have a face with grizzly bear claw marks across it to match the claw marks now left across your hind end! She really got you good, and this time it will be my honor to be a 'frontier doctor' on your miserable carcass and I hope I can hurt you as much as you did me when you tried fixing my nose," Big Hat said with just a slightly devious smile on his face.

Having had enough problems for the day, the men left what beaver were in their traps along the rest of their trap line and returned to their campsite. As they did, one of the men rode standing up in his stirrups all the way back to their camp, for obvious reasons… Then after consuming five cups of rum, Bear Scat lay over a sitting log as Big Hat broke out his leather needle and twine so he could sew up Bear Scat's backside. After pouring some rum into the washed-out one-inch-deep slashes across his bottom, Big Hat sewed up the four 'claw-slashes' to much howling from the now rum-soaked trapper laid over a sitting log, who was also being held down by a laughing David Hager…

For the next week, Bear Scat stayed back in camp watching their livestock, cooking meals, fleshing and hooping all the beaver that were caught on a daily basis, as his hind end began the process of healing up enough so he could ride once again, as Big Hat and David continued running the trap line. Finally his deep claw marks across his bottom had scabbed over enough so Bear Scat could ride, although somewhat uncomfortably, once again. With that, Bear Scat was released from all the camp's duties as he happily joined his brother trappers finishing out their trapping season come ice-up with the arrival of winter in all of its fury.

Two weeks after the arrival of the deep winter ice and the end of beaver trapping, Big Hat, Bear Scat and David built three, hell-for-stout meat poles right next to their campsite. The following morning, after a previous evening of casting more .52 caliber balls for their lead-eating Hawken and Lancaster rifles, setting a fine edge to their knives because buffalo hair had such a dulling effect on their blades, and filling their powder horns, the three trappers dressed for the weather and ventured forth on a buffalo hunt. Since a small herd of about 150 buffalo had moved in right next to their campsite and with such an opportunity so close at hand, the trappers made ready to avail themselves of such a great-eating gift from Mother Nature.

Saddling up their riding horses and affixing packsaddles to their four mules, the three men ventured forth out onto the snow-covered prairie heading for the herd of quietly feeding buffalo. Finding several low hills to hide behind in order to ride up even closer onto the unsuspecting buffalo, the men lay low in their saddles like the Indians did, as they slowly moved within range of the animals so as not to spook them. Finally leaving their horses behind on the back side of a hillock, the men crawled up to the top of the hill carrying their three extra rifles and laid out not 40 yards from the unsuspecting feeding animals below. Laid out along the hilltop, the three men looked over at each other as if saying with their eyes "Are you ready?" and then in unison, fired three quick shots into the unsuspecting feeding buffalo below. Then laying aside their first rifles, the men picked up their reserve rifles and once again fired three more shots into the now getting-alarmed buffalo, as they began smelling the blood from their dead and dying brethren and began slowly moving out of the area away from the thundering rifles, puffs of smoke and the increasing smells of blood.

Then as the perils of the frontier had 'taught' the men, they all dropped below the hillside, took the time to reload all of their rifles and then walked back up to the hilltop to look over the death and destruction they had wrought on the small herd of buffalo once feeding quietly below. As they happily did, they topped the rise and observed six stilled forms of dead buffalo lying below them on the windswept prairie, and about 30 Indians riding 'hellbent for election' towards those three trappers standing out in front of god and everybody else after doing the shooting and topping the rise!

With several loud and excited 'whoops', the hard-charging Indians, realizing they were about to count 'coup' on three isolated men, as if on command, separated into two bunches and rode around the small hillside holding the three trappers and surrounding them in the maneuver! The first bunch coming around the back side of the hill ran into the trappers' horses and mules, and immediately ran them off and away as prizes from the battle soon to come! Meanwhile, the other bunch of Indians swarmed up the hillside at full gallop figuring they would kill as many of the men as they could in the first fusillade and then ride right over those trappers who remained alive with their horses!

BOOM—BOOM—BOOM! Went three shots fired by the now surrounded trappers, clearing three of the hard-charging Indians from their saddles as they stormed up the small hillside! Then three more quick shots from their reserve rifles closely followed, as the sharpshooting trappers used their reserve and hastily reloaded rifles for their second round of defense! Once again, three more hard-charging Indians dropped from their saddles, being struck in their centers of mass by the half-ounce lead balls from the deadly accurate shooting of the now very desperate and trapped trappers! When that happened and finding almost half of their number had fallen to the sharpshooting trappers, the charge of Indians storming up the front of the hillside faltered, whirled and at full gallop, stormed off the hill as if the devil was on their tails, full well knowing what was coming next as the desperate trappers began pulling their pistols and were now stoically awaiting their fates!

Then as if on command, the desperate trappers dropped to the ground to reduce their silhouettes, withdrew their pistols and killed two Indians and another's horse from that group of warriors now storming up the back side of the hill after running off the trappers' livestock! That alone caused the hard-charging Indians to stop and mill about in confusion because of the straight-shooting trappers, only to once again feel the sting of three more shots being fired from the trappers' second pistols, which at such a short range between the shooter and the 'targets', three more Indians fell to the snow-covered ground to move no more!

Moments later, that group of Indians, surprised at the desperate battle the trappers were waging and the accurate shooting they were pouring into their ranks, broke and galloped back down the hill in order to get out of the trappers' gun range! When that happened, all three trappers hurriedly began reloading their rifles and pistols like their lives depended upon it and 'they' did! As the surprised Indians milled about out of range out on the prairie trying to decide what to do in light of the straight-shooting trappers, the group of Indians from behind the hill streamed off and joined up with the first batch of Indians in order to hold a parley among their depleted ranks deciding what to do next. Having eleven of their own cleared from their saddles by the straight-shooting trappers, partly out of desperation and partly out of being such accurate shooting Mountain Men who had been in tight situations before, the Indians hesitated over their next move.

When they did, there was a flurry of reloading activity back on the hilltop until all three trappers now had two reloaded rifles and two pistols each ready for the next charge. Then they figured they would be down to knives and tomahawks for however long that lasted... However, they had eliminated eleven of the 30 Indians who had surprised and confronted them, but the trappers knew the remaining 19 could quickly overwhelm them if they came at them en masse, so they just hoped for the best and expected the worst. Especially in light of what David Jackson had told Big Hat months earlier about not being taken alive by the Southern Ute Indians unless one wanted to die a slow and painful death!

Then the chance for death the trappers had stared in the face when confronted by the 30 Indians that had just attacked them, was multiplied! On another hillside, a second group of 20 or so Indians popped up in plain view of the trappers! They now knew that when the two forces of Indians combined, they would be quickly overridden, killed and scalped... in fact, as the outnumbered trappers looked on in horror at the arrival of another band of Indians, they also observed that those Indians had captured all of their previously stampeded livestock and now had all of their horses and mules in tow... Seeing what they were seeing, Bear Scat realized that he would never see his brother again, Big Hat was beginning to wonder if he had made the right decision in following Bear Scat on his mission to find his long-lost brother, and David, ever the odd one, wondered if he would live long enough to ever be able to eat another of Bear Scat's wonderful biscuits...

Then something out of frontier character occurred! The first group of Indians below them began milling around like they were in some sort of confusion after observing the arrival of the larger band of Indians on the horizon. It was then that the Indians that had attacked them earlier began streaming below the trappers on their horses as if they were going to come at the three men from the back side of the hillside upon which the trappers perilously occupied. When that happened, that got five more of the streaming-by Indians cleared from their saddles and another Indian's horse shot out from underneath him as the desperate trappers put their accurate shooting with their rifles to work once again! That Indian who just had his horse shot out from under him by a trapper's errant shot, ran alongside another horsed Indian and leaped up onto the back of that man's horse and the entire group instead of attacking again, unbelievably began riding out of sight and sound...

Turning and reloading for the next Indian charge from the larger second group, the trappers could see the new arrivals streaming their way as they calmly walked their horses right at their position on the hillside single file. Not understanding what the hell was happening because of such unusual behavior, the three men said nary a word but finished reloading their rifles and waited for the next expected massed attack from the now approaching and larger group of Indians. Finally the second group of Indians stopped just out of shooting range of the straight-shooting trappers and sat there quietly on their horses looking on, as a single warrior left their group and walked his horse directly at the three grouped trappers desperately holding the high ground.

Once the approaching Indian rode within the range of the accurate shooting trappers, he stopped and raised his right arm in the universal Plains Indian sign of peace. "What the hell is he doing?" said Big Hat as he nervously fingered his trusty Hawken, not one to trust any Indian under the circumstances they had previously experienced and were now facing anew.

"What have we got to lose?" said Bear Scat. "It is obvious that he wants to talk, so I say we let him talk. But if he tries anything funny, he will get what the rest of that earlier group of Indians got."

"It is your hair, Bear Scat. If you want to walk down and see what he wants to say, I will cover you. But if he even looks at you in the wrong way, I am going to send a ball his way that will spill enough of his guts that even the little people will have a hard time making a meal of it," said Big Hat through seriously gritted teeth.

With that, Bear Scat raised his right arm in the universal sign of peace and with a fully cocked Hawken in hand just in case things went from bad to worse, left his friends on the hilltop and began a slow walk down to the lone warrior still sitting stoically on his horse in the deep cold of winter. Walking up to the Indian sitting quietly on his steed, Bear Scat stopped 20 yards away from him saying in the sign language of the Plains Indians that Big Hat had taught him, "Good Morning, what do you want?"

"Which of you is called 'White Eagle' by my Brothers, the Lakota?" said the warrior in English, as he sat quietly on his horse.

Surprised by what the man had just said in clipped English, Bear Scat then remembered back to the honor Lakota Chief Buffalo Calf had bestowed upon him before he and his protective group of warriors had separated from the trappers just outside St. Louis. An honor bestowed because of what he and his fellow trappers had done for his band of warriors by providing them with an abundance of provisions for their return trip home, and he in particular for rescuing the chief's only son who almost drowned in a Bull Boat on the Missouri River many months earlier. That honor bestowed being he had been renamed from Bear Scat to the name "White Eagle" by the Lakota Chief. Chief Buffalo Calf had also advised that he would send runners from his band to other bands letting them know about White Eagle as a "Brother Lakota", to be treated accordingly and if discovered among other white man trappers, they were to be considered friends of the Lakota and the individual so honored could be easily identified by the five white eagle tail feathers tied into his horse's mane!

Stunned over what he was hearing from the man sitting high atop his horse, a man who had yet to crack a single smile, about the name that had been given earlier by a Lakota chief, Bear Scat responded by saying, "I am the one called White Eagle who was so named by Lakota Chief Buffalo Calf."

"My warriors and I, upon hearing all the shooting, came over to see what was going on. When we did, we captured a horse wearing the sacred white eagle tail feathers in its mane. A sign according to Chief Buffalo Calf of the Lakota that the rider of that horse is called White Eagle and is to be treated with respect like a Lakota Brother. I am called "Bear-Who-Wanders" by my People of the Minneconjou Lakota." With those words of introduction and Bear Scat now remembering the white eagle tail feathers woven into his horse's mane and what they were to signify to any Lakota or Northern Cheyenne Indian, reached out and shook Bear-Who-Wanders' hand.

Then Bear Scat said to Bear-Who-Wanders, "I must go and tell my fellow trappers to lower their rifles. I will tell them that Bear-Who-Wanders and his fellow warriors are our friends and upon seeing the white eagle feathers in my horse's mane when they captured him, have come to rescue us from the bad Southern Ute Indians who were attacking us." Bear-Who-Wanders nodded his head in understanding over Bear Scat's words, especially when he looked up towards the hilltop holding the two remaining trappers who were still holding their rifles in the 'ready to fight' positions.

Still shaking his head in amazement over the day's turn of events from the earlier violence generated by the attacking Utes to now being saved by the Minneconjou Sioux, Bear Scat walked back up to his fellow trappers who had been staring at the powwow taking place below their hilltop with one of their own and a lone Indian with questions written all over their faces over what had just occurred. Then there were even more questions on their faces as they saw this second group of Indians showing no signs of hostility, slowly coming their way leading the trappers' horses and mules back to them after their having been run off by the hostile Southern Utes with just the specter of the Lakota's surprise appearance on the battlefield! Once back with his fellow trappers, Bear Scat explained to them what had just happened and about being rescued from certain death by a band of nearby buffalo-hunting Sioux warriors who had heard the story about White Eagle, had remembered the story upon capturing the trappers' horses and mules, and had ridden over to investigate what all the shooting was about!

The rest of that morning was spent with the Sioux warriors and trappers feasting on the warm buffalo livers from the six buffalo the trappers had killed earlier before being attacked by the Ute Indians. That was after the Sioux had scalped and mutilated all of the dead Southern Ute Indians the trappers had killed earlier... Then with the mules loaded to the gills with fresh buffalo meat which was still dripping droplets of blood every time the pack animals took a step, the trappers and their new friends returned to the trappers' campsite. Upon their arrival back at camp, Bear Scat hurriedly loaded up two coffee pots with water and previously roasted green coffee beans and set them on the hanging irons to boil on a newly built fire. Then out came the roasting stakes, slabbed with generously sized chunks of buffalo meat and set over the fire to cook, as he began making biscuits using all three of his Dutch ovens for their newfound friends. Indian friends, who if like the rest of their kind, seemed to have a penchant for Bear Scat's Dutch oven biscuits and like David Hager, lots of them...

Once the coffee was ready, the three trappers using all of their cups and bowls which were utilized as drinking cups because there were so many Indians all wanting the white man's hot coffee all at the same time, served the strong trapper's coffee in shifts to the cold Indians along with slabs of partially roasted buffalo meat, a favorite among the Indians as well as the trappers, and Dutch oven biscuits slathered in honey, which was very much appreciated by their new Indian friends.

Come early afternoon, everyone had eaten their fill and as the Lakota made ready to leave and resume their own buffalo hunt, Bear-Who-Wanders came over to bid Bear Scat good-bye saying, "White Eagle, you and yours are welcome anytime at my band's winter camp which is located on the Green River where it enters the valley. If you and yours come, we will kill and eat much buffalo meat together as friends." He then mounted his horse and with that and a wave, the sub-chief and his warriors rode off in the direction from whence they had come earlier in the day when they had stumbled upon the battle between the Southern Utes and trappers, and ultimately rescued the three white men trappers.

Come the following morning bright and early, Bear Scat left their dugout, attended to a call of nature, let their livestock out to pasture once they had been hobbled, and then started his cooking fire so he could make breakfast. About then, Big Hat emerged from the dugout with a look of urgency on his face and quickly headed for the cottonwood grove behind their dugout to take care of his urgent call of nature. As he did, Bear Scat whipped up his biscuit making dough and just grinned. Grinned because the day before when he and his fellow trappers were feeding all of their Indian friends, Bear Scat remembered that Big Hat had not only previously binged on fresh raw buffalo liver, but had eaten several pounds of partially cooked buffalo meat around the campfire as well. Bear Scat could not remember when he had seen anyone eat so much raw liver and then consume so much buffalo meat just hours later. However by doing so, it appeared Big Hat was now suffering the consequences of putting away so much of the rich and great-tasting meat...

Meanwhile out in the distant cottonwood grove, Big Hat comfortably rested his bottom over a small log that had been placed up off the ground over a latrine, and rid his body of at least a portion of the more than five pounds of raw liver and partially cooked buffalo meat he had consumed from the day before. As he did, he dreamingly watched a small herd of buffalo moving and grunting their ways through the cottonwood grove not 30 yards from where he was taking care of his urgent call of nature. In so doing, he was so engrossed in watching the feeding herd of close at hand buffalo that he failed to pay any attention at all to his surroundings as he had taught Bear Scat in their early days of association to constantly do when out on the frontier.

Little did Big Hat realize that there was a grizzly bear not yet in hibernation and still hungrily looking for a meal. As such, the bear was carefully stalking the nearby small herd of buffalo quietly feeding along in front of where Big Hat was 'taking care of business' in ridding himself from several pounds of previously consumed buffalo meat. As the great bear continued his careful stalk of the nearby buffalo herd hoping for an easy meal to aid him in his coming hibernation, his nose intercepted another foreign smell. An intriguing foreign smell that moved his senses away from that of the buffalo quietly feeding nearby to another close at hand scene of a 'thing' sitting on a nearby cottonwood log making a very interesting 'smell'. Turning his attention to the new and interesting smell, the great bear moved away from stalking the noisy herd of buffalo to that of the quiet and unmoving 'thing' sitting on a nearby log making a very interesting smell…

Big Hat, totally involved in 'taking care of the business at hand' and at the same time closely observing the interesting behavior of the nearby feeding buffalo now just a few scant yards away from where he quietly sat, had unfortunately turned off the rest of his survival senses. Occurring simultaneously, the grizzly bear carefully and quietly, cautiously step by step in the fresh six inches of snow, continued approaching the 'thing' making the interesting smell from behind! However, the smell of 'man' was ever-present and the bear in making its approach to the 'thing' sitting on the log, was now elongated as he could make his great body stretch in an attempt to get as close to the mystery smell as possible without touching it or being detected. Even though the bear was the ultimate predator of the land and feared no man or beast, it still found caution in his approach to the 'thing' sitting on the log, a 'thing' like he had never before experienced in his young life. But if what he was approaching was good to eat, he meant to add it to his empty and growling belly to aid him in his long period of hibernation soon to come…

Seconds later, Big Hat felt a still questioning cold and wet nose pressed onto his 'last part over the fence'! Surprised over the 'cold-nosed sensation' pressing against his 'unsuspecting' bottom and snapping his survival senses once again into play, Big Hat lost his interest in the nearby feeding buffalo who were all now looking his way as if now sensing danger and quickly spun around on his sitting log. There just inches away from his bare and defenseless bottom on all fours stood the biggest grizzly bear he had ever seen on the Western frontier, and its dark and beady eyes were eyeballing him with as much surprise as any bear could get on his face over never having experienced a human's bare smelly bottom before!

"YEEE-HOW!" went Big Hat, as he exploded off his cottonwood log rising almost four feet into the air. When he exploded off his log in terror over what was just inches away with his buckskin pants draped around his ankles, Big Hat in a huge surge of adrenalin tore his pants in two at the crotch with his first escape step taken! What was still remaining in his body that 'needed out', came out with such force that the bear found his head covered with what he had been so curious about when he had made his cautious and stealthy approach towards the mystery 'white-bottomed thing' quietly sitting on the log!

Then the bear's primal instincts of 'chase' kicked in, as the 'white-bottomed thing' awkwardly fled away from him with half of a buckskin pant leg madly flopping around the ankle above each foot! When that surprise movement exploded off a nearby log, the buffalo stampeded away in alarm with their tails held high into the air as they now had also smelled a great and dangerous bear close at hand as well. However, the 'thing' was closer and more slowly moving away and it was that which the bear tore after with a vengeance!

"YEOWWEE—YEOWWEE!" screamed Big Hat, as he stampeded back towards camp and the safety it offered with a buckskin pant leg wildly flopping off each ankle. However, regardless how fast he sprinted for the safety his dugout offered, he was more than aware that the bear was rapidly gaining on him with each leap it took! Meanwhile back at the campfire, Bear Scat was just taking a boiling coffee pot off its hanging iron and attempting to set it off to one side on a cooling rock when he heard a terror-filled voice of Big Hat renting the air and sounding in loudness like it was quickly coming his way from behind the dugout!

All of a sudden, around the north end of their dugout stormed Big Hat with a look of terror spelled clear across his face that said it all! Seeing that look of terror on Big Hat's face, Bear Scat quickly set the coffee pot down on the cooling rock, sprinted for his nearby rifle lying against a sitting log, and swung it to his shoulder just in time to see a huge grizzly bear rounding the end of their dugout in full pursuit and close behind the bare white hind end of Big Hat! Then for just an instant, Big Hat's eyes registered even more terror when he took a look at Bear Scat aiming his rifle at what appeared to be RIGHT AT HIM INSTEAD OF THE IN-HOT-PURSUIT BEAR!

Yelling and screaming, "DON'T SHOOT ME—FOR HEAVEN'S SAKE, DON'T SHOOT"! Big Hat came storming his way with both pant legs just a-flapping from both ankles towards Bear Scat! About then, David, hearing all the yelling and commotion near the front of their dugout, staggered out the front door of their dugout still about half-asleep. When he did, he had chosen the wrong moment to make his outside appearance just as the great bear tore by him chasing Big Hat, and IN SO DOING, violently brush-blocked a totally surprised David Hager! David had just closed the dugout's door and was immediately smashed back into the sturdy log structure serving as an entrance point, knocking the trapper senseless from his impact with the door's heavy log framing!

BOOM! went Bear Scat's rifle, as Big Hat felt the wind and heard the "ZIPPP" of the bullet which whirred by him so closely that he heard the sounds of "Angel's Wings"! That was when Big Hat's fleeing body lunged right over the blazing campfire and plowed right into Bear Scat with a tremendous impact! In fact, the impact of the collision between the two men was so violent, that both of their bodies were then hurled over a nearby sitting log and into the woodpile with a bone rattling "CRUMP"!

In the meantime, the great bear, shot right through the left eye by Bear Scat, died instantly from the impact of the half-ounce, .52 caliber lead slug! In so doing, his speeding body just moments earlier chasing Big Hat hoping for 'lunch', continued on with such velocity, that he too plowed right through the campfire, scattering the hanging irons, pots and pans, and blew the scalding contents from the still cooling coffee pot clear over himself and the two trappers trying to scramble out of the way from where they had ended up smashed together in the woodpile! That scalding coffee then lent wings to the two scalded trappers, especially the bare-assed body of Big Hat! It seems that when the boiling coffee blew over the trappers, Big Hat's bare backside was that portion of his body that was splashed the most with at least a gallon of boiling hot coffee! When that hot coffee hit Big Hat's exposed backside, he jumped like a 'bug on a hot rock' and even God, busy and as far away as he was, heard him howl clear to the Heavens!

Somewhat later after things had settled down, David had recovered from being 'brush-blocked' and violently slammed into the heavy log structure of their dugout by the brutish-sized bear hurtling by earlier in his chase after Big Hat. Big Hat's scalded backside had cooled off somewhat in the cool of the winter morning but not before leaving a mess of tiny water blisters on his 'saddle-side'! Lastly, Bear Scat had managed to fix up his cooking area and an hour later was now busily making breakfast, and primary on the menu and roasting steels busily spattering away over the fire were numerous skewered portions of a winter-fattened grizzly bear! That while the rest of the freshly butchered-out monster-sized critter was now swinging slowly in the cooling breeze on their meat pole in readiness for many future meals... Speaking of meals, moments after the great bear's carcass had been roped up onto the trappers' meat hanging pole, a family of gray jays had discovered the fat-laden skinned-out carcass and were making the most of it in the winter's cool air. Additionally, a fresh grizzly bear hide lay draped over the woodpile awaiting being scraped, stretched and tanned for sale as a valuable bear robe at the upcoming summer rendezvous. Lastly, Bear Scat made sure that he thanked Big Hat for bringing such a mountain of great-eating winter fat-laden grizzly bear to breakfast...

Several days later found the three trappers armed to the teeth with every firearm they possessed, either being carried or strapped to their four mules in case there was a repeat of crossing trails with more members of the Southern Ute Nation looking for their now long-dead and scalped brethren and their bad attitudes. However, no Indians were encountered that day and the three trappers, out to kill more buffalo since the Lakota Indians had eaten up most of their supplies of fresh meat, killed another six fat cows. Several hours later, the best portions of the meat from the buffalo just killed had been loaded into the mule's panniers for transport back to camp, and then wolf traps had been set out around what remained of the buffalo carcasses in the hope wolves would find the carcasses, as well as 'fill' the trappers' wolf traps... A winter of wolf trapping, buffalo hunting for fresh meat, wood gathering, and packing into traveling packs of the many taken fall-trapped beaver became the daily regimen. However now, the three trappers having learned their lessons carried all of their weapons anytime they were out and about in plain view of the locals with their bad attitudes when it came to the trespassing trappers...

Some months later, spring beaver trapping began and once again the men moved into their individual duties while on the trapping scene. Big Hat as usual, remained horsed at all times because of his bad case of arthritis and excellent shooting skills, acted as a sentinel and provided the first level of protection to the other two men working in the water and on the ground nearby. Bear Scat, true to his nature and now an experienced Mountain Man, did all of the beaver trapping-related work, scouting out the trap sites, setting the beaver traps and emptying of the same. Since he was the youngest of the trio of trappers and able to better withstand the rigors of walking about in the icy and deep trapping waters, that was his chosen assignment. David Hager on the other hand, being the best of the three men when it came to the beaver-skinning duties, happily drew those assignments.

That spring trapping season the men saw little in the way of active Indian sign and continued trapping with lessened concerns regarding those kinds of dangers. Other than the bone-chilling immersions up to one's waist in the icy cold beaver ponds, occasionally running across a stray, bad-tempered grizzly bear too close for comfort or a late spring snowstorm with its wet, heavy and chilling snows, spring trapping continued unabated. Then when back at camp, Bear Scat drew the cooking duties because of his expertise, while all of the men were responsible for the care and tending of their livestock, wood gathering, harvesting fresh meat supplies, and the pelting of the beaver hides and tanning of the wolf skins.

Come the late spring when the beaver went out of their prime, the trappers' traps were pulled and the men began preparing for traveling to the much-anticipated Green River Rendezvous to be held at Horse Creek that summer, as had been so indicated earlier by one David Jackson, fur company owner. For the next week, the three trappers took all of their beaver furs, folded them with the fur side in and with protective tanned deerskins for each pack, placed around 60 *'plus'* to a bundle and using a homemade chain, pole and sapling press, compressed each bundle of furs into packs weighing about 90-100 pounds. Then tightly tying and lacing the tanned deerskins around each pack of *'plus'* for the protection they offered, they were set aside for later hauling by their mules, two packs per mule, to the rendezvous for sale. Once at the rendezvous, each pack would then be sold at 'Mountain Prices' which would hopefully fetch around $300-600 per pack of Made Beaver (adult-sized beaver). Then the money derived from the sale of the pelts and wolf furs would be used to purchase, once again at 'Mountain Prices', supplies needed for the next year's trapping season (goods so priced were marked up anywhere from 700-1,000%). Once again, those high markups for provisions reflected the business concerns of potential loss of the furs being transported back to

St. Louis to theft from Indians, damage from horse wrecks, and changes in fur prices from purchase at the rendezvous to sale in St. Louis. Historically, some entire caravans returning to St. Louis were wiped out by hostile Indians and all of the furs and livestock stolen, hence the 'Mountain Prices' being charged by the fur companies while afield!

One late spring morning as Bear Scat prepared breakfast, Big Hat, just back from his morning trip to rid from his body that which plugged him up, sat down on his sitting log and just looked thoughtfully into the campfire. After a few moments, Big Hat said, "Bear Scat, we need to make ready to head for Horse Creek to our north and the Green River Rendezvous. I am not sure of the exact time the rendezvous will be held but as near as I can figure, now is the right time to be there and on-site. But first we need to dig a cache and hide that which we do not need to take on this trip. Way I figure it, we still have plenty beaver in this area and feel we need to return to this site after we re-provision at the rendezvous and continue trapping until we catch all the beaver in this area that we can. Once we have caught most all of the beaver out from this area, then we can move on to a new trapping area but not before, since we know this one so well and the trappings are so good."

About then David Hager staggered out from their dugout, walked over to the fire, poured himself a cup of coffee, and took a long sip of the still boiling hot liquid. After taking a sip of the coffee and then smacking his lips to alleviate the burning feeling from drinking something too hot to drink he said, "Now by dammit, I think I will live. Now what is this talk about digging a cache and hiding what we do not need to carry to the rendezvous I just heard about while walking over here?"

Bear Scat then said as Big Hat poured himself more coffee, "Big Hat says we need to come back here at the end of the summer rendezvous and continue trapping in this area, because we still have a lot more beaver to catch before they are all trapped out and then we can up and move on to new trapping grounds. That being the case, he also feels we need to dig out a cache site and leave what we will not need for the trip to the rendezvous at Horse Creek. That way upon our return, all we have to do is open up our cache site, recover that which we left behind and commence our trapping and living operations like nothing has happened. By doing it that way, all we will be packing to the rendezvous will be our *'plus'* and a light load of what we need in order to subsist along on the trail, thereby making travel for our livestock and us somewhat easier."

"I agree. From what I have seen, there are still hundreds of beaver remaining in this area and we haven't even begun to reduce their numbers except for those living just around our campsite. I too say we return here at the end of the summer rendezvous and continue trapping in this area until we catch everything that we can. Besides, we have a fine home here in our dugout and I say we come back, and that way I don't have to shovel another mountain of dirt in order to make another dugout somewhere else," said David with a big grin, hoping to be able to duck any more heavy work shoveling another dugout's worth of dirt.

"Well, if that is the group's feeling, I say we get at digging a cache so we can store what we have and need not haul clear back to Horse Creek," said Bear Scat, as he looked over at Big Hat to see what else he might have to say about the matter of staying for another trapping season. Hearing nothing negative regarding the matter coming from Big Hat, Bear Scat continued saying, "Besides, if we are lucky enough to find my brother at the rendezvous, maybe we can convince him to join our group and by so doing, adding one more trapper and his gun to our family down here for the protection that would provide."

"Well, then it is settled. I say we dig into that sandy clay flat over yonder and make that our cache site. The way I figure it, that high ground over there by those trees is away from any floodwaters, dry and would make an excellent cache site. Besides, it is next to that grove of cottonwoods and that would make it easier to hide from prying eyes with all that grove's tree leaves on the ground in the way of leavings. With that kind of groundcover, that would make it easier to hide our cache site from the Indians once we have it dug, loaded with our gear and covered up. That way, no damn Indian would find it, dig it up and steal what he wanted of our unused provisions," said Big Hat.

Later that afternoon found the three trappers hard at work digging a deep cache hole and lining the same with dry limbs and leaves to reduce the chance of spoilage or rusting of any of the goods stored therein. Two days later found a deeply dug cache hole lined with dry tree limbs and leaves, and supported from inside with saplings cut from the cottonwood grove to keep the roof from caving in. Then as Bear Scat removed the few cooking items and provisions he would need for the journey and time spent at the rendezvous, Big Hat and David carried more goods over to the cache site and situated them within for later retrieval when they returned from the rendezvous.

While Big Hat and David continued hauling the trappers' goods from their dugout over to the cache site, Bear Scat built up a fire in order to cook up their evening meal. As he did, up on the row of hills above the trappers' dugout, a herd of buffalo stampeded along after being alarmed by a pack of wolves looking for a meal comprised of a sick or weak buffalo or maybe even a calf. When they rumbled by shaking the ground on which he stood, Bear Scat looked up from his cooking detail to look at the herd passing nearby with all of their tails held up over their rumps in alarm. He just smiled over being a trapper and not that of a wolf, and having to drag down one of those dangerous beasts with one's teeth and not have the use and aid of his trusty Hawken rifle to take care of business.

"HELP, HELP!" Bear Scat, upon hearing those shouts for help looked up from what he was cooking and all he could see in the direction of those shouts was a cloud of dust rising up into the air. When he saw that cloud of dust rising into the air, his heart almost stopped. The cloud of dust was right where Big Hat and David Hager were putting the finishing touches to their cache and loading it full of provisions not necessary for their trip to the rendezvous grounds later in the month!

Dropping what he was doing, Bear Scat grabbed his nearby rifle off a sitting log and sprinted for the site of their new cache. Running up to where its entrance had been, all he could see was Big Hat on his hands and knees digging like a mad man with his hand and a shovel in what remained of a cache entranceway! FOR AN INSTANT, BEAR SCAT JUST FROZE OVER SEEING THAT THEIR ENTIRE CACHE HOUSE ROOF HAD JUST COLLAPSED! Then yelling from Big Hat broke his frozen movement and dropping his rifle, fell to his knees and began frantically digging as well, because now he realized what the problem was involving the collapsed cache site! David Hager, who had been loading their provisions into the cache, was nowhere to be seen! It was now obvious that he had been inside when the entire thick roof had collapsed from the vibration of the earth's trembling caused when the nearby buffalo herd had stampeded by after being chased earlier by the wolves!

Until it got too dark to see, Big Hat and Bear Scat dug with their shovels and hands until their fingers bled trying to get their friend and fellow trapper out from under the tons of earthen roof that had collapsed upon him when the herd of buffalo had thundered by up on a nearby hillside! Unable to see in the fast-falling darkness exactly what they were doing and being thwarted at every turn by the brush, limbs and saplings they had used to 'feather' their cache site, the two exhausted trappers finally laid down their shovels and tiredly headed for their campsite. With the use of a fire steel, Bear Scat got a small fire going as Big Hat went into their dugout and brought forth their last keg of rum and several cups. The two trappers had no supper that evening other than numerous cups of rum trying hard not to think of the inevitable back at their collapsed cache site...

Daylight the following morning found two 'thick-headed' from all of the rum consumed the previous evening trappers digging once again for all they were worth and did so with sinking hearts! Come late afternoon, the crushed body of David "Are there anymore biscuits?" Hager was finally recovered! It was obvious from his crushed skull that he had died instantly when the tons of roof dirt had collapsed upon his unsuspecting self as he loaded provisions deeply into the cache. That evening, no supper was had as more cups of rum sorrowfully flowed over the sad loss of their friend and fellow trapper...

The next morning, the two trappers buried their friend on the hillside above their dugout where he could overlook the beaver trapping waters located below. Ironically, his grave was dug in the middle of a 200-yard-wide path of torn-up ground caused by a thundering herd of buffalo being chased by wolves from the day before. That same herd of buffalo that had caused the collapse of the cache's roof that had crushed and killed David Hager in the prime of his life... However, there was a good reason for burying David under such ground torn up by all of the earlier passing herd of buffalo. When they had finished with the gruesome task of burying their friend, there was little evidence of his whereabouts. By so doing, hopefully no Indians would see the disturbed ground above the actual burial site and realizing something was buried there, dig it up, steal his clothing and desecrate his body.

For the next three days, Big Hat and Bear Scat dug into the collapsed cache site and removed the rest of their previously cached provisions. Realizing the previously collapsed cache site would be investigated by any curious Indians passing by, a new cache site was dug alongside the old one, figuring the Indians would only carefully examine the ruins of the old site near a previously used dugout and not be looking for another one cleverly hidden and located right alongside the old site.

Three days later found Big Hat in the lead and Bear Scat bringing up the rear of a caravan of horses and mules heavily loaded with provisions and packs of beaver *'plus'* and other animal skins heading for the confluence of Horse Creek and the Green River for the 1833 Rendezvous to be held during the month of July.

CHAPTER NINE: THE GREEN RIVER RENDEZVOUS OF 1833

Arriving during the last days of June at Fort Bonneville in the Green River Valley was one Jacob Sutta, older brother to Elliott Bear Scat Sutta, leading five horses packed with beaver *'plus'*, followed by his long-time partner Wild Bill McGinty, also leading five horses heavily packed with packs of beaver *'plus'*. Riding up to the front gate of what was euphemistically called Fort Bonneville, Jacob hailed the guard and moments later he and his partner were admitted into the inner grounds of the rather smallish fort of log and mud buildings and home to the frontier's St. Louis Fur Company.

The two trappers tiredly dismounted their horses and were soon surrounded by St. Louis Fur Company fur graders, who immediately began unloading the trappers' horses, breaking down their packs and beginning the process of grading and counting the two men's *'plus'*. As the fur company graders began their arduous work, both Jacob and Bill warily watched the process of the grading and counting of the fruits of their labors for the past year while trapping up in the "Bighorns". Three hours later the grading and counting process was completed and Jacob was given a line of credit for those furs at the trading post's store and warehouses.

Jacob and Bill, not having had a drink of whiskey or rum for over two months ever since those provisions had run out back at their campsite, then headed for the fort's store where such spirits were kept and closely guarded, so they could purchase some whiskey with their newly earned credit from the sale of their furs. Tying their livestock up at the store's rail, both trappers went inside, sat down at a real table for the first time in almost a year, ordered supper and several 'horns' of rum. Soon the warmth from the fiery rum could be felt throughout their bodies, as the two men ordered several more drinks just as their supper arrived. When the supper had arrived, Jacob leaned back in the first real chair he had sat upon in over a year and proposed a toast with his partner for their very successful year's beaver trapping season. That and for having held onto their hair throughout, even though they had several dangerous and deadly run-ins with the local Blackfeet Indians out on the trapping grounds.

After supper and a number of drinks, the men adjourned to the fort's livery and had their horses grained, watered and lodged. Removing their rifles and saddlebags, Jacob and Bill made for the lodging quarters provided by the fort's Factor for upper class trappers such as Free Trappers Jacob Sutta and Wild Bill McGinty. There they spent their first night's sleep under a roof instead of the stars. Something the two Free Trappers did for the first time in months without the fear of worrying about being attacked by a hungry grizzly bear or a mess of Indians maddened over the fact the trappers were trapping and hunting buffalo on what were considered sacred Indian lands.

The following morning after having a welcoming breakfast with Fort Bonneville's St. Louis Fur Company's part-owner Robert Campbell, the two men adjourned to the livery where they arranged to have all of their 14 horses' (four riding and ten packhorses) old horseshoes removed and shod with new ones for the coming trapping season. Then it was a day-long 'shopping' trip over to the fort's warehouses selecting those provisions the two trappers figured would carry them through the coming trapping season. Six hours later and satisfied with their purchases of needed provisions, Jacob and Bill settled up with the trading post's Clerk and still had some credit left over from their previous trapping season. Having the Clerk and his *Engagés* haul their selected provisions over to where they were staying in a bunkhouse reserved for Free Trappers, Jacob and Bill then headed over to the company store for another home-cooked meal prepared by the cooks working for the St. Louis Fur Company.

After the two trappers had supper and a number of cups of rum, they decided they would head for their room and catch up on some much-needed sleep. THAT WAS WHEN IT HAPPENED! Stepping out from the company store, Wild Bill McGinty, seeing four new trappers arriving from the field with their caravan of horses and packed mules, grabbed Jacob's arm and hustled him back into the store and out of sight from the arriving fur trappers.

"What the hell is the matter with you, Bill?" asked Jacob Sutta in surprise over his partner's almost frantic actions.

Without a word being spoken, McGinty ran back to the building's front window and peered out at the four rough-looking and just-arriving Company Trappers like he had just seen a ghost! "Jacob, we have to get the hell out of here and fast! See those four Company Trappers just arriving? Well, back in Kentucky a number of years ago I killed their father! Their father and I were in the moonshining business and after a rather large sale of our liquor, my partner, their father, took all of the money from the sale of our liquor and gambled it all away. I hunted my old partner down and demanded an explanation as to why he had stolen my share of the money from the sale of our whiskey. Instead of coming clean with an explanation, he drew his knife and knowing his ability with a 'blade', I drew my pistol and shot him dead afore he could cut me up with his 'pig-sticker'. Ever since then, those four boys have been a-hunting me, swearing since I had killed their Pa they were going to kill me regardless of why I did what I had to do! Knowing that, I went west and joined up with you and we have been trapping for the last seven years together. They somehow found out that I went west to become a fur trapper and I guess they also came west hunting me. That being said, those boys are killers of the first degree as their reputations so attest back in Kentucky, and they aim to do me in if they ever find me. Knowing that, I have tried staying out of their ways and until now, have been successful. However, fate has placed the five of us together once again and there will be a killing of either me or them for sure if we stay here. Since I don't want to drag you into my business any more than I already have, we must leave or face those four killing sons-a-bitches. I am sorry I didn't share that tale with you earlier in our relationship, but figured I would get lost to those four boys by coming out west and just figured no use in bothering you with that story," said Bill McGinty somewhat shamefully. Shamefully because he knew if those four Travis Brothers ever saw Jacob and himself together, they would kill the two of them straightaway without any questions being asked.

"Well, I am sorry we have to leave this rendezvous so early. And in so doing, not get a chance to see some of our old friends and celebrate along with them for the rest of the month this 'shindig' lasts, over the fact that we all have kept our hair, brought in a mess of fine Made Beaver and have weathered another year out here in God's country. But if that is how you are thinking, then I say we load up our livestock and head back out into the Bighorns tomorrow right at first light afore them rascals get a rifle's sight on either of us and begin shooting for all their worth," said Jacob Sutta with a tone of finality in his voice.

The following morning before most of the celebrating fur trappers had gotten their legs under them after a night of heavy drinking, celebrating, hell-raising and were wandering about, saw Jacob Sutta and Wild Bill McGinty on their heavily packed horses heading out the front gate for their cabin back in the beaver-rich Bighorns without staying but four days at the Green River Rendezvous of 1833. That they did because of the 'bad blood' existing between Wild Bill McGinty and the four Travis Brothers over the killing of their father years earlier in Kentucky by Bill

McGinty over the theft of his share of the moonshine money owed him by old man Travis! Little did Jacob Sutta realize that his younger brother Bear Scat Sutta, who was looking for him, was but one day out from his arrival at the Green River Rendezvous of 1833!

******

One day after Jacob Sutta and his partner Wild Bill McGinty had left Fort Bonneville and the Green River Rendezvous of 1833 on their way back to their cabin in the Bighorns, Big Hat and Bear Scat rode through the front gate of the fort and the St. Louis Fur Company's trading post! There true to a tradition he had started, Robert Campbell just returning from the field and part-owner of the St. Louis Fur Company, met the two arriving Free Trappers with a cup of fiery rum for each man just as they lit down from their horses. After a few short directional instructions, the unpacking of the horses' fur bundles, grading and counting of their year's beaver trappings by the company's Clerks began. As the *Engagés* and Clerks performed those functions, Big Hat and Bear Scat carefully watched over the proceedings, making sure the counting and grading assessments matched their previous assessments of the numbers and quality of their furs.

That evening, Big Hat and Bear Scat with fur company credit slips in hand from their successful year of beaver trapping, were escorted into a vacant room in the company's bunkhouse reserved for arriving Free Trappers after they had cared for their valuable livestock. Ironically, it was the same room that Jacob Sutta and his partner had just vacated the morning before, as they beat a hasty retreat back to their familiar beaver trapping grounds to avoid a confrontation with the four, mean as snakes, Travis Brothers. Four brothers who were on the lookout at the rendezvous with a killing look in their eyes for Wild Bill McGinty for killing their pa...

The following morning after having breakfast as the special guests of Robert Campbell, Big Hat and Bear Scat saw to their livestock. There they arranged to have them housed in the fort's stable, grained and watered daily, and had all of their old horseshoes removed and all of their horses fitted with new ones so they would be ready for the coming trapping season. Following that and several days of celebrations later with other fur trappers and old friends, the two men made their ways to one of the warehouses and began the selections of what they figured would be the needed provisions for the two of them for the coming trapping season.

While at the warehouse selecting provisions for the coming trapping season, Bear Scat asked the Clerk assisting them in the purchasing process if he had ever heard of a fur trapper named Jacob Sutta. Without looking up from his sheet recording what Big Hat and Bear Scat were selecting for purchase with the credit from the sale of their beaver and wolf skins, the Clerk just shook his head in the negative. Then looking up, the Clerk advised that there were several other Clerks who had been assisting other trappers procuring their coming year's supplies, and that he would ask around to see if any of his counterparts knew the name of such a trapper. However he further advised that the trappers from the field and the Shoshone Indians arriving daily for the July rendezvous were just in their early stages of arrival and after a week or so with more arrivals, that he, Bear Scat, might have better luck in looking for that 'Jacob' fellow he was looking for at that time. Disappointed over the lack of good news but hopeful for better information of his brother from some of the other Clerks or other arriving trappers, Bear Scat dropped his searching for Jacob for the moment. He later joined Big Hat in some of the ongoing rendezvous celebrations, especially the fur company-sponsored shooting matches for a keg of rum to be awarded to the best shooter.

Later that evening while drinking with Big Hat's old friend Jim Bridger, who had won the 'rum keg shoot-off' and making it known that he and his partner Bear Scat were looking for a couple more reliable and experienced partners, Jim lit up like a coal oil lamp with a long wick. "Boys, I got just the trappers in mind that you are two looking for. I know two damn good trappers and straight shooters who I have trapped with previously over in the Bighorns. They just lost their two long-time partners to the Arikara Indians along the Missouri. As such, they have now moved over into this neck of the woods and away from such killing sons-a-bitches swarming all over their old trapping grounds further to the east. The big fella of these trappers I have in mind is called "Little Griz" Johnson because of his size and abilities when it comes to a fight against the odds. He stands over six-and-a-half feet tall, is strong as a bull, a damn good trapper even though he has the 'arthritis' pretty badly from wading in cold waters most of his life setting out beaver traps, and is an eager eater when it comes to chow time. His quiet as a snake moving across a damp field partner is one called Oliver "One Shot" Barnes. Now One Shot is not one to mess with as his name so indicates. Aside from me and "Old Betsy" here, I think One Shot is the best shooter in this here neck of the woods bar none! But as I swear on my dear mother's grave, they are 'true-blue', damn good trappers, as right as rain and good men to have in camp and on your side when the chips are down or a grizzly is looking you in the eye. We were going to have a get-together this evening and if you two be up to it and interested, swing on by my camp when it gets dark and I will introduce them to the two of you. That-away, you fellas can look one another over and see if you want to pair up for the extra protection that would provide for all of you by having four guns speaking for you when things go crossways instead of only the two you lads presently carry," said Bridger.

Later that evening, Big Hat and Bear Scat strolled over to Bridger's campsite amidst all kinds of surrounding happy yelling by freshly arriving trappers, other trappers 'whooping it up' after a round or two of rum, sounds of trappers firing their rifles into the night air in celebration, and a number of camped nearby Shoshone Indian dogs barking their heads off at every damned thing, real or imagined. Walking into the light of Bridger's campfire, Big Hat and Bear Scat immediately observed a giant of a man skewering huge chunks of buffalo meat on metal roasting stakes over the campfire. *That has to be Little Griz Johnson,* thought Bear Scat as he stepped into the light from the roaring campfire at Bridger's campsite. When Bear Scat and Big Hat strode into camp, Bridger arose from his sitting log near his campfire and introduced his old friend Big Hat to Little Griz and One Shot. Then Bridger turned saying, "This here fella and partner to my friend Big Hat, is for some reason called Bear Scat. I am not sure how he got such a handle but it sure has to be one hell of a story, were the truth of it to be told."

The four men shook hands all around and then Bridger invited them to sit and partake of some freshly roasted buffalo and several cups of rum from the keg he had just won in a shoot-off with a horde of other trappers, including Bear Scat who finished third. Big Hat and Bear Scat happily accepted Bridger's food and drink offer since both had been so busy getting their provisions squared away that neither had eaten all day. For the next four hours, 'greased' with many cups of rum, Big Hat, Bear Scat, Little Griz and One Shot got acquainted and found themselves immensely enjoying each other's company. Finally come the dawn, the men feasted again on freshly roasted chunks of buffalo along with additional cups of rum around Bridger's campfire. The four new friends and trappers agreed to meet again come noon at the fur company's eatery, have lunch and talk over the possibility of joining forces in the coming year's trapping season and the shared logistics of doing so.

Bear Scat, not used to drinking so much rum at one sitting, was glad to finally flop down in his bed in the bunkhouse and did not move one whit until Big Hat woke him up and reminded him that they were to meet Little Griz and One Shot for lunch. Walking over to the company store and eatery somewhat later, Bear Scat found himself almost floating along as he walked because of the lingering effects of the many previously consumed cups of rum from the evening before. He made a mental note that in the future he would drink less rum and talk more in order not to feel so fuzzy-headed the next day and unsure of his 'floppy' footing...

For the next four hours over lunch, the new friends talked over who would be bringing what to the table if a foursome of trappers was formed and seeing that was possible, made a division of the duties each man would shoulder once they were afield. With that and agreeing to form up into one trapping unit, the men shook on the deal and then separated to go their several ways in order to complete their final acts needed for the preparation as a group for the coming trapping season. Being that Bear Scat and One Shot both liked to cook, they formed an alliance and headed over to the fur company's warehouse to add more materials needed when it came to cooking for four men versus just two, with one of their group being an extra big eater. Soon both men were into selecting more spices, green coffee beans, 'carrots' of tobacco, a lot more flour, dried beans, dried apples and raisins, bags of rice, two extra Dutch ovens, as well as several new brass pots. The brass pots were selected by Bear Scat because when the grizzly bear had 'thundered' through their camp chasing Big Hat earlier in the year, it had been headshot by Bear Scat. However, the charging dead bear's momentum after being shot carried it right through Bear Scat's cooking area and its heavy body had slammed into the brass pots around the campfire, smashing all of them flatter than a beaver's tail. Hence Bear Scat purchasing three extra brass cooking pots to replace those smashed flat by a 'flying' dead grizzly bear.

Both men settled up with the Clerk accompanying them regarding their purchases, and then headed out from the warehouse to meet with Big Hat and Little Griz over at the livery to see how the work was progressing with the shoeing of all of their livestock. Walking out the door of the warehouse, Bear Scat accidentally bumped into another fur trapper entering to purchase needed provisions as well. Bear Scat, without really looking at the man entering the warehouse, excused himself for bumping into the stranger and then their eyes suddenly fixed upon each other...

Bear Scat found he was looking into the eyes of what he remembered as his former friend Muskrat! The one and same man, along with the rest of his party of trappers, who had abandoned bear scat out on the prairie during a heavy nighttime thunderstorm after taking everything he owned including his horse! In so doing, leaving Bear Scat afoot in a land of Indians and not knowing where to go, how to get there and with no food or other means, to die!

Bear Scat blinked in the bright daylight after leaving the darkened warehouse in order to make sure what he was seeing was what he thought he had seen. Muskrat on the other hand, hardly believing what he was seeing coming out from the warehouse, blinked to make sure he was not seeing a ghost! Not seeing a ghost, because he damn well knew that the greenhorn trapper from his original party, one Elliott Sutta, had died out on the prairie either at the hands of Indians or from starvation! *But sure as God made green apples, there was the man he had helped to leave out on his own in a sea of grass with plenty of wind to die,* he thought as he gave a quick shake of his head in disbelief!

What occurred during the next few seconds became like a slow motion blur to both men! Muskrat and Bear Scat were so close together at that moment in time that Muskrat quickly drew his pistol from his sash, thrust the end of its barrel forcefully onto Bear Scat's cheek and pulled the trigger before bear scat had the time to even blink over what was occurring! "CLICK!" Went the loudest sound Bear Scat had ever heard, as Muskrat's pistol forcefully stuck into the flesh of his cheek for a killing shot had misfired!

In one fluid movement, Bear Scat drew his sheath knife and rammed its blade deeply into Muskrat's lower belly! As he did, Muskrat's face revealed surprise over his pistol misfiring and then reflected an even stranger look over the instant sharp burning pain, as the blade of Bear Scat's knife ripped into Muskrat's lower intestines and then was forcefully ripped upward through the man's belly until the blade slammed against the man's breast bone!

"UUUMMMNED", groaned a dying Muskrat, as he grabbed Bear Scat's extended hand holding the gutting knife and then falling backwards, fell away from the knife as his intestines spilled out through the knife tear in his buckskin shirt and onto the ground in a bloody coil at his feet! As his ripped-open insides spilled out onto the ground, the man's partially digested breakfast spilled out as well!

BOOM! Went a pistol being fired from the man walking directly behind Muskrat upon seeing his friend mortally knifed and falling backwards towards him! In that shot quickly taken, the lead ball missed Bear Scat's face and blew off his right earlobe! Dropping his knife and grabbing his burning and now madly bleeding and painful earlobe, Bear Scat got a quick look at the man shooting at him through the cloud of black powder smoke from the shot fired by the man just feet away from his face! In an instant, Bear Scat recognized that the man doing the shooting was none other than Bear, the leader of the group of fellow trappers he had once befriended and because of his greenhorn status and frontier innocence, had seen to it that everything he owned was stolen in the dead of night and then had him abandoned out on the prairie to die!

BOOM! Went a surprise rifle blast from behind Bear Scat fired by one shot and as that bullet struck its target, Bear Scat, even through his pain and surprise of being shot in the ear along with the unexpected roar of a rifle being fired from close behind him, saw Bear's head explode into a spew of blood, bone and gray matter all over four other hard-looking trappers who were trailing the now dead man to the warehouse for supplies! Those four trappers trailing Muskrat and Bear, all new members of bear's trapping group as it turned out, collectively went for their rifles! This they did once the surprise had left them of having Bear's essence from being headshot at such a close range splattered all over the bunch of them!

However almost immediately, all four of those trailing trappers lowered their rifles slowly to the ground, as they now faced a determined Bear Scat and one shot facing them off with their four drawn and cocked pistols quickly pulled from their sashes!

About then, Robert Campbell, part-owner of the St. Louis Fur Company, arrived on the scene upon hearing the discharging of rifles and pistols near his warehouse holding huge stores of barrels of highly explosive black powder! "HOLD 'ER RIGHT THERE!" Campbell shouted, as he ran up to the two groups of trappers facing off from one another! "PUT THOSE DAMN GUNS DOWN OR ELSE WE ALL STAND A GOOD CHANCE OF BEING BLOWN FROM HERE TO KINGDOM COME IF ANY STRAY BULLETS HIT THOSE BARRELS OF STORED BLACK POWDER DIRECTLY BEHIND THE LOT OF YOU IN THAT WAREHOUSE!" yelled Campbell in a desperate tone of voice.

With those words of caution ringing in everyone's ears, both Bear Scat and One Shot slowly lowered their pistols as Campbell had ordered. That was when the four trappers who had previously lowered their rifles to the ground upon seeing Bear Scat and One Shot drawing down on them with their four cocked pistols, quickly made a move to pick up their rifles once again and resume the fight!

"DAMN THE FOUR OF YOU! THE FIRST MAN WHO LAYS A HAND ON HIS RIFLE I WILL KILL RIGHT HERE AND NOW," shouted Campbell, as he drew his own pistol from his belt and leveled it at the four trappers reaching midway down for their rifles! When he did, the four trappers quickly stepped away from their rifles lying on the ground and moved a short distance away to avoid being killed by a very mad and serious Campbell. "I told the four of you to stop this foolishness around so many kegs of gunpowder. Since the four of you ignored me, you can all pick up your gear and leave this here fort immediately. If any of you care to challenge me in this order, I will see to it that my men shoot the first son-of-a-bitch disobeying my order for all of you to leave. You stupid son-of-a-bitches could have blown this fort to Kingdom Come had one of your stray bullets hit any of those 40 kegs of gunpowder stored there in this warehouse. With that, I don't need your kind around this here fort! So pack up your gear and whether or not you have your next year's supplies, the four of you are banished from this fort and don't ever come back while I am in charge or I will have you shot! The four of you can just get your supplies from someone else and while you are at it, you can sell your furs there as well..."

About then, four *Engagés* from the fort arrived at a dead run carrying their rifles and headed for their boss to see what he wanted them to do under the circumstances. "You men, go and get a couple of horses over here and haul these two dead son-of-a-bitches off and drop them in any gully away from the fort and our horse and mule herds for the wolves and bears to clean up. Also, one of you men follow those four trappers who were just leaving. They have been ordered to pack up their gear and leave the premises and see to it that is exactly what they are going to do." Turning, Campbell said, "Alright, would you two care to tell me how all of this started and the explanation had better be good, or you will be going the same way those four son-of-a-bitches are heading as well, namely off this fort's grounds!"

Bear Scat placed both of his now un-cocked pistols back behind his sash, turned his head back towards his new partner still standing behind him saying, "Thanks, One Shot, for backing me up."

"Well, it looked like you were a bit outnumbered and needed some help. Plus since we are now partners it just seemed the right thing to do," said One Shot with a wicked little smile on his face, pleased over his rifle shot placement on such short order directly into the forehead of Bear, who looked like he needed a damn good killing to his way of thinking, and got one...

Turning, Bear Scat looked back at Campbell saying, "Where do I begin? Well, here goes. Several years back after my folks died in a tornado and having no living kin other than my older, fur trapper brother Jacob, I decided to come west and try my luck at finding him and learn the trade as a trapper as well. I unfortunately hooked up with the man I stabbed after he tried to kill me here this morning and one of his partners, the one One Shot headshot after he shot me in my ear. They were already in the trapping trade and had come to St. Louis to trade in their furs for the higher prices they would bring in that fur center versus out in the field at Fort Union.

I unfortunately and not knowing any better being a greenhorn, hooked up with them and we came north heading for Fort Union and the trapping fields further to the west. En route one night and while camping during a fierce thunderstorm, the entire group of five men took everything I had and quietly left me behind. When they did, that left me out on the prairie with only 13 bullets for my rifle, not knowing where I was and which way to go in order to get to Fort Union. In short, they left me out on the prairie to either be killed by Indians or starve to death. Well as you can see, they didn't succeed and here I am. However, I vowed to kill every one of those men if I lived long enough and ever located them. As fate would have it, the two remaining men from that group who tried to kill me I found this morning right here. The other three of that original group, as near as I could tell, were killed by the two dead men we killed this morning while they were trapping up on the upper reaches of the Porcupine River some time back. This morning, I met face to face with the man I knifed, one who called himself "Muskrat". We stumbled into each other in the doorway as I was leaving the warehouse and he was entering. He recognized me, immediately drew his pistol before I could react, stuck it onto the side of my face, pulled the trigger, and luckily it misfired. In turn, I drew my sheath knife and gutted him! However his partner, a man who called himself and was called by others "Bear", upon recognizing me and realizing his death was also near if I was given just half a chance, drew his pistol and shot for my head, hitting me in my ear! However, my partner here, One Shot, killed Bear after he tried to head shoot me but only managed to blow off my earlobe. Then the four you just expelled from the fort went for their rifles to shoot the two of us, but we got the drop on them with our pistols. That was when you arrived and put a stop to any further bloodshed and the rest is history."

"Well, that certainly explains why the shoot-out here at my warehouse this morning. I would say that you are now square with those who set you adrift out on the prairie without any real chance at survival and that leaves only you to settle up with either the devil or your Maker for what went on here today. As for those other four I just ran off, I would keep my powder dry and my eyes peeled any time in the future you are around any of them. Say, earlier you mentioned that you were looking for your brother, a man named Jacob my Clerk told me. That wouldn't be Jacob Sutta per chance would it?" asked Campbell.

"Holy Cow, is he here at the fort? If so, do you know where he is camping so I can go find him and then with what is left of my family, we can be reunited?" excitedly asked Bear Scat, as he wiped some more blood from his profusely bleeding ear off his neck and the shoulder of his buckskin shirt.

"You are several days too late. Jacob Sutta and his partner Wild Bill McGinty arrived here at the fort during the last few days of June and for some reason, skedaddled back to where they came from right after resupplying just a few short days after arriving. Hell, they didn't even join any of the rendezvous celebrations going on afore they left," replied Campbell.

"Do you know where they went?" excitedly asked Bear Scat.

"Hell, Boy, I don't even know where they were trapping. But I do know they brought in one hell of a mess of Made Beaver wherever they had been trapping. Maybe Bridger knows where they were trapping. He seems to know just about everyone and where they are staking out their trapping grounds," replied Campbell.

Later that evening, Bear Scat and One Shot sat around Bridger's campfire and related to Little Griz and Big Hat what had occurred that morning back at the warehouse. Big Hat just smiled over what Bear Scat had done in avenging what had been done to him early on by Bear, Muskrat and company. He was also grateful One Shot had been along, otherwise his friend and fellow Mountain Man would have been killed. Sitting back on his sitting log, Big Hat took another deep drink of Bridger's rum and found himself at peace over what he had been teaching Bear Scat over the many months and around the many campfires they had shared since they had been together, about surviving on the frontier as a fur trapper.

However there was one disappointment for Bear Scat that evening that surfaced. That was, Bridger did not know where Jacob Sutta had been trapping or to where he had returned for the next trapping season... But a number of cups of Bridger's rum soon made that disappointment fade off into the night air as Bear Scat, at Bridger's request, began making his brand of Dutch oven biscuits from Jim's hoard of supplies. As Bear Scat began mixing up the biscuit dough and preparing the Dutch ovens for the baking event to come, he found himself all of a sudden staring hard at Big Hat who was sitting just a few feet away on a sitting log by the campfire.

BIG HAT WAS AIMING HIS HAWKEN RIFLE RIGHT AT BEAR SCAT! Freezing in what he was doing around the Dutch ovens, Bear Scat could hardly believe his eyes as he slowly stood up and faced what appeared to be his sure death at the end of Big Hat's rifle from just a few feet away for whatever reason he knew not! Big Hat was aiming his rifle right at Bear Scat and its hammer was now in the full cocked mode! The next thing Bear Scat observed coming right at him almost in slow motion was a cloud of black powder smoke enveloping his body, hearing a loud explosion and feeling the concussive force of a speeding lead ball zipping right beside him so closely that he could feel the shock wave ripple his buckskin pants! Jumping back in alarm over what he felt was a surprising attempt on his life by his friend Big Hat, Bear Scat took two more steps and then froze once again. This time he could see Jim Bridger scrambling for his rifle as well and having survived over what he had thought that he was being shot at by Big Hat, Bear Scat knew he could not survive being shot at by the straight-shooting Jim Bridger if that was coming next...

Then Bear Scat became aware of more unusual sounding shooting in the other close at hand trappers' campsites! That shooting broke his 'frozen in place' stance and sent him sprinting for his rifle lying against a nearby sitting log. Grabbing his rifle and now seeing Big Hat hurriedly reloading, Bear Scat figured out that Big Hat had not been shooting at him but at something else that was dangerously close behind him! Whirling around to face what he figured had to be danger from attacking Indians and taking a quick look, Bear Scat did not see any Indians but did spot a huge timber wolf fleeing through other trappers' camps, biting several unfortunate trappers as he fled among them!

By now, the entire camping ground occupied by about 300 trappers at the rendezvous was roaring with the sounds of shooting, yelling and shouts of warning over a rabid wolf that was attacking any trapper who came within biting distance. (Author's Note: About a dozen trappers were bitten by a rabid wolf during the 1833 Rendezvous at Horse Creek! Before the rendezvous had ended, several trappers so bitten had run off into the forests acting strangely, never to be seen again, and several other trappers so bitten by that same rabid wolf, either died en route St. Louis with the returning fur caravan, died in the field later on from the effects of rabies, or just disappeared in the field never to be seen ever again.)

About then, Jim Bridger strode up alongside Bear Scat saying, "Bear Scat, our friend, Big Hat just saved you from dying a horrible death. That there wolf in camp with the froth-covered mouth probably had rabies and was stalking you, when Big Hat shot at him just mere feet away from where you were standing and making your biscuits with your back turned to him!"

With those words over what had just occurred, Bear Scat took a quick look over at Big Hat who was still reloading his rifle and grinned. *No matter where he turned, it always seemed that Big Hat was either teaching him something or 'pulling his irons from the fire',* thought Bear Scat thankfully. That evening after the other shooting around the trappers' campsites had died down and the wolf-biting incidents had died away, even more rum flowed in Jim Bridger's camp in celebration for surviving another of the dangers found out on the frontier.

By July 24th of that year, the Green River Rendezvous had petered out, and any trappers who were continuing their trade for at least another year had provisioned up and were returning to their trapping grounds of choice. Additionally, those trappers who had enough of the hardscrabble life of that of a trapper and the dangers associated with living on the frontier and were quitting the trade, had hired on as guards on the fur caravan that was returning to St. Louis with that year's $60,000 take of furs from the 1833 Rendezvous. (Author's Note: The time spent as a fur trapper on the frontier has been reported to only be about 2.7 years. After that, horse wrecks, grizzly bears, accidents, freezing to death, drownings, death on the end of an arrow shaft or a speeding lead ball, or the trappers just walking away from the hardscrabble life, accounted for that of such a short life span as a trapper. For those engaged in other parts of the fur-trapping industry such as Clerks, *Engagés*, blacksmiths and the like, their associations with such a demanding trade were noticeably longer because of a less dangerous and exacting type of life lived.)

CHAPTER TEN: NEW PARTNERS AND "BEAR'S" DEADLY LEGACY

The 25th of July in 1833, found Big Hat in the lead of a caravan of horses and three other fur trappers heading southwest to their old trapping grounds in the lands of the Southern Paiutes. In the middle of the fur trappers' caravan rode Little Griz and One Shot, trailed by Bear Scat bringing up the rear with his heavily loaded horses as well. Big Hat made sure the caravan of trappers and heavily loaded horses were not hurried in order to avoid injury to them being so heavily loaded. That or initiating an unnecessary horse wreck common among heavily loaded pack strings when the heavy packs shifted or badly chafed the backs of the animals carrying them.

Several days later come dusk found the caravan pulling into Big Hat and Bear Scat's old dugout campsite. Just as Big Hat pulled into the area of their old horse corral, his riding horse and the five trailing packhorses he was leading loaded with supplies began acting up like they were walking in and among a nest of snakes. Finding it difficult to control his normally very steady riding horse in the face of frontier surprises, Big Hat quickly realized danger was at hand and immediately led his horse and string of pack animals away from the area of the dugout and corrals! When he led his horse train away from their campsite, the other trappers realizing he did so for a good reason, followed suit. Moving their horse train about 100 yards away from the dugout and up onto the hillside above their old camp, Big Hat spotted the possible reason the horses were so skittish. Handing his horse's reins off to Little Griz, Big Hat stepped lightly from his saddle and began walking along the ridgeline away from the still very nervous string of horses over what they were scenting in the air.

After walking about 20 yards distant from the string of trappers and their horses, Big Hat paused and looked down at the ground. There before him was a freshly dug large hole in the ground where he and Bear Scat had buried their old friend and fellow trapper David Hager, after he had been crushed to death when their newly built cache house roof had collapsed upon him. Aside from a few scraps of buckskin clothing, the burial site was empty and its occupant dug up and totally consumed by what appeared to be a grizzly bear! Then it dawned on Big Hat why the horses had been so nervous when the caravan had approached their old campsite. Walking back in the gathering dusk, Big Hat had One Shot dismount and together the two trappers walked off the ridgeline and headed towards the front entrance to the dugout. Making an approach towards the dugout with its heavy log door hanging on just one leather strap acting as a hinge, with their rifles held at the ready, purposely making lots of noise in case the bear that had eaten David's entire body might be living inside, the two men cautiously approached the dugout's opening. As the trappers walked even closer to the dugout's entrance, their noses due to the strong stench in the area, told them that a grizzly bear had taken up residence in their former dugout home and the living site was to be cautiously approached. However after making lots of 'human' sounds and throwing a number of rocks inside the dugout area in order to purposely disturb anything living inside, it was determined by the men that the site had been abandoned by whatever bear had been living therein earlier. Then with a shout and a wave of his arm, Big Hat let it be known it was now safe for the other men and their still nervous horses to come down off the ridgeline. However he advised the men to get off and lead their horses into their corral so no one would get injured in a horse wreck if the animals spooked once again.

Once the men were all together again, they jointly entered the dugout only to find that a grizzly bear had temporarily made the dugout's living area his home while Big Hat and Bear Scat had been at the rendezvous. But for some reason, the grizzly had since abandoned the dugout living site and was nowhere to be seen. With the mystery of the nervous horses smelling the old close at hand presence of a grizzly bear now solved, the four men set about making the site livable for themselves. While Bear Scat built a fire in the outside cooking pit area, Big Hat and One Shot cleaned out the refuse left by the bear inside the dugout. In the meantime, Little Griz began unpacking the horses, stacking the packs off to one side, hobbling the horses and letting them out to graze, while the other men made the living area once again shipshape for the trappers' living that was soon to come.

As Bear Scat continued making preparations for the men's supper, the rest of the trappers began moving all of their packs and supplies into the dugout for protection against any evening thunderstorms, hungry critters or theft from passing Indians come nightfall. Not forgetting that Little Griz was an 'eager eater', Bear Scat made sure there were ample chunks of buffalo meat roasting away on skewers taken from an earlier-killed buffalo, the coffee pot was full and steaming away, and he had three Dutch ovens beginning the process of baking his signature, special occasion cinnamon-laced biscuits. Additionally, he had placed an ample supply of pinto beans into one of his newly purchased brass pots to begin soaking for the following day's supper, along with another brass kettle soaking and plumping up a mess of dried raisins, rice and apples for a special Dutch oven compote desert for the morrow's supper as well.

The men worked long into the evening setting up their campsite, cutting and hauling firewood, hauling water, graining their horses, unpacking their provisions, and conveniently arranging those that would be needed for meal makings in the days to come. Then with

Big Hat leading the way and showing Little Griz and One Shot where their old cache site was located when they had left the first time for the rendezvous at Horse Creek, had those two men dig it up and return all the items so cached to their dugout for future use as well. Finally, calm and the evening's darkness settled over the trappers' campsite as they finished their supper and finally bedded down in the dugout with its outside log door's leather hinge finally repaired, old grizzly bear smell and all...

The next morning the trappers were up early since they figured they had a full day ahead of them continuing to make their camp livable for all concerned. As Bear Scat performed his duties around the campfire, Little Griz had hung his mirror on one of the cottonwood trees near their horse corral and was beginning to shave. As he did, Bear Scat filled the air once again full of those smells associated with roasting buffalo meat on metal skewers, boiling coffee and the Heavenly smell of Dutch oven biscuits wafting through the air every time Bear Scat lifted the cast iron pot lids checking for degree of biscuit browning.

Meanwhile, over near their horse corral, Little Griz leaned down over his wash pan, splashed the warmed water over his face, lathered up his shaving brush with soap, and commenced applying its soapiness to his craggy and still dirty face so he could shave. Bending over once again, he lay down his shaving brush on a corral rail, took up his straight razor, checked his face in his mirror to make sure he had soap everywhere on his whiskers for the shaving to come, blinked and then blinked once again. There filling his mirror looking from immediately behind him was the face of a very large and curious grizzly bear staring quizzically at the crazy antics of one of those 'human-smelling things'! Whirling around to make sure of what he was seeing in his shaving mirror, Little Griz observed about a 750-pound, nine-foot-tall grizzly bear standing on his hind legs not ten feet away quietly sizing 'the human-smelling thing' up!

"YEEEOOOWH!" yelled Little Griz, forgetting all about looking beautiful, whirled himself around, took three clumsy steps sideways, tripped and fell flat on his heavily soaped face in the dried horse manure scattered inches deep around the corral! Then in a panic and trying to get up so he could run, all Little Griz could do was explosively dig with his flying feet and hands in the dried, loose horse manure in such a manner that he literally coated the face of the grizzly which had now moved dangerously even closer to the flailing hind end of Little Griz! Finally gaining traction on the soil under the loose manure, Little Griz managed to get to his feet and forgetting his near at hand rifle, took off running for Bear Scat and his cooking fire for the assistance a fellow trapper could render under such circumstances.

Simultaneously hearing Little Griz's terrified howling and caterwauling, Bear Scat looked up from tending his biscuit making duties just as Big Hat and One Shot hearing the same verbal 'hell-raising', came charging out the door of their dugout! Bear Scat, upon seeing Little Griz storming his way with flailing arms, a funny looking soapy face all covered with dried horse dung and right behind him, a now mad-as-hell charging and fast-gaining MONSTER-sized grizzly bear with wide open mouth just feet from the fleeing trapper's hind end, froze for just a second! Then upon visualizing such a surprising and dangerous unfolding situation, Bear Scat dropped the lid of his Dutch oven he had been holding and took off running for his nearby rifle leaning against a sitting log! In his hurry to get to his rifle, Bear Scat running by the edge of the cooking fire, hooked his foot on one of the stuck in the dirt and angled metal buffalo meat cooking skewers and fell flat on his face in a cloud of dust, ashes and wood chips!

Meanwhile, Big Hat, racing out the front door of their dugout and upon seeing what was happening with Little Griz, quickly turned to run back inside the dugout and retrieve his rifle. When he did, he was flat knocked asunder onto his backside and blown clean out the front door by the bodily impact of One Shot, who was charging right behind trying to respond to Little Griz's frantic and terrified bellowing! 'Back at the ranch', when Bear Scat had hooked his foot onto the angled into the ground cooking skewer calmly roasting a huge slab of buffalo alongside the blazing fire, he had jerked it out from the dirt and had flopped the steaming-hot cooking slab of buffalo meat and metal skewer onto his bottom, as he frantically tried crawling towards his nearby rifle in order to save Little Griz from a fate worse than death itself! It took just a long second for the sizzling hot and greasy three-pound slab of buffalo meat and hot metal skewer to make 'themselves' more than felt through Bear Scat's buckskins covering his previously bear claw-raked and now scarred and still sensitive hind end! "YEEEOOOWH!" yelled Bear Scat, as he forgot all about grabbing his rifle to aid his friend and ended up grabbing his now steaming hind end instead to remove the hot and still sizzling slab of meat and more than hot metal skewer laid across the cheeks of his 'last part over the fence'! However, when Bear Scat grabbed the steaming hot chunk of roasting buffalo meat and the hot metal skewer to remove it from his 'complaining hind end', it 'grabbed' him right back as well!

In the meantime, Big Hat and One Shot, one on top of the other lying out on the dirt in front of the dugout trying to unscramble from one another, looked like two bear cubs in a sack trying to get out! By now the horses, upon seeing a charging and badly smelling grizzly bear right in their midst, began jumping the corral's side rails and shouldering their ways out through the closed gate, scattering gate logs every which way to Sunday! Suffice to say, the grizzly bear that had dug up David Hager earlier and had eaten him and then subsequently had later discovered a quiet unoccupied dugout below the ridgeline in which to digest his gruesome meal, now found himself surrounded by a mad world of things out of kilter in his previously quiet world! Taking into account all of the pandemonium happening all around him and all at the same time as well, the bear stopped his charge after Little Griz in mid-stride, then fled off into the nearby brush below the trappers' camp. In so doing, it left only a small cloud of dust as evidence that things had gone badly wrong back at the 'shaving tree', and that it was best in that bear's world having never previously experienced a live human being before, to leave such noisy and confusing 'badly smelling things' alone…

Later back at the dugout, Big Hat found that he had a severely bloodied nose as a result of his collision with One Shot. On the other hand, One Shot had a badly blackening eye, where after colliding with Big Hat, had been blasted and fallen face first onto the metal corner of the butt stock of his rifle and in so doing, had messed up his 'shooting eye' in the process. Looking over at Bear Scat's 'wreck' caused by a hooked foot under a roasting skewer alongside the campfire, found that he had a greasy burn blister on his already bear-damaged hind end, and a badly swollen burned right hand from grabbing the still cooking chunk of meat and the hot metal cooking skewer! Little Griz on the other hand, in his urgency to escape a mauling and maybe even worse, had charged in terror through the cooking area knocking over the brass pots of soaking beans, raisins, rice and apple slices and in the process, had painfully lifted off his big toe's nail when his moccasin-covered foot had collided with one of the heavily loaded brass pots! Suffice to say, that evening's meal was quietly consumed with a minimum of talk in order to hide a maximum amount of embarrassment for all comers, except for the earlier 'hell-raising' grizzly bear down by the beaver ponds who was currently happily, and quietly I might add, munching a beaver it had just caught…

The next morning after a hearty breakfast, the four contrite and somewhat worse for wear trappers set to enlarging their corral in order to accommodate the extra horses Little Griz and One Shot had brought to the group. Two days later, a much larger and stouter corral had been constructed, much to the satisfaction of the men involved. Then it was off to do one of the things all of the men loved doing, namely hunting buffalo. Finding a feeding herd was fairly simple because all they had to do that morning of the hunt was to follow the pulverized trail out on the prairie a large herd of buffalo had left from the evening before, along with the numerous 'buffalo chips' dotting the prairie. Moving in behind a small set of rolling hills, Bear Scat and One Shot being the group's best shooters, crawled to the crest of the hills and with Big Hat and Little Griz hurriedly reloading the shooter's rifles, soon had 12 buffalo shot down from the small herd when they went into a 'stand' once the shooting started. Then the work began after the men had eaten their fill of raw buffalo liver taken from two of the cows. As Big Hat and Little Griz butchered out the choicest cuts of lean meat, Bear Scat and One Shot loaded all the panniers full of the bloody slabs of meat onto their packhorses. When all of the packhorses had been loaded with all of the rich lean buffalo meat they could carry, plus the four best cow skins and one pannier partially full of buffalo brains, the trappers mounted up and headed back to their dugout for the important processing work to be done before the meat spoiled.

For the next two days, the four trappers cut most of the buffalo meat into thin strips and hung it from their previously built smoking racks. Then while Big Hat tended the meat smoking process, the rest of the men kept him in rotten cottonwood they had collected from the groves of nearby trees because that type of wood created the densest smoke. In between trips collecting and hauling smoking wood for their meat and jerky smoking racks, the men scraped the four staked-out cow buffalo hides down to the root hairs, and with brains and water from the spring near their horse corral began the brain-tanning process of the hides. Then once the brain-tanning process had been completed to the men's satisfaction, the hides were smoked over their smoking racks as well, to make them supple when made into buffalo robes to be used by the trappers during the harshest of winter weather. Robes which were welcome when the men were out and about doing the fall and spring beaver trapping and during their winter wolf-trapping escapades as well. Once the meat had been sufficiently smoked or made into jerky, it was placed into previously brain-tanned deerskins and hung from the support beams and poles in the dugout for future use when out on the trail come winter.

Upon completion of the meat processing, the men turned to making small mountains of cast bullets for their various calibers of rifles and pistols. Once that vital chore was completed, knives, axes and shovels were sharpened and their collection of beaver and wolf traps were smoked to help reduce the 'man' smell. Lastly, the four men set to felling as much dead timber they could find, then carried and dragged the logs back into their camp for the coming winter when the deep snows made wood hauling not a labor of love but one of necessity.

With the fall beaver trapping season upon them, the four Free Trappers spent one evening making sure they had filled at least two powder horns apiece from their kegs and had placed plenty of percussion caps, fire steels, extra lead balls, and bullet 'worms and reamers' in case one had a misfire and needed to remove the stuck ball, into their 'Possibles bags'.

The following morning with a cold nip in the air, the men hastily finished their breakfast, eager to mount up and begin their fall beaver trapping season in earnest. Big Hat knowing the beaver trapping location he figured they should start their fall trap line, led the way. He was followed by One Shot and Little Griz trailing their packhorses carrying panniers full of shovels, spools of trap wire, 20 traps, axes and a small saw to be used in cutting the trap's 'dead wood', deep water anchor poles (precludes the beaver from chewing on them). Bringing up the rear was Bear Scat who provided cover in case they were jumped by Indians from the rear of their little caravan, a historically favorite attack method used by many bands of Plains Indians for the confusion it caused among the ranks of those being attacked.

Once on the newly selected trap line site, it had been previously determined among the trappers that Bear Scat would be the one responsible for the selection of trapping sites, trap setting and beaver removal. Those reasons being that Bear Scat was the youngest and did not suffer so much from being arthritic from many previous years of wading up to his waist and immersion in the often icy beaver trapping waters as did Big Hat and Little Griz. Plus he was very good at what he did when it came to trapping beaver. Since One Shot and Big Hat were very good shooters and

Plains Indian savvy, they were selected to always remain horsed and on guard against Indian incursions and any problems that occurred from wild critters, while Little Griz and Bear Scat attended to the on-the-ground trapping duties. Little Griz was also to provide Bear Scat any support needed while setting the traps and be the trapper providing him the dried wood anchor poles cut from the nearby willow thickets or cottonwood groves for each trap set. Additionally, Little Griz was the best man with a skinning knife and was selected to do all of the skinning of the beaver trapped in the field.

On that day as Bear Scat walked along the watered areas selected by Big Hat for setting out their strings of traps and looking for fresh beaver sign, Little Griz walked along behind him carrying the traps and tools he would need in order to make proper beaver trap sets. Watching from atop his horse, Big Hat smiled over just how smoothly the team of trappers worked together, a testimony to all the men's previous experience as trappers to his way of thinking and their love for what they were doing. Shortly thereafter, Bear Scat began making numerous trap sets in the beaver-rich area. In fact, there was so much fresh beaver sign in the area they had selected in which to set their traps, that just six hours later Bear Scat had set out all 20 of their traps and was in the process of scouting out their next day's beaver sets as well!

Stopping in between two sets of rolling hills in a grove of cottonwoods, the four men rested and feasted on jerky as they watched the nearby antics of a small herd of buffalo trying to keep two prairie wolves at bay and away from their young of the year. All of a sudden from around the base of a nearby hill stormed a stream of horseflesh and humanity, as a band of 23 Indians rode right into the small herd of now surprised buffalo standing off the two wolves and began shooting! Losing all interest in eating their pieces of jerky because of the possibility of danger at hand, the trappers immediately went for their rifles lying across their laps and almost as if on cue, took up their reins with their other hand and simultaneously melted back deeper into the grove of cottonwoods taking their pack animals with them. From there and away from prying hostile Indian eyes, the trappers quietly dismounted, moved their horses even deeper into the grove of trees and prepared for battle in case they were inadvertently discovered by the Indians now killing buffalo nearby out on the prairie.

For the next four hours, the trappers remained trapped in their grove of trees as the successful Indian hunters began butchering out the 18 buffalo they had just killed. Like the trappers, the Indians stopped their hunt after putting the 18 buffalo down and began gathering around two buffalo, eating chunks of raw and warm liver from the dead animals. Then all of a sudden, the hidden trappers' problems were compounded. Into view streamed a number of Indian women, children with their dogs and horses pulling travois from around the nearby base of hills! Soon there was a general celebration among the Indians, as the eating of raw livers, barking dogs, butchering of buffalo, the loading of meat upon the travois, and numerous dog fights over the scraps of meat tossed their ways, continued throughout the remaining afternoon.

Soon more problems arose over the closeness of the Indians to the trappers still remaining hidden and basically trapped within the grove of cottonwood trees. Several of the Indian women came over to the grove of trees to relieve themselves and with that, the trappers were forced to move even more deeply into the trees in order to avoid being discovered. It was then that Big Hat gathered the men around him saying, "We need to leave this grove of trees. I fear those Indians will later in the day move into this grove of trees and camp for the night. With 18 buffalo down and them not wanting to waste any of the meat, I am sure that will require all of them to camp out for the night. That means they will camp out somewhere near the dead buffalo not yet butchered in order to keep the wolves and coyotes from coming in and eating some of their kill. I think we had best sneak out through the back side of this grove of trees and beat a hasty retreat into another hiding place far away from here if at all possible. Especially if their men discover our fresh shod horse tracks in the same grove of trees in which they choose to camp for the night."

With those words of frontier wisdom, Big Hat could see acknowledgement in the other men's eyes over what he was saying, which was further evidenced in their support for his idea when all of them moved without being asked any further to gather up their horses, and began sneaking out through the rear of the grove of trees they now were hidden within. Unfortunately, there was too much open prairie all around them and the trappers could only move about 200 yards further down a waterway into another grove of cottonwoods in which to hide. There they dragged a number of old dead logs into a pile, so if discovered the trappers would have some form of cover from which to hide behind and defend themselves. Then all they could do was wait to see what kind of a hand they would be dealt from fate were their shod horse tracks discovered in that first grove of cottonwoods...

Sure as Big Hat had predicted, right at dusk the group of Indians moved into the grove of cottonwoods they had been hiding in earlier and set up their camp. Soon the trappers could see the light from several of their campfires and hear lots of happy sounds of talking and laughing coming from that area. Suffice to say, the trappers spent a rather miserable night in the late fall's cold night air having come not prepared for an overnight and since they had eaten what little jerky they had brought with them, supper was not on their evening's menu either. Additionally, it was not yet cold enough to keep the mosquitoes at bay and without the benefit of a smoky campfire, the men suffered horribly as did their livestock being so close to a heavily watered area!

Come daylight the following day and the warming air, the trappers suffered more of the same, especially with the dense clouds of hungry mosquitoes. Come noontime, the Indians had cleaned up all they wanted and could pack away of the dead buffalo from the day before's hunt, and once again in a stream of humanity and horseflesh returned from whence they had so surprisingly come. Waiting in hiding for a couple more hours to make sure some sort of Indian straggler would not catch them leaving the area, the previously outnumbered men finally headed back in the direction from whence they had come. However in so doing, Bear Scat was able to check his previous day's sets of beaver traps since it was not wise to advertise one's presence in country by leaving a number of dead beaver hanging in traps in the beaver ponds as evidence of the close at hand presence of the much-hated white man...

As it turned out, there was a dead beaver in every trap and two had been partially consumed by what appeared to be mink or river otter. As such, those partially consumed beaver were useless and tossed off to one side since their pelts had been so damaged in the scavenging process. Also, the traditional first day's trappings which usually entailed bringing several of the larger and fatter beaver carcasses back to camp for a celebratory first day's trapping supper was foregone. Since the animals had hung in the traps too long before being removed, the trappers figured they would not be good eating, so they were just skinned out and the carcasses disposed of along the waterways for the other land predators to find and consume. Once the traps had been checked, the dead beaver removed and skinned, the carcasses dumped on-site, the horses loaded, and the trappers headed for their hidden campsite, it was long after dark. But returning by the light of the stars, moon and the good night vision of their horses, the men were able to do so without further incident. Then as Bear Scat, the designated camp cook, started a campfire and began making supper for the very hungry men, especially Little Griz, the other three men removed any excess fat and meat from the remaining undamaged beaver skins, stretched and hooped the same using limber willow limbs from their stockpile. Following those activities, they were treated to a dinner of Dutch oven biscuits, hot coffee, a warmed-up pot of pinto beans laced with wild onions, and a raisin cobbler. Sitting around the campfire late into the evening nursing cups of coffee and rum, the men itched and scratched their numerous mosquito bites from the evening before and cussed the critters causing such irritations. But they also were very pleased with their catch of beaver, only two of which were considered juveniles and the other 16 being considered Made Beaver!

Without further interruptions in their fall beaver trapping operation, the four trappers harvested so many beaver that they had to take one day off and store their extra hoard of beaver *'plus'* in their old cache site because there was no more storage space in their dugout! Shortly thereafter, 'Old Man Winter' covered the land with his white cloak of snow, blew his bitter temperatures into every nook and cranny and with that, the men pulled their beaver traps ending their fall trapping season because the ice was too thick to easily trap under. Then there was a flurry of activity as the four men headed into the nearby groves of cottonwood trees with their axes and saws and brought forth more short logs, and hauled them with their teams of horses back to their cabin for their winter woodpile in case the winter's blasts were longer and colder than expected. Following that, the men sallied forth once again on a buffalo hunt and brought back to their campsite the best parts of ten buffalo for their meat supply. Most of the now near-frozen meat was hung under their meat poles, and between the always present gray jays and magpies along with the four trappers, meat was had by all. As for the remains of the buffalo not taken back to the men's dugout and camp, wolf traps were cleverly arrayed around each of the kill sites waiting for the unwary wolf to make his final fatal mistake on the frontier. The rest of that winter was spent wolf trapping and hide processing, deer hunting and the processing of those hides to act as covers on their bundles of beaver *'plus'* once en route to the up and coming 1834 Rendezvous, buffalo hunting, the casting of more bullets for what seemed to be their always 'hungry' rifles, woodcutting for their winter woodpile, and more buffalo hunting for fresh meat because such meat was preferred by the four trappers over any other kind.

One morning come late spring found Bear Scat and One Shot around the campfire rattling their Dutch ovens, pots and pans, with Bear Scat grumbling over a badly cut finger received while trying to slice up and skewer several chunks of half-frozen buffalo meat fresh off one of their ever-present meat pole carcasses for roasting over the open fire. About then, Big Hat came back from taking his 'daily dozen' over at their latrine, walked over to his sitting log by the campfire, poured himself a steaming cup of 'trapper's coffee', and said to Bear Scat, "Fix up a good and hearty breakfast for all of us. I think with most of the ice having melted out from the deeper watered areas near the beaver houses, we need to get our gear together, see if we can't set a few beaver traps and catch some of those really prime beaver who have wintered under the ice growing heavier coats for us to take and then sell at the coming rendezvous at Hams Fork. What do you think, Bear Scat?"

Bear Scat just grinned over hearing Big Hat's all-too-familiar spring trapping words announcing he was ready to shake off his winter 'trembles' and get on with catching some beaver. "I kind of figured one of these mornings you would come bursting forth like new leaves of the year on the cottonwoods and announce you were ready for more beaver trapping. Me, I think I could wait until summer when the water and mud is not so dang icy cold, especially when I am the one walking around in those still frigid spring waters like a damn fool setting the traps," he said, with an "I can't wait to get to trapping either" smile spread clear across his face.

"You had better roll out Little Griz so he and you can begin saddling and loading out our packhorses for the day's events to come. While you are doing that, I will see to fixing something up that will stick to our ribs in case we get stuck out there like we did last fall when the Indians were killing buffalo right in front of where we were hidden in that grove of cottonwoods," said Bear Scat, as he got out his flour mixing bowl for his Dutch oven biscuits soon to come.

After eating a hearty breakfast made around roasted buffalo steaks, the four trappers gathered up the last of their traps and trapping gear for the day and headed out. That morning as usual, Big Hat led the contingent of trappers with One Shot and Little Griz herding along their pack animals behind and Bear Scat bringing up the year. Since the trappers had trapped out most of the beaver near their campsite, that morning found the men venturing about three miles further from their camp following the many waterways before Big Hat signaled they had arrived in their newest beaver trapping waters.

Stopping near a number of larger beaver-dammed and ponded waterways, Big Hat sat there on his horse for a few moments surveying the potential trapping areas lying out before him. Then waving Bear Scat forward, he quietly waited further surveying the area's beaver trapping potential until his partner had arrived on his horse. "What do you think of starting our trap line in these large ponded areas to our front and running it along the waterways extending further to the northeast?" asked Big Hat of his fellow trapper, Bear Scat.

"Well, I certainly see a larger number beaver houses all over the place not to mention all the other sign, so it is pretty obvious there surely are a lot of beaver in this area. But from what I am seeing, the water looks a whole lot deeper than I am used to trapping in from years past," replied Bear Scat, as he stood up in his stirrups so he could see further along the waterways under consideration.

"Yes, we would be trapping in deeper water but from the looks of all the beaver houses in these waterways and all of the feeding and beaver slide signs, I would think we stand to harvest a slurry of beaver and probably a whole lot of larger-in-size adults as well," said Big Hat, as he too examined the watered areas around them by standing tall in his stirrups so he could see better as well.

"Then let us get cracking and I intend to start right over there by that fresh beaver slide next to that clump of willows," said Bear Scat, as he dismounted and then slipped out from his buckskin pants and moccasins. Walking back to the first packhorse, Bear Scat lifted out one of their beaver traps from a pannier and then removed a small bottle of castoreum from his 'Possibles bag' and began walking over to the beaver slide with its many fresh beaver tracks in the mud showing mute evidence of recent use. "WHOOO-EEE!" Bear Scat yelped, when he waded out into the much deeper and icy spring water, especially when the water level reached his crotch and hind end for the first time! Then carefully feeling his way along in the deeper water and mud until he was opposite where the beaver slide area entered the water, Bear Scat found a small but solid bench of ground just about four inches under the water near the slide and then laid down his previously set and ready-to-go trap. Taking his hands, he swirled the muddy water around and over the trap until he had swirled enough muddy water over the trap to hide it from the wary eyes of any approaching beaver. Walking out the length of trap chain carefully and then looking up at Little Griz in an acknowledging way, Bear Scat caught a stout anchor pole tossed to him. Turning, he then walked out into waist deep waters sucking in his wind all the way due to the depth and cold of the waters. Once at the end of the trap's chain, he hammered in his anchor stake with the trap's end ring attached. Then the naked from the waist down Bear Scat hustled his way out from the deeper waters and began walking along the edge of the next waterway looking for more active beaver-use sign in which to set another trap. Two more hours of trap setting found Bear Scat arriving at a very large and much deeper beaver pond whose bottom was covered with pond grasses. As he ventured into those beaver-rich waters, he could see more active dams, beaver slides near the willows, numerous beaver houses along the far length of the waterway, and even a few beaver swimming unconcernedly nearby as long as he did not make any sudden moves. That time he stayed immersed up to his waist as he walked the full quarter-mile 'mud-deep' waterway, never leaving the waters as Little Griz would set the trap and using the length of the chain, swing the trap out over the deeper waters into the waiting hands of Bear Scat. Then he would toss the anchor poles he was cutting as he went along out to Bear Scat in the waters and the next set would soon be made. By now the icy waters had numbed Bear Scat's feet and legs all the way up to his now immersed hind end! But his work continued until he had set his last trap in the pond's deeper waters and then he began making his way towards the shore, stumbling occasionally in the deep and sticky mud. Finally crawling up onto a grass-covered bank, Bear Scat could immediately feel the warmth of the air on his numbed parts as he lay there in the warming grasses getting his breath. About then, Big Hat, Little Griz and One Shot rode up to where Bear Scat lay on the grassy knoll getting his wind and when they did, they all sat there in their saddles looking down at their fellow trapper in wide-eyed amazement!

"Don't just sit there! Would someone bring me my dry pants and moccasins so I can get dressed and warm up a bit?" asked Bear Scat, as he continued lying there stretched out on the warm grassy bank with his eyes closed in relief over now being out from the frigid waters. Not a single one of his fellow trappers moved but just sat there high atop their horses and stared down at their half-naked fellow trapper in apparent disbelief! "What the hell is the matter with you guys?" said Bear Scat looking up at his friends. "Would someone please bring me my pants and moccasins so I can get dressed and begin to warm up?" asked Bear Scat as he sat up and looked up once again at his fellow trappers. When he did, he noticed that every one of his friends was just sitting there and looking all funny-like at him as he sat there on the warm grass. Scrambling to his feet, Bear Scat turned facing his friends saying, "Yeah, I know. I am not 'built' like the rest of you but if someone does not fetch my pants and moccasins, it will be a cold day in hell before I make another raisin and rice compote for you ungrateful wretches come suppertime."

The three trappers, seemingly oblivious to Bear Scat's words, continued staring down at him with looks of disbelief spelled clear across their faces! Then Bear Scat got pissed, jumped up and started to walk back to his horse and fetch his own clothing and when he did, he became aware that from the waist down he appeared to be as black as coal! Taking a closer unbelieving look at what was originally his nakedness, Bear Scat saw that he was totally covered with long black leeches! Thousands of them! So much so that he could not see one bit of his white skin! Shocked over what he was seeing, he just stood there dumbfounded for a moment, then in terror began slapping and trying to scrape off all the black wiggling evil-looking things! His frantic movements trying to dislodge all the thousands of leeches fastened to his lower body immediately brought his previous disbelieving in what they were seeing compatriots flying off their horses and with their now drawn gutting knives, began scraping off the wiggling vile bloodsuckers!

Now hopping around in pure panic, Bear Scat kept trying to brush off the leeches. However, they did not brush off but had to be individually picked off with fingers or scraped off with the men's knives! Then it got even trickier when the men in their hurry to aid their afflicted friend began removing those leeches attached to Bear Scat's privates or those that were deeply attached into the crevices of his hind end! After many frantic moments with the three trappers all trying to aid their leech-afflicted friend at the same time, finally there he stood in all his glory, covered with that of his own blood that had oozed out from the cut-off leeches but finally, mostly leech-free...

Taking a quick dip back into the beaver pond to wash off all the blotches of blood covering his body, Bear Scat immediately scrambled free from the leech-infested waters and finally was able to dress himself and begin warming up once again. Then came the dawn! Tomorrow he would once again have to enter such waters and remove any beaver trapped or even just to remove the traps once and for all, since he decided he would not trap in those waters ever again... Unfortunately, riding back later over the first part of their trap line, the men found a number of dead beaver already hanging lifelessly in their traps. So once again Bear Scat had to partially disrobe and enter the deep waters in order to retrieve those dead beaver. However, since he had to go back into those leech infested waters, Bear Scat tried a different tactic. The first time in which Bear Scat had set their traps and unaware of the leech-infested waters, he had slowly wandered along looking for trapping sites. Having learned a valuable lesson in not moving around so slowly, Bear Scat hustled his way out to the trapped beaver, quickly released it, re-set the trap and then hustled his way out of the water. That tactic worked because in all of his frantic movement, the slow swimming leeches did not have enough time to attach themselves to his naked lower body and the problem was solved. By the end of that memorable day, they had trapped 11 beaver after making their earlier sets, and those pelts along with four entire adult beaver carcasses were brought back to camp. There a thankful to be out from those frightening waters Bear Scat, put together the group's traditional celebratory beaver meat-laced supper, as the remaining three men scraped and hooped the hides from those beaver caught that day.

Those days following, until the trappers had trapped out all of the beaver from the "Leech Pond", Bear Scat made sure he did not remove his pants prior to running the trap line in the deeper waters. He just took along an extra pair of pants and wore his old ones when in the heavily leech-infested waters. That combination of wearing clothing and moving fast when setting and tending the traps proved to be the answer to having a 'shaggy wool-like covering' of black leeches attached to one's body. Two weeks later, the trappers had trapped out those heavily leech-infested waterways and then they had moved on to newer beaver trapping waters. When they did, they discovered areas that were less leech-infested and their beaver trapping procedures returned to normal.

For the remainder of that month, the four trappers trapped the waters in their new trapping area hard. In so doing, they took great numbers of the very territorial beaver and soon had trapped out those new waters for several miles around. Realizing the law of diminishing returns had set in with the demise of the beaver availability, together with the beaver seasonally going out of prime, the men finally pulled their traps and called it quits in that area. Then it was time to hoop and dry the last of their trappings, bundle the same, wrap them with their protective brain-tanned deerskin hides, and begin preparations for heading to Hams Fork and the celebration of the 1834 Rendezvous. (Author's Note: All rendezvous were held in the summer months when the beaver were out of prime and not trapped, plus it made for easier traveling.)

******

Free Trappers Ken Douglas, Abraham "Abe" Dickinson, Joseph "Pike" Johnston, and Peter "Mill Wheel" Jefferson, last partners with renegade Free Trappers Bear and Muskrat, two trappers who had years earlier left Elliott "Bear Scat" Sutta out on the prairie to die, were getting desperate. After getting into a fight with Bear Scat and One Shot at the St. Louis Fur Company warehouse in Fort Bonneville, along with their partners Bear and Muskrat who were killed in that fight, those remaining four trappers of 'Bear's Legacy', had been run off from that trading post by Robert Campbell, the fort's Factor and banned from trading there evermore! When that 'banning' had been so ordered and they were cast out from the only trading post around for many miles, the four now desperate trappers found themselves destitute of their most-needed supplies. Being low on food staples, powder, lead, traps, and horse supplies, the four now renegade Free Trappers from 'Bear's Legacy' were forced to not only live off the land, but began preying upon and killing other trappers discovered working the area's beaver waters and stealing their supplies, horses and furs, which were then traded to the friendly Indians for needed staples in order to survive.

One afternoon while out hunting buffalo so they would have something to eat for their supper, Ken Douglas, Abe Dickinson, Pike Johnston, and Mill Wheel Jefferson, the four trappers banned from Fort Bonneville, occasioned upon an obviously trapped and dead floating beaver in a ponded area. Quickly realizing the nearby presence of white trappers, the four now renegade trappers melted off into a grove of cottonwood trees where they could lay in wait and watch the area of the trapped beaver awaiting their owners' return. They knew it would just be a matter of time until the white trappers came by to run their trap line, so the four trappers rested

301

their horses and let them put on the feed bag. Meanwhile, while three of the men slept in the warmth of the afternoon sun, Mill Wheel Jefferson stood lookout 'like a snake in the grass', watching over the area of the previously spotted floating dead beaver from the cover of the cottonwood grove.

Long about four in the afternoon, Mill Wheel spotted four trappers running what had to be their trap line when they were observed removing the dead beaver from the trap, resetting the trap and then one of the trappers skinned the beaver out at their catch site. Observing the trap-tending action, Mill Wheel woke up the rest of his bunch of men so they could observe what was going on at the trap site as well. When he did, Ken Douglas, the group's leader, took one look at the ongoing action at the trap site and quietly began chuckling out loud over what he had just observed. "What is so funny, Ken?" asked Mill Wheel.

"You aren't going to believe this, but that tall one on the bay horse and the one removing the beaver from the trap are the same two who killed our partners Bear and Muskrat back in Fort Bonneville! In fact, the same two who got us thrown out of Fort Bonneville by that bastard Campbell! I say we watch them and when they leave, cut their trail and see where they are holing up. Maybe then we can have a little 'get-together' and square things up like we didn't get the chance to do back at Fort Bonneville when they killed our friends Muskrat and Bear," said Ken Douglas with a wicked little smile crossing his lips...

******

Bear Scat awoke with a start! Lying still and not moving anything but his eyelids and eyes like his now long-dead father had taught him when something didn't seem right out on the frontier, he continued moving only his eyes back and forth looking for what had awoken him so suddenly. In the darkness of their dugout, Bear Scat saw nothing out of the ordinary. Even his ears detected nothing out of the ordinary through the sounds of Little Griz's loud snoring. For the next few minutes, Bear Scat saw or heard nothing that alarmed him and then he wrote off his sudden awakening by his 'sixth sense' as just nothing more than an over-reaction to something that he had eaten the evening before. Realizing he was now wide awake and facing another busy day getting ready to leave their trapping area for Hams Fork and the upcoming rendezvous, he quietly rose so as not to awaken the others, dressed and started for the door so he could go outside, get a fire going and begin getting breakfast ready for his always hungry group of men.

Bear Scat dressed and then took two steps towards the front door of their dugout when his 'sixth sense' began stirring within his body once again! Now thinking maybe Indians had located their dugout and were about, Bear Scat reached over and felt the cold steel and comforting wood on the forestock of his Hawken rifle. Starting once again quietly for the door with rifle now in hand, he once again paused. Returning to his sleeping area, he picked up and placed one of his pistols behind his sash and stuck his tomahawk behind his back into his belt. Then feeling foolish about going out armed to the teeth, he justified the tomahawk in his own mind saying to himself that he could use its always sharp blade if for nothing else to hack off a hank of buffalo from their meat pole for the men's breakfast meal.

Then once again he headed for their front door but before exiting, looked through a chink in the log door to see if any danger existed close at hand in the outdoor cooking area. Seeing nothing of danger that caught his eye, he began blaming his now growling hungry stomach for the unusual awareness coursing through his body that morning. With that, he opened up the front door to their dugout, took another cautious look around and then moved towards the firepit so he could get a fire going from some of its still hot coals. However as he did, his Mountain Man-experienced senses allowed for his practiced eyes to sweep the immediate area around their campsite looking for anything out of place or unusual. All he observed making any kind of movement was a pair of magpies exploding off part of a buffalo carcass hanging from one of their meat poles, when his movement outside the dugout disturbed their breakfast.

Laying his Hawken against a nearby sitting log by the firepit as he always did, he glanced around one more time and then began searching with a short stick in the bed of ashes in the firepit for any sign of live embers. Finding a few live embers in the firepit's bed of ashes, he added some grass and small twigs to the glowing coals and moments later, had a small flame going and then more and heavier sticks followed until his fire was becoming respectable. Walking over to their meat pole, Bear Scat removed almost the entire backstrap from the partial buffalo carcass hanging there and lugged it back to his log table, laid it out and began slicing off a number of steaks to soon find their ways onto the ends of a number of metal roasting stakes. Then he greased two Dutch ovens up with some bear grease from a stoneware jug sitting underneath his table in preparation for making biscuits. Walking over to their little spring by the corral, Bear Scat filled up their soot-covered coffee pot and headed back to the fire now more than making itself known and felt. Taking the coffee pot, he hung it on a cooking rod hanging over the fire so it could boil, and then turning to one of his brass pots, dumped several large handfuls of green coffee beans into it and set it over the fire to roast. Once the roasting of the green coffee beans had been accomplished, they were removed and placed into the bottom of a cast iron pot and using the blunt end of a well-used limb, he began crushing the beans into granules. Once finished, those granules were poured into the now simmering coffee pot to boil into the strong brew all of his crew of trappers loved, called 'trapper's coffee'.

Twenty minutes later, smelling the coffee aroma wafting through the air, the front door of their dugout opened and out walked One Shot yawning as he went. Without a word, he walked over to the horse corral and urinated. Then he walked over to their spring, splashed several handfuls of the cold water on his face, wiped his buckskin shirt over his face and hands and then headed for the cooking fire.

"Morning, Bear Scat. Is the coffee ready?" asked One Shot.

"Help yourself. It is more than ready and it will mend everything that ails you from a 'broken heart to the crack of dawn'," said Bear Scat with a grin over the funny he had just made.

About then, Little Griz exited the dugout and standing there, stretched his muscular arms and yawned widely enough to make even a grizzly bear ashamed to compare yawns. Last to exit the dugout was Big Hat, taking careful short steps because it was obvious to Bear Scat that his arthritis was devilling him again that morning something awful.

BOOM! went the sound of a heavy rifle being fired from close at hand, and Bear Scat saw Little Griz's head explode into a bright red spew like someone had just shot into a watermelon! Big Hat, standing right next to Little Griz, was spewed with Little Griz's essence in such a volume that he instinctively threw up his hands to avoid more of the 'spew', then ducked! Just as Big Hat ducked the flying spew from Little Griz's exploding head, a .52 caliber bullet meant for his head narrowly missed and smashed into the heavy log door of the dugout, throwing wooden splinters every which way! In fact, that bullet had passed so close to Big Hat's head that he instinctively dropped to the ground like he had been hit. Then with his survival senses now surging through his body, Big Hat reacted like the experienced Mountain Man that he was and quickly scrambled back inside the dugout for the safety it offered!

However, things were happening so rapidly and surprisingly around him that Bear Scat just stood there like a dummy! In that same instant, One Shot, who had been taking a sip of his coffee, was shot right through his coffee cup and had his head exploded into a bloody spew, sending its essence all over Bear Scat standing just a few feet away! When One Shot's liquid essence spewed all over Bear Scat, he found himself reacting like an experienced frontiersman and no longer standing there in amazement like a dummy over what was happening all around him. Dropping to one knee just as a bullet meant for him whizzed right through the space where he had just been standing microseconds earlier, he grabbed his Hawken and broke running for the nearby timber in a running crouched-over position! As Bear Scat broke and ran for cover into the nearby stand of timber, his brain was steaming with the facts over what had just happened. Four quick rifle shots had just been fired indicating there were at least four assailants surrounding their campsite. One Shot and Little Griz were dead as a result of being head-shot. That meant that only he and Big Hat remained alive in the face of superior odds against them. Lastly, whoever was doing the shooting, were damned good shooters and experienced in the art of ambush!

Then realizing why his 'sixth sense' had 'lit' him up earlier in the morning and mad at himself for not listening and applying the teachings his father had given him earlier about depending upon one's 'sixth sense', he found that his 'Red' was now up! Whoever was doing the shooting had just killed two of his friends and had tried killing off Big Hat and himself as well! All of a sudden, Bear Scat found the bile boiling up inside him like it had when he realized he had been left years earlier out on the prairie to die by his so-called friends. Right then and there with his 'Red' up, he coldly dedicated what was left of his life to finding and killing those who had been so foolish in doing to him and his friends that which they had just done...

Figuring the shooters would think he had just escaped and had run off in fear, Bear Scat quickly turned once he was in cover and began stealthily making his way through the timber back towards and from whence all the deadly shooting had come. In so doing, Bear Scat came not like a bull in a china shop but returned like a weasel on the hunt for a small mouse! Just then he saw a man that he recognized from their altercation back at Fort Bonneville with Bear and Muskrat slipping through the woods looking for him and reloading his rifle as he came! The man was none other than one of the four trappers who had wanted to fight, but had been stopped by Campbell back at the fort's warehouse and was now slowly working his way through the brush and timber tracking Bear Scat as he came, like an Indian would do. Only to Bear Scat's way of thinking, he was now the hunter not the other way around! About then another shot was fired and it had come from inside the dugout. *That meant that Big Hat was still alive and back in the fight, and that was a good sound to hear!* thought Bear Scat.

Then several more shots were fired at the front of the dugout and another one was fired back from inside as well. The moment when that shooting had occurred, the trapper from Fort Bonneville who had been cold tracking Bear Scat, raised up his head over some brush to see what had just happened back at the dugout. When he did, a tomahawk quickly looped its way through the air and its blade slammed into the back of the head of the man who just moments before had been cold tracking Bear Scat! With only a soft groan, the man dropped onto the forest floor and after a number of jerking movements with his legs indicating the dying of a being was occurring, he then moved no more!

However, the thrower of the tomahawk was moving silently like a snake across wet grass toward the man just killed with the well-thrown tomahawk. Presently, the tomahawk was pulled with some difficulty from the back of the dead man's skull, wiped off on the man's buckskin shirt and then reinserted back into the thrower's belt for later use should the opportunity occur. Then Bear Scat turned and began moving like a mink through a marsh as he worked his way around through the timber towards where the shooting had originally emanated. As he did, one Abe Dickinson began cooling out in death after being hit in the back of his head moments earlier with the blade of an accurately thrown tomahawk, thanks to Big Hat's earlier frontier teachings of his pupil Bear Scat...

Realizing no one was showing themselves and to move any further towards their locations was dangerous, Bear Scat quietly crawled into a dense clump of brush and partially hid himself under the bark from a nearby rotten log. Then Bear Scat lay there waiting for darkness or for someone else to show himself within a killing distance. He still had his Hawken but it was only good for one shot and then he was down to just his pistol because his 'Possibles bag' with his reloading materials had been left behind in his hurry to escape the flying bullets. Realizing he was one against at least three very committed assassins and excellent shooters, he 'held his milk' and waited for his chance to even up the odds!

With darkness came movement around the downed log as Bear Scat, with all of his survival senses on the alert, rose to his knees and searched the darkness for any signs of nearby movement signifying danger was nearby. Seeing none and quietly crawling just a few inches at a time, Bear Scat crawled towards their horse corral from whence had come the earlier deadly shooting, figuring he would lay in wait in that area and let the horses' nervous shuffling around cover any noises he might make. Two hours later, Bear Scat had quietly crawled the 30 yards to the horses' corral and now hid near a stack of riding and packsaddles.

Around midnight, bathed in the faint light of a quarter-moon, Bear Scat waited quietly for any sign of movement. His eyes had now adjusted to the faint lunar light and moments later, he saw movement near the horse corral that was not that of the horses therein! Soon two human-like forms became discernible as they were obviously in the market for stealthfully stealing some horseflesh as well as killing the horses' owners. Once again, Bear Scat found the killing bile rising up inside him as he waited for a close at hand killing opportunity. Moments later that opportunity arose as the nervous horses, sensing a stranger moving around in their midst, began shuffling nervously around in their corral. With 20 horses shuffling around in the corral, that allowed Bear Scat to slowly stand up alongside a cottonwood tree and continue his deadly wait. He didn't have long to wait as a shadow of a man moved stealthily towards a waiting Bear Scat without the realization that the 'Grim Reaper' was close at hand. When the 'shadow' passed in front of Bear Scat's tree and place of hiding at arm's length, the flash of a tomahawk's blade was barely discernible in the moonlight, as it found a resting place deeply in the man's brain case with a bone-crunching sound that was covered by all the horses' nervous shuffling in the corral. When the tomahawked man had quit wiggling, one Pike Johnston began cooling out in the same manner as had Abe Dickinson killed by the same tomahawk's blade earlier!

About 30 minutes later, Bear Scat heard a soft calling whisper from out of the darkness of, "Pike? Pike, where are you?" "URRGGH," went the quiet sound of a man gurgling his last, as a knife blade flashed in the quarter-moon's light, ripping clear through the soft tissue of one's throat and scraping against the victim's spinal column with such force, all the man could do was gurgle out his essence all over Bear Scat as he held up his most recent kill in a standing position until he quit wiggling. Then Bear Scat slowly and quietly let the dead man named Mill Wheel Jefferson, who had come looking for his accomplice in crime Pike, slump to the soil at his feet. When he did, Bear Scat felt the man's hot blood spraying all over his feet and running into his moccasins!

Come first light, Bear Scat found himself carefully looking through the trees by the south end of the horse corral at a stranger behind a tree holding a rifle at the ready and looking all around as if he was looking for something, or maybe someone! Finally it was obvious the stranger could not stand the silence, began quietly saying, "Pike, Mill Wheel, Abe! Where the hell are you guys hiding?"

Those desperate searching words were all Bear Scat needed. Counting the stranger calling out for his three now dead henchmen, that made number four of the original shooters to Bear Scat's way of thinking. Bear Scat had originally felt there were only four shooters based on the number of shots initially fired at his bunch of trappers and remembering back to the four trappers back at Fort Bonneville with Bear and Muskrat, that last stranger calling out made number four of the mystery shooters!

Free Trapper Ken Douglas and ringleader of the four men who had killed One Shot and Little Griz, and had shot at Big Hat and Bear Scat, soon found the answer to his rather plaintive calls for his fellow partners in crime. Bear Scat's .52 caliber soft lead slug fired from his Hawken rifle tore through Ken's ear and when the spew of his essence had finished drifting windward, all that remained of his exploded head was his quivering lower jaw still attached to the rest of his body as it hit the ground! It was plain to a now calm and relaxed Bear Scat that Douglas and his friends would not have to worry about being banned from Fort Bonneville and facing supply problems ever again...

Laying down his now empty rifle and taking his pistol out from his sash, Bear Scat slowly walked out from his hiding place in the grove of trees next to the horse corral and carefully looked all around, making sure there was no more danger close at hand. After a few more minutes of looking all around, Bear Scat realized the danger had passed with the killing of the last stranger in the grove of trees. Whereupon Bear Scat then softly called out, "Big Hat, do not take a shot at me. The four shooters are no more. It is safe to come out from the dugout now." Then standing there with his pistol still at the ready, Bear Scat saw the door to the dugout slowly open and his friend Big Hat carefully peering out making sure everything was alright for him to come out from hiding.

"They are all dead, Big Hat. It is safe to come out," said Bear Scat, as he went back, picked up his rifle, walked over to the outside cooking fire and retrieved his 'Possibles bag'. He then quickly reloaded his rifle just in case, as his father had always taught while on the always dangerous frontier... As Bear Scat reloaded his rifle in case some sort of danger was to rear its ugly head again, he thought, *I should have killed those four trappers back at the Fort Bonneville warehouse when I had the chance. If I had, One Shot and Little Griz would be alive today.* No matter how he thought about what had just transpired during the killings of his two friends by those four trappers who were friends of Bear, 'Bear's Legacy' would haunt him the rest of his life...

The rest of that morning was spent in respectfully burying their two fellow trappers and friends up on the hilltop where they could 'look out' across the sometimes harsh and unforgiving land that they loved so much. Then Bear Scat and Big Hat roped up the four dead assailants and dragged their bodies off away from their camp with their horses so they would not attract any hungry grizzly bears, and left them aboveground so the critters could fare well 'around the dinner table'. Following that, Bear Scat set the coffee to boiling over the campfire, staked out some chunks of buffalo meat to roast away and made a single Dutch oven full of biscuits. Suffice to say, it was a sad and quiet breakfast meal had that morning by the two sad but thankful trappers and close friends that morning...

Four days later found Big Hat in the lead of a caravan of heavily loaded horses carrying bundles of beaver furs. In that caravan were also the four riding horses of the four killers who had come to Big Hat and Bear Scat's camp and in so doing, ended their careers as Mountain Men Free Trappers... Big Hat was followed by Bear Scat leading the men's now extra riding horses left by the deaths of One Shot and Little Griz, a total of 20 horses in all! In so doing, he provided rear cover for the two trappers' fur caravan headed for Hams Fork and the 1834 Rendezvous, with mixed feelings of sadness and yet anticipation of a new day, maybe with the reunion of his brother...

Elliott "Bear Scat" Sutta, Mountain Man

CHAPTER ELEVEN: HAMS FORK RENDEZVOUS OF 1834, THE SNAKE RIVER COUNTRY

Several days later, Big Hat and Bear Scat arrived at the front gates of Fort Bonneville leading 20 heavily packed horses, trailed by extra riding horses. With their arrivals came the traditional welcoming cups of rum for Free Trappers from the St. Louis Fur Company's Factor, Robert Campbell. When Campbell handed the cups of rum to Big Hat and Bear Scat, his searching and questioning eyes 'ran down' the long caravan of packed as well as the riderless riding horses, looking for fellow fur trappers and friends, One Shot and Little Griz. Then as Big Hat maneuvered the packed horses over to the fur company's waiting sorters and graders in the fort's courtyard, Bear Scat dismounted by Campbell and related the sad story of the two trappers' deaths.

Campbell just shook his head upon hearing the story of his friends' deaths and then remembering back to the fatal incidents at his warehouse and the four troublemaking fur trappers he had banished from the fort's grounds, said, "I always knew those four men were 'bad seeds'. They came into my fort with the smell of death about them and when they joined up with those Muskrat and Bear fellows, I knew that someday nothing good would come of it." Then shaking his head still in disbelief over what Bear Scat had just told him about the deaths of One Shot and Little Griz, he took both Bear Scat and Big Hat's now empty cups, walked over to the standing keg of rum for all arriving Free Trappers to partake from, and refilled both cups once again, clear to the brim…

Upon his return with the cups full of rum, Campbell turned to Bear Scat saying, "Say, are you still looking for that Jacob Sutta fellow? Because if you are, you will have your work cut out for you this year because of the way the rendezvous sites are scattered up and down the valley. As such, it appears we are having trappers arriving at the three sites on a daily basis."

"Yes I am," replied Bear Scat, now livened up a bit upon hearing Campbell's question regarding the matter of his much sought-after brother whose paths the two of them kept crossing and missing each other.

"Well, as I said, you will have your work cut out for you this go-around. The general rendezvous is going to be held at Fort Bonneville this year. However, several other competing fur companies are in the area as well this year hoping to cash in on the more than abundant fur crop. The American Fur Company is located about five miles below us on the Green River, and the Rocky Mountain Fur Company is located about five miles below where the American Fur Company is located, also on the river. That being said, trying to find your brother at either of the three fur company locations along a ten-mile stretch of big country along the Green River may be a bit of a chore. Especially in light of the reported bad blood between your brother's partner Wild Bill McGinty and the four Travis Brothers, who as I understand from other trappers are still on the hunt for the reported killer of their father over a moonshine deal gone sour way back in Kentucky," said Campbell.

"However, that issue of finding your brother can be addressed later. For now, once my graders and sorters complete the counting and grading of your furs, you two Free Trappers are invited to have supper with me this evening. Now I know the two of you are tired and need to see to the care of your horses at the fort's livery, but once that is done, plan on staying in the fort's bunkhouse since I see the two of you do not have any tenting material on your packhorses and upon that I insist. Supper will be around seven at the big house and don't be late, because my cooks will be baking several pies and if I remember correctly, Bear Scat had one hell of a sweet tooth the last time he had supper with me," said Campbell with a toothy grin.

After their furs had been processed and the two men had the credit slips from the fur company, they headed for the fort's bunkhouse reserved for Free Trappers. There they unloaded their sleeping furs and then headed for the fort's livery stables for the needed work to be done with all of their horses, since the men had not as of yet decided on selling any surplus horses they had. Once there, Big Hat and Bear Scat made sure their horses were all slated for re-shoeing for the coming year's trapping season. However before they ordered the re-shoeing, the two men sat down and discussed their next year's trapping plans. They had jointly decided that they would not return to the country they had previously trapped for the past two years. For the most part, the men decided they had trapped out most of the beaver in that area and did not feel returning for a third year in the same area would be profitable. Additionally, since they had not decided where they would head next when it came to beaver trapping territory, the two trappers decided they would for now keep One Shot and Little Griz's entire horse herd and their killers' riding horses, 'just in case' for some reason they would need the extra horses for wherever they decided they would trap next. Little did they realize what a wise decision that would turn out to be! Then they made sure the men at the livery doing the horseshoeing would see to it that Big Hat and Bear Scat's horses were shod first, so they could be used right away in their search for Bear Scat's brother Jacob Sutta, at either of the three rendezvous sites. A search that would take the two trappers to the Rocky Mountain Fur Company's or the American Fur Company's locations along the Green River where other parts of the 1834 Rendezvous were also being held.

Later it was off to Campbell's home for a grand supper, one which was traditionally reserved for arriving Free Trappers or other dignified guests so honored and invited by the St. Louis Fur Company Factor. That evening Big Hat and Bear Scat were treated to roasted buffalo hump ribs, fried potatoes and onions from the fort's garden, homemade bread fresh from the cook's ovens, homemade butter and wild plum jam, and all the apple pie the two men could 'fathom'. Suffice to say, Big Hat and Bear Scat made sure that Campbell knew they really enjoyed what they had for supper, based on the 'small mountain' of great home-cooked food they managed to put away...

Then Big Hat and Bear Scat got the surprise of the evening! As the three men sat in the Grand Room of the Factor's house smoking cigars and drinking fine rum after supper, Campbell raised an issue that was obviously dear to his heart saying, "Big Hat, you and I have known each other now for at least eight years. During that period of time, I have come to know you as an honorable and good Christian man, as well as one hell of a good trapper. With that in mind, I would like to ask you and Bear Scat, since it will take the two of you to hopefully carry out my plan, for a favor of great importance to me."

After saying those words, Campbell paused letting those words sink into the two trappers' inner beings but more importantly, being the good judge of character that he was renowned for, wanted to personally 'read' the men's reactions to his obviously 'seeking and most important' request. Reading in the faces of the two trappers exactly what he was looking for and without waiting for further validation of what he had seen, Campbell began. "Big Hat and Bear Scat, I have two wayward sons who need to spend some time 'before the mast' so to speak in nautical terms, experiencing what it takes to become a man on this here frontier. I realize the dangers that exist out there on a daily basis being a fur trapper and I am willing to take that chance, even if it means I may lose one or both of my sons to the elements. As the two of you can see, I am willing to take chances in the losses of their lives, if it brings into their 'beings' the heart, soul and ethic I feel they will need to succeed as men. And fathers of their own sons and daughters and good Christian men who will someday carry my good name into their own world," quietly uttered Campbell.

Upon hearing those words, Big Hat's slightly rum-soaked brain spun into a higher level of mental processing than it had been just moments earlier, rocking along after a most satisfying supper, enjoying the comfort of a warm house without any sign of near at hand danger, and the satisfaction of sitting in a deeply comfortable chair instead of a hard sitting log around a smoking campfire with his face and hands covered with hordes of mosquitoes...

Bear Scat's mind on the other hand, upon hearing and understanding the deeper 'meanings' in Campbell's conversation, instantly spun back to his days of starvation when he was compelled to eat partially digested paddlefish eggs from bear scat, only to be rescued by Big Hat and through his many hours of teachings and training, had found his way as a person and experienced man of the frontier... Possibly the same, only the circumstances being different, in the way of a life's prospect proposal for his two sons, if Bear Scat was correctly reading the meaning and direction Campbell was now heading in his ongoing discussion.

Reading the questioning looks now spreading across the faces of Bear Scat and Big Hat, Campbell paused for a moment with his next words and then sallied forth like the man on the mission he was. "I know I am asking a lot of the two of you but I respect you Big Hat, and have come to respect you Bear Scat, as well, and in so doing feel a need to ask of you what I would hesitate to ask of any others that I see in the fur trade at this fort. Will the two of you take my two young sons and either 'make' God-fearing men of them for me and their mother, or just let me know where their remains reside for time immemorial under this great land of ours? Additionally, it is also with the understanding that if they are killed by whatever means, my two sons would be given a good Christian burial under a pile of rocks so that the grizzly bears can't dig them up and eat their remains."

"Mr. Campbell. May Bear Scat and I have an evening alone to talk about what you have asked of us? I ask for this favor of you because of the gravity of what you are asking of us," said Big Hat quietly. "It is all that we can do out there just to survive, make a living trapping beaver and keeping our own 'top-knots', much less looking out for someone else who is very important because they are kin to one of our good friends."

"I understand. Tomorrow the two of you will have breakfast with me if you please and then at that time, I would like to introduce the two of you to my sons. 'Win, lose or draw', I would like the two of you to meet my sons. If the two of you decide to honor my request, we will have even much more to talk about tomorrow. But for now, I ask you for this favor based on my trust in the two of you, and because of the loss you recently suffered when One Shot and Little Griz were killed. As you both realize, my request is timely and practical. Both of my sons are crack rifle shots and as the two of you know, four rifles are better than just those from the two of you in this land of ours when the going gets rough. I am just saying…," said Campbell with a sly grin, knowing what he was talking about was as solid as a river rock…

Later that evening after several more cups of very fine rum supplied by Campbell, Big Hat and Bear Scat sat on the edge of their beds in the bunkhouse talking into the early morning over their friend and Factor's very personal request. Finally the two men retired to their beds for what sleep remained of the morning's hours. But as it turned out, sleep that morning for the two of them was fleeting. Both men found sleeping on a bed with metal springs uncomfortable, so they removed all of their bedding and slept on the floor like they had been doing for the last two years on the earthen floor of their dugout.

The following morning, Big Hat and Bear Scat found themselves sitting behind plates of steaming hot pork sausages, sourdough biscuits and fresh fried chicken eggs by the 'barnyard' in number... That repast was followed by piping hot wild plum pies fresh from the cook's wood stove, and coffee that was once again so weak, a respectable horseshoe would not be found 'standing up' in such a thin brew...

After breakfast and adjourning to the large sitting room of the Factor's home, Campbell without further ado asked straightaway if the two men had enough time to discuss his unusual request regarding the 'manning-up' and training of his two sons. Big Hat taking another sip of the weak coffee, a coffee that was not at all like the 'trapper's coffee' that Bear Scat routinely made around their campfire, said, "Mr. Campbell, do you seriously understand what you are requesting of me and my partner?"

"Yes I do! I did so fully aware of what I am asking of the two of you to do for me, and also that tomorrow out on the frontier is never guaranteed. On this frontier as a fur trapper, one is looking at living in extreme cold, many missed meals, numerous mean-assed critters wanting to take a bite out of your hide, drowning in river crossings and wading around in deep beaver ponds, freezing to death, along with a steel-tipped arrowhead or a speeding lead ball is more than likely the 'next sunrise' that many of you trappers will be facing. But my sons need leavening and will only get what I am seeking for them from those of you who have been there, done that and have survived. I would do for myself what I am asking of the two of you if that was possible. But as you can see, I have my hands full here just running the fur company's business. So with all of that in mind, I am forced to rely on my friends to do what a father really needs to do when it comes to raising a couple of his sons."

"Then with that realization on your part and I assume at the behest of your Missus, Bear Scat and I have decided we will support you in your wish to treat your sons to a baptism of life's reality out on the frontier. We will do that with the hope that what we bring back to you will have a heartbeat and the will to face the rest of their lives with a knowing and understanding smile," replied Big Hat quietly...

"Thank you, thank you, Gentlemen! Now I would like to have the two of you meet my sons, Dan and Tom Campbell. But before I do, I expect to hold up my end of the bargain in this mission and sacrifice I am asking of the two of you. Since the two of you will be caring for and teaching my sons, I will allow the two of you free hand in their raising, as well as a free run of my warehouses when it comes to outfitting your provisions for your next year's trapping season for a party of four instead of just the two of you. Whatever you will need is yours for the taking. Just make sure you purchase plenty of what you will need in the way of foodstuffs, because both of my kids are over six feet tall, weigh over 200 pounds each and eat like Clydesdale horses would from an oat bucket! Additionally, I expect the two of you to teach them everything they will need to know about the trapping end of the fur trade. I need you to do so because someday they will be replacing me in the St. Louis Fur Company if it is God's will. So as the two of you can see, it is imperative that both of my boys learn the trade from the ground up from those who know it the best and will share their experiences with them."

The rest of that morning was spent with the four men, once they had been introduced, getting to know one another without the 'hovering' presence of their father and Factor. Big Hat and Bear Scat quickly discovered Dan and Tom very likeable but dumb as river rocks, when it came to knowing what they were getting themselves into and what they would eventually need to do and learn in order to survive! The only positive mechanical aspect of the boys' previous training had been that which they had learned from their father regarding the function, repair and use of firearms. As the two trappers soon learned, Dan and Tom knew firearms forwards and backwards, including teardowns, repairs and as their dad had reported, they were very accurate and accomplished shooters. But that was where their skill level in their lives ended when it came to surviving out in the wilds while out on the frontier. As Bear Scat soon discovered to his dismay, neither boy had ever been on a horse in their 21 years of life! Their mother had coddled them when it came to horses because her father had been killed in a horse wreck and as a result of that issue, had forbidden the boys to ever ride a horse. In short, their coddled lives involved riding around in carriages whenever they wanted to travel somewhere back where they lived in St. Louis!

For the next three weeks of the 1834 Rendezvous, Big Hat and Bear Scat spent their times not in the usual celebrations with other trappers, but in the preliminary training and preparation of their two new partners and getting to really know them and their shortcomings. As it turned out, there was a plus in that aspect of their training and getting to know one another. The boys' newness in the care and riding of horses gave Bear Scat the opportunity to ride back and forth between the two other spread-out competing fur companies at the rendezvous other than just that of the St. Louis Fur Company, looking for his 'will-o'-the-wisp' brother. In so doing, that riding back and forth also gave Dan and Tom daily experience in riding and getting used to their individual horses, as well as learning all of the little quirks found in the world of horses. As they did, Big Hat spent time working with other trappers searching out their knowledge of the many trapping areas not trapped out or covered with a passel of mad at white men Indians in the nearby mountain ranges. This he did because as of yet, he and Bear Scat had yet to decide in what part of the country they would be moving into next to trap beaver.

******

Jacob Sutta and Wild Bill McGinty arrived at the American Fur Company's location five miles below Fort Bonneville around four in the afternoon their first day of arrival at the 1834 Rendezvous. Pleased to have finally safely arrived at the rendezvous, they quickly discovered that their 'just arrival' pleasure was short-lived. Pulling into the lower end of the American Fur Company's location, who did they see but older brother Bud Travis drinking with a bunch of other fur trapper friends and whooping it up!

321

Discovering the oldest of the four Travis Brothers, the head of the clan on the hunt to find and kill Wild Bill McGinty, promptly caused Jacob and Wild Bill to turn their horses southward toward the location of the more distant Rocky Mountain Fur Company before they were spotted! Making all haste while travelling towards the most distant part of that year's rendezvous grounds, the two trappers rode deeply into the darkness in order to quickly arrive at the Rocky Mountain Fur Company's location. However, to avoid any further run-ins with the Travis Brothers, the men quietly scouted out the rest of that camp's fur trappers on the lookout for any signs of trouble in the form of the presence of the Travis Brothers' campsite at that particular trading site. Finding none, the two trappers set up their camp at the outskirts of the main camp's site. The next morning found Jacob and Wild Bill having their furs graded, sorted and counted out for the credit in trade they would bring. Then in all due haste, they traded in their fur credits for the provisions they would need for the coming trapping season to make sure they could quickly leave the rendezvous if any of the Travis clan arrived on-site unexpectedly. The morning following found the two men at the temporary livery having all of their horses reshod for the trapping season ahead and several of their horses' teeth floated as well. Then it was back to their campsite for a night's sleep away from the center of the rendezvous campsite and any adverse prying eyes.

As they did, Jacob thought about facing off with the Travis Brothers. In so doing, Jacob figured it best to settle up the old issue with that involving his partner so they wouldn't have to be on the run at every rendezvous they attended and constantly looking over their shoulders all the time. However after thinking through the face-off issue and looking at two to one deadly odds, finally won out in the common sense department and settled the issue of survival after confrontation over such uneven and deadly odds. In short, Jacob gave up his idea of facing off with the Travis Brothers as producing the same odds of survival when facing off with a bull moose in rut with just a stick... The next morning with packed horses loaded to 'the gills' with a year's supplies, Jacob and Wild Bill slipped out from the rendezvous site and headed back to their cabin in the Bighorns where they still had beaver trapping and numbers 'a-plenty' and the Brothers Travis in known scarcity...

******

Two days later, Bear Scat, Dan and Tom rode into the Rocky Mountain Fur Company's rendezvous site, which at the time was in full swing celebration mode. Aside from much evidence of drunkenness, fist fights, whooping, Indian wife swapping and yelling, along with several ongoing horse races and wrestling matches, Bear Scat was unable to find anyone who knew of the whereabouts of Jacob Sutta, Wild Bill McGinty or anything else regarding those two men's whereabouts. With those few trappers at the Rocky Mountain Fur Company's campsite in full celebration, finding out anything further about his 'will-o-wisp' brother appeared to be a lost cause. With that and plenty of other things needing to be done in preparation for the coming trapping season, Bear Scat turned his mount back to Fort Bonneville with Dan and Tom in tow, figuring he would return at a later date and inquire again as to the whereabouts of his brother at that portion of the rendezvous.

******

Eight days of travel later, Jacob and Wild Bill arrived at their cabin in the Bighorns and after unloading all of their provisions and storing the same, began preparations for their fall trapping season with a buffalo hunt for their winter's meat supply being first on their list of things that needed doing.

******

Days later back at Fort Bonneville, fellow trappers Big Hat, Dan, Tom and Bear Scat sat on their beds in the fur company's bunkhouse and began formulation of their plans for heading out into new beaver trapping grounds come the end of the rendezvous. Big Hat began their discussions over several cups of rum informing the men of what information he had gleaned from visiting the plethora of fur trappers at the Fort Bonneville rendezvous grounds and campsites. While visiting his old fur trapping friends, Big Hat had discussed new trapping areas and pertinent geographic information that pointed to reported rich beaver trapping grounds located further to their northwest in the Snake River country. That Snake River country so described by Big Hat's fur trapper friends was reported to be largely untrammeled by anyone trapping beaver, other than the local, mean as a stepped on snake, Northern Cheyenne Indians. However, Northern Cheyenne Indians or not, the more Big Hat described the possible new beaver trapping area and its reported large numbers of beaver just waiting to be trapped, the more interested Bear Scat became and the more excited Dan and Tom became over the soon to be new adventures in their lives.

But before any further plans could be made to head for the Snake River area, Big Hat figured he needed more information and directions on how to access that specific beaver trapping country in the area of the Snake River. On the other hand and in light of Big Hat's findings, Bear Scat figured there were preparations needed in acquiring their provisions for a year afield, which including a much-needed 'clothing acquisition trip' for Dan and Tom who were still dressed in the clothing of the 'English'. The following morning, Big Hat returned to the campsites of some of his former trapper friends for more travel-related information and directions, as Bear Scat set out on his important mission getting Dan and Tom properly clothed for the rigors of life the young men would soon be facing in beaver trapping country.

Taking Tom and Dan with him after breakfast, the three men rode into a camp of friendly Shoshone Indians camped on the Fort Bonneville grounds, and directly to two tipis in particular known to him for meeting his particular needs of the moment. Entering one tipi with Dan and later the other with Tom, soon found the two young men stripped of all their English clothing and being measured by Indian seamstresses skilled in the making of buckskin clothing for the rendezvous' white fur trappers. An hour later after the Indian women had taken all the measurements needed for the two very tall for that day and age white men, off they went now fully dressed back in their English clothing to one of Fort Bonneville's warehouses to address the next part in their preparations. As they did, Tom asked Bear Scat why he had ordered new buckskin clothing from the Indian women for the two men when they already were wearing their own good clothing and didn't need any other clothing. Bear Scat stopped his horse and as his two charges reined up alongside saying, "The world of a trapper is a hard one. It is not only hard on the men who choose such a profession, but is hard on everything that person wears that is English-made as well. Your English clothing will last only a short period of time while afield and then what are you to do as it begins falling apart on your body? Knowing that from my own experiences when I became a trapper, that is why we just visited the Indian women and had them measure the two of you for a new type of clothing that is better suited for that of the life of a trapper. That in mind, both of you will soon be outfitted with buckskin clothing from head to toe that will better suit your trade and the land you will be living in. That is necessary because clothing made from animal skins will outlast any English clothing ever made. Plus it resists being torn by brambles and is resistant to mosquitoes being able to bite through like they can on English cloth. However there are drawbacks to wearing animal skins instead of warm wool like the English wear in colder weather. In the summer months, wearing buckskins makes one hotter than all get-out and when wet or in the winter months, offers little in the way of warmth. But wearing tear-resistant clothing made from animal skins will allow the trapper to at least remain clothed when afield. So in the warmer weather trappers will wear the lighter English shirts, and in colder weather will use heavy capotes or buffalo robes in order to keep warm. However come wintertime we will wear our warmer English shirts under our buckskin shirts for the extra warmth it provides. As both of you will soon come to realize, riding a horse in the wintertime is a rather cold affair. That being the case, we must dress warmer come the cold weather and by wearing several shirts, that helps in keeping one much warmer." Hearing no further questions coming from his two young charges regarding the clothing changes, the three men continued on to the warehouse Bear Scat had selected to begin outfitting their group with the needed provisions for the coming trapping season away from any easy resupply sources.

Stepping into Bear Scat's first warehouse of choice with a fur company Clerk who had been awaiting their arrival, in went the three men. Bear Scat, right off the bat, headed for the firearms section of the facility. When he arrived at that section of the warehouse, he saw the wide grins of anticipation from Dan and Tom over the things that were familiar to them. It was apparent they were now in a section of the warehouse that the two men most appreciated and understood. There Bear Scat selected four .52 caliber Lancaster rifles for Dan and Tom. Handing the men their new rifles, Bear Scat could see questioning looks spread across their faces of "Why do we need two rifles each"? Bear Scat then said in 'answer' to the questioning looks he figured he was getting, "In the field we always carry two rifles apiece. We will always be outnumbered by Indians or animals larger in size that require a 'heap' of killing. Since each rifle is a single shot, by carrying two that just gives one an extra shot to get himself out from trouble and just maybe survive to trap another day. Besides, rifles are always misfiring or there is a horse wreck which ends up with a non-functioning rifle in the hands of the trapper. Hence the extra rifle we always carry in case our primary firearm of choice is not functioning. You will also soon see that each of you will be armed with two pistols of the same caliber as are your rifles. Once again, we do so in order to provide the greatest amount of protection that we can in case we are jumped by a mess of hostile Indians or a mean-assed grizzly bear at close quarters. In short, the more firepower we carry close at hand, the better our chances are of surviving whatever the frontier tosses at us. Asides, if Big Hat and I do not come back with the two of you intact, your father will 'string us up just for our mangy hides'," said Bear Scat with an easy smile over the 'funny' he had just uttered.

Then continuing, Bear Scat said, "Both of you have already noticed that our rifles and pistols are the same caliber. Big Hat and I have found that the heavier caliber rifles and pistols shooting the heaviest lead ball is the best for stopping power. We have found that is the best survival medicine if you are trying to kill a close at hand hard-charging Indian, bison, grizzly bear or bull elk and keep your hide intact. Additionally by having the same caliber weapon, that just means we only need to carry fewer bullet-making mold blocks or tools servicing or tending to those weapons. And by all of us shooting the same caliber weapons, if we get into a long and sustained fight with Indians and one of us runs low on lead balls, we can get some from each other and continue the fight. Lastly, by going with just one caliber of firearm, that makes our powder selection simpler in choosing just one burning-rate of propellant and just varying our amounts of powder charges for our guns, instead of having to carry several, always clacking together and noisy powder horns with different powders of varying strengths and burn rates." Seeing the quizzical looks disappearing with that explanation, Bear Scat moved on with the procurement lessons best learned by Dan and Tom if they wanted to be successful in the trapping world.

Then it was off to the pistol section of the warehouse and after previously explaining the selection of several handguns for each man, handed two pistols to each man that possessed the more reliable percussion-type ignition systems like that of their rifles and were each caliber '.52'. Then without a word, Bear Scat began selecting extra rifle and pistol parts for field replacement repairs, tools to service the weapons, several powder horns for each man, extra rifle ramrods because of their tendency with hard use to break, bullet pullers, bullet screws, several spools of brass wire to repair cracked rifle and pistol stocks, and a single mold block for each man that was .52 caliber as well. Once again, Bear Scat got questioning looks from Dan and Tom over his selection of just one bullet-making mold block for each of them. Grinning because the two new partners were showing wisdom in their questions asked or displayed on their faces, Bear Scat said, "I only purchased one mold block for each of you. That is because weight is a carrying factor for our horses when we go afield for a year at a time. The horses can only carry so much weight, so we try to keep their loads at that which is only necessary. In our case, Big Hat and I already have our mold blocks of the same caliber as yours are and if you lose one for whatever reason, you can use one of ours."

By now, Dan, Tom and the Clerk had begun making small mountains of supplies on the warehouse floor as Bear Scat continued selecting more and more items the four men would need for a year afield without having any access to an easy resupply trading post or fort. Those piles of supplies were soon joined with eight ten-pound lead canisters of powder and 20 tin boxes of percussion caps for their percussion cap ignition system rifles and pistols. Continuing on, Bear Scat headed over to the stacks of lead pigs. There he selected 100 pounds of the lead pigs and added them to the ever-growing piles of selected provisions. Then moving over to the bins holding hundreds of cast lead balls, Bear Scat selected 200 precast, .52 caliber balls and had the Clerk sack them up in a canvas bag and placed in the stacks of provisions as well. Once again, Bear Scat ever the teacher said, "Once afield, we will be using the precast lead balls when we travel to the Snake River country. However, once there and in need of more lead balls, we will use our axes and cut chunks off the awkward-sized lead pigs so those smaller chunks can fit into our smelting pots to be melted. Once melted, we will use a ladle to dip out the molten lead and pour the lead into our bullet molds. Once they cool off, we knock off the lead 'sprew' from the tops of the mold blocks and there we have our bullet. Since Big Hat and I already have bullet-making equipment in our provisions, we need not purchase any additional smelting pots, mold blocks, ladles and the like. Remember, we need to keep our weight the horses are carrying to a minimum as much as possible for the trip ahead." Lastly, Bear Scat selected several cloth bags full of greased wads for their firearms upon which to seat their bullets in the barrels of their weapons to reduce the friction once the bullet had been fired.

Then it was off to the bladed items in the warehouse. On the way over to the bladed section of the warehouse, Bear Scat explained to Dan and Tom the absolute value of edged weapons to the men. There he impressed upon each of his new charges that edged weapons like gutting knives, skinning knives, boning knives, axes and tomahawks were of equal value for their survival as were firearms, to both the white man and Indian alike out on the frontier. As such, they were to be carefully cared for and guarded diligently against loss, theft and any other form of destruction. On the way, Bear Scat scooted over to the bins holding various sizes and styles of whetstones. There he selected a number of the sharpening devices for their axes, saws, knives and shovels. By now, Bear Scat could see that Dan and Tom's heads were just swirling over all of the items needed for a year afield, along with the short lectures as to why the need and values of each and every item. What Bear Scat was doing in teaching the young men regarding the frontier necessaries was what their father Robert Campbell, had hoped for when he turned his two sons loose into the trusted hands of Big Hat and Bear Scat, and now his sons were getting the opportunity to learn the fur trade from the bottom-up in 'spades'…

Walking over to the knife sections of the warehouse, Bear Scat picked up two Thomas Wilson cutting and gutting knives. Handing a knife each to Dan and Tom said, "Men, these knives are made in England of the finest Sheffield steel. They not only hold their edges the best of all the other brands of knives out there but are the strongest knives going. Guard them with your lives, because someday your lives may very well depend upon having those knives as one of your possessions. Now pay attention to what I am doing next. Note that I am selecting more than one kind of knife. Once afield, we will be using cutting, gutting, skinning and general purpose knives every day of our lives. Each knife type has a different function and once we get to where we are going in the field, Big Hat and I will teach each of you how to handle and care for each type of knife. Once again, they are one of the more valuable things you will carry every day when working as a trapper. Guard them with your lives, especially when around any kind of Indian. It seems that every time we get around Indians, a number of our knives end up 'disappearing'. So learn to watch your knives like a hawk, because everyone out in the field realizes just how valuable they are and you will find yourselves using them many times a day doing what needs doing." With that, Bear Scat took the two new members of their party aside and showed them the different types and styles of Thomas Wilson knives and then selected what he figured they would need and the numbers of each for the coming year. (Author's Note: For my 'history buff' readers, the fabled 'Green River' brand of knives did not arrive on the scene and into the hands of the trapping fraternity until 1837. Hence the story line using the real McCoy, 'Thomas Wilson' knives made from Sheffield steel.)

Next, Bear Scat walked over to that section of the warehouse holding all kinds and styles of animal traps from the dainty marten-sized traps to the giant-sized and toothed grizzly bear traps. There Bear Scat pulled out one of the general five-pound sized beaver traps and said, "This is the size and weight of beaver trap Big Hat and I have used over the years. However we prefer the St. Louis-style custom-made trap and have a number of them already. Therefore, we will not be buying any new traps because we already have plenty. Again, remember the weight issue and our horses. Each trap weighs about five pounds with their chain which helps in drowning any beaver so trapped, and we only set out six to eight traps per trapper. As it is, it is not long before we are carrying and handling over a 100 pounds of beaver traps every day! Keep in mind that beaver trapping is truly an art form. Once we get into the field, I will teach both of you the best ways to make beaver sets with traps like these. Before all is said and done, you both will be so tired of walking through the cold and sometimes icy water and the deep and foot-grabbing mud, the two of you will shy away from any such endeavors and look for lighter work in the future, like running a section of a fur company like your father!"

Then away went Bear Scat to the clothing section of the warehouse where he selected wide-brimmed hats to reduce the sun's glare, two heavy capotes per man sized to fit, several dozen pairs of socks also sized to fit, wool gloves, belts and the like. In each selection, Bear Scat made sure that Tom and Dan understood the value and reasoning for selecting such specific and necessary items. Then when he began selecting sewing needles, awls, thread, buttons, bolts of cloth for clothing repairs and the like, the two larger in size than most men with bear paw-sized hands and pickle-sized fingers gave Bear Scat a disbelieving and askance look over what they obviously considered were the rightful tools of a woman...

Once again, seeing such questioning looks over the items being selected, Bear Scat said, "Both of you will discover that when all of this coming fur trapping adventure is finished, the two of you will have wished you would have watched your blessed mother more closely when she had to sew up your clothing. Yes, we do a lot of needle and thread work while afield, especially if we don't want to walk around all bare-assed naked and the like and the target for every damn mosquito in the country. If we aren't patching up our clothing, sewing on a button or two or repairing the leather on our saddles and the like, we aren't doing our job. So before this year is finished, both of you pickle-fingered fellows will be adroit with needle and thread or you will look like a rag-merchant," said Bear Scat with a knowing grin based on the several years he had already lived afield...

Then Bear Scat walked the Clerk and his two new partners over to those items utilized by horses and mules in the fur trapping trade.

Arriving at that rather large section in the warehouse, Bear Scat turned and said, "Before the two of you finish up with a year afield beaver trapping, you will come to respect that of your beast of burden lugging your rather large carcasses around and up and down every mountain we choose to traverse. Without your horse on the frontier, you are a 'dead man walking'. First of all, this country is so big that without your horse, you will either starve to death or die of thirst on your 'walk-about'! Then if that is not enough of a worry, without your horse, and a good horse at that, you will be the target of every hungry and mean-assed grizzly bear or angry Indian mad over your trespassing carcasses on their sacred lands. So best you learn to ride well and be outfitted with the best equipment that money can buy, and gear that fits you well and is adapted for what you need it for," said Bear Scat with a damned serious look over the advice he was now giving to Dan and Tom!

"Mr. Clerk, would you please step over here and using these wooden 'saddle horses', form fit each of these two rather large men to a saddle that is fit to the size of their frames. Please make sure they are properly fitted to the size of the saddle selected and that the length of their stirrups can be properly adjusted to these two long-legged 'galoots'. Then when you have finished, I will spend time with them on the type and use of saddle blankets, proper cinching techniques, fitting a bridle, care of 'sored' up animals from the improper placement of saddles and packs on the horses and the like," said Bear Scat, as he took a chair and with a practiced eye and tuned ear, watched and listened to the instructions being given by the fur company's Clerk to Dan and Tom who by now were all ears and eyes… Once the Clerk had worked his 'magic' with the two men and had seen to it that the saddles and other gear met Dan and Tom's specifications, their newly purchased equipment was placed alongside the ever-growing mountain of other provisions recently selected.

Satisfied over the men's riding procurements, Bear Scat added a number of new saddle blankets, packsaddles, panniers, bridles, spurs, extra leather strapping, and additional sets of horseshoes to the growing pile of provisions as well. Since Big Hat and Bear Scat still had their farrier tools and extra horseshoe nails, files and such, no further like in kind supplies were additionally purchased. However, the importance of having such items while in the backcountry was impressed upon Dan and Tom, who by now were all 'eyeballs, assholes, false teeth and tea kettles' in the listening and committing to their memories what was being said or advised department!

About then, the group of trappers and fur company Clerk shopping for their supplies in the warehouse for a year of living in the backcountry were joined by Big Hat, who had finished his business with his fur trapper buddies regarding the geography and routes into the Snake River beaver trapping country. When Big Hat walked into the warehouse, he found Bear Scat and company heading for the section of the warehouse holding the foodstuffs. Without saying a word, he walked close to the group and remaining standing off to one side and out of view, observed Bear Scat in action as the experienced Mountain Man he had developed into over the years was doing what he figured needed doing for the coming year's beaver trapping and survival successes.

Turning and facing Dan and Tom, Bear Scat said, "Alright you two, what kind of foods do you like and dislike? Remember, we are always looking at the weight issue of what we are packing into the backcountry on our horses and now I am adding one other thing for the two of you to commit to your memories. We eat what we take and we try to take foodstuffs into the backcountry that are lightweight and will last for a year without spoiling when properly stored and cared for. So talk to me. What are your likes and dislikes, but don't forget that meat from Mother Nature's cupboard is always the centerpiece of our meals, and that we try and work other things around that single food item that makes us happy and keeps the 'big guts from eating all the little guts'."

Dan and Tom just looked at each other and then Dan who was the oldest by one year said, "Bear Scat, me and my brother will eat just about anything. But we do love our mother's homemade pies and biscuits. But other than that, we both are big meat eaters, so get what you and Big Hat will eat and we will eat the same and fall in behind the two of you when it comes to what kind of 'grits' are selected."

Pleased with what he was hearing from his two new partners, Bear Scat turned and without any hesitation based on his experience and being the camp's main cook, said to the now two Clerks who were helping them, "Here is what I need, Boys. Dan and Tom, you two lads step in and give those Clerks a hand because we need to keep moving, otherwise Big Hat will fire the lot of us for mooching around and not keeping busy." When Big Hat heard those words, he had to smile over Bear Scat's antics and work ethics. It was now very plain to Big Hat that all of his work in teaching Bear Scat that which was needed in order to survive out on the frontier as a Mountain Man had not been lost on him or time wasted spent in so doing...

Standing in the middle of the foodstuffs section of the warehouse, Bear Scat's roving eyes fastened onto those items needed for a year in the backcountry for four men saying, "I need 200 pounds of that number one grade fine wheat flour, 200 pounds of dried pinto beans, 100 pounds of rice, 100 pounds of salt, 50 pounds of black pepper, 150 pounds of brown sugar cones, 300 pounds of green coffee beans, 50 pounds of dried raisins, 50 pounds of dried apples, two sacks of red pepper flakes, 20 pounds of shaving soap, 20 'carrots' of tobacco, four kegs of your first proof rum, six tins of bag balm, three jugs of honey, two jugs of that finer grade of bear grease for my biscuit making, two sacks of cinnamon, one sack of white pepper, and that should do it for starters," said Bear Scat, as he put his shopping list back into his buckskin shirt pocket for safekeeping. As he did, he couldn't help but noticing how the two Clerks, Dan and Tom were sweating over selecting all of the food items that Bear Scat had barked out and then stacked said items into separate piles for later loading. Finally Bear Scat said to the lead Clerk who was aware Bear Scat and company had been given 'carte blanche' when it came to shopping in the company's warehouses, "I will come back for any items I have forgotten that I need later on before we leave." With those words, Dan and Tom breathed a sigh of relief as they rested themselves on a couple sacks of flour after being 'run hard and put away wet' over the movement of all the items Bear Scat had ordered from the warehouse stocks over to their own pile of goods placed off to one side.

Then without saying a word, Bear Scat walked over to another nearby section of the warehouse holding dried eagle skins used in the trade with the various groups of Indians who came to the fort to trade their furs, robes and bearskins. Digging through the stacks of whole, dried eagle skins, he finally selected a large dried skin of that of an adult bald eagle. Cradling the skin carefully so he would not break any of its tail feathers, Bear Scat tenderly laid it on top of a pile of previously selected supplies. As he did, he caught the curious looks coming from not only the company Clerks but those from Dan and Tom as well.

Turning and facing those men with the questioning looks as to why a white man had selected a bald eagle skin, Bear Scat said, "It is kind of a long story. Years ago when Big Hat and I were cast out upon the prairie further east of here, in those travels we came upon a young Indian boy in a sinking Bull Boat on the Missouri River who was about to drown. I jumped in and saved the young Lakota boy and as I did, both Big Hat and I found ourselves being quickly surrounded by a large number of hostile-looking Lakota warriors! They took us prisoner but as it turned out, because I had rescued the only son of a great Lakota warrior chief name Buffalo Calf, they treated the two of us with respect and dignity. In fact, because I had saved the young Indian boy named Buffalo Horn, we were fed, clothed and treated with great respect by the whole band of Indians. Then Chief Buffalo Calf presented Big Hat and me with three horses out of gratitude for saving his son's life and bid us farewell as we continued our journey onto Fort Union. Once there, we were refitted and spent a year further west trapping on the Porcupine River. Eventually we worked our ways back to Fort

Union and then decided to travel to St. Louis to seek my long-lost brother who was also reported to be heading in that direction as well."

Then Bear Scat stopped talking, took a deep breath and then began once again with the rest of his rather unusual story by saying, "Big Hat, two other trappers and I then headed for St. Louis to trade in our furs for higher prices than the Mountain Prices that we could get for them at Fort Union. While on our travels heading south through the land of the dreaded Arikara Indians, we were once again surprised and surrounded by about 30 Lakota Indians led by Buffalo Calf, war chief for the Lakota. Upon recognizing Big Hat and me as the saviors of his one and only son Buffalo Horn, the war chief decided to escort us four trappers through the Arikara country so we would be able to safely arrive in St. Louis. But before the Lakota left us when we were almost safely to St. Louis, Buffalo Calf was discovered one morning tying bald eagle tail feathers into the mane of my riding horse. When I asked him what he was doing, he advised that henceforth I would be known to his people as White Eagle and not Bear Scat. He also advised that he would send runners to the other bands of Lakota and his Brothers, the Northern Cheyenne Indians, that I was to be considered a Lakota Brother and accorded safety through any Lakota or Northern Cheyenne lands henceforth. As a gesture of his goodwill for saving his son, he tied white bald eagle tail feathers into the mane of my horse so other Lakota and Northern Cheyenne could see from a distance that the horse wearing such special feathers of respect was being ridden by White Eagle, friend to all the Lakota and Chief Buffalo Calf."

Running down on his story once again, Bear Scat paused, took another deep breath as if that would help in the storytelling, and began again by saying, "Lately, I have noticed that the white bald eagle tail feathers tied into my horse's mane were getting a bit ragged, and several became untied and had fallen out along the way. So I picked out this bald eagle skin and plan on removing all my horse's old tail feathers and will tie in these newer feathers for whatever benefit it will bring me and those around me, if we ever run across Lakota or Northern Cheyenne Indians who see that White Eagle sits atop the horse wearing the feathers tied into its mane, and maybe they will let us safely pass."

After telling that story, Bear Scat noticed that everyone who had been listening to his story was now respectfully as quiet as a 'mouse running across a ball of cotton'. Embarrassed over opening himself up and telling that story and then the respectful silence that followed he said, "Alright, you guys. We need to get all of our supplies carted up to the front door of this warehouse, get those supplies recorded in the company's records, and then bring our horses over and begin the packing of those supplies back to our bunkhouse for safekeeping." After leaving the warehouse and heading over to the livery so they could get their newly shoed packhorses, load them up with their just-acquired supplies and cart them over to the bunkhouse for safekeeping, Bear Scat remembered one item that he had forgotten to select. As the other three men began packing their horses over at the warehouse, Bear Scat returned to the food section of that facility and selected a large sack containing beeswax candles to be used in any cabin or dugout they would construct at a later date once up on the beaver trapping grounds for light during the evenings or on dark winter days. There they would be most helpful, especially when doing the delicate fleshing, defatting and 'hooping' work on the fresh beaver pelts.

Following breakfast the next morning found Bear Scat standing by his favorite riding horse dutifully removing the old bald eagle tail feathers from his horse's mane and tying ten new white eagle tail feathers into the animal's mane for all to see. When finished and while standing back and examining his handiwork, Bear Scat was satisfied that any Lakota or Northern Cheyenne Indian spotting those ten white eagle feathers flapping in the horse's mane would know that 'White Eagle' was atop that horse and to be respected as one of their Brothers...

One week later found Bear Scat, Dan and Tom at the two tipis of the Shoshone women who had been commissioned to outfit the brothers in the proper frontier outerwear. Since those women were renowned at the rendezvous as makers of fancy beaded clothing for any Free Trappers who had enough Made Beaver, vermillion or glass beads to trade for such finery, Bear Scat had availed himself on behalf of the brothers for such specialized outfitting. Once there, Dan and Tom were stripped naked once again by the Indian women and then fitted into two full buckskin sets of shirts and britches. Additionally they each took away from such a clothes transformation venture three pairs of beautifully beaded moccasins. Two pairs of the moccasins were for normal wear and one pair each of the heavier ones for winter footwear. Once Dan and Tom were fully dressed in the 'garb of the land' and seated atop their riding horses, Bear Scat had to shake his head and smile over what he was seeing. The clothing of the fur trapper now being worn by Dan and Tom, because it was so clean and new, fairly glowed in the sunlight. In fact both men looked like 'golden-hued trappers' in the light of day. The two men looked like they were made of gold because their new and clean buckskin outfits had yet to be exposed to the life of a trapper. Exposed to rain, snow, smoke from the many campfires one sat around, gutting out buffalo, deer or elk, and being covered with tallow, blood and stomach juices from the many animals butchered, grease from the many beaver skinned on a daily basis, and lastly from wiping greasy hands numerous times upon the now golden-colored garments until they turned dark chestnut brown from the many collective elements smeared across them over time. Once afield for any amount of time and their golden looks would soon turn to a weathered and soft dark brown look routinely found as a badge of courage signifying rugged Mountain Men of the fabled beaver waters, craggy mountains and buffalo meat partially cooked just the way most men of the mountains loved it…

The last week of the 1834 Rendezvous was a whirlwind of activity on the part of Big Hat, Bear Scat and trappers-to-be Dan and Tom Campbell. There were last meals to be shared with friends and fellow trappers, last-minute requisitioning of supplies, final adjustments made to newly acquired packsaddles, last meals as Free Trappers as guests with Factor Campbell, saying last good-byes to fellow trappers already leaving the rendezvous, and adjustments made to loaded packs soon to be hauled over the many rugged miles into the beaver trapping backcountry.

Finally came the long-awaited morning of departure from Fort Bonneville. After a last breakfast with St. Louis Fur Company Factor Robert Campbell and his last words with his two sons who were also heading out, Campbell motioned Big Hat and Bear Scat over to where he was standing watching the final departure preparations in the making. There standing alongside the two Mountain Men trusted to teach his two sons the way of the West, Campbell looked into the faces of the two trappers saying, "Please bring them back to me and their mother in one piece. Bring my two sons back in one piece and wiser as to the fur trade and as honorable 'Men of the Mountains', please."

Big Hat and Bear Scat, very much aware of the new responsibility they had now shouldered in taking under their 'wings' backcountry novices Dan and Tom, quietly nodded their understandings as to what was expected for their friend and now worried father Robert Campbell. Then without further ado, Big Hat took the lead, trailing five heavily loaded horses, followed by Dan and Tom each trailing five heavily loaded horses, as Bear Scat, ever the guard against surprise attack by Indians, brought up the rear of the trappers' caravan trailing five heavily loaded horses as well. Following loosely along behind the string of trappers' horses were One Shot and Little Griz's faithful mares, which Big Hat and Bear Scat had wisely not sold when they arrived at the rendezvous a month earlier. For some reason, the two men just decided they would keep their previously killed friends' horses as extra riding stock, in case one of them lost their favorite riding horse somewhere along the trail due to being attacked by critters, an unfortunate horse wreck, or theft from Indians as they headed out into the coming year's newest trapping grounds. However, as the long horse caravan of 26 valuable animals headed out, Campbell quietly realized with a certain amount of dread in his heart, that such a tantalizing livestock string represented nothing more than a 'target' for every horse-poor Indian in the country to try and raid...

For the next five days, Big Hat slowly led the men in a northwesterly direction as he had been instructed to do by several of his trapper friends back at the rendezvous, to a place they had named "Moose Flat" when they had travelled through the same country during an earlier time. There they camped for the night but not before they had unloaded all of their horses, hobbled the same so they could graze near the campsite, and then stacked their packs full of provisions and saddles in a defensive circle in case of attack from Indians. The following morning, late by the time they had allowed the horses to feed and then repacked all of their supplies, found the trappers on the western edges of rugged Hoback Peak. (Author's Note: The same area in Wyoming in which the Author and his father hunted elk from horseback in 1971. The one and same area in which the Author noticed a trap ring on the end of a chain half-buried in the duff of the forest as he rode by elk hunting one morning. Dismounting, the Author pulled on the ring and chain only to unveil an old and rusty beaver trap partially buried in the soil! A beaver trap that probably had fallen unnoticed off a packhorse by a Mountain Man riding by on the same trail many years earlier! That trap was unfortunately later stolen from the Author by the outfitter's camp cook when I was out on the trail hunting. Left back at camp in the bottom of my duffle bag, its loss was not noticed until I returned home at a later date...)

Slowly picking his way across a talus slope on a narrow trail and then around a jagged rocky finger of basalt, Big Hat paused and turning in his saddle, looked back to see how his two novices were navigating the dangerous talus slope behind him with their strings of horses. When Big Hat did, he was instantly knocked off his horse by a just-as-surprised and now aroused grizzly bear coming around the same basalt outcropping from the opposite direction! Down into the canyon plunged Big Hat's horse after being charged, spooked and then body-slammed by the now enraged bear! In that explosion of spooked horse and enraged bear,

Big Hat was tossed skyward, but managed to grab onto a stony protrusion on the rockface on his way over the cliff's face! In so doing, that lucky handhold precluded him from following his horse dropping into the abyss of the canyon below, bouncing off the rocks as the mare fell! Hearing his rifle clattering off the rocks below him, wiry strong Big Hat managed to keep his head, drew his pistol and hanging onto the rockface with his other hand, shot the now enraged bear in the face from less than six feet away! However, all that did was smash out a mess of teeth and enrage the bear even further, especially after seeing his 'dinner' sailing over the cliff and then being painfully shot in the mouth by a badly smelling 'human thing'!

Meanwhile behind Big Hat, still in the dangerous process of crossing the talus slope's narrow trail with their horses, novices Dan and Tom found themselves in the middle of a rodeo with their riding and packhorses! In a rodeo with their riding and packhorses smelling and observing the great, now standing and roaring forth grizzly bear above them and just yards away! With the bear making his angry presence known above them, Dan and Tom's heavily loaded horses were desperately trying to turn around on the narrow trail on the steep talus slope where good footing was scarce to find and not having much luck in the process. In that 'rodeo', inexperienced Dan and Tom, instead of stepping off their horses on the uphill side and trying to kill the bear with their rifles, were instead hanging onto their bucking mounts' saddle pommels for dear life!

Bear Scat, bringing up the rear of the caravan of horses and trappers, upon seeing the melee above him, quickly dismounted in a much-practiced move and in so doing, took his trusty Hawken rifle along with him. Bear Scat's experienced backcountry horse, although nervous with the bear's smells now filling his nostrils, managed to stand there shivering in fear, trusting his master had the upper hand in such a dangerous situation. **BOOM!** went Bear Scat's rifle and microseconds later, the bear forgot about his lost horse dinner in the canyon below, and concentrated on the burning in his face from being hit with a ball from Big Hat's desperately fired pistol and now from the deeply burning pain in his broken shoulder! Bear Scat, true to his experienced form, had fired at the bear's front shoulder in an attempt to break him down and in so doing, take his killing urges off the close at hand Big Hat still desperately hanging onto his rockface for fear of following his horse to his death below in the canyon as well!

That first shot was quickly followed by a second **BOOM!** as Bear Scat hurriedly retrieved his Lancaster rifle from his first packhorse in line, which was also quickly fired at the bear. Big Hat heard a loud "THWACK" from his barely hanging on position on the rocky face, as the Lancaster's .52 caliber lead ball smashed into the bear's face just below his right eye, dropping him instantly dead onto the narrow trail into a crumpled, quivering in his death throes, pile!

For the next few minutes after seeing the bear lying lifeless in among them, the trappers began the process of getting control of their horses before they 'followed' Big Hat's horse into the nearby deep canyon below as well. As they did, Big Hat, now safe from the close at hand bear, scrambled up the rockface onto the narrow trail. Then realizing his Hawken rifle had lodged itself into a rocky crevice below him, crawled back down over the edge of the cliff face, retrieved his rifle and then crawled back up to the wide spot in the trail now occupied by a very dead grizzly bear thanks to Bear Scat's accurately placed second shot into the head of the bear... (Author's Note: At one time in early America, the grizzly bear was estimated to number around 100,000 individuals and whose range extended as far south as northern Florida! Today the grizzly bear numbers a shade over 1,000 individuals in the 'Lower 48' and at the time of this writing in 2017, is protected by the federal Endangered Species Act of 1973, and a number of state laws. Today in the United States, the grizzly bear is found primarily in the States of Montana, Wyoming and Alaska.)

That evening at a place Big Hat's trapper friends back at the rendezvous had previously geographically described and had named "Station Creek" just to the northwest of the deadly ground around the western side of Hoback Peak, the four trappers made their camp for the evening. Once again in a practiced move, all the horses were hobbled and let out to graze. That was, minus Big Hat's original riding horse. A horse attacked by a grizzly bear back on the Hoback Peak trail which had shied off the narrow trail in alarm over being attacked by a grizzly bear and had fallen several hundred feet to its death into the canyon below. Once control had been established back at Hoback Peak, Dan and Tom walked down into the canyon and retrieved Big Hat's saddle, bridle and saddlebags from his now dead horse, which ironically now represented dinner for the next hungry grizzly bear that came along…

Once the saddle and its accessories had been retrieved and brought back to the top of the trail on the site of the bear attack, Bear Scat brought in One Shot's favorite riding horse which had been brought along in case a spare riding horse was needed, saddled and became Big Hat's riding horse, now that his other horse was 'bear bait' ready for the 'eating' at the bottom of the canyon. Following that bit of excitement, the men decided they would spend the next several days at the Station Creek site to rest up their horses, let them put on the feed bag, and give Big Hat the opportunity to recover from his scare and sore back received when he had been 'exploded' off his horse and fell over the ledge onto which he had been riding on the narrow trail. Additionally, when his Hawken rifle had also gone over the side of the cliff, it had landed on some rocks, busted off its hammer and broke the spring in its lock. So after rifling through one of their packs, Bear Scat had recovered the extra rifle and pistol replacement parts that he had procured from the warehouse just in case someone of their group had a rifle broken or busted up, and made the necessary repairs of Big Hat's main and preferred use rifle. Then Bear Scat, the designated camp cook because of his skills around the campfire, calmly broke out his cooking implements from another of their packs and began roasting tender chunks of grizzly bear meat from the freshly butchered bear on their roasting steels. As the 'mean-assed' grizzly bear's steaks now roasted away, Bear Scat, as if nothing exciting had happened earlier in the day, made up a batch of biscuit mix for their evening's supper. Then recovering his Dutch ovens from several other packs, he greased the same with some fresh grizzly bear fat and began heating up the frontier's version of a cast iron oven for the biscuit baking process soon to follow.

Following that welcome respite at Station Creek, two more subsequent days of travel found the men in the earlier rendezvous trappers' self-described Snake River country. There the trappers found themselves in a much welcome area, thick with numerous beaver ponds, watered areas, heavy patches of willow which was the beaver's favorite food, numerous beaver houses, and much evidence of beaver tree-cutting activity along the many secondary waterways dotted with nearby cottonwood trees. After further looking around, to Big Hat and Bear Scat's way of thinking, they had found where they wanted to be for the coming trapping season. Now they just needed to find a suitable location to build a cabin that possessed water, good grazing, firewood supplies, out of the north wind's path, and was somewhat out of the way to 'eyes' other than their own.

Locating their temporary campsite in a finger of trees near a meadow so the horses could graze, the men laid out their numerous packs in a defensive circle in a cluster of pine trees. Leaving Big Hat back in their camp because of his still sore back from the grizzly bear attack, a sore back aggravated even more by riding horses, to guard their camp, the other three men set out looking for a suitable permanent campsite. Riding throughout the rest of that day along the northward length of the Snake River, the three men led by Bear Scat were unable to locate what they figured was a suitable permanent campsite. Returning later in the day back at their temporary campsite, the men were surprised to find a campfire already made and a freshly killed mule deer hanging on a temporary meat pole back in camp! That evening after supper, the men discussed what they had observed throughout their day's travels. They advised Big Hat that there were elk and deer aplenty and even small herds of buffalo feeding along many of the valley's meadows. However, with no real suitable location discovered that was central to their anticipated beaver trapping activities, one that was watered with a goodly supply of drinking and horse water, adjacent close at hand fuel and grazing area, they had come back to camp empty-handed and disappointed.

The next morning, the three men departed once again after their morning meal and headed south that day along the Snake River looking for a suitable campsite. Around noon judged by the sun's location, the three men found what they were looking for. All along their travels that morning, they had traversed along many watered areas all of which held numerous signs of beaver activity. Rounding dual fingers of trees ending at the edge of a very large beaver pond, the men observed a sheltered draw at the head of which two separate fingers of trees originated from a heavy stand of pine and Douglas firs. Running down the middle between the two separated fingers of trees was a spring-fed creek emanating from below a large rockface at the head of the draw they were closely examining as a future campsite. Dense grass-lined meadows shadowed both sides of the creek and vast meadows ran both north and south alongside the nearby beaver pond and adjacent watered areas. Quietly sitting on his horse and examining the vastness of the potential grassy feeding areas for their horses, Bear Scat knew such areas would more than provide the needed food source they needed for their large horse herd.

Riding their horses up into the head of the long draw bordered by the two fingers of trees, the men saw that the spring-fed creek was more than adequate for all of their needs. Then Bear Scat spotted a flat spot at the edge of the trees next to the rockface that would be more than adequate for a cabin at least 20 feet in length and some 15-20 feet wide. Immediately adjacent the potential cabin site were also numerous pine and Douglas fir trees suitable for cutting and building a substantial cabin. Then Bear Scat noticed that up on the timbered hillside was a burned area from a previous lightning strike that covered about an acre of dead timber in size. To his way of thinking, there was their dried wood supply and one that was no more than 150 feet from where he figured would be their new cabin site. As Bear Scat's experienced eyes continued quietly studying the area for what they needed in a living space, he located not far from where the creek exited the ground from beneath the huge rocky face, a site for a corral that would be suitable enough to house their rather extensive horse herd. He also noticed that such a corral site would be out of sight from anyone riding along the lower beaver ponds at the ends of the two fingers of trees. Lastly, if a cabin was built where he figured one should be situated, it could be very easily defended against anyone caring to cause the trappers any harm.

Sitting there on his horse and looking around one more time making sure he took in all the positive aspects of their possible new homesite in order to respond to Big Hat's expected line of questions once they returned, he thought, *There is one more thing that I need to do in order to meet the request of Factor Campbell and that was to teach his two sons everything about the fur trade from the ground up, starting with the proper cabin site selection.* Turning in his saddle so he could face Dan and Tom who had been quietly sitting there on their horses looking all around as well, Bear Scat began explaining to the two young men what he had been looking for in a new homesite. As he did, he took the time explaining the positive and negative aspects of what he was considering and finally, why he had chosen this location for their new home. As he did, he could see both Dan and Tom really paying attention to what he was saying and committing to their memories what a trapper must look for in a good homesite. A homesite that would be safe from attack, meet their animals' needs for nearby horse feed and lots of it for such a large herd like they had, the availability of good cabin-building wood and fuel for their outdoor and eventually indoor fires, the importance of a quality supply of fresh drinking and horse water, and lastly a good field of fire if they were ever attacked by hostile Indians.

Upon finishing with his homesite location justifications for how he had made his selection, he could see in Dan and Tom's eyes something deeper than just a simple comprehension of what was needed for survival out on the frontier. If Bear Scat was correct in what he had been reading in the two men's eyes of recent, he had better be careful. He wasn't sure but he felt that he could see a look in the two brothers' eyes indicating more than just a simple interest in what they had just learned from an experienced Mountain Man. To Bear Scat's way of thinking based on his ability to read people, the two brothers were almost 'displaying looks' that 'read' they were liking what they were seeing, loving the life they were now experiencing more and more ever day where it was them pitting themselves against the wilds and looking forward to what the world had in store for them in the future. *Damn,* thought Bear Scat, *if Big Hat and I are not careful, we might just be returning to Factor Campbell two dyed-in-the-wool and loving it as a future lifestyle, fur trappers!*

Returning back to their temporary campsite later that afternoon, Bear Scat, Dan and Tom dismounted, unsaddled their horses, hobbled the same and turned them out to water and graze. Big Hat, one who had trained Bear Scat and now almost able to read his every move, after greeting the men, remained silent in order to hear the good news soon to be forthcoming. Good news because Big Hat could almost read in Bear Scat's actions that he soon would be the recipient of good news. He wasn't wrong in his 'read' when moments later, Bear Scat, with a smile as wide as the mighty Mississippi River splashed clear across his face, approached his mentor and the recognized leader of their group of trappers, obviously with something important to say.

"Well, as I suspect you already know, we three found a great site for our new home for the rest of the trapping season. It is located just a mile or so from where we now stand, is central to our new trapping grounds, is secluded and as you have trained me, it has good water, good grass for the horses, has firewood aplenty and is out of the worst of the winter weather," said an obviously happy to be reporting Bear Scat. Upon hearing such a good report, Big Hat just smiled and then said, "What's for supper? I hope it might include some of those sugared and cinnamon-coated biscuits you are known to make once in a while…"

By noon the day following, all the horses had been packed and found the four trappers strung out in a caravan of 'horseflesh and humanity' heading for their new homesite. However, unknown to the trappers, three sets of 'dark eyes' watched their every move… Then those three sets of 'dark eyes' rode along out of sight from the trappers riding in the meadows below, but stayed close enough to see where the trappers turned at the two fingers of trees and headed up into the head of the draw until they rode out of sight… Then the three sets of 'dark eyes' rode off out of sight.

Dismounting at the head of their secluded draw, Big Hat's practiced eyes swept the area of homesite selection and found the seclusion, good supply of water, available horse feed, and wood supply more than meeting his expectations. To his way of thinking, *he had trained Bear Scat well.* In a now practiced move when in Indian country, the four men hurriedly unloaded their pack animals and arranged their numerous packs in a defensive circle just below the huge rockface at the head of their draw. That necessary move of precaution now out of the way when in Indian country, Big Hat and Bear Scat walked off the proposed area of their new cabin. The cabin site's dimensions decided, Bear Scat paced off a short distance from the soon to be built cabin, removed a shovel from one of the packs and began digging a firepit central to the front of their proposed cabin. As he did, Dan and Tom began hauling in large rocks from the nearby spring-fed creek in order to line the outdoor firepit. As Bear Scat, Dan and Tom tended to the building of the firepit, Big Hat, sore back and all from the recent grizzly bear attack, began dragging in armloads of dry firewood for that evening's cooking fire. Then removing a single buck saw from another set of packs, Big Hat walked just a short distance behind their proposed cabin site and began cutting down a dead Douglas fir tree. After 'felling' the tree, Big Hat began cutting up the downed log into short sitting log sections. Upon completion of that task, Bear Scat, Dan and Tom, now finished with building the firepit, hauled down the sitting log sections and positioned them around the firepit for use by the men when eating their meals outdoors during good weather.

Finished with those chores, Big Hat and Tom removed their rifles from their saddle scabbards and headed up into the timbered area behind their proposed cabin site looking for the first mule deer they ran across. In the meantime, Bear Scat and Dan unpacked the men's sleeping furs and arranged their bedding behind the defensive circle of packs. Then the two men began unloading Bear Scat's cooking ware and other meal-making implements and hauled the same over to the location of the outdoor firepit. While Bear Scat began making preparations for their evening meal, Dan built a fire so Bear Scat would have sufficient coals for his Dutch ovens when it came time for making biscuits. About a half-hour later as the fire began making sufficient coals and with Bear Scat smearing the two Dutch ovens with some bear grease from one of the jugs purchased from the warehouse, the two men were somewhat startled upon hearing not one rifle shot, but two in close succession!

Realizing both Big Hat and Tom were excellent shooters but still being a little concerned, Bear Scat and Dan brought their rifles in closer to their outdoor cooking fire and laid them along two near at hand sitting logs ready for quick retrieval in case the two shots fired earlier meant Indian trouble. However, about a half-hour later, back to camp returned Big Hat and Tom with big grins, both dragging a field-dressed adult doe mule deer. As Tom and Dan assembled a meat pole in the timber next to their campsite, Bear Scat began expertly removing the backstraps from both doe deer. He did so because he remembered the earlier words from Factor Campbell that both of his rather large sons 'ate like a pair of Clydesdale horses from an oat bucket' after a hard day's work!

Come dark and after a fine supper of freshly roasted venison, along with sugar and cinnamon-coated biscuits and 'trapper's coffee' liberally laced with some fine rum, the men brought in their horses, double hobbled them and tied them to a double-roped, near at hand picket line. Following those precautions, the trappers retreated to their sleeping furs realizing tomorrow would mean the start of a number of hard workdays ahead. However, before nodding off, each man placed his rifle near at hand alongside his sleeping furs, with a pistol at the head of where he slept just in case any sign of trouble reared its ugly head...

Just before daylight the next morning, Big Hat, Dan and Tom awoke to the sounds of Bear Scat rustling around his now roaring campfire as he began preparing breakfast for the group of men. Then the unmistakable smell of coffee wafted throughout the campsite, and that brought the men out from under their warm sleeping furs and over to the nearby spring-fed creek. There the men washed up, shaved and with sleep still riding the outer edges of their souls, walked over to the campfire. There they had cups of boiling hot coffee that was strong enough to dissolve a mule's shoe thrust into their hands by a smiling Bear Scat. That was soon followed with freshly roasted slabs of mule deer and Dutch oven biscuits plated up and handed out as well. Soon the only sounds heard around the campfire that morning were those of hungry men eating like they knew they had a hard workday lying ahead of them and the crackling of a good wood fire.

The rest of that day, only the sounds of a single buck saw sawing, the crashing of falling trees and the ringing sounds of axes 'limbing' the trees filled the air. Those same sounds would be repeated throughout the next four days as well. Come day five found Big Hat with shovel in hand scraping out the rough dimensions of their cabin to be and smoothing out the cabin site's ground. As he did, he was visited throughout the day by heavily sweating Bear Scat, Tom and Dan, driving horse teams into the proposed cabin site area hauling green logs precut for their new home. Four days later found the cabin's walls pre-cut, notched, placed and in the process of being 'chinked' by Big Hat, as the other three trappers returned to the forested area behind their cabin to cut roof poles. After those roof poles had been dragged down in sufficient number to roof the entire cabin, Big Hat sent the men back into the forested area to cut even smaller poles for what he called 'his surprise'. Following that, the single front door and windows were cut out from the newly walled-in cabin and the roof's last timbers laid. That was followed with panniers filled with dirt hauled over to the cabin and placed until the dirt was about two feet deep across the entire roof to preclude anyone from attacking their cabin and trying to set fire to their roof, as well as being deep enough to keep out any rains or melting snows. Then for the next three days, Bear Scat, Dan and Tom spent their days in the burned-over area above their cabin caused by an earlier lightning strike, cutting dry Douglas fir trees and dragging the logs down and placing them out in front of their cabin as their winter woodpile. However, the men made sure the log pile was arranged in such a fashion so no Indians could use them as cover when attacking the cabin from the front. As the three men continued working on the woodcutting detail, Big Hat stayed back at the cabin saying someone needed to watch over the horses and their packs against anyone slipping in and stealing the same. However, every time the men came down the hill with a load of horse-drawn logs, they found Big Hat banging and making other suspicious noises from inside their new cabin. Then when they tried to investigate what Big Hat was up to, he good-naturedly ran them off and told them to get back to work because the fall trapping season was almost upon them and they soon needed to be getting ready for those activities...

Finally when the men came in for their evening meal, Big Hat unveiled his surprise. Inviting the men to go inside their cabin and look around, the men did so. There they discovered why Big Hat had stayed back when they were doing the backbreaking work of cutting and hauling down their winter wood supply. Each man discovered that Big Hat had made wooden bedframes with horse halter rope stretched across the bedframes which acted as 'bedsprings'. In so doing, now each man would not have to sleep on the ground inside the cabin but could sleep warmly above the hard-packed soil. Additionally, Big Hat had made a pole table and chairs, as well as log shelves along the cabin's inside walls to hold some of their provisions up off the floor so they would not spoil from dampness or invite rodent damage! Upon closer examination, the men also discovered a number of pegs driven into the cabin's walls to hold clothing, guns, 'Possibles bags' and any other items needing to be up off the cabin's dirt floor!

Talk about surprised, the men were elated! However, then the really important work began. Every pack had to be brought into the cabin for safekeeping away from the rodents and weather, sorted out and placed onto the shelves or pegs to prevent loss. Then the four men built a shed-like attachment with log flooring onto the side of their cabin overlooking the nearby horse corral, so all of their leather goods could be placed inside to prevent damage from the rains, snows, salt-hungry porcupines eating the sweat-soaked leather, or theft from Indians.

Finally the last big project had to be undertaken, that was building the horse corral. Back to the forested area went the trappers turned 'lumberjacks' to cut more wood for the poles and rails needed for a stout horse corral that could hold their 25 horses. Three days later, the horses now had a safe and secure home as well. The trappers had seen to it that the horse corral had been built in such a location that the structure was cleverly placed below that portion of the creek the men used for drinking, washing and shaving. By letting the creek flow through the middle of the large corral, that also precluded the men having to take the horses to the water source every night and morning so they could drink.

When Bear Scat, Dan and Tom were busy with building the horse corral, Big Hat was busy building two heavy duty meat poles in camp sufficient to hold elk or partial buffalo carcasses, and two large meat racks to be use for smoking and drying meats for jerky. When he had finished with those vital chores, Big Hat took their pack of tanned deerskins that had been used to protect their packs of furs while being transported to the 1834 Rendezvous and after building log frames, stretched the hides over the frames so they could be used as window coverings on the cabin's three window openings. Since the deerskins had been shaved and tanned, they were thin enough to let in some light through the window frames and yet keep out most of the cold winter air and the rains or snows that followed. Then with the faint amount of light the deerskins allowed through the window frames, in combination with the use of the heavy duty beeswax candles Bear Scat had purchased back at the fort's warehouse and the light from their fireplace, there would be plenty of light inside the cabin at night to do what needed doing. So much so that when the weather was nasty making outside work a misery, the trappers could continue fleshing out the beaver hides and hooping the same while inside the candle-lit cabin. That plus the light coming from the fire in their fireplace would more than provide any light needed during the winter's dark hours or during the long winter nights.

The day after the men had finished building the corral, meat poles, smoking racks and installing the specialized deer hides onto the now hung window frames, Big Hat emerged early and was sitting beside the outside cooking fire while Bear Scat began preparations for making breakfast with the last of the camp's deer meat. "Bear Scat, be sure and fix up a big breakfast for all of us today. Then make sure you have a big pot of pinto beans soaking away so we can have some beans and roasted buffalo for our supper tonight," said Big Hat.

With those words, Bear Scat turned saying, "Big Hat, I don't have any buffalo meat for supper tonight. In fact, this is the last of the deer meat in camp. Someone needs to go out and kill us some more meat or you guys will be relegated to just beans and biscuits for our supper tonight," said Bear Scat, as he poured more coffee into Big Hat's coffee cup at the end of his extended arm and hand.

"Well, that 'someone needing to go out and kill some more meat' is us," said Big Hat with a grin. "I think it is time that the four of us go out and kill a number of buffalo. We are fast approaching our fall trapping season and we damn sure will be in need of a mess of jerky, especially with the eager eaters we have in Dan and Tom," said Big Hat with an anticipatory grin over the day's coming events.

Without a word, Bear Scat got a big grin of anticipation on his mug as well, wiped his deer tallow-covered hands off on his buckskin shirt and then trotted back inside their cabin. Moments later out he came with a bag of pinto beans, a sack of red pepper flakes and a small sack of black pepper. Dropping those items off on a makeshift table Big Hat had made for him, Bear Scat headed off for their spring carrying a large heavy brass bean pot in hand. Soon back he came and then spent the next 20 or so minutes picking out the bug-chewed beans, sticks, clumps of mud, and other non-eatables from the bag of dried pinto beans that had found their ways into the bag when they had been harvested and sacked up. Then into the pot went the good beans with a handful of wild onions picked from a rocky hillside just the day before, along with generous helpings of black pepper and red pepper flakes. With that, the pot was then set off to one side of the firepit to soak.

After breakfast, the four trappers set about readying themselves for the upcoming buffalo hunt with keen anticipation and the thoughts of richly marbled, partially cooked buffalo meat swirling around in their heads come suppertime. Putting the panniers on their four stoutest packhorses, the trappers streamed out from their secluded home about an hour later in high anticipation of the hunt to come. They did not have to travel very far, maybe a mile, when they came upon a small herd of buffalo calmly feeding in the rich grasses alongside a beaver pond. Four shots later and four cow buffalo breathed no more, as the men advanced upon their kills. Following tradition, Bear Scat opened up the side of one of the cows, removed a large chunk of still quivering liver, cut off a smaller chunk and handed the remaining lobe to Big Hat. As Bear Scat 'wolfed' down his chunk of the raw, mineral-rich liver, Big Hat cut a chunk off the lobe of liver and passed it onto Dan. Then as Big Hat happily ate big bites from his chunk of raw liver, he watched Dan holding his first slab of warm buffalo liver to see what he was going to do with it. Without batting an eye, Dan cut off a chunk with his knife and handed the remainder of the liver to his brother. As he did, Bear Scat, having finished eating his first chunk of raw liver, was once again fishing around inside the cow and cut off another large chunk of the still bloody liver. When he looked up, it was just in time to see Dan spew a line of raw buffalo liver-laden vomit all over Big Hat and his brother Tom! When he vomited up the raw liver just consumed, Big Hat jumped like 'a bug on a hot rock', not expecting such a reaction from the normally staid Dan. That was when Tom, still holding his slab of raw liver and not really sure what to do with it, upon seeing his brother puking all over everyone close at hand, reflex-puked up the remains of Bear Scat's previously made breakfast all over his unsuspecting brother!

With that, Bear Scat with buffalo liver blood-smeared lips and chin began roaring with laughter! Bear Scat laughed not over the two novice trappers' reaction to eating still quivering raw buffalo liver but the fact of the picture it presented. No longer were the two brothers all golden-looking in their new buckskin outfits. Now the more than soiled buckskins they were wearing were beginning to take on the rich looks like those worn by real trappers! The rest of the morning was spent butchering out the four buffalo and loading the chunks of their rich meat into the horses' panniers. Then the four men mounted up and headed for their campsite so they could process their meat into thin strips for the smoking process yet to come needed to make jerky. Once back at their camp and while Bear Scat was cutting up some previously gathered mountain mahogany limb wood to be used in the meat smoking process, he broke out laughing once again. Looking over at Dan and Tom, Bear Scat found both men still looking the color of grass over the raw liver issue as they cut up the buffalo meat into thin strips as Big Hat had so instructed. Additionally, Bear Scat noticed that both boys' puke-covered buckskins were covered with flies! It seemed the flies preferred landing on the puke-covered buckskins of the two brothers over that of the fresh buffalo meat! *Yes,* Bear Scat thought, *Dan and Tom will make fine Mountain Men someday down the line...and even their new buckskin outfits are beginning to show that as well...*

For the next five days the trappers spent their time in camp making up mounds of buffalo jerky, tending the smoking fires so they would not get too hot and scorch the meat, and keeping the black-billed magpies and gray jays off the meat racks, eating and pooping their way on the buffalo meat as they slipped in to grab a piece of meat off an unattended meat rack and then speed away. Just as fast as the meat was processed and cooled, Big Hat and Dan placed it into tanned deerskin bags and hung it from the pegs in their cabin for later use during the colder winter weather. Finished with the jerky making, Bear Scat and Tom headed down to the watered areas below their campsite and there the two trappers cut 20 four-foot-long anchor poles out of dry willow wood to be used when the trapping started. Wooden poles which were to be used to run through the ring at the end of the beaver trap chain and act as an anchor out into the deeper waters. In the dried pole-cutting process, Bear Scat explained to Tom and Dan that after the trap had been set, its chain would be extended out to the anchor pole in the deeper water, have its ring slipped over the pole and tied off on the pole to avoid any trapped beaver from swimming off with the trap. Bear Scat could see the quizzical look Tom was giving him so he explained even further that a beaver when trapped would try to swim out into deeper water to escape. When it did, the animal could only swim as far as the end of the trap's chain allowed, which was anchored to the dry pole sunken into the bottom of the pond. That would preclude the beaver from escaping, and eventually tiring from trying to swim off with a valuable five-pound trap on its foot, would drown from exhaustion.

Following that activity, Bear Scat and Tom found the time to smoke their beaver traps in dense rotten cottonwood wood smoke (makes the most smoke) to rid the metal of the man or other beaver smells. Then all the men had to do besides killing a few more buffalo for meat was wait for the fall's colder weather to descend upon them, so it would start the process of the beaver's fur coming into prime with the advent of colder water and weather. As each fall morning grew colder and colder, Bear Scat waited expecting Big Hat to burst forth from their cabin and announce today would be the day to start the fall beaver trapping season.

Like in times past with Big Hat, Bear Scat would find himself the camp's cook one morning and then come the next day the main beaver trapper of the group, after Big Hat announced it was time to begin either fall or spring trapping. Setting the pot of boiling 'black as the devil's soul' trapper's coffee on a flat rock next to his morning fire to cool off a bit, Bear Scat saw Big Hat emerging from their cabin, looking skyward, seeing his breath in the air and then briskly walking over to the outdoor cooking fire like a man on a mission.

"Bear Scat," he announced in loud tones, "set us up with a hearty breakfast because we all are going out beaver trapping this morning." Then he poured himself a steaming cup of the coffee which was as black as a lump of coal and as thick as an oil seep, took a sip and then said to Bear Scat, "Just the way I like my coffee, stout enough to mend a broken heart or fix the crack of dawn!" Then with a 'bellow', Big Hat called for Dan and Tom to hurry up and get dressed because today they were going to get a lesson on how to trap beaver! Little did he realize all of them would soon get more than they bargained for when it came to life's lessons in wilderness living...

After finishing up their breakfasts and loading their saddlebags with handfuls of rich-tasting buffalo jerky, the four men commenced loading their panniers on two 'hell-for-stout' packhorses. Into those panniers went 20 heavy beaver traps, a shovel, short- and long-handled axes, spools of heavy duty twine used to tie down trap chains onto the anchor poles, 20 four-foot anchor poles cut from dead willows, a whetstone, and two extra fully loaded Lancaster rifles carried by their packhorses just in case things did not go right out on the beaver trapping grounds with the local Indians…

Mounting up, Big Hat verbally directed from his lead position in the caravan of trappers that Dan and Tom were to trail the two packhorses behind him, and that Bear Scat would bring up the rear of the caravan because of his excellent 'shooting eye' and experience when it came to defending against any kind of attacks from the rear. Once everyone was lined out, Big Hat set off for the beaver-loaded waters just below their campsite. Moving slowly between the two fingers of trees leading to the beaver waters, Big Hat all of a sudden found himself being drawn up short and confronted by an Indian! Slowly riding out from the southernmost finger line of trees, a lone Indian warrior boldly rode his horse into the trappers' line of sight and travel! Then that Indian turned his horse so he could obviously confront Big Hat and the company of trappers heading his way. Big Hat, the most skilled frontiersman of the group, narrowed his eyes under his broad-brimmed hat in order to more carefully examine the Indian's dress so he could determine what tribe he was from. By so doing in determining the nature of the man's dress, Big Hat could determine the degree of danger now confronting him based on the tribal affiliation of the warrior confronting his group. But as he did, he continued riding towards the Indian as a show of courage, which most tribes of Plains Indians respected. However as Big Hat did, the dark eyes of the Indian confronting the trappers narrowed, as he too was carefully examining the potential threat he also faced with the oncoming trapper…

Then out from the two fingers of trees 'quietly melted' 15 more heavily armed warriors, who quickly rode around and surrounded the four trappers and their horses before they could do anything to protect themselves by setting up a defensive firing circle! Then the lone Indian confronting Big Hat and his fellow trappers raised his right arm in a universal gesture of peace, but all four trappers also noticed that the 'surround' of Indians about them continued looking as if they were ready in an instant to do battle with the trespassing trappers!

Then all of a sudden, a murmur of surprise rippled throughout the ranks of the Indians surrounding the four trappers! When that happened, the lone Indian, as if understanding what his fellow warriors were murmuring about, rose up in his stirrups and looked back towards the last trapper in line who was Bear Scat. Then all of the Indians still surrounding the four trappers began excitedly talking in their native tongue among themselves! When that was occurring, Big Hat looked back and then all around him at the now excited Indians surrounding his little party of trappers. It was then that Big Hat, who understood five different Indian languages, rose up in his stirrups and looked back at Bear Scat, who was nervously fingering his now fully cocked Hawken rifle as if ready to go to 'war once the bugle sounded'!

"Bear Scat," said Big Hat, "let the hammer down on your rifle by holding it up high into the air and letting the hammer down from its full cock position. These Indians are friendly. Hell, Bear Scat, all they can talk about is 'White Eagle'! It appears your name has reached clear across this land of ours all the way to these people. Near as I can tell, these Indians are Northern Cheyenne, 'blood brothers' to the Lakota! That being the case, Chief Buffalo Calf who renamed you White Eagle on our earlier trip to St. Louis several years back, was good to his word. He apparently sent runners to other bands of the Lakota and their Northern Cheyenne Brothers about you and how you are to be respected for what you did. Appears you saving Chief Buffalo Calf's only son has just saved our bacon once again, because the Northern Cheyenne like the Blackfeet, have declared all-out war on the white man trappers trespassing on their sacred lands. So let the hammer down on your rifle and ride up here so you can be alongside me when I start talking in 'sign' to this warrior in front of us because I am better at that then speaking in their native lingo."

Dan and Tom, not remembering the 'White Eagle story', looked on in disbelief over what was transpiring as Bear Scat rode forward to be with Big Hat. Once there, Big Hat parleyed with the lone Indian warrior blocking their way, which he discovered through the use of sign language was named "Little Robe". When Bear Scat had ridden forward and stopped alongside Big Hat, he was surprised when Little Robe reached over and touched him. Then in sign, which Bear Scat had learned from Big Hat early on, was told by Little Robe, "That White Eagle and his friends were welcome in the land of the Cheyenne and could travel without any fear from his people."

Then Bear Scat upon seeing those 'words' signed, undid his belt holding his coveted 'J. Russell' knife made from the finest Sheffield steel and handed it, beaded holder and all, to an amazed Little Robe over such a gesture of friendship. Little Robe, upon receiving the cherished frontier symbol, held it high over his head so all of his warriors could see the important gift just received and let out a triumphant yell, which was echoed by all of his braves. Then Little Robe undid his own knife, reached over, handed his cheaply made Indian trade knife to Bear Scat and then clasped the trapper's arm and hand in friendship! Then with another yell, Little Robe and his warriors 'melted' off into the finger of trees obviously on another mission they deemed important. As the four trappers sat there on their horses in amazed silence, they watched the band of Cheyenne warriors riding off until they were heard or seen no more riding through the trees.

Then Big Hat said, "Damn, Bear Scat, you talk about luck. Those damn Indians just happened to run into us by surprise and were ready to do battle with us to the death. If it hadn't been for you rescuing Chief Buffalo Calf's son in that Bull Boat sometime back, and all of those more than obvious white bald eagle tail feathers a-fluttering from your horse's mane, we would more than likely be all cooling out here on this very ground as I speak."

With those words, Bear Scat tied Little Robe's cheaply made trade knife around his waist saying, "I thought we were going beaver trapping. Damn, Big Hat, we are burning daylight and if you expect me to be able to find good trapping sites and get all these 20 beaver traps set, we best get a-going afore it gets dark on us. If that happens, don't expect me to be a-making all of you galoots my special first day of fall beaver trapping biscuits for supper in the dark."

With that and a proud grin over what Bear Scat had done in the way of gifting his knife to Little Robe, Big Hat headed his crew for the nearest beaver pond so they could begin their fall trapping season. Arriving at a large beaver pond with a huge beaver house sitting out in the middle, Bear Scat dismounted and handed the reins to Dan saying, "Dan, you remain seated while I set the traps. You are the better shooter between you and your brother, so I need you to remain seated and be on the lookout for any kind of trouble because once I am in the water, I am pretty defenseless. I still expect you to watch what I am doing as per your father's request, but for now remaining on guard for any sign of trouble will be your main duty when I am trapping since I will not have my rifle for defense. Tom, you bail off your horse and come with me. I will show you what I do when determining where to set my traps and you will be my helper. Additionally, you will be our skinner since you seem to have the best hand when it comes to using your knife. Besides, all I now have for a knife is Little Robe's poor excuse for a knife and if I am guessing right, it is dull as hell. Remember what I taught the both of you back at the warehouse. Make sure you get good equipment, especially when it comes to your knives. Also remember I had the two of you pick out extra of everything important in case of losing a valuable piece of equipment to a horse wreck, loss or theft from an Indian. That is why I also purchased several J. Russell knives myself and when we get back to our cabin, I will swap out Little Robe's knife for the extra J. Russell knife that I also purchased. Now, Dan, pay attention and watch from your horse as to what I am doing and how I set my traps. From atop your horse, you can watch me in what I am doing as well as act as a lookout in case any trouble arises. Besides, Big Hat is also going to act as a lookout and that way, he doesn't get his rheumatism all riled up by wading around in the cold water setting or tending to beaver traps. Tom, you can start by handing the reins of your horse and packhorse to Big Hat. While I am looking for a suitable trap site, you can bring me one of those dry wooden poles we cut earlier, a trap and a hand ax so I can get to the business at hand and make my beaver sets."

For the rest of that morning and into the early afternoon, Bear Scat set his beaver traps as Tom and Dan watched the experienced Mountain Man doing one of the things that he did best. By early afternoon, Bear Scat had set his last trap in the Snake River's beaver-rich country. Then taking some time to eat some jerky and drink a little water, Bear Scat commenced with other aspects of training his two novice trappers in the art of beaver trapping.

As Bear Scat expected, once the highly territorial beaver smelled the strange castoreum he was using as a scent-bait by each beaver trap, they would come exploring to see who the 'new' beaver was in the area. Mounting up after their 'jerky break', Bear Scat led the trappers in the reverse along his newly set trap line. Sure as shooting, six traps back from the last set, a dead beaver already floated in the trap. Once again, Bear Scat waded out, removed the dead beaver from the trap, reset the trap in its original site, and walked ashore with his catch, a rather large adult beaver weighing about 70 pounds! Once ashore, Bear Scat commenced showing Tom how to make the correct cuts in the dead beaver's underbelly hide, so the value of the hide would not be reduced with the slip of his blade. But only after retrieving a whetstone from one of the panniers and setting an edge to the more than dull knife Little Robe had gifted him earlier before he used it to skin the beaver. He also made sure he was keenly aware that if he messed up in his use of his knife, he was costing the group money or credit back at the next rendezvous. By the time Bear Scat had worked most of the afternoon with Tom on the correct beaver-skinning procedures, he had figured it out and had the process down pat. Then Bear Scat turned Tom loose on his own skinning beaver but not before keeping four large beaver carcasses out for their traditional supper on their first day of fall trapping for good luck in trapping the rest of their fall season.

When the four men finally headed back to their campsite at the end of that first day of trapping, they did so with ten fresh beaver *'plus'* in their panniers, along with four unskinned beaver in another pannier for their evening's supper! With a catch for the day of 14 beaver out of 20 traps set, Big Hat was more than pleased with their choice of fall beaver trapping waters along the Snake River and its many adjacent watered areas. However on their ways back to their campsite, Bear Scat stopped the group along a long line of willows growing at the edge of a long waterway, and the men cut green willow limbs and filled the remaining panniers with 'hooping' materials for their fresh beaver hides to be hooped come that evening.

Back at their campsite after Bear Scat had replaced Little Robe's cheap trade knife with his last high quality J. Russell knife, he commenced making supper. As he did, Big Hat continued Tom and Dan's instructions around the firepit on how to carefully flesh out and hoop fresh beaver skins so the important drying process could begin. Meanwhile, in celebration of their first day of fall beaver trapping, Bear Scat went all out in his supper preparations as tradition would have it. After boning out the four large beaver brought home for supper's meat, Bear Scat coated the chunks with salt and black pepper, and skewered the fatty and meaty chunks on his roasting steels. Then draining a previously set aside Dutch oven full of rice to soak and plump up, Bear Scat filled the mixture with scrapings from a number of brown sugar cones, cinnamon, nutmeg and enough raisins to satisfy even the biggest sweet tooth in his group, who just happened to be Big Hat. Then that mixture was set over a low fire on a hanging iron to slow cook and plump up the raisins in the process. By then it was time to make his special celebration of their first day trapping Dutch oven biscuits, slathered in cinnamon, sugar cone scrapings and riddled with raisins. Taking one of his brass bean pots, Bear Scat roasted up a mess of green coffee beans over the fire and when they were sufficiently roasted, crushed the same in the bottom of the pot with a rounded stone, and then commenced making his brand of damn strong and eye-opening trapper's coffee. As the smell of freshly brewing coffee began filling the evening air, so did the smells of roasting chunks of beaver meat, cooked fat drippings and pungent wild onions cooking away on the skewers. Stirring his now thickened, cooked aromatic rice and raisin mixture and satisfied with his Dutch oven biscuits for doneness, Bear Scat pulled the fat-dripping meat skewers from the open fire, turned to call his partners for supper, only to find every one of them quietly perched on their sitting logs wearing grins of anticipation over what was soon in coming. Soon the only sounds heard around the cabin that evening were that of a crackling outdoor fire, humming clouds of mosquitoes, and of men doing what they did best when it came to eating great food out in the night's cool air on the frontier... (Author's Note: Can any of my readers out there tell that the Author likes to cook?)

For the next two months until the ice became too thick to easily trap beaver from underneath, the four men developed into a smoothly working team. Dan and Tom, contrary to their father's work ethic concerns, turned out to be not only first-rate trappers in and of their own right once they had learned the art, but especially close friends with Big Hat and Bear Scat as well. Happily, the men now found moving around inside their cabin somewhat problematic because of the numbers of drying *'plus'* stacked along the cabin's inner walls and the bundles of furs already packed, covered with their protective tanned deerskins and stacked two deep for transport come the time to head for the next rendezvous come summertime!

With the arrival of the winter's bitter cold in the northern latitudes and the extreme difficulty in trapping beaver beneath the ice that followed, the men pulled their beaver traps and retired back to their cabin. With fall beaver trapping done for the year, it was time to pack in some more winter meat and with that, the men went forth and killed six of the excellent cow buffalo feeding nearby. Knowing what to expect in such a hunt, they took along six of their packhorses and loaded all of them with as much meat as they could carry, then headed back to their cabin and their soon to be filled meat-hanging poles. However not before setting out a number of wolf traps around each buffalo's carcass on their kill sites, hoping to catch any hungry and unwary wolf frequenting the area and not watching where it was placing its feet.

For the next month when the winter weather allowed, the men successfully ran their wolf and marten trap lines. Then one fine but cold winter morning, Big Hat decided they would not only run their wolf and marten traps, but would also kill a few buffalo from one of the always available herds roaming in the area. Later that morning after a casual breakfast, the four men streamed out from their campsite trailing four packhorses. Just below a low ridgeline a mile distant from their cabin, Bear Scat had all the men stop by their first wolf trap set alongside the carcass of a previously killed buffalo to remove a single wolf from one of their traps. Killing the wolf with a heavy Douglas fir limb so as not to ruin the hide with a bullet hole and carefully removing his hide before it froze in the sub-zero temperatures, Bear Scat cleverly reset his trap near a string of frozen intestines, and then the men headed out to their next wolf trap site by another previously killed buffalo also being used as a bait station for any unwary wolves not watching their foot placement.

Riding along a nearby ridgeline exposed for all to see in friendly Northern Cheyenne country, the men observed nine Indians heavily dressed in winter clothing on another distant ridgeline, almost as if paralleling them. Immediately upon seeing the line of trappers riding away after setting another trap, the Indians began riding their way like they were on a mission. Seeing that kind of suspect movement by the now oncoming Indians, Big Hat motioned Bear Scat to come forward in their caravan so as the Indians got closer, they could see Bear Scat's horse's mane with the fluttering white bald eagle tail feathers and recognize the heavily winter-dressed trappers as friends and welcome neighbors. Drawing up their horses just below the ridgeline, the trappers waited for the oncoming Indians to arrive so they could identify themselves, parley and share some of their jerky with the still unidentified 'Men of the Plains' riding their way.

As the now hard-riding Indians got closer, Bear Scat rode forward of the rest of his trappers so the oncoming Indians could more easily recognize him and his horse as that of White Eagle, a friend of the Lakota and Northern Cheyenne. **ZIPPPP—BOOM!** was Bear Scat's reward for riding forward to greet the oncoming Indians, as he instantly felt the close at hand wind of a flying bullet 'snapping' closely by his head, along with the quickly followed sound in the cold winter air of a rifle being fired at him! **BOOM— BOOM—BOOM—BOOM!** went four more quickly fired rifle shots from the hard-charging Indians at the trappers sitting behind Bear Scat, as the scream from one of the trapper's packhorses went down after being hit in the shoulder! For a second, Bear Scat just sat there on his horse in shock since they were clearly in friendly Northern Cheyenne Indian territory and hoping no one else of his party had been hit in that fusillade of shots being fired in his direction! Momentarily stunned in the reception he and his fellow trappers were now receiving, Bear Scat's practiced survival response then quickly kicked in and with a fluid positioning movement with his Hawken rifle, fired and cleared one of the oncoming, apparently hostile Indians from his saddle with a well-placed shot directly into the man's chest! With the impact of that bullet hitting the man in his center of mass, his arms were flung upward as was his recently fired rifle, and then he was swept off his horse from the bullet's impact and rolled backwards over the animal's rump, disappearing under the hooves of the rest of the still oncoming riders' horses! Bear Scat's shot was followed by three more being fired simultaneously from behind him by Big Hat, Dan and Tom, as they cleared two more now close at hand Indians from their saddles and rolled a third Indian rider from off his mount and slamming him hard to the frozen ground as his horse was cleanly shot out from underneath him!

By then the remaining hard-charging Indians were upon the four trappers, shooting their pistols or swinging their tomahawks with a violence borne of desperation after having four of their own cleared from their saddles and now being confronted by four very determined, straight-shooting trappers not giving one inch of ground! The first arriving Indian of their group bailed off his hard-charging horse and right into the arms of a surprised Bear Scat, exploding him and his attacker clear off Bear Scat's horse in an explosion of colliding bodies! Down the two desperate men went to the ground in a flurry of flying snow, stomping horse hooves, a swinging tomahawk, and a now empty Hawken rifle being smashed into the face of the madly yelling Indian by a now fighting mad and aroused Bear Scat!

Fortunately for Bear Scat, the Indian's tomahawk aim was slightly off-kilter caused when their two horses collided, striking Bear Scat in his right shoulder and burying its blade deeply into only flesh and no bone! However, when the Indian swung his tomahawk at the trapper's head, an anticipating Bear Scat side slipped the most dangerous blow from the Indian's blade and managed to roll the attacker around and then they both hit the ground in a flying cloud of snow and dust upon being unhorsed! Upon being unhorsed, Bear Scat found himself on top of the struggling and fighting man! "OOOOPPHF!" went the wind out from the Indian after having Bear Scat's weight landing forcefully on top of him and that proved to be the second to last breath he expelled, as Bear Scat's knife found itself hastily drawn and deeply plunged into his attacker's vitals! The Indian attacker, upon feeling the long-bladed gutting knife in Bear Scat's hand forcefully being driven into his vitals just below his breast bone, let out a low groan and then expelled his final breath. When the dying Indian breathed his last, Bear Scat could smell the stink of a partially digested breakfast, as the two men's faces touched during the exact moment when his assailant joined his ancestors, the 'Cloud People'...

Forcefully shoving off from the dying man, Bear Scat lunged to his feet to join the life or death struggle going on around him, only to be immediately run over by one of the attacking Indian's horses, knocking him to the ground and painfully cracking one of his ribs! But by now, Bear Scat's adrenalin was raging and upon hearing and seeing the rest of the wild battle swirling around him just feet away between his friends desperately fighting for their lives with the remaining Indians, he lunged back into battle with his tomahawk in one hand and his knife in the other!

Into a mass of trappers' and Indians' swirling horses, swinging tomahawks, flying buttstocks from now empty rifles, spews of snot and blood flying through the frosty morning's air, along with recently discharged clouds of black powder smoke from hastily fired pistols hanging heavy around the combatants, lunged a maddened Bear Scat! Grabbing the closest Indian's long braid from behind, Bear Scat gave an almost inhuman jerk downward! In so doing Bear Scat pulled the man off Dan and in one fluid motion, chopped his tomahawk down into the front of the Indian's skull! When he did, Bear Scat had swung so violently in his adrenalin-fueled state that he buried the metal of his tomahawk out of sight into the man's skull and snapped off its blade where it joined the handle! That was when 'the lights went out', as Bear Scat was struck from behind with a rifle butt and fell beneath the Indians' and trappers' madly milling horses' legs and hooves...

When Bear Scat finally came around somewhat later from having what turned out to be an Indian's rifle stock violently bashed into the back of his head, all he could see were fuzzy images of a bloody-faced Big Hat, a bloody-faced Dan, and a seemingly untouched Tom leaning over him peering down with grave looks spelled across each man's face. Then Bear Scat, after taking a faltering look at his world now fuzzily unfolding around him, blinked letting everyone know he was alive. Tom with a big grin and much to the relief of everyone said, "Hell, he ain't hurt. He is just pretending just so he can get some sympathy from the likes of us."

Finally the 'fuzzy' began leaving Bear Scat's ringing head as he slowly sat upright and looked around. Lying on the ground around him were three dead horses and six dead Indians whose bodies were still emitting steamy vapors from their bloody wounds into the sub-zero winter air. Lying back out on the prairie a few yards distant was the Indian who had his horse shot out from under him earlier. A closer look revealed that he appeared to be on his last legs after having been slammed to the frozen ground at a high rate of speed from his horse, which had been moving at full gallop before being shot out from under him and killed in the process!

Looking back up at the three trappers staring down at him once the fuzziness began leaving his head, Bear Scat saw that Big Hat's face had a long, madly bleeding gash from what appeared to have been a tomahawk swipe and in so received, had busted out four of his lower jaw teeth and opened the wound up clear to the now glistening jaw bone! As for Dan, he too had been swiped by a tomahawk but with obviously just a glancing blow. In Dan and Big Hat's cases, the wounds were not life-threatening but being that they were head wounds, they were bleeding like that of a liver cut out and pulled from the carcass of a freshly killed buffalo to be consumed as is on the spot! As for Tom, he had a powder burn alongside his face from a close at hand shot taken by his attacker. He also had a tomahawk slash along his right shoulder where he had ducked and in the ensuing moment, knifed his attacker in the stomach! In fact, Tom's attacker was still withering around on the ground in intense pain just a few feet away. Tom, upon seeing that his friend Bear Scat was alright, turned and quietly walked over to the attacker he had just painfully knifed in the guts. Reaching down, Tom grabbed his badly wounded attacker by the man's long hair braid, lifted the man's head upward and then calmly slit his throat clear to the neck bone with his knife! Tom then let his attacker fall back to the ground to bleed out and then quietly walked back to where Bear Scat now sat upon the ground, saying nothing and acting as if he had done nothing more than killing a snake...

Big Hat, after removing some of the heavy winter clothing from the dead Indians, identified them as "A bunch of murdering Blackfeet on the prod far from their home further to the north."

With that pronouncement, the trappers used some of the Indians' inner clothing to bandage up their still bleeding wounds and wiped the blood from each other. Still holding his sore side with the cracked rib after being horse-stomped, Bear Scat, along with the help of Tom, pulled the eight dead Indians off into a pile by the ninth and dying Indian who had been violently dumped from his horse during the start of the battle. Then the trappers rounded up the remaining five valuable Indian horses and tethered them to a rope removed from one of their packhorse's panniers so they would not wander off.

Still feeling a bit dizzy after being cracked on the back of his head by an Indian's rifle stock, Bear Scat without saying a single word, walked over to one of their packhorses and removed three wolf traps from its pannier. Then after asking Tom to bring a hand ax and a number of iron stakes to help him set the traps, Bear Scat walked over to the pile of dead Indians stacked up around the one dead Indian's horse killed earlier in battle. There he commenced setting out the three wolf traps he had brought around the pile of dead Indians to the looks of surprise from the other three trappers... Then as Tom drove in the iron stakes to hold the traps from being dragged off by a hopefully soon to be trapped wolf, Bear Scat returned to his packhorse for their remaining three wolf traps. Once again, he set those wolf traps around the pile of dead Blackfeet Indians he was now using as bait for any hungry wolves who happened to be in the area and had a 'hankering' for the taste of human flesh! Standing back and examining his work in concealing the wolf sets from the eyes of any suspicious wolf happening by, Bear Scat quietly said, "If that pile of dead Indians does not attract a wolf or two, then this country is barren of such critters and we need to move on with our traps." Big Hat, Dan and Tom, still surprised over Bear Scat's use of a rather unusual type of 'wolf bait', said nothing... After all, a prime adult wolf pelt was bringing the same price from the fur buyers at the rendezvous as that from a Made Beaver, or anywhere from $4-6 per pelt!

Having set the remainder of their wolf traps, the men mounted up and a sorry-looking lot they were but they were all still alive. From there, they went on to check the rest of their previously set wolf traps before heading back to their cabin. Hours later back at their cabin and in the light of their candles and light from the fire in their fireplace, after cleaning out the now crusted blood from everyone's injuries with the point of his knife after soaking it in rum, Big Hat set about with needle and thread closing up everyone's wounds from the fight with the Blackfeet. But not before cleaning out each wound with a touch of their rum poured directly into the open wound, followed up with a liberal dollop into the belly of the one being sewn up... Then it was Bear Scat's turn with the thread and needle with Big Hat saying since he was the oldest, he was allowed two cups of rum instead of one like all the rest of the men had imbibed... Bear Scat also advised that since Big Hat would howl the loudest among the four of them, he hoped by letting him have two cups of rum, maybe his howling would not be so loud as to attract another mess of 'Blackfeet Indians on the prod' or awaken God from one of his well-deserved sleeps after worrying some of His 'children were not getting along'...

The next day all four 'sored-up' trappers ventured forth to once again check their previously set wolf traps. When they approached the traps set about the pile of dead Indians, all of the men had trouble controlling their horses because of the heavy smell of wolves trapped around the site in the cold winter air. As it turned out, an entire pack of wolves had tried to feast on the pile of dead Indians and six of the pack had been trapped! After dispatching the six wolves with a club and a knock to their heads and skinning out the same, all six wolf traps were once again set around the dead Indians' bodies. Two days later, the trappers ran their wolf traps once again and found four more wolves trapped around the gruesome 'bait station'. After dispatching all of those wolves and skinning out the same, the men pulled their traps from their grisly bait pile. This they did because it seemed every crow, raven, black-billed magpie, gray jay, coyote, fox and badger had found the pile of dead Indians and had helped themselves to the free meals as well. In so doing, the critters had scattered the nine dead Indians and the dead horse all over the place, and the trappers figured the Indians had paid enough for taking on the trappers. So the four trappers pulled their traps and went elsewhere with their wolf trapping. However every time any of the trappers looked upon one another, they were reminded of that day when figuring they were being approached by friendly Northern Cheyenne Indians and had to learn a valuable lesson the hard way. That lesson being the frontier was never what it appeared to be on the surface and if one wanted to survive, every situation had to be evaluated individually and accordingly with rifle at hand and at the ready. As for Big Hat, he eventually ended up pulling his four worst busted-up teeth because of the problem their shattered crowns were giving him when he tried to eat with such a damaged mouth. So with his knife and fingers, he dug out the tomahawk-busted teeth and in so doing, used that bit of work to cleverly justify an extra cup of rum...

Spring finally came that year without the four trappers running into any more serious Indian problems. But with the changing of the seasons came their spring beaver trapping and the vast amount of work that entailed. As expected come their first day of beaver trapping, Big Hat, sore mouth and all from all of his pulling of damaged teeth in the fight with the Blackfeet, exited their cabin, looked skyward checking the weather for the day and yelled at Bear Scat to 'set a breakfast table' that would hold the trappers for the first long day of spring beaver trapping that lay ahead.

After a hearty breakfast fit for four hungry trappers, Big Hat led the caravan of trappers from their homesite out into another new beaver trapping area. That he did because they had trapped out all the beaver near their cabin and were now being forced to set their traps further and further away to the north each week of trapping that was to follow if they wanted to continue their beaver trapping successes.

Once again upon arrival in the chosen place to set their traps, Bear Scat was their primary trap setter with Big Hat and Dan remaining horsed while he once again set their 20 beaver traps. Tom on the other hand, remained as Bear Scat's 'right hand', supplying him with the necessary trapping materials and performed all of the subsequent skinning of their catches. Working as an experienced team, beaver after beaver was eventually pulled from the traps after being expertly placed by Bear Scat. In the meantime, just because Big Hat was avoiding being immersed in the cold spring waters setting traps because of his bad case of arthritis, he earned his keep by keeping the men safe from animal and Indian alike, as well as keeping a sharp eye 'turned' towards selecting the best beaver trapping waters they encountered. Over a period of several spring months of trapping before the beaver went out of being in their prime fur-wise, the four trappers trapped an additional 413 beaver! However by then, they had pretty much trapped out all but a few of the beaver in their area and Big Hat determined that the time was right to move on to another more populated area.

Back at their cabin, the men were 'trapper poetry in motion' when it came to finishing up their field work and making preparations for their return trip to the 1835 annual Rendezvous to be held at "Malachite's Hole" on the Green River, where the 1833 Rendezvous had been held several years earlier. In the process of preparing to attend the rendezvous, broken riding gear was inspected and repaired as necessary, worn packsaddles were re-strapped with new leather strapping, rifles and pistols were checked and adjusted so they would be in excellent firing condition for the arduous travel expected ahead in returning to the rendezvous, all dried furs were bundled up for travel, horseshoes were inspected on all of their animals and replaced as was necessary, and lastly all of their provisions were prepared for loading since the men would be trapping in another geographic area come the fall beaver trapping season. Not a day went by now that they were making ready to return to the rendezvous that Bear Scat did not think about the possibility of reuniting with his brother at the upcoming rendezvous. He had missed meeting his brother on the previous rendezvous but he just knew this would be the one time and event that would finally bring the two of them back together. Then if he had his way, never again would the two of them be separated until the 'Grim Reaper' came a-calling for them...

CHAPTER TWELVE: THE 1835 RENDEZVOUS AND TROUBLE COMES IN "FOURS"!

Sitting around their campfire one evening, Jacob Sutta, older and long-lost brother of Elliott "Bear Scat" Sutta, looked over at his partner Wild Bill McGinty saying, "Bill, I have an idea on how to possibly avoid crossing swords with those damn Travis Brothers, who are out to kill you for something you legitimately did in killing their father when he cheated you out of a big sum of money the two of you made in the moonshine business back in Kentucky. What say instead of heading down to the rendezvous at Malachite's Hole this summer and facing the chance of running into that gang of four killing Travis Brothers, we forego making that trip and take another route to a different trading post?"

Upon hearing his partner speaking relative to a deadly issue that had been troubling him as the rendezvous date crept closer and closer, Wild Bill McGinty looked closely at his fellow trapper and long-time friend with a close scrutinizing look upon hearing him speaking to that very concern. Here they were ready to take their load of beaver furs to the summer's coming rendezvous so they could re-supply for the coming year as trappers, and yet he had a killing 'hanging fire' in the offing, either his or those of the Travis Brothers who were after him, staring him dead in the face! A 'killing' that just as easily could leave him dead and magpie bait, if his sworn enemies the deadly Travis Brothers' trails ever crossed at the much-needed supply-providing upcoming rendezvous. "I'm listening," said Wild Bill McGinty with a squinty-eyed and jaundiced look over his partner's proposal that could just possibly reduce any chances of a bloodletting, be it either his or those of his enemies...

"What say the two of us, instead of heading down to the summer rendezvous at Malachite's Hole in the Green River Valley and the possibility of running into those damn killing Travis Brothers, that we fool them entirely. What say the two of us head on down using the "Bad Pass Trail" along the western side of the Bighorn Canyon and head for the Shoshone River where it meets the mouth of Grapevine Creek? That way we can miss the dangerous rapids and falls found in the river in the Bighorn Canyon. Along the way, we can kill a mess of buffalo, skin them out and when we arrive at our Grapevine Creek destination, make a couple of Bull Boats, load them with our bundles of beaver *'plus'*, turn our horses loose so they can fend for themselves and then float down the Shoshone, Yellowstone and Missouri Rivers until we reach Fort Union. Once there, we can trade in our furs, buy new horses and still have a lot left over to pay for our provisions for another year of trapping out here in God's country. By getting our next year's provisions that way, we sure as hell can avoid the Travis Brothers who will more than likely be at Malachite's Hole for the Green River Valley summer rendezvous. The only other option is we can hope they run into a speeding lead ball or a mess of Blackfeet arrows and maybe that would take care of our problems. But barring that for which I have little hope, I say we give that idea of mine a try and in so doing, avoid me having to break in and train another partner if those Travises were to get lucky and get a ball into your miserable carcass," said Jacob with a big grin.

Two weeks later found Jacob and Bill at the mouth of Grapevine Creek putting the finishing touches to their two recently built Bull Boats. That evening they loaded both boats brimful with their remaining provisions and furs. All of their saddles, bridles, packsaddles, horse blankets and the like went into one Bull Boat, and all of their bundles of furs were loaded into the other. Then after turning all of their stock loose to fend for themselves in the wilds, the two men feasted on buffalo hump ribs before crawling into their sleeping furs early, for the morrow would more than likely turn out to be a long and Bull Boat-learning day. Daylight the next morning after a light breakfast found the two men getting used to the individual handling characteristics of their heavily loaded and somewhat clumsy Bull Boats, as they floated slowly down the Shoshone River en route the Yellowstone and Missouri Rivers on their way to a distant Fort Union. (Author's Note: Historic Fort Union is located in extreme northwestern North Dakota and at one time was a major fur trading hub for local tribes of Indians, Company and Free Trappers alike.)

Thirteen days later, the two tired trappers turned 'Bull Boatmen' moored their boats alongside a dock on the Missouri River at the base of a trail leading up to Fort Union. By late that afternoon, their furs and equipment had been hauled by wagon into the inner courtyard of Fort Union and while Jacob and Bill sipped cups of First Class Rum, the fort's Clerks were busy counting and grading their furs. Later that evening, as Free Trappers and tradition called for, they had been invited to have supper with the fort's Factor, Mr. McKenzie. The following day found Bill and Jacob looking over the fort's horse and mule herd, as they busily made the necessary livestock selections for their coming trapping season since they had released all of their horses earlier to the wild. The next day found the two trappers in the fort's several warehouses making their selections of needed provisions for the coming trapping season. For the next several weeks, the two trappers found themselves mingling with other Free and Company Trappers and other old friends in the fur trapping profession, having the usual good time in and among their own kind at the summer rendezvous celebrations. That they did without having to constantly look over their shoulders for the hotheaded and mean-spirited Travis Brothers... Of course, Jacob was also now miles away from his desperately looking younger brother, who was back at the summer rendezvous in Malachite's Hole, located in the faraway Green River Valley.

******

Come the morning of their departure from the Snake River country because they had depleted the beaver resources in that immediate area and needed to re-provision at the upcoming rendezvous for the coming trapping season, Bear Scat and his fellow trappers had been up early as they made ready for the long and hazardous trip. Bear Scat had chunks of buffalo meat merrily sizzling away on metal skewers hanging over the fire, two Dutch ovens baking and turning out biscuits every three minutes, and an apple cobbler emitting squirts of steam out from under its heavy cast iron lid, filling the air around the campfire with glorious smells. In the interim, Big Hat, Dan and Tom were packing fur bundles and unused provisions along with their sleeping furs atop the patiently standing ready to be loaded pack animals. Finished with the packing of all of their animals, including the five extra Indian horses they had laid claim to after the fight with the Blackfeet in the late winter months, the men then curried and saddled their own riding stock. In fact, it was a good thing they had the extra Indian horses because each animal now sported three packs of beaver furs each. Extra beaver furs the men had trapped during their very successful spring trapping season that now adorned the Indians' horses.

Then with scalding cups of trapper's coffee handed each man as he arrived at the campfire around his sitting log, Bear Scat began filling the men's metal plates with heaps of steaming chunks of buffalo meat and biscuits. As it turned out, Bear Scat had made extra biscuits which the men later placed into their saddlebags for eating while traveling out along the trail. Then onto the men's soon emptied plates went a mound of still steaming apple cobbler made especially in celebration of a successful trapping season, one in which none of the men had lost their hair, and their numerous packs of furs which spoke volumes to the men's successes as beaver trappers. Even after a big breakfast of buffalo meat and biscuits, Bear Scat was amazed at how fast the sticky sweet cobbler disappeared into the men's mouths and found its way to their stomachs! After breakfast, Bear Scat cleaned up his cooking and eating gear while the men checked their cabin one last time making sure they had loaded everything. Then they adjusted all their livestock's cinches and the like in preparation for the long day ahead over a rugged and dangerous mountain trail leading them back into the Green River Valley, home to the 1835 Rendezvous.

As the men departed from their old cabin lived in during the previous trapping season, they all looked back for one last look. Then they fastened their eyes on the trail and surrounding countryside looking for any signs of danger as they traveled along. After all, they still had a long way to ride trailing a valuable horse pack string in Indian country that could be just as dangerous on any given day as any cornered grizzly bear. But they now were heading for another rendezvous with old friends, many good times, a return to a worried father and mother who had not heard from their two loaned-out sons for months, and possibly with a reunion of Bear Scat with his long-lost brother Jacob. A long-lost brother for whom he had been looking for a long time in which to reunite and become a family once again!

Days later, the four Free Trappers tiredly pulled into the dedicated rendezvous site already noisy with many smaller ongoing celebrations, reunions, feasts, shooting-fests, wife swappings, hell-raising and most of all, the much-anticipated rounds with cups of fiery rum, whiskey and revelry. Revelry after a year of isolation in a wilderness where over a quarter of their beaver trapping kind rested their bones every year along the way due to horse wrecks, drownings, being killed by critters, or just being swiped off one's horse by a speeding lead ball or a steel-tipped arrow! Revelry which in a month's time would leave most trappers dead-broke or in debt for the coming year to the fur companies, or at worst, leaving one's bones moldering in the ground or crippled up as a result of losing a fight or quarrel among one of their own drunken kind commonly found among such periods of revelry...

Riding into the rendezvous area, the four trappers observed right off the bat over 40 lodges from the distant Nez Perce and Flathead Indians camped in their sacred circles with their tipi openings facing the rising sun. Further north along the Green River were several hundred Shoshone Indian tipis surrounded by dozens of small horse herds, barking dogs, gaily dressed and beautiful women, and clumps of happy children playing in and among the 'structures of the Plains'. (Author's Note: The fur trappers of the Rocky Mountains considered the Shoshone women to be the best looking and most desirable as wives among all of the mountain tribes.) Then center to the huge encampment were hundreds of smaller campsites denoting Company and Free Trappers and their smaller herds of horses, clustered about with over 300 gaily dressed fur trappers moving about in noisy celebration. To the four entering trappers after many months of almost total wilderness silence and isolation surrounding them on a daily basis, the human noises emanating from such a huge encampment almost hurt one's ears there was so much ongoing activity. So much so that it even made the men's horses unused to such activity begin acting all nervous-like for the first few days on-site!

(Author's Note: The 1835 Green River-Horse Creek Rendezvous was reportedly one of the largest on record with over 300 Company and Free Trappers, over 2,000 Shoshone Indians, 40 lodges of Nez Perce and Flathead Indians in attendance, and even a small party of Hudson's Bay Company men! Over $60,000 in furs were traded, equivalent to over a $1,000,000 in today's dollars! A Made Beaver (adult) which was the standard unit of trade, brought about $4 a pelt (Mountain Prices), and the entire rendezvous only lasted about 30 days before the people attending began heading back to where they had originated from to begin harvesting their winter meat supplies of buffalo or began preparations for the fall beaver trapping season.)

Moving their pack train in and among a number of their own kind, Big Hat directed his group of trappers to a quiet spot along Horse Creek with a goodly supply of high water mark driftwood located nearby. There they set up their campsite. However it was apparent to Big Hat and Bear Scat that Dan and Tom were anxious to depart the scene just as soon as their camp was laid out and return to their father Robert Campbell, Factor for the St. Louis Fur Company. Robert Campbell, the one and same man who had previously requested of Big Hat and Bear Scat to take his two wayward sons, introduce them to the fur trapping side of the fur trade industry and either make men of them or leave their bones out on some far hillside in the wilderness. Shortly thereafter, Dan and Tom rode off to reunite with their demanding father and fill him in on their recent adventures as partners with fellow Mountain Men Big Hat and Bear Scat.

Seeing the developing storm clouds in the northwest, Big Hat set about raising their tipi and dragging their sleeping furs, rifles and such into it so they would not get wet. Then he covered all of their packs just removed from their pack animals and placed a tarpaulin over them to keep them dry as well. As he did, Bear Scat scurried around, digging a firepit, gathered in several armloads of dry driftwood, set his fire, and began making supper preparations from the remaining buffalo meat and biscuit 'makings' that remained in their provisions larder. When Bear Scat's brand of trapper's coffee began a low boil, he shouted for Big Hat to come over and eat while the oncoming rainstorm held off, allowing them to eat around a dry campfire and without taking their weekly bath a day early.

That evening, with the oncoming threat of a summer thunderstorm hanging low in the northwest, Bear Scat put away all of his cooking implements, hauled in several more armloads of dry driftwood into their tipi, made sure their horses were double hobbled and well-tied onto their picket line so they would not spook off during a lightning storm, and then disappeared into the warm and dry confines of their tipi as the first large and cold drops of rain spattered off its buffalo hide covering. That evening among the howling winds, drenching rains and frequent flashes of lightning, Big Hat and Bear Scat slept comfortably in their tipi, secure at the rendezvous from any of the normal wilderness dangers.

Awakening the following morning to the sounds of raindrops still dripping off the nearby tree leaves, Bear Scat exited the tipi into the cool, clean smells found on the prairie after a drenching thunderstorm. Standing outside in the morning's cool dampness, Bear Scat looked skyward as Big Hat had taught him to do on a daily basis in order to ascertain what the weather would be for the day and saw nothing but a blue sky developing. With that he went back inside the tipi, brought out an armload of dry driftwood previously stashed and shortly thereafter with his fire steel began a campfire to boil some of their remaining coffee and make some of his special biscuits with lots of sugar, cinnamon and the last of their raisins to salve Big Hat's sweet tooth.

Later that morning as Bear Scat and Big Hat repacked their pack animals with their bundles of furs so they could be walked over and presented to the St. Louis Fur Company's Clerks to grade, sort and count, the men were surprised by the sounds of the arriving horses of Dan and Tom entering their campsite.

"Hey, Big Hat and Bear Scat! Father wants to see you two for supper this evening. He also wants to invite you to have breakfast with him and us tomorrow if you two are willing," said Dan with his usual characteristic big face-wide grin.

Big Hat looked over at Bear Scat, as if to read what his face was 'saying' as to the requests just made and 'reading' what he figured was his partner's answer, and said, "We would be honored to sit at your father's table, especially if he has his cooks make up a pie or two which the two of us really favor," said Big Hat with a hopeful grin. Later that morning, Big Hat and Bear Scat turned in their beaver, wolf and marten pelts to the St. Louis Fur Company Clerks and had them sorted, counted and graded under the watchful eyes of Big Hat and Bear Scat. Then taking their 'chits' regarding the value of their pelts and now credit line with the St. Louis Fur Company, Big Hat and Bear Scat mingled with more of their own kind and tipped more than a few cups of First Class Rum in celebration of a very successful trapping season. However as they did, both men closely listened to other trappers' discussions on where the hordes of beaver were best located, and especially discussed with a number of their friends whom they trusted as where best to head to next for the coming trapping season since they had cleaned out the beaver in their most recent location on the Snake River. But the one troubling theme they continued to discover among their friends and fellow trappers was that since 1830, the beaver were getting harder and harder to find because so many had already been trapped out of existence in and near to the Green River Valley and many of the adjacent mountain areas...

That evening, Big Hat, Bear Scat, Dan and Tom were seated at the table with St. Louis Fur Company Factor Robert Campbell. Looking out over a crowded supper table, one like they had not seen the likes of for many a month, they saw serving plates heaped with roasted buffalo, a huge wooden bowl of mashed potatoes from the fort's garden topped with gobs of real butter, several bowls of cooked turnips and peas also from the garden, two loaves of homemade bread fresh from the oven as noted by its Heavenly smells, roasted whole onions on skewers, and three pies, two of which smelled like apple, Big Hat's favorite! Bear Scat could not remember when he had seen such a spread outside of his mother's kitchen when he was a young man, before the tornado took her and the rest of his family save his brother Jacob...

"Don't the four of you just sit there looking all lost and such over what to do when so much food is on the table and ready for you to eat. That food is for you and is a show of my appreciation for first of all taking my boys and making them into the men they have become, and for bringing them back to their mother and me alive and in one piece. Now between mouthfuls of good grub, Big

Hat and Bear Scat, tell me what the hell the two of you did to my sons in order that they have apparently turned into 'Men of the Mountains'? When you do, don't leave anything out because you two did for me what I had hoped for and then some. In fact, both boys want to continue trapping in the future and I will let them do so after they spend some time back in St. Louis with their mother, who is worried sick that I sent them out into the frontier to die or be killed off by those damn savages," said Campbell with a thankful smile.

When Campbell's big grandfather clock struck midnight that evening, Big Hat and Bear Scat were still telling stories on what had happened over the last year to the boys and the group in general. However, Campbell stopped the storytelling when his clock struck midnight and advised that he expected to meet with a large number of trappers in the morrow bringing in their furs. Being that many of them would arrive all liquored-up, he figured there would be some disagreements over the quality of some of their furs and figured he had best be on hand to assist his Clerks when those troublesome occasions arose. With that and more than enough cups of rum under their sashes, not to mention a mountain of some of the best food they had eaten in many months, Big Hat and Bear Scat wandered off back to their camp for some more much-needed rest.

The next morning found the two trappers seated once again around Campbell's table enjoying a monster breakfast which included real pork sausage, homemade wheat bread slathered with freshly churned butter, real chicken eggs, and all they could eat at that. Additionally, Big Hat and Bear Scat almost foundered on the number and variety of homemade pies Campbell's Chinese cooks had made special for them. In fact when the two men had eaten their fill and were making ready to leave, Campbell, still pleased over what the two trappers had done for his sons, insisted that each man take a freshly made pie along with them back to their camp, once again in appreciation for what they had done for his sons.

Suffice to say, Big Hat walked out with a wild plum pie and Bear Scat one made from fresh crab apples…

Leaving the Factor's campsite with more than full bellies and a still oven-warm pie apiece, Big Hat and Bear Scat were rudely confronted by the four liquored-up Travis Brothers, who had been quietly awaiting their departure from Campbell's table so they could intercept the two Mountain Men with a series of questions and slightly veiled threats! Stopping abruptly and in surprise once physically confronted by the four obviously testy Travis Brothers who obviously had been drinking, Bear Scat almost dropped his pie! Stumbling as he was forcefully bumped by Bud Travis, the oldest and most hotheaded of the Travis Brothers and then having to take another step forward in order to grab his falling pie, BEAR SCAT HAD IT SLAPPED FROM HIS HANDS!

Then with Bud's face shoved almost physically into Bear Scat's with a breath smelling sourly of whiskey, Bud said, "Are you the son-of-a-bitch who is looking for his long-lost brother? The long-lost brother who is called Jacob Sutta? The one and same trapper who befriended and partnered up with Wild Bill McGinty, the one and same killing son-of-a-bitch who killed our Pa years back in Kentucky?"

Taken aback by Bud's rude and aggressive behavior, Bear Scat took one step back in surprise and after a moment's hesitation forcefully replied, "I am Elliott Sutta, called Bear Scat by my friends, which for your information does not include you and yours. If you ever again do to me what you just did in causing me to lose my pie or anything else like that, you can count on getting your ass handed back to you in such a manner you will have a hard time taking a dump!"

With those words, Bud doubled up the fist in his right hand and started to swing on the smaller-in-size Bear Scat. However, Bud stopped in full 'stride' with his swing when he instantly found a .52 caliber horse pistol shoved up under his chin with such force that the front sight of Bear Scat's handgun tore the skin under his neck open, causing it to bleed profusely!

385

That was when the remaining three Travis Brothers, surprised by Bear Scat's unanticipated immediate response to their elder brother Bud's physical actions taken against the trapper, began swinging up their rifle barrels as if to shoot Bear Scat! That was when the wild plum pie held by Big Hat was splattered against Clem Travis's face blinding him from any further immediate and deadly action with his rifle. Brother Jordan Travis then found Big Hat's Hawken rifle thrust against his cheekbone with such force, that he was knocked to the ground and lay there stunned! Pierce Travis's eyes expanded to almost the size of metal dinner plates, when starting to swing up the end of his rifle barrel in order to shoot Bear Scat, found Bear Scat's second pistol shoved into his 'shooting eye' with such force, that it immediately went black from the barrel's impact!

The next few moments of silence over a deadly confrontation between four mean-as-snakes brothers and two trappers just trying to mind their own business, was only broken by the sounds of a Western meadowlark's signature melodious call... "Now," said Bear Scat, "I want all of you to know I don't care what kind of feelings all of you have for or against Wild Bill McGinty. That is among the four of you and McGinty. However, as it relates to my brother Jacob and any of your actions, if any of you care to be skinned alive and left out for the black-billed magpies to feast upon, then you go ahead and make your move! However if you do and I find out what you have done, when I get through with you, even God will look away and not be able to recognize you! Do we have an understanding among the four of you of what I will do if any harm comes to my brother?" quietly asked Bear Scat, with more than just a trace of destiny in the tone and tenor of his voice for any who chose to ignore those words...

Lowering their rifles, the four Travis Brothers gathered into an ugly-looking clump of bested trappers and with glaring eyes and a cryptic tone of voice, Bud Travis said, "This ain't over. You just opened up a sore that won't heal until we have avenged our father's death! Let it be known to the Heavens that if your brother stands in the way of the four of us killing Wild Bill, then he will suffer the same fate and even more so after what has happened here today and that goes for you and your partner as well!"

Upon hearing that deadly threat coming from Bud and realizing its implication, Bear Scat slammed his pistol barrel up alongside Bud's head with such crunching force that he dropped that brother like a sack of spuds onto the ground and the man moved not one twitch! Then swinging both barrels of his pistols so he covered two of the three remaining standing Travis Brothers while simultaneously loudly cocking both weapons, Bear Scat narrowed his eyes and coldly said, "Who is next?"

"Damn, Bear Scat!" said Big Hat. "Leave at least one of those killing son-of-a-bitches for me...!" With that deadly move made by Bear Scat, the remaining three Travis Brothers slowly lowered their rifles all the way to the ground. Then using the ends of his pistol barrels to gesture what he wanted done next by the three standing Travis Brothers, Bear Scat quietly waited until they removed their pistols from their sashes, along with their knives and eventually their tomahawks from their belts and laid them down on top of their rifles. Then Bear Scat said, "Now, walk away from me and don't let me see any of your faces ever again. Because if I do, I will kill you on sight and if you think I can't do that, just try me on for size! Just remember, when I see any of you ever again, your last thought on this earth will be asking yourself is that a .52 caliber lead slug heading right for my shooting eye?"

With those words, the three Travis Brothers dragging their older and now totally disarmed brother as well, sullenly staggered away, all the while casting many vicious looks back at Bear Scat and Big Hat indicating this 'hoorah' was not over by a long shot... "Damn, Bear Scat, I think that is not the last of those four that we will see. No two ways about it, we have just made enemies for life out of that bunch of back-shooting sons-a-bitches," quietly said Big Hat, realizing that he had just thrown his hat into the deadly 'McGinty feud ring' along with his partner, come hell or high water...

Then Bear Scat slowly placed both of his pistols back into his sash after letting their hammers back down along with his flared temper. Without another word, Bear Scat gathered up the rifles left on the ground by the Travis Brothers. Gesturing with a nod of his head, Bear Scat had Big Hat pick up the remaining knives, pistols and tomahawks and to follow him. Walking over to a still burning and recently abandoned trapper's campfire, Bear Scat laid all four of the Travis Brothers' rifles across the open flames and Big Hat following the lead of his partner, laid all the remaining handguns, knives and tomahawks on the fire as well. Walking away, the two men soon heard the rifles and pistols 'cooking off', as the heat of the fire destroyed all of the Travis Brothers' valuable weapons! Word soon spread throughout the rendezvous of the confrontation between the four Travis Brothers and Big Hat and Bear Scat, and how the two outnumbered trappers had backed down the 'mean as a stepped upon snake in the hot sun'Travis Brothers. Word also spread among the many experienced trappers over such issues among their own kind at the rendezvous, that the battle started that fine day was not yet done until the 'devil had his due' somewhere on down the line...

The next day word quickly spread throughout the rendezvous that the Travis Brothers had resupplied themselves with needed provisions, including new firearms, knives and tomahawks, and had hurriedly left for parts unknown, apparently fearing Bear Scat's deadly threat. However Big Hat being the experienced Mountain Man that he was, made sure Bear Scat truly realized that the two of them had made bitter enemies and more than likely they would all meet again and maybe the circumstances would not turn out quite the same...

That night after the confrontation with the four Travis Brothers, Big Hat, fearing Bear Scat needed some time to come down from his 'killing high', took him over to Jim Bridger's campsite in order to visit his friend, the highly respected and famous trapper. Heading over about suppertime, Big Hat and Bear Scat were surprised to find Big Hat's friend sitting on a log next to his camp and not wearing a buckskin shirt. As Big Hat and Bear Scat came closer, they could see a number of other trappers gathered around Jim Bridger and another man standing closely behind him doing something to Bridger's back. Once the two trappers walked up to Bridger so Bear Scat could say 'hello', they saw what was happening. As they did, an unknown man, later discovered to be Dr. Marcus Whitman, was in the process of cutting open Bridger's shoulder from the back side! As Bridger's blood ran darkly down his white back skin, Big Hat and Bear Scat saw that the doctor was cutting in and around an old, bent-tipped steel arrowhead that Bridger had received years earlier in a fight with the dreaded Blackfeet! The arrow's wound had healed over time and now the muscle tissue had grown around the steel arrowhead, making the doctor really do some significant cutting of Bridger's tissue in order to remove the recently getting bothersome arrow from its resting place in the fur trapper's shoulder. Once removed and without Bridger making one single whimper as the arrowhead was being cut out from his shoulder, the doctor reminded Jim to keep the wound clean with splashes of high proof rum every now and then so the wound would heal. Bridger turned and quietly said to the good doctor, "Meat don't spoil in the mountains!"

That evening, Big Hat, Bear Scat, Jim Bridger, and a number of other friends feasted on buffalo hump ribs as most trappers preferred for their main course, namely rare. During a supper conversation, Bridger turned to his friend Big Hat saying, "Them Travis Brothers are mean ones. Best watch your backs, my friends, because if I know them from past experiences and word of mouth from other trappers over the years, they still have deadly business with the two of you and that Wild Bill McGinty fella. That being said, I dare say they won't rest until they have kilt the likes of you or are dead themselves as this here buffalo is that we are eating upon..."

For the next eight days, Big Hat and Bear Scat moved among many of their friends at the rendezvous eating, drinking, celebrating and finding who had disappeared among their kind into the vastness of the wilderness leaving their bones behind, and who had beaten the odds and remained aboveground for the foreseeable future. As they did, Bear Scat kept looking for his brother in the crowd of assembled trappers and at every opportunity, asked around to see if anyone had heard of him, seen him or knew of his whereabouts. After over a week of looking and asking, Bear Scat finally gave up any hope of seeing his brother at the 1835 Rendezvous because the event was already beginning to wind down, and every day trappers were heading back to their choice of trapping grounds for the coming trapping season. However on day eight of his search, Bear Scat ran across three trappers who had trapped in the Bighorn Mountains and remembered running across Wild Bill McGinty and his partner, a man named 'Sutta'! But that was the extent of their knowledge of Bear Scat's long-lost brother and he had to settle for that bit of information. However in that bit of information, Bear Scat realized that his brother was at least still alive during the last fall trapping season in the Bighorn Mountains and settled for that thread of comforting hope for a future reunion.

For the next three days, Big Hat and Bear Scat spent their time and credit with the St. Louis Fur Company, gathering up the supplies they would need for the coming trapping year. Additionally since they had lost Dan and Tom, their previous trapping partners to a keelboat heading down to St. Louis to spend some much-needed time with their much-worried mother before they headed out again as fur trappers as Bear Scat had thought they might, they now looked for new and compatible partners. However new partner 'pickings' were scant, as Big Hat found anyone so contacted either too heavy a drinker, not reliable as to their work ethics, or were questionable trappers of merit. In the end, Big Hat and Bear Scat figured they would probably have to venture forth as trappers to wherever they would trap in the future without any new partners unless they could find quality partners at the rendezvous, and fast...

As Big Hat and Bear Scat continued looking around for new partners for the protection additional numbers would represent once afield, they also questioned many trapper friends regarding the trapping potential in the distant Wind River Mountains. A final supper and discussions with their friend Jim Bridger clinched Big Hat and Bear Scat's choice of new trapping grounds. At that supper, Bridger advised that in his earlier travels, he always found many beaver in the Wind River waterways, and also discovered in his travels that the Shoshone Indians were mostly friendly to white trappers just as long as they respected their Indian counterparts and their culture. Later that night back at their camp, Big Hat and Bear Scat discussed what Bridger had advised and decided that trapping in the Wind River Mountains located to their north and east, although sight unseen, would be their coming year's trapping destination of choice.

CHAPTER THIRTEEN: TRAPPING IN THE WIND RIVER MOUNTAINS AND COMING OF AGE

After having one last breakfast with their friend Robert Campbell, Factor for the St. Louis Fur Company, Big Hat and Bear Scat took their leave and headed for their fully loaded pack string and patiently waiting riding horses. Mounting up, they bid their friend Campbell good-bye and headed their caravan to the northeast toward the fabled Wind River Mountains, bolstered with the directions given them by wilderness explorer and trapper Jim Bridger. By tradition among them, Big Hat led the way trailing an extra riding horse and a fully loaded pack string of four horses. Riding behind Big Hat rode Bear Scat trailing an extra riding horse and four fully loaded packhorses as well. In both cases, the extra riding horses were lightly packed, carrying an extra Lancaster rifle in a scabbard, as well as an extra pistol in a close at hand and handy holster, in case extra weapons were needed in case of attack by a hard to kill grizzly bear or hostile Indians. Additionally, each trapper sported a Hawken rifle across his saddle and wore two pistols each in their sashes. As for their remaining horse herd of 17 horses, Big Hat and Bear Scat had sold the lot to the St. Louis Fur Company for a handsome profit. A handsome profit now represented in a letter of credit at the St. Louis Fur Company carried in Bear Scat's saddlebag for over $1,700!

For the next five days following Jim Bridger's instructions, Big Hat and Bear Scat traveled in a northeasterly direction toward the Wind River Mountains and the North Fork of the Little Wind River near a body of water named Raft Lake, so named and geographically described by Bridger as their destination of travel. However, throughout their travels after the first day after leaving the rendezvous site, Big Hat kept looking off to the south in the direction they had just traveled like he was looking for something or someone. At their campsite on their second night of travel during their supper of venison from a buck deer killed by Bear Scat, Big Hat casually asked, "Bear Scat, do you get the feeling that we are being followed?"

Looking up from his piece of deer meat he had been chewing upon, Bear Scat asked, "What makes you think that?"

"I don't know but my sixth 'sense' says we are being followed. But by damn, I haven't seen 'hide nor hair' of anyone riding the ridges or following along way back on our trail. But I have been surviving in this country long enough to know that when my senses are acting up like that, one had better damn well pay attention or they can expect an arrow or a speeding lead ball at the next juncture in the trail," said Big Hat, as he looked out past the light of their campfire into the darkness as if expecting someone to show his hand and validate his internal 'sixth sense' concerns.

"I have had the same feelings ever since we left the Green River Valley as well. I don't know if it is just other trappers leaving the rendezvous going to where they want to trap in the fall and spring coming up behind us or not. But either way, I have been keeping a sharp eye 'skinned' every time we pass along a series of ridges or the like looking for that someone to show their hand," said Bear Scat, as he went back to worrying his piece of deer meat knowing there was nothing he could do in the dark of night about anyone possibly tailing them. But he too had that gnawing feeling in the back of his mind that the two of them were being quietly and sinisterly tailed as they headed into the backcountry…

With those concerns still alerted but put to the back of their minds, the two men in the days following concentrated on watching the terrain traveled over looking for the landmarks Jim Bridger had so clearly described to the two of them days earlier in which to follow. As they did, the two men couldn't help but notice the wildness of the land they were traversing and the numbers and herds of wildlife of every kind they continued experiencing. Additionally, true to Bridger's descriptions, the land was full of numerous waterways and at every turn in the trail, Big Hat and Bear Scat saw extensive signs of beaver going about their everyday life's activities.

Finally arriving in the previously described vicinity of what they suspected to be Raft Lake, they found Bridger's descriptions to be uncanny as to his accuracy in its geographic layout and surroundings. Almost immediately adjacent the lake, Big Hat and Bear Scat discovered a small glen in among a stand of Douglas fir trees bordered by a lush meadow that was bifurcated by a deep and swiftly flowing stream. Riding deeper into the glen, the two men quickly discovered that the tree cover surrounding the area blocked the general view of the location from any wandering sets of eyes, making it a perfect site for a secluded cabin and set of corrals. Riding up to a small bluff of sandstone, Big Hat dismounted, stretched his tired frame, rubbed his sore knees that came from riding a horse, turned to Bear Scat riding up alongside where he stood, and said, "How about this site for our home for the trapping season?"

Dismounting and rubbing his stiff knees from their long ride that day, Bear Scat slowly turned completely around and let his practiced set of eyes examine his surroundings. In that quiet examination, he observed their site was completely blocked from view by anyone riding along the many adjacent waterways, there was horse feed aplenty, the nearby stream's water flow was sufficient for man and horse alike, a cabin site alongside the sandstone bluff allowed for a three-walled cabin to be built using the bluff as its fourth wall, there was timber all around for building the cabin, and a more than adequate supply of firewood nearby. Turning to Big Hat, Bear Scat said, "I say we unpack our horses, hobble them and let them out to water and feed. Then we need to 'walk off' our cabin site and start building our horse corral adjacent to it so we can keep a sharp eye on our horses at all times. Then while you are digging corral postholes, I can set up our outside campfire site, drag in some sitting logs and begin making ourselves at home," said a smiling Bear Scat realizing he was 'home' once again.

For the next two weeks with only breaks for killing a buffalo for food, the two trappers cut green timber to length, made their cuts and set the logs to making a three-sided cabin with a 'fourth side of the cabin wall' being the steep side of the sandstone bluff, precluding having to cut and construct a fourth wall to the cabin. Once the cabin walls were up, roof timbers were cut, additional stringers laid and then numerous armloads of sagebrush cut and laid densely on top of the roof's stringers. Following that, Big Hat and Bear Scat took their shovels and from atop the sandstone bluff above their cabin, shoveled dirt down on top of their sagebrush-covered structure until at least two feet of dirt covered the cabin's entire roof. In so doing, the two trappers made sure the layer of dirt on the roof was sufficiently deep enough to keep the rain, snow and cold out, and the heat from their mud and stone fireplace in during the much-anticipated severe northern clime's winter months.

With their cabin almost completed, the two men moved in all of their packs, saddles, provisions and remaining equipment for safekeeping from damaging afternoon thunderstorms and incidental theft from wandering Indians. Then as Bear Scat finished digging the rest of the corral's postholes, Big Hat cut to proportion all of the corral posts and side rails for the corral. Two days later, their riding and packhorses were then confined to their new corral, which featured being built over the stream running through their glen so they could water at will. Then as Bear Scat dug out and stoned in a site in the stream adjacent their cabin and above the horse corral for their drinking water, Big Hat busied himself with putting the finishing touches to their cabin. This he did being a carpenter learned in his younger years as an indentured servant.

Once finished with building a small stone enclosure in their stream for drinking, bathing, shaving and use as wash water, Bear Scat joined Big Hat in putting the finishing touches on their new home. First the two men built framed structures for their sleeping areas, then addressed the chore of cutting out two window openings on the front side of their cabin and another window opening on the end of their cabin that faced the horse corral site. The purpose of the end window allowed the men to keep a careful watch over their livestock without it being obvious. The window opening at the end of the cabin also facilitated shooting anyone who tried to steal any of their livestock. Following that, the door and window openings were framed and 'shuttered' with tanned and shaved deerskins stretched over the framed window openings. That way, some light could be emitted through the thinned deer hides and most of the cold, rain and mosquitoes kept out.

As Big Hat put his carpentry skills to work building their log front door, Bear Scat commenced locating and cutting down the dead pine and fir trees surrounding their cabin site. With their single buck saw, he bucked them into manageable lengths, and using two of the packhorses gentle enough to pull together as a team, dragged the logs down to the outdoor firepit. These he planned on using for their winter's supply of available firewood when the snows became too deep to easily traverse on wood hunting details. Following that, the two men built several meat hanging poles near the horse corral and adjacent the outdoor firepit. Big Hat then began building their meat smoking racks adjacent their cabin so it would be easier to watch over and keep the birds and bears away from the valuable smoking and drying meat supplies. Meat supplies that would then be used come the winter months as jerky when out on the trail trapping and hunting deer, elk and buffalo. Last but not least, Bear Scat built a small shed-like structure near the corral side of their cabin in which to house their riding and packsaddles out of the weather so there would be more room inside their cabin, and could keep the sweat-soaked leather goods away from the porcupines looking to feast upon for the much-desired body salts. That shed made for more room inside their cabin for when the men began trapping, drying and housing their furs inside their cabin for safer keeping.

Finally one morning as Bear Scat was putting the finishing touches on his biscuits and beans breakfast, Big Hat finished with his daily washing and shaving duties, ambled over to their outside firepit and sat down on his sitting log. When he did, Bear Scat poured a cup of coffee and handed it to Big Hat as he traditionally did. Taking a sip of the 'dark as a devil's heart' style of trapper's coffee that Bear Scat made, Big Hat said, "Damn, just as I like it, black as the devil's heart, hot as a volcano, and thick enough to stand up a large-sized mule shoe inside my cup without it tipping over."

Bear Scat then shoveled several scoops of his steaming bean and venison meat mixture onto a tin plate with a couple of his Dutch oven biscuits, and handed it to Big Hat. He then scooped out a mess of beans and meat on his plate for breakfast as well. Sitting next to their propped-up rifles for the safety that offered against any surprise attack, both men were soon lost in the morning's quiet as they enjoyed what the good Lord had given them as their bounty that fine day.

"Bear Scat, what say today we go and kill a couple of buffalo so we can have a goodly supply of meat on hand for our meat smoking racks and meat poles?" mumbled Big Hat through a mouthful of beans and biscuits.

After pulling a deer hair out from his mouth that had found its way into his bean and venison breakfast, Bear Scat said, "Sounds great to me. Besides, we have been working so hard lately it would probably do us some good to kill a nice fat cow buffalo and then pleasure ourselves on a hank of fresh buffalo liver for the goodness it has to offer."

"That being the case, best we after breakfast get our horses saddled up along with several packhorses and get cracking so we aren't burning daylight. Best we do so because as you know, once we get a couple of them beasts down, we have a heap of work getting the meat butchered out in the field, hauled all the way back here and then begin processing it for the smoking racks," said Big Hat as he finished off the last of his beans and biscuits. Rising from his sitting log, he then tossed his plate and fork into the pan of hot water sitting alongside the fire so they could be washed.

That afternoon as Bear Scat sighted his rifle so his bullet would hit the quietly feeding beast of the Plains behind the shoulder, Big Hat stood behind him with another rifle in hand for a quick hand-off. That way two cow buffalo could be quickly killed from the small herd where they stood out in the open with easy access once the killing was done. However as Big Hat stood ready for the quick rifle hand-off, he continued looking all around at his surroundings because his 'sixth sense' told him they were being watched. Once Bear Scat had fired his first shot knocking down the cow he had been aiming at and upon handing his now empty rifle back to Big Hat, the necessity of quickly firing and killing a second buffalo in an easy to get to area overrode Big Hat's concern over being watched. Forgetting for the moment his 'sixth sense' concerns, he took the now empty rifle in one hand and quickly handed a fully loaded one to Bear Scat for his second shot. Taking the now empty rifle, Big Hat quickly reloaded the weapon being the experienced Mountain Man he was, knowing that danger was always around the next tree in the wilderness, plus he still had the nagging sense that they were being watched...

After Bear Scat had reloaded his fired rifle, he then walked down to where the two dead cows now lay as the rest of the small herd rumbled off, holding up their tails into the air they routinely did when aroused or disturbed. As he did, Big Hat delayed following him down to the two dead buffalo. Once again following his 'sixth sense', he looked all along every tree line looking for what was still concerning him. He knew that Bridger had told him that they would be deep in Shoshone Indian territory, but they were generally friendly when it came to their interactions with the white man trappers. Still they were Indians, so he made sure the tree line was clear of any danger and then walked down to where Bear Scat was in the process of opening up the side of one of the cow buffalos just below its last rib, in order to extract a chunk of the still warm and quivering raw liver for both him and Big Hat to consume on the spot. Moments later, both trappers had blood-smeared mouths and chins as they hungrily gobbled down the warm and raw buffalo liver for the wonderful treat it represented! Then after eating more of the same until they were satiated, the hard butchering work began.

Later back at their cabin, the men tiredly dismounted, unsaddled their riding horses, hobbled them and set them out to pasture. Then the remaining quartered portions of the buffalo were removed from their pack animals and hung from their meat poles. Following that chore, the pack animals were unsaddled, hobbled, curried down and let out to pasture as well. Putting their saddles into their sheltered structure next to the cabin so they could dry out and be up off the ground so the porcupines in the area would not be eating at the leather strapping for the horses' body salt it offered, the horse blankets were then tossed over the corral railings to dry out.

Bear Scat took one of the buffalo's backstraps and placed it on the log table next to his cooking area adjacent the firepit, and then began helping Big Hat in cutting the rest of the rich buffalo meat into thin strips and hanging the same from the smoking racks. After Big Hat built a smoking fire beneath the hanging strips of meat on the heavily loaded meat racks, Bear Scat returned to his firepit and built a cooking fire. By now twilight had descended upon the two trappers as they scurried around in the last vestiges of daylight to get the last of their work done before darkness set in.

As Big Hat tended to the smoking fire to make sure it only smoked and did not cook the meat hanging from the meat rack, Bear Scat mixed up his biscuit dough and stirred his pot of beans and rice heavily laced with red pepper flakes for their supper. Then laying out the backstrap on his log table, Bear Scat cut and skewered the meat after heavily lacing it with both white and black pepper as the men liked to have their meat spiced. After supper, the men brought in their livestock and placed them inside their corral and then adjourned to their cabin for some much-needed sleep. However both men found sleep problematic, because the noises the horses made that night continually milling around and making nervous sounds kept the men continuously coming outside their cabin with rifles in hand expecting a grizzly bear causing the disturbance. However no bears were sighted or smelled and the men finally managed to fall off to sleep. But not before each man lay there for several hours as 'sixth senses' continued stirring within their bodies and souls...

Fall seemed to arrive earlier that year and found Big Hat and Bear Scat still unprepared for the rapidly onrushing fall trapping season. They still had their beaver traps to smoke, beaver trapping areas to scout out for early morning and late evening activity on the part of the rodents, a small mountain of .52 caliber lead balls to cast and bag up, powder horns to fill, edges to set on skinning and gutting knives, a mound of willow branches to harvest in order to hoop the beaver skins once they were brought back to their cabin for hooping, and the like.

Sure as shooting, as Bear Scat was preparing breakfast one morning, out from their cabin walked Big Hat like a man on a mission. First he went into the woods behind their cabin and took care of his daily 'business seeing a man about a horse'. Then he walked over to their creek, washed his face, shaved, wet and combed his hair, then came back to where Bear Scat was cooking breakfast and watching his partner's antics out of the corner of his eye all at the same time.

"Bear Scat, make us a good breakfast this morning. I say we hit the beaver trapping trail and begin our fall trapping season. The weather has turned cold enough, the water is colder than all get-out and I have seen a lot more beaver activity as they are cutting down just about every willow and young cottonwood in sight, swimming across their ponds and placing what they just cut down deeply into the mud of their winter food caches. That tells me we need to catch as many of those critters as we can afore we ice up and the fall trapping season is over. I will saddle up our horses and pack animals with the panniers and the tools that we will need for the day's activities. You get our chow ready and holler when it is done, because I could eat one of our horses this morning now that I am 'emptied' out and all hollow inside for want of some victuals," bellowed a happy Big Hat, pleased to be alive and doing what he loved doing the most.

Bear Scat just grinned because he had been expecting Big Hat to come bursting forth from their cabin any day now and announcing he was ready to begin their trapping season. Well, that had been the much-anticipated morning and he now found himself more than ready to get on with the beaver trapping as well. Shortly after a breakfast of biscuits, hot coffee, beans, buffalo meat and roasted skewered wild onions, the men loaded their riding horses' saddlebags with several handfuls of jerky. Then they made sure they carried several filled powder horns and that their 'Possibles bags' carried a larger number of pre-cast rifle balls than they normally did, along with fire steels, bullet screws, extra tins of percussion caps, wadding and spare rifle lock parts. Following that, into the pack animals' panniers went 16 St. Louis-style beaver traps weighing about five pounds each, a shovel, two hand axes, a whetstone, and 16 pre-cut four-foot-long dried willow poles to be used as trap anchors out in the deeper water once the traps were set. Lastly Bear Scat, since he was the one doing all of the trapping, made sure he was carrying two corked bottles of the foul-smelling liquid called castoreum, to be used on the scent sticks placed directly over the trap's pan once set.

Leaving their secluded and hidden from sight glen, the two trappers led by Big Hat headed out for the previously selected beaver waters to be trapped first during the start of their fall trapping season. Watching all around for any signs of trouble, the two men arrived at the first set of beaver ponds and when they did,

Bear Scat bailed off his horse and leading the same, began examining the edge of the pond for fresh signs of a well-used beaver slide or batches of willows showing signs of recently being harvested by beaver. Locating fresh beaver sign, Bear Scat returned to one of the packhorses carrying the beaver traps in one of its panniers, grabbed one, his hand ax and a four-foot wooden anchor pole all in the same motion. Soon thereafter Bear Scat had made his first set, swirled muddy water over the trap to hide it from sight of any arriving beaver, scented his lure stick over the pan, and then anchored the end of the trap's chain into deeper pond water onto the four-foot wooden pole driven into the bottom of the pond. Then leaving Big Hat in the saddle to follow and remain on the lookout for any signs of danger, Bear Scat headed for his next trap site. Since there were only two trappers instead of four like they had been the year before, it was decided that only eight traps apiece would be set. That had been decided because of all the work it took to find good trap sites, set their traps, scout out new trapping sites for the next day, skin out all they trapped and then when back at their cabin, flesh out their pelts and hoop the same for beginning the drying process.

It had also been decided that whenever a beaver had been trapped, Bear Scat would retrieve the same so Big Hat would not have to get his rheumatism all worked up by wading in the cold water, hand the critter off to Big Hat and he would do all of the skinning. That way, Bear Scat could walk around outside of the cold water warming up his legs while Big Hat skinned the beaver and as he did, even though walking all around trying to warm up, could be the team's lookout while Big Hat was skinning. Then they would reverse their roles once the trap-setting commenced again.

Four hours of hard trap-setting work later and Bear Scat had successfully set all 16 of their traps. Then as he dried out some and warmed up, the two men sat on a log in a small grove of aspen trees eating some of their jerky and mused over old times after they had met, when Bear Scat was discovered by Big Hat picking paddlefish eggs out from bear scat to avoid starving to death. Once Bear Scat got the feeling back into his feet and legs after wading in icy cold water all morning, back the two men went retracing their tracks along their previously set trap line. As luck and good trapping, scouting and trapping techniques would have it, the men discovered on their return trip that they had already caught nine beaver in their 16 previously set traps! Yes, Jim Bridger had been right about his comments that the Wind River area was rich in beaver.

Following tradition, Bear Scat loaded three large beaver carcasses for their evening meal into one pack animal's pannier. Then as he walked around warming up his feet and legs and acting as their lookout for any signs of danger, Big Hat skinned out the rest of their catch that day. When finished, the men headed for home and the work that still remained in caring for the fresh pelts back at their cabin. Back at their cabin, Big Hat skinned out the three whole beaver they had brought back with them for their traditional supper on their first day of fall beaver trapping. Then as Bear Scat began preparing a special supper of roasted heavily fatted beaver, fresh Dutch oven biscuits, a cast iron pot full of rice, pinto bean and wild onions, coffee, and a special Dutch oven apple cobbler made from dried and previously soaked apples for their first successful day of the fall trapping season, Big Hat saw to the skinning and hooping duties on the day's catch. They later celebrated in fine style with a supper made just for 'kings of the wilderness', especially when several cups of First Class Rum were imbibed later on in the evening when all of their day's work was done and there was time to sit around their outdoor fire, talk, laugh, drink rum and swat mosquitoes, almost like 'father and son'...

From the middle of September until the last week in October, Big Hat and Bear Scat toiled at their beaver trapping activities. The trapping was so good on their new beaver trapping grounds that soon the men found the bundles of dried furs almost filled all the available spaces in their cabin to the roof! So much so that by the end of the third week in October, Big Hat and Bear Scat had amassed 268 beaver pelts! This and they still had several more weeks of productive beaver trapping until freeze-up in the fall trapping season, and then they still had the spring beaver trapping season ahead of them and the furs that would bring in! That being the case, Big Hat figured they would amass another 300-plus beaver providing there was not a winter kill of their beaver, giving them at least 568 *'plus'* for their season or a record catch for the two men operating by themselves! That would be a stunning accomplishment since most single trappers of the era only averaged between 120-140 beaver per year! *Yes, Bridger had been right when he had advised the two trappers that the area he was sending them to was full of beaver,* thought Big Hat...

The next morning the men awoke to find 'the frost on the pumpkin'. As Bear Scat hurried along making a hearty breakfast using the last of their most recently killed buffalo, Big Hat loaded their horses for the day's beaver trapping activities. Like the now 'well-oiled' team that they were, the two men headed out after breakfast and soon they were hauling in beaver after beaver from their newest trap line. As they had done in the past weeks, Bear Scat did all of the trapping and when he was out of the now icy cold water attempting to warm up and acting as a lookout for any signs of danger, Big Hat did all of the skinning of the beaver carcasses back on land. Once again, due to Bear Scat's expertise as a trapper plus working in a beaver-rich area, almost every trap checked was discovered to be filled with an adult-sized beaver! Finishing that day with 14 beaver discovered trapped when the trap line was initially run and another seven gathered up upon the return trip, the men could hardly believe their luck. Heading home before Bear Scat froze out after being immersed in the icy cold waters for so long, they hustled their horses so that he could undress back at the cabin, get into some dryer clothing and then sit by the inside fireplace for a spell and warm up.

Entering their secluding circle of trees surrounding their glen and riding up to their corral, Bear Scat all of a sudden noticed that the rest of their horses in the corral, instead of looking at the two trappers as they arrived home, were all looking at their cabin.

Starting to say something to Big Hat over the odd behavior of their remaining livestock in the corral, Bear Scat was startled to see their cabin door quickly slam open and their two front deerskin window coverings being simultaneously flung aside, and then as if almost in slow motion, seeing puffs of black powder smoke erupting from the door and window openings! **BOOM—BOOM—BOOM— BOOM!** went four quick shots blowing Big Hat, who was closest to the cabin, from his saddle, as Bear Scat in the same moment had the reins shot out from his hands and heard the "ZIPPP" of a bullet and a blast of wind come so close to his head, that it spun his wolf skin cap into the air! For a split-second, Bear Scat just sat there on his now nervously 'crow-hopping' horse as he watched Big Hat crash to the ground from his horse, and was keenly aware of the patch of now bright red color on his partner's buckskin shirt splashed all over his chest! For some reason, Bear Scat instantly realized that his great friend and almost father-figure had more than likely been killed outright before he had hit the ground, and he wasn't far behind if he continued sitting on his nervous horse out in the open as he was…!

Spurring his horse forward towards the open cabin doorway and now feeling a towering rage rising up inside, a feeling that occurred every time he found himself in a killing mode because of deadly circumstance swirling around him, Bear Scat saw a familiar figure standing framed in the cabin's doorway. Then he saw that same familiar figure reaching for a pistol in his sash since his rifle was now empty. Spurring his horse right up to the front door's opening, Bear Scat saw Bud Travis leering at him as he drew his pistol. Without a moment's hesitation, Bear Scat's rage reached a fever pitch as he with one hand leveled his Hawken rifle, pulled its trigger and exploded the 'leer' off Bud's face with a bullet strike between the eyes! Realizing his rifle was empty and NOW thinking back to both his and Big Hat's senses early on telling the two of them that they were being followed, Bear Scat now knew what that 'sixth sense' had been trying to tell him. It was now clearly apparent that the Travis Brothers had been 'dogging' Big

Hat and him from the beginning after their run-in back at the rendezvous! That being the case, that meant that since he had just killed Bud Travis, there were still three Travis Brothers out to kill him and unless he moved on and out of the way quickly, he would be lying alongside Big Hat!

With his killing rage roaring in his ears and almost reaching a crescendo, Bear Scat spurred his horse around the side of their cabin and raced it up into the surrounding timber until he was out of harm's way for the moment. Then bailing from his horse and sprinting back towards the dense brush behind the north side of the cabin, he reloaded his Hawken on the run. Below him he could see the remaining three Travis Brothers standing by the side of the cabin all hurriedly in the act of reloading their rifles as well! However they were no way as quick at reloading as was Bear Scat, as he calmly stopped running through the forest of trees after reloading his rifle, quickly placed a percussion cap on the nipple of his rifle, whipped the stock to his shoulder, and in his killing but controlled rage over what had been done to his friend Big Hat, deliberately shot Clem Travis in the pelvic region so that he would die a very slow and horribly painful death! Clem screamed upon having Bear Scat's .52 caliber lead ball smash into his intestines, explode his bladder and blow a huge chunk of bone out through the back of his pelvic girdle and through his left buttocks!

Seeing Clem Travis writhing on the ground and screaming in pain distracted brothers Jordan and Pierce for just a moment from continuing to reload their rifles. In that moment of distraction over seeing their brother gutshot, gave Bear Scat the needed opportunity for him to quickly melt out of sight and gun range into the timber surrounding the cabin. In so doing, giving Bear Scat the edge because he now had all three remaining Travis Brothers trapped inside the cabin without any avenue of escape except into his deadly line of fire out the front of the cabin...

Running over by their spring box and kneeling behind a boulder, Bear Scat began reloading his Hawken once again knowing he now held the deadly upper hand. Bear Scat held the upper hand because he now controlled any exit from the cabin by the Travis Brothers due to his just-assumed commanding view and open field of fire. As he continued hurriedly reloading, hearing the unholy screaming coming from within the cabin by a badly gutshot Clem Travis, Bear Scat chanced a quick look over at his friend, Big Hat. Big Hat lay where he had fallen, only now his buckskin shirt was nothing but a mass of blood, letting Bear Scat know for sure that his friend was no more... He also discovered that his towering rage was no more, as he had since settled down into a cold, calm and dedicated killing mode that he knew was soon to be exercised again and again...

Soon the groaning and screaming coming from within the cabin from Clem Travis began waning in frequency and loudness. That was when Bear Scat heard a muffled pistol shot from within the cabin and with that, the groaning sounds quit altogether. It was apparent to Bear Scat with the sound of that pistol shot that one of the Travis Brothers had just shot his brother to put him out of his misery! *They haven't even seen misery yet!* thought Bear Scat to himself, as he watched the sun slowly sinking down behind the mountains to the west... **HELL WAS COMING AND HE WAS RIDING A BLACK HORSE!**

With the falling of darkness and no sign of sound or movement coming from the two brothers still trapped within the cabin, Bear Scat slowly made his way over to their packhorses still standing by the corral. Once there, Bear Scat removed his spare Lancaster rifle from the packhorse just in case a need arose for its use. He then remembered that was a survival technique that Big Hat championed when he was still alive, just in case one ran dry with his personal rifle in a time of need. *Thank you, Big Hat,* thought Bear Scat, as he once again quietly scurried over to an even better observation spot, one from which he now TOTALLY commanded any movement whatsoever from within his cabin, namely from his location right alongside their front door! Then like the cold killer he had become seeking revenge for killing his friend, he waited like a rattlesnake alongside the cabin's door jam, ready to strike...

Long about midnight, a motionless Bear Scat heard what he figured was labored breathing coming from someone just inside the front doorway of the open-doored cabin and a 'someone who was just inches away from a date with his Maker'! Moments later a darkened form slowly stepped out from the doorway of the cabin and just stood there silently, as if looking and listening for any sign of the trapper they had failed to kill in their first fusillade of shots. Little did that person realize he was so close to Bear Scat that Bear Scat could feel the body heat emanating from the man and could smell his sweat of fear! The next thing that person standing in the doorway heard was the 'swish' of a violently swung tomahawk just microseconds before its blade smashed through his mouthful of teeth and lodged deeply into his spinal cord! A soft crumpling sound immediately followed, as the man's body hit the front step of the cabin and began thrashing around in its throes of death!

"Pierce!" screamed a now terrified Jordan Travis and then he was heard rushing over to the body in the darkness which was still thrashing around on the cabin's door stoop. When that darkened form heard movement moving across the cabin's floor and materialized over Pierce Travis's body, a brilliant flash and explosion immediately followed! This as Bear Scat's Hawken exploded away the darkness inside the cabin for just a moment, revealing the last Travis Brother's head erupting like a melon when the Hawken's big lead slug hit him just below his cheekbone from a distance of only two feet away!

With the firing of that fatal shot into the last of the evil-minded Travis Brothers, Bear Scat reloaded his rifle in the darkness with a calmness born from many years living on the frontier under the practiced hand of a Mountain Man. He then walked over to the outside firepit and with his fire steel started a fire. The rest of that night, Bear Scat sat by his fire thinking over what had just happened, the grave loss of his dear friend Big Hat, and the fact that he was now ALONE IN THE WILDERNESS! Additionally, Bear Scat sat there that night tending the fire in order to make sure a hungry grizzly bear did not enter his camp and carry off Big Hat's body before he could be buried like the Christian man he had been...

The next day after unpacking all of his packhorses, Bear Scat took a shovel, dug a grave next to their cabin and with tears unashamedly spilling down his face and splashing all across the front of his buckskin shirt, buried his friend and mentor. Then he removed the Travis Brothers' bodies from the area, dragging them into an adjacent aspen grove of trees and left them aboveground for the wolves, ravens and bears to feast upon. Returning to the cabin, Bear Scat cleaned up the messes of blood and brains scattered about, making it livable once again. Then it dawned on Bear Scat that the Travis Brothers had arrived by horse and he needed to locate such valuable animals and include them in his corral. An hour later found Bear Scat leading the Travis Brothers' four riding horses and THEIR EIGHT HEAVILY LOADED PACKHORSES back to his cabin. There Bear Scat found himself unloading 12 bundles of beaver furs from six of their packhorses and stashing them inside the already cramped cabin space, along with his numerous bundles of furs as well! In so doing, Bear Scat marveled over how well the Travis Brothers had done, based on their 12 bundles of furs just unpacked, during their fall trapping season. Then Bear Scat spent the rest of the day fleshing out and hooping all of the beaver pelts he and Big Hat had trapped the last day before they had been ambushed back at their cabin by the Travis Brothers. By now exhausted from all of his labors and wildly fluctuating emotions, Bear Scat made up a batch of Dutch oven biscuits and when they were baked, ate the entire batch since he had not eaten anything in the last 20 hours of his life, a life now turned upside down and looking at a very lonely existence as a single trapper out in the wilderness!

Sitting there by his campfire, Bear Scat quietly took stock of his situation. He was now alone in a fierce and unforgiving land. He had just lost his best friend and mentor to a violent death. Looking over at his crowded corral, he could see that he was now the owner of 24 valuable horses, a number of such magnitude that he would find it almost impossible to manage trailing them to the next rendezvous when he decided to leave the area. He was now the owner and a rich man of over 1,200 *'plus'* of beaver furs from the Travis Brothers' horde of 720, not to mention the 568 that he and Big Hat had amassed during their portion of the current fall trapping season! Lastly, he still had 16 beaver traps out catching beaver, which was way more than he could adequately tend to or process those catches come the end of the day! Then it dawned on him, how was he to run a trap line and at the same time all by himself, provide for his protection from any attacks by grizzly bears or Indians? With such a swirl of issues running through his brain, Bear Scat was soon found walking over to his cabin, bringing out one of the kegs of rum, sitting down by the fire and in the crushing silence and intense realization that came from abruptly finding himself totally alone in the wilderness, drank himself to sleep alongside his campfire…

The next morning, Bear Scat awoke shaking from the cold and being thoroughly wetted from the morning's dew after lying passed out outside all night. Crawling to his feet somewhat unsteadily, the fuzziness in his eyes did not dissipate when he observed a very crowded horse corral with livestock impatiently stomping their feet and constantly moving around within their confines wanting to be released so they could feed! Staggering over to the horse corral and pulling a set of hobbles off the rails, Bear Scat began hobbling his horses and releasing them one at a time so they could feed in the glen's vast meadow. Upon finishing with his horses, Bear Scat found that his head had cleared somewhat, especially after he had dunked his head into the cold creek's waters over at his spring box! Wiping the water off and rubbing his still aching head from all the rum imbibed the night before, Bear Scat walked over to his firepit and finding some live coals, soon had a roaring fire going. In so doing, he also found that a cup of their fiery rum sure helped steady his shaking hands and the ringing sounds in his head as he worked around the campfire…

Then Bear Scat remembered he still had 16 beaver traps that had not been tended since his shootout with the Travis Brothers! Retrieving his saddle horse and one packhorse from their meadow, Bear Scat saddled and packed the same and with a saddlebag full of jerky, headed out to his trap line. As he did, in addition to checking his surroundings for any signs of danger, he kept looking around as if expecting his friend Big Hat to appear wearing his always infectious grin, beat-up old floppy hat and reminding him to remain on the alert… As luck and his trapping skill would have it, every beaver trap that day held a dead beaver! Bear Scat realizing the amount of work he was now facing, reduced the number of traps on his trap line from 16 to just eight being run daily. Come dusk that first day as a lone Mountain Man and trapper, Bear Scat dejectedly rode back into his cabin's glen. However now more alert than ever, he saw that his horse herd was still feeding in the meadow. Tying up his packhorse, Bear Scat then herded his horses into their corral, shut the gate and then removed their hobbles. Unloading his packhorse's pannier full of freshly skinned beaver pelts, he hauled it over to his cabin, sat it down and then headed for his firepit. After getting his fire going, Bear Scat roasted a skinned-out beaver carcass in the round and ate like a starving man who hadn't really eaten anything substantial in the last 48 hours! Then under the candlelight in his cabin, Bear Scat fleshed and hooped his day's trappings and set them out along the inner walls of the cabin to dry. Without even cleaning up, he dropped emotionally and physically exhausted into his sleeping furs and did not wake until late in the morning the following day.

Thus began a dizzying routine of horse care, trap tending, trap setting, skinning the day's catch, providing his own protection, remaining aware of his surroundings, fleshing and hooping his daily catches, cooking and eating whenever he could until the fall trapping season freeze-up occurred. With that respite, Bear Scat found the time to quit eating so much beaver meat, and hunting down and killing a much-needed meal change found in that of a buffalo. However when he did, he found the tears of loss streaming down his face once again when he opened up the side of a cow buffalo just killed for a chunk of liver, and every time feeling the heavy load of such a personal loss in his friend Big Hat. Especially now that he was not there to share such a delight as the two of them had done so many times in the past. Then every time thereafter when he killed a buffalo and opened up the side of the animal for the treat of fresh liver, a heavy feeling of loneliness and the thoughts of being all alone would always overcome him with an almost physical-feeling rush...

Winter that year seemed to drag on and on, especially without anyone other than the horses to talk to. Additionally, Bear Scat found himself restricting his wolf trapping to just setting his traps around a freshly killed buffalo for the meat it offered him back at camp. No longer did he just shoot a buffalo in order to have a bait station around which to set his wolf traps. That he did since there was always other work that needed doing now that he was all alone. Those duties always involved cutting wood from their woodpile for his cabin's fireplace, hobbling horses so they could graze and then making sure they were placed back into his corral each evening, making a small mountain of bullets, packing all of his dried beaver hides into bundles so they could be safely transported to the 1836 Rendezvous because he still had to be able to procure provisions for his next trapping season if he could find a good partner, equipment always needed repairing, he needed to make new clothing for himself for the coming spring trapping season, and he still had to cook his meals. Thus ended the lonely winter of 1835 for Elliott "Bear Scat" Sutta, Mountain Man...

One morning early in the spring of 1836, Bear Scat found himself cooking his breakfast at his outside firepit and preparing for the beginning of his spring beaver trapping season. Then all of a sudden while making up a batch of biscuits and smelling the strong aroma of his coffee boiling, his mind wandered back to earlier and better times. As those thoughts of yesteryear took him back to those better times, his eyes slowly swung to the front door of their cabin. Then his thoughts came flooding back to that first spring in his life as a Mountain Man. A spring event in which Big Hat would come out from the door of their cabin happily announcing that today would be the first day of their spring beaver trapping season. Then he would come down to the firepit where Bear Scat would be preparing breakfast, looking for his morning's coffee made Bear Scat-style. Bear Scat coffee that was 'black as the devil's heart and thick enough to stand a mule shoe upright in the cup without it falling over'. Then he would let the cook know to fix a big breakfast because 'he was hungry enough to eat his own horse'... Once again Bear Scat felt the heavy pall of loneliness flooding over him like a wet buffalo robe, and he found his eyes misting up over the loss of a friend who was more like a father-figure than just another human being. Shaking those hurtful thoughts from his mind, Bear Scat quietly finished making his breakfast without looking over at the cabin's front door... Quietly sitting on his sitting log and eating what he had prepared, he began running through his mind all the preparations that he had made for this first day of spring beaver trapping.

He was going to trap a new area that he had recently scouted out and found it to be loaded with many signs of beaver activity. He had smoked the eight traps he planned on using which was a normal complement for a single trapper, had checked the shoes on his riding and packhorses to make sure they weren't loose, stuffed his saddlebag with jerky, and loaded his panniers with all of his needed beaver trapping supplies. Pouring out the remains of his cup of coffee into the fire, Bear Scat stood up, stretched, picked up his nearby rifle off his sitting log and walked over to his previously saddled riding horse. Moments later, off Bear Scat rode to his new beaver trapping grounds to begin his first day of the spring beaver trapping season as a lone trapper. That, care for his livestock, fleshing and hooping of his daily catch of beaver pelts, and meal-making without much enthusiasm began the routine of the lone Mountain Man as he continued in his much-loved trade as a fur trapper for the first month of the 1836 spring trapping season.

CHAPTER FOURTEEN: A GRIZZLY BEAR AND ALONE NO MORE...

After breakfast one morning into that second month of his spring beaver trapping season, Bear Scat saddled up his horse, loaded the panniers on his packhorse with needed trapping equipment, and headed out to check his trap line. Looking skyward as Big Hat had taught him in order to check the weather for the day, Bear Scat only observed fluffy white clouds slowly passing overhead against a backdrop of a velvety blue sky. A soft breeze was blowing from out of the northwest and the morning's temperature was such that he was looking forward to the day, spring cold waters to wade in or not when it came time to check his traps and recover any beaver carcasses.

As it turned out, it was one of those kinds of days in which a trapper reveled in. Every trap set had a beaver and in each instance every beaver was an adult or soon to be a Made Beaver, the standard unit of trade at any rendezvous. Resetting each trap in the same location because of the heavy beaver activity in the area while keeping a 'sharp' eye tuned to his surroundings, Bear Scat finished by around noon. That included running his entire trap line that day as well as skinning his entire catch. Letting his two horses feed on the rich mountain grasses, Bear Scat walked around trying to warm up after being immersed in the cold beaver pond waters all morning long. As he did, he feasted on some of the last pieces of jerky that Big Hat had smoked and put up into their tanned deerskin bags that hung from the rafters in his cabin. Savoring the smoky taste of the semi-hard piece of buffalo jerky, Bear Scat let his mind wander back to the days when he and Big Hat had roamed the marshes after the fabled beaver. Moments into reminiscing about his past relationship with a man he had come to love as a father, Bear Scat once more felt a tear sliding down the side of his nose before dropping onto the front of his buckskin shirt, leaving a dark blotch on the leather...

Finishing his jerky, Bear Scat mounted his horse and began the trip back along his previously set trap line rechecking his traps for any just caught beaver. As anticipated, three of the traps already held a dead beaver in their steel jaws. Dismounting and wading out into the cold beaver pond waters with his rifle in hand, he all of a sudden felt a cold chill running through his body as he became aware that his 'sixth sense' was once again roiling around inside of him! Stopping his travel across the ponded waters after his trapped beaver, Bear Scat looked carefully all around at his surroundings. First he checked the dense patches of willows looking for a disturbed and maddened cow moose charging out at him in an act of defending her calf. Seeing nothing of the kind, he slowly turned all around carefully examining the rolling hillsides and adjacent ridgelines looking for lines of Indians riding along or watching him. In so doing, he saw only a golden eagle making lazy circles in the sky above a far ridgeline, *probably looking for a jack rabbit lunch,* he thought. Checking one more time, realizing how many times his 'sixth sense' had been right and finding nothing out of the ordinary, he relaxed. Turning, he once again traveled over to his trap and the drowned beaver. Transferring his heavy rifle from his right hand to a position up under his armpit so his hands would be free, he emptied the beaver from the trap and carried both back to its original trap site. Tossing the heavy beaver up onto the bank, Bear Scat laid his rifle down alongside the beaver within easy reach in case its use was called for and then reset his trap in its original trap site one more time.

Crawling out onto the bank from the beaver pond, Bear Scat unsheathed his skinning knife and just minutes later, his experienced skinning technique had a beaver carcass in one hand and a fresh pelt in the other. Tossing the beaver's carcass off to one side for the critters to find and eat after Bear Scat had cut off the beaver's tail from the pelt, he then tossed both into his packhorse's pannier. This Bear Scat did so the pelt could be fleshed and hooped later back at the cabin and the tail to be roasted over the fire for its warmth-giving fat later during his supper.

Mounting his horse and still mindful of his earlier 'sixth sense' urgings, Bear Scat took a few moments to once again check his surroundings for any signs of danger. Then his now 'sixth sense'-searching mind could only recall fresh tracks of a grizzly bear sow and what appeared to be a couple of almost grown cubs at the edge of the circle of timber concealing his cabin's location. However they appeared to be heading for the remains of an old buffalo carcass, one that he had shot a week earlier for fresh meat, located several hundred yards away from his cabin. Putting that to the back of his mind, Bear Scat rode on towards his cabin. There he had a number of beaver pelts to flesh and hoop, his horses to let out from their corral, hobble and let out to feed, and then fix his supper when he was free from his other daily chores.

Rounding the lower end of the tree line surrounding his secluded glen, Bear Scat picked his way through the timber and out onto the south end of the glen below his cabin. As he did and looking momentarily back at a small fawn that he had spooked out from its bed in the timber when his horse had almost stepped on it, his attention was quickly brought back to the glen when his horse gave a whinny of other horse recognition. When he did, HE INSTANTLY WENT FOR HIS RIFLE LYING ACROSS HIS LAP AS HE SPOTTED AN INDIAN SITTING ON A HORSE NEXT TO HIS HORSE CORRAL! For an instant, Bear Scat thought the Indian was in the process of looking at stealing his valuable horses! Then he remembered Jim Bridger's words back at his camp at the previous rendezvous regarding the fact that where he was sending both him and Big Hat to trap beaver in the Wind River Mountains, that was home to the Shoshone. To his way of thinking and based on his historical knowledge, Bridger considered the Shoshone Indians friendly to the white man trappers and not to be concerned about being attacked by such people unless one did them wrong. With Bridger's words ringing in his head, Bear Scat relaxed a bit but only just a bit. He still was not as good as Big Hat had been on instant recognition of an Indian and one's potential aggressiveness based on the manner of one's dress, so Bear Scat kept his hand on his rifle, just in case.

Spurring his horse just slightly, Bear Scat ambled towards the unknown Indian as his 'sixth senses' reared their heads once more! With that, Bear Scat cocked the hammer on his Hawken without making such an offensive move noticeable if the Indian was to look at the oncoming trapper. Now within 30 yards of the rather smallish Indian rider without being noticed, Bear Scat tightened his hand around the wrist of his rifle and quickly cast his eyes down to his sash to make sure both of his pistols were still there and riding close at hand comfortably within reach.

"URRRGHHH!" roared a HUGE sow grizzly bear from near the head of the corral from behind the cover of the spring box, unseen previously by the Indian, the horse being sat upon or even the corral full of horses! Right behind the hard-charging sow grizzly bear were her two almost fully grown cubs following their mother's lead! Before the Indian, whose full attention had been focused on the corral full of valuable horses, could react to the charging bear, the sow grizzly had closed the distance, grabbed the Indian rider's horse's head in her jaws, and had bowled the horse and its rider over onto the ground! When the Indian's horse slammed onto the ground, it let out a muffled cry as the great bear crunched down upon its head with its jaws and in the process, pinning the Indian rider under the now dying horse!

For just a second, Bear Scat sat there upon his horse stunned over the grizzly bear exploding onto the scene and then found himself quickly unhorsed, as his terrified horse now reacted to the three foul-smelling and close at hand grizzly bears. Grizzly bears who were now in the process of jointly mauling and ripping the dying horse to pieces! Just as Bear Scat staggered to his feet after having the wind knocked out from him when he hit the ground after being bucked off by his horse, HE HEARD A WOMAN SCREAM! Bear Scat then realized that the smallish in size Indian now struggling to get out from under the dead horse and just feet from the mouths of three grizzly bears savagely tearing the horse apart, was a young Indian female!

Sucking hard trying to get his wind back, Bear Scat without thinking broke for the woman pinned under her horse, just as one of the sub-adult grizzly bear cubs realized the struggling human with her left leg trapped under her dead horse was also a food source! With that realization, the 300-pound cub made an aggressive move towards the Indian woman tightly pinned under her horse! As the cub came in for the kill on the pinned woman, **BOOM!** went Bear Scat's Hawken, as the big .52 caliber slug struck the sub-adult bear in the neck, causing it to cry out in pain just before it rolled off to the side and died! If the act of killing the Indian's horse was not enough of a savage action, the plaintive cry of a dying cub certainly initiated another one! Dropping the horse's head from her crushing jaws upon hearing her cub crying out in pain, the female grizzly bear instantly reared onto her hind legs to her full eight feet in height over the dead horse. The killing-mad grizzly bear, upon hearing her cub crying out in pain just before it died and sensing the nearness of Bear Scat now trying to pull the trapped female Indian out from under her dead horse, let out a terrifyingly sounding roar! That was instantly followed by a charge when she dropped to all four feet and made a quick rush for Bear Scat, just as he managed to pull the terrified Indian woman out from under her horse and toss her off to one side and away from the action. Now free from being pinned under her horse, the young

Indian woman took off running like a scared deer, as Bear Scat turned and faced the maddened and charging grizzly bear who was so close at that moment in time that Bear Scat could smell her sour-smelling breath!

In a blur brought on by the terror of the moment, Bear Scat quickly drew one of his pistols and in one fluid movement cocked its hammer and JUST managed to force the gun into the gaping mouth of the female grizzly bear as she collided with Bear Scat! **BOOM!** went the sound of a muffled handgun going off in the bear's now closed mouth over Bear Scat's right hand! The bullet flew truly, breaking the bear's spine and killing her instantly! However, her great weight in her furious charge carried the bear over the top of Bear Scat, almost crushing him with her weight in the process! As a stunned and terrified Bear Scat tried to crawl out from under the female grizzly in her death throes, the bear vomited up her stomach contents all over his head and face, causing him to gag and cough violently!

Gagging and vomiting all in the same reflex action, Bear Scat found himself now confronted by the second sub-adult grizzly bear weighing about 350 pounds, standing over him just as it grabbed him by the front of his buckskin shirt. With an upward rip of his head, the bear violently dragged Bear Scat out from under the dead female bear and tossed him off to one side! Bear Scat hit the ground so hard from being so violently tossed that he lay there on the ground for a second stunned. Then seeing the bear coming for him and before he knew it, the grizzly had bitten down for Bear Scat's head and only a quick move out of the way saved the trapper's life! However, the bear was not finished and in his second attack, it bit down HARD on Bear Scat's left shoulder with a crunching bite! Then the bear ripped Bear Scat upward by his shoulder just as Bear Scat fired his remaining pistol into the so close at hand bear that one could smell the burnt bear hair from the pistol's muzzle blast! However, being jerked all around by his left shoulder, Bear Scat's shot went wild and instead of going into the head of the bear, struck the bear in its shoulder. That wounding only infuriated the bear even further and he grabbed Bear Scat once again in his previously bitten-into shoulder, violently jerked him up off the ground and with a violent toss of its head, tossed Bear Scat some 20 feet! Bear Scat, landing with a hard "CRUNCH" on his now twice badly bitten left shoulder, even in his blinding pain was now going for his gutting knife held in his belt with his previously bitten right hand, when he was grabbed by the bear once again, violently shaken and finding that explosion of pain so great, that his world went black! But not before his dulled senses clearly heard in the recesses of his brain the close at hand sounds of **BOOM—BOOM—BOOM!**

Sometime later, Bear Scat first heard voices way off in the distant recesses of his mind speaking in a tongue that he did not understand. Then in intense pain, he blacked out once again! Later when he began coming around for a second time, he was lying on his back and looking skyward into the afternoon sun through a vision that was so fuzzy, it appeared his eyes were covered with a red film of blood. But just before he blacked out once again after trying to move, only to have the pain in his left shoulder flood over him in a blinding flash, he could hear a number of men's voices talking and sounding like they were speaking from being inside a wooden barrel partly filled with water. The next time Bear Scat came around, he found himself looking up into the most beautiful face of an Indian woman that he had ever seen... She was wiping the bear's vomit off his face, head and neck and was speaking to him in soothing tones in a language that he did not understand. THEN HIS HEART ALMOST STOPPED! He saw out of the corner of his eye a number of Indians removing armloads of everything from his cabin and loading all of his goods, provisions and bundles of furs onto a number of horses standing nearby! Then he saw another bunch of Indian boys removing all of his horses from the corral and herding them away! Figuring the Indians were robbing him of everything he possessed, he tried sitting up to object, when the intense shoulder pain once again flooded over him and his last remembrance of his world was the beautiful face of the young Indian woman laying him back down on the ground, and then everything in his world went black followed by a roaring sound in his ears!

The next thing Bear Scat remembered was a gradual light coming into his eyes, the roaring sounds in his ears were gone, and he could feel the cool all over him where he was lying on something soft. As his senses gradually began slowly coming back into consciousness, he realized he was lying on a bed of animal skins and was looking up into the insides of a darkened tipi. To his surprise, he had been washed up, was free of the grizzly bear's acidic vile-smelling vomit, and he was as naked as a baby robin! Trying to sit up, he immediately felt a crashing and burning pain in his left shoulder where the bear had bitten him several times, and had violently tossed him off to one side after ferociously biting down on his shoulder! Additionally, in trying to use his right hand to push himself up off from his sleeping furs, he felt instant pain as well! Then looking over at his right hand, he could see that it was colored black, purple, yellow and red, and was swollen three times its normal size! Bear Scat then remembered in the fight with the bears, he had in one instance, thrust his pistol into a bear's mouth with his right hand and the bear had viciously bitten down just as he had pulled the trigger, killing that bear! Lying back down until the pain had somewhat subsided, he then became aware of someone pulling aside the flap of the tipi he was in and could hear the quiet 'swishing' sounds of someone in a dress walking by him. As the person walked in behind his head where he could not see who it was, he was clearly aware of the soft rustling sounds a tanned animal skin skirt would make, in addition to the quiet, almost tinkling sounds an elk's ivory-toothed upper garment would make when bodily movement rattled the teeth together.

Then a beautiful young Indian woman quietly and in a fluid movement, knelt down beside him with a bowl of some kind of wonderful-smelling food. Then all of a sudden, Bear Scat recognized the young Indian woman kneeling down beside him. It was the same Indian woman he had found looking at his horses just before the grizzly bear had attacked. The same Indian woman he had pulled out from under the side of her dead horse just before one of the sub-adult grizzly bear cubs tried to attack and kill her!

Bear Scat's amazement must have been really noticeable because the young woman reached down and put her index finger over his lips as if 'telling' him not to try speaking just now. Realizing what she was trying to tell him, Bear Scat relaxed and then found a spoonful of some wonderful-smelling food was pressed to his lips in a sign for him to eat. That he did and found that he was famished. Little did Bear Scat realize that he had been lying in that Indian tipi for over a week, out of his head in pain, infection and inflammation from the almost bone-crushing bites and deep puncture wounds made into his left shoulder and right hand by two different grizzly bears!

For the rest of that week, Bear Scat found himself under the personal care and attention of the young Indian woman he had rescued. During that time, she fed, washed and applied some stinking and burning kind of poultice to the almost-putrefying deep puncture wounds in his shoulder and onto his right hand on a daily basis. After another two weeks of such care, Bear Scat was healing up sufficiently enough allowing him to be able to sit up without passing out from the pain in his badly bitten shoulder. However he found himself very weak, prone to throbbing headaches and lingering soreness from the rampant infections he was suffering from the various bear bites on his left shoulder, right hand and his chest where he was first bitten and tossed off to one side like a rag doll.

It was during one of those sitting-up sessions that he remembered all the strange Indians removing all of his possessions from his cabin, including his numerous bundles of *'plus'* as well as making off with his entire horse herd! Feeling a panic setting in over the loss of everything he worldly owned now that those remembrances came to mind, he figured he would try communicating with the beautiful young woman who was nursing him back to health regarding those losses. Finally one day after repeated attempts at communicating with the young woman, all of which ended up in obvious frustration for both parties, she put her finger to Bear Scat's lips, then got up and walked out from his tipi. Confused over her actions, Bear Scat tried to get up on his own and walk out from the tipi, and find someone with whom he could communicate in an attempt to discover what had happened to all of his worldly possessions. That was the last thing he remembered as the terrible burning pain instantly came back the moment he tried to stand and he immediately pitched forward and passed out.

When Bear Scat awoke, he found himself back on his bed of furs and sitting alongside him was an older Indian man quietly watching him. "Good Morning. You had a bad day and night after you tried to walk, so we decided to let you sleep as long as your body needed to. I am called "Medicine Pipe" and I am a holy man for the Wind River Band of the Shoshone People. My English is not so good, so you must listen carefully to my words, for I speak for Chief Gray Wolf of the Wind River Band of the Shoshone People since he does not speak in the tongue of the white man." Medicine Pipe then paused and holding a small bowl of smoking sagebrush leaves, began wafting the smoke over his body and that of Bear Scat as he mumbled some sacred words known only to him and his People.

When he finished with the ceremony involving the smoking sagebrush, Medicine Pipe commenced speaking to Bear Scat once again in broken English saying, "You have done a good and brave thing, White Man. Chief Gray Wolf's oldest daughter discovered your trapper's cabin many days ago and rode in to look at your horses. There her horse was attacked by a mother bear. She tells us that she was knocked under her horse, her horse was killed by the bears and then The Great Spirit sent you to save her life. However in that great battle between you and the three bears, you were injured after saving her. My People were nearby returning from a buffalo hunt and came to see who was doing all the shooting after the chief's daughter ran to us asking for help. There our braves found you in the jaws of the Great Bear and killed him in order to save you. Our People brought you here to heal up which is going to take a long time. As a way of saying thank you for saving Chief Gray Wolf's daughter "Kimama", or "Butterfly" in the language of the white people, our braves took your horses and what you had in your cabin and brought them here so bad Indians or a grizzly bear did not take or destroy them. Your horses are with our horses and are being watched over by our "Young Chiefs"." (Author's Note: The term "Young Chiefs" used by many American Indian tribes denoted young boys.) They will be returned to you when you are able to leave our people and go back to yours. The things in your cabin that you valued were also brought here and are stored in the empty tipi next to yours. There they will stay guarded by our braves until you are able to leave and also take them to your people, and trade them for more of the things that white men find important."

Then Medicine Pipe could see the wonder in Bear Scat's face over his command of the English language and said, "I can see in your eyes that you are wondering why I speak in the tongue of the white man. Years ago, the Great Chief who lives far to the east and rules all of your people sent your Captain Lewis and his people to spend some time with us on their trip to where the sun sets in the Big Waters. Some of us escorted them through our mountain passes of the deep snows since they did not know the way. During those times, they spoke the words of the white man to me and I learned what they were saying because I felt it important to do so. When they returned many moons later, I once again learned more and was finally able to speak in the white man's tongue. True to his word, your Captain Lewis sent a "Black Robe" back to my people to teach us the ways of our friends the white man. That is how I came to be able to speak and listen to you in the tongue of the white man." With those words of comfort and explanation, Bear Scat lay back down on his furs and was soon fast asleep, as Medicine Pipe seeing he needed the rest, spoke the words of the white man no more that day and quietly left Bear Scat's tipi.

******

When the beaver went out of prime in the Bighorn Mountains, Jacob Sutta and Wild Bill McGinty began the arduous job of packing all of their beaver skins into bundles for transport to the 1836 Rendezvous to be held at Horse Creek in the Green River Valley. After six days of work folding, bundling and wrapping their furs in tanned deerskins to protect the furs during the long transport, Sutta and McGinty were pleased with their efforts and year's catch. They had another good year and were looking forward to attending that year's rendezvous, meeting old friends, tipping a cup or two of rum, checking around to see who still 'had their hair and who had lost theirs', take on new provisions, and then head out to locate new trapping grounds since they had exhausted the numbers of beaver in their latest trapping area. However, there was still the issue of the Travis Brothers and their deadly mission of wanting to kill Wild Bill McGinty for what they considered was a major wrong done to their family. With that problematic issue hanging in the air, both men were now looking at a fur-trading trip more than likely traveling clear across to Fort Union once again, instead of going to the Green River Rendezvous in the hope of dodging the four deadly brothers.

Sitting around their campfire that evening and quietly sipping a cup of rum, Bill after looking into their crackling campfire for many long moments, finally turned and said to Jacob Sutta his longtime partner, "Jacob, I am tired of running from the Travis Brothers for something their father did that was wrong and not I. True, I shot and killed him after he lied to me as to where my share of the moonshine money had disappeared, but I gave him every chance to settle up with me and he chose not to. In fact, he drew first on me when confronted, and then he shot and tried to kill me over the money he had stolen from me but in so doing, missed. However I did not miss and he died as he had lived, a liar and a thief."

Then looking back into the fire as if to once again gather his thoughts, Bill turned facing Jacob and said, "This year we will go to wherever they are holding the rendezvous. I am tired of running from nothing that I did that was wrong. True, I killed a man and the Travis Brothers' father, but only after he had cheated me out of my money and only after he tried to kill me. So I say we go to the rendezvous in the Green River Valley instead of going clear over to Fort Union on the Missouri River. If I am killed there by the Travis Brothers, so be it. But I am tired of running away from those four boys. Now I don't want you to get involved because you had nothing to do with this feud. So if and when the shooting starts, I don't expect you to get involved. Just bury me if I am killed under a lot of dirt and rocks so the wolves, coyotes or grizzly bears don't dig me up and eat me. There is no way I want to end up being an animal's scat out on the prairie somewhere..."

Seeing that his partner had 'run down' on what he had to say, Jacob Sutta just looked at him and said, "We have been partners for many a year now and through a lot of 'thick and thin'. I don't plan on now or ever for that matter stepping back and letting you handle any kind of a load that the both of us should share. Bill, if and when the shooting starts, I will be there by your side. That way, we will either settle this matter once and for all time, or lay side by side out on the prairie as animal scats after they have dug us up and eaten their fill of what they wanted of our better parts."

Two weeks later, Jacob Sutta and Wild Bill McGinty rode into Horse Creek near the confluence of the Green River in the Green River Valley to attend the 1836 Rendezvous in style. (Author's Note: Near the current-day town of Daniel, Wyoming.) However, both men sported two pistols apiece in their sashes, a rifle across their riding horse's saddle and an extra rifle in a scabbard on the first packhorse in each man's string of heavily loaded animals just in case they 'ran dry' in any kind of a shoot-out...

However, for 'some reason' that year, the Travis Brothers did not show up at the 1836 Rendezvous held in the Green River Valley at that Horse Creek location... So Jacob Sutta and Wild Bill

McGinty relaxed and celebrated along with their friends, doing what all trappers did after spending a full year out in the western wilds trapping beaver and seldom seeing another white man for over a year at a time. At the end of that rendezvous, Jacob and Bill traded in their furs, took on the coming year's provisions and disappeared back into the wilds of the wilderness doing what they did best, namely trapping beaver, eating buffalo and enjoying a lifestyle that only God could have created for the men cut of that 'kind of cloth'...

Also for 'some reason', that was the first rendezvous in a long time in which Big Hat and his partner Bear Scat Sutta, who always seemed to be looking for his long-lost brother, namely one Jacob Sutta, mysteriously did not show up either...

******

For the rest of 1836 and into the early spring of 1837, Bear Scat never left Chief Gray Wolf's Wind River Band of Shoshone Indians. As it turned out, his wounds from his fight with the three grizzly bears remained infected longer than he figured, oozing pus from the many deep puncture wounds for weeks on end. Additionally, Bear Scat found that his left shoulder was more badly damaged than he thought and turned out to be so stiff that he initially could not adequately shoulder a rifle in which to defend himself against his human or animal foes, or speed load the same while on the run. As a result, Bear Scat found himself under the almost constant care and attention of Chief Gray Wolf's oldest daughter, Kimama, as he began the slow process of healing from his wounds. He also in the same period of healing began vigorously rehabilitating his left shoulder with all kinds of exercises so he could get back the use of his left arm in order to be able to shoulder his rifle, and in so doing, provide for himself as well as defend himself in a land known for many times finding death and danger at every turn in the trail.

During that period of time regaining back his strength and eventually the full use of his left shoulder and arm, Bear Scat found himself on many long rides and sitting a number of long afternoons under the shade of trees getting to know Chief Gray Wolf's oldest and beautiful daughter, Kimama. During those many sessions, he also found himself learning the beautiful Shoshone language from Kimama, and he in turn was teaching her the language of the white man. Soon the rides became longer and longer, and Bear Scat found that under Kimama's care his healing took a turn for the better, and soon a very special relationship began developing between the two of them past the healing and horseback-riding stages...

It wasn't long before Chief Gray Wolf's band of people began noticing the close personal relationship developing between the fur trapper healing up from his deadly fight with three grizzly bears and the chief's oldest daughter. Soon the 'talk' of that personal developing relationship began among the People and reached the chief's ears. Coming back from another one of their long rides in March of 1837, Chief Gray Wolf sternly met the couple at his tipi, dismissed his daughter abruptly and asked Bear Scat to accompany him into his tipi. By now having learned many of the histories and traditions of the Shoshone culture, Bear Scat entered the chief's tipi, moved to the east once inside as visitors were expected to do, and quietly sat down. The chief then curtly dismissed his wife from inside the tipi and after she had left, sat down opposite Bear Scat. When he did, for the longest time the chief said nothing but just sternly looked at the trapper sitting across from him. Bear Scat, realizing what now might be at stake, made sure his cold-eyed stare did not leave the chief's eyes for even a second...

In the Shoshone language which Bear Scat could now fluently speak and understand, Chief Gray Wolf finally began talking by saying, "Kimama is my oldest and most beautiful daughter. I have heard my people talking about the two of you and have seen with my own eyes how the two of you look at each other. What are your intentions with my daughter, White Man, as I am told by my people who is called "Bear Scat" in name by his own people?"

Caught off guard over the chief's surprisingly pointed question but not letting any of that surprise show, Bear Scat stoically continued looking at the powerful chief for a long moment in time. Finally Bear Scat quietly yet courageously after finding his courage from deep within his soul, said, "Great Chief Gray Wolf, I have come to love your daughter very much. She has nursed me back to health from my fight with the three grizzly bears after I saved her life and since that day, she has stood by my side with love and care. After all our times together these many moons, we have had many long talks and I believe she feels the same love for me that I feel for her. We both have come to realize that The Great Spirit brought us together in the battle for life with the three grizzly bears. We both also feel The Great Spirit challenged the two of us with the bear attack to see if we both would be worthy of each other. My intention is to marry your beautiful daughter if that is at all possible. Yes, I will love her with all of my heart, forever, if our joining together in marriage is your will."

For the longest time, the chief just sat there looking sternly at Bear Scat over his just-spoken words. Then Chief Gray Wolf said, "Are your wounds healed up enough where you can support and protect her if she needs protecting?"

Bear Scat stared hard right back at the chief realizing the Shoshone highly valued courage saying, "Chief Gray Wolf, I have healed completely and am as strong as I ever was and can now run and shoot like I did before my fight with the bears, thanks to The Great Spirit and the care from Kimama. As for caring for her, I am a fur trapper and a good one. The bundles of furs being kept for me in the tipi where they are being stored speaks to my ability to more than provide for your beautiful daughter and the love of my life. In fact, in the white man's money, I will be a very rich man once I get all of my furs to a rendezvous where they can be sold." As Bear Scat spoke those words, he knew them to be true. He had a small fortune in furs between what the Travis Brothers had carried with them prior to their fight at the cabin and those furs amassed by Big Hat and himself. Additionally, he still carried in his saddlebag letters of credit from the American Fur Company for $13,032 and the St. Louis Fur Company for $1,700 from previous rendezvous' fur and horse herd sales! So no two ways about it, he knew the chief was aware of the bundles of valuable beaver furs stored in the tipi, which spoke to his ability to provide for his oldest daughter. With those words of assurance, Bear Scat was hoping in his heart the stern chief would find it in his heart to allow his daughter to marry him.

For the longest of time, the chief continued staring at Bear Scat as if looking for any kind of a flaw in the white man seated before him. Then he asked, "Bear Scat, in your many long rides and times away from the eyes of my people, have you already 'taken' her?"

Bear Scat, surprised at that very personal question and knowing how much the Shoshone valued chastity, he made sure the chief clearly understood the truth in what he was about to say when he emphatically uttered the word, "NO! Nor do I intend to 'take her' unless you give your blessing AND we are married in the eyes of The Great Spirit first!"

With those words, Bear Scat saw the first vestiges of a slight smile on the weathered face of the great warrior chief of the Shoshone. Then the wise chief quietly said with just a slight smile creeping across his weathered face, "Bear Scat, how will you pay for her?"

Caught off guard over what amounted to the chief's subtle blessing if he was to ask for Kimama's hand in marriage and remembering the Travis Brothers had brought four riding horses to the battle at the cabin plus eight packhorses, Bear Scat paused for a moment with his answer. That he did because he knew how much the Shoshone valued good horseflesh and one who bargained wisely. Since the Shoshone had taken all of his horses at the end of the fight with the bears and knowing he needed most of them just to take his hoard of furs to the rendezvous, he could not squander any of his animals in payment for Kimama if he wanted to get all of his furs to the traders. However, the number of horses offered for the hand of his daughter had to be honorable as well. So in Bear Scat's response to the chief's horse flesh question, he said, "You may select any four horses from my herd if I may have your daughter's hand in marriage. The rest of my horses I will need just to take all of my furs to be sold, so that I might provide for her as you have provided for your wife and children."

In his response, Bear Scat had cleverly provided the chief a handsome price for the hand of his daughter in marriage. Plus, by throwing in that last bit about needing all the rest of his horses so he could transport his valuable furs to the rendezvous in order that they could be sold so he could provide for his daughter, he figured would more than persuade him from asking for more horses when his daughter's lifestyle was at stake...

Upon hearing that response, Chief Gray Wolf quietly rose, walked over to where Bear Scat was sitting and told him to rise. When Bear Scat stood, the chief put his hands on Bear Scat's shoulders saying, "You shall have Kimama as your wife for the four horses of my choice from your herd, just as long as that is her will."

With those words, Bear Scat's heart literally skipped a beat! Kimama was beautiful and one of the most wonderful, kind and accomplished women he had ever met. He had fallen in love with her over their months together and wanted to marry her so badly, but he had yet to even ask her! *What would she say as to her choice of husband being a white man instead of one of her own kind?* he thought with a hopeful but now slightly sinking heart over the reality now at hand. He now began to become concerned that maybe he had spoken out of turn...

Walking outside the chief's tipi, the chief was met by the chief's wife and all three of his daughters. There they all stood somehow understanding that a very important meeting was being held between their father and Bear Scat. A meeting in which the possibility that Bear Scat, the white trapper, was going to be asked by their father about his interest in the chief's daughter and maybe even their forthcoming marriage! With that in mind, they had all gathered around the tipi's opening flap waiting in suspense over their stern and protective father's decision and final outcome of his meeting with Bear Scat. When the dour old chief exited the tipi, all the faces on the four women waiting outside fell like a sack of rocks in disappointment over the solemn look on his face. However, when Bear Scat exited the tipi and the chief publicly acknowledged how positive the meeting had been by putting his hands on Bear Scat's shoulders once again like he was a long-lost son, the four women squealed in delight!

Kimama immediately ran into her father's arms crying great tears of joy! So much so, her tears of joy left dark blotches on the front of Chief Gray Wolf's beautifully beaded buckskin shirt. Then Kimama left his arms and flew into those of a much-surprised Bear Scat! Once there, Kimama stained the front of Bear Scat's buckskin shirt with her tears of joy over her father's acceptance of the love of her life as well. By now, a large number of Chief Gray Wolf's band began gathering around the unusual activity going on around the front of his tipi. Those numbers of his band grew even larger when it became apparent that the wife of the chief, now in his arms was crying tears of joy, as was Kimama who was still in the arms of Bear Scat. Then Chief Gray Wolf held up his right arm in order to get the attention of everyone who was looking on at all the unusual activity saying, "Let it be known that I have given permission to the white trapper we all have come to know as Bear Scat, to marry my oldest daughter Kimama!"

Upon hearing those words, many members of his band who had seen and suspected the developing relationship between Bear Scat and Kimama, voiced their approval with their sounds of much joy and great happiness over Bear Scat's acceptance into the Wind River Band of the Shoshone. The next two weeks were a whirlwind of cultural and cleansing activities, as the Wind River Band of Shoshone prepared for the marriage of Kimama and Bear Scat. The band's holy men prepared Bear Scat for the ceremony of becoming a member of their tribe and made sure he was cleansed in the process according to Shoshone customs and traditions. Meanwhile other braves began making preparations for the great wedding celebration and feast that was to follow. In addition, a new tipi was constructed off to one side of the main camp for the two newly married members of the band to be, so they could have their privacy...

Come the day of his marriage to the beautiful Kimama, Bear Scat could hardly wait for the wedding ceremony and all of the blessings from the holy men to be completed. In preparation, Kimama and her sisters had gotten together and had made Bear Scat a brand new set of fitted buckskins to get married in. After the short traditional Shoshone marriage ceremony, a great feast followed with much eating of specially prepared foods, singing and dancing among the band's members. Finally, while the wedding's celebration events were still ongoing, Bear Scat and Kimama quietly slipped away from the celebrants and ran to the tipi especially constructed with new buffalo hides for the two of them. Entering the tipi, Bear Scat and Kimama were surprised at all the trappings made and left for them inside. A central firepit had been built and blessed with sacred sagebrush burnings, a bed of buffalo and river otter sleeping skins had been arranged, and specialty foods and jugs of water were arrayed around one side of the tipi for the newlyweds.

Bear Scat, surprised over what Kimama's mother and sisters had prepared for them, stepped into the center of their new tipi, all backlit inside from the numerous fires back in the village where the wedding celebrations noisily continued unabated. After looking all around at the gifts in amazement, Bear Scat turned back towards his new bride. There he saw in the dim light of their tipi that Kimama was gesturing for him to come and sit on the sleeping furs. Surprised over her gestures, Bear Scat walked over and sat down on the deeply comfortable bed of sleeping furs. When he did, Kimama turned and quietly faced him. She then began taking off her beautiful white, tanned bighorn sheepskin shirt all bedecked with rows and rows of elk ivories and numerous beaded lines of blue and red glass beads. Lifting off her shirt and letting her long black hair fall over her full naked breasts, Bear Scat found himself finding it hard to breathe. Then Kimama untied the leather thong holding up her beautifully adorned and expertly tanned, bighorn sheepskin skirt and let it slip away down to her feet, revealing a beautifully tanned and lithe body, almost magically illuminated inside their tipi by the many campfires glowing back in the main camp... Then Kimama slipped out from her moccasins, stepped out from her dress lying on the floor of the tipi, and quietly stood there for her new husband to acknowledge her full and beautiful presence. Bear Scat had never seen such beauty and looking on at his new wife's full presence, found it even harder to breathe! Standing, he disrobed from his wedding clothing and stood there facing Kimama. When he did, she quietly slipped into his open and waiting arms and when she did, Bear Scat had never felt anything so warm, soft and desirous in his life! Lying down on their wedding bed of soft animal furs, Bear Scat felt his new wife 'melting' into his waiting arms and he never imagined life could be so meaningful, exotic and special between two people who were not talking. Finally Bear Scat was lost in love and not alone anymore...

Elliott "Bear Scat" Sutta, Mountain Man

CHAPTER FIFTEEN: A NEW PARTNER AND TRAPPING THE WIND RIVER

Come the last part of June in 1837, Bear Scat got a bad case of 'itchy feet' and began his preparations to attend the 1837 Rendezvous in the Green River Valley along Horse Creek, that location of which had been previously determined by the trappers and traders during the 1836 Rendezvous. The previous week, Bear Scat had several braves from Chief Gray Wolf's Wind River Band bring in his horse herd, minus the four horses the chief had selected as payment for giving him the hand of his daughter Kimama. Then Bear Scat began going through his provisions left over after his earlier fight with the grizzly bears and began organizing which supplies and bundles of beaver *'plus'* would be packed by which packhorse. Additionally, he had selected out from his horse herd Big Hat's always reliable buckskin and had designated that fine horse would heretofore belong to his new wife Kimama, so she could ride in style. Also from the time of their marriage until the present, Bear Scat had been teaching Kimama not only how to shoot a rifle and pistol, but correctly and quickly load the same. In so doing, he was amazed just how fast Kimama had picked up the self-defense techniques when it came to protecting herself with her own weapons. In fact, she had become after a short period of time, not only an accomplished user of weapons but had taken to her new horse like none other Bear Scat had ever seen. In short, Kimama was not only a truly wonderful wife but rapidly becoming an accomplished partner to Bear Scat as well.

Then one day as Bear Scat was continuing his preparations to travel to the 1837 Rendezvous, he observed his father-in-law Chief Gray Wolf walking towards the new couple's tipi. Pausing in his packing and preparation labors, Bear Scat greeted Chief Gray Wolf warmly as he was also greeted. It was then that he got a welcome surprise. Chief Gray Wolf advised Bear Scat that the women from his band had requested of their men that they go to the 1837 Rendezvous as well, so they could procure new cooking pots, beads, calico and other goods of the white man. That being the case, the tribal elders had decided to move the entire band down to the rendezvous site in the Green River Valley, and spend a month trading and visiting with members from other attending Shoshone bands of Indians. Besides, they had camped long enough in their current location and sanitation was now becoming problematic, so it was time to move.

Two days later there was great excitement in Chief Gray Wolf's camp as the braves returned from a buffalo hunt with great stocks of meat. Then the smoking and meat-drying fires burned brightly for the following week as the meat was processed and prepared for travel. Three days later after all of the meat stocks had been cared for, there was even greater excitement in camp, as the tipis were dismantled by the women and the horses and dogs were packed with tipi covers, poles and household goods needed for the upcoming trip. Then with the chief and tribal elders leading the way and the mounted braves providing protection along the sides, the long caravan of excited people began a trek southward towards the previously selected site for the 1837 Rendezvous. Four days of travel later found Chief Gray Wolf's band of Shoshone riding into the rendezvous site all dressed up in their finery amidst numerous barking dogs, excited voices from all the children, and a dust cloud from the many loaded horses, as well as the rest of their horses from their horse herd being herded along behind the main caravan!

Moving the band into an unoccupied portion of ground along Horse Creek where there would be a goodly supply of clean water, good grazing for their horse herds and plenty of buffalo chips and driftwood for their cooking fires, Chief Gray Wolf's band settled in among the hundreds of other attending Indians, Mountain Men and members of the American Fur Company attending the rendezvous.

Very soon thereafter, the women had set up their tipis, the horse herd had been let loose in a designated area away from everyone else's horses, and numbers of Indian women and their children were scurrying about gathering in driftwood from the Green River and Horse Creek, as well as blankets loaded with buffalo chips being carried back to their individual campsites. As the women and children continued setting up their campsites, the men began mingling with Shoshone tribal members from other bands, racing their horses, visiting, and trading in their buffalo robes and beaver *'plus'* with American Fur Company representatives.

Bear Scat, true to his band of Shoshone, helped Kimama set up their tipi in their designated tribal camping area and began unloading their horses, much to the negative and sometimes derisive remarks from braves of different bands for doing women's work. However Bear Scat just shrugged off their derisive comments for doing women's work, full well knowing that in his culture the men always helped the females of his race, unlike the surrounding Indian men in their cultures. Kimama on the other hand, tried to get her man to go off and visit other members of his race instead of doing 'women's work', all to no avail. Finished with the work around their tipi, Bear Scat hobbled all of his now unpacked horses and kept them close at hand, so they would not mingle with the other horses belonging to trappers and bands of Indians. Only then did he begin walking around the huge campsite of trappers and hundreds of attending Indians looking for his brother Jacob. However there were so many people in attendance, along with other ongoing activities, horse races, shooting contests, trading of Indian wives by a number of trappers, crowds gathered all around several trappers in wrestling matches, and folks drinking, fighting and other hell-raising, that he finally gave up in frustration looking for his brother and returned to his tipi. There he figured he would try looking for his brother Jacob on another day when things had settled down and all arriving trappers that were still coming to attend the event had finally arrived.

The next day way before daylight to avoid having to fight through the crush of other trappers wanting to sell their furs at the American Fur Company trading sites, Bear Scat loaded all his packs of *'plus'* and with Kimama at his side, set out to trade them in. Five hours later, his *'plus'* had been sorted, counted and graded by an American Fur Company Clerk who was amazed over how many furs Bear Scat had brought in to trade. In fact he had so many furs to be sorted and graded, that he had been assigned two company Clerks to complete the task. In the end, Bear Scat was credited with 1,031 Made Beaver and 336 smaller beaver *'plus'* valued at $5,132. Mountain Prices! The other American Fur Company Clerks were aghast at the number of beaver pelts he had single-handedly brought in since 200-400 *'plus'* brought in had been the average per trapper! Bear Scat did not mention that a great number of those *'plus'* had been caught by the four now-dead Travis Brothers, in addition to what he and Big Hat had trapped together. He just figured it was none of the Clerks' business since he had single-handedly settled the issue between him and the Travis Brothers, and just let all explanations as to his total presentation of beaver *'plus'* quietly 'ride off into the prairie winds'…

The whole time he spent with the American Fur Company Clerks in the fur-counting and grading process, Kimama had quietly looked on with rapt attention at an activity she had never ever seen performed before. Even when all was said and done, she did not have any idea that her man was now a very rich man in that day and age. With a company credit document in hand for the value of all of his furs, Bear Scat gathered up his pack animals and with Kimama, rode over to where all of the American Fur Company's wares were on display on log tables or scattered about on buffalo skin rugs for potential buyers to view and purchase. Moving over to the sections displaying fancy blankets, red and blue glass beads, cooking implements, mirrors and the like, items normally purchased by the trappers to woo the visiting Indian women or for their own Indian wives, Bear Scat dismounted. Then walking back to Kimama, he reached up and proudly filled his arms with 'his woman'. Setting her down, Bear Scat told Kimama to look around and anything that she saw that she liked to take it because it was hers! For the longest time, Kimama's dark eyes searched Bear Scat's eyes trying to understand, in looking deeply at him, the meaning of what her husband had just advised. Bear Scat, seeing the confusion in his wife's eyes took her by the hand over to several wooden barrels holding strings of brightly colored glass beads and told Kimama to take whatever she would like of the white man's goods because when she did, it would be hers. Kimama hesitated for a moment upon hearing those words, then Bear Scat took her right hand and thrust it into the barrel and told her once again to take whatever she wanted. Kimama did not need any further urging in the matter and with a smile, filled both hands with strings of red and blue glass beads made originally in Europe. Bear Scat then 'shepherded' Kimama over to the company trading section holding women's mirrors, combs and brushes. There he once again told Kimama to take what she wanted and finally she got the idea of what was expected of her. There she took enough combs, brushes and mirrors for all of her sisters and mother. From then on, whenever Bear Scat took her to various display sections set up by the traders of trade items and told her to take what she wanted, she was not bashful. Soon Bear Scat and a company Clerk both had their arms full of selected items by a very happy Kimama. Very soon after Kimama started 'shopping', Bear Scat had a packhorse fully loaded with bags of hard candy, several bolts of red calico, combs, mirrors, brushes, ordinary red cloth, an assortment of various colored beads, and other like 'fancies'! When Kimama's 'shopping' trip was completed, Bear Scat found he still had almost $5,000 remaining worth of credit with the American Fur Company!

Settling up with the company Clerks, Bear Scat took his American Fur Company credit chit designating his remaining balance, placed it into his saddlebags and led his now empty packhorses, save one loaded with Kimama's selections which she led, back to their tipi. There a very happy Kimama placed all of her 'white man' treasures in the tipi and then ran into Bear Scat's arms and made sure he understood that she was very happy over what her man had just purchased for her... That evening while having supper over at Chief Gray Wolf's tipi, Kimama shared a number of her treasures with her two very surprised sisters and mother. When she did, Bear Scat could not help but notice the signs of approval spread all across the chief's face regarding his new son-in-law's ability to provide for his oldest daughter...

Still seeing trappers arriving daily with their pack strings from the field reminded Bear Scat that he needed to renew his efforts in looking for his brother Jacob. Taking leave of his wife Kimama one afternoon, after explaining the situation to her regarding that of trying to locate his brother, Bear Scat set out once again searching in among the trappers' camps looking for his brother's camp. For two days he went about quietly looking for his brother. In so doing, he also failed to find a single one of his old friends in and among the camps of trappers and Indians! It became readily apparent to Bear Scat that a lot of his friends had not survived the trapping ordeals and had either 'lost their hair' or were bear scat lying somewhere out on the vast prairie or in the deep timber of the mountains they had loved so much...

Still needing to resupply for the coming trapping season, Bear Scat finally gave up looking for his brother and spent the next two days purchasing those needed supplies for the coming year as a trapper afield. Upon completion in his quest to resupply, Bear Scat found that he still had a little over $3,000 credit remaining from his sale of beaver *'plus'*. Finished with his re-provisioning of mostly foodstuffs and spices since he still had all of his cooking gear, traps and weapons, Bear Scat acquired an adjusted letter of credit to be eventually redeemed at the American Fur Company warehouse in St. Louis. Then walking over to his horse, he tucked that document safely away in his saddlebag for future use if he ever got out of the fur trade, took Kimama and decided to head for his old family farm back in Missouri. Upon placing that letter of credit for the American Fur Company for $3,000, he also added it to his other letters of credit from the American Fur Company and the St. Louis Fur Company. Yes, Chief Gray Wolf, your new son-in-law could provide very well for your oldest daughter...

Two days later and before the rendezvous ended, Chief Gray Wolf's band of Shoshone left the rendezvous for their winter quarters. Since they needed to return so they could stock up on buffalo meat before the winter snows flew across the land, the entire band left the Green River Valley, as did Bear Scat without finding his brother at the 1837 Rendezvous... But before leaving, the trappers and the traders had decided the 1838 Rendezvous would be held in a small valley along the Wind River. (Author's Note: The 1838 Rendezvous was held near the town of current-day Riverton, Wyoming.)

******

Wild Bill McGinty and Jacob Sutta, determined to face the music with the four Travis Brothers if it should arise, turned their horses and trailing pack strings into the site of the 1837 Rendezvous along Horse Creek in the Green River Valley. As they did, both men cocked the hammers back on the rifles lying across their laps figuring if the Travis Brothers noticed them, they would come storming right at them shooting all the way. Little did the two trappers realize that Jacob's younger brother Bear Scat, had removed the Travis Brothers' threat in 1835 after a fierce shoot-out at his and Big Hat's cabin, where Big Hat had lost his life.

As Bill and Jacob turned their horses and loaded pack strings into the rendezvous site, they observed a long line of Shoshone

Indians trailing their huge horse herd and their heavily packed animals heading to the northwest towards what was to be their winter's encampment site. Little did Bill or Jacob realize that in among that horde of horseflesh and humanity was Jacob's little brother Bear Scat Sutta! Bear Scat on the other hand, seeing the two really late arriving fur trappers at the rendezvous from a distance of over a 100 yards away while traveling among his people heading for their winter camp, hardly gave them more than a passing glance. He had given up on finding his brother at the 1837 Rendezvous after several hard days of searching and in the end, did not give the two newly arriving fur trappers hardly a second glance...

******

Back at Chief Gray Wolf's Band of Shoshone's winter encampment site, Bear Scat helped Kimama set up their tipi, then he hobbled his riding and packhorses. Once hobbled, the remaining packhorses were unloaded and turned out so they could pasture nearby. Bear Scat then built up an outside cooking fire site while Kimama arranged their belongings inside their tipi. That evening during supper, Bear Scat announced to Kimama that if he was going to do any successful trapping during the fall trapping season, they would have to leave within the next several days or so in order for him to stake out a trapping site, set up their winter encampment and build a horse corral for all of their valuable riding stock and pack animals.

Kimama looked over at Bear Scat for a long moment upon hearing those words of leaving her people and then said, "I will go wherever my man goes. I just need to inform my mother and father that we will be leaving soon so you can trap and provide for us. They will be sad as will be my sisters but they will understand."

That evening, Bear Scat and Kimama went over to Chief Gray Wolf's tipi and told Kimama's parents that they would be leaving soon in order to locate a good trapping site, set up their campsite, build the horse corral and begin trapping. Kimama's mother was visibly upset over hearing those words that her daughter and new son-in-law would soon be leaving, but Chief Gray Wolf's face remained impassive-looking as if cast in stone over hearing those words and realizing he soon would be losing his oldest daughter. But in his heart he knew Bear Scat was making sure he could provide for her as was the chief's desire, so a small part of him was also pleased.

Two weeks later found Bear Scat leading one riding horse and eight packhorses as he headed eastward towards the Wind River's trapping grounds. Behind him came Kimama trailing an extra riding horse and following were another eight heavily packed horses. Two of the packhorses were dragging tipi poles and the rest were packed with buffalo skin tipi covers, sleeping furs, foodstuffs, cooking gear, a single keg of rum, two kegs of powder, lead bars for bullet casting, panniers filled with trapping gear, tanned deer hides for covering bundles of furs while traveling, and the rest of the stock animals bringing bundles of winter and summer clothing.

After several days of slow travel so Kimama could get used to trailing so many horses, the two of them finally arrived on the western shore of what is today named "Bull Lake". Seeing many beaver dams, conical beaver houses and much sign of the beaver's favorite food, namely young cottonwoods, aspens and willows scattered throughout the watered areas, Bear Scat drew up his horse and let his experienced eyes search the area for a suitable campsite. An hour or so later, he had located a small flat near a dense stand of pine and Douglas fir timber that would block most of the soon to be felt north winter winds. Picking up his reins, Bear Scat rode over to the specific area of consideration for their new homesite and upon further quiet examination, decided that was where they would erect their two tipis. In so doing, that left ample room to build a large nearby horse corral that would be out of sight in the timber, there would be firewood aplenty and the horses would have ample water and grazing nearby. Then Bear Scat had to smile inwardly to himself. It was just as Big Hat had taught him, make sure one has lots of nearby firewood, good cover from wandering eyes, ample horse feed close at hand, nearby water, and out and away as much as possible from the north winds that would come howling his way come the winter months...

That evening after they had eaten their supper, Bear Scat and Kimama slept out under the stars on their new homesite, as their hobbled horse herd quietly fed in the meadow nearby. Daylight the next morning, Kimama was up early cooking their breakfast, while Bear Scat dragged down firewood for their outside campfire from the nearby forest. The rest of that day was spent in part erecting the two tipis they had brought, one for sleeping and winter use and the other for storage of their furs once caught, horse equipment and reserve food supplies. Then Bear Scat went into the nearby forest once again and began cutting down pole wood so he could construct a proper horse corral. By week's end, Bear Scat had dug the postholes, set the posts, assembled the rails and built a hell-for-stout gate, thereby finishing their horse corral. Then he set about walling in a firepit with stones, hauling in two sitting logs for placement around their outdoor cooking firepit, and cutting and hauling in numerous loads of dry firewood for current day and coming winter use. Then Bear Scat spent two days digging out their nearby spring, lined it with rock so they would have a nearby reliable source of water for their personal use and plenty of water for the horses. Throughout his work efforts, Kimama pitched right in giving her husband help wherever he needed it. Where the work was too dangerous or heavy for her to get involved or lift, Kimama acted as their lone armed sentry while Bear Scat strived to build their winter campsite so it served all of their needs. Lastly, Bear Scat constructed a meat hanging pole right in camp and several meat smoking racks next to their living tipi, so they could keep a close eye on the meat in order to preclude any predators from helping themselves.

The following day right after breakfast with a nip in the fall air, Bear Scat and Kimama went forth and after stalking a small herd of buffalo, Bear Scat shot and killed two cows. After Bear Scat and Kimama had feasted on a portion of one of the cow's fresh liver, the hard work began of butchering up the buffalo into quarters for manageable transport back to their campsite before hungry wolves or a grizzly bear winded the smell of fresh blood, investigated and came calling. That evening while Bear Scat cooked a supper of fresh roasted buffalo and biscuits, Kimama began cutting the rich buffalo meat into thin strips for smoking and later bagging up the jerky made from such meat processing. For the next four days, Kimama kept a low heat-high smoke fire going under the many pounds of drying and smoking meat, while Bear Scat kept busy cutting additional smoking wood and hauling it to Kimama so she could keep a good smoking fire going. Plus Kimama drew the job of keeping the gray jays, black-billed magpies and chickadees from feasting on the meat hanging on the smoking racks as well…

******

Wild Bill McGinty and Jacob Sutta, finding the 1837 Rendezvous free from the troublesome four Travis Brothers, who unbeknownst to them had been killed by Bear Scat in 1835, celebrated like all the other trappers after having survived another year on the frontier trapping beaver and other fine furs like river otter. For the next week after trading in all of their furs and re-supplying for another year of fur trapping, Bill and Jacob made the rounds in the camps of their fur trapping friends enjoying their camaraderie, as well as discussing better places to trap beaver other than their now previously trapped-out area. Several close friends suggested to Bill and Jacob that they give the upper reaches of the Wind River a try during the next beaver trapping season. After much discussion and a number of cups of rum shared with each other, Bill and Jacob decided they would give the upper reaches of the Wind River a try during the coming fall trapping season. However each of their friends advised they had stayed away from such an area because of the occasional bands of Blackfeet Indians that came down from their native lands far to the north on raids killing trappers, stealing their horses, furs and provisions. Then the Blackfeet would melt back into their own northern territory and sell the stolen furs to the Hudson's Bay Company for rifles, powder and whiskey.

Satisfied with their decision of exploring and then trapping on the Upper Wind River and confident in and of themselves in their ability to defend themselves and what was theirs against any Blackfeet incursions, Bill and Jacob left the rendezvous and headed to the northeast for the earlier described upper reaches of the Wind River country. However, two weeks into their travels and after making a selection for a cabin site for the fall and winter trapping seasons but before they could get a horse corral built, they were raided by four Blackfeet Indians in the dark of the night! Before all had been said and done, the Blackfeet Indians had slipped into Bill and Jacob's new campsite, stolen two of their riding horses and quietly disappeared, which down the road started another mystery chapter in Bear Scat's life... Fortunately Bill and Jacob, like many trappers of the era, had brought along a spare pair of riding horses in case their original horses had been stolen or crippled up and could no longer be ridden. Unfortunately, in Jacob's saddlebags rode an outstanding credit document from their most recent fur sales at the 1837 Rendezvous for anytime redemption at the American Fur Company's fur house back in St. Louis for $3,050! Undeterred over their loss of their two riding horses from the four far-ranging Blackfeet Indians and the loss of the American Fur Company credit redemption certificate held in Jacob's saddlebags, the two trappers established their fall and spring beaver trapping campsite. Following that, the two trappers began their fall trapping season in the northernmost portion of the Upper Wind River area, miles above that area being trapped by Bear Scat and Kimama.

******

One morning Bear Scat emerged from their living tipi, stretched his arms overhead and then noticed his breath in the frosty mountain air. Just like Big Hat used to do to him, Bear Scat called for Kimama to come out and get some breakfast going because it was time to get ready for the fall beaver trapping season. Turning, Bear Scat was surprised to see Kimama standing right behind him with a smile on her beautiful face as she looked at her husband and just shook her head as she found herself enjoying what was his joy. While Kimama began their breakfast, Bear Scat went over to their storage tipi and withdrew eight St. Louis-style beaver traps and hung them on their smoking rack. A short time later he was burning some old rotten cottonwood bark so the traps would take on the smoke smell and rid themselves of the 'man' smell.

Later that day with Bear Scat in the lead being trailed by Kimama riding her buckskin and leading a packhorse carrying a set of panniers, the two headed for a number of previously scouted-out beaver ponds heavily used by beaver. Arriving at what he considered a likely trapping site, Bear Scat slid off his horse, handed its reins to Kimama and began walking the pond's shoreline looking for good beaver sign of a well-used 'slide'. Finding what he was looking for, Bear Scat walked back to their packhorse and advised Kimama to keep a sharp lookout for any on the prod grizzly bears or Indians. Kimama was also cautioned by Bear Scat that he was to always be advised if she ever observed any Indians nearby watching them. Then he caught himself with what he had just said. *He was married to an Indian,* he thought with a grimace over what he had just said and the cautionary way in which he had said it...

Walking the bank of a large beaver pond, Bear Scat discovered a slide that had been used recently. Kneeling down, he discovered a number of large beaver pawprints in the soft mud of the well-used slide area. Walking back to his packhorse, he withdrew a beaver trap, a pre-cut four-foot wooden deep water anchor pole and his hatchet. Heading back to the slide area, Bear Scat soon had a trap set and was in the process of driving in his four-foot wooden anchor pole in the deeper water at the end of the trap chain when he noticed that Kimama was intently looking at something on a distant ridge. Since she didn't say anything or look alarmed while sitting upon the back of her horse acting as a sentry against any form of danger, Bear Scat continued with anchoring the end of the trap chain onto the wooden pole now driven deeply into the pond's muddy bottom.

For the rest of that morning, Bear Scat went about his trap-setting duties while Kimama acted as Big Hat used to do on the lookout for any signs of danger. Finished with setting all eight of his traps, Bear Scat commenced walking along the many waterways still to be trapped looking for additional beaver sign. This he did so that when he had trapped out the beaver in his first area, he would have previously scouted out another beaver trapping area in mind in which to go without delay. Then Bear Scat commenced walking back along his newly set trap line checking his previously set traps. As luck would have it, four of his previously set traps already contained a dead beaver!

It was then that Bear Scat had Kimama dismount and then he taught her how to correctly skin the beaver just caught. As it turned out, Kimama was a quick learner and by beaver number two after being shown how to properly skin beaver, began doing it on her own! By the time she and Bear Scat had come to dead beaver number four in their traps, Kimama was skinning beaver almost as well as Bear Scat could do it. Like in the old days and keeping with a first day of trapping tradition started by his old friend and mentor Big Hat, Bear Scat kept two of the largest and fattest of the four beaver just trapped as the meat dish for that evening's supper.

Back at their campsite that evening, Bear Scat started their cooking fire while Kimama continued fleshing out the rest of the fat and hooping the beaver caught that morning. There Bear Scat found that he did not have to show her how to do such things because she and her sisters had done so many times previously, when her father brought beaver and other animals home to be skinned, fleshed out and hooped in her earlier days for the drying that followed. (Author's Note: Most beaver, wolf, marten, river otter, muskrat and any other fine furs were early on trapped and traded to the fur companies by the many Indians living in America at that time. The Mountain Man fur trappers, once the American white man really got involved in the fur trade during the years of 1807-1840, numbered ONLY approximately 1,000 afield in any given year! It only stands to reason that such a small number of Mountain Men only accounted overall for a small percentage of furs taken, when considering the hundreds of thousands of Indians involved in one way or another in the trapping, shooting or catching of fur bearers. Basically, in early Canada and the United States, trapping for the fur market was mostly done by the Indians so they could trade what they considered was a common item, namely an animal's skin, for white man's goods, which they considered a luxury and in the end, helped in changing their cultures from that of being an honorable 'red man' to one almost wholly dependent upon the white man. It was not until later years that the white man killed and brought in more hides than the Indians when they commenced killing the buffalo in major numbers. That the white man did until the buffalo were almost shot into extinction from their one-time many millions down to just a few remaining hundred! With the demise of the vast herds of buffalo went the Indian cultures and ways of life as well!)

Supper that evening prepared by Bear Scat in celebration of their first day of successful trapping during the fall trapping season was hot coffee, only not as strong as he used to make it out of deference to Kimama's weaker tastes, Dutch oven biscuits slathered in honey, roast beaver skewered over the campfire, and a rice and raisin mixture cooked in another Dutch oven, flavored by scrapings from their sugar cones and cinnamon. In their ensuing supper conversation that evening, Kimama told Bear Scat about the four Indians trailing two saddled riding horses that she had seen watching them earlier in the day! When she did, Bear Scat dropped the hot piece of roasted beaver he was mouthing, almost choking in the process!

"Kimama, why didn't you tell me? Anytime you see anyone, you need to tell me about what you are seeing!" said an exasperated Bear Scat over the possible danger that could have represented.

"I didn't think it was important. I thought they were just some of my father's Shoshone braves out hunting. Besides, they did not come over and bother us when they saw us trapping beaver, so I didn't think it was important to tell you and have you stop setting traps," she innocently advised.

"What did they look like?" asked Bear Scat, with an edge in the tone of his voice showing more than just deep concern.

"I don't know. They were just four Indians trailing two other riding horses with white man types of saddles," she innocently continued.

"Damn, Kimama! In the future if you see any Indians of any kind you are to let me know and right away!" said a concerned Bear Scat with a more than discernible edge to the tone of his voice.

"Well, there is no use for you to get so concerned. They were just probably four Indian braves from my father's band who recognized me and just kept riding on because they knew I had married a white trapper and what we were doing was to be expected," said Kimama with a defensive edge now forming in her voice over being questioned so sharply by Bear Scat. Then becoming truly upset because she had angered and disappointed her husband over something she considered immaterial, she abruptly rose and strode indignantly off to their living tipi without finishing her supper...

Bear Scat just sat there and watched his wife storm off to their living tipi and closed the flap abruptly. For the longest time, Bear Scat sat there fuming over his wife's lack of caution. After all, she had been the one on guard so they would not get ambushed by Indians, an angry grizzly bear or a dangerous bull moose in rut! Realizing he had better let Kimama cool off, Bear Scat just sat there by his fire and listened to the sounds of nightfall around him. Then he realized his horses, although hobbled, were still out in the meadow feeding way past their normal feeding hours. Cussing himself for letting that horse-feeding problem late at night occur because of the flare-up between him and Kimama, Bear Scat grabbed his rifle from his sitting log and walked out from the light of his campfire into the moonlit darkness in order to round up his livestock and bring them back into their corral where they would be safer for the night.

Since the horses had been allowed greater feeding latitude, they did what horses will do and wandered further off into the far end of their meadow after the better grasses. About an hour later, Bear Scat had finally rounded up all of his horses and was in the process of slowly herding them back into his camp since all of them had been hobbled and could only hop-walk so fast. All of a sudden as he got closer to their camp, Bear Scat noticed that the head of his favorite horse was pointing towards his camp and his ears in the darkness appeared to be pointing forward as if trying to listen for something strange or unusual ongoing at his distant campsite...

Bear Scat stopped his herd of horses from moving forward out of caution over his horse's alertness, and when they had quietly stopped and commenced feeding again, Bear Scat switched his Hawken rifle from his right hand into both hands so it could be held at the ready position just in case his horse had sensed danger of some sort. That he also did as his 'sixth sense' began roiling around inside his being for some reason! Standing there in the darkness a short distance from his camp, Bear Scat listened for all he was worth and heard nothing out of the ordinary other than the noises his horses were making as they pulled up and ate grass nearby. After about another ten minutes of hearing nothing out of the ordinary, Bear Scat relaxed just a bit and once again began slowly moving his horses towards his camp.

THEN HE HEARD IT! A low muffled moan of pain was heard coming from his campsite and then nothing else followed in the ways of any other strange noises. However his 'sixth senses' were now storming around inside him like spring floodwaters running down a narrow stream! Realizing something was not right, he left the horses quietly feeding out in the meadow and began sneaking the final 30 yards towards his camp from whence the low moan had originated. As he did, he looked all around his still burning campfire and saw nothing out of the ordinary before he stepped into the edge of its light. Then as he crept closer towards the tipis, he heard the low moaning sounds once again and it was coming from inside his living tipi! NOW HE KNEW SOMETHING WAS DEAD WRONG BUT HAD NO IDEA WHAT WOULD BE CAUSING THOSE MOANING SOUNDS OF DISTRESS! Resting his rifle against his buckskin shirt, he silently cocked his rifle, just in case. Then reaching down into his sash, he pressed both of his pistols against the softness of his buckskin shirt and silently cocked both of them! By so doing, when he cocked his rifle and his two pistols, the hard metallic 'click' not normally a wilderness sound, would not be heard since it rested against his soft garments.

Then in the faint light of a small fire burning inside his living tipi for the warmth and light it offered, BEAR SCAT SAW THE DANGER! Moving around inside his living tipi, Bear Scat saw the faint outline of a standing man backlit by the small fire! THEN HE SAW THAT THERE WERE SHADOWS OF TWO MEN, NO, THERE WERE THREE! Then he heard the moaning sounds again only louder that time! Then Bear Scat saw another man's shadow rise up from the ground of his living tipi and then one of the standing men's shadows disappeared down towards the ground! Then he heard even more groaning! It then dawned on Bear Scat with a rush what was going on! The four Indian men that Kimama had observed when he was out in the water setting beaver traps earlier in the day were now in his tipi! Then from the groaning and the men's shadowy telltale movements illuminated from the small fire inside the tipi, appeared to be indicating with the men's up and down movements, were 'having their way' with the beautiful Kimama!

With that realization, Bear Scat found an instant rage surfacing from within him that almost got the better of him by having him storm right into the tipi and start shooting! But then his common sense and well-honed survival instincts took over. When they did, that helped in calming down his rage and made him clearly understand that there were four of them inside the tipi, and if he did not do what needed doing right, in all probability Kimama would be killed along with him and that would not solve the issue as far as he was concerned!

Moving up to the side of his tipi as quietly as a snake sliding across wet grass, as much as it hurt him over what was happening to his wife, he paused. Bear Scat waited until the Indian currently having his way with his wife was finished. Then Bear Scat waited until that man stood up and then during that moment of distraction when the men were deciding who 'was going next', Bear Scat made his move! Taking his always razor-sharp gutting knife in his right hand, he placed its blade against the side of the tipi buffalo skin, took a deep breath and then made a man-sized tall cut into the side of the tipi wall in a heartbeat! Instantly dropping his gutting knife, Bear Scat burst into the crowded inside of the tipi and with his rifle shot the first Indian he came across facing away from him, dropping him in an instant with a shot into the center of his broad back! He then quickly dropped his rifle, jerked both pistols from his sash and headshot the next two Indians who had turned in surprise over his instant entry, only to look down at two exploding pistol barrels from less than two feet away! When face shot, both Indians fell over backwards on top of a naked Kimama lying flat on her back on the sleeping furs after being painfully raped by the first two Indians! The last Indian standing quickly reached over for his rifle lying on the ground of the tipi, only to have Kimama's hand quickly placed over it causing him to struggle with her before he could get his rifle raised and into a shooting position. In that moment of struggle, his rifle was finally jerked away from the intruding hands of Kimama. With that action, the largest of the four Indians whirled to shoot from the hip at a close at hand Bear Scat, only to be felled with a tomahawk chop into the frontal portion of his skull that was so violent, Kimama was splashed with the man's bright red blood splatters from head to toe!

Leaving his tomahawk firmly planted into the front of the dead Indian's skull, Bear Scat, raging with a mountain of adrenalin flowing through his system over the killing moment just experienced, reached down and bodily lifted naked Kimama up from lying under two dead Indians headshot just seconds earlier! When he did, Kimama melted into Bear Scat's arms crying like a child over what had just happened to her! As she did, Bear Scat kept a sharp eye on the four men lying on the sleeping furs of his tipi making sure none of them moved while they were on their way to joining their own tribe's 'Cloud People'! It was some time before Kimama's body wracked with emotion from that horrible moment in time, finally stopped shaking from what she had just endured.

During those intense emotional moments from which his wife was suffering, Bear Scat, trying to come down from his emotional killing high, let his mind run through the events described by Kimama earlier in the evening. She had seen the four Indians from a distance watching her sitting upon her horse out in the middle of the wilds, motionless. *Thinking she was all alone and so distracted, they must have overlooked Bear Scat setting traps out of sight in the brush at the edge of the pond. Thinking the Indian woman was all alone, the four men must have decided they would find her later in the evening after they had made camp nearby and then 'take her for their own',* thought Bear Scat. *That would be the last time those four Indian men would ever do such a thing,* he coldly thought with a great degree of satisfaction.

Carrying a still sobbing Kimama in his arms, Bear Scat deposited her into her sleeping furs and covered her up to cry off her life's nightmare. Then he grabbed each of the four dead men and dragged them out from their living tipi. Laying the four dead men alongside their firepit so he could look at them more closely, Bear Scat could clearly see from the men's dress in the light of his campfire that they were Blackfeet Indians. Young Blackfeet Indians who appeared to be in their late teenage years obviously far south of their homeland, a homeland they would never see again.

Probably on their first raid outside of the boundaries of their homeland to count 'coup', and one of their inexperienced and last such ventures, he thought with cold satisfaction. Walking over to his corral and aided by the light of a newly stoked-up campfire, Bear Scat cut his riding horse out from the rest of the horses in the corral, saddled him up and then led him outside the corral. Taking his rope, he looped it around two of the dead Indians' necks, mounted his horse and began dragging the two dead men off and away from his camp. Several hundred yards away in a distant aspen grove, Bear Scat left the two dead Indian men for the critters to enjoy. That act was repeated one more time, leaving the four men now deposited in the aspen grove, all together as they had been in life, so shall they be in death...

Riding back towards the light from his campfire, Bear Scat left his horse tied to the corral and then entered his tipi. As he expected, there was blood everywhere from the killings that had just taken place. Additionally, the acrid smell of freshly ignited gunpowder hung heavy inside the tipi. Opening the flap to his tipi and that of the cut he had made with his knife in its side wall, Bear Scat let it air out, as he then quietly lay down beside the love of his life and after an hour of lying there and hearing her finally deeply sleeping, fell asleep as well.

The next morning, Kimama was up early, stoically building a fire and starting breakfast as if nothing out of the ordinary had happened to her the night before. As she did, Bear Scat removed all of their goods from inside their tipi and laid them off to one side. Then he dismantled his 'tipi of death' and moved it over closer to their horse corral under a number of cottonwood trees for the shade they would offer during the summer months. Bear Scat just figured there was no use in having a tipi located in other men's blood, so it was moved and all of its 'bad ghosts' and memories were left behind on that dark and bloody ground as well...

Finally moving over to his sitting log by the fire, Bear Scat waited for Kimama to speak first. She chose not to speak that morning and so the two ate their breakfast in silence. After breakfast, Bear Scat packed one of his packhorses and prepared to leave by himself to run his trap line. A trap line that he had to run daily in order to remove any dead beaver before any grizzly bears did it for him. That was when Kimama quietly saddled her horse with some difficulty, picked up her own Lancaster rifle that had at one time belonged to Big Hat, checked it to make sure the percussion cap was still on the nipple, shoved a pistol under her sash, mounted her buckskin, and then rode it over to where Bear Scat was sitting on his horse looking on in amazement at her actions. Kimama then reached over and took the packhorse's reins from his hands, then looked up at Bear Scat with a steely-eyed look saying, "I go with my husband…"

First thing on Bear Scat's mind was to locate the horses ridden by the four men he had just killed. An hour of backtracking and searching finally located the young Indians' six horses tied to a picket line. Without a word, Bear Scat dismounted and released the horses so they could wander as they saw fit. That way if anyone came looking for the four boys and discovered their horses wandering out on the prairie by themselves, they could not trace the missing boys back to Bear Scat for any reason. The rest of that morning found Bear Scat running his trap line, removing the dead beaver tossing them up onto the bank, resetting his traps and then moving on. With each dead beaver, Kimama gracefully slipped off her horse and skinned out the beaver, while Bear Scat moved around near her carrying his rifle acting as their lookout as he walked about trying to warm up after his immersion in the cold beaver pond waters. However there was little or no conversation between the couple as the morning went on. Upon Bear Scat's return trip along his trap line checking for any freshly trapped beaver, he noticed that Kimama's eyes were NOW constantly watching all around them for any signs of danger or anything unnatural or out of place. It was apparent to Bear Scat that she had learned a valuable lesson about survival, at great cost, one about being extremely vigilant when on lookout while he was defenseless walking around in a beaver pond in waist deep water tending his traps… At the last beaver pond by one of its fast running outlets of water, Kimama reined up, slipped off her horse, disrobed and as Bear Scat stood guard, she bathed to remove the 'stink' off her body from her previous evening's bad experience. Upon finishing, she dressed, mounted her buckskin horse and without a single word began riding back to camp like nothing out of the ordinary had occurred…

On their way back to their campsite, Bear Scat shot a mule deer and an hour later, it had been skinned out and hung from their meat pole back at camp. As Bear Scat cut out one of the deer's backstraps, Kimama came over, removed it from his hands and then walked back to the fire to prepare it for their supper without a single word being spoken between the two of them. That night after they had eaten, Kimama walked over to their new tipi location and went inside without saying a word. Moments later she emerged from the tipi naked as a baby bird and stood there by its opening flap. "Bear Scat, come here and let us celebrate our new homesite's location!" said a now smiling Kimama… Bear Scat had no trouble finding his tipi's newest location. He also had no problem locating the love of his life in the shadowy darkness of their new home… It was obvious the previous night's bad experience was now considered just that and to be forgotten as their lives continued on…

Throughout the rest of that fall trapping season, Bear Scat and Kimama trapped the Wind River, catching 338 beaver! Then come ice-up, Bear Scat removed all of his traps and he and Kimama retreated to their campsite, only to occasionally come out to haul in more wood for their cooking and warming fires and hunt buffalo in order to add to their meat supply. However, care for their large horse herd was becoming another matter. Their large horse herd had pretty well eaten down to the ground most of the good feed in the meadows nearest their campsite, necessitating Bear Scat to take them into other more distant meadows so they could feed. One morning in late spring before the ice had left the beaver waters so that Bear Scat could once again resume trapping during the spring trapping season, he was in the process of bringing his horse herd back to his corral after allowing them to graze in a far distant meadow.

Turning his herd of horses into his meadow where he was camped, he all of a sudden was alarmed to see some 20 or so fresh sets of horses' tracks ahead of him leading right up to his campsite! Kicking his horse in its flanks, Bear Scat hurriedly pushed his horse herd towards his corral. Since the corral gate was still open, Bear Scat pushed his horses into the corral, bailed off his horse and closed the gate. Then seeing the unidentified horse tracks continuing on towards his two tipis, he ran towards them. Yelling for Kimama as he ran towards the living tipi and not seeing her emerging from within, his heart sank. Hoping all the horse tracks were from some of Kimama's father's Shoshone warriors, Bear Scat threw back the flap to the tipi and his heart sank even further!

Quickly looking inside, Bear Scat saw that Kimama was gone, as well as were most of their personal belongings as well! Then seeing a number of moccasin tracks in the muddy spring ground leading over to their storage tipi holding all of their fur bundles and supplies, he ran over to see if Kimama was possibly there. Throwing back the flap on the tipi, Bear Scat saw that a large portion of their supplies was missing, as were all of his bundles of beaver *'plus'* and no Kimama! Racing back to his horse corral, Bear Scat mounted his horse and began following the fresh unidentified horse tracks leading away from his campsite and off to the north. As he did, his thoughts as to what had happened darkened. *Whoever the riders were, they badly outnumbered him and why had they come?* As he sped along, Bear Scat found himself cussing himself for only carrying 20 bullets and enough powder in his powder horn for shooting about ten of them! Racing along following the fresh tracks, Bear Scat saw that from the spacing of the tracks, the riders of those horses were not in any big hurry to leave the country. *That fact bode well for him to catch up to them,* thought Bear Scat as he redoubled his pursuit of those who now obviously had Kimama and all of his furs. *If those riders were not in any kind of a hurry and he was, he soon would be upon them and then he would have to find a way to successfully confront such a horde of riders,* thought Bear Scat darkly as he raced along. But as he raced along in pursuit, his eyes darted ahead to every bit of cover possibly hiding an ambush, as Big Hat had taught him so long ago.

That evening as darkness settled over the Wind River country, Bear Scat finally saw a faint flicker of light from a fire dead ahead in a dense stand of timber! Dismounting and tying off his horse, Bear Scat began sneaking into the timber holding the light from a flickering fire from the camp that he suspected were holding the mystery riders since that is the direction in which their horses' tracks led. About an hour later after stalking towards the shadows of men moving around the campfire, Bear Scat finally got into a position whereby he could observe the men without being observed and in so doing, got surprised! Instead of 20 or so mystery riders, Bear Scat saw only six of what appeared to be fairly young Blackfeet Indians moving around their campfire! With a grin of relief over a lesser number of adversaries that he would have to deal with, Bear Scat relaxed just a bit. Then he came to realize the six Indians had only been a small raiding party traveling through Shoshone territory on a horse and trapper's fur stealing raid, instead of a 20 or so larger and more devastating Blackfeet war party.

Then Bear Scat saw his wife Kimama! She was cooking supper for the six Blackfeet men and did not look any too happy. But at least she was still alive and soon to be back into the arms of Bear Scat or he was going to know the reason why. About then, Kimama began serving the six now seated men around their campfire and as she did, one of the men ran his hand up under her dress to the raucous laughter of the other five men. That move got the man with the wandering hand a pot of hot venison stew instantly dumped on his head by an irate Kimama! The scalded man immediately jumped up as the other men sitting around the campfire quickly moved away from the venison stew-pot fracas. Reaching out, the scalded man after wiping away the stew off his face, grabbed Kimama by the front of her throat with his right hand and in an instant began violently shaking and choking her! As Bear Scat instantly raised his Hawken rifle to kill the man choking her, Kimama was dropped to her knees as her adversary continued choking her for what she had done with the venison stew. Just as Bear Scat's finger pulled his 'set trigger' and then tightened on the trigger of his rifle as he sighted in on his wife's attacker's head in the campfire's light, Kimama's arm lashed out in desperation! Although being choked to death, her survival instincts kicked into play as she instantly reached out, grabbed her assailant's knife from his waist belt, quickly drew it and violently drove its long blade upward into the man's genitalia! With that knife strike, the attacking man let out a scream, grabbed his genitalia with both hands and dropped screaming to his knees bleeding profusely from his groin! Now face to face with a still gagging Kimama from being almost strangled, the attacker now found his own knife being plunged deeply into his right eye by a very angry Kimama! The dying man's scream of pain now energized the other five Indians into action upon seeing one of their own being mortally wounded by the woman they had captured earlier in the day and had planned on jointly 'pleasuring' later in the evening.

A heavyset Indian with a large protruding stomach quickly stepped over to Kimama who was still kneeling trying to get more air into her lungs, grabbed a handful of her long black hair, jerked her head back and with his hastily drawn knife, went to slit Kimama's bared throat! Kimama, now in even more desperation for her own life, took the knife she had just used to disembowel one man and being off balance with her head being jerked back so far, reached backwards with her knife towards the man behind her trying to cut her throat. As she did, she desperately drew its blade across his much-protruding belly lying against her head! With a scream of agony and holding his now spilled-out madly bleeding intestines with both of his hands, he dropped to his knees and then in extreme pain, fell flat on his stomach! When he did, Kimama turned and plunged the knife she was holding between his shoulder blades and in so doing with such emotional force, severed the man's spine! The disemboweled man made no more sounds, only just quivered in his death throes as he now began bleeding out!

In an instant, another Indian picked up his rifle off a nearby sitting log, swung it over to shoot Kimama, only to have the whole front of his face shot off by Bear Scat! With that surprise shot coming from out of the darkness, the remaining three Indians quickly moved for their rifles lying against a nearby sitting log, grabbed them up and turned to face the area of darkness from whence the rifle shot had come. **BOOM!** went the bellowing sound of a pistol from 20 feet away, as the loud sounding "THWACK" of a soft lead bullet expanded itself upon hitting the closest bare-chested man square in the center of his chest! When the heavy lead slug tore into that fourth Indian, the impact-energy from that bullet being fired from such close range staggered the man backwards, sprawling him dead across their blazing campfire! Moments later, the smell of burning flesh began permeating the campsite, but was not smelled by the remaining two Indians from camp, who were now running through the darkened forest in terror as fast as their legs could carry them away from the surprising close at hand assailant hidden in the darkness of the forest!

Before stepping into the light from the smoking campfire burning human fat and flesh, Bear Scat had the survival sense to calmly but quickly reload his rifle and then his pistol, in case the still armed but fleeing Indians decided to return to do battle. Then when he finally stepped into the light of the fire, he quickly found his arms filled with a surprised and sobbing but very brave Kimama. However, as Kimama filled his arms, Bear Scat could see that she still retained the bloody knife she had taken from one Indian and had used it to kill not only him but one other of her captors as well...

Pulling the burning Indian from the fire and rolling his smoking and stinking body out from the campsite so they wouldn't have to smell it, Kimama and Bear Scat then dragged him and the other three dead men from the campsite. Then as Kimama began roasting pieces of deer meat over the fire so the two of them would have something to eat before they left, Bear Scat looked around the Indians' campsite. Therein he found 21 horses tied to a long picket line! Scattered around the horses in several piles, Bear Scat found his bundles of stolen beaver *'plus'* and 14 other bundles of beaver furs taken from other unknown trappers who were now probably dead! Additionally, he located all of the supplies that had been taken from his storage tipi as well. Not knowing where the two Indians who had escaped being killed had fled to and how far away or close they now were, after Bear Scat and Kimama had eaten they loaded up all of the horses with the bundles of furs along with the rest of their stolen supplies and they headed for their distant campsite. Later after leaving the latest killing field, Bear Scat picked up his riding horse that had been hidden in the timber and then with the horse herd's unique abilities for seeing fairly well when traveling in the dark, the two of them and the horse herd rode throughout the night, eventually arriving at their campsite by dawn later the following morning. However, all along the long way back to their campsite Bear Scat had been doing some very serious thinking. *Ever since he had become a Mountain Man, even with Big Hat in company, he had been in battle after battle for his survival or the survival of a loved one. Those battles had been fostered by thieving white men, white men and fellow fur trappers out to kill him, hostile Indians or just Indians out on raids stealing furs or valuable provisions. Additionally, he had lost friends in those battles and almost his wife of less than a year! Maybe, just maybe, he ought to think about giving up the fur trade, taking his wealth and returning back to his home in Missouri before falling victim to a speeding lead ball or a steel-tipped arrow point,* he thought... With those thoughts seriously running around in his head, Bear Scat began thinking maybe he would enjoy quietly farming back on his Missouri farm after all...

Early the next morning found Bear Scat waist deep in a beaver pond retrieving a trapped and dead beaver. On the bank sat a very alert Kimama with Big Hat's Lancaster rifle in hand watching all around for any sign of danger, and that time nothing escaped her eyes! Meanwhile, Bear Scat walked out from the beaver pond's cold water with the dead beaver and placed the animal and trap into one of the panniers of their packhorse. For the rest of the morning, that same routine was followed. That is every beaver and trap were tossed into a pannier and if any beaver trap turned up empty, it too was collected and tossed into the pannier as well.

In short, Bear Scat had decided to pull off from his entire trap line, break camp and head back to the safety of Chief Gray Wolf's main camp for the protection it offered against any incursions from the much-dreaded Blackfeet Indians ranging far south into the Shoshone's tribal homeland. That and because Bear Scat now had redemption certificates from several fur companies back in St. Louis worth thousands of dollars! He was also now in possession of 14 additional bundles of beaver furs that he had taken away from the six Blackfeet who had kidnapped Kimama, which numbered around 840 pelts! Additionally, Bear Scat and Kimama had amassed 338 of their own trapped 'plus'! Lastly, they were now in possession of 21 horses over and above the four riding and 16 packhorses they possessed of their own original stock, with many being taken in battle! In short, Bear Scat and Kimama were holding 1,178 beaver 'plus' valued at anywhere from $4-6 each, and 21 horses that could be sold at the next rendezvous for what the always-hungry horse market would bear!

With that in mind and a fortune in horseflesh that was very attractive to any Indian or fur trapper in country in need, Bear Scat figured he would not gamble any further with what he had. He would just take them at the first opportunity and head for the nearest form of protective cover, namely Chief Gray Wolf's band of Wind River Indians some several days distant to the west. But now he had to get there...

That evening back at their camp, Bear Scat took all of their horses and herded them to a distant meadow so they could feed and make ready for the long trip ahead. Meanwhile back at their campsite, Kimama skinned out their most recent catch, cooked up

465

a number of the beaver for their supper and in between, fleshed out the valuable pelts and hooped the same. Upon Bear Scat's later return, they quietly ate their supper thinking about what lay ahead and then began breaking down their two tipis, stacking their bundles of furs for transport and packing the rest of their personal gear for the next day's trip. That evening, the two of them slept out under the stars and by around four the next morning, found the two of them loading up their horses with tipi poles, bundles of furs and personal gear. By noon that day all packed and ready to go, Kimama led the string of packed horses and Bear Scat followed, bringing up the rear for protection and herding the stragglers along. In front rode Kimama now carrying Big Hat's much-coveted Hawken rifle and wearing his two pistols in her sash. Behind her trailed a second riding horse sporting Big Hat's old Lancaster rifle in a scabbard for quick retrieval in case an occasion arose calling for extra firepower. Bringing up the rear of that huge caravan trailed Bear Scat. He too carried his beloved Hawken rifle and wore two pistols loaded with buck and ball. Trailing Bear Scat was his reserve riding horse toting two extra rifles, just in case he was jumped by any hostile Indians lusting after their valuable horse herd or a grizzly bear looking for a free lunch. As Bear Scat trailed along herding any straggling packed horses stopping to feed along the way, he had to smile. Leading the way back to her people was the love of his life and a wife who was the equal of any trapping partner he ever had. His trapping partner had gone through some troublesome times, but now she had learned 'the way' and even though a female, was every bit as accomplished as any partner ever was...

Long about dusk, Kimama still leading the way of the slow-traveling horse herd stumbled upon an encampment of about 20 Indians cooking their suppers! Recoiling in surprise and fearful over what she had just stumbled into upon seeing that multitude of Indians, she stopped in fear right out in the open! Before Bear Scat and Kimama could do anything in their defense, they were completely surrounded by about 20 or so howling and yelling

Indians on horseback who were just as surprised as were Kimama and Bear Scat!

Then all of a sudden, one of the braves rode 'lickety-split' right up to a still stunned Kimama, grabbed her up into his arms and unhorsed her! When he did, Bear Scat swung his rifle up and lined up his sights onto the brave who was now riding off with Kimama in his arms! It was then that Kimama, yelling in laughter over what she was experiencing, waved back at Bear Scat saying, "Bear Scat, don't shoot! I am in the arms of "Bear Claw", my younger sister's husband!" As it turned out, it was a good thing she had shouted when she did because Bear Scat had already pulled his rifle's set trigger, was swinging a lead on the Indian carrying off Kimama and being the excellent shot he was, that kidnapping Indian was a golden eagle's tail feather thickness away from joining his 'Cloud People'! It was then that Bear Scat quickly pulled his finger off the trigger!

As it turned out, Bear Scat and Kimama had ridden into a camp full of Chief Gray Wolf's braves out hunting the closest herd of buffalo to their nearby encampment in preparation for a tribal winter's meat hunt! Soon there was much celebration over seeing that the chief's oldest daughter and her white man husband were alright. There was even greater astonishment over the fact that the two of them were herding along a horse herd numbering over 40 valuable animals! That evening, there was great rejoicing in Bear Claw's camp, not to mention a great deal of relief to be among extra friends when trying to control an almost unruly-sized herd of horses with just two people...

The next day, Bear Claw detached six of his braves to ride along and help Bear Scat and Kimama get their huge herd of horses and personal gear safely back into Chief Gray Wolf's main winter encampment. Needless to say, Bear Scat found great comfort in having the extra help and in thoughtful relief that he was not quicker on the trigger when an unrecognized Bear Claw had joyfully swooped Kimama off her horse and had ridden off with her in his arms... Two days later, Bear Scat and company rode into

Chief Gray Wolf's encampment to many joyful sounds of barking dogs, excited children and many womenfolk walking alongside Kimama, excitedly talking with her as she proudly rode along with 'her man'! Then Kimama spotted her father Chief Gray Wolf, rode on ahead to meet him, bailed off her horse when she was near and ran right into his arms. Suffice to say, when Bear Scat finally rode up to the great chief, the looks on his face were not sullen as they had been during their first meeting, but all smiles over seeing his daughter back alive and with her, her more-than-successful husband as evidenced by his huge valuable horse herd and the numerous packs of valuable furs. Yes, it was evident that Kimama or 'Butterfly's' husband was able to provide a good life for the chief's oldest daughter...

CHAPTER SIXTEEN: THE END OF THE QUEST AND A 'FORTUNE' OF LIFE IS DISCOVERED IN ST. LOUIS

For the rest of 1837 and into 1838, Bear Scat and Kimama stayed with her people in Chief Gray Wolf's encampment. There Kimama visited daily with her family and other Shoshone people, while Bear Scat hunted buffalo, elk and deer with Bear Claw and other Shoshone warriors. However, come early summer, Bear Scat was once again getting 'itchy feet'. The 1838 Rendezvous was upcoming and going to be held at the confluence of the Wind River and Little Wind River or "Popo Agie" River. There he hoped to be able to sell those horses taken from the six Blackfeet who had kidnapped Kimama the year before, as well as his furs. Also while there at the rendezvous, he would once again attempt to locate his older brother Jacob, and possibly join up with him as trappers or the two of them return to Missouri as farmers on their old home place. Barring once again not finding his brother, in light of the dangers on the frontier, consider his decision if he wished to continue his life as a trapper in light of losing his best friend, all the other frontier dangers and that of almost losing his beloved wife. That or just call it quits and with his money from the sale of the valuable horses and his furs, return by himself with Kimama to his farm back in Missouri, settle down and raise a family. (Author's

Note: Historians have discovered that most white trappers died or quit after trapping only 2.7 years on the frontier due to its rigors and/or dangers!) After all, Bear Scat was now a rich man for that day and age. He still possessed a $1,700 Certificate of Redemption from the St. Louis Fur Company from a previous rendezvous for money he did not spend, in addition to a Certificate of Redemption from the American Fur Company for $3,050 that he discovered in the saddlebag of a horse that he had recovered from the Blackfeet, who had earlier stolen that horse surprisingly from his brother. Those certificates alone made him a fairly wealthy man in that day and age, when an average yearly income was $300-400 per year! Then he still had the profits to come from the sale of his valuable horse herd recently captured from the Blackfeet who had kidnapped Kimama, as well as from the upcoming sale of over 1,100 beaver *'plus'* at the upcoming rendezvous which would bring him anywhere from $4-6 a pelt! With those monies, Bear Scat figured if a safer life farming was what he desired, he would pretty much be set for life once back on his old Missouri farmstead, currently being watched over by a neighbor and close friend...

For several evenings back in their tipi, Bear Scat discussed with Kimama what he had been thinking about regarding trapping or farming. Smiling at her 'wanderlust' husband, Kimama said, "I will go with my husband wherever he goes." Following those discussions, Bear Scat began making preparations to travel to the site of the 1838 Rendezvous on the Popo Agie, in the hopes of seeking the whereabouts of his brother and selling his horse herd and his furs. Riding out to his horse herd that was kept separate from the rest of the tribes' horses by the Young Chiefs, Bear Scat selected out the ten best packhorses. This he did figuring he would need ten horses in order to carry the 20 packs of beaver *'plus'* at 60 beaver pelts per pack weighing about 90 pounds per pack. Then he selected another four riding horses which included Kimama's favorite buckskin, along with another four packhorses for their cooking, sleeping furs and other necessaries, for a total of 18 horses in his combination pack and riding string. Realizing that size of a pack string might be a bit unmanageable for just Kimama and himself to handle, he enlisted the help of his brother-in-law Bear Claw and one other warrior friend named "Elk" to help out. Satisfied over his planning efforts, Bear Scat began making the final preparations to attend the 1838 Rendezvous.

Around the middle of June in 1838, Bear Scat, Kimama, Bear Claw and Elk headed easterly from Chief Gray Wolf's encampment towards the reported rendezvous site near the confluence of the Wind River and the Popo Agie (Little Wind River). Four days of travel later found the group entering the rendezvous site that was supposed to be somewhat of a secret, so the American Fur Company would have the advantage in trading with all of the Mountain Men when they arrived. However when Bear Scat and company arrived, there was already a surprise Hudson's Bay Company trading contingent there as well! As expected, there was competition and acrimony between the Canadian and American trading companies. So much so that the two companies sold their trade goods at very high Mountain Prices and purchased the furs from the trappers at the very lowest prices possible in order to make a huge company profit. (Author's Note: The major reason for trading companies buying low and selling their goods at such high prices was because of the risks the trading companies took in bringing supplies into the deepest and most dangerous parts of the frontier. The trading companies were faced with so many dangers from primitive man and beast, that their losses in men and material just trying to get to the rendezvous sites required them to always buy low and sell high in order to be able to guarantee that they could be able to pay back their investors in St. Louis and make a profit for themselves as well.) Drawing from his previous experience trading at a rendezvous, Bear Scat quickly discovered that his furs would be much more valuable sold in St. Louis than sold to either of the two fur companies represented at the 1838 Rendezvous. Those concerns were further buttressed when setting up their campsite immediately adjacent Jim Bridger's campsite, allowed the two now very disgruntled trappers to discuss the situation facing them. In short, they could pay outlandishly high prices for any goods they purchased which they needed if they were to remain trapping for the coming trapping season on the frontier, or they could make the long and hazardous trip through Indian country to St. Louis, sell their furs for about twice the price of that being offered at the 1838 Rendezvous, and then purchase their needed provisions for about half the price in St. Louis than that being required for purchase in the mountains.

As Bear Claw and Elk partook of the festivities at the rendezvous with friends from other Shoshones in attendance, Bear Scat and Kimama looked among the many campsites for his older brother Jacob. After three days of fruitless looking and asking around, the consensus of information received was that Jacob had not been seen or recognized in years and more than likely had, like many others of his kind, 'gone under'!

Disgruntled over not being able to locate his brother, the last living member of his family other than himself and very much aware of the outlandishly high purchase prices for provisions and low prices being offered for beaver *'plus'* at the rendezvous, Bear Scat returned to his campsite and drank more than one cup of rum upon his return... Later that evening, Jim Bridger came over to Bear Scat's campsite to tip a cup or two of rum with the somewhat dejected Bear Scat. As Kimama served Bear Scat, Jim Bridger, Bear Claw and Elk their evening meal of roasted buffalo, Dutch oven biscuits and coffee, she overheard the two trappers discussing a new plan that made her very apprehensive!

Mouthing a particularly large chunk of freshly roasted buffalo, Bridger said to Bear Scat, "Between the two of us we have a pile of very fine furs. However, to sell them here at the rendezvous will be like getting scalped and then skinned alive by a mess of them Blackfeet killing sons-a-bitches. I would like to propose that the two of our camps join together and head for St. Louis. There we can trade in our furs at a good price and procure our needed supplies for the coming trapping season for a lot less than these bastards are wanting to charge us at this here rendezvous."

When Kimama heard those words from Jim Bridger, she almost dropped the Dutch oven in which she had been serving the men freshly baked biscuits! To Kimama's way of thinking, to do as Bridger suggested would place all of them in danger. Kimama was not sure where this 'St. Louis' place was, but she had heard a lot of talk about that place from Bear Scat since they had been married. She also knew that to go there would more than likely take them through the territory of the mighty Sioux Nation. A nation of Indians who were bitter enemies of the Wind River Shoshone! Standing there with the heavy cast iron Dutch oven in hand and trying to get her heart to work once again after hearing those words regarding traveling to St. Louis with their furs, she listened intently as Bridger began speaking once again.

"Bear Scat, together our party of trappers would be such that most Indians would think twice before attacking such a large group. So with that kind of a trip in mind and with our 'long-shooting' Hawken rifles and keen eyes, we should be safe in our travels. That is unless they came at us in overwhelming numbers, then I guess we die in the country we love doing what we love doing, like a lot of our kind have done before us and will continue to do so until they 'go under' as well..."

Bear Scat quietly sat there with his plate of food getting colder and colder by the moment and then after a long pause thinking over Bridger's proposal, said, "You know, Jim, that might not be a bad idea. I have been mulling over in my mind what I wanted to do with the rest of my life. I have spent the last few years as a trapper searching for my brother out here on the frontier, in order to tell him what has happened to our family back in Missouri and decide what the two of us can do once joined back up. I have not been successful in my ventures of trying to locate my brother, other than finding a redemption document belonging to him in a saddlebag on a horse stolen by a Blackfoot Indian. A 'find' that more than likely means he has 'gone under' at their hands when they stole his horse! That has been the sum total of my success looking for the last of my kin. Ever since my marriage to Kimama whom I love with all

473

of my heart, I have come to realize that maybe living out here on the frontier with all of its dangers, deadly weather elements, mean-assed critters waiting to attack and eat oneself, and discovering at every rendezvous the number of my friends who have 'lost their hair' and have 'gone under' gets larger each year, I have been thinking. I love this country, its quiet and unspoiled natural beauty, its sunsets and sunrises, its challenges to me as an individual and its many rewards for those of us who survive. But I am now realizing that I am tired of being cheated out of what I have earned the hard way. Cheated out of my bounty by someone only paying low Mountain Prices for our hard work in trapping, and then turning around and making me pay high Mountain Prices for the goods I need in order to survive another year on the frontier. I think I am obliged to provide more for my wife other than freezing to death in the cold waters or long winters and for what children we will have in the future. Count me in, Jim, and may the good Lord help us to be successful in this here endeavor of what you speak!"

With those words from her husband, Kimama's heart skipped a beat and then she remembered she loved him very much, was his wife and would trust and go with him forever, no matter where he went or what he did. Drawing in a deep breath, Kimama began serving the men the rest of the biscuits she had in the Dutch oven. But as she did, she was hoping The Great Spirit would be riding along with them wherever they went and watching over them in whatever they chose to do...

Then almost as an afterthought, Bear Scat said, "However, Jim, I have one small problem with what you are proposing and what I have decided to do. Bear Claw and Elk as you well know, are Wind River Shoshone. Asking them to go with us through the land of their enemy the Sioux and risk their lives is not the right thing to do. They will have to return to their people, and that means Kimama and I will have to be the ones somehow doing the 'wrangling' of our rather large horse herd. That will be a problem, especially if we are attacked and those attacking us are trying to run off our horses. Just trailing that number of horses to St. Louis will be more than a bit of a chore. Throw a hungry grizzly bear or attacking Indians into that mix, and there is no way Kimama and I can keep control of all of our horses and valuable furs which they will be carrying."

Jim, upon hearing of Bear Scat's concerns, thought for a moment in silence and then said, "I have an idea. I know of six other trappers who are also looking at going south to St. Louis to trade in their furs. What do you say that I look into what they are going to do and if they still feel that way. If they still plan on leaving out from this here rendezvous for St. Louis, I will ask them to throw in with us. That way, with those six trappers added to our group, you would have some extra help in herding your horses along with the rest of us."

Bear Scat, now mouthing with some difficulty one of Kimama's hot biscuits, nodded his head in the affirmative over Jim's suggestion and then dropped his biscuit when it met his tongue, which immediately 'objected' over the biscuit's baking heat being fresh out from the Dutch oven sizzling on his tongue...

The next day with the preparations of the trip to St. Louis being set into motion, Bear Claw and Elk made ready to go back to Chief Gray Wolf's Wind River Band of Shoshone. In so doing, Kimama spoke to Bear Claw making sure he relayed the travel to St. Louis information to her family and that she would try to stay in touch. Then with many tears flooding her eyes, Kimama watched her brother-in-law leave her life. Sensing his wife's deep emotions over what he was about to do, Bear Scat walked over to her, gathered her up in his arms and held her until Bear Claw rode out of sight. Finally Kimama removed herself from Bear Scat's arms, turned and with still glistening eyes said, "I love my husband very much and will go with him wherever he goes." With those words, Kimama turned and went back to her camp duties. When she did, Bear Scat found that his eyes glistened as well over what she had just said... That afternoon Bear Scat slipped away from his campsite and rode over to the Hudson's Bay Company trading site. There he traded a Made Beaver *'plus'* for a dried adult bald eagle skin. Riding back to his campsite, Bear Scat took apart the white tail feathers from the tail portion of the eagle's dried skin and quietly began weaving each white eagle tail feather into the right side of his horse's mane. Upon completion, he burned the rest of the eagle's skin in a sacred sagebrush fire according to Shoshone tradition. Kimama, looking on, did not question her husband as to why he was fastening ten of the adult bald eagle's white tail feathers into his riding horse's mane. Just watching her husband carefully weaving each tail feather into the right side of his horse's mane told her what he was doing was somehow very important and she did not ask...

Three days later with Jim Bridger in the lead with his horses, followed by Bear Scat and Kimama and trailed by six other trappers and their caravan of heavily loaded horses, they rode quietly out from the 1838 Rendezvous. Riding south along the Beaver River until they came to the Sweetwater River, they then turned easterly following the Sweetwater. Passing Independence Rock, the caravan continued on until they arrived at the Platte River. As they traveled easterly along the Platte, the trappers' caravan made about 25 miles per day, only stopping at night where there was good grass for their animals, wood for their campfires and clean drinking water.

Two more weeks of travel found the group camped along the Platte one evening, with Jim Bridger leaving camp and riding his horse out onto a distant hill where he sat there looking all around until dark overcame him. Come dark, Bridger quietly returned to camp, unsaddled his horse and without fanfare joined the rest of his group for dinner. During supper Bridger appeared very introspective and after lighting up his pipe, addressed the group saying, "For the last day, I have been seeing a lot of unshod pony tracks. Right now the direction of travel of those tracks appears to indicate they are doing nothing more than hunting buffalo. However, we are now in Arikara country and they can be killing sons-a-bitches if we are not careful and let our guards down. Starting tonight, we will take watches around the campfire and by our horse herd. My thinking is that if they see the size of our horse herd or get on our trail realizing the tracks are from shod horses, they will be a-coming for them and us. That happens and we will have our hands full, no two ways about it. So starting right after we are through here this evening, I want all of our horses double hobbled. That way there is no way they can sneak into our camp after dark and easily run our stock off. Next, make sure our picket pins are driven deeply in solid ground and our picket ropes are well-tied. Additionally, use a double knot when you tie off your horses so they will be harder to untie and be quickly led off in the dark of night. Lastly, on your second weapons like your reserve rifles and all of your pistols, you need to load them with buck and ball. If the Indians attack us, they will do so in surprise, in numbers and hope to overrun us after you have fired your first shot at them with your principal rifle. If they do try and overrun our group after you have fired your first shot, they will run into your buck and ball being fired from close range, and that should discourage many of them from continuing the attack after your second and third rounds of shooting. Oh, one other thing. Kimama is a beautiful woman. She is also Shoshone, a lifelong enemy of the Arikara and Sioux. I would suggest that she put some man's clothes on so they can't see that she is a woman. For if they do and they somehow surround us, they will want her as part of any bargain in letting us go so they can 'pleasure' her. That would be a fate worse than death, Bear Scat! You know from your many years in the mountains, all of them will want to bed her. I suggest if you see that we are about to be overrun by the Arikara, that you shoot Kimama, as opposed to letting her fall into their evil hands for a fate that is worse than death and one no woman should ever have to endure…"

With those words, the men began changing out their secondary weapons to buck and ball and when done, began double hobbling all of their livestock. Suffice to say, in light of what 'Man of the Mountains' Jim Bridger had said, little deep sleep was had by the group that night… For the next two days, Bridger and company continued their travels making about 25 miles a day. As they did,

477

they came across numerous herds of buffalo, elk, some bighorn sheep and large numbers of antelope, as well as a number of roving grizzly bears seeking out any animal carcasses they could find. However, on day three of their travels after Bridger's warnings, the group was spotted by a number of what Bridger identified as the dreaded Arikara! True to form, the small band of Arikara began tailing the group, but not before dispatching one of their braves to more than likely head out and bring back more of their kind so they would have overwhelming numbers if they decided to attack!

That night Bridger and company posted double guards, as the small group of Indians who had been slowly tailing them camped just a short distance away, as evidenced by the light of their campfire. Dawn the next morning found Bridger and company on the trail still heading for the distant city of St. Louis, Missouri. However by the middle of that day, instead of being trailed by just six Indians, they were now being trailed by an additional 18! Bridger had his group bunch up their caravan even more closely than the day before for the better defensive posture it presented if they were to be attacked, which in turn let the trailing Indians know the trappers were prepared to fight if attacked! One of those 'trappers' dressed like a man had her long hair all tucked up inside a wolf skin hat. She also carried Big Hat's Hawken, a Lancaster rifle tied to her trailing riding horse for quick retrieval, two pistols loaded with buck and ball in her sash, and knew how to accurately use them! That 'trapper' also carried a long-bladed gutting knife that she had used to dispatch two Blackfeet Indians who had kidnapped her months earlier, in case the Indians following them got close enough to become overly 'friendly'!

Rounding a bend in the Platte, Bridger noticed that the 24 Indians that had been trailing alongside his small party of trappers had melted away into the rolling hills of the prairie! About an hour later as the trappers walked their horses over a small rise in the rolling prairie, they discovered the 24 Arikara Indians had now arrayed themselves into a 'U'-shaped formation to their front, thereby effectively blocking the fur trappers' route of travel!

Stopping in as good a defensive position as they could find under the circumstances, Bridger rode forward with his right hand raised in the universal sign of peace. However, a single rifle shot fired into the ground alongside Bridger's horse by the Arikara stopped Bridger in his tracks, as the group of Indians now quickly circled their horses all around those of the trappers! Riding back to his group, Bridger had the men hurriedly unpack a number of their bundles of furs and stack them in a small ring around the trappers and their horses, to act as a defensive barrier if and when the Indians attacked. For the next few minutes the Indians rode around and around the trapped trappers yelling and evilly gesturing at the small group of now trapped fur trappers!

Then all of a sudden the Arikara charged in towards the trappers from all sides and in so doing, were met with a blistering wall of rifle fire from the accurate shooting trappers, dropping six of their number! However, the stacked bundles of beaver *'plus'* saved the trappers from any deaths or wounds, as the Arikara bullets smacked harmlessly into the bundles arrayed around the trappers. With that, the Arikara pulled back and began shooting into the huddled group of trappers from a distance and in so doing, managed to drop three of the trappers' horses, killing them outright! However once again, the trappers suffered no personal casualties thanks to their defensive barriers of fur packs.

That afternoon, the huddled group of trappers ate jerky and carefully observed what was happening all around them. Come the dusk found the Arikara had split up into smaller groups and had circled the trappers pinning them in, as was evidenced by four surrounding campfires. Dawn the next morning appeared to herald a day of low clouds with the heavy smell of moisture in the air. Looking out over the prairie, Bridger and Bear Scat could see they were still surrounded by the Arikara camps. Then Bear Scat and Bridger discussed the option of attacking several of the smaller groups of Arikara come nightfall. That they discussed because after another day without food and water, some of those still heavily packed animals would start suffering intensely.

Then all of a sudden, the surviving Arikara gathered into a group and appeared to be looking at something occurring further to the north of their position. Moments later, the Arikara quickly left the field of battle with the trappers for places unknown... Suspecting a trap, Bridger had all the men repack their animals and make preparations to get under way and leave the area once it was determined to be safe to do so. Then in so doing, try to find a better defensive position with some form of water for the group and their animals. All of a sudden looking out across the prairie, Bear Scat froze in his tracks! There to the north streamed a number of Indians heading their way! That time, the number of Indians appeared to be in excess of 30 or so, and they were heading across the prairie right at the small group of trappers at full speed!

The trappers once again hurriedly unloaded their pack animals and used their bundles of furs as some sort of a barricade, when this new bunch of Indians and the intentions they represented made themselves known! Like well-trained soldiers, the oncoming group of Indians rode directly at the trapped group of trappers and then at the last minute, split into two streams of horseflesh and humanity, completely surrounding Bridger and company! Using their standing horses and bundles of furs as a defense against any incoming rifle fire, the trappers prepared for the fight of their lives, especially now being completely surrounded and outnumbered by at least three to one!

It was then that two riders who appeared to be the leaders of the group, rode out from the mass of the other surrounding Indians, dismounted and one of them, using what appeared to be a captured Army telescope, began looking intently at the group of huddled trappers. That he did as his partner excitedly kept pointing at the surrounding group of trappers, making many hand and arm gestures of excitement! Then the Indian with the looking glass hung it back around his neck on a thong, mounted his horse and began slowly riding right at Bridger, Bear Scat and company. As the lone Indian got closer, Bridger was heard to utter, "They appear to be Sioux from the looks of their dress. That being the case, I can see why the Arikara turned tail and ran. The Sioux are deadly enemies of the Arikara and have been known to kill and eat the hearts of such enemies."

Then the Indian riding towards the trappers, stopped, dismounted and began walking towards the trapped men with his right arm raised in the universal sign of peace. That was when Bear Scat let out a yell, laid his rifle down and excitedly walked out from his huddled group towards the oncoming Indian to the amazement of his countrymen and wife Kimama! Within moments, the two men met AND EMBRACED! Turning, Bear Scat yelled, "Lower your rifles. These Indians are my friends!"

With those words, the two men began walking back towards the huddled trappers, who by now had bewildered looks spilled clear across their faces over what they were witnessing! Here they had been surrounded by the Arikara and now the even deadlier Sioux. The Arikara had shot at them earlier in an attempt to kill the trappers and steal their horses and goods. Because of the straight-shooting trappers and their firm resolve, the Arikara had not been successful. However, here they were once again surrounded by an overwhelming number of Indians and yet this group according to a happy-faced Bear Scat was now being called their friends. There were a lot of incredulous and questioning looks spelled clear across everyone's faces back at the 'trappers' surround' to say the least...

Walking up to the trappers, Bear Scat explained to the still on-guard group saying, "This is Buffalo Horn my friend, son of Buffalo Calf, a great Sioux chief. I rescued a younger Buffalo Horn from drowning when his Bull Boat began sinking in the Missouri River and he couldn't swim, years ago when Big Hat and I were partners heading for Fort Union. His father, Buffalo Calf, took Big Hat and me in when he discovered we were starving and wandering around on the prairie without any horses after being abandoned by our former friends. He later provided us with horses and supplies and allowed us safe passage to Fort Union. A year or so later, Buffalo Calf escorted a group of us trappers heading for St. Louis to trade in our furs and did so, escorting us safely through Arikara country. Out of respect for me saving his only son from drowning, Buffalo Calf named me White Eagle in honor of my deed. He did so, renaming me from being called 'Bear Scat' to that of 'White Eagle', and as a 'naming sign and honor', wove the white tail feathers from a bald eagle into the mane of my horse as a symbol of peace among the Sioux and Northern Cheyenne Nations. It was those white bald eagle tail feathers fluttering from the mane of my horse that Buffalo Horn spotted through his looking glass, and that is why his braves did not attack and kill us for trespassing on their lands. He is honoring his father's pledge that whenever I walk upon their lands, I may safely do so, as well as any kind who are with me."

That evening after killing a cow buffalo, the trappers and their Sioux Indian friends feasted on raw buffalo liver, then roasted hump ribs, coffee and Dutch oven biscuits slathered in cinnamon and sugar, a favorite of the Indians. The next morning after another group breakfast of buffalo, coffee and Dutch oven biscuits cooked over 'buffalo chips', the two groups parted company. Buffalo Horn and his warriors to continue hunting buffalo, and Bridger, Bear Scat and company to continue on their way to St. Louis to trade in their furs and restock their provisions for the coming trapping season after spending some time in St. Louis celebrating.

Six more weeks of travel without further incident, other than being blocked for a full day until a huge herd of buffalo had crossed in front of the trappers, whereupon they safely arrived in St. Louis! Riding their heavily loaded horse caravan down Front Street, Bridger stopped and asked a civilian where their fur houses were located. After getting instructions as to the several fur house locations in the city, the caravan once again headed into the city-center so they could sell their furs, locate a boarding house for some good home cooking, perhaps a hot bath and then several hours of sleep in a real bed, without the fear of stepping on a rattlesnake, surprising a sleeping grizzly bear in his day bed, or running into a high speed bullet or arrow point from an irate Arikara Indian. Riding through town, Kimama found her head looking from side to side like it was on a swivel, gaping at a whole new world of wonder. There were huge wooden structures like she had never seen before, the streets were full of more white people than she had ever seen, the noise of the living city was almost too much for her ears, then she was almost blasted off her now skittish horse when a nearby docked steamboat blew its noonday whistle. She saw live hogs running around in the streets, and the smell of the white man's civilization hung thickly in the air and was almost overwhelming after living in the clean air out on the frontier!

Finally arriving in front of a huge yellow building with a large sign proclaiming, "THE AMERICAN FUR COMPANY", Bridger swung the caravan's horses over to the structure's front hitching rails and was immediately met by a Company Clerk. Within moments, the fur caravan was led around behind the building and there it was met by a dozen fur counters and graders. For the next four hours, Bridger, Bear Scat and the rest of their party haggled with the Company Clerks over the grades of the beaver *'plus'* being counted and graded.

At the end of the fur counting and grading session, each trapper was given a credit slip from the American Fur Company to be drawn from the First Mercantile Bank of St. Louis for what was owed each trapper for his furs. In Bear Scat and Kimama's case, they were handed a credit slip to be drawn from the bank for $6,479 for their 1,178 beaver *'plus'* at an average value of $5.50 per fur! With that purchase information, Bear Scat just smiled. He smiled because the 'Mountain Prices' being paid at the rendezvous were only $3 per pelt versus the $5.50 he had just received from the American Fur Company! Then before the day was done, Bear Scat collected on his previous American Fur Company redemption certificates of $13,032 and $3,000 from fur sales, another American Fur Company certificate for $3,050 which was his brother's discovered in the saddlebag of a stolen horse, and $1,700 in credit from the St. Louis Fur Company for his earlier horse herd sale. Those five redemption certificates totaled $27,261! No two ways about it, Bear Scat was now a very rich man in the coin of the realm for that day and age where the living wage for the average man ran from $300-400 a year!

After placing all of their stock animals in "Marshal Davis's Livery" for safekeeping and care, which was next door to "Ma Sylvia's Boarding House and Eatery", Bridger and company started up the steps to the boarding house and eatery for a welcome meal. A welcome and clean meal served in civilization unlike one normally served out on the trail all covered with specks of dirt, flies and bits and pieces of buffalo chips… However, at the front door of the 'clean as a hound's tooth' eatery stood two hell-for-stout young men closely resembling the size and strength of a couple of draft horses, named Clifton and Thomas Davis, sons of Marshal and Ma Davis. "Hold 'er right there, Boys," said Clifton, standing in front of step-climbing Jim Bridger, Bear Scat, Kimama (still dressed like a man), and the rest of their party. "Before you chaps go inside my mother's place of business, you need to kick any hog crap picked up on your boots or moccasins walking through these streets, and remove all of your percussion caps from the nipples of your pistols and rifles before entering. My Ma runs a respectable place of business here and all of you are more than welcome. But we have rules here at this here establishment and if you wish to partake of the good food and hospitality, you must follow our rules," said Ma Sylvia's 'stout as a horse' son Thomas! Then Thomas caught himself upon seeing Kimama removing her wolf skin cap and letting her long dark hair fall about and over her shoulders. "Holy Cow, I am sorry, Ma'am, I didn't know you was a 'she'. But you are just as welcome, just as long as you remove the percussion caps from your rifle and pistols," said a very embarrassed Thomas Davis over his earlier mistaken gender identity of one of the trappers confronted on the front steps.

Smiling over Thomas's identification error, Kimama removed the percussion caps from her guns, wiped off her moccasins and was graciously allowed to enter the eatery ahead of the men. Once inside, it took the group a few moments to adjust to such a noisy place full of happily eating people and an establishment smelling of good home cooking! Sitting down at a long table, all nine of Bridger's group were soon overwhelmed by the service at Ma Sylvia's. First and foremost, the group was confronted by a pert and pretty Betsy Davis, younger daughter to Ma Sylvia. Soon coffee was at everyone's plate and fresh blackberry pies now gloriously graced their table, as the men dove right in after ordering a breakfast of such proportions that it would have fed an entire ship's crew based along the docks of St. Louis!

Soon a monster-sized breakfast was served to the group, and soon all one could hear were the men wolfing down cooking like they had not seen since they had left their beloved mothers to go into the fur trade out on the frontier years earlier. Kimama on the other hand, was picking at her food since she had never seen some of the likes of what she was seeing on her plate. But the more she ate, the more she was taking a liking to this style of home-cooked white man's type of food…

Then Bear Scat slowly stood up from the table and in so doing spilled the cup of coffee he had been holding in his hand! When he did, everyone at his table quit eating, trying to figure out what the hell Bear Scat was looking at so intently. FOLLOWING THAT, BEAR SCAT KICKED HIS CHAIR NOISILY BACKWARDS ONTO THE FLOOR AND TOOK OFF RUNNING ACROSS THE MAIN FLOOR TOWARDS THE REAR OF THE DINING ROOM LIKE A MAN GONE CRAZY! "**JACOB!**" YELLED BEAR SCAT! With that bellow from Bear Scat, the entire eatery went silent out of fear of the unknown being caused by a buckskin-clad Mountain Man running through the eatery like a crazy man! Then a number of the patrons rose from their seats almost as if in their defense, when they saw Bear Scat running towards a table at the back of the room holding two other buckskin-clad 'Mountain Men' and a beautiful Shoshone Indian woman quietly eating their breakfasts!

With that loud shout heard from clear across the spacious dining room, Jacob Sutta looked up from his breakfast, only to see his younger brother Elliott Sutta, running right at him! Recognizing his younger brother running right at him, a surprised Jacob stood up, only to be bowled over when Elliott ran full speed right into the arms of his long-lost brother! "CRASH" went the two brothers into the wall of the dining room, as other nearby patrons rose from their tables, with some even going for their knives in order to defend themselves if the two mountain men now rolling around on the floor just a-hooting and a-hollering started a general brawl in the eatery!

However a general 'hurrah' was not in the cards as Thomas and Clifton, upon hearing the ruckus ongoing in their mother's eatery, burst through the front swinging doors and ran to what they figured were two crazy 'Mountain Men' fighting it out! However by the time the Davis Brothers got there to break up the fight, they found the two 'hell-raising' patrons yelling, laughing, crying and talking all at once as they held each other like two grizzly bears locked in mortal combat! Suffice to say, it took more than a few moments to calm things down, get everything back under control and settle down all the rest of the breakfast-eating patrons once an explanation was offered to all, along with an apology by the two Sutta Brothers. Once an explanation was offered to all the seated customers, a loud cheer went up and soon the two Suttas found the table where they were still standing and not wanting to let each other go, crowded with a number of congratulatory drinks from other nearby customers!

For the rest of that morning and into the afternoon, Bridger and Elliott Bear Scat Sutta's table was joined by Jacob Sutta and Wild Bill McGinty, as everyone learned about the history of the two brothers, their family and Elliott Bear Scat Sutta's years-long vision quest to find and join his brother. There were tears when Jacob discovered that his parents and younger sister had been killed in a tornado years earlier, and a number of tears of amazement and joy shed when both Sutta Brothers discovered they had married Shoshone Indian women! As it turned out, breakfast slid into suppertime at Ma Sylvia's, since there was much catching up to be done and happiness in doing so. In fact, Ma Sylvia upon hearing the stories about the two now-found brothers, saw to it that the entire group ate free that day, as were their drinks in celebration of the brothers' reunion...

That evening after Bridger and his trappers left the group for more drinking and celebrating with Wild Bill McGinty, Jacob, Jacob's wife Shani or Shoshone for "Wind", Elliott and Kimama retired to Elliott's bedroom so they could talk and get to know one another better. Finally about midnight with the two wives fast asleep on Elliott's bed, the men woke up their wives and adjourned to their own bedrooms. However they agreed to meet the following morning, and over breakfast discuss what they wanted to do with the rest of their lives. However just before they parted for the morning, Jacob looking at Elliott said, "When we get back together, you need to tell me the story behind all those claw marks across your face and why you only have one ear lobe..."

After a long breakfast and much discussion, including the stories as to why Elliott only had one ear lobe and all the claw mark scars on the side of his face, Jacob and Elliott took their wives shopping for anything they wanted from the white culture, since both men had sold their furs and were now very well off in that day's coin of the realm. Later that afternoon, Wild Bill McGinty joined the group for supper. There he was told that the two brothers were quitting the fur trade, returning to their Missouri farm, settling down, raising a family and wanting to become gentlemen farmers. Bill congratulated both brothers over their decision to quit the often-times dangerous fur trade and then advised that he had been offered a partnership with Jim Bridger. With that offer and in light of the brothers' life-changing decision, he was going to accept Bridger's offer and return to the fur trapping trade and his beloved frontier for whatever that lifestyle would bring.

It was during that conversation of teaming up with Bridger that the name of the Travises came up and when a cloud flew across Elliott's face, Jacob asked him what was wrong. Elliott shared his story about the ambush at their cabin and the following shootout he had with the Travises and the deadly outcome. When he did, Wild

Bill's face lit up like a candle and he said with relief, "Thank goodness that chapter in my life is over! Thank you, Elliott, for solving a problem really not of my doing that has been hounding me all these many years. I guess I owe you a drink for taking care of that problem for me and in so doing, allowing me to not always be looking over my shoulder for those killing sons-a-bitches sneaking up on me."

That evening after a happy parting with his lifelong trapping partner Wild Bill McGinty, the Suttas returned to Elliott's room, while Kimama and Shani tried on the new clothes their men had purchased for them that day so they would be as well-dressed as were their white counterparts. As it turned out, both Kimama and Shani were about the same age and had instantly taken a liking to each other, just like the 'sisters' they would soon become. With the direction of their new lives decided, Jacob and Elliott made plans for leaving St. Louis and returning to their parents' old farm now being tended by a close family friend and neighbor. There they planned on building their homes on their parents' old place so they would never be separated again, and farm the rich bottomlands as gentlemen farmers in the future. That they planned on doing since they both were now well-off thanks to the fur trade and what it had provided for the two of them, besides their two new wives.

CHAPTER SEVENTEEN: THE BIG BUCK AND FINALLY "HOME"

Two weeks later, the Sutta Brothers and their wives arrived at the farm of their family friend near the town of Weldon Spring just west of St. Louis. After meeting with the current family friend who was now farming their old farm and informing him regarding the brothers' future plans of farming the land themselves after their friend had removed that year's crops after they had matured, the two former Mountain Men departed for their old homestead. There they unloaded all of their pack animals kept from their days as Mountain Men in front of the old family barn, and while Jacob helped the wives take all of their belongings into the barn for safekeeping, Elliott set up an outside firepit for cooking their meals. Later the two brothers gathered in their horses from grazing nearby and put them into the old barn for safekeeping. That they did because as Mountain Men, to do differently might just mean one woke up the next morning only to find all of his valuable horses missing or stolen. That was especially so in Missouri in that day and age, because the country was almost overrun with ruffians and renegade Indians. After their first evening meal back on the old farm in years, the two families adjourned to the back of the barn and settled down in the old horse stalls now being used as their temporary living quarters until their new homes could be built.

The next day bright and early, the Suttas went into the nearby town of Weldon Spring, contracted with some local builders and carpenters to build their new homes, and then headed back to their farm in order to tend to their horses and further clean out the old barn so it would make a better living quarters. Later that day, the builders and carpenters arrived and after meeting with the brothers as to where they wanted their new homes built and to what specifications, they turned their labors to exploring the families' nearby forest for the right kind of cabin-building timbers needing harvesting to provide the lumber and logs for their two new homes. That afternoon, the families' forest sang with the sounds of saws, the ringing of axes and the crack of whips as teams of oxen brought out the freshly cut hardwood timbers from the woods and piled them up at each new homesite to be used for later construction.

The timber harvesting, cutting to size and hauling went on for two more weeks before the log homes began appearing from the ground up, as the two happy Mountain Man turned farmers and their families rejoiced over the progress being made. One late evening as their suppers were being prepared, Jacob suggested to Elliott that perhaps he could go hunting the next day in order to kill a deer and refresh their dwindling meat supply currently hanging in the cool of their barn. Elliott nodded in the affirmative to his brother's suggestion and then all of a sudden, a 'dark and deadly' memory flooded over him like an ocean's wave to the point that he almost became physically ill! In that moment of time thinking back, he realized that he had been 'there' before in times earlier as a young 16-year-old, when his father had suggested he go forth into their family's forests, kill a deer and bring it home to augment their dwindling meat supply. Hunting he did shortly thereafter as suggested with his father's borrowed rifle and had killed a monster buck deer, only to have a tornado suddenly appear out of the northwestern sky! A mid-summer's day tornado, that swept down upon him leaving him battered and bruised, took his big buck into the roaring sucking air, and then subsequently moved over his parents' home, destroying it in the process and 'taking' them as well as his baby sister! As those 'dark' memories flooded back over Elliott like it was only yesterday, he suddenly felt his 'sixth senses' awakening and then a physical coldness began sweeping over him in the mid-summer Missouri heat!

With those dark and hurtful thoughts from a time long past flooding over him, Elliott did not sleep very well that night... However, their two families needed fresh meat and he was up way before daylight as he had often done as a 'Mountain Man' on the frontier, and headed off into the families' forests on a deer hunt in the Missouri morning's cool darkness... The same kind of a morning when he was only 16 out hunting a deer to replenish the family's meat supply, when the tornado almost swept him away...

An eerily reddish-orange orb of a sun rose ominously over the great State of Missouri that morning and soon the summer heat and humidity across the land became almost palpable. Off in a distance, a ten-point white-tailed deer still in velvet peacefully feasted under a huge spreading oak tree on the plentiful mast scattered around at the base of the tree dropped from the previous fall's natural harvest. Then all of a sudden, the quietly feeding deer's head shot up into the air in an alertness that came from living in an often-times predator-rich environment! That and 10,000 years of survival genetics went into that alertness, moving the deer from quietly feeding under an oak tree into a now and all of a sudden, highly alerted and statuesque presence. Every sensory nerve in the seven-year-old buck deer was now being utilized in an effort to detect what his innate survival senses were 'telling' him.

The early morning's breezes wafting across the landscape did not bring him anything out of the ordinary other than those smells normally associated with his feeding presence in the field under the great oak tree. His eyes which only saw in black and white, not color, did not provide any early warning signs of movement in his surroundings other than that of the softly rustling grasses, tree leaves and bushes in the face of an oncoming summer storm. His 'mule-like' shaped ears, developed over the last 10,000 years to provide hearing acuity of the highest level for his species, especially when danger was near, brought him no such suspicious evidence or early warnings. The only out of the ordinary element that the great buck deer's body could foretell was that there was a great storm brewing far to the northwest, if he correctly 'read' the barometric pressure changes now swirling around him. Being of 'white-tailed deer' genetics and possessing the collateral highly developed survival instincts associated with that species, the great buck carefully examined his nearby brushy surroundings at the edge of the meadow once again for any signs of danger. Then a slave to his empty stomach, he set carefulness and caution aside in favor of consuming more of the flavorful and abundant mast scattered around his feet. Lowering his head once again, he adroitly picked up another of the energy-rich acorns with his lips, moved it with his tongue to his molars and with a satisfying 'crunch' began enjoying the nut's rich flavor as he began quietly eating once again.

THUD! went the impact of a .52 caliber lead ball fired from a nearby Hawken rifle, striking just behind the great deer's right front shoulder. As the high-speed lead ball tore through the deer's skin and flesh, it finally lodged deeply into his lungs in an explosion of destructive energy! The surprising explosive impact of the mushrooming speeding lead ball dropped the massive-in-size deer to the ground in a heartbeat! Then a microsecond later, a chemical surge of adrenalin initiated by the physics of the ball's impact pumped into the deer's heart and spread throughout his circulatory system in two rapid heartbeats. With that chemical's surge into his bloodstream, the great buck found the power to leap back to his feet, took two lunges away from the "**BOOMING**" sound of a rifle and the whitish-black, black powder cloud of smoke surging his way from some nearby elderberry bushes. Two giant leaps later and after one backward kick with his hind feet, the giant buck deer dropped dead!

Twenty-one-year-old Elliott Sutta, son of Adam and Edna Sutta, small Jewish Missouri homesteaders, felt the comforting recoil of his old reliable Hawken rifle being fired against his shoulder. That assuring recoil after hearing the report of his rifle being fired at a massive white-tailed buck told him after his long and arduous sneak upon the feeding monster-sized deer right at daylight had been successfully carried out. Jumping to his feet in excitement and looking past the small drifting away whitish cloud of black powder smoke from his rifle, Elliott saw his quarry the massive white-tailed buck lying on the ground kicking his last!

Remembering his dad's earlier survival teachings learned during his former military years on the frontier fighting Indians, instead of running over to his kill site in the excitement of the moment, Elliott took the time to quickly reload his rifle. As he did, he continued looking all around for any signs of approaching hostile Indians or Missouri border ruffians who had heard him shoot and might be coming his way to investigate who was doing the shooting. Additionally, he alertly watched for any signs and listened for any sounds of an approaching through the brush black or grizzly bear. Like in kind sounds from predators conditioned to hearing anyone shoot, smelling death in the wind and then somewhat later because of their alertness, being 'treated' to a warm gut pile. For the next ten minutes of so after reloading his rifle and standing still as a stone surrounded by brush at the 'ready' just in case any sign of danger reared its head, Elliott did as his dad had also taught him regarding surviving sometimes in a savage wilderness. That being delayed danger could still be coming his way after he had made it known that he was nearby in country, so best to always remain alert longer than one figured necessary before exposing one's exact location after shooting. Finally, Elliott in his excitement over his kill could stand himself no longer and trotted out from the cover of his position to examine the great beast he had just slain! Standing over the body of the deer, Elliott's heart skipped a beat in the excitement of just his second monster white-tailed buck deer taken in his life!

Looking down once again, Elliott saw that the animal he had just killed was huge, weighing in around 350 pounds! Upon closer examination, Elliott could see from the bullet's entry point that he had made a clean kill and one that his dad, if he were still alive, would be very proud of. Now their two families back at the barn would have enough excellent-eating deer meat to last them for a number of days.

It was only then that Elliott realized after the excitement of the hunt, that with the increasing winds blowing across the landscape and the ominous blue-black low hanging clouds quickly forming overhead, that a huge and dangerous-looking storm front was developing to the northwest! The same kind of storm just like the one that had earlier in his life spawned a tornado that killed his parents and baby sister! Then those same dark foreboding thoughts from the evening before and his 'sixth sense' of dread came roaring back, after his brother had requested he go on a deer hunt and bring back some fresh meat, as his father had so requested years earlier, only to later die from the tornado!

Finally getting his wits back about him and really intelligently looking skyward for the first time, Elliott saw that a fierce thunderstorm was coming his way and he best make haste in gutting out his massive buck! Then 'both' of them had better retreat to some form of cover to avoid getting drenched with the oncoming deluge of rains, hit by lightning or both! Then the previous night's foreboding thoughts came back with a rush once again, as he began hearing the sounds of 'a thousand angry thunderstorms' all rolled up into one, and it sounded like its fury was coming his way! Then what he saw next caused his 'sixth senses' to roil around inside him like a herd of stampeding horses! Elliott could now see the beginning of a tornado's funnel cloud beginning to form beneath the ugly blue-black clouds that were now rolling his way! Stunned over what he was seeing coming his way, he had a flashback to his earlier days deer hunting when a like funnel cloud roared across his dad's farm, destroying all living things and only leaving the barn standing! Then his mind exploded with the thought that kimama, his brother and his wife were now possibly in mortal danger from another potential family-killing tornado!

Stepping away from his prized buck deer, Elliott started to take off running for his distant tied-off horse in the hopes of reaching it and riding back to the homestead in time to warn everyone still sleeping in the barn of the coming danger! However, Elliott's hopes were not to be realized. Just as he turned to run, a bolt of lightning hit the great oak tree he was standing under, the same one the deer had been quietly feeding under just moments before Elliott had shot him! There was a huge white flash in his eyes and a loud sounding explosion in his ears, as a huge bolt of lightning hit the tree, blowing its massive top to pieces! When that happened, a chunk of the exploding treetop flew through the air striking Elliott in the head and the lights went out!

The next thing Elliott saw when he came to was his horse standing nearby peacefully grazing in the meadow. Rising painfully up on his elbows, Elliott became aware that the sun was shining and the air was heavy with humidity from the now long-past storm, which he found refreshing. Then remembering a tornado forming below the ugly blue-black oncoming storm clouds before he was knocked out, he rose to his feet. As he did, he expected to see a path of destruction left by the tornado as he had seen when one had traveled through his farmstead years earlier, destroying everything in its path. Looking around, he saw nothing of the kind of damage like he had seen after the first killer-tornado had passed through his farm years earlier. The land was intact, the birds were once again singing and after the storm had passed, breezes were now softly moving across the land. Mounting his horse and riding to the south end of the meadow, Elliott could see off in the distance that the old barn was still standing and he could faintly hear the ringing of axes in the nearby forest cutting timbers to fit into the log walls of the two new homes being built on the homestead. As near as he could tell from the people walking around by the barn, everything and everyone was alright. Then he remembered his massive buck deer was still lying out under the destroyed great oak. Riding back to the deer, he could see that it was starting to bloat. Seeing that, he dismounted and began field-dressing the big deer so it would not go to waste. After all, he had been sent out to get fresh meat for the two families, hadn't he? A half-hour later, he had the deer field-dressed, loaded upon his horse and was walking him down towards the construction crew working on the two homes for the new families of Jacob and Elliott Sutta and their two now pregnant Shoshone wives.

Then all of a sudden, Elliott 'Bear Scat' Sutta stopped dead in his tracks, as another intense feeling physically flooded over his body and roared through the annals of his mind! The old forebodings that had flowed over him the day before and throughout his life during troubled periods of time were now gone... Standing there quietly in the beautiful Missouri countryside, Elliott 'Bear Scat' Sutta finally realized he was now one with his surroundings, Kimama and himself. He had dreamed of what America could be and had been a living part of those dreams. He then understood that 'his' was the beginning of an American story, where the best part of a good man stays forever, and he was now finally home...

ABOUT THE AUTHOR

Terry Grosz was born in June 1941, in Toppenish, Washington. He graduated from Quincy High School in 1959, and attended Humboldt State College where he earned his Bachelor of Science Degree in Wildlife Management in 1964, and his Master of Science Degree in Wildlife Management in 1966. He was a California State Fish and Game Warden from 1966 until 1970, based first in Eureka, California, and then in Colusa, California, in the Northern Sacramento Valley. He then joined the U.S. Fish and Wildlife Service in 1970, and first served in California as a U.S. Game Management Agent and then as a Special Agent until 1974. In 1974, he was promoted to Senior Resident Agent over the States of North and South Dakota where he served until 1976. In 1976, he was promoted to Senior Special Agent and transferred to Washington, DC. There he served as the Endangered Species Desk Officer and Foreign Liaison Officer until 1979. In 1979, he was transferred to Minneapolis, Minnesota, where he served as the Assistant Special Agent in Charge until 1981. In 1981, Terry was promoted and transferred to Denver, Colorado, as the Special Agent in Charge over the wildlife resource-rich eight-state region of the Service's Region 6, encompassing over 750,000 square miles in the States of North Dakota, South Dakota, Nebraska, Kansas, Montana, Wyoming, Colorado, and Utah. He retired from the U.S. Fish and Wildlife Service in 1998, after a 32-year career in state and federal wildlife law enforcement.

In 1999, Terry began his second career as a writer, with the publishing of his first wildlife law enforcement true-life adventures book titled, *"WILDLIFE WARS",* which won a National Outdoor Book Award in the Nature and Environment category. He has since had 13 additional wildlife law enforcement adventure books published, titled, *For Love Of Wildness, Defending Our Wildlife Heritage, A Sword For Mother Nature, No Safe Refuge, The Thin Green Line, Genesis of a Duck Cop, Slaughter in the Sacramento Valley, Wildlife's Quiet War, Wildlife Heritage On The Edge, Wildlife Dies Without Making a Sound (volumes 1 and 2),* and *Flowers and Tombstones of a Conservation Officer (volumes 1 and 2).* Additionally, he has written nine Mountain Man and Western historical novels, titled *Crossed Arrows, Curse of the Spanish Gold, The Saga of Harlan Waugh, The Adventures of the Brothers Dent, The Adventures of Hatchet Jack, The Adventurous Life of Tom "Iron Hand" Warren, Josiah Pike, Hell or High Water,* and *Elliott "Bear Scat" Sutta, Mountain Man.*

Additionally, Terry has a two-hour movie film credit on the reality-based TV series of "Animal Planet" titled, *"WILDLIFE WARS",* filmed in 2003 and released nationwide, based on a number of Terry's true-life wildlife law enforcement adventures during his career as a state and federal wildlife officer.

Terry has earned many awards and honors during his lengthy career, including the U.S. Fish and Wildlife Service's Meritorious Service Award in 1996 -- Recognized as one of the "Top Ten" employees of the U.S. Fish and Wildlife Service under Service Director Frank Dunkle -- The first federal employee to be honored with the "Guy Bradley Award" presented by the National Fish and Wildlife Foundation in 1989 -- Colorado Conservationist of the Year Award in 1984 -- The Conservation Achievement Award for Law Enforcement from the National Wildlife Federation in 1995 (the first law enforcement officer so honored by that organization) -- Special Achievement Award for Law Enforcement Excellence from the U.S. Department of Justice in 1998 -- Distinguished Alumnus, College of Natural Resources, Humboldt State University, 1995 -- Humboldt State University Distinguished Alumnus Award, 2008 -- Distinguished Achievement Award from the Native American Fish and Wildlife Society, 1992 -- Received the Service's highest Annual Performance Ratings under five different supervisors from 1983-1998 -- Unity College in Maine awarded Terry an Honorary Doctorate Degree in Environmental Stewardship in 2002.

Terry resides in Evergreen, Colorado, with his high school Sweetheart and Bride of 55 years.

Find more great titles by Terry Grosz and Wolfpack Publishing at http://wolfpackpublishing.com/terry-grosz/

Made in the USA
Monee, IL
16 December 2021

85797904R10296